THE 13TH REALITY

BOOKS 3 & 4

DON'T MISS THE REST OF
THE 13TH REALITY
SERIES!

✳

The 13th Reality
Books 1 & 2

The Journal of Curious Letters

The Hunt for Dark Infinity

THE 13TH REALITY

BOOKS 3 & 4

THE BLADE OF SHATTERED HOPE

THE VOID OF MIST AND THUNDER

JAMES DASHNER

ILLUSTRATED BY BRANDON DORMAN

Simon Pulse

New York   London   Toronto   Sydney   New Delhi

SIMON PULSE

An imprint of Simon & Schuster Children's Publishing Division

1230 Avenue of the Americas, New York, New York 10020

This Simon Pulse paperback edition July 2015

The Blade of Shattered Hope text copyright © 2010 by James Dashner

The Blade of Shattered Hope interior illustrations copyright © 2010 by Brandon Dorman

Originally published in hardcover in 2010 by Deseret Book Company

Published by arrangement with Shadow Mountain

The Void of Mist and Thunder text copyright © 2012 by James Dashner

The Void of Mist and Thunder interior illustrations copyright © 2012 by Brandon Dorman

Originally published in hardcover in 2012 by Deseret Book Company

Published by arrangement with Shadow Mountain

Cover photograph copyright © 2015 by Yolande de Kort, Christine Amat/Trevillion Images

All rights reserved, including the right of reproduction in whole or in part in any form.

SIMON PULSE and colophon are registered trademarks of Simon & Schuster, Inc.

For information about special discounts for bulk purchases, please contact Simon & Schuster Special Sales at 1-866-506-1949 or business@simonandschuster.com.

The Simon & Schuster Speakers Bureau can bring authors to your live event. For more information or to book an event contact the Simon & Schuster Speakers Bureau at 1-866-248-3049 or visit our website at www.simonspeakers.com.

Cover designed by Gail Ghezzi

Interior designed by Tom Daly

The text of this book was set in Adobe Garamond.

Manufactured in the United States of America 0615 OFF

4 6 8 10 9 7 5

Library of Congress Control Number 2015938659

ISBN 978-1-4814-5702-6

These titles were previously published individually by Aladdin.

CONTENTS

✳

THE BLADE OF
SHATTERED HOPE

For Ben and the rest of the Egans.

So many memories—

most of them embarrassing,

all of them good.

ACKNOWLEDGMENTS

＊

I'd like to thank the following people for being really awesome:

My wife, Lynette.

My agent, Michael Bourret.

My editor, Lisa Mangum.

Chris Schoebinger and everyone else at Shadow Mountain.

Emily Lawrence and all the good people at Simon & Schuster for believing in this series enough to publish the paperbacks.

My incredibly supportive author friends: J. Scott Savage, Julie Wright, Sara Zarr, Anne Bowen, Emily Wing Smith, Bree Despain, Brandon Sanderson,

Aprilynne Pike, and everyone in the Rockcanyon and Storymaker groups.

Angie Wager, for believing in my potential from the very beginning.

The people behind *Lost*. Best. Show. Ever.

The geniuses who invented cheddar cheese, potato chips, iPods, movies, books, and really soft couches. Oh, and lamps. I really love lamps.

But most of all, I want to thank you—the reader. Thank you for being here.

PROLOGUE

✳

THE LAKE

Bryan Cannon looked at the catfish—its bone-like whiskers, its slimy skin, its dark, unblinking eyes—and he saw death. For the creature, of course, not himself. Dinner would be fine and tasty tonight.

The day was beautiful. A slight coolness crisped the air, balanced perfectly by the brilliant sun shining down on Bryan's boat, sparkling off the waters that surrounded him, dancing like fairies of light. Too bad this fish wasn't enjoying things as much as he was.

Bryan had caught the fish in the little body of water in which he floated—called, quite pretentiously, *Lake* Norman. But if that tiny spit of rain-washed sludge was classified as a lake, then Bryan's toilet at home constituted a big pond. He chuckled to himself, as he often did at his own jokes, and spiked another squirmy worm onto his hook. Bryan shifted to get comfortable then he cast the line.

His small canoe rocked at the movement, sending gentle waves rippling across the lake's surface. He watched the outermost wrinkle, enjoying how it traveled along like it didn't have a care in the world. Bryan always loved it when he could keep his eyes trained on the tiny wave until it actually hit the shore. It wasn't as easy as it sounded, and his eyes watered with the effort.

There it goes, he thought, getting smaller and smaller, smaller and smaller . . . there! It hit right over by that sandy—

Splash!

A disturbance in the water, right where the lake met the shore. Then another splash, a huge one, that sprayed droplets all over the small beach. Bryan had been staring right at the spot, so he knew no one had jumped in.

Yet another splash. Then another. It looked like some kid thrashing about with his arms, trying to douse all of his friends in the face. Bryan used to love doing that when he'd been a kid.

There was only one problem. There wasn't a kid anywhere in sight. Or an adult, for that matter. Nobody.

The disturbance continued. Curious, Bryan laid his fishing pole along the length of the canoe and reached for his paddle. Never taking his eyes off the white-water display, he lowered the tip down into the lake and began paddling his way over to check things out. He figured only one of three things was possible.

One, they had themselves a ghost right here in Lake Norman.

Two, some vicious sea monster had found itself a way to the lake from the ocean.

Or three, Bryan Cannon had finally flipped his lid and gone bonkers.

The closer he approached, the worse the splashing. Great cascades of water shot up everywhere—five, ten feet in the air. A curtain of spray unfurled next to him as he rowed along, the water soaking him and sluicing down the sides of the boat. For the first time, terror crept through Bryan's innards, and he realized it might not have been the smartest thing in the world to come so close to whatever *thing* was under the water.

He stopped paddling, slowing to a drift. As he did so, the splashing abruptly ceased. In a matter of seconds, the surface of the lake grew relatively calm, the small waves lapping against his canoe the only evidence anything had happened at all. If anything, the sudden stillness only scared Bryan more. He stared at the spot.

Something started rising out of the water.

Bryan shrieked as he saw what looked like an upside-down glass bowl break the surface of the lake like a bubble, shimmering like wet crystal. The bubble formed into the rough shape of a head, although there were no eyes or nose or mouth. Rising higher, the thing had a neck, and then shoulders, all made out of water. Up and up it rose, *forming* itself, growing out of the lake's surface like a demon rising from its grave. Before long, a human-shaped creature of water stood in front of Bryan, floating on clear feet, the sun casting spectrum-colored glimmers of light as it shone through the apparition.

Bryan sucked in a huge gulp of air, ready to let out the biggest scream of his life. But before he could do it, the watery ghost held up its arms and a sudden wave of water exploded from under its feet, crashing forward and down toward the canoe. Hundreds, maybe thousands of gallons of water, slammed on top of Bryan like a deluge from ancient and angry gods.

Bryan Cannon would never eat a catfish again.

~~~~~~~~

If the waterkelt had a brain, it might've been impressed with its display of power. If the creature had a heart, it might've felt ashamed for causing the death of an innocent person. It had neither, so it simply walked its way to the shore and up into the surrounding trees, leaving behind a wet and muddy trail.

It knew where to go and what to do when it got there. So did its companion, which had been created on the other side of the lake. Their bodies sparkled and flashed in the sunlight like glistening quicksilver as they marched toward their duty.

Only their creator, Mistress Jane, understood the irony of the situation as she observed from a place very far away. Water, the basic element which sustains all human life, was about to be used for quite the opposite.

First stop, the Higginbottom house.

And then—revenge.

PART 1

THE DARK BASEMENT

CHAPTER 1

✳

TWO VERY
DIFFERENT MISSIONS

Sato shivered, then grimaced. His rain-soaked clothes felt icky against his skin; it felt as if an army of leeches clung to him for dear life. He'd stood in the open for barely a minute, trying to figure out where he'd arrived exactly. Drenched already, he looked about, confused.

The air had the feel of twilight, though he knew it was almost noon in this Reality. The reason for the darkness floated above him—massive, heavy clouds of gray-black that were emptying their contents on his sopping-wet head. The clouds seemed close enough to touch. George had warned him that this Reality was a dreary, dreadful place where it rained constantly. Sato couldn't have agreed more.

But he saw no tombstones, no plaques planted in the ground to mark graves. He stood on concrete—or something like it. Hard and flat, the ground was dotted with regularly-spaced holes to drain away the water as quickly as it fell. Sato was glad for that. He didn't relish the idea of standing in a deep pool of water.

Why do I always get stuck with these jobs? Sato thought to himself. If it wasn't a windy, snow-swept mountaintop insane asylum, it was a rainy parking lot supposedly full of dead people. Fun stuff.

He noticed a small, square building about forty feet away, a scarce shadow in the wet darkness. No lights shone from any windows or outdoor fixtures. Seeing nothing else in any direction except the flat expanse of hole-dotted pavement, Sato walked toward the dark building.

As he sloshed his way across the ground, he wished he had a companion with him. Grumbling alone was no fun. Why hadn't George at least given him an umbrella? Maybe next time the red-faced geezer would send Sato to the middle of the ocean without a boat, or maybe to the desert without water, or skydiving without a parachute.

Sato shivered and kept walking, his socks soaked through from the rain. The squishy chill felt like he was smashing hundreds of iced shrimp below his feet. If no one answered at the building, he'd send the signal immediately for Rutger to wink him back. They might have found their first dead-end in Sato's latest mission.

A mission that creeped him out and left him in awe at the same time.

Oh, man, Tick, he thought. *What in the world does this all mean?*

As Sato got closer to the building, he noticed it had absolutely no markings of any kind—not a door, a window, or anything else he could see. It was made up of the same drab, no-color material of the ground, but smooth and unblemished. It was a perfect square, maybe ten feet in height and width.

He walked right up to the cube and put his hand out. Rain cascaded down the sides of the building in sheets, and when his hand made contact with the cool, hard wall, the water parted and washed across his skin, down his arm, and spilled onto the ground in tiny twin falls. Sato pulled his hand away and whipped it back and forth in a futile attempt to dry himself.

He was just about to call out the inevitable "Hello?" when he heard a loud thump and felt the ground tremble below his feet as if some giant beast from the underworld was trying to break free from its lair with a massive hammer. It happened only once, but Sato's feet tingled from the vibration of the impact. Surprisingly, he didn't feel afraid. Not yet, anyway.

There was a loud hiss, muted by the pounding rain, and then the wall directly in front of him began to move outward, toward him.

Sato felt anxiety grip his heart for the first time since arriving, and he stepped back, almost turned to run. But he quickly collected himself, reminding himself that George must have known where he'd been sending him after all. He had nothing to be afraid of.

He realized that it was only the bottom edge of the wall that was moving, swinging out and upward like an old-fashioned garage door. To his left and right, the side walls were doing the same, the groan of metallic hinges a faint squeal in the background. A soft light shone out from an unknown source, turning the thousands of raindrops into silvery sparkles. Sato could see through the cube to the other side where the fourth wall opposite him was opening up like its counterparts. Seconds later, the four walls locked into position parallel to the ground, and all movement stopped with a loud clank. Just a few feet above him, a wide shelter from the weather had formed, the doors and middle sections together now shaped like a square cross supported by four large metal pillars.

His fear gone, Sato stepped out of the rain toward the middle of what used to be a closed building and was now just a really fancy covered patio. He half-expected to see a picnic table or maybe a barbecue grill, but what he found instead surprised him greatly.

A hole.

A round hole, with a spiral set of stairs leading down into its depths and an iron handrail fastened to the wall. The light he'd noticed before was coming from somewhere at the bottom of the hole. Everything in sight was surprisingly dry. A small metal sign was bolted onto the floor right next to the first step, and several words had been stamped onto its surface:

GRACE OF HER HEART CEMETERY

A prickle of fear raised bumps on Sato's flesh, but reason calmed his nerves soon enough. In a place where rain was the norm, it made perfect sense for the dead to be buried in some kind of vault or tomb instead of within the spongy, soaked, muddy earth. Dead people would be floating all over the place if they'd made that mistake. It was a cemetery after all—a normal, peaceful, full-of-bodies graveyard.

And over the last few weeks, Sato had become very used to graveyards.

Blowing a breath through his lips, he squeezed as much water as possible out of his clothes and hair, then set off down the stairs. With each step, an audible squish sounded, inexplicably making him want to laugh. Step by step, round and round, he descended into the hole. With every full circle he made, he saw a square light set into the wall, casting a warm glow—literally. Things heated up quickly and considerably.

After what felt like ten or so floors, Sato reached the bottom of the stairs and stepped through an open doorway. Unable to hold back a gasp of wonder, he gaped at the massive chamber in front of him. Row upon row of metal containers stretched as far as he could see, fading away into a shadowy mist in the distance. Large pillars supported the roof thirty feet or so above him, standing like iron angels guarding the dead.

For that's what filled the room. The dead. In metal caskets, stacked five high, with barely enough room between them for Sato to walk. Sato calculated there had to be thousands of deceased in the underground cemetery. Thousands upon thousands.

It took him four hours and forty-five minutes to find what he was looking for.

The casket looked like every other one in the vast tomb. Made from a dark steel, the slightest shade of silver prevented it from being utterly black. The final resting place of two other souls lay on top, two more beneath, with hundreds to either side. A dirty bronze plaque named the person whose body was inside the casket. Sato reached forward and wiped away the dust, more out of respect for the dead than anything else; he could read the words imprinted on the tarnished plaque just fine.

This was the seventh Reality in which he'd read such words.

It was the casket for Atticus Higginbottom.

〜

Frazier Gunn had grown weary of prisons.

He'd now visited eleven of them, each one more foul than the one before it. Dirty. Grimy. Full of people with no self-control, no humanity. Full of thieves and murderers.

Now, walking down the dark, damp, smelly stone tunnel, escorted by two massively strong Brazilian guards with machine guns, he wondered how much more of this he could take. It didn't help that Mistress Jane had refused to tell him the purpose of the mission he'd undertaken, only the whats and wheres. The hows. None of the whys.

He'd long since gotten over the shock of finding his prey in prison, each and every time. Without fail, his searches had ended at some sort of jail, penitentiary, detention center, or, in three memorable cases, a hospital for the criminally insane. Always in shady institutions run by shady men and women. Always in places where the right price could buy you anything. Were there places in the Realities where this was *not* the case? He doubted it.

They came to a wooden door, heavily bolted and reinforced with a thick chain and lock. The guard to his right grunted something in Portuguese, but Frazier understood him well enough. He reached in his pocket and pulled out a thick wad of cash, obtained that morning at a local bank, in the local currency. He was amazed how easy it was to come up with money when you had someone as powerful as Mistress Jane backing the operation.

When the guard reached for the cash, Frazier pulled his hand away.

"The prisoner," he said, keeping his voice as empty of emotion as possible. "Get me the prisoner."

The man grunted again. Frazier was fully aware that these two brutes could simply take the money and leave him for dead. But he'd been sure to fill their heads with hopes of future deals, future bribes, future money-making opportunities. They'd be idiots to jeopardize such possibilities. It was, of course, a complete lie. Frazier would never, not in a million years, return to this country in this Reality, certainly not to this wretched cesspool of lowlifes. He needed one thing here, and one thing only.

After a long stare-off, the guard finally pulled out his jangly ring of keys and unlocked the chain and the three bolts of the door. He swung the door open, the hinges squealing like tortured rats, then disappeared inside, making it clear with a scowl that Frazier should wait for him to return. Frazier was more than happy to wait, having seen more than enough prisoners and jail cells in the last few weeks.

He stood next to the other fellow, a sour-faced, bearded giant of a man, who looked at the floor and never spoke a word. Frazier could only imagine what darkness lurked inside the man's brain, what memories haunted his dreams at night. For the slightest of moments, Frazier felt sorry for the man.

Several minutes passed, the only sounds that of breathing and a constant, echoing drip of water somewhere down the tunnel. Finally, the guard returned with the prisoner for which Frazier had paid handsomely. The eleventh such prisoner, the eleventh such bribe. And, according to his boss, worth every penny.

The woman stepped forward, still shackled at the wrist. Her black hair was a nest of greasy strings, her torn clothes were filthy, and her long fingernails were crusted with black dirt. For a moment, she refused to meet Frazier's eyes. Irritated, he reached forward and put his hand under her chin, tilting her face up so he could get a good look.

Despite her pale complexion, the smudges of grime, the cracked lips, and the way her skin seemed to squeeze the sharp bones of her skull, he had no doubt, none whatsoever. She was still beautiful to him.

Frazier handed the money to the guard, who then passed over the key to the chains around the prisoner's—the *former* prisoner's—wrist. Frazier nodded once, curtly, then took hold of the woman's arm.

Without saying a word, he turned and escorted the Alterant of Mistress Jane down the long and dark tunnel.

CHAPTER 2

✳

THE KYOOPY QUIZ

O kay," Mr. Chu said, leaning both his elbows on his desk at school and staring down at the open physics book. "If you get this one right, you are The Man. That's capital T, capital M."

"Hit me," Tick responded. Even he could hear the tiredness in his own voice. He'd been studying with Mr. Chu for more than an hour, question after question. Tick was schooled at home now since Master George had insisted that it was too dangerous for Tick to be out and about with classmates and the general public every day. But enough time had passed that Tick had finally convinced his parents and Master George to let him visit Mr. Chu three times a week in the afternoons. Any break from the house was welcome, even if it did involve his former teacher grilling him with questions about physics. Mr. Chu glanced up before continuing, a grin spreading across his face. Tick faltered a moment, hating how much the man looked like his Alterant from the Fourth Reality. Like Reginald Chu. The *evil* Reginald Chu, who was stuck—uncomfortably, Tick hoped—in a place called the Nonex. Too bad Master George didn't have a clue as to where the Nonex was, or what it was, or anything else about it at all.

"Okay," Mr. Chu said, speaking slowly. "How does the wave-particle property paradox contradict the theorems related to radiation damping and nonlinearity in the pilot wave interpretation of quantum mechanics?"

Tick slumped back in his chair. He barely understood the question, much less knew the answer. Figuring his brain had finally gone to sleep, he murmured, "I give up. My head's not working right now."

Mr. Chu laughed, and any remnant of his Alterant was wiped away in a flash. "I was just kidding. I'm not sure the question even made sense, actually."

Tick couldn't help but feel relieved. He needed to understand quantum physics and all the sciences in order to figure out what was wrong with him. He had an extremely dangerous influence over Chi'karda, the force that ruled the world of quantum physics—or QP, as Mr. Chu liked to call it—and Tick had very nearly killed himself and countless others when his Chi'karda had gotten out of control just a few months ago.

Since then, he'd been careful not to get too excited or too angry. So far nothing bad had happened—except for the time he'd sent his poor dad flying across the room and through an upstairs window. If it hadn't been for that bush . . . Well, needless to say, the bush didn't survive, but his dad—whose weight was classified somewhere between pudgy and ginormous—did. Though he had complained about a hurt back for weeks, sending Tick on countless runs to the kitchen to get him cookies and milk to enjoy during their video game battles.

"Tick?" Mr. Chu asked, snapping his fingers.

Tick realized he'd been staring at the floor, completely lost in his thoughts. "Oh. Sorry. I was just thinking about something."

Mr. Chu yawned, then closed the science book with a loud thump. "Well, you've got a lot to think about. Any problems lately?"

"No." He looked into his teacher's eyes, trying to see if he could read anything there. The man had been through just as much as Tick had, and Tick worried about him. "What about you? Have you . . . gotten over it?"

"Gotten over what? Being imprisoned by a bunch of thugs, forced to torment you and your friends, almost killed? What's there to get over?"

Tick shook his head, trying not to look sad, but knowing he did. Thinking back to what had happened in the Fourth Reality, and everything that led up to it, always made him sad. He didn't even really understand why—or at least he told himself that. After all, they'd escaped. They were safe. All seemed fine in the world.

But deep down, he knew why he felt sad. He knew all too well.

It was her. It was Mistress Jane. What he'd *done* to her.

"Tick," Mr. Chu repeated, snapping his fingers again. "What's buzzing in that brain of yours?"

"I didn't mean to hurt her," Tick said, almost whispering. His heart felt like a squishy pile of mud. "I don't even know exactly what I did to her. For all we know, I killed her."

Mr. Chu stood up, shaking his head. "Enough of that." He picked up the book and slid it inside Tick's backpack, then held the pack out toward him. "Seriously. You shouldn't feel one ounce of guilt for something that happened completely out of your control."

Tick didn't respond, just reached out and took his backpack, slipping the straps over his shoulders.

"I'm not even going to talk about it with you anymore," Mr. Chu continued. "Maybe that's making your subconscious mind think it's something you *should* feel guilty about, something you should come to terms with, seek forgiveness for. Well, it's not. As soon as blame the wood for killing with fire."

"Huh?" Tick asked.

Mr. Chu shrugged. "Sorry. It was the best I could come up with."

For some reason, that made Tick feel better. "I'm fine, I guess. It's just that . . . she seemed like maybe she was starting to feel bad about being so evil. I thought maybe she was going to change, maybe even help us."

Mr. Chu put two fingers together and swiped them across his lips like pulling a zipper.

Tick rolled his eyes. "Fine. Well, thanks for helping me study. I'll see ya next week."

"Sounds like a plan. Study the chapter on natural electricity's role in physics carefully. A lot of things build off that information."

"I will. See ya."

"Take care." Mr. Chu smiled then, and he looked nothing like his diabolical twin who had almost driven billions of people permanently insane.

Tick turned and headed out the door, deciding at the last second to swing by the city library to check his e-mail before going home. He was looking forward to the best weekend ever—his sisters Lisa and Kayla had gone to stay with their cousins in Seattle until Monday night. Uncle Ben and Aunt Holly had two daughters the same ages as Tick's sisters, and the two families swapped weekends between Deer Park and Seattle about every five months.

No girls for three whole days. Well, unless you counted his mom, which he really didn't.

Peace and quiet. Books, junk food, and video games. It was gonna be great.

⁓

Mrs. Sears, the librarian, was in her usual good mood, greeting Tick with that lilting laugh of hers as the gray cleaning pad she called her hair wiggled back and forth on her head. She asked him about the pros and cons of homeschooling, the latest books he'd been reading, and how he'd been faring against his dad in the latest installment of his favorite video game, Football 4000. But every time he answered a question, he eyed the long line of computers, trying to give her a hint.

Finally she nodded toward an empty chair and said, "Well, I know why you're here. Go on, and I'll find you a good book before you head out. Deal?"

"Deal," Tick responded, already moving away.

He was logged into his e-mail in no time. Just as he'd hoped, there was a letter from Sofia and one from Paul. Jackpot. Paul's had been sent first, addressed to both Tick and Sofia, as usual. Tick opened Paul's e-mail and began reading.

Dudes,

Okay, I'm bored. When the highlight of your day is
getting an e-mail from some chick in Italy about
how she hurt her pinky toe in a vicious spaghetti
sauce can incident, you know it's time to change
things. Where in the world is Master George?
Yeah, I know we almost died and all that in the
Fourth, but better that than getting up at the
crack of dawn for school and then sitting around
all afternoon eating cheese puffs. I can't watch TV
anymore. Too boring.

Tick, how's that whole power thing of yours
working out? Melted any bad guys recently?
Dude, I was thinking we could present you to the
world as the first human microwave oven. We'd
be rich, and the ladies would swarm. Think about it.
We'll split it 50–50. You do the cooking, I'll do the
promoting.

Sofia, when you gonna bring us out to Italy?
Don't give me any junk about money. Just ask ol'
Pops to slip you a few bones to buy us airplane
tickets. I'll even bring you some hot dogs. No,
make that corn dogs. Yeah. Corn dogs and Italy.
Now that's living.

I'm out. Any time you start mentioning corn dogs, you know it's time to end the e-mail. Later. Call us in, Master George!

Paul

Still snickering, Tick closed the e-mail and opened Sofia's, which had been sent soon after Paul's, despite the time difference.

Dudes?

Did you really start that last e-mail with "Dudes"?!?!? Promise me you'll call me a dude next time I see you. Oh, and "chick from Italy"? You're getting awfully brave, Rogers, what with an entire ocean between us. Next time we meet, you might want to wear something made of metal.

I'm kind of bored too. Things with my parents seem worse than ever. All my old friends just seem stupid now. I hate how clueless they are. They have no idea what kind of stuff is going on out there.

I wish I had a funny joke. But once Paul says something that's actually funny, I'll try harder.

Seriously, though, I do think you guys should
come to Italy. I'll ask Frupey about it. Maybe this
summer. Of course, I hope we're doing something
as Realitants by then.

See ya.
Sofia

Tick looked at his watch and realized he should
probably get home. His mom worried her head off
every time he left the house these days. Deciding he'd
just write his friends from home later, he logged off,
checked out the book Mrs. Sears recommended, then
headed out the door.

Just a few minutes later, he was walking down the
long road toward his neighborhood, surprised that he
was already sweating.

It was almost spring, but it was still too early to
be *hot* in Deer Park, Washington. Since his escape
from the Fourth Reality, Tick had seen his birthday
come and go—he was a manly fourteen years old
now. Thanksgiving, Christmas, the New Year, and
most of the winter had passed as well; April was just
a few days away. Tick had heard less and less from

Master George in the last month or so. It gave him an uneasy feeling. He wondered if it was the calm before the storm.

He wondered about Mistress Jane, too. He'd give anything to know what had happened to her. Whether or not she was still alive. And if so, whether or not she was okay. He dreamed about her at night, reliving those terrible moments in Chu's palace when he'd sent a world of chaos at her body and attacked her with thousands of flying shards of metal.

For some reason, he'd lately had dreams where one of his sisters—sometimes Lisa, sometimes Kayla—replaced Jane and suffered the terrible onslaught instead, screaming in agony. He woke up in a sweat every time, and seeing it play out that way humanized the ordeal, made it more real. No matter what she'd done in the past, Jane was still a person, just like Lisa and Kayla.

His actions haunted him, consumed him with guilt. He wished—

Womp!

Tick stumbled to the ground, crying out as one of his elbows banged against the rock-hard dirt of the road's shoulder. He twisted onto his back, fear ripping through his body. He searched around with his eyes, tried to figure out what had happened. It'd been like a wave of hardened air had slammed against him, knocking him down with a sound like the thump of a million bass drums . . .

Womp!

He braced himself as a massive surge of energy swept across the road and past him. He expected his hair and clothes to whip in the wind, but nothing stirred. He almost felt the energy . . . *inside* his body. As if someone had injected charges of lightning into his bloodstream.

Womp!

Tick squeezed his eyes shut. He felt a surge of heat in his chest, an intense pressure that enveloped his body, then it disappeared. Terrified, he scrambled to his feet, stumbling in a circle as he searched around him. There was nothing unusual in sight, nothing out of the ordinary.

Womp!

Tick took a step backward, wrapping his arms tightly around him, tensing as the wave of force hit again. With each surge of energy, he felt heat within his heart and veins, like a raging fever. Heat. Pressure. Squeezing. But only for an instant. Then it was gone again.

Gasping for breath, he stood as still as possible, peeking through squinted eyes, waiting for it to happen again. His mind churned, trying to imagine what it could be. In some ways it felt like the attack of

Chi'karda he'd had when everything had gone crazy in
Reginald Chu's research chamber.

Similar, but different.

This wasn't coming *from* him. He was feeling it
coming from *somewhere else.*

A blast of panic shot through his nerves. From
somewhere else . . .

Womp!

The wave hit again. Tick sprinted for home.

CHAPTER 3

✳

A STRANGE GUEST

Lorena Higginbottom sat in the chair where she always waited for Atticus to come home from his visits with Mr. Chu at school. Her constant worrying over the boy had done strange things to her. She couldn't sleep, couldn't concentrate. She rarely laughed anymore. Sometimes—not often, but sometimes—the worry turned into utter misery, engulfing her like a horrible, *eating* cancer.

Her boy. Her one and only boy. Mixed up with the Realitants and plagued with a burden of power that no one understood yet. Something was terribly, terribly wrong with him.

She'd gone through all the usual phases. The denial,

the blame, the guilt, the despair. She'd run the whole gamut of emotions over the last few months, and it had all come to a head this morning. When her husband, Edgar, had left for work, and Atticus had disappeared into his room to study, she'd sat in her room, crying, *sobbing*, a sorry sack of gloom and grief. It had taken every ounce of willpower in her body to pull her anguish back inside and hide it away. But she did, for Atticus's sake.

With a smile on her face, she'd seen him off to his appointment with his former and favorite teacher. She'd been sitting in her chair ever since, counting down the minutes until he returned. *I should've gone with him,* she thought, just as she did every single time Atticus left the house. But she couldn't. She knew that. She and Edgar had long since agreed that they couldn't exist in a constant state of terror and fear. Atticus needed time alone, time to grow, time to learn how to bear his burden. Still, he was only a child, only fourteen . . .

A rattling sound from the back of the house snapped her mind alert.

Like a shot of pure caffeine, adrenaline rushed through her body, and she jumped out of the chair before any thought had time to form. Wondering why Atticus would come home the back way—and feeling the slightest fear that it might *not* be him—she ran out of the room and down the hallway, into the kitchen, toward the door leading to the patio behind their home.

The rattling noise continued. Someone was pulling at the knob, twisting it back and forth in vain because it was locked.

The trickle of fear turned into a gush; she pulled up just short of the patio door.

"Atticus?" she called out.

No answer. But whoever was out there quit trying to open the door.

"Atticus?" she repeated, louder.

Still no answer.

The door had a large window, currently covered by the drawn yellow curtain. Alarmed, she grabbed the side of the stiff material and pulled it back an inch, peeking outside.

The thing standing on her back patio wasn't her son.

⁓

When his house finally came into view, Tick somehow found another burst of energy and ran faster. The loud thumps and waves of energy had stopped, but he couldn't rest until he made sure everything was okay at home. A fresh spurt of panic squeezed his insides, and he picked up the pace yet again.

He was only two houses away when he noticed a car coming down the road from the other direction. His heart skipped a beat when he saw that it was his dad's.

Then his heart almost stopped beating altogether when the car suddenly accelerated, the engine screaming, the tires squealing. The car swerved off the road, over the curb, and onto his front lawn. It shot across the grass until it reached the driveway, picking up speed instead of slowing down.

Tick watched in horror as the car slammed into the garage door with a thunderous crunch, then disappeared in a pile of shredded wood and dust.

In her head, Lorena couldn't reconcile the thing she saw through the door's window with any semblance of reality she knew or felt. It looked like something out of a science fiction movie—a man-shaped, shimmering ghost made out of clear liquid, its rippled surface glistening. The face had no features, but it seemed to be looking at her all the same.

For a bare instant, she actually considered unlocking and opening the door. The creature seemed so harmless, so peaceful, the water rippling like the gentle, lapping waves of a Caribbean beach. But her hand froze halfway to the latch, and a shudder of fear snapped her out of her hypnotized state. Her mind kicked into gear, reminding her that creatures made out of water were not normal, that although she'd lived a life believing only in things that were *normal,* not supernatural, seeing this creature probably changed things forever.

The sparkling water creature she saw through the window could *not* be a good thing. And most likely, it had something to do with her son.

She stepped back, her hand rising involuntarily to her mouth as the shock of her visitor hit home. Somehow she knew that something terrible was about to happen.

The creature's watery hand reached out and grabbed the outside door handle, rattling it again. Lorena couldn't actually see the knob from her angle, and she wondered how the thing grasped objects if it was made only out of liquid. Then better sense told her that now probably wasn't the best time to figure out the physics of the situation, and that she'd better run.

But just as she took a step away from the door, the creature *melted* right in front of her, the water crashing to the pavement outside with a loud splash. It was as if a force field or an invisible membrane had been holding the thing together, and it had been abruptly taken away, leaving nothing to hold the body together. She realized she'd been holding her breath and sucked in a huge gulp of air in relief. Whatever it had been, whatever purpose . . .

Her thoughts were cut short when movement down by her feet caught her vision.

In the thin space between the door's lower edge

and the short strip of wood that kept out the wind and bugs, a three-foot wide sheet of water began pouring through and onto the kitchen floor. A puddle formed in a matter of seconds, somehow deepening into a narrow pool on the flat linoleum surface.

Before Lorena could react, a horrendous crash rocked the house, the sounds of crunched metal and shredded wood thundering through the air like a sonic boom.

Even as her hands rose to cover her ears, even as the beginnings of a scream formed somewhere in the back of her throat, Lorena saw the puddle at her feet bubble and churn, swirling, coalescing into a bulbous glob, like a huge see-through water balloon about to burst.

And then the glob rose toward the ceiling, slowly re-forming its human shape.

The scream finally escaped Lorena's mouth.

"Dad!"

Tick had faltered when the car hit the house. He was too stunned to move. Of all the things he'd expected to see when he came home, it wasn't this.

He shook himself out of his daze and ran for the mangled mess of the garage. A hissing sound came from within, the engine letting out its last, dying breath. Smoke and dust billowed out, attacking Tick's lungs with a vengeance. Coughing, he kicked at the loose metal and broken boards, digging his way in to see if his dad was okay.

"Dad!" he yelled again.

He'd just moved a big chunk of something heavy when the front door to the car popped free, a horrible metal groan screeching through the air as his dad forced it open all the way.

"Dad! What's going—"

Tick's voice stuck in his throat when he saw the large body of Edgar Higginbottom stumble out of the car and fall onto the garage floor.

He was covered in . . . goo. Clear goo.

Frozen by fear. Not able to move. Your mind screaming at your legs to run, but your legs not listening. This was why Lorena had left the Realitants long ago, hoping she'd never have to experience it again.

She stared as the mysterious, impossible thing formed, water sluicing upward from the floor, defying the law of gravity in the process. Legs, then torso, then arms, finally a head. The entire process took less than twenty seconds, but it looked unnatural, like a time-lapse film of a geological event that had taken thousands of years.

When the creature finished re-forming, the watery demon stood silent for a long moment, staring at her despite the lack of eyeballs or even eye sockets.

Lorena stared back, frozen as much by stubborn disbelief as fear.

Without warning, the creature moved toward her.

CHAPTER 4

＊

DEATH BY WATER

Tick's dad thrashed about on the garage floor, the thick layer of transparent goo that covered every part of his body bouncing and wiggling like jelly. The gel-like substance was never more than an inch thick in any one spot, but it enveloped Edgar from head to toe. Most alarming was the clear mask covering his face.

The man obviously couldn't breathe. More than a year ago, Tick had almost seen his dad die; he felt the same horrible panic now.

"Dad!" Tick yelled again. He knew screaming wasn't going to help no matter how many times he did it. He had to *do* something.

He knelt down beside his squirming dad, who kept

grabbing and tearing at the gel on his face, ripping sections away from his mouth to catch a quick breath only to have the goo be replaced almost instantly. When Tick saw his dad's hands rip at the stuff and saw the way it splashed and wavered, he realized it wasn't goo at all.

It was *water*.

Somehow, some force had captured his dad in a man-sized pool of water.

And it was killing him.

Something trembled inside Tick, fluttered, as if a raven had magically appeared inside his stomach and was trying to escape. Heat surged through his veins. Pressure built up behind his skull, pushing outward, hurting. He closed his eyes, rubbed them.

His . . . *problem*. He knew it was his problem. The stress of the situation had ignited his inexplicable reservoir of Chi'karda, causing it to erupt inside him. It was just like what had happened in Chu's palace. It was starting all over again. But he couldn't afford to lose control now.

No, he told himself. *Not this time. I have to save Dad.*

He took several long breaths and concentrated, probing his body with his thoughts, reaching out to something he didn't comprehend. Repressing it, pushing it away. Calming himself. He imagined the Chi'karda surge as a cloud of orange mist—as Mistress Jane had shown him months ago—trapped within his rib cage. Mentally, he made the cloud dissipate, weaken, flow out of him. Go somewhere else. Somewhere safe.

He had no idea what he was doing. He'd spent months trying to understand the power within him, make it a tangible thing. He'd spent months failing. But urgency won out. He felt his heart slow, felt the heat cool away, felt the pressure release.

It was gone. Tick opened his eyes, looked down, focused.

His dad's face was turning purple.

⟋⟍

Lorena's screams were drowned out in a sickening gurgle as the cold wave of water crashed into her. The creature had leaped into the air and dove for her face, forming into a thick stream and slamming into her like a sudden burst from a fire hose. She shook her head, spitting and coughing, and grabbed at her face. Instead of washing off her and falling to the floor, the liquid seemed to stick, enveloping her head and neck in a mask of water. It crept into her mouth, into her throat. She gagged, spit again. She wiped frantically at her face, but it did no good.

The terrifying situation had created a crisp sense of clarity in her mind, and an idea formed somewhere in the dark factory of her thoughts. A very bizarre idea.

She turned and bolted for the garage. With every step,

she felt rivulets of water running down her torso, the creature capturing her inch by inch. She knew she wouldn't be able to move once the thing had control of her legs.

The garage. She had to reach the garage. She made it out of the kitchen and into the short hallway with coat hooks and shoe racks. The door was only a few feet away.

The water reached her knees. She felt herself slow a bit.

She lurched forward, reaching for the door that led to the garage. One arm had been taken completely over, and the other had only a second left before its fingers would be swallowed by the possessed water. The liquid encasing her arms made it harder to control her movements, but the creature seemed mostly focused on her head. She found the handle. She twisted the knob and pulled. An instant later, the wet monster had consumed her fully.

Lorena fell forward and toppled down the three stairs that descended into the garage. Ironically, the thick layer of water cushioned her fall.

⁓

Tick slapped at his dad's face with cupped hands, like a dog digging for a bone. Each swing caught a little pool of water and sent it flying, but more instantly sloshed back in, and the displaced splashes somehow flew back onto his dad's body like metal shavings returning to a powerful magnet. Every once in a while their combined efforts would clear just enough water for his dad to take a quick breath, but Tick knew they couldn't keep it up much longer.

The garage door that led to the inside of the house banged open.

Tick looked up and saw his mom. Fully encased in water just like his dad, she fell down the short staircase and crashed onto the floor with a wet flump.

"Mom!" Tick cried, scrambling over to her and falling on top of her. He could only hope his dad could find enough breaths to survive.

His mom clawed at the water around her nose and mouth. She kept trying to say something, but all that came out was the garbled mess you hear when someone talks to you while submerged in the swimming pool. Her eyes were open, fixed on Tick through the crystal-line, shimmering layer of water. She wasn't panicked, but definitely trying to communicate something.

Tick forced himself to stay calm. Reaching forward, he placed his hands on either side of her face. She got the message, and remained completely still. With a quick jerk, Tick slid his hands across her mouth, swiping away a huge section of water long enough for her to get one word out.

He didn't know what he'd expected, but it sure wasn't the two syllables that came out of her mouth in a gargled scream.

"Vacuum!" she yelled.

At first, confusion engulfed Tick. He thought surely his mom's mind had snapped under the pressure of being possessed by a blob of water. But then he realized it was quite the opposite. She'd been the only one to actually come up with a solution.

He turned his head to look over his shoulder, across his dad's heap of a wrecked car, and focused on the huge beast of a machine that sat next to some tools and cleaning supplies on an old wooden workbench.

The MegaVac. The thing looked like R2-D2 with a big hose.

And it could suck water out of rock.

Tick got up and ran around the front of the crashed car and over to the workbench. He reached up and grabbed the heavy, squat yellow cylinder with its thick, snaking hose attached. He dragged the vacuum toward his mom, whose face was darkening into a sick blue color.

"Mom!" he yelled. "Keep swiping at it!"

He reached her and flipped the switch on the MegaVac.

It didn't turn on.

For one agonizing second, despair crushed Tick.

But then he realized the stupid thing wasn't plugged in. He scrambled for the long black cord, found its end, then crawled over to an outlet and pushed the big plug in. A heavy roar kicked in behind him. Tick scooted back over and knelt down beside his mom, grasping the end of the vacuum hose like the mouth of a deadly cobra.

The thing worked like a beauty.

He stuck the hose on his mom's mouth and watched with elation as the vacuum sucked up the water with no problem. The MegaVac had been a birthday present for his dad two years ago, and Edgar had excitedly given a demonstration to the family on how the beast could make *anything* disappear into its glorious, hard-plastic belly, be it cereal bits or gallons of floodwater. It was the closest thing to a black hole that the Higginbottoms would ever experience, he'd said.

Tick wanted to shout in victory as he realized even a supernatural creature made of liquid couldn't resist the monstrous sucking power of a MegaVac, lord of all vacuums.

He finished cleaning the water off his mom, her soggy hair and clothes the only sign she'd been encased by a water monster just moments before. Tick's dad was only a few feet behind him, and twenty seconds later, the vacuum had sucked up his captor too.

Tick leaned back, panting as his mom and dad

gasped and spit, doing their best to recover from the ordeal. He thought of Lisa and Kayla in Seattle, and had an almost overwhelming feeling of relief that they hadn't been here. The odds of Lisa—and especially little Kayla—surviving something like this . . . Tick quenched the horrible thought before images formed that might never go away.

He looked over at the body of the MegaVac, which now contained two—what exactly were those creatures?—within its belly.

A worry hit him. He didn't want to turn off the vacuum for fear the creatures would find a way to seep back down the hose. "What should we do? Do you think we killed them?"

His dad laughed, a mere sputter between heavy breaths. "I say we flush the suckers' guts down the toilet. That oughtta do it."

And that's what they did.

CHAPTER 5

✳

A MOTHER'S LOVE

Sofia leaned forward against the railing of the balcony outside her bedroom, resting her elbows on the smooth stone as she looked out over her family's estate toward the east, where the sun slowly rose above the horizon. The orange glow sparkled on the waters of the Adriatic Sea in the distance. A cold breeze blew past, stirring her black hair and sending chills across her arms and down her back. Though she enjoyed the cold—it was just pleasant enough to keep her awake, keep her alert and alive—she pulled her jacket tighter.

She missed Tick and Paul. She missed Sato. Master George, Mothball, all of them. Even Rutger.

Days dragged like weeks now. Their adventures in the Fourth seemed like a million years ago. She knew it was crazy to want something to happen again, considering they'd almost died, but ever since she'd returned home, returned to school, and gone through the motions of a normal life, she'd been utterly bored out of her mind.

The Realitants were her true friends now. Yes, Frupey the Butler was good to her, kind to her, ready to fulfill any command she spoke, but he was paid to do that. She had her parents, of course . . .

"Sofia?" said a soft voice.

Startled, Sofia whipped around to see her mom standing behind her—as if she'd snuck up on her. Arms crossed, her mom rubbed her shoulders through her fur coat, looking cold and miserable.

"I'm sorry if I scared you," her mom said. In Italian, of course. How Sofia missed speaking in English with Tick and Paul.

"It's okay," Sofia replied, turning back to the railing and her previous position so her mom wouldn't see the roll of her eyes. Of all the days to come up here. She couldn't remember the last time either one of her parents had stood on this balcony atop their mansion. And Sofia wasn't in the mood.

Her mom stepped up beside her and leaned forward just like Sofia, almost mockingly copying her. "I've been meaning to talk to you about something.

Ever since you . . . came back. Ever since I realized how close we came to losing you."

Not this, Sofia thought. *Please, not this.* "Mom, I'm not quitting the Realitants. I don't care what you say. It's too important."

Her mom stiffened, then relaxed. "I don't care for that tone, young lady. I'm your *mother.*"

Sofia was shocked but quickly tried to hide it. Her mom never showed the slightest hint of parenting or discipline. Almost not knowing how to respond, Sofia muttered an apology.

"In any case," her mom said, "that's not what this is about. Your father and I recognize that this . . . Realitant thing is something you will do, either with our consent or without it. Which is why I want to make sure you understand something. I think it will show you how much we care about you, despite what you may think."

Sofia couldn't help but be intrigued. It'd been years since they'd had such a conversation. "What is it?" She didn't look at her mom, but kept her eyes on the distant, brightening horizon.

"Well," her mom started, then hesitated. "It's hard to know how to say it, so please hear me out. Your father and I never intended for you to be born. I mean, we'd made a decision early on to never have children. We never meant to have you."

Sofia almost choked on the lump that blossomed in her throat. "*That's* what you came up here to tell me?"

"Now, now, I told you to hear me out," her mom quickly responded, patting Sofia's arm. "Listen to me—we never intended to have you or any child, but you came anyway. Unexpectedly. And even though it was against all of our plans, even though it hindered your father's career and made it difficult for us to travel and accomplish the goals we'd set out before getting married . . . Well, I think you can see that despite all that, we accepted it and raised you and have always provided you with whatever you needed. And, above all else, we made sure to love you."

Sofia shifted her hands so she could grip the edge of the railing, squeezing hard to prevent her arms from shaking. Something terrible formed in her chest, something bulging and hurtful and full of bad things. It seemed to reach through her heart, through her throat, grabbing her mind and soul, begging her to cry. That was it. Every piece of her wanted to bawl her eyes out, sob until she felt nothing.

But she refused. She didn't understand how she did it, but she refused to let the tears come. There was no way she would let her mom see such a thing and misinterpret it, think that she'd finally bonded with her only child. Mistake her tears for love.

Concentrating with all her might, Sofia forced the

heavy feeling away and took control of her emotions. Finally, she relaxed her hands.

"Well?" her mom said after a long few seconds. "Do you understand? Is everything okay now? Better?"

"Yes," Sofia said, pushing the word out of her mouth, praying it was over and her mom would walk away.

"That's wonderful." She patted Sofia's arm again. "You know I love you, right?"

"Yes, Mom."

"And you love me?"

"Yes, Mom." That's all Sofia could manage. Just those two words. She clung to them, hoped they'd be enough to end this conversation.

"And your father?"

"Yes, Mom."

"Great. I'm so glad we had this talk. Aren't you?"

"Yes, Mom."

"Okay, then. Your father and I are going away for a few days. We'll be leaving tonight. Bye, now."

And with that, she turned and walked away.

Sofia thought about the fact that they hadn't even hugged. She knew it should bother her as much as everything else, but it didn't. Sadly, it didn't bother her at all.

When she was absolutely sure her mom wasn't coming back, Sofia finally gave up the internal battle and decided to let the tears flow.

But nothing came.

An hour passed. Maybe more. She couldn't really tell. She felt like she was in a haze, numb to the world. Eventually the cold got to her, and she went inside, though in some ways, the house felt chillier.

For a while she wandered the large house, completely ignoring the paintings and vases and tapestries and wood paneling and plush carpet that marked it as a mansion. She wandered, dreading her afternoon lessons with Lolita the private tutor. Sofia longed for the weekend, for two full days of nothing and no one—even though she knew she'd spend it sulking and checking the computer every two minutes for e-mails from Tick or Paul.

She entered the massive kitchen, all marble tile and shiny silver appliances, hoping a snack from the fridge would jump-start her from the doldrums. Frupey—his blond hair slicked back as usual—and the head cook were there, planning meals for the few days Sofia's parents would be gone. When that was the case—which was often—Frupey and the cook schemed to make dinner a little more tasty for Sofia, a little less healthy. Sometimes they even spoiled her with hot dogs, a secret she'd never dare tell her friends back in America.

"Sofia," Frupey said when he noticed her. "I was just going to come for you. I've received word that you have a friend coming within the hour."

Sofia felt a tinge of excitement, and the dull blahs inside her vanished. A friend? Her immediate thought was it had to be a Realitant. Maybe Mothball or Rutger.

"Really?" she asked, trying not to sound too eager. "Who is it? And what do you mean you *received word?*"

"Well, it's rather strange." Frupey stood straight, arms clasped behind his back. Ever the butler. "A metal tube came flying through a window. It thoroughly shattered the glass and required quite the cleanup. Based on your stories of, well, you know, your new friends, I thought it must be from the adventurous science people."

Sofia's heart soared. It *was* them. She couldn't wait to give Master George a hard time about his less-than-apt abilities at placing his message tubes when winking them.

"What did it say?" she asked. "Where is it?"

Frupey bowed and pulled a small piece of white cardstock from his jacket pocket and handed it over to her.

She snatched it out of his hands with a quickly murmured thank you and read it:

```
Sofia, we'll be there straightaway
to pick you up. Within the hour.
It's most urgent!

MG
```

Unable to hide a grin, and now thrilled that her parents were leaving, she ran from the kitchen without another word to Frupey so she could pack a few things for her trip.

Master George came alone.

Sofia had been standing on the large brick porch for thirty minutes, the strap of her bag digging into her shoulder, staring down the long paved drive, waiting anxiously. When she spotted the old man shuffling along with an almost comical, hurried gait, she sprinted out to meet him.

"Why didn't you just have me go to the usual cemetery?" she asked when she reached his side.

Master George stopped walking, bent over and put his hands on his knees to catch a few deep breaths.

"I don't mean to wink you back to headquarters for now," he finally responded. "Believe it or not, I've left Sally in charge of the Barrier Wands back at headquarters. I came to pick you up personally so we could travel together to our next location."

"Which is?" Sofia urged. She could hardly stand the anticipation; the desire to get away from her large and dreary house was almost overwhelming.

Master George stood straight again, fixing his gaze

on her. His ruddy face framed eyes full of concern. "Sofia, I don't quite know how to say it. We've received an . . . invitation. A very odd one, at that."

"Really? From who? For what?"

"Let's just say it frightens me greatly. Come on. We need to make our way back to the cemetery so we can wink to Florida and pick up Paul. I'll explain along the way." He turned and started down the drive.

Sofia, baffled but full of excitement, followed.

CHAPTER 6

FINGER ON THE PULSE

Tick suspected he'd probably think the whole incident hilarious a few years down the road. They'd killed two monstrous water creatures with a vacuum cleaner and a dozen toilet flushes. But that night, lying in his bed, all he could think about as he stared at the dark ceiling was how close it had been. What it was like to see his mom's face behind that deadly mask of water and his dad's big body thrash around on the floor. What it was like to see his parents—both of them— almost die.

It hurt. It haunted. And he couldn't get the images out of his mind. People always used the phrase "too close for comfort," and after all he'd been through, and more than ever tonight, he understood what that meant on a very deep level. Especially when he considered how lucky they were Lisa and Kayla had gone away for the weekend. He knew there'd be no sleep for him tonight. Even if there were, it'd be full of nightmares.

Sighing, he rolled over onto his side and looked at the closet. The door was shut. He hadn't consciously thought about it before, but he was pretty sure that door had been closed every night since the Gnat Rat had shown up and attacked him. Compared to the things happening to him now, that incident almost seemed funny. Almost silly.

Compared to his . . . problem.

That was the word he'd started using when referring to whatever was wrong with him. Somehow, for some reason, he had a natural surplus—an *extreme* surplus—of Chi'karda, that quiet force that explains and controls the world of quantum physics and therefore everything in the universe. The fact that Mistress Jane had pulled it out of him, shown it to him, burned the visual in his mind forever, only made it more terrifying.

He had enough Chi'karda inside him to power a Barrier Wand. He had enough to disintegrate a spaceship-sized weapon of metal. Enough to destroy one of the largest buildings in all of the Realities. He'd said it before, and he felt it now, for the millionth time.

He was a freak. A dangerous, out-of-control freak.

But then he felt the slightest glimmer of hope,

almost like a visible light in his shadowed room of nighttime. In the garage, when he had started to lose control, he'd been able to pull back, make it stop. The more he thought about it, the better he felt.

He'd stopped. He'd controlled the power. That was a huge thing. The realization hadn't really hit him until now—he'd been too preoccupied with the aftermath of the attack by the water creatures—but the Chi'karda had almost exploded within him, and he'd made it go away!

Tick sat up in bed, wrapping his arms around his knees. He had to tell Sofia and Paul. And Master George, of course. He looked over at the digital clock on his desk and read the time—just a few minutes before midnight. No way he could wait until morning.

Swinging his legs off the bed, he stood up and headed for the computer downstairs.

The house was dark and silent, the faint swooshing of the refrigerator the only sound. Tick knew his odds of making it downstairs without his dad hearing him were tiny, but he tried all the same, creeping along on his tiptoes, hitting all the quiet spots in the floor and on the stairs he'd scouted out long ago. If Dad did come down, surely he'd understand why Tick wanted so urgently to tell his friends about what had happened.

And to make sure nothing had attacked them.

Once in his e-mail program, and after feeling a little disappointed that he had no messages waiting for him, he created a new one for Paul and Sofia. He started typing.

Hey guys,

I don't even know where to start. Crazy day.
Horrible day. Worst day since that stuff in the
Fourth. Guess I'll just tell it how it went.

It started while I was walking home from school
after my normal visit with Mr. Chu. (Sofia, I
know you hate him, but he's not the same guy
as Reginald. He was being controlled when he
kidnapped us. Get over it!)

Anyway, I got hit by this weird feeling, like a huge
electrical charge, like some kind of invisible power,
hitting me in waves. Then things got worse.

Tick went on to tell them about the run home, finding his parents under attack by the water creatures, fighting the things, killing them with the vacuum. Flushing them down the toilet.

He winced when he typed that part, already imagining the response from Sofia. It was like handing your enemy a thousand rounds of ammo so they could shoot you with more ease. And glee. She'd have a field day with that stuff.

He paused for a moment, wishing he could make the fight sound tougher, scarier. Like it had been in real life. In an e-mail, it sounded completely stupid. Might as well write, *Hey guys, you should've seen how I wielded that vacuum cleaner! I was invincible!*

Groaning, he continued typing.

Well, it was a lot worse than it sounds. Trust me. I just wish I knew where they came from, what they were, and who sent them. And what those weird waves of power I felt were. Has anything happened to you guys? We better be extra careful, really be on the lookout.

I think we should talk again on the Internet phone-thingy Sofia's butler helped us all set up. Since tomorrow is Saturday, what about in the morning (for me)—9:00? Let me know.

Tick
Realitant First Class

Tick always signed his e-mails that way, purely for one reason: it bugged the heck out of Sofia. He clicked

SEND, then sat back and folded his arms, watching the screen as it confirmed the message had been sent on its way.

His thoughts wandered. He saw his mom, encased in water, writhing on the floor. His dad's face growing purple. Remembered the terror of those few moments in the garage, before they were safe. He felt as if his heart had turned to lead.

What if it happened again? Almost certainly, it would. Something like it. Or worse.

A yawn leaked out, almost surprising him, and he snapped out of his stupor. Stretching his arms high above his head, he stood up from the chair, then leaned forward to shut down the computer. Once finished, he turned to head up for bed, already dreading the dreams that might await him.

Womp.

Tick sucked in a breath, reaching out to grab the back of the desk chair. The burst of energy had swept across him, throwing off his balance. Once he was sure he was stable and could stand, he looked around him, searching his surroundings. All he could see were shadows draped across more shadows, a faint light coming through the windows, another small glow from a nightlight down the hall. But the house was mostly dark, and everything seemed a great hiding spot for a monster ready to spring for him.

Womp.

Again. This time he realized how much *smaller* the energy wave was than those that had hit him earlier that afternoon on the road home from school. It had only been remembering that experience that sent terror pumping his heart when he'd felt the burst of energy this time. He calmed, just a little.

Womp.

Definitely smaller. Weaker. Whatever the word was. Barely there, almost a vibration. A sound that was not quite a sound.

Womp.

A pulse. That described it better than anything else. He was feeling a pulse of energy, sweeping through the air, through his skin, rattling his insides like a tuning fork. He could sense its source, just like he'd be able to tell from which direction he heard a radio or piano playing.

Womp . . . womp . . . womp . . .

Again and again.

It was coming from the basement.

CHAPTER 7

*

BENEATH

Tick's racing heart eased when he realized the pulse was far less powerful this time, felt less dangerous. But having it come from the basement—the unfinished, cement-floored, dark and cold basement? That was way worse than a closet.

He had to investigate. He had no choice on the matter. He was a Realitant, and he'd brought this danger—if it *was* a danger, and it didn't take a genius to jump to that conclusion—to his family, to his home. Responsibility for that hung like a huge sack of rocks, draped with ropes across his back. Despite what he'd experienced so far with the mysterious power within him, despite what he'd done to Chu's palace and the weapon called Dark Infinity, despite what he'd done to—

70

He cut off the thought. The point was, he didn't *feel* powerful. Not in the least. Having a gun does you no good if it's missing the trigger.

Womp . . . womp . . . womp . . .

But none of that mattered. Something weird pulsed in his basement, and he was going down there to figure out what.

He realized his hands were clasped tightly into fists. If he'd had long nails, his palms would be bleeding like geysers. He forced himself to relax, flexing his fingers and taking several deep breaths. Then he headed out of the room, down the hall, toward the door to the basement.

He hesitated in front of it, as though the black shadows of the hallway clung to him like a gluey mass. He stared at the knob, a stub of gold that was the only spot of color in the darkness. The throbs of the unseen force continued, a small vibration in his skull.

He opened the door and stepped through it onto the landing of the stairway that led below. If he'd thought it had been dark before, the bottom of the stairs was a lightless abyss. He fumbled for the switch, found it and turned on the light, banishing the shadows. Before him lay the wooden staircase, surrounded with bare white walls with a cement floor at the bottom. He couldn't see anything else yet.

Womp . . . womp . . . womp . . .

The pulse strengthened slightly, calling to him from the basement. He had the sudden and terrifying thought that maybe he'd been hypnotized, that he was acting irrationally. He stopped before taking the first step. Was he nuts for even thinking about going down there? The first time he'd felt this energy pulse, something terrible had happened.

But he had to do it. He had to. He wondered if he should get his dad, but pushed the thought away. The hairs of his arms standing on end, he started down the stairs. Even treading lightly, each footfall still made a deadened thump. He wished the steps had carpet. He descended further, running his right hand along the wall, making a soft scraping sound, almost a swish.

Womp . . . womp . . . womp . . .

He reached the bottom, then darted toward the long string that fell from the ceiling, attached to a single lightbulb. He pulled the string, waiting in dread to see what the light would reveal. When the bulb clicked on and the room brightened, nothing seemed out of the ordinary. The single room in the half-basement was maybe twenty feet wide, and Tick couldn't see anything out of the ordinary.

The room was cluttered with boxes, bags, plastic tubs full of old clothes, a horizontal pole holding up dusty coats on hangers, a rack of shoes which hadn't been worn in years, a pile of Christmas decorations that hadn't quite been put away yet. He wondered if his mom even knew her wonderful and faithful husband had neglected that duty for months now.

But the pulsing continued, stronger now, though nothing like what he'd felt on the street. Still, it was powerful enough that the energy surrounded him, throbbing, and he couldn't tell from which direction it came.

Womp . . . womp . . . womp . . .

He slowly turned in a circle, scanning every inch of the room with his eyes. Boxes, tubs, junk. Nothing else.

The pulse stopped. Cut off.

It didn't slow, didn't fade. It stopped, abruptly. A powerful silence filled the air. Tick's skin tingled, as if it had grown used to the almost comforting vibrations of the energy waves and wanted them back. He heard his own breathing as he continued to turn, and for some reason that creeped him out. He felt stuck in one of those nightmares where you *know* you're dreaming, but you can't wake up.

His instincts came to life, telling him to get out of there. He—

"Atticus. Higginbottom."

Tick turned sharply toward the sound, stumbling backward until he hit the stairs. His knees buckled, and he sat down on the third step. He sucked in a breath, feeling as if something had been shoved down his throat, clogging it. The barely female voice that had spoken his name had been monstrous. Dry. Raspy. Painful. As if every syllable sent waves of flame through its owner's body. And it was slightly . . . muffled.

He couldn't see anyone in the basement. He swept his head back and forth but saw nothing. No one. His hands gripped the lip of the step beneath his legs.

"Two words," said the horrible voice. "A name. How different my life would be if I'd never heard them uttered."

Tick concentrated on a certain spot, a dark shadow behind a pile of boxes he hadn't noticed before. Probably another project his dad should have organized and put away months ago. But there was enough room back there for someone to stand. To hide.

"Who's there?" Tick asked, relieved his voice came out with no cracks. Relieved he could talk at all.

"An old friend," came the reply, the harsh voice softening to a bare whisper, like the crackling of dead leaves in the distance. "Someone who wanted to *be* your friend."

Tick knew his mouth was open. He knew his eyes were wide, full of terror. Every inch of him screamed that he should run. He should book it up the stairs and yell for his parents to call the police.

It was her. It was *her*.

He couldn't move his eyes away from the tall length

of shadow. Something moved in the darkness. A human figure formed, then stepped into the light. A robe of dull yellow covered every inch of her body, the hood pulled up and over her head, almost hiding the face.

Except there was no face. At least, not a human face. The figure wore a red mask of metal, its features pulled into a smile that somehow looked more frightening than a scowl of anger.

"Mistress Jane," Tick whispered, his senses having turned numb. He knew it was her before she nodded ever so slightly to confirm what he'd said. So he hadn't killed her after all.

But that mask. And her voice. What *had* he done to her?

He waited for her to speak, to explain why she'd come. But she only stood there, completely still, her hands hidden within the folds of her robe. The red mask was impossibly shiny, almost as if it were molten metal. Liquid. Wet.

One of the eyebrows twitched, moving half an inch up then back down again. As he stared, the smile on the mask slowly melted into a frown, into a grimace. The eyebrows slanted with unspoken rage.

How did she do that? Tick could feel blood rushing in his temples, in his neck. What was she going to do to him?

Still, she said nothing. She didn't move.

Tick couldn't take the silence anymore. "Jane . . . Mistress Jane . . ." He was stuttering, searching for words. If his hands hadn't been firmly holding on to the stair beneath him, they'd have been trembling uncontrollably. "I promise I didn't mean to do whatever I did to you. I lost control—I don't even know what I lost control of. My mind wasn't working right. I don't know what happened."

He paused, hoping for a change on that mask. If anything, it looked angrier.

"I'm sorry," he continued. "I could tell by the way you . . . screamed, that, um . . ." He looked down at the floor. "I know I hurt you. I'm sorry. I didn't mean to."

When he lifted his eyes again, he almost cried out. She was three steps closer to him, the mask as scary as ever, the rage evident on the sparkling, deep red surface.

"I'm sorry," he said again, barely getting it out.

"Stop talking," Jane said, her raspy voice muffled but strong, creating a dry whisper of an echo in the room. "Don't say another word until I give you permission. Do you understand?"

"Ye—" Tick stopped himself. He nodded.

Mistress Jane stood still, her robe unruffled. She reminded Tick of a statue. A very angry statue with a red face. "I don't want to hear your apologies. Your excuses. Don't insult my pain by refusing to take responsibility for your actions. You know the nature of Chi'karda. You know the nature of your heart. You did this to me by your own choice. It couldn't have happened against your will. Your conscious . . . current . . . evident will." She spat out the last few syllables.

Tick felt awful. It wasn't so much the words she'd used. He felt the meaning of them more in the tone of her voice. Worse, he felt the truth of it. Shame and guilt blossomed like diseased flowers in his lungs, making it hard to breathe.

"I—" he began.

"I DIDN'T ASK YOU TO SPEAK!" she screamed, her body shaking beneath the robe, the first movement Tick had seen in several minutes. Terror pinched Tick's nerves.

Then, as if it came from another world, one in which he used to live but could barely remember, he heard footsteps upstairs. Urgent footsteps. The basement door opened above them.

No! he thought, even as he turned to look up the stairs, ready to tell his parents to run.

But when he saw who stood in the doorway, confusion and surprise almost burned away his fear. He blinked, forcing himself to swallow.

It was Sofia.

CHAPTER 8

QUITE THE CROWD

Shocked to see her, Tick stood up and fully turned around, facing the stairs, his eyes riveted on one of his best friends. He could almost forget he had the most dangerous woman in the Realities standing behind him.

"Sofia?" he asked, his voice cracking.

"Is she down there?" she responded in a whisper, gesturing with a nod.

Tick was completely baffled. "How do you . . ." He didn't know how to finish or what to ask first. What was going on?

"Is *she* down there?" Sofia repeated, her emphasis leaving no doubt who she meant.

Tick jabbed a thumb over his shoulder. "Yes!" he

snapped in a loud rasp. "She's standing right behind me!"

"Bring them down," Mistress Jane said. "They're late."

Tick wilted, hoping against hope that maybe the woman would have gone away when she realized they had company. How had she gotten to Tick's house in the first place? Only inanimate objects should be winkable to his house and its relatively low amounts of Chi'karda. And what happened to that pulsing thing? He felt completely unsettled, like the old dream where he walked into class at school dressed in nothing but his underwear.

At the top of the stairs, Sofia leaned back out the door and seemed to be talking to someone. Then she popped back in and started down the steps, each footstep a thump. To Tick's complete surprise, others followed her.

Master George, dressed in his fine, dark suit, redfaced and dry-skinned as usual, as if he'd been standing in a windy desert for hours. Behind him came Paul, an inexplicable grin on his face. Next was Tick's dad, then Tick's mom, both of them looking bleary-eyed and disheveled as if they'd just been awakened.

Tick could only stare, his mind trying to convince himself he must be dreaming. When Sofia reached the bottom step, he absently moved aside and let her pass, then Master George and Paul, both of whom patted him on the shoulder as they walked by. No one said a word, and it was impossible to read anything from the look in their eyes. There was fear there, but only a little.

His dad stopped beside him, then his mom. They both put their arms around him as Tick turned toward the middle of the basement. Everyone stood in a semicircle, facing Mistress Jane in her yellow robe and red mask, which was now empty of expression, neither angry nor happy. For what seemed like the hundredth time, Tick felt relief that his sisters had gone to Seattle for the weekend.

The whole situation was just too bizarre, and he finally found his voice.

"What's going on here?" he asked to no one in particular. He felt like he was on one of those hidden-camera TV shows where they play pranks on people. He half-expected a cameraman to step out of the shadows any second.

"Ask her," Sofia said almost viciously as she pointed at Jane.

"Yes, my good friend," Master George added. "Ask our host."

Tick looked at Jane, surprised. She'd *arranged* this?

Jane didn't move as silence settled in the room, anticipation palpable in the air. Tick stared at the shiny surface of her red mask, trying to understand what was happening. He stood huddled with his parents in his basement, next to his two best friends and the leader of the Realitants, staring at a woman in a robe and mask, who could probably kill them all without breaking a sweat.

Time stretched as they waited for Jane to speak, to give an explanation. Tick wanted to scream, wanted to—

"I sent my waterkelts as a little opening exercise to our meeting," Jane finally said, her voice scratchy but calm and cool. "Though I'm very disappointed they didn't kill at least *one* of your parents, Atticus."

Tick said nothing, fighting the urge to run at her.

"Anyway," Jane said, "you're probably wondering why I've brought you all here."

No one replied, but Tick's thoughts ran wild. She'd brought them all to his *basement?*

The face of Jane's mask remained expressionless. "I knew Atticus would have the hardest time getting permission to leave due to his . . . unusual gift. That's why we're here. That's why I sent you the note this morning, George. I'm glad to see you're still capable of performing simple tasks. Though I wanted the boy Sato here as well."

Tick glanced at Master George, who was visibly struggling to contain his contempt for this woman. "The boy is on a mission at the moment," the old man spurted, unable to sound composed. "Be glad we came at all. I'll have you speak your mind and be done with it. Remember, you've given your word this will be a diplomatic meeting. A peaceful meeting."

Jane's mask grinned, though the lips never parted. "Frightened, George? Scared of what your old pupil may do? You can thank the boy"—she nodded at Tick—"for making your fears relevant. You should definitely *be* afraid."

"What is this nonsense?" Master George demanded.

"How did you get here?" Jane asked him.

Master George shifted on his feet. "What do you mean?"

Jane's smile vanished almost instantly, the mask frowning. "George, don't make me repeat questions a child could understand. How did you *get* here?"

"What does it matter? I fetched Paul and Sofia, then we winked to the forest a mile or so from here and walked the rest of the way. *Why?*"

"The forest?" Jane repeated. "Ah, yes, the forest. I sensed a pool of Chi'karda there. Perhaps an old cemetery, its wooden grave markers long turned to dust. I hope you walked briskly—good exercise I'm sure. Looks like you need it."

"What is your *point?*" Master George snapped.

For the first time, Jane pulled her hands from out of the folds of the robe where she'd had them hidden. No one in the room could hold back a small gasp at the sight of them, especially Tick. He felt his mom's arm tighten around his shoulders.

Jane's hands were hideously red and flaky, covered with scars. Small shards and slivers of golden metal seemed fused to her skin. She folded her fingers together delicately, then rested her hands on her midsection. When Tick finally tore his eyes away from the terrible sight and looked at her face, he saw a horrific grimace of pain. Intense, aching pain. But then it was gone, replaced once again by the expressionless mask.

Jane must have noticed Tick's own look of horror. "See something disturbing, Atticus? What, you don't like my hands? You don't think they're pretty? Wouldn't like to hold them, go for a stroll?"

Tick felt as though his insides were melting. He'd spent the last few months wondering what had happened to her, wondering if she was dead. He'd been consumed by guilt for what he'd done. Seeing Jane's hands for himself now, he made the only logical conclusion he could. She wore the robe and mask because the rest of her body looked the same as her ruined hands.

He wanted to run. He wanted to sprint up those stairs and run away forever.

Jane seemed to sense his thoughts. "No, Atticus. For what you've done to me, you will be by my side.

You'll make restitution, and you'll help me accomplish what I set out so long ago to do. That's the only way I'll forgive you."

Tick felt his mom tense again, and he couldn't stop her before she spoke.

"Now listen to me, Jane," she said. "My son isn't responsible for what happened to you any more than my left foot is. We've heard every detail of that day a million times over. He can't control what's inside him. You tried to *kill* him. What did you expect!"

Jane's mask moved fiercely to rage. "I did *not* try to kill him! He knew I was trying to release his Chi'karda. I wanted to stop Chu from driving every last person in the Realities insane. I told him that—he knew it!"

"That's a load of horse poop!" Tick's dad suddenly yelled, making Tick jump.

"You're an adult, Jane," his mom continued, surprisingly calm and collected. "You should've known what his reaction would be. Everything that happened to you was your own fault. You—"

"Shut up!" Jane screamed, her whole body trembling from the effort, the mask full of hate and anger.

Tick felt his mom and dad take a step backward. He went with them. The other Realitants did the same. A storm of emotions raced through Tick. He wanted to cheer for his dad yelling at Jane; he loved his mom more than at any other moment in his life for standing up for him, for acting so brave and leader-like. And he hated Jane. Hated her.

But laced through all the other emotions was fear. Pure, unsettling fear. Something terrible was going to happen. He knew it. And deep down within him, he felt the stirrings of his power, massing like a storm. Scared of what might happen, he forced the power away as he'd done earlier in the garage. If only he could learn how to use it . . .

After a long moment, the echo of Jane's command faded away, and silence clouded the room. When she spoke again, it was very quiet. "You'll all be coming with me. I want you to witness something."

"Coming with—?" Tick's dad began, but when Jane's arm shot out and one of her hideous fingers pointed at his face, he shut his mouth.

Jane lowered her arm and folded her hands once again. "I remember in old movies, how the villain always said, through mad laughter, that he had a diabolical plan. As if anyone actually *used* such a word as diabolical."

She stepped forward, the face of her mask smoothing back to normalcy, though Tick didn't feel the tension in the room lessen, not one bit.

"But," she continued, her voice icy and soft, "it's the only word I can think of for what I have planned. My plan is, indeed, diabolical. For you, Edgar, slow-witted as you seem to be, that means terrible, horrible, awful, treacherous, and unspeakably nasty. Understand?" Her eyebrows arched.

Tick wanted to punch her for being so cruel to his dad, but did nothing. Next to him, his dad merely nodded. Tick hoped it was out of fear and not shame or embarrassment at her accusation.

"Yes," Jane said, with a slow smile. "A diabolical plan. And every one of you is going to witness it."

CHAPTER 9

*

DEAD TICKS
EVERYWHERE

This was the eighth time Sato'd seen it now. A tomb for Tick.

Every place was unique. The wording was a little different every time, and the dates varied, but they all meant the same thing.

Tick's Alterants were dead. All of them, by the looks of it.

Sato hoped this latest discovery would finally be enough to satisfy George and let him end gallivanting all across the Realities. Tick was alive in Reality Prime, but Sato had personally witnessed his friend's grave in eight of the remaining twelve. Did George really need him to go through with making sure the other four were the same? Knowing George, Sato thought with a sigh, probably yes. Just to make sure.

Sato stood in a vast field in the Fifth Reality, dawn still a couple of hours away. He'd woken up in the middle of the night back at newly repaired Realitant headquarters in the Bermuda Triangle—Sato still missed going for walks in the Grand Canyon—and hadn't been able to go back to sleep.

So he'd made Rutger roll his round body out of bed and wink him here to the Fifth Reality. He wanted to get the trip over with and be done. He was looking forward to getting back earlier than usual and having plenty of time to rest and relax. Maybe play cards with Mothball and Sally, though those two turned vicious when the stakes got high. Especially if the pot reached a whole bag of M&Ms.

The air had winter's bite of cold—the place was far in the north with a high altitude—but he'd worn his thick coat and gloves, so he actually felt great, refreshed and full of life. Beaming his big flashlight this way and that, he'd slowly made his way across the huge cemetery, checking each and every tombstone.

It was easy to tell this was Mothball's world. Each grave was a good couple of feet longer and wider than he was used to, and the markers had an almost disturbingly humorous edge to them: "Plank, please don't come back and haunt us—you have stinky feet." "Toolbelt, you were a wonder in life, despite your gigantic nose." "Snowdrift, who died with a smile on her face, even after falling off that cliff."

The strangeness didn't completely surprise him, knowing Mothball. She had a very unusual sense of humor. But there was just something wrong about giggling out loud like a little kid, over and over, in the middle of a dark graveyard.

He finally found Tick's marker after almost two hours of searching. Standing before it, he focused his flashlight on the large, rounded tombstone:

Here lies Atticus Higginbottom
Dead at the sad age of seven.
Atticus, you had more gas than
any normal child should,
but we still miss you terribly.
Rest in peace, our sweet, sweet son.

Sato clicked off the flashlight and stood in the dark for several minutes, surprisingly touched by the eulogy. It was impossible to separate these Alterants from the people you knew—hard not to imagine that lying beneath you was the person you'd grown to care for. In many ways, it was the same person. Although he didn't quite understand how it worked yet, this boy who'd died of who-knew-what was just Tick along a different path. He'd probably been similar in personality, looked the same though much taller, had the same drive to help others—just like Tick had saved Sato's life twice now.

And even though Sato had been grumpy with George more than once about this mission, in some ways it had helped him appreciate the fact that his friends—who were few in number—were alive and well, not dead like this poor kid. But it also made him sad, imagining another version of Tick dying so young. George said they didn't quite know why these major Realities still followed the same general pedigrees and lineages despite having such vastly different histories, but there had to be a big reason for it.

It worked geographically, too. Tick's Alterants had all been born in the same place and buried in the same vicinity. And, as far as Sato knew, Tick's parents were always named Edgar and Lorena and he always had two sisters, Lisa and Kayla. Strange stuff. Interesting how it all worked. Lately George thought he was on the verge of a breakthrough.

It had something to do with soulikens, a phenomenon the old man was trying desperately to figure out. He rarely talked about it, claiming all his information would get jumbled up and confused if he tried to explain it. Once he could lay it before them piece by piece, in a rational and comprehensible discussion, he'd immediately gather the Realitants to do so—something he'd been promising for months.

Soulikens. All Sato knew was that it had something to do with the electricity that existed within the human body. Actual and real electricity. Words like *signals* and *impulses* and *imprints* were thrown around, but never enough at once to make any sense of it. The Realitants would just have to be patient and wait for George to get it all together inside his thick skull.

But Sato had learned some things on his own, and as he stood in the darkness, enjoying the cool air, the quiet, the peace he always felt in a cemetery, he thought about one of them. Electricity was an essential physical element in making the heart pump. It seemed impossible that the human body could create electricity, but it was true. And the fact that the heart—the most important organ and the symbol of so many things in life—depended so greatly on it meant . . .

Well, he didn't know what it meant. But it had something to do with soulikens, and something to do with his mission to find dead Alterants of Tick. Except every time Sato tried to put the pieces together, it got jumbled and confusing. No wonder George was so insistent that he couldn't talk about it yet.

Sato felt a headache coming on. He reached into his pocket and pushed the little button that signaled he was ready to wink back to HQ.

A nice, long morning nap. That's exactly what he needed. Folding his arms and shivering at the cold that had seeped through his thick coat and chilled his skin, he waited for Rutger to bring him home.

A minute passed, then two. To his surprise, two people appeared in front of him—one short and fat, the other tall and skinny. He didn't need to shine the light on them to know who they were, but he did anyway.

Rutger threw up one of his pudgy arms to block the brightness. He held a Barrier Wand in the other. "Point that back at your feet, Sato! I'd like my eyes to last another decade or two!"

Sato didn't budge, hoping they couldn't see the big smile that flashed across his face.

Mothball, towering over her best friend and standing like a pile of sticks thrown together at the last minute with glue and draped with loose-fitting clothes, merely squinted. "Master Sato, best be puttin' down your torch there. 'Less you're wantin' to have a nice-sized pair of fists box them sad little ears of yours."

Sato did as she said, snapping back to the reality of the situation as he did so. Why had they come? Something had to be wrong. A trickle of panic wiped his grin completely away.

"Wait," he said. "What are you guys doing here? What happened?"

Rutger, temporarily blinded by Sato's trick with

the flashlight, was making his way forward, waddling along on his short legs and reaching out with his free hand to make sure he didn't bump into anything. "Calm down, you worrywart. Everything's fine."

Mothball's eyes seemed to have already adjusted. She made it to Sato before Rutger was even halfway there. "The wee man is right, Master Sato. No need for your worries. Just come to give ya a bit of a break, we 'ave. Thought we'd come and visit me mum and dad. Let ya see what real nice folks are like here in the Fifth."

Sato felt a strong surge of relief, which made him worry that maybe he was worrying too much. *Oh shut up,* he told himself. "Serious? We're going to see your parents?" He was surprised at how much the idea lifted him.

"Right ya are," Mothball replied. "'Long as we can get our guide here to quit stumbling about like an eyeless toad. Come on, Rutger, set your dials and switches and get on with it."

Rutger grumbled something too quiet to make out, then held the Barrier Wand up, concentrating. "A light, please?"

Sato shined the flashlight on the Wand, then asked, "Where do they live? Around here?"

"No, grumpy cheeks," Rutger responded as he turned a dial or two, his tongue caught between his lips. "We're going to wink to another cemetery near them. It's a good ten thousand miles from here, so hold your hats."

"I'm not wearin' a ruddy hat," Mothball said.

"It's an *expression*," Rutger huffed. "All right, we're ready to go, and I'm locked on to all of our nano-locators. Here we go."

Without another warning, Rutger pushed the button on top of the Wand. Sato heard the metallic click and felt the familiar tingle on his neck, and then everything changed.

It was daytime, the sun above almost blinding. Sato shielded his eyes, and at first he thought that what he saw in front of him was a trick of the light on his mind. But then it came into better focus, and he had no doubt.

Several people were trying to kill each other with swords.

And they were dressed like clowns.

CHAPTER 10

RIBBONS OF ORANGE

Tick couldn't believe how quiet Paul and Sofia had been since coming down the stairs—especially Sofia. The girl could never keep her mouth shut. And Paul—he had to be terrified to stay so silent. And his face showed it. Tick thought about how many weeks he'd been dying to see these guys, and now that they were here, he'd give anything to send them safely away.

"What do you mean?" Master George asked Jane after a long period of silence, Jane seemingly content to let her pronouncement sink in. "What plan are you talking about, and why would you want us to witness it?"

Tick had been trying to look at the floor, avoiding the menacing mask on Jane's face. But his eyes kept drawing back to it, fascinated at its almost magical ability to change expressions. Upon Master George's question, it melted into compassion, almost sadness.

"You have always known my wishes," she said in a flat voice, as if beginning a long lecture. "My ways and means may have changed—certainly my abilities have—but I've never wavered from my lifetime mission, George. And that is to see the suffering of countless Alterants end. To create one and only one Reality, where the strongest of each one of us can live, and where we can stop the torturous splitting of worlds."

"I've never heard you put it quite that way before," Master George said. "I remember your talk of a Utopia, a paradise, a place where all can be happy. The way you describe it now sounds more like the wishes of an evil, insane, power-hungry monster. What's happened to you, Jane?"

She paused to let him speak, but then acted as if she hadn't heard a word he said, continuing her lecture without missing a beat. "The first step of my plan is not going to be easy. I hardly expect any of you to understand what I do or to give it your blessing. But I couldn't possibly care less. For what the lot of you have done to me, I don't expect to let most of you live long enough to see the end come to pass."

She paused, turning her head to look at each person in the room. "But you all will see what I plan for tomorrow. You'll see it, and you'll know my power once and for all."

Master George wouldn't quit pushing. "Jane, this is madness."

"Madness?" she repeated. "I tried it your way, the *Realitants'* way. And look what I got in return." She motioned to her face and robed body with her hideous hands, then held them up for everyone to see. "The irony is, that by ruining me physically, you've helped me more than you know. Not only can I channel my abilities more acutely than ever before, but I've been reminded of what I knew from the beginning. That the only way to accomplish anything is by taking the hard road, the harsh road. The sometimes cruel and hateful road. Never before has it been so true that the ends will justify the means. I'll never stray from the path again. Never."

Tick felt heat simmering inside him as she spoke, growing and intensifying with every word. Though he didn't really know the specifics of what she was talking about, he could hear the evil in her voice, the horrible intent of her words. He could almost *feel* it, just like the pulse that had brought him down here in the first place. The pulse. What had that been?

"As you can see," Jane continued, "I'm learning more each and every day about how to use the gifts that have been given to me. Take the waterkelts, for example. You'd be amazed at how easy it is to manipulate the molecules of our favorite liquid."

Tick's anger grew, heat boiling in his chest. And despite his better judgment, this time he didn't stop it. Jane had obviously noticed.

"Atticus, are we going to have a problem?" she asked coolly. But he thought he heard the slightest trace of concern, and she definitely took a small step backward. She feared him; he knew it.

"Tick," his dad said next to him, turning toward him and gripping him by the shoulders. "Are you feeling it again? Push it away, hold it back, do something." The worry creasing his face tore at Tick's heart, so he looked away, back at Jane.

His mom squeezed his arm, then whispered in his ear. "Atticus, pull it back. Go through the breathing exercises. Son, we're not going to let her hurt—"

"I won't listen to another word she says!" Tick screamed. He was losing control and felt his body trembling. He had to *do* something. "We can't just let her talk like this to us!" His skin burned. He looked at his arms, half-expecting to see blisters and smoke. But all was normal.

"Atticus—" his mom said.

She stepped away from him, as did his dad. Tick looked over at Sofia and Paul, their eyes wide. They were scared of him. They were *all* scared of him. He noticed Master George's hand had slipped into his pocket, fingering something there. Tick knew it had to be another shot of whatever Sofia had used to knock him out in Chu's mountain office building.

Tick didn't know what to do. He felt the heat inside him, the power, weaken a little. He looked back at Jane, hoping to reignite it. She hadn't moved, but her mask was pulled back in fury.

"You can't stand against me," Jane said. "Not now, not after what you did to me. Stop now, or you'll spend the rest of your short life regretting it."

"What did I do to you?" Tick spat back at her. "You tried to kill me!"

"What did you do? What did you *do?*" Jane stepped forward, closer than before, regaining her ground. "You took the strongest parts of the most powerful weapon ever created by man and melded them with a woman already equipped with a control over Chi'karda never seen before. That's what you *did,* Atticus. Your selfish, cowardly act will end up being the very thing that will allow me to win."

"It . . . will . . . not," Tick said, concentrating with every ounce of brain power he could muster, trying to sense, to feel, to grasp the boiling Chi'karda within him. He remembered last year when Jane had pulled it out of him in a cloud of orange sparkles, a mist of tangible power. He tried to visualize it the same way, tried to *touch* it.

"Stop it," Jane warned. "Stop it *now!*"

"Atticus," his mom pleaded. "She's right. Now's not the time!"

"Tick, pull it back before you kill yourself!" Sofia yelled.

The others shouted similar words at him. Master George pulled what looked like an ordinary pen from his pocket. But Tick couldn't stop. He couldn't let Jane do anything to harm his friends and family.

He turned his attention back to her, focusing again on the burning power within him, holding on to it in a way he could've never described to anyone. Then he threw it at Jane. Screaming, he leaned forward and threw the power at her, pushing it away from him in a rush of energy and invisible flame.

A thunderclap shook the room as Jane stumbled backward, fiery sparks exploding all around her. Boxes tumbled, people fell to the ground. There was shouting and yelling. Somewhere, glass shattered. Another thunderclap, a thump of booming sound, shook the whole house. Streaks of orange mist swirled throughout the basement like ribbons of sunset, slashing this way and that. Tick felt as if lava flowed in his veins and thought his head might explode from the pressure.

Still, he kept *pushing,* kept aiming every bit of his strength at Jane.

She didn't fall. She planted her feet against the

onslaught. Her red mask raged. Thunder continued to blast the air in repeated bursts, filling the world full of noise. A loud, piercing, terrible *noise* that only fed Tick's fire.

But then, somehow, through all that sound, he heard Jane's voice, as crystal clear as if she'd spoken directly into his ear in a silent room. It took a moment for her words to register, for him to comprehend exactly what she was saying, but when it clicked, when he realized what he was jeopardizing, what he was risking, he immediately pulled it all back, all of it. He had no idea how he did it, but in an instant the power vanished, sucked back into him and quenched like a candle in a rainstorm.

Jane had said four words.

"I have your sisters."

CHAPTER 11

✳

LATITUDE AND LONGITUDE

Frazier Gunn walked through the thick forest, trying his hardest to ignore the humidity that tried to suck the life out of him and fill his lungs with heavy water. Every breath seemed an effort, and every inch of clothing clung to his skin. He was miserably uncomfortable.

And then there were the insects: almost microscopic gnats that swarmed in small packs around his nose and eyes, tiny dragonflies that appeared to love the darkness and warmth of the human inner ear—at least that's where they kept trying to get to, wasps and bees. But the mosquitoes were the worst—big as moths and drinking up his blood like miniature vampires. With his free hand, he swatted the latest one to land on his neck, then looked at the greasy dark smear on his palm. Disgusting.

His other hand was occupied, gripping a makeshift handle on the end of a thick rope, which dangled away behind him to its other end, tied loosely around the neck of a woman. He didn't want to hurt her, but he couldn't have her running away, either. Her long, black hair was matted against her face and head, and her clothes were soaked with sweat, but she kept Frazier's pace, never uttering a word of complaint.

Yes, she was a criminal, but she was also an Alterant of Mistress Jane. She looked just like her except for the long mane of hair. But it was the same face, the same—

Frazier faltered in his steps, almost tripping over a big root. He'd forgotten—just for the barest of moments—that his boss no longer had the beauty and grace that had distinguished her for so many years. She'd yet to show him her face, but he'd seen enough—just her *hands* were enough—to know that the Higginbottom kid had done something truly horrific to her body. The poor woman Frazier dragged along behind him was a goddess compared to Mistress Jane now.

The thought saddened and angered him in equal parts, and when they rounded a massively thick oak tree, he accidentally jerked on the rope. The Alterant yelped behind him and stumbled to the ground, gurgling out a choke as the noose tightened. Frazier quickly got her back on her feet and apologized, though he knew it was empty and cold. He kept thinking of her as his boss, and he had to stop it.

On they went, hiking their way through the hot, wilted, miserable forest.

Frazier was exhausted. The only other person in the Realities to whom he'd dare entrust this assignment was Mistress Jane herself, and she obviously couldn't do it. If two Alterants met face to face, bad things happened. Reginald Chu had discovered that little gem of information himself, and now he was stuck in some place Frazier hoped he'd never see. The Nonex. What a stupid name.

It wasn't just the humidity and the heat that had Frazier so tired. It was more the fact that he had to do the same thing twelve times—taking each Alterant to the exact same location in each of their respective Realities, leaving them chained and secure, but with enough food and water to survive until the plans were complete. He'd already finished with ten; two more to go. But only a handful of Realities had GPS equipment in the air, so most of the time he had to use maps and human guides to find the latitude and longitude coordinates. It was a real pain in the bahoonkas.

This world had the satellites and the technology, for which he was extremely grateful. Having a group of jabbering guides and a backpack full of maps didn't sound like something he could handle right now, trudging through the dense, suffocating woods. The Blade component strapped across his shoulders was plenty heavy enough, and sweat poured down his body in streams. He looked at his GPS navigation watch— the one he'd, um, taken for free from a poor sucker back in Carson City, the closest patch of civilization to this wretched place. They were close to the destination now.

Frazier squeezed his way through a clump of thin, gangly trees into a wide patch of vegetation. His spirits lifted slightly. Maybe they were past the thickest part of the forest. Kicking and pounding down with his foot, he pushed his way through the thick, clinging growth, leading the Alterant and moving ever closer toward the exact latitude and longitude of the Blade location. By the time he saw another grove of gigantic trees looming up ahead, his watch beeped, once, long and loud.

They'd reached the fifty-foot radius point.

If he hadn't had a prisoner behind him, tied and bound to him and watching his every move, he would have dropped to his knees and howled at the sky in delirious joy. Of the now eleven times he'd made this journey, this one had been the most difficult. It was the heat; it had to be the heat. He felt utter dread knowing he still had one more Reality ahead of him. But, for now, he allowed himself some elation, at least a little. Even if he did keep it on the inside.

"We're here," he said, making sure he didn't allow the relief to trickle into his voice. "I need a minute to set up. Don't try anything. Or, um, I'll have to, um, kill you." Of course, not in a million years would he do that—the Blade operation was way too important, and it couldn't happen if even one of the Alterants died—but *she* didn't know that.

"Where's here?" the woman asked, her voice hoarse and scratchy. "Why won't you tell me anything?"

"Because you don't need to know." Frazier walked a little way farther until they were in the rough middle of the designated area. He let go of the rope, giving the prisoner the evil eye as he did so, knowing she'd get the message. He swung the Blade component off his shoulders, unhooked the leather straps, and let it thump to the ground in front of him.

"I've dealt with people a lot worse than you," she said in a raw whisper.

Frazier barely heard her. He was down on his knees, studying the Blade. Or, more accurately, a *part* of the Blade. One of thirteen parts, it was a beautiful piece of work. Made of the blackest stone—a substance that did not even *exist* in any Reality, at least not naturally—it had no measurable shape or dimensions. Twisty, curvy, and slightly elongated, it was like a beautiful, abstract sculpture, with dozens of thin strands connecting two bulky end pieces, all of it harder and stronger than the toughest metal or stone. And blacker than the deepest, starless night.

Jane had *made* this. She'd created it. He'd begged her to explain how she'd done it, explain what the material was, explain the science behind it. But she always refused, saying it was on such a deep and complex level he'd never understand. A lot of it, she finally told him, came about purely on instinct, a result of her digging through the wonders of quantum physics and spacetime. But on several occasions, when she otherwise seemed asleep or lost in thought, he'd heard her whisper two words:

Dark matter.

He was sure of it. She'd said *dark matter*. Whether or not it had anything to do with the Blade, he couldn't be sure. He certainly had no idea if what lay in front of him now was made of dark matter or contained it somehow. But his gut told him that his boss had stumbled upon a discovery that would alter the Realities forever if she ever chose to share it with her fellow scientists. But that, he knew, would never happen.

Dark matter.

He shivered, and feeling the chill in the brutal heat ripped him out of his wandering thoughts. He snapped his head up to look at the Alterant, who stood quietly, everything from her face to her hands to her clothes seeming to wilt toward the ground, a display of misery.

He felt truly sorry for her, and knew it was because of how much she looked like Mistress Jane.

"I'm sorry this has been so rough on you," he said, positive she'd think he was up to something and not being sincere. He didn't care. "Sometimes I lose myself in the amazing things we're trying to accomplish. Sometimes I . . . forget that the people we hurt along the way are human."

The woman stared at him, disgust wrinkling up her face. Then she spat on the twisted black stone. "You can take your sick voodoo toys and shove 'em up your nose. Go ahead and kill me. Do whatever. I don't care."

Frazier couldn't take his eyes off her for a long moment. She looked so much like his boss, it hurt his heart to hear her say such things. He felt a sudden surge of something between pain and love. He wanted to go to the woman, hold her, kiss her. In that instant, he didn't want to hurt her like this.

"Get your ugly eyes off me," she said. "I've seen rats who look more intelligent than you."

That ended his brief flare of weakness. He reached out and grabbed the rope around her neck. He stood up and made her sit on the roughly flat surface of the Blade's top bulky section. The thin strands of hard, black stone twisted and curved their way down until they connected with the bottom section. They looked like a clump of wires. Maybe, he thought, somehow that's what they were.

"Sit there and don't say another word," he said as he wrapped the rope around her body twice and then strung the rope through the tight spaces between those strings of dark rock. Once he'd tied that off, he took a set of metal shackles from his pack and clamped them around the Alterant's ankles, securing them to a couple of strands that bent out more than the others. There was no way she could get away, and the stone was far too heavy for her to drag and shuffle along in tiny steps.

Everything was set.

"Are you going to leave me here?" she asked, having lost her bravery from a minute before. "Let me die?"

"Yes and no." He loved giving that answer, loved seeing the perplexed look that came over the Alterant's face when he said it.

"What's that supposed to mean?" she responded.

Frazier placed the prepared sack of food and water next to her feet. "Just answering your question." He stood up, then turned and started to walk away.

"*Wait!*" she screamed. "Please! I can help you. I'm the best of the best! Please don't leave me here! *Please!*"

Frazier didn't respond. He found it was better that way. He just kept walking, knowing it'd be easier to make it to the winking point without a huge block of stone on his back and dragging a prisoner behind him. Ignoring her desperate pleas, he reached the end of the swatch of vegetation and reentered the vast forest.

The Blade of Shattered Hope was almost complete.

PART 2

THE BLACK
TREE

CHAPTER 12

✳

SWEET DIGS

Mothball had to grab Sato and physically pull him away from the spectacle. The sight was just too hard to believe and had put him in a daze. Luckily the fighting clowns didn't seem to notice them.

"Come on," she yelled at him, dragging him across the field as easily as a sack of raked leaves. "Soon as those lugs take notice we've got one the likes of you, we'll be the ones they be fightin', not themselves—bet your buttons. Come *on!*"

Sato finally got his feet under him and regained his composure, walking quickly alongside Mothball as Rutger struggled to keep up. "What *was* that? Who are those people?"

"Bugaboo soldiers," she replied. "Nasty people, they are. Completely insane."

Sato forced out a chuckle. "They're dressed like *clowns* and trying to stab each other with sharp swords. What makes you think they're crazy?"

Mothball seemed to miss his sarcasm. "Not right in the head. Been crazy ever since the war ended, not knowing what to do when there's no one to fight. Rutger, chop-chop, little man!"

Sato turned to see Rutger a good twenty feet behind them, pumping his short little arms as he tried his best to run. "Slow *down!*" the short man yelled. "Before I croak!"

They topped a small, sparsely wooded rise and headed down the other side. Once they were out of sight from the odd group of battling clowns, Mothball finally stopped and allowed Rutger to catch up. The poor man's face was bloodred—a cherry on top of a black ball. Sato expected a blur of insults and smart remarks from Rutger, but it was all the guy could do to breathe, heaving air in and out.

"I still don't get it," Sato said. "Who *are* those people?"

Mothball rolled her eyes, in a rare bad mood. "'Tis a long story and no time to tell it. Once we make it to me mum's house, you can ask your questions. Can we go now?" She loomed over Rutger with her hands on her hips.

The robust little man looked up at her. "How far?"

"Just 'round the bend up yonder," she answered, pointing toward a small paved lane that came out of a forest to their right and went over the next hill. "We can stop runnin', we can. I 'spect them Bugaboos'll be quite occupied for a spell. Come on." She headed off for the road.

Sato looked at Rutger. "Do *you* know anything about these Bugaboo soldiers?"

Rutger shrugged, a movement that shook his whole body. "Enough not to bug Mothball about it. She has a *long* history with those nutsos. Let's just get to her house and then we can talk about it."

"Whatever," Sato muttered, consumed with curiosity. Sword-fighting clowns were bad enough, and the fact that Mothball was scared of them only made it worse. He felt a disturbing chill that made him shudder. "Let's go."

Rutger started off down the hill, and Sato followed.

The road led to a cluster of homes surrounded by an enormously tall wall of roughly mortared stones. In fact, everything about the neighborhood was tall: the houses, the trees, the carriages and their horses. And once he got past the sheer size of it all, Sato was amazed at how medieval everything looked.

What kind of a world had Mothball grown up in?

She seemed to sense his thoughts. "Don't ya worry, Master Sato. Plenty of fancy things in this Reality—cars and tellies and the like. We just enjoy livin' the old-fashioned way 'round these parts."

"Just be glad they have fridges and real toilets," Rutger muttered.

They made it to the wide opening of the border wall, where a massive iron gate was closed and locked to prevent anyone from entering.

"Can't be lettin' in the Bugaboos," Mothball said. "Gate stays closed every minute, 'less you say the password." She took a deep breath, then yelled in a slow, booming voice, "Donkey hoe tea!"

Sato wasn't sure he'd heard right. "Did you just say *Don Quixote?* Like the book?"

Groans and creaks of metal filled the air as the gate swung inward.

"No, never 'eard of that one," Mothball responded as she stepped forward to enter. "I said *donkey . . . hoe . . . tea.* Chooses three random words, it does, and every day's different."

Sato hurried to keep up with her, Rutger hustling along right behind him. "It? What is *it?*" A loud clang announced the gate had closed again.

"Old Billy's fancy 'puter that runs the place. The gate, the lights, the whole bit."

Sato couldn't help but be fascinated by this Reality.

Up until now, he'd seen only the cemeteries of Tick's Alterants, and he was excited to have a break and meet more people, see if they were a lot like Mothball.

A gravel path led them from the entrance through a greener than green patch of grass, speckled with red and yellow and purple wildflowers. A slight breeze picked up, running across the grass in waves, bringing a sweet scent along with it. It hit Sato that the temperature was perfect here—not too cold and not too hot. For the first time in a while, he had the urge to kick back and relax, take a long vacation. And right here in his tall friend's neighborhood seemed like the perfect place.

With a deep sigh, surprised at his sudden good mood, he followed Mothball as the path intersected a wide, cobblestone road, running away from them for at least half a mile, both sides of the road lined with those ancient-styled houses. Made of large rocks and roughly hewn brick, the homes would have looked almost like natural formations that had stood for a thousand years, except for the countless boxes of flowers hanging here and there, the roofs thatched with bundles of long grasses, the multicolored windows, and the brightly painted wooden doors—mostly reds and yellows.

And the yards. Sato was used to his home country of Japan, where the small homes sat almost on top of the streets and had maybe just enough room for a tiny tree and a single bush. But these houses had huge yards, filled with green grass and finely groomed bushes and majestic trees. And gardens. Lots and lots of gardens, growing every veggie and fruit known to man, by the looks of it.

As they walked down the street in silence, Sato had the feeling that if he'd been born in this Reality instead of his own, he would've grown up the happiest person ever. How could anyone be grumpy in a place like this?

Then he remembered those psycho people dressed up like clowns and fighting each other with swords. The big stone wall and locked iron gate. Maybe life here wasn't so blissful after all.

"Which one's yours?" Sato asked. "And where is everybody?" He'd yet to see one other person.

Mothball absently pointed somewhere up ahead. "Just a bit farther. And most folks are off to town, doin' their jobs and such. Thems that ain't are havin' afternoon tea in their parlor, I 'spect."

"I don't think my feet will ever forgive you," Rutger said through heavy breaths. "We need to bury a bunch of dead people in your backyard so we can wink straight there next time."

"Mayhaps we'll start with you," Mothball replied.

Rutger barked a fake laugh. "Well, the way my heart's beating, you just might be right! I've probably lost ten pounds already."

"Walk another few weeks straight, and maybe you

can fit through me mum's door without me kickin' ya in the ruddy bottoms." She laughed, a rolling stutter of thunder that lifted Sato's spirits even more.

"You guys are the weirdest best friends I've ever met," Sato said. "Maybe you should just go ahead and get married."

"Married?" Mothball roared. "What, and have little monster babies with my ugly face on little balls of fat? Methinks I'd rather marry a horse."

"Feeling's mutual!" Rutger countered.

"Would eat a lot less, that's for sure," Mothball murmured.

"And wouldn't complain at your incessant gibbering!"

"Smell better, too."

"You know what they say—sometimes a husband and wife look like brother and sister. You and a horse—well, perfect!"

Mothball scratched her chin, acting like she couldn't hear him. "There'd be horse patties lyin' 'round about me flat. Might get a bit messy."

"Okay, this is getting creepy," Sato interjected. "Where's your house?"

Mothball stopped, then threw her arms up and clapped once as she looked at the large home to their right. "Well, bite me buttons, here we are!"

The house and yard looked a lot like the others,

though the front door was pink. Mothball's proclamation had barely ended when the door swung open and a gigantic woman with a huge mop of curly black hair on her head came rushing out to greet them. Her clothes were the same style as Mothball's—loose, dull colors, hanging off her skin-and-bones body like drying laundry. Or maybe *dying* laundry.

"Me love!" the lady yelled as she ran down the stone steps, all gangly legs and arms making her look as if she might collapse into a heap of sticks at any second. "Oh, me sweet, sweet love! Been 'specting you, we 'ave!"

She reached Mothball, and they squeezed each other tightly, circling around, both of them crying. Sato looked away, uncomfortable at intruding on something intimate and personal. When they finally let go of each other, Mothball pointed straight at him.

"This here's Master Sato," she said proudly. "And, of course you know Rutger, me best friend."

"Ah, yes, yes," her tall mom replied, the enormous smile she'd worn since opening the door still there. Sato noticed her teeth were just as crooked as her daughter's, but much whiter. "So good to see you again, Rutger. And you, Sato, welcome. My name is Windasill, and I'm so happy to say we've finally met. I've been waiting for months."

"Really?" Sato said, surprised.

"Of course." She looked at Mothball, a slight look

of confusion on her face. "You didn't tell him?"

Mothball shrugged, clearly embarrassed.

Sato couldn't imagine what was going on. "Tell me? What didn't you tell me?"

Instead of answering, Mothball nodded at her mom.

Windasill grinned again and curtsied—quite the display from someone so big. "You do look just like him, I must say. A wee bit shorter's all." Then, inexplicably, she started crying, the stifled sobs accompanied by tears streaming out of her eyes.

Now he was beyond confused. "What are you *talking* about? What's going on?"

Rutger answered for them. "Sato, you're the Alterant of Grand Minister Sato Tadashi, who was the supreme ruler of this entire world—in this Reality anyway."

"*Was?*" Sato repeated, not knowing how to react to the strange revelation.

Mothball's mom answered, right after spitting on the ground. "Bugaboos killed him last month, they did, just weeks after he took office. Sacrificed hundreds of blokes to break through security and get to him. He was the most respected leader we've had in ages, despite being so young. Gone and dead now."

"Why . . . why'd they kill him?" Sato asked. He had an uncomfortable feeling this was leading somewhere he wouldn't like. Mothball's answer confirmed it.

"They thought he was you."

CHAPTER 13

✳

SLEEPLESS IN THE DARK

rip.

Drip.

Drip.

That was all Tick could hear, and it was driving him crazy. The others were asleep, and even though the soft sighs and snores of their slumber floated through the air, all his mind could focus on was that stupid dripping water.

Drip.

Drip.

Drip.

Everything had happened so fast after Jane revealed that she'd kidnapped his sisters, Lisa and Kayla. The news shocked every bit of surging power out of him, and he'd collapsed to the floor in defeat, knowing he couldn't take the risk she might be lying. He couldn't risk their lives. Not them.

As soon as he'd given up, Jane had winked them all away. He didn't know how she did it, or who helped her, but one instant they'd been in his basement, and the next they were here, in some kind of cell made of gray stone, damp and cold and dark, with that maddening drip of water as a constant companion. The only light was faint, coming from somewhere down a long hallway outside the bars of their prison.

They'd been there for hours and hours. Every question in the world had been asked, every nook and cranny of the room examined, and they had shouted and screamed for help until their voices went hoarse. Then exhaustion crept in, and now everyone was asleep.

Except Tick. He huddled with his back against the hard, cold wall, his arms wrapped around his knees, his hands clasped in front of him. He felt empty, like his mind and heart had become a complete void of space, sucking every last bit of strength and will away. Jane had his sisters—but who knew where or how or why. And he was here, with his mom and dad, his two best friends, and the leader of the Realitants, all of them captured and helpless.

He'd tried several times to summon even the smallest trace of the power he'd felt against Jane in the basement of his house, but nothing came. Just emptiness. He floated in a void. A yucky, blecky, hopeless void.

"Tick?"

The voice startled him. He put his hands down to the ground, ready to spring to his feet. But a second later he realized it was Sofia, just a few feet from him, lying down with her head resting on her folded arms. She pushed herself into a sitting position and looked at him. He could barely see the features of her face, but they didn't look as sad as he would've expected.

"Still here," he replied. "Did you actually fall asleep?"

She yawned in response. "Think so. Had a bad dream."

"I wish *this* were a bad dream."

"Yeah."

"Dude, I finally snooze and you guys wake me up." Paul was getting to his feet, rubbing his eyes. He made his way over to sit next to Tick and Sofia. "You think the geezer and your mom and dad are actually sleeping?"

"I hope so," Tick said. "They're old—they need it."

"Actually," Sofia whispered, "the younger you are, the more sleep you need. Just for the record."

Tick wasn't in the mood for her smarts. "Whatever."

"So what do you think she's up to?" Paul asked. "Jane the Beast, I mean. And what's the deal with that robe and mask, the scratchy voice? Tick, you're the only one who's met her before—did she talk like that? Did she have that mask?"

Tick shook his head and was happy to realize he didn't feel any guilt at what Paul had just said. In fact, he wished she'd died. "Remember when I broke apart Dark Infinity and attacked her with it? I think it burned her and melted stuff all over her. Kind of like it . . . fused them together."

"And maybe it made her more powerful, too," Sofia added. "Maybe she somehow kept the powers of Chu's weapon. How else could she have winked into your basement *and* winked us all here?"

"Huh?" Tick asked. "How do you know *she* did it? Not someone with a Barrier Wand?"

Sofia pointed in front of her as if Jane were standing there. "Because I was staring at her the whole time. As soon as you quit trying to do whatever you were doing with your orange hocus-pocus stuff, she reached out with her hands and swept them through the air, like she was picking up a big pile of leaves and throwing them. Then I felt the tingle, and next thing I know, we're here."

"What *were* you doing to her, anyway?" Paul asked.

The question hit Tick like a thump in his chest. He hesitated, not knowing what to say.

"Hello?" Paul pushed. "Earth calling Atticus Higginbottom."

Tick shifted to get more comfortable. "I don't know, man. It's hard enough to understand it in my brain, much less explain it to you guys."

"Well, try," Sofia said. "If we can help you figure out these freaky powers of yours, we might get out of here someday."

Freaky powers, Tick thought. Did she have to say it that way? After a long pause, he cleared his throat and resolved to tell them everything. "Every time I've had an . . . episode, I feel this heat in my chest and gut, something burning inside me. I've been able to push it down a couple times recently and make it go away."

"Hey," Paul said, "at least that's progress over what you did at Chu's shack. Maybe you're learning to control it."

Tick nodded. "Maybe. Anyway, in my basement, I kind of panicked when Jane started talking, and when the heat came, I didn't stop it. I . . . encouraged it, tried to hold on to it, make it grow. It was like I had these mental hands, trying to clasp invisible fingers around an invisible . . . something. I don't know—I can't describe it. It took a lot of focus and concentration. Then, I just mentally threw it at her. I guess I attacked her just by thinking it and wanting it."

Paul and Sofia stared at him, apparently at a loss for words, a minor miracle with those two.

"Anyway," Tick continued, "it felt really good. I

still think I'm a long way from controlling it anytime I want to, but this was about a billion times better than what happened a few months ago. Back then it was like somebody had ripped my spirit out of my body, and I couldn't do anything about it."

"What *is* the power?" Paul asked. "I mean, you're doing some crazy stuff here, dude."

"It's Chi'karda, brainiac," Sofia answered. "We know that much. For some reason Tick has a ton of it."

Paul shook his head. "I know it's Chi'karda—at least, that's what Master Georgie boy over there thinks." He pointed to the snoozing man, who looked a little ridiculous all dressed up in a prison cell. "But what does that *mean?*"

"What do you mean, what does it mean?" Sofia said.

"I mean, what does it mean?"

Sofia blew out a loud breath. "I don't know what it means."

"Man," Tick said, "we are really making progress here."

They stayed quiet for a while, and then Sofia broke the silence. "Well, we can leave the science side of it to Master George and the Realitants. We just need to help you learn how to control it so we can use it. As a weapon."

"Yeah," Paul agreed. "How about right now? I don't think I'm up for hanging around here much longer."

Weapon. For some reason that word gave Tick the chills. He didn't want to think of himself as a potential killing device. "It doesn't matter right now. I can't feel anything, not even a flicker."

"Maybe you need to be ticked off," Paul said. "Here, let me kick you in the—"

"I'm good, thanks." Tick scooted away.

"Just start thinking about stuff," Sofia suggested. "Think about Jane and what she's done to us and how we're sitting in this prison. Think about your . . ." She didn't finish, looking at the ground as if she'd just confessed something horrible.

Tick felt tears glisten his eyes. "You were going to say *sisters*. Think about my sisters."

Sofia looked up at him, then nodded.

"Maybe that's why I'm so empty," Tick said, hearing the gloom in his own voice. "She threatened to hurt them if I try anything, so my subconscious won't even let me get close to trying."

"Man," Paul said, "guess we shouldn't expect you to, then. Too risky."

"What *are* we going to do?" Sofia pleaded.

Master George stirred to their right, grunting as he rolled over and pushed himself into a sitting position. He let out a huge yawn while rubbing his eyes. "Goodness gracious me, how long have I been sleeping?"

"Couple hours," Tick said.

"I had the strangest dream," the leader of the Realitants said in a groggy voice. "I was in your basement, Master Atticus, and I saw a person in a big rabbit suit. It was a very creepy bunny. Quite disturbing. I woke up just as the person started to take off his head. What I would give to have seen the face beneath the mask."

"It's symbolic," Sofia said. "Jane wears a mask now. I'm sure it's her you would've seen."

"Uh, what about the whole bunny thing?" Paul asked with a slight snicker.

"Well," Master George began, clearing his throat, embarrassed. "I was, er, a bit frightened of bunnies as a child."

Tick shocked himself when he laughed out loud. So did Paul.

"Poke fun if you must," Master George countered, though he had a smile on his face. "You try falling into a cage filled with a dozen hungry rabbits and see how—"

A loud metal clang cut him off, and they all turned to see the iron-grilled door to their cell swing open. Standing behind it in the hallway was Mistress Jane, still dressed in her yellow robe and her expressionless red mask. There was a cart next to her, loaded with several plates of steaming food.

"My, you all look cozy," she said. "I've brought you

something to eat. I can't have you starving to death before our big plans come to fruition." She pushed the cart into the cell then swung the heavy door shut again. Its clanking ring echoed like some haunted musical instrument.

She turned to walk away, apparently done with them.

"Where are we?" Master George shouted at her.

Jane stopped, but did not look at them. "You're in the Thirteenth Reality, George. Though it won't be called that much longer."

She started walking again, and soon was out of sight.

CHAPTER 14

✳

QUESTIONS WITHOUT ANSWERS

Mothball's dad was actually shorter than his wife, and, impossibly, even nicer. His dark hair and the angled features of his face would have looked hard and cold except for the permanent smile breaking it all up. He ushered Sato and the others into the huge living room, where they all sat down with cups of steaming hot tea. His name was Tollaseat, and he wore a bright red sweater with his drab-colored pants. He looked about as unfashionable as a person could possibly get.

As for the inside of the house, it was finely deco-rated. Bookshelves made of a dark and shiny wood were everywhere, some of them stocked with leather-bound books, others with various porcelain sculptures, dishes, and other knickknacks. The furniture all seemed a little fancy, with frilly carvings and flower prints and lacy stuff here and there. But at least the chairs were comfortable, and the soft carpet was easily three inches thick. Over a huge fireplace—which looked like it could burn an entire forest in no time—hung a portrait of an old woman just as tall and awkward-looking as Mothball and her mother.

"So," Tollaseat said, his voice like a massive tolling bell, "Sato, my friend, I can't tell you how nice it is to finally meet you."

"Thanks," Sato said, nodding with a curt smile. He couldn't quite settle down, trying desperately to come to terms with his connection to the recently murdered ruler of the Fifth Reality. Why would a fifteen-year-old kid be the leader of an entire planet? It was just too bizarre. And if those Bugaboo soldiers—what a ridiculous name!—really wanted him dead . . .

Rutger cleared his throat. He was perched on a chair, his short legs dangling like a little kid's. He glanced sidelong at Sato. "You'll have to excuse our new Realitant friend. He's not one for a lot of words. I'm sure he's very happy to meet you too."

"Ah," Tollaseat scoffed, waving at the air with both hands. "No bother, really, no bother at all. We're simply thrilled to have the lot of you come and sit a spell. No need for jabbering and such."

Sato had to figure this out. "Could someone please explain to me about my Alterant? How could these psycho clown soldiers possibly think I'd come to this world and become the . . . what did you call it?"

"Grand Minister," Windasill said quietly, as if indulging a child taking a quiz.

Sato snapped his fingers. "Yeah, that. How could they think I'd become the Grand Minister of the Fifth Reality? And why would they want to kill me in the first place?"

Mothball was sitting directly across from him. She leaned forward and put her elbows on her knees. "We think the Bugs and Mistress Jane have gone off and made some type of nasty arrangement. Mayhaps done it quite some time ago. And we reckon old Jane put out the scoop on you and your friends. Looking for revenge, she was. Just happens that your Alterant became our Minister, and the Bugs thought maybe we'd planted you. Replaced Sato Tadashi in a swap. Like we'd wanna ruddy take over the Reality or some such nonsense."

"They must be the dumbest people in the universe," Rutger muttered.

"No, no, my friend," Tollaseat said, shaking his head. "Crazy, vicious, bloodsucking tyrants, maybe. But not dumb. That I can promise ya."

Sato ran a hand through his hair, not sure which bothered him more: that his Alterant just happened to be the ruler of an entire planet, or that a group of crazy clown soldiers wanted him dead. Scratch that, he thought. The second one was definitely worse.

"Wait a minute," he said, just realizing something that should've been obvious from the start. "How could they possibly think that guy was me? Wouldn't he have been way taller?"

"Not really," Tollaseat answered. "Most of us chaps here in the Fifth don't hit our growth spurts 'til we hit drinkin' age. That not the same in your neck of the woods?"

Sato shrugged his shoulders wearily. "This is weird," he said, as if those three words summed up everything. Maybe they did. "I really feel like I'm missing something. And why'd you guys bring me here if you knew all this?"

Mothball's face scrunched up into a look of apology. "Sorry 'bout that. Really I am. Never thought we'd run into the Bugs. They 'aven't been about much lately, according to me parents. Thought their troubles with these parts was quite well and over."

"Quite true," Tollaseat added. "Had our wars with 'em blokes back when Mothball was a wee one, but not seen 'em much since. No idea why they're up in the deadie fields today. Strange, really."

Sato folded his arms and stared at the floor. Staying here much longer didn't sound like a good idea. "Well, maybe we should go back to headquarters. If those clowns want to kill me, I'd just as soon not be hanging out a couple of miles from them."

"Leave before supper?" Tollaseat exclaimed, shooting up from his seat. "Not a chance. I've got all three ovens runnin' top heat, cookin' a feast like you've never seen before, young man. Bugs 'ave no idea you're 'ere, I'd bet me left shoe. You just sit there and enjoy yourself with me wife and daughter while I go ready things up."

Windasill reached out and patted Sato on the knee. "I married the best cook in the entire valley, I did. Good thing me blood runs fast and hot, or I'd look like poor Rutger sitting over there."

Sato felt his eyes widen. He glanced quickly over at Rutger, who didn't seem fazed in the least by the rude comment.

"I'd rather be down close to the ground," the man said. "Safe and balanced, fat and happy. Lot better than looking like a bunch of dusty bones with clothes."

Windasill laughed, the nicest sound Sato remembered hearing in a long time. "Oh, Rutger, we do love you so. Every last inch of you—and that's saying quite a lot." Giggling, she left the room, presumably to help her husband in the kitchen.

Once she was gone, Sato sat up straighter and glared first at Rutger, then Mothball. "This is crazy. Is all that stuff true?"

"Right as rain," Mothball replied. "What's all the fuss? We'll have our dinner and be on our way, we will."

Rutger rolled forward until he plopped off the chair and onto his feet. "If anything, you're safer than ever. They think they killed you, remember? Calm down, and let's go eat. I'm—"

"Let me guess," Sato interrupted. "Starving."

"How'd you know?"

"Come on, funny bunnies," Mothball said, standing up on her tall legs. "I could use a bite to eat myself." She reached down and swatted Rutger on the back before moving toward the kitchen, her best friend right on her heels.

Sato stared at their backs until they disappeared out of the room. How weird had his life become? He was standing in a house that made him feel like he was four feet tall, in an entirely different world, about to eat dinner with three giants and a man shaped like a big beach ball, in a place where his twin had been the leader of the entire planet and had been assassinated by insane men dressed like clowns.

Could it get any stranger?

Refusing to answer that question, he walked quickly out of the room and toward the wonderful smells wafting from the kitchen.

CHAPTER 15

✳

THE TWELFTH BLADE

Frazier Gunn stared down at the twelfth Alterant of Mistress Jane.

She was huge. And she was the last of them.

This one had been living a normal life in a small village in the Fifth Reality, where quirks of evolution, diet, and climatic factors had led to an unusually large race of humans. He guessed the woman sitting in front of him, now safely chained to the twisty black stone of the twelfth Blade component, had to be almost eight feet tall, and skinny— like she'd eaten nothing but lettuce her whole life. Crooked teeth, no makeup, stringy black hair.

And yet, even then, she was beautiful. Despite the tears streaming down her face, despite the constant begging, despite the disgusting way she wrung her hands and wiped snot from her nose with her fingers, she was beautiful to him. Maybe it was just the resemblance to Jane. He hadn't seen her in days and missed her terribly. Maybe it was his longing for how she'd looked before the terrible Atticus Higginbottom incident. Maybe it was a lot of things.

But he was wasting time. He had to get back to the Thirteenth.

"Please," the woman whimpered for the thousandth time since being dragged from her garden. With her size and surprising strength, Frazier had been forced to use the Stunning Rod Jane had created for him, jolting the Alterant every so often to remind her to cooperate. It'd been a long and grueling trip. But nothing could dampen his spirits now—it was over. The hardest mission of his life was finally over.

Now the exciting part would begin.

"Please don't leave me here," the Alterant said between loud sniffs. "I 'ave children, I do. Me husband's away. None to take care of the wee ones."

Frazier leaned over, looking her square in the eyes. "Please be quiet." He dropped a pack of food and water at her feet then straightened and turned to walk away, moving as quickly as he could so he wouldn't have to hear her wailing pleas for help. He knew he should've told her what a good cause she was participating in, how eventually great things would come from Jane's plan with the Blade of Shattered Hope. But he couldn't bring himself to do it. He was too tired to speak anymore.

He topped a rise and quickly went down the deep slope. The woman's screeching, painful cries finally faded into the background. Capturing her had been the worst by far, maybe because she was the only one who hadn't had some kind of criminal or shady background. Of course, the pitiful lady didn't know this, but she had very good reason to feel such hopeless desperation.

Of the twelve Alterants of Mistress Jane, this one in the Fifth would be the only one to die. Well, this time around, anyway.

Mistress Jane stood at her favorite spot in the entire Lemon Fortress—maybe her favorite spot in all of the Realities. The open window of her room overlooked countless miles of forests, fields of green grass and wildflowers, and the snowcapped mountains in the distance. The beauty of it was overwhelming, even as seen through the eyeholes of her mask.

Normally she'd take it off, but she expected Frazier to report at any minute. And despite several months having passed since her entire body had been scorched and mutilated by Higginbottom, she had yet to let anyone see her true self—only her hands, so they'd know something horrible had happened. But she was still too ashamed, too embarrassed to reveal any other part of her now-hideous body. *Especially* her face. A face that had once, she thought proudly, been very, very beautiful.

A face that now looked like the scarred surface of a planet too close to a boiling sun.

At least the pain had subsided somewhat. With her increased powers over Chi'karda, she'd spent many days experimenting until she'd finally been able to manipulate her nervous system, a complex network of seemingly infinite human "wires." In the beginning she could only reduce the pain when she concentrated, focusing in deep meditation. But as the weeks passed, she'd come to learn to do it on instinct, and life had become much sweeter. More conducive to fulfilling her long-awaited plans.

But, unfortunately, she was still a long way from changing her appearance. For now, she had to settle for the robe and the mask to hide herself from the world, even from her closest friends.

Friends, with an "s" at the end? She was being far too generous. Only one person in all the Realities considered her a friend—Frazier.

Speaking of the devil, she heard a knock at the door.

"Come in," she said, sending out a wave of Chi'karda to dissolve the door, something she'd done a thousand times—much more satisfying than merely pulling it open, and a task that was much easier now with her supercharged abilities over the realm of physics.

She looked over from where she stood next to the window, and after Frazier had stepped through, she imagined the billions of tiny particles that made up the wood of the door coming back together. She *pushed* a mental surge in that direction, and with a buzzing swoosh, the door appeared as it had seconds before, unblemished and whole.

With another mere thought, she made one of the eyebrows on her red metal mask arch upward. "Is it finished?"

Frazier walked over, obviously trying his hardest not to smile, but it was there anyway, especially in his eyes. "Yes, Mistress. The twelfth one is in place, secured in the Fifth. All of them have nanolocators and monitoring devices injected within their bodies. The observation area is alive and chirping as we speak. All we need now is—"

"I know what we need!" Jane snapped, flowing her mask into anger. "Honestly, Frazier, sometimes you act as if all this were your idea, your plan. Keep speaking to me like I'm some lowly wretch, and I'll end your service to me—swiftly and painfully, I assure you. I don't care who you are or what you've done for me."

She regretted the words even as they flew out of her

mouth, hating the look of sincere and utter hurt that melted the poor man's face. But they had to be said. Once again, Frazier had shown traces of . . . confidence. Too much of it. She couldn't allow it. Confidence led to insubordination and betrayal. Always.

"I'm sorry, Mistress," Frazier muttered, his eyes downcast, his hands folded in front of him. "I'm only excited to see our—um, I mean, *your* plan—come to fruition."

There it was again, even after she'd rebuked him. *Our* plan—he'd actually said it! As much as it would hurt her, and as much as it would cause even more loneliness for her, she had to distance herself from him. Now more than ever.

"Very well, Frazier. Have a seat." She gestured toward the couch by the fireplace, then followed behind him until he sat down. She sat in the armchair directly across from him. The stone hearth to their right was dark and cold.

Bringing her mask back to a smooth, calm expression, she crossed her legs under the loose folds of her robe, instinctively suppressing the pain with her power the instant she felt it. "Let's be clear. All twelve of my Alterants are currently chained to the Blade devices, in each Reality, including Prime, within the specified ranges of the needed coordinates?"

Frazier nodded, his face now pale. *Ah,* she thought.

She *had* gone too far. When the man got too frightened, he became useless. Somehow she needed to learn how to hold back.

"Are you certain they're undisturbed?" she asked, trying to speak with a soothing voice. For all his tendency to fear her, he usually melted back to stupefied worship easily enough. "They're all alive and well?"

He only nodded again, but some of the color had returned to his face.

"Any potential problems?"

"Well, Mistress," he said, croaking a bit on the last syllable. He cleared his throat. "The coordinates in each Reality were in pretty remote areas, except for two. Your Alterant in Prime is in a basement, and in the Seventh, in the bottom floor of a parking garage. I left a couple of Sleeks in each of those locations to guard against potential intruders. As long as we stay on schedule, we should be okay."

Mistress Jane nodded slowly, pleased. If Frazier was correct, all the pieces were in place and everything else was up to her. All she needed was the Blade Tree, her witnesses, a quick wink to where she needed to go, and a few minutes of the most intense concentration she would ever embark upon.

She stood from the chair and held a hand out to Frazier. "Then I think we're ready to induce the Blade of Shattered Hope."

Frazier took her hand without the slightest hesitation, even though the hideous scars and melded chunks of gold were plainly evident. His touch warmed her, and the fact that he had no reservations or prejudice against her new nature . . .

That meant something. She felt ashamed of how she'd treated him earlier.

"Frazier," she said, pulling him up from the couch so he stood in front of her, just inches away. Her mask flowed into the most sincere smile she could conjure up in her mind. "You'll be by my side when we do this. Agreed?"

A trickle of . . . something pricked her heart when she saw tears glisten his eyes.

"Yes, Mistress," he said. "I'd be more honored than words can say."

"Good. Then let's go change the Realities once and for all."

CHAPTER 16

A DIABOLICAL PLAN

When Tick woke up, his parents had disappeared from the prison cell.

At first, he didn't quite notice, his mind still numb from sleep. Almost absently, he scanned the dimly lit room from left to right, expecting them to be *somewhere*. Huddled in a corner, maybe. Or hidden behind Master George, Paul, or Sofia, still dozing. Veiled in a shadow to which his eyes hadn't adjusted quite yet.

But then it hit him. They were gone.

His body jerked to full awareness like a bucket of water had been dumped on his head, and he jumped to his feet. "Where's my mom and dad? Where's my mom and dad!"

The others stirred, his shouts waking them.

"Huh?" Paul said groggily.

Sofia was looking around the room, much like he'd done just moments earlier. Master George grunted as he got to his feet, also searching with his eyes.

"Goodness gracious me," he said. "Where could they have gone off to?"

"We would've heard the door open," Sofia said. "No way we could've missed that."

That familiar panicky feeling threatened to consume Tick. "Where could they be?" He ran over to the bars of the cell, gripped his hands around the cold iron. "Mom! Dad! *Mooooom! Daaaaad!*"

First his sisters were taken, hidden in any one of who-knew-how-many horrible places. Now his parents were gone. "This can't be happening," he murmured, whispering it over and over. Then, "I'm gonna stop her. Once and for all, I'm gonna stop her."

"Calm down, Atticus," Master George said, hurrying to his side and placing a hand on his shoulder. "Remember the whole point of why Jane took your sisters. To *prevent* you from doing anything reckless."

For the first time since they'd left the basement of his house, Tick felt the surging boil of Chi'karda within him, burning and growing. But he also knew that Master George was right—he couldn't take a risk. Not now, not yet. Closing his eyes and concentrating

146

with all his might, he pushed the power away, urged it to cool and dissolve.

"Why would she have taken my parents?" he asked when he felt the episode was safely over. "Why now?"

"I'm sure we'll find out soon enough," Paul said. He stepped up next to Tick and squeezed his arm. "Sorry, dude. Seriously, though, we'll figure this out. We've been in worse shape, haven't we? We're like superheroes, man—we'll win this time, too."

Sofia walked over and hugged Tick, squeezing him tightly. Surprised, it took him a second before he squeezed back.

"Paul's an idiot," she said as she let go and stepped back. "And he never knows how to say anything. But he's right. We'll get your family back, don't worry. There's no way she'll . . . hurt them. Then she'd have nothing to threaten you with. I think she's terrified of you."

"Terrified?" a voice asked behind him.

Tick spun around to see Mistress Jane standing in the hallway, her red mask glaring at them with eyebrows raised.

"Where are they?" he shouted at her.

"They are safe for now," she replied, her face melting back into that non-expression she wore most of the time. "I decided there were too many of you to keep track of. Plus, your parents have been winked to a different location than where your sisters are. I now have double collateral to hang over your head. I sense even a spark of Chi'karda surge out of you, and one of them dies. On and on until they're all dead. If something bad happens to me, they all die at once. I trust you'll not test me on this."

Tick fumed more with every word that popped out of her mouth. It took all his concentration to keep the warmth from igniting to pure heat inside his chest. But he also felt a slight glimmer of hope. Based on what she'd said, it seemed like she couldn't sense his surges of Chi'karda as long as he kept them at bay. Maybe, when the time was right, he could let the power build and build, unleashing it all in one powerful explosion before she could react or send a message to anyone.

What am I thinking? he thought. *I don't even know what I'm talking about. I can't control this stuff.* It was just as likely he'd kill himself and his friends as it was he'd kill Jane.

"I'll take your silence as a sign that you understand the situation." Jane's arm shifted slightly, and the lock on the door sprung open with a loud click. The metal hinges groaned and squealed, and the door swung open. "And the same goes for any one of you. Try anything, and Tick's family will suffer the consequences. If we run out of Higginbottoms, we'll just have to do some hunting for Pacinis and Rogers. Or perhaps the tall ugly woman and her little pet, the ball of fat named Rutger. Do we all understand one another?"

When no one responded, Jane's scream pierced the air like a burst of thunder. *"Answer me!"*

"Yes," Tick said quickly, as did Paul and Sofia. The best she got out of Master George was a firm nod.

Jane stepped through the door and into the cell, standing very close to Tick. "We will be winking to a specific location here in the Thirteenth. Frazier has set up several spinners and monitors so all of you can best witness what happens today. When it's over, you'll spread the word, and we can begin the process of my taking over the Realities and putting the Utopia Initiative into full swing."

Master George laughed, a slow, condescending chuckle. Tick braced himself for Jane's reaction. He didn't see what was funny. Though he didn't know what she was talking about, her words had been like icy daggers scraping down his spine. She had something terrible planned, no doubt about it.

But Jane didn't explode with her usual anger. "Laugh all you want, George. Giggle, chortle, snicker, whatever pleases you most. A couple of hours from now, when you see what I do, you may never make such jolly sounds ever again. The Blade of Shattered Hope, George. Soulikens. Dark Matter. These are things you aren't even close to understanding yet."

Master George's face now showed no humor whatso-ever. It burned red, almost as if he wore his own mask. "Words, Jane. Anyone can say fancy words, trying their best to sound smarter than others. You keep telling us you have this *diabolical* plan. Well, then, what is it?"

Jane paused before answering, the corners of her metallic lips curving upward slightly. "I'm going to destroy the Fifth Reality."

Master George huffed. "Destroy it? What kind of nonsense is this? A mess of atomic bombs come across your path recently?"

Jane's mask turned a darker shade of red, something Tick hadn't thought possible. However, her expression didn't change. It was still set in that mocking half-smile. For a long time, she just stared at Master George.

"Jane," he finally said, "I worry your mind has slipped down a slope from which it can't be saved."

"You mistake my silence, George," Jane replied. "I'm surprised, actually. I'm baffled that you could be so short-sighted. So . . . *stupid.*"

"What exactly is *that* supposed to mean?"

"Do you really not understand my power over Chi'karda? Even before my . . . *union* with the core of Dark Infinity, I almost had the ability to do what I plan for today. Now, it will be done with absolute certainty."

"Well," Sofia chimed in, "quit talking about it and tell us what your big bad plan is."

Tick winced. She and Master George weren't being smart about this. Couldn't they see that Jane was deadly serious? Ticking her off even more was a very, very bad idea. But when Jane responded, her voice was as calm and collected as anything Tick had ever heard come out of her mouth.

"The Blade of Shattered Hope will collect every souliken from my Alterants, channel them into the necessary components, and ignite the dark matter within. The Blade will then *slice* the Fifth Reality from existence. Forever." She paused, then took a step forward. "Let me say it slowly for you, George. The Fifth will . . . be . . . no . . . more."

CHAPTER 17

✳

TALE OF THE
IRON POKER

As Sato devoured his third helping of the duck dumpling stew, he realized he'd gone at least five minutes without thinking about the whole nonsense of his Alterant being the ruler of a Reality before being murdered. There is something about tasty food that tends to wash your troubles away. And Tollaseat's food was, without hesitation or doubt, the most excellent stuff Sato had ever put in his mouth.

"This is good," he mumbled between bites, probably having said those three words a dozen times by now. "This is really good."

"Glad ya like it, I am." Tollaseat leaned back in his chair and puffed on his pipe. He'd lit it after eating

152

only one helping, and seemed to be enjoying every second of watching Sato eat like a starved hyena.

"Quite good, it was," Mothball pitched in, folding her arms and looking very satisfied.

Surprisingly, even Rutger—who was propped up on at least three pillows and a very large book—was finished, wiping his mouth and laying the napkin on his bowl. "Sato, I had no idea you could stuff your face like that. You'd make my mama proud."

Windasill grinned as she leaned forward and reached for the ladle in the big pot of stew. "Care for another helping, Master Sato?"

Suddenly, as if a switch had been flicked inside of him, Sato realized he was terribly, horribly, awfully full. He dropped his spoon and looked up, hoping the feeling that he might explode at any second didn't show on his face. "No, thanks. I think I might've taken one bite too many."

"Oh, rubbish," she said through an exaggerated frown. "There's always room for more duck dumpling stew. Isn't there, my sweet?" She glanced over at Tollaseat.

Mothball's dad puffed out a big cloud of wispy smoke. "Methinks the lad's proven himself quite nicely, me love. Let him rest up an hour or two. Then we'll bring out the *desserts*." He emphasized the last word in a roar with his wide eyes twinkling. He put the pipe back into his mouth and chuckled lightly.

The thought of dessert almost put Sato over the edge. "Sounds great," he managed to get out.

"Tell us a story," Mothball said, looking at her dad. "Been quite some time since we've 'eard you make somethin' up 'bout the war years, it 'as. Sato 'ere might enjoy your boastin' for a while." She looked over at Sato and winked. "Won't quite know what's true and what's not, but it's fun to listen to, ya can trust me on that one."

Rutger pounded the table. "I second the motion. After a meal like that, a body needs to hear a good tale or two."

Tollaseat scrunched up his face into something very serious, looking around the room at each person in turn. "Wanna hear a story, do ya?"

"Yeah," Sato said at the same time as everyone else. He was surprised at himself, but he suddenly wanted nothing more than to hear this tall, kind man tell stories about the old days, even though those old days would be very different from days in Reality Prime.

Tollaseat leaned back, his chair creaking, and shifted so that the elbow supporting his pipe-holding hand rested on the other arm. He took a puff or two then started talking, swirls of wispy smoke slowly drifting toward the ceiling.

"Back when I was a wee lad, barely ten and six—that's sixteen to you, Master Sato—just when the growin' pains started stretching me arms and legs, life was sweet and terrible. Sweet in that me mum and dad were alive and well, the crops were growin' right sprightly, and I'd just met me future love"—he nodded toward Windasill—"at the August Festie. But it was terrible, too, yes indeed. That ruddy summer marked the worst we'd had yet with the Bugs, it did."

He coughed and reached out for a sip of water before taking another puff from his pipe. "Late one night, I was sleepin' nice and cozy in me bed, dreamin' of good days to come. Mayhaps dreamin' about Windasill, even. Most of the fightin' with them nasty Bugs was off in the far country, ya see—just frightenin' tales and rumors to the likes of us, it was. But we knew things were quite bad, and that blokes like myself might have to run off and get to soldierin' and whatnot. But that night, all was well when I put on me long johns and dozed to the soft sounds of the breeze and the stream out back.

"But then came the knock on the door." He leaned forward, putting his elbows on the table. "Woke me right up, it did. I remember sittin' up, perkin' me ears. Heard the footsteps of me dad, heard the door creak as it swung open, heard the murmurs of conversation, though I couldn't make out any words. Then . . ."

He trailed off, a glazed look coming over his face. Sato felt his own face redden in embarrassment. Maybe the old man—

Tollaseat slammed his hand against the table. Dishes rattled and his pipe went skittering across the floor. Windasill quickly jumped up to retrieve it and returned it to her husband. As she sat down again, Sato waited breathlessly for what Tollaseat might say next.

"Can't quite say what sound it was I 'eard next," Mothball's dad continued. "A groan. A sigh. Maybe a bit of a whimper. But for some reason, it sent me brain spinnin' with alarm. I jumped from me bed and scrambled out to the main room. Right there in front of me, a ruddy Bugaboo was on top of me dad, his hands raised, claspin' the biggest sword you ever did see. Mum came in right then and screamed a sound you'd never believe 'less your own ears were there to 'ear it. If I'm honest with ya, which I am, 'twas that sound— me mum splinterin' the air with all the anguish in the world—that made me move. Even more than seein' me dad 'bout to meet the pointy end of a sword."

Sato leaned forward, sure he'd never been so captivated in his life.

Tollaseat barely paused between sentences now. "Acted, I did. Ran straight for the hearth—the ashes still glowin' hot—grabbed the iron poker me own Uncle Kent forged, gripped it with both of me ruddy hands, swung it up, and charged that Bug. Saw the fear in that loonie's eyes. Saw them widen and turn into pools of pure white. He started to say somethin', started to move, started to swing down with his arms and his sword. I screamed and swung that blessed iron poker. I swung it with every bit of strength cloggin' me pores and joints. I swung it straight for the Bug's face."

He paused then and took a long pull on his pipe. Scanning Sato and the others at the table, he finally blew out a stream of smoke. He looked down at the table, his eyes full of shadowy memories.

"What happened?" Sato whispered, unable to help himself.

Tollaseat, still staring at the empty plate in front of him, answered in a haunted voice. "I missed him. Completely missed the ruddy buzzard."

Sato swallowed heavily, slumping in his chair.

"Killed me dad, the Bug did." Tollaseat finally glanced up, his gaze resting on Sato. "But I saved me mum. I was able to run off the Bug. Swore the rest of me life to hunt them down, one by one, 'til every last one of them buggers was dead and rottin'."

The pipe went back into his mouth, and complete silence settled on the room. After a long minute, Sato looked at Mothball, her eyes moistened with tears, and then at Rutger, who was probably unaware he was still nibbling a biscuit. Both of them were staring at Tollaseat. After a moment, it became evident the story was over.

"Thank you for sharing, dear," Windasill said,

patting her husband on the arm. "'Eard it a thousand times, I 'ave, but I marvel at your courage every time. Never forget you saved your mum that day, dear. Never forget."

"Wish I could've met Grandpa," Mothball said, a choking clog in her voice. "But 'tweren't for you, Daddy, I wouldn't've spent me whole childhood with Grandma. Thanks be to ya, Daddy. Thanks be to ya very much."

Sato was stunned. He'd expected a story more along the lines of a fairy tale, maybe a funny or an embarrassing moment. But Tollaseat had just shared probably the most terrifying, pivotal moment of his life. And Sato had absolutely no idea what to say. He stared at his plate, feeling the heavy weight of all the food he'd eaten.

"Right cheerful, don't ya think?" Tollaseat said, a smile breaking through the gloom on his face. "Not quite sure why I told that story. Meant to tell somethin' else, I did. But it just popped out of me mouth."

"Important we remember," Mothball offered, giving her mom an uncomfortable look.

"Yes, me sweet," Tollaseat replied. "Reckon I wanted Master Sato 'ere to understand why them Bugs aren't just a joke, even though they look it. Crazy, they are. Vicious little rats. But underestimate 'em, and you'll be lookin' up at ten feet of dirt soon, you will. Be wary while you're about these parts, is all I'm sayin'."

Sato merely nodded, still unable to speak. He didn't know why, exactly, but that story had touched him, made his heart ache with sorrow. And then it hit him why.

Sato, too, had seen his father killed right in front of him. Burned to death by Mistress Jane's flying flames. Maybe that was worse than seeing your dad stabbed by a sword. Maybe not. It didn't matter. Something came over him in that moment.

He stood up. "Mister, um, Master . . . Tollaseat?"

Mothball's dad lowered his pipe, looked at Sato with dark eyes, and Sato somehow knew the old man had already figured out what he was about to say.

"I want to help," Sato said, trying to sound like an adult and hoping no one laughed. "I want to help your people fight the Bugs."

CHAPTER 18

✳

TOWERS OF RED

Tick," Master George whispered. "I need you to listen to me very carefully. And do me a favor."

Jane had brought them to a room several levels above the prison cell in which they'd been held captive. She'd left a couple of guards at the door. The creatures in full armor were human in shape but all comparisons ended there. Tick hadn't gotten a good look, but he swore he saw horns or tusks coming out of their shadow-hidden faces and large bulges on their backs.

"What?" Tick asked.

In response, Master George handed him a small, metal tube.

"What's this?"

"What do you *think?*"

Tick looked over at Paul and Sofia, hoping they were listening. But both of them were trying to look through a grime-covered window. "Is it a message for somebody?"

"Precisely," George whispered.

"For who?" Tick asked. "And what do you want me to do?"

"It's a message for Sally. It's short, but he should get the point. I want him to gather the Realitants so they'll be ready on a moment's notice. For what, I have no idea—but he needs to get them to headquarters straightaway."

That made perfect sense to Tick, but he had a bad feeling about this all the same. "And . . . what does that have to do with me?"

Master George looked at him, his eyes shifting slightly back and forth. "Well, er, well, I need you to . . . wink it to Sally."

"*What?*" Tick rasped, way too loudly.

Sofia noticed. "What are you guys talking about over there?"

"Never you mind," Master George answered, surprisingly harsh.

Sofia, of course, completely ignored him and walked over, dragging Paul with her. "No secrets, boss. What's going on?"

Tick couldn't remember the last time he'd seen

Master George look so perplexed. His face was red, eyes darting around the room, sweat trickling down his temples. "Someone's going to *hear* us!" he exclaimed in a half-shout, half-whisper.

Tick didn't like it that Master George had asked him to use his power in the first place. Only a half an hour ago, Jane had threatened to kill his family one by one if she sensed him using Chi'karda. "How am I supposed to wink the message? Even if I could, even if I had a clue how to do it, I can't risk Jane finding out."

"Yes, yes, I *know*," Master George said, throwing all the frustration he could into the last word. "But perhaps you can risk it when she's . . . occupied with whatever she has planned. If we don't gather the other Realitants to help us, it may all be quite moot anyway."

Tick slid the message tube into his pocket. The old Brit was being coy, but Tick knew exactly what he was *really* trying to say. "So you think it's okay to sacrifice my family for the greater good. Let them die if it'll save the world. Worlds. Whatever." Tick couldn't believe how bitter he sounded. To make it worse, Master George had a *point*. But not one Tick could accept.

For the hundredth time, he felt an overwhelming, gloomy sorrow squeeze his chest and lungs. His sisters. His mom and dad. Jane had them. No matter what, he had to save them. No matter what.

But how?

"Tick?" Sofia asked, jolting him back to reality. "You okay? What does he want you to do?"

"We need to stop talking about this," Master George said. "Right now!"

"Dude," Paul said, "what are you two freaks talking about?"

Tick looked at him and shook his head. "It's nothing—George just wants to get a message to Sally." He turned his attention back to Master George. "Don't you have a way of talking to him? Through your nano-locator or something?"

Master George shook his head. "I think she's done something to us. Shielded us somehow. I've tried making contact several times. Nothing."

"Since when is Sally in charge?" Paul asked. "Rutger finally explode or something?"

"Maybe he ate one of his own Ragers," Sofia added.

By the looks of it, Master George was not amused. He turned his back to the three of them and walked over to a corner.

Sofia elbowed Paul in the arm. "Way to go, smarty."

"You, too, Godzilla," he replied. "Your comment was worse than mine."

Tick couldn't remember a time when he'd been *less* in the mood to listen to his friends fight. "Guys! You think this is all some kind of stupid joke?" As soon as the words were out, he regretted them. Especially when he saw the look on their faces—shock, mixed with a little hurt.

"What crawled up your pants and started biting?" Paul asked.

"Tick's right," Sofia said, her eyes never leaving Tick's. "His family's been taken. I can't imagine . . . what that must be like. We need to take things more seriously."

She looked away, and Tick saw an expression he couldn't quite identify come over her face. Regret? Longing? Whatever it was, it was something to do with *her*, not him. He thought about all her comments in the past, the subtle remarks here and there about her family—none of them very nice. Maybe she was wishing she had parents and siblings whom, if taken, she'd worry about as much as he was worried about his. The twisted thought added to his sadness.

"Well, we still have to be ourselves," Paul said. "Tick, dude, sorry, but if we get all mopey, then we might as well just give up and die. You know I don't think this is all a joke, man. Give me a break."

Tick looked at him, surprised at the angry tone of his voice. Paul was always laid back, taking what came at him. Even his sparring words with Sofia were always filled with obvious jest.

Tick shook his head. "Okay, whatever. This is all stupid anyway. We're sitting here in a soap opera while

Jane's planning something *diabolical*. What are we gonna do?"

Master George was still in the corner, but he turned around to face them. "We need to stay on our guard and look for the first opportunity that comes along. I've no idea what that may be, and I've no idea what we'll do. But something will come along, and we *must* be ready."

"What about Tick's family?" Sofia asked.

Tick had been wondering the same thing, but reality hit him then. He didn't know what it was—maybe it was the distressed look on Master George's face, maybe it was something in what he'd said. Either way, Tick realized a heavy truth. This wasn't just about him and his parents and his sisters. Jane was planning the single worst thing to ever happen to humans in the history of the universe. At least, that's what it sounded like. Her plan involved destroying an entire world full of people.

Could he really put his family above that? If it really came down to choosing between them and dozens, hundreds, thousands, even millions of lives, what would he do? What *should* he do?

He wanted to scream. No one should have to make decisions like this, especially not a fourteen-year-old kid. In that instant, his hatred for Jane changed into something more powerful, more acute. Every single molecule in his body wanted her dead.

"Tick?" Paul asked. "What are you staring at?"

Tick realized his eyes were focused on a greasy, dark smear on the stone on the opposite wall. He shook his head, scrambling the thoughts in his mind. "Sorry. Just thinking."

Master George walked back to him and the others. He held a hand out and squeezed Tick's shoulder. "Master Atticus. I give you my word that I will do everything in my power to help save your family. I will give my life, if necessary. But in return, you must promise me that you'll look at the bigger picture and do whatever it takes to stop Jane before she does something apocalyptic. I know her, my good man, and when she says she'll destroy the Fifth Reality, she means it. She has no reason to boast with lies. We're talking about billions of lives, Atticus. Billions."

Tick couldn't meet his gaze. He couldn't promise himself or anyone else that he'd be able to make the right choice if it came down to that. All he could see in his mind were his parents, Lisa, and . . .

Kayla. Thinking of little Kayla just about shattered his heart.

Unable to do anything else, he nodded.

"Very well," Master George said. "We can only take things step by—"

tingle

"—step."

In the small blip of time between his last two words, everything changed. As Tick was looking at their leader and listening to him speak, he felt the familiar tingle shoot down the back of his neck. The room around them disappeared, replaced by red rock.

He noticed the others spin around, just as he did, to see where Jane had brought them with her strange winking powers. They were in the middle of a desert, towering spires of stone standing all around them, jutting up from a natural rock wall that more or less encircled them. Tick couldn't see one plant, not one weed, or anything close to the color green or even brown. Everything was reddish-orange, jagged and rough, all sharp corners and cracks and crevices. Desolation.

The sun was behind a massive tower of stone, but the heat was suffocating. Tick already felt himself sweating.

"I don't see any tombstones," Paul muttered, and Tick couldn't tell if he was being sarcastic or making a very good point.

"Realities help us," Master George said. "If she can wink people to anywhere she wants so easily . . . Let's hope a lot of poor saps were killed here at some point in history."

"That's a cheerful thought," Sofia said.

Just then, Mistress Jane appeared in front of them. As always with winking, there was no puff of smoke, no flash of light or sound. One second she wasn't there, and the next second she was, dressed in her usual yellow garb and her shiny red mask. Her face was pulled into a genuine smile. It gave Tick the creeps.

"Looks like I miscalculated a bit," she said. "Guess I'm not perfect after all. We need to be on the other side of that."

She pointed at the stone face to their right. The wall was maybe forty feet high, with several spires of rock stretching toward the sky from its top edge. Though it had a menacing feel to it, the slope didn't seem too steep, and Tick thought they could probably climb it pretty easily.

"Follow me," Jane said as she headed in that direction, lifting up the bottom folds of her robe as she walked and carefully avoiding chunks of rock strewn about the desert floor. "And remember, Atticus—don't try anything."

When neither Tick nor anyone else made a move, Jane stopped. Her body stiffened, and some kind of unspoken warning seemed to flow from her, back at them like a misty spray of poison. She didn't need to say a word.

As one, Tick and his friends stepped forward and followed her.

CHAPTER 19

✳

THE BLACK TREE

The heat was stifling, an invisible fire that suffused the air of the world, filling Tick's lungs with every breath he took. Once they reached the slope of the red wall, he realized it was much steeper than it had originally looked. Amazed at how easily Jane scooted up its face, he determined to do just as well.

Grabbing rocks that blistered with heat and finding footholds aplenty in the cracked and creviced stone, he found climbing wasn't so bad. About halfway up the wall, he looked down to see Paul and Sofia right below him. Master George was struggling a little, mainly because he was trying to keep his suit from getting dirty, but the darker patches of sweat under his arms revealed that his suit would need a good wash anyway—though Tick doubted they'd be seeing a Laundromat on the other side of this wall.

What am I thinking about? Tick asked himself as he continued to climb. Laundry? Sweaty armpits? He needed to stay focused.

Jane reached the top ridge above him and disappeared from sight, kicking a trickle of rocks down the slope with her last steps. Tick squeezed his eyes shut until the rocks passed; a couple of pebbles nicked his forehead. He pulled himself up the last few feet and stood on the top edge of the wall, taking in the sight before him. Sofia thumped the back of his leg.

"Scoot over, Tick," she said. "Give us some room here."

Tick stepped forward, too focused on the strange setting below him to respond to Sofia. The ground slowly sloped from where he stood, leading to a wide depression surrounded by squat, scraggly trees that barely clung to life, their sparse leaves more brown than green. Scattered across the dusty ground of the natural bowl formation were several groups of people, each group focusing and working on various stations that couldn't possibly have looked more out of place.

Computers and monitors covered tables scattered around the ground. Other platforms held large, silver machines he'd never seen before, each one loaded with odd appendages and dials and switches. Several viewing screens had been set up, tall and square and white, perched precariously on metal stands. Tick feared the slightest wind would topple them over. In the middle of each screen, Tick saw something he recognized: a small metal rod attached with a suction cup.

Spinners. Devices from the Fourth Reality, spinners used some kind of laser technology to project pictures and video. Jane had said she wanted them to witness something, but Tick hadn't thought they'd be watching it like *that*.

Sofia and Paul were standing next to him now, scanning the area as he was. Master George finally made it to the ridge as well. Tick heard him grunting and gasping for breath behind them.

"What's that in the middle?" Paul asked, pointing.

Tick looked, and when he saw what Paul was pointing at, he couldn't believe he'd missed it before.

It was a statue of a tree, maybe four feet tall, and made of the blackest material Tick had ever seen. There was no blemish to its darkness, no dust, no flash of light or reflection. Every inch of it was pure black. The trunk of the tree was about a foot thick, and its limbs shot off starting halfway up, branching out over and over until the outermost tips were as thin as toothpicks.

"That's plain weird," Sofia said.

"What could she possibly be doing with all this

junk?" Paul asked. "Especially a stupid sculpture of a tree?"

Master George had finally caught his breath. "Whatever that tree is, I suspect it's the most important thing down there. It gives me a very bad feeling."

"It's so black it doesn't seem real," Sofia said.

Tick noticed Jane had walked all the way down to the outermost group of people next to a row of computers but was now coming back. Her red mask still had that creepy smile, like she was a kid at Disneyland and having the time of her life.

"Come down!" she called. "I've got chairs for you!"

Tick exchanged looks with Paul and Sofia. Jane sounded way too cheerful, way too nice. That scared Tick almost more than when she screamed at the top of her lungs.

"Off we go," Master George whispered, giving the three of them a gentle push from behind.

When they made it to the bottom, Jane gestured toward a man holding four folding chairs in his hands, two in each. He had black hair and unusually thin eyebrows, and he wore a faded red T-shirt and jeans. As he started setting up the chairs, Jane introduced him.

"This is Frazier Gunn, my most loyal servant. He'll be in charge of ensuring you all witness today's events. I'll be too busy to see to it myself. But let me make this clear—if you cooperate, no harm will come to you or the

Higginbottom family. However, one sign of trouble, and Frazier . . . has his orders."

Tick's hatred for her burned inside him, and he had to suppress a rising tide of Chi'karda. He pushed it away, feeling an icy chill settle in his gut. Completely dejected, he numbly walked to one of the chairs and sat down, saying nothing, ignoring everybody. All he could see in his mind were images of his family.

"That's the spirit," Jane said. "The rest of you sit down. The show will begin shortly."

"What *is* the show?" Master George asked, not having moved an inch at her command.

"Sit, George," Jane replied. "You'll see soon enough."

Paul and Sofia sat down on either side of Tick, their faces looking half confused and half angry, and maybe a little curious as well. Tick couldn't help but wonder what they were thinking. If the roles were reversed, would he think them selfish if they refused to fight Jane because they didn't want to risk the lives of their families? He hoped not.

"Hey," Paul whispered as he leaned toward him. "Look at that tree. It almost looks like it's made of liquid or something. Does funny things to my eyes when I stare at it."

Tick moved his eyes in that direction. The black sculpture was fascinating this close up. The tree was deeply dark, its details crisp, the edges finer than they naturally should be. Every branch, from the thick parts where they connected to the trunk to the needle-thin tips, which looked sharp enough to impale rock, almost seemed to move in an unseen breeze, tricking his vision as he scanned the sculpture from top to bottom, side to side.

"It *is* weird," he finally said to Paul.

He felt like he wasn't looking at something in the real world. It reminded him more of animation, something done with the most advanced computer technology available. It made him queasy; he finally looked away. Jane's workers bustled about the area, checking dials and switches, typing on keyboards, adjusting the screens. But no one came within a few feet of the black tree. No one even appeared to look at it.

Maybe they are as terrified of it as we are, Tick thought. What could it possibly be?

Actually, one person *was* looking at it. Jane stood on the edge of the temporary complex, almost hidden from his sight by one of those movie screens. Arms folded, her mask showing that unreadable expression, she seemed to be concentrating on the tree. Tick would've given anything to see her real face at that moment, or better yet, to read her thoughts. What was going on here?

"Tick," Sofia said quietly.

"What?" He cringed—he hadn't meant to sound so harsh.

Sofia's head snapped around to glare at him. "Okay, you know what, *Atticus?* I know they have your family, and I know you're stressed to the max. But being rude to us isn't gonna help anybody."

Tick knew she was right, and for about three seconds hated her for it. "Sorry," he finally muttered.

"It's fine. Listen, what can you do with this power of yours? The Chi'karda. We haven't really had much chance to talk about it."

Paul leaned forward to put his elbows on his knees, looking their way. "Yeah, man, it seems like you learned a lot more about it since last time you gave us an update on e-mail."

Tick shook his head. He didn't really want to talk about it, but he forced himself to do it, hoping he could get his mind off his family. "It's crazy. I feel this really warm burning in my chest, like hot air is swirling around in there. In my basement, I concentrated on it, tried to picture things in my mind. Like it was something I could grab with my hands—my pretend hands, I guess. Then I threw it at her. It was all mental—just like acting out images in my head."

"I couldn't really tell what was happening," Sofia said. "I felt something, like a big surge of energy or electricity. And I could tell Jane was struggling against an invisible wall of whatever. But it wasn't like you were shooting balls of fire."

"Yeah," Paul added. "Why can't you just shoot balls of fire? That'd be nice."

Tick ignored that, trying to decide if he dared say what he'd just thought. "Well, there might be something."

Sofia gave him a puzzled look. "What?"

"You know how she keeps saying she can sense when I use the Chi'karda?"

Sofia and Paul both nodded.

"I think she might be bluffing."

"Really?" Paul asked. "Why?"

Tick tapped his chest. "There have been a few times when it swelled up inside me, and I had to fight it off. She never said a word about it."

"Maybe she can't sense it unless you actually use it," Sofia suggested. "Or throw it, or whatever it is you do."

"Yeah," Tick said. "Still, maybe I can play with it a little bit. Test it out a little and see if she says anything. I bet she'd give me a warning before she actually did something to my family."

Paul grunted. "Dude, you sure you wanna risk that?"

Tick looked at him, surprised at how glad he was Paul had asked that. He hoped Sofia felt the same. He hoped they understood how careful he had to be.

"No, but I think I have to try. Next time I can trigger

something in here"—he tapped his chest again—"I'll try it a little."

Sofia looked like she was about to respond when a loud humming sound cut her off.

Tick's hands instinctively covered his ears. It wasn't so much the volume of the sound as the *vibration* of it. A deep, thrumming toll, like a massive bell had been struck just feet away. The noise had an underlying buzz, too, as if the same bell had upset a nest of gigantic wasps.

"What is that?" Paul shouted.

Tick didn't know for sure, but it seemed like the source of the horrible sound was coming from . . .

He saw dust and pebbles bouncing on the ground. He had no doubt.

It was coming from the black tree.

CHAPTER 20

DISTURBANCES

It took a lot of persuading, but Sato finally convinced Mothball and Rutger to accept Tollaseat's offer to stay overnight and return to headquarters the next morning. They were anxious to get back and hear about the results of some secret meeting Master George had run off to, but agreed that one night wouldn't hurt.

But the promise of a warm fire in a cozy house, and the promise of more desserts from Tollaseat—maybe even a story or two—sealed the deal. And Sato loved the idea of sleeping in one of the gigantic—and soft—beds upstairs. His cot back in the Bermuda Triangle always made him feel like he'd slept on a concrete floor.

They'd just sat down in the living room, plates

of cheesecake balanced on their laps, cups of hot tea steaming on the end tables, and a large fire crackling in the brick hearth, when Rutger brought up for the tenth time what Sato had said earlier about wanting to help in the fight against the Bugaboo soldiers.

"What made you say that?" Rutger asked, not caring that his mouth was full of cake. "You were just being nice, right?"

"I thought it a very kind gesture, indeed," Windasill said. She held her cup right below her lips and blew across the hot tea.

"Why do you keep asking me about it?" Sato turned to Rutger. "It just ticks me off that they've done so many bad things. I want to help. Why is that so hard for you to get?"

"I just meant—"

"Isn't that what we're about?" Sato snapped. "The Realitants? Aren't we supposed to help people?"

Rutger's eyes widened in surprise. "Well, yes. Of course it is."

"Then quit asking." Sato forked a bite of cheesecake into his mouth, then took a sip from his cup.

He had no idea why he felt so edgy and irritated. He shouldn't feel embarrassed that the real reason he wanted to help was because of Tollaseat's story about watching his own father be killed. No one had been there to help Sato when the same tragedy had happened to him. He felt obligated, but not in a forceful, guilty way. It was more that he felt a connection to Tollaseat that wouldn't go away.

For the first time, his feelings solidified into one easy statement in his mind: He wanted revenge. And by fighting the Bugs who had killed Tollaseat's father and were connected with the woman who had killed his own father, maybe he could find it.

"Sorry, Sato," Rutger said. "I didn't mean it as an insult. The opposite, actually. I was impressed, and that made me curious as to what was behind it. I'll shut up now."

"That'd be perfect," Sato said, trying to soften his words with a smile, trying to return to the good mood of his earlier determination to fight the Bugs and his excitement at spending the night in the Fifth Reality. "Seriously, I mean it, though. Tollaseat, I'm going to get permission from George to come back and help. Whatever I can do."

Tollaseat bowed his head in a deep nod. "I'm quite honored, Master Sato. I'll ask around town for ways you . . ."

He trailed off, slowly lowering his cup back to the small table next to his chair. He looked confused.

"What is it, dear?" Windasill asked.

"What?" He focused on her. "Oh, well, I just had a thought. People will see that Sato here is a dead ringer for our deceased leader. Don't know how we can get around that."

"Makes a good point, he does," Mothball said. "Sato, not sure we can be doin' that. Quite risky. Might make folks talk and wonder."

Sato couldn't believe he hadn't thought of that very problem. How would that work to have someone come along who was the Alterant of your dead leader? He felt a pit of disappointment open up in his stomach.

"No matter," Tollaseat said, waving his hand in the air. "Think on it, no rush. Things have been quite cool of late, not too many problems with the ruddy Bugs. Mayhaps when you get a bit older, look a bit different, when it's . . . less obvious you're not from these parts and couldn't be him."

Rutger suddenly chuckled.

"What's so funny?" Mothball asked.

Rutger shrugged. "Could be quite a sight. Those clowns seeing their victim come back from the dead. Maybe they'd—"

A loud, horrible crash and the crunch of shattered glass cut him off. Sato jumped up, looking over in time to see hundreds of shards from the big window that overlooked the front yard blow inward, the glass bouncing and clinking off furniture as it fell to the floor.

Mothball's mom yelped; Tollaseat called out something, but Sato couldn't tell what he'd said. Rutger, who had been the closest to the window, seemed too shocked to move. Pieces of glass glittered in his hair and on his shoulders.

Everyone stared at the empty window as if waiting for someone to jump up and explain what had happened. In the silence, Sato heard the distant sounds of glass breaking in other parts of the house. Then, from outside, came a low, repeating pulse of noise, some kind of deep buzz or static, surging in short waves. He almost *felt* it more than heard it with his ears.

"What's going on?" Sato asked. "What is that noise?"

"No ruddy idea," Mothball answered.

The sound grew and intensified, making Sato's head hurt. "What shou—"

He fell to the floor as the whole house started to shake and tremble.

Tick sat still, transfixed by the humming, throbbing black tree. Its waves of energy were almost visible to some sixth sense he didn't quite understand. Since the noise had started, none of his friends had said a word, and Tick was sure they were as mesmerized and scared as he was.

The man Jane had called Frazier Gunn was walking from screen to screen, flicking the thin metal bar of each spinner that was attached to the exact center. He moved on without even waiting to make sure the spinner worked. As if by magic, and certainly by a technology Tick didn't understand, the metal rods spun faster and faster, despite the seeming lack of any motor.

A shimmering silver disk, maybe four inches wide, appeared. Once the spinner hit full speed, a much larger, red-tinted projection shot out, creating a wide, hazy circle that covered most of the screen behind it. Only the white corners of the squares were visible. Tick knew that soon those red circles would turn into video feeds, as clear in quality as any movie he'd ever seen.

Just as Frazier flicked the last spinner, Mistress Jane came over to Tick and the others, seemingly done with whatever she'd been doing to make the menacing black tree hum as it did. She stopped a few feet in front of their line of chairs, her red mask looking somewhat weary. She stared directly at Tick.

"I'm going to explain everything to you," she said, her voice tight. Strained. "And this isn't some example of the bad guys telling the good guys the whole *diabolical* plan just in time for them to escape and save the day. No, I *want* you to know. Every last detail. Once you do, and once you witness the extent of my power, I'll set you free so you can tell the other Realitants and spread the word throughout each world. Everyone must know what I'm capable of, and the reasons why it must happen."

She paused, and the eyes of her mask, dark and deep, never wavered from Tick. "Correction. I'm going to set *most* of you free to spread the word. Atticus stays with me."

Tick stood up, not sure where the courage came from. "What? Why? You promised you'd let me and my family go if I didn't try to stop you."

Jane's scarred hand shot out from beneath the folds of her robe, her palm outward. At the same instant, Tick flew backward, hit by an unseen force that thumped him in the chest. He fell into his chair and toppled over, banging his head against the dusty, hard ground. Shaking it off, he scrambled to his feet and picked up his chair. Glaring at Jane, he took a seat, hating himself for being such a wimp. Not an ounce of Chi'karda flickered inside him.

Jane's mask was a sneer. "I never made any such promise of letting *you* free, Atticus. Only your family. Now stay silent, or I'll get rid of one of your sisters."

Tick gripped the sides of his chair to stop his hands from shaking. He had to do something. This wasn't right, letting this woman treat them this way. He had to do something!

Jane continued with her speech as if nothing had happened. "What you'll be witnessing today is the first fully functional use of the most mysterious substance in the universe. Most scientists throughout the Realities don't even know what it *is,* much less how to use it."

"What are you talking about?" Master George said.

Jane didn't take her eyes off Tick, answering her former boss without so much as the courtesy of a glance. "George, as usual, you speak to me with your condescending, I-know-more-than-you-do arrogance. Now shut up."

Tick looked over at Master George, shocked at how childishly rude Jane's command had been. The old man glowered, his face redder than ever, his lips quivering despite being pressed together so hard they were almost white. But he didn't say anything.

"The Blade Tree before you," Jane continued, her expression still angry, "is made from the substance I was trying to tell you about before being so rudely interrupted. No tool of modern science could've accomplished such a thing as creating this object, I assure you. It took my ever-growing skills—fostered from my connection with the Thirteenth Reality—along with the additional powers granted to me by being unified with Chu's Dark Infinity, and an understanding of physics only my innate brilliance combined with a lifetime of study could accomplish."

She leaned closer to Tick. "Think on this, Atticus. As great as my gifts over Chi'karda have become, I could not have done this without the catalyst and boosting power of Chu's failed mechanism. In many ways, you are my partner. Think on that as you see what's about to happen."

She knelt down before him, reached out her disgusting right hand, and placed it on Tick's knee. Even through his jeans, he could feel the roughness of her palm, the tiny pricks of metal jutting out from her skin. Though every instinct told him to get up, scream, and run as far away as possible, he refused to cower away from her.

Jane's mask melted and flowed into an evil grin.

"Yes, Atticus," she said in a mockingly gentle voice. "Think on what you did to me as you watch billions of people in the Fifth Reality die."

Tick had hoped deep down that she hadn't meant it when she'd said her plan was to destroy an entire planet. But the demented tone of her next statement erased all doubt—and hope.

"Billions, Atticus. Billions."

CHAPTER 21

✳

THE UNLEASHING

The constant, terrible, pulsing waves of sound increased in volume, rattling Sato's skull as the earthquake's intensity slowly escalated.

He crawled toward Windasill, unable to get back to his feet. The house shook like a ship at sea, thrown about by massive waves and wind. Things crashed all around them: lamps, dishes, picture frames, decorative trinkets of glass. Their remains littered the floor, sharp and vicious. Sato picked through the wreckage, ignoring the pricks of pain, the feel of moistness on his palms. He refused to look down, hoping it was sweat, not blood.

He'd seen Windasill fall but hadn't heard a peep from her since. With no idea where Mothball, Rutger, and Tollaseat had gone off to, Sato could only think to try to help where he could. Windasill.

He rounded an overturned cabinet, the large wooden drawers spilling out. Windasill was on the floor, lying on her side, a trickle of blood running from her mouth. Her eyes were closed, but her chest rose and fell with deep breaths.

"Windasill!" he yelled. When she didn't respond, he lurched forward. He felt like he was trying to move with three extra arms and legs. Thumping to the floor next to her, he smashed his nose against the ground. Somehow, despite the world shaking all around him, he got his arms around her and lifted her head into his lap as he sat up.

"Windasill!" he shouted again.

A moan escaped her, and her eyes flickered open. "What's happening?" she whispered.

Sato wouldn't have understood if he hadn't been able to see her lips mouth the words. "I don't know!" he shouted back. "I—"

"Sato!"

Mothball's voice. He turned his head to see her and Rutger at the front door, the two of them clutching the doorframe as their bodies swayed back and forth, constantly bumping into each other. He could see past them to the trees whipping in the wind. The sky was dark, only a few stars barely bright enough to flicker.

How had he gotten here? He thought he'd been moving toward the kitchen, toward the back of the house. "Where's your dad?" he yelled, completely disoriented.

"Out in the yard! Come on!" Mothball let go of the doorframe and stumbled toward him, her tall body losing the balance battle as she toppled to the floor, almost on top of her mom. She quickly got her hands and feet under her and began helping him with Windasill.

Like three drunken sailors, they got up, shuffled to the door, glass crunching under their feet with every heavy step. Rutger did what he could, reaching out and holding on to clothes, pulling, pushing. Soon they were all outside, where at least the danger of a house falling down on top of them was eliminated.

Sato drew in ragged breaths, his chest heaving as he released Windasill into Mothball's care. He spread his feet in the grass of the front yard, putting his hands on his knees to keep his balance as best he could. The earthquake rumbled on, distant sounds of destruction wafting through the night: crunching wood and breaking glass, alarms blaring and people screaming.

Sato couldn't believe what he was seeing. The trees seemed to be jumping up and down. The yard looked like a bed of thin grass growing on a lake, rippling in waves that made him queasy. The road and driveway did the same, cracking and crumpling.

Through it all, suffusing it all, was that sound, thrumming and humming and buzzing, like horns and bees and gongs amplified a thousandfold. Sato's head felt split in two, pain lancing into his eyeballs. He'd lived in Japan most of his life and endured a dozen or so earthquakes. But nothing like this. Not even close.

All he could think was that the world was coming to an end.

⁓

"Dark Matter," Jane said after letting her statement about killing billions of people sink in. She was acting as though she'd merely announced she was having layoffs at the fangen factory. Tick realized he was more scared of Jane's insanity than he was of her powers over Chi'karda.

"What do you mean, *dark matter?*" Master George asked. "You can't possibly expect me to believe your fancy tree statue is made of dark matter. Impossible. Utterly impossible, and you've now proven yourself quite mad. As if we needed any further proof on the matter."

"Dark matter," Jane repeated, as if she hadn't heard Master George. "It makes up more than seventy percent of the universe and yet, until recently, no one could determine its nature. I'll spare you hours of lecture and say this—by combining the powers of Chi'karda with the non-baryonic dark energy, I can eliminate the electromagnetic forces holding the Fifth Reality together. I can ignite extreme entropy. In other words, I can dissolve it into floating atomic gunk."

Tick knew a little about dark matter, mostly from a couple of books he'd read. But they had been science fiction stories that didn't really explain what it *was* exactly, just made up some cool uses for it. Destructive uses. Cataclysmic destruction. If Jane was serious about what she could do with it . . .

"The connections between my dark matter components are already strengthening, channeling through the hub of the black tree, magnified by my Alterants, each one of whom is set up in her own Reality, in these same coordinates. The soulikens are strong in these Alterants of mine, just as I knew they would be. Our genetic makeup is almost perfectly compatible. Any one of them could have done what I have done in the Thirteenth, if only they'd been given the opportunity."

Her voice grew quiet. "The Chi'karda is flowing, my friends, flowing on a scale I doubt you could scarcely comprehend. Soon the dark matter will be linked, and the Blade will do its slicing."

Dark matter. Alterants. Soulikens. Chi'karda. Blade. Jane's words bounced around inside Tick's mind, trying to sort themselves into something that made sense. But it wasn't working. He felt completely confused and out of his league. Jane was up to something monstrous.

Mistress Jane finally looked away from Tick, taking in each of his friends one by one with her mad gaze. Then she settled back on him. "I don't expect you to comprehend the workings of the Blade of Shattered Hope. Just know this, and know it well so you can spread the word: the Blade is a series of dark matter components, linked by my Alterants to create the greatest flow of Chi'karda since the beginning of time and space. And when I tap into that power and give the order to *sever* the Fifth Reality, the dark matter will consume the Fifth like a black hole. The Fifth will cease to exist—along with every man, woman, child, beast, insect, and plant living there. *That* is what you are about to witness."

Tick couldn't hold back anymore. "How can you do something like this? You're always spewing this garbage about wanting to do good, but now you suddenly think it's okay to kill billions of people?"

"Yes, Atticus, you're absolutely correct."

She turned and motioned to the closest screen, where moving images had now appeared in the spinner's projected circle. A woman sat huddled on another odd black sculpture—this one had a solid top and bottom connected by dozens of curved, twisty rods. The lady was dirty and appeared to be terrified and hungry, but Tick could tell she was an Alterant of Jane. He remembered his time with the "real" Jane at Chu's mountainous palace. This lady had the same black hair, the same eyes, the same face.

Tick looked at the other screens and saw similar video feeds. More Alterants, more black sculptures. Each woman had her own unique attributes, but there was enough there to see that all of them were Jane's inter-Reality twins. In one of the video feeds, the image shook, as if the person holding the camera was doing some kind of jig. The Alterant was screaming uncontrollably, trying to free herself from the chains binding her to the dark black object below her. Then the other video feeds started to shake as well, one by one, worsening every time Tick looked at a new screen.

"I've learned my lesson," Jane said, "about walking softly and kindly as I try to achieve my dream of a Utopian Reality. I'll tread lightly no longer. The people of the Fifth will die, yes, but it is for the good of mankind. In the long run, we will all be eternally grateful for their sacrifice."

Master George's whole body trembled with rage. "How could even your twisted, sickened mind stretch a tragedy of such proportions to something that will achieve good? You've lost your soul, Jane."

Jane's hand whipped out again, her palm facing George. But she paused, then slowly withdrew it back into her robe. "Yes, you may be right. But if I'm willing to sacrifice billions of lives, wouldn't it be logical for me to also be willing to sacrifice my soul? I don't care what guilt I must endure, what internal torment I must suffer for the rest of my life. Only one thing matters, and I *will* see it achieved."

"Why are those places shaking?" Paul blurted out, pointing to the screens. Every image now showed a world that seemed to be suffering from massive earthquakes. The Jane Alterants jerked about, still chained to the black sculptures that had toppled over on their sides.

"The Chi'karda is building, that's why," Jane answered, her voice so calm it made Tick mad. "Each Reality will see its own effects from the Blade's purge of the Fifth, but in the end, they'll suffer minimal damage. And all of my Alterants will survive to move on to the next phase of my plan. All except for the one in the Fifth, of course."

Tick was filled with turmoil. Though he didn't entirely understand what was going on, he felt an overwhelming responsibility to do something, to at least *try* something. He looked down into his lap, where his hands were clasped, squeezing them together so hard his fingers drained of blood. Maybe, if he could just reach for a trickle of Chi'karda . . . experiment a little . . .

"It's time for me to bend the Blade to my will," Jane announced. "Move from your chairs and die, as will Atticus's family. Frazier's watching. Remember to keep your eyes on the spinners. If your abilities to spread the message of what you witness today aren't sufficient, there'll be no reason for me to keep you alive."

Without waiting for an answer, she turned sharply and walked away, back to a spot before the black tree.

Tick barely saw her go. He was still looking down, concentrating on his hands. He didn't know exactly why, but it helped to have a spot for his eyes to focus on as he mentally probed his mind and heart and body, searching for a spark of Chi'karda. Something small, he told himself, something Jane won't be able to sense . . .

"This can't be for real," Sofia said next to him, though he barely heard her over the sounds of the humming tree and through his efforts to think. "She can't possibly do something like this."

"She's doing it," Paul said. "Look at her. She's a nut job."

Tick finally closed his eyes, squeezing his mind as he tried to latch on to that mysterious something within him. He pictured Jane, focusing on his hatred of her. He pictured his family. He tried to think about what his heart must look like, pumping blood to his veins. It always started there, the warmth—

There. He could feel it. A spark. A little surge of heat. Like a flickering flame.

Just as he'd done before in his basement, Tick reached for the warmth, mentally grasping it with unseen hands.

He didn't fully comprehend how he was doing it, but he threw all his energy into doing it anyway.

But then Master George said something, and even though Tick heard it only from a distance, as though it had been spoken through a thick wall, the words sliced through his concentration. The flame of Chi'karda, small to begin with, went out completely.

Tick opened his eyes and looked at Master George. "What did you say?" he asked, practically shouting to be heard over the thrumming of the tree.

The old man hung his head sadly. "It's true, I'm afraid. I believe Sato, Mothball, and Rutger are in the Fifth Reality even as we speak."

CHAPTER 22

LIGHTNING AND FLAME

Terror. Panic. Fear.

Those were words Lisa associated with disaster movies and scary books. News stories of dangerous lands thousands of miles away. History lessons of wars past. In her sixteen-and-a-half years of life, she'd never considered that one day those words might describe part of her own life, her own experience. Though she tried to be brave for her sister, she couldn't keep herself from crying every few minutes. Kayla's tears were a constant.

They'd been in the small room for at least a full day, maybe longer. Sparsely decorated, it held only two hard wooden chairs and a small bed with a table and lamp next to it. Drab wallpaper covered the walls, and ugly brown carpet covered the floor. There were no windows.

She had no idea how they'd gotten there. She'd been sleeping in her bed, dreaming about something icy crawling down her back, and then she woke up in this room, lying on the floor with Kayla right next to her. Since then, food had been brought to them by cruel ladies who refused to answer any of her questions and who glared at the two girls as if she and Kayla were hardened criminals.

Kidnapped, imprisoned, hated for no reason. It was all terrifying. The worst part was not knowing anything. She and Kayla mostly huddled together on the bed, hugging and consoling, sharing their tears. Lisa had no idea how many times she'd said the words, "It'll be okay," but it had to be at least one hundred.

She knew this had something to do with her brother. No one had told Lisa anything directly, but she knew about the Realitants and how Tick was special to them, helping them in some way. And somehow it had all led to this.

Come save us, Tick, she thought. *I know you got us into this mess. Now come get us out!*

Someone knocked hard on the door, just once, then opened it. Lisa had already started scooting as far away from the door as possible, dragging Kayla with her to the other side of the bed.

It was the older of the two ladies, her gray hair

pulled into a tight bun, her pale face full of hard-lined wrinkles. "Might wanna see this," she said gruffly. Then she opened the door wider and stepped to the side, nodding toward the hallway.

"See what?" Lisa asked warily. "You want us to come out there?"

The old woman let out an exasperated sigh. "Yes. Come on, I'm trying to be nice, you little ingrate. Such a historic moment—wouldn't want you to miss it."

Lisa squeezed Kayla's arms, then moved to get up from the bed.

"No!" Kayla shouted.

"It'll be okay," Lisa said softly, taking her sister by the hand. She hated saying those words again. "Come on."

Kayla looked up at her with moist eyes, then slowly slid off the bed and followed Lisa, their hands still clasped. They walked to the doorway and into the hall. From there, the woman led them down a set of stairs and into a living room that was as ugly as the rest of the house, all dull colors and boring furniture. Several other ladies were sitting on chairs and a worn-out sofa. Every pair of eyes was glued to a television set on a small table.

When Lisa saw and heard what was coming from the TV, she almost forgot how terrified she'd been just moments earlier. It was a news program, a man's tight voice narrating as the view switched from one scene of destruction to the next.

Fires. People trapped under cement, bloody and crying. Sirens. Shaky film of a large building, the horrendous crashing sounds booming from the television speakers when the structure crumbled to the ground. A massive car wreck. Smoke everywhere.

At first, Lisa was too shocked to read the words flashing across the bottom of the screen or hear exactly what the reporter was saying. But then she focused. The scrolling words accompanying the images made it clear the disasters were happening in different parts of the world. Paris. London. Berlin. Moscow.

Wait, she thought. Those cities were all in Europe and spread apart by hundreds and hundreds of miles. What could possibly be happening?

"The earthquakes are still rumbling as we speak," the reporter was saying. "They've already shattered all known records in terms of length of time, and they still continue, as you can tell from the shaky video footage. All of Europe and Asia seem to be affected by these quakes. Mass panic is spreading out of control."

Lisa felt an entirely new fear grip her. It made what she'd been feeling back in that prison of a room seem silly. That fear had been about just her and Kayla, trapped in a room, but otherwise safe and sound. This was something else. And whatever it was that was happening, Lisa knew the world would never be the same.

"What's going on?" Kayla asked, her small voice breaking Lisa's heart.

"I don't know, sweetie. I don't know."

The last word had barely left her mouth when the lights suddenly went out. The TV made a popping sound as the screen went black. Kayla screamed, and the ladies in the room started bustling about in the darkness, each of them calling out things that jumbled into a chorus of panicked nonsense.

The room started to vibrate.

The floor trembled.

And then the house shook like someone had picked it up and thrown it.

Tick couldn't take it anymore. He had to do something.

As the black tree hummed and throbbed its pulses of energy, as people ran about adjusting computers, as Mistress Jane stood completely still, her expressionless mask pointed at the tree, as Paul and Sofia and Master George fidgeted in their chairs, Tick leaned forward, closed his eyes, and searched once again for the flame of his Chi'karda.

With mental hands, he probed and picked and prodded.

There it was—a puff of heat.

He found it much more quickly this time. Encouraged, he threw all his thought and concentration into the warmth, grasping it, tensing his body as he imagined himself enveloped in the heat, consumed by it. Once again, he had no real clue what he was doing, but he did it anyway. Somehow, with his mind and heart, he became one with the Chi'karda. He felt it spread through his organs and veins and skin. Felt himself burn.

Ordering the power to stay, to wait, to hold, he opened his eyes.

Everything was as it was before, except for one small change. He saw things more clearly, more crisply. He heard sounds more distinctly, each one somehow separated from the other, each one crystal clear. He sensed vibrations in the air, particularly from the black tree, its power tickling across his skin with every throb.

He looked at Jane standing in front of the tree, probably throwing her powers into the Blade of Shattered Hope, maybe even close to flicking the final switch and severing the Fifth Reality. Tick turned his gaze back to the black tree. Its darkness was so deep, its edges so finely detailed, he had a hard time believing his own eyes. His vision had gone beyond anything he thought possible—maybe this was what they called four-dimensional sight. Maybe five or six. Maybe infinity.

None of it mattered. He had to act. He'd convinced himself of this without realizing when or how, but he had to try. His family would be safe. He'd make sure of it. He'd do whatever it took.

Focusing as deeply as possible on the trunk of the black tree, he imagined a pinhole in the imaginary barrier he'd created within him. With his eyes wide and his hands gripping his knees, he released the slightest bit of pent-up Chi'karda. He felt an almost untraceable amount of heat leave his body.

A trickle, nothing more.

And not knowing what else to do, he focused all of his thoughts into one distinct line of words, saying them over and over in his mind, projecting them at the same spot where he'd aimed the Chi'karda.

Stop the Blade. Stop the Blade. Stop the Blade.

Sato ran, though he fell down with every fourth or fifth lunging leap forward.

The others did the same, stumbling and bumbling about like they'd just been granted the gifts of legs and were trying to figure out how to make them work. Rutger was having the hardest time of it. Sato swore he actually saw Rutger *roll* forward like a ball a few times.

Mothball stayed by her friend's side, helping him

along as best she could. Tollaseat and Windasill worked together, pushing and pulling and balancing each other. Sato was on his own. He kept his head down and ran.

The earthquake continued to rage, shaking the entire world and everything on it. Crashes and clangs and breaking glass sounded like small explosions. The air reeked of sulfur and gas and burning wood. Screams came from every direction, from young and old, male and female.

And even though neither Sato nor anyone else knew where they were running to, there didn't seem to be any choice. You ran from terror, and that was that.

A booming crackle sounded to his left, splitting the air just as he caught a flash of bright light on the edge of his vision. He snapped his head around, but it was too late. The light was gone. It had been like a bolt of lightning.

Another one exploded in front of him. He barely had time to register the jagged line of brilliant white before he closed his eyes, hoping he wasn't blinded for life. Electric thunder rocked the air and shook the ground. Sato fell on his face and rolled three times, feeling rocks bruise and batter his body.

Another lightning strike, somewhere to his right. Another one way behind him. Each one was an explosion of light and energy and sound.

He got to his hands and knees, searching the area

for his friends. He caught sight of Mothball sprawled across Rutger, scrambling to get up. No sign of her parents.

Sato stood up, lurching back and forth as the land continued to shake and tremble violently. Lightning was striking everywhere, long, crooked bolts of white fire hitting the ground in quick flashes instantaneously with the world-crushing sound. He held his hands up to his ears, wondering if he'd ever be able to see *or* hear again.

A brief pause in the lightning storm was as sudden as it was welcome. Sato squinted against the bright blurs of afterimages obscuring his vision as he headed toward Mothball. He had taken a few steps before he realized something very strange. The screams had stopped. So had the yelling and crying.

In disbelief, he scanned the area, shocked that he couldn't see anyone. Nobody. Nowhere. Only Mothball and Rutger. Where had everyone else gone?

He cupped his hands around his mouth to yell something to Mothball. "What's—"

A massive bolt of lightning shot from the sky, landing exactly on top of his two friends.

Sato threw his arm up to block the light, then looked as soon as it was gone. Barely able to see, he ran desperately toward the spot.

But even with his burned-out vision, he could tell

Mothball and Rutger weren't there. They were gone. Completely gone.

Not even charred remains or blackened, smoking skeletons were left behind. And, oddly enough, the grass wasn't burning or even disturbed as far as he could tell. It was as if his two friends had just disappeared.

Maybe they've been winked away, he thought with an unexpected rise of jubilation. Maybe someone had saved them at the last second. In his present state of shock and panic, the idea didn't seem so far-fetched. Anything was possible, right?

As if in answer to his question, the world around him suddenly turned white, a blanketing sea of complete and utter brilliance that engulfed his body even as the air singed with burning heat.

Sato felt his body erupt in flames.

CHAPTER 23

✳

A THREAT REVERSED

Lisa's only thought was to find Kayla and keep her safe.

The house shook and rattled around her, the echoes of wood groaning and cracking, glass breaking, and the terrible ladies screaming. Darkness pressed in, and the air filled with a choking dust. Something smelled burnt.

Lisa crawled forward on her knees, fighting to keep her balance. She didn't understand why Kayla wasn't crying or yelling for her. They'd been standing close together when the earthquake began, but lost each other in the first chaotic seconds.

"Kayla!" she shouted. "Kayla!"

No one answered, but Lisa heard a distinct whimper to her left, a miracle considering the sounds of destruction surrounding them. She shuffled in that direction and bumped into the small body of her sister, who was curled up into a ball, shaking with sobs.

"Kayla," Lisa whispered. "It's okay, sweetie, it's okay. Come on. We need to get out of the house."

"No, no, no," Kayla murmured.

Scared the house might collapse on them at any second, Lisa put her arms around Kayla's body and lifted, grunting with the effort. She staggered to the right, running into a table, then to the left, hitting a wall. Squeezing Kayla tightly to her body, she moved forward, taking heavy and careful steps so as not to fall down. The light was dim, but she could see a hallway leading to the front door, which was open and hanging crookedly on one hinge. The whole house jumped as if it had grown legs.

"Let's get out of here!" she yelled as she decided to go for broke and sprinted for the door.

With a wobbly run, she made it to the opening and stumbled outside, falling into a clump of bushes. Tiny, sharp branches scratched her as she squeezed her arms even tighter around Kayla, trying to protect her. She kicked with her legs and used her elbows to maneuver their way out of the bushes and onto the front lawn.

The sounds of things breaking inside the house had been replaced with horrible, world-shattering cracks of thunder. Constant flashes of light illuminated their surroundings. Lisa saw people running, more people falling. The air smelled like burning plastic and tasted like . . . electricity. That was the only word she could think of.

Then, forty feet away, a bolt of lightning arrowed down from the sky and exploded around a woman in a bulb of pure incandescence. Lisa squeezed her eyes shut, though it was too late. When she opened them, she was completely blind, seeing only blurs of white in front of her.

Not knowing what else to do, she hugged Kayla and smoothed her hair, crushed by how the little girl's body shook with sobs and terror. How could this be happening? *What* was happening?

The air around them exploded with heat and electricity. Pain ripped through Lisa's body, and her arms suddenly closed on empty air.

Kayla was gone.

Tick didn't know what he'd done.

He felt as though a chunk of his insides had somehow been squeezed through his skin and catapulted toward the black tree, engulfed by the pure darkness.

He fell from the chair, gasping for breath. His link to Chi'karda had vanished, replaced by a cold emptiness.

"Tick!" Sofia shouted, jumping out of her chair to kneel next to him. "Are you okay?"

Tick rolled over onto his back, looking up at her. "Yeah. I'm fine."

Paul stood and reached down to grab Tick's arm, then heaved him to his feet. "What happened?"

Tick shook his head. He couldn't have answered even if he felt like talking. He had no idea what had happened and began to worry that he'd done something really stupid.

"Take your seats," Master George snapped in a tight whisper. "She's coming."

Tick quickly sat down, as did Paul and Sofia. Sure enough, Mistress Jane was almost to them, marching with determined steps, her red mask showing an anger that made Tick's heart want to stop.

"What did you do?" she screamed into Tick's face. "What did you put in the Blade?"

Tick leaned back in his chair and looked up at her, embarrassed and terrified. "I don't know," was all he could get out.

Jane's chest heaved up and down beneath her robe. "You . . . don't . . . know?"

Tick shook his head, dread exploding within him. What had he done? What had he been *thinking?* She was going to kill his family. He knew it. She was going to kill them!

"I felt a surge of Chi'karda slice into the Blade," Jane said, her breath still quick. "It had to come from you. What did you do? If I have to repeat the question again, your youngest sister will be killed. Then the other one. Speak."

Tick fought the panic thrusting up his throat, threatening to choke him. He had to have lost his mind. How could he have been so stupid to try something when he didn't even know how to control it or what he was doing?

"What did—" Jane began.

"Wait!" Tick shouted. "I . . . I just . . . I tried to use my Chi'karda. I don't know what I was thinking. . . . I'm sure it didn't do anything!"

"What did you expect?" Master George said, coming to Tick's defense. "You tell us you're about to kill billions of people, and you expect the boy will sit there quietly? He has something you don't, Jane. Morals!"

Jane's head slowly swiveled around until her eyes paused on Master George. "Enough talk. Frazier!"

The man was at her side before the ring of her shout had faded away. "Yes, Mistress?"

Jane returned her gaze to Tick, the features of her mask melting into a void of expression. "Order the Ladies of Blood and Sorrow to kill the younger girl. Now."

"No!" Tick screamed, vaulting to his feet as Frazier walked away. He felt like an arrow had just sliced through his chest, tearing a jagged rip across his heart.

Jane's hand shot out from her robe, her palm flat and facing Tick. A thump of solid air slammed into his body, throwing him into the air. He flipped backward and landed on the ground behind the row of chairs. Jolts of pain made him shudder as he turned his head to look back toward Jane.

"Stop it!" Sofia yelled. She stood up as well, her hands clenched into fists at her side. She rocked back and forth on her feet as if contemplating whether or not to attack Jane. "How can you be such an evil—"

Jane's hand flicked toward Sofia and sent her body shooting through the air to ram into one of the screens that currently showed a burning building. Sofia and the screen crashed to the ground with a clatter of clanging metal rods and ripping cloth.

Tick pushed himself off the ground, groaning from soreness. Anger lit his insides like liquid flame, and he knew his Chi'karda was welling up again, threatening to explode out of him. Kayla. All he could think about was Kayla. What could he do . . .

Movement by the chairs grabbed his attention. Paul had been sitting still, obviously waiting for the right moment. Just as Jane turned away from Sofia, Paul leaped from his chair and tackled Jane. He grabbed her around the waist and pushed her to the ground, falling on top of her. They'd barely landed when Paul suddenly shot straight up into the air, hovering ten feet above Jane. Then his body flew away until he slammed into another screen, with the same result as Sofia's unwanted flight.

Jane got to her feet, brushed the dust and dirt from her robe, then looked at Master George. "You want to try something, George? Here, let me go ahead and save you the trouble."

She pushed her hand toward the old man. He flew up and backward over the chairs, landing on his stomach just a few feet from Tick. He didn't move, lying flat with his arms and legs twisted at awkward angles, his face on a rock. There was blood.

Tick couldn't take it anymore. This woman was evil. She was too evil.

He got to his feet, staggering a little until he caught his balance. Then he held up a hand and pointed a finger at Jane.

"Listen to me," he said, his voice straining from the internal effort of holding back the Chi'karda burning within him. "If you kill my sister—"

"What?" Jane snapped, taking a step forward. "What, Atticus? What will you do?"

"Then I won't care what happens anymore," Tick said. "If you kill Kayla, I won't care about anything. I'll build up this Chi'karda until it's a million times stronger than it was back at Chu's mountain. I'll build and build, and then I'll let it all out. I'll throw it all at you."

Jane shook her head. "So selfish, so . . . *weak*. You can still save your other sister and your parents. And you can help me achieve great things in the Realities, if you'd just grow up and see things with a bigger perspective."

Tick hated her. Oh, how he hated her. "Don't say another word to me! Tell him not to kill my sister. Now!"

"No."

She said it so simply, so nonchalantly. But Tick couldn't back down—he had to reverse the threat here. The power burned and boiled inside his chest. "I'll count to three. Stop Frazier, or I'll throw it all at you. Every ounce of it. Even if it kills me."

"No," she said again.

The Chi'karda was starting to overpower him. He felt his hands begin to shake. He quickly stepped forward and gripped the back of a chair to steady himself. "One," he said as calmly as he could.

Jane did nothing, just kept staring at him with a blank expression on her mask.

"Two," Tick said. Fear filled him. He didn't know if he had the courage to go through with his threat.

"Three," Jane said for him.

Tick's fingers tightened on the chair. He looked down to see that they'd actually sunk into the metal, warping it. He had to do this. He had to—

"Mistress Jane!" a man's voice yelled.

Tick's head snapped up to see Frazier run frantically around the computer tables, heading straight for them.

"Mistress!" the man shouted again. "Something's wrong!" He pulled up, panting with deep breaths.

"Speak!" Jane yelled back at him.

Frazier held his hands up to his ears as if his head were about to explode. His eyes were lit with panic. "They're all gone—all of them. Everything's gone crazy with the earthquakes and lightning . . . but there's no doubt. I can't find them anywhere. None of them!"

"What are you saying?" Jane insisted.

Frazier turned to look at Tick. "His sisters. His parents. They've all disappeared."

CHAPTER 24

✳

COLORED MARBLE TILES

The scream had barely escaped Sato's mouth before the excruciating pain vanished, gone in an instant. It didn't fade or slowly feel better. One second he felt like his entire body was on fire, horrible burns eating away at his skin, the next second he was perfectly fine. He collapsed to the rock-hard ground anyway, the mental shock of the pain bad enough. The air around him was gray and dull, twilight's last moments before full night.

On his back, he held up his hands even though he dreaded what he might see. Blood and red blisters at best. Black, charred flesh at worst. But instead, in the faint glow of the light around him, he saw smooth, healthy skin, not a blemish or a scrape or a bruise.

What had happened? He remembered the earthquake, then bolts of lightning striking everywhere, and people disappearing when struck. Then the world had lit up, exploded in fire, as if he himself had been . . .

Sucking in a gasp, he sat up, then scrambled to his feet. He turned in a slow circle, looking all around him. With each second, with each revolution, his eyes grew wider and wider. He saw no sign of the homes and trees and stone walls of the Fifth Reality. He'd been taken to another place. Even though the light was dim, he had no doubt of it.

He stood on a vast, flat ground made of a hard substance and checkered with large squares of differing colors. It seemed to stretch in every direction as far as he could see, with no breaks of any kind. He knelt down and felt the floor. It was cool to the touch. Marble, maybe. The light wasn't strong enough for him to see if the floor had the familiar pattern of that stone.

He stood back up and looked above him. Though the marble floor beneath him would suggest that he was inside a building of some sort, no other evidence supported it. No roof hung above him—just blank, unblemished air. No stars, no clouds, no planes in the sky. The perimeter around him was just as gray and lifeless. The floor went on forever, with no walls or fences or trees. No mountains in the distance. No furniture.

That was all; a marble floor with countless squares of color, stretching to infinity in every direction and a lifeless sky that seemed the definition of *nothing*.

I'm dreaming, he thought. Or maybe he was dead. Though he'd never learned much about religion and the afterlife, he couldn't help but think of the possibility that he'd died and was in some sort of waiting room for souls. Certainly no place like this existed in the real world, no matter which Reality.

He heard a humming sound behind him and turned quickly to check it out.

Twenty or thirty feet away, a figure lay crumpled on the floor. It was a girl with curly blonde hair, her clothes filthy and torn. She had black smudges on her bare skin. She looked to be about his same age. She twitched a little and let out a low groan.

"Hey!" Sato yelled, cringing when it came out so harshly. "Are you okay? Do you know where we are?"

The girl glanced at him when she heard his voice, her eyes filled with fear. "Hello?" she called back weakly.

Sato ran to her, sure he must be in a dream after all. He approached her and knelt on the ground, putting a hand out to touch her shoulder softly.

"You okay?" he asked again. "I don't know how we got here."

He looked around again, scanning their surroundings to see if anything had changed. Still nothing but colored marble tiles going forever and a sky of dead air. He returned his attention to the girl.

"My name's Sato," he said, hoping the girl would snap out of her daze and help him understand what was going on. She looked up, and he saw tears streaking down her cheeks.

"I'm Lisa," she said, stifling a sob. "Have you seen my sister?"

⁓

At first, Tick felt the slightest hint of hope at Frazier's words, but it didn't last long. He remembered the horrible images of destruction on the screens, recognizing that the man had said his sisters and parents had vanished *after* mentioning earthquakes and lightning.

There was nothing good about that. Maybe they'd been trapped under rubble. Maybe they'd been struck by lightning. Maybe no one could find them because they were dead.

No! he shouted in his mind. His insides still boiled, the heat of his Chi'karda flaring up even stronger at the depressing thoughts of what might have happened. He didn't know if he'd ever felt so scared and completely hopeless. Useless.

Jane had stayed quiet for a long moment after Frazier's pronouncement, staring at the man with a blank expression. Then she turned to Tick.

"Then they're probably dead already," she said coolly. "How fitting it would be if it was *your* disobedience, Atticus, your arrogant, reckless use of Chi'karda that ended up killing your family. I hope you can live with that."

Tick barely heard the words. He couldn't hold back the Chi'karda anymore. He'd let it go too far, and now it was too late to stop it. His insides had become a roaring inferno.

Something seemed to rip deep inside of him, and he screamed from the pain. He fell to his knees, wrapping his arms around himself. Trying to escape it, he curled into a ball and screamed again, as loudly as he could.

Everything *changed*.

The dusty desert around him vanished, replaced by trees.

The power and burning disappeared, as did the pain, and everything was perfectly silent, except for his quick and heavy breaths.

He was in the middle of a forest. And he was alone.

CHAPTER 25

✳

SILVER-BLUE LIGHT

Tick didn't move for a long time.

The forest was dark, only the slightest traces of moonlight seeping through the thick canopy of branches above him, dappled here and there on the ground. He heard nothing but a few insects and the very distant sound of a dog barking. The woods smelled fresh and pungent, the scent of the pine trees closest to him by far the strongest. It made him think of Christmas.

Which made him think of his family, which pulled at his heart like a huge rock had been tied to it and dropped to his stomach. He ached for them, and he didn't know how he could survive if they'd been hurt or killed. For now, not knowing anything for certain, his mind only allowed him to hold on to hope. He didn't let anything too dark settle on his thoughts. They *could* be alive. There were a million possibilities for such a thing, and he held on to that.

He had to get going. He had to figure out where he'd been sent. Had he actually winked himself? That seemed the only logical explanation, but the instant he'd arrived in the forest, the flames of Chi'karda had burned out, leaving him empty. He was cold, and not just because the air in the forest was cool and wetly crisp, as if a storm might be coming. He also felt the chill of fear.

He stood up and turned in a slow circle, scanning the woods. He saw only trees, some thin, some thick, all of them crowded one after the other until they faded into obscure shadows. He closed his eyes to focus, but again, he heard only the insects and that frantic dog, still in the distance. Unless some super spy was nearby, watching him in silence, he was alone.

What *had* happened? His experience with winking kept the situation from being completely bizarre, but had he really done it to himself? Or had it been Sally back at headquarters? He doubted that since no one else came with him; also, it would have made much more sense to wink him to Master George's compound in the Bermuda Triangle, not to the middle of the woods.

A lot of questions, no answers, and it was cold. He shivered, rubbed his arms, and told himself once again that he needed to get going. But the worry that he'd go in the wrong direction kept his feet glued to the forest floor.

Go, he thought. *Just go. That way.*

He stepped forward, but stopped when the sound of crunching ground cover startled him. He took another quick look around him. Nothing.

Shaking off his childish worries, he walked forward resolutely, moving aside tree branches and stomping down weeds. The crick-crash with every step filled the air with echoes until it almost seemed like someone *was* following him. He realized he was acting a little ridiculous and feeling way too paranoid. Refusing to slow again for another look, he kept going through the trees.

He'd just squeezed through two big oaks when he definitely heard something behind him: a quick but loud moan, as if some giant had awakened with a stomachache. Sucking in a breath, Tick spun around, throwing his arms out to catch his balance on the thick trees. There'd been an odd glimmer of light behind him, he was certain. But it disappeared the instant he saw it.

Silence returned, thicker than before. The moan must have spooked the insects, because they'd quieted as well. Tick felt a sudden burst of claustrophobia, there in the darkness with the trees pressing in around him.

Childish or not, he was officially scared. That stifled groan had sounded otherworldly, like a . . .

Well, like a ghost.

He turned and ran, not taking the time to be careful anymore. Branches slapped his face, and twigs and leaves scratched his skin. He didn't stop, dodging the obstacles as best he could.

Ooooooohhhhhhhhhhnnnnnnnnnnn . . .

There it was again—the low moan. It was still behind him, but this time it lasted much longer. A flicker of terror, like icy water shooting up his throat, made him cough and wheeze. He wanted to look back. Every instinct *screamed* for him to look back, but he knew he'd have to slow down to do that, or he'd run right smack into a tree. Weaving, dodging, ducking, he ran on.

A flash of silvery light gleamed from behind him, illuminating the woods. Unable to fight the urge to look, Tick stopped, put his hand against a pine tree, and turned around. Once again the strange glow vanished as soon as he saw it, but he'd caught a glimpse of wispy brilliance, as if streamers of fog had magically transformed into a cloud of almost blue light.

Ooooooohhhhhhhhhhnnnnnnnnnnn . . .

The sound came again, along with another few flashes of the silver, misty beams. There was something oddly *metallic* about the light, making Tick think of aluminum or steel. And then it was gone.

Tick turned and ran again, swearing to himself he

wouldn't stop again until he found a person, a building, something. A policeman or a ghost hunter would be great.

Because of the darkness, he had no idea he was at the edge of the forest until he broke through the last line of trees. A sharp but short hill sloped up, and he stumbled and fell before he could slow down. His face smacked into a clod of dirt. He spit the gritty stuff out of his mouth as he scrambled with his hands and feet to move up the hill.

He reached the top, pumping his legs and flailing his arms until he found his balance and could run again. His feet slapped pavement—a road. It took another few seconds for Tick to realize where he'd been sent. Or where he had sent himself. A mixture of relief and confusion consumed him, almost making him stop again.

But he didn't stop; he didn't even slow down. He knew exactly where to go, and a fresh surge of adrenaline lifted his energy and spirits.

He was in Deer Park, Washington, on the road leading to his neighborhood, a path he'd walked thousands of times in his life. The why and how ceased to matter in his mind. Something creepy was behind him, and his house was in front of him.

He ran for home.

As Tick rounded his mailbox and shot up the driveway, he couldn't help but feel a trace of déjà vu. His thoughts went back to his very first wink, when he'd gone to the cemetery as instructed and performed the strange initiation ritual he'd had to figure out from the twelve clues sent to him by Master George.

When he'd winked that night and felt that cool tingle down the back of his neck, the first of many more to come, he thought it hadn't worked. Sullen and heartbroken, he'd headed for home only to discover he'd been sent to an alternate Reality, one in which a strange, nasty old man lived in Tick's house.

What if that old man was there again? Or another one?

What if Tick had been winked to another Reality, and his Alterant was in the house, sleeping or sitting at the computer or about to come outside? Though he'd been totally unconscious in the Fourth Reality, Sofia and Paul had told him about what happened when the two versions of Reginald Chu met. There had been an earthquake, a wave of air, and the Reginald from the Fourth had disappeared, gone to some place Master George called the Nonex.

What if that happened to Tick when he opened the door?

Then, despite the darkness, he noticed the crashed garage door from when the water creatures had attacked his parents. His doubts washed away, and he ran up to the bushes lining the house and dropped to his knees, searching for the fake rock that contained a spare key. The key had been missing before when he'd unknowingly been winked to an alternate reality. This time he found it, and, pulling the key from the rock, he ran up the porch steps and unlocked the front door. He went inside and flicked the light switch in the hallway. Nothing happened.

He walked into the kitchen, the moonlight seeping through the windows just enough to aid his way. The lights there didn't work either. He paused and listened for a minute. Nothing, not even the sound of the fridge or the heater.

So the power was out. Maybe nearby areas had been hit by the same devastation he'd witnessed on the screens back in the Thirteenth.

Based on what little he could see, he no longer had any doubt this was Reality Prime, and that this was his very own house. Just to make absolutely sure, he made his way back to the stairs and went up them to his room, feeling carefully along the wall in the dark. Every bit of furniture, the blankets on the bed, the wall decorations—everything was exactly as he last remembered seeing them.

He felt a little disappointed. Deep down he'd been hoping to find his family here, even though he knew it was a long shot. Jane had taken them, but then Frazier had said they'd disappeared. Tick had hoped the same thing might have happened to them as what had happened to him. He'd hoped they had been sent back home too.

Bad thoughts drifted through his mind, images of all the terrible things their vanishing from Jane's captors might mean.

To get his mind off it, he knelt down on the floor and reached under his mattress. After feeling about, he found what he'd been looking for and pulled it out, then sat on the bed. Though he couldn't see it very well in the pale light coming through the window, he knew every detail of the object anyway. His *Journal of Curious Letters.*

Yes. Unless this was a Reality that had split from Prime very recently, he at least knew he was in the right place. But what in the world was he supposed to do now?

He set the book on the table by his bed and kicked up his legs onto the bed, not bothering to take off his shoes. He lay back on to his pillow, hands clasped behind his head, and stared at the ceiling. Odd-shaped shadows from the moonlight slanted from corner to corner, dark and menacing. He closed his eyes.

Sleep. Could he really sleep despite all the terrible things going on that very instant? He didn't know, but he needed it for sure. Surprising himself, he relaxed, feeling the first trickles of sleep edge his mind.

A minute passed. Two. The darkness was deep. No sound except a slight breeze pushing branches against the outside of the house. Something smelled good, like the fresh scent of laundry detergent and dryer sheets. All of it seemed to pull him down into the bed, as comfortable as he ever remembered being. Almost feeling guilty, he sank into the welcome pool of slumber.

Ooooooohhhhhhhhhhnnnnnnnnnnn . . .

This time the sound came from the hallway right outside his room, a miserably haunted, ghostly moan. Tick shot up in bed, his feet swinging to the floor. A silver-blue light glowed through the space under the door.

So much for sleep.

CHAPTER 26

✳

MANY FACES

He heard the sound again. Then again. And again. Each time it was only a few seconds apart. The moan had such a creepy, deathly feel to it that prickles of goose bumps shot up all over his body, and he felt like every hair on his head reached for the ceiling. This was a new kind of terror—something very different from the constant worry of being killed or hurt, something he'd almost become accustomed to.

No, this was like a real-life ghost story. He was in a horror movie.

He quietly stood up and walked over to the window, carefully stepping on the non-creaking spots of his bedroom floor. He looked through the glass, wondering if he'd have the courage to jump out. The moon cast its pale glow on the yard outside, making the trees look dark blue and creating shadows in which he could imagine every monster from his every nightmare hiding, waiting.

Oooooohhhhhhhhhhnnnnnnnnnnnn . . .

Tick turned around to face the door. His mind felt hollowed out. How had it come to this? An hour ago he'd been in the middle of a desert in the Thirteenth Reality, watching Mistress Jane destroy an entire world. Now he was back in his house, in the dark, staring at a sheet of silver-blue light panning across his floor. He saw that it wavered with flashes and glimmers of shadow as though the source of the light was a gigantic TV out in the hallway, showing an old black-and-white film.

He didn't want to face whatever was out there. He turned back to the window and unlatched the lock. After pulling up the window, he unhooked the screen. He stuck his head out to look at the ground twenty feet below. If he could land in that clump of bushes . . .

Behind him, the moan took on a different pitch, stuttered. Then something sounded almost like a cough, followed by an odd crackle. Tick couldn't help but look back at this new noise.

Tendrils of bright white electricity danced around the doorknob, sparking and zigzagging like small bolts of lightning. It had a charged sound to it, like the monster-making machines in the old Frankenstein movies. There were dozens of small sparks casting flashes of light all over the room.

Tick was pretty sure he had stopped breathing and didn't know if he would ever start again.

The lightning and electricity intensified, spreading out and growing larger until they covered the entire door and the walls around it. A glow of silvery light formed in the middle, growing brighter and brighter until Tick couldn't see the features of the door or his wallpaper. Just a globe of metallic blue.

He realized he was in some sort of a trance. He was about to turn away and jump out the window—he'd take the broken leg or arm instead of whatever this was—when the entire display in front of him collapsed into an oblong and upright shape, standing maybe six feet tall. Crackles of electricity still danced along the surface, but they seemed more controlled, swirling around the oval body of light.

Then, to Tick's shock, a large face appeared in the middle of the light. It was a young woman, her features shimmering but smooth, and her expression showing a small struggle, as if she was concentrating on a difficult task. But then she was gone, replaced by another face. This time it was a man, his features rigid and angled. Then another face formed—a young boy. Then another one—an old woman, her wrinkles lines of blue against silver. A second later, a younger woman appeared, this one with a round face and eyes.

More faces appeared, each one lasting only a few moments before another took its place. Boys and girls, men and women, all ages and all races. They all had that same look of intense effort, their eyes focused on Tick, sometimes with their tongue bit between their lips.

Tick realized he'd relaxed. He was breathing normally and no longer felt the urge to jump out the window. If this thing was a ghost, it didn't seem very scary. After all the studying and intense reading of science and its inner workings he'd done over the past months, his rational mind had finally taken over. What he saw before him had to be some kind of explainable phenomenon, and his fear had been replaced by excitement to find out what it was.

The faces continued to change, one after the other, all types and ages. The light cast from the glowing oval shimmered and danced in the room, which had an even more relaxing effect on Tick. He stepped over to his desk, pulled out the chair, and sat down, never taking his eyes off the apparition.

The morphing faces seemed to relax a bit. When a young Asian man appeared, the lips of his mouth parted. He transformed into an African-American woman, and her lips began to form a word. When the sound finally came out, traveling across the room for a very shocked Tick to hear, it came from a teenage

boy. Then a fat man. Then a beautiful woman. Then an old man. Face after face, image after image, their lips remained in sync as the odd phenomenon began to speak. The voice never changed, however; it was deep and charged with energy, laced with crackles of electricity.

"Atticus Higginbottom," it said. *They* said. "We need to have a very serious talk."

⌒

Sato had learned a lot about Tick's sister. There wasn't much else to do when you were stuck in a place that stretched to infinity in every direction with nothing to see but colored marble squares. They'd walked for a while as they talked, but eventually had given up, deciding they were just as well off sitting and waiting for something to happen as they were wandering about aimlessly.

"I'm sure your sister is safe," he said after a long lull in their conversation. "Somehow those bolts of lightning sent us somewhere else. Here. Maybe other places. Maybe totally random, I don't know. But the more I think about it, the more I think it has to be something like that. If the lightning had been killing people, it would've left behind charred bodies."

Lisa nodded absently, staring down at her finger as

she traced the lines in the red marble square on which she sat cross-legged. "Charred bodies. Pleasant."

"How much do you know about the Realitants?" Sato asked.

"Most of it," she replied, looking up at him. She'd stopped crying, but her eyes were still puffy and red. "I tried to keep living my normal life and pretend it was just something for Tick, something I didn't have to worry about. I have my friends, you know? I have my own life. My mom and dad tried hard not to put all their attention on Tick and his fancy Realitant stuff, but they couldn't help it. I don't really blame them. I was happy to kind of ignore it all. Guess I have no choice now."

She pulled up her legs to wrap her arms around her knees. "This has something to do with Tick, right? It can't be a coincidence that I'm his sister and was kidnapped and then sent here by a bolt of lightning."

"I'm sure it has something to do with Tick and Mistress Jane," Sato said. "Our boss had a meeting scheduled with her, and I'm sure it all went to pot right about then."

"What's really happening? I've never been in an earthquake before, but I'm pretty sure what I just went through wasn't normal. Especially with all the lightning."

Sato shook his head. "I don't know. We're not sure what happened to Jane after the crazy stuff in the

Fourth Reality, but if she survived, I'm guessing she's one ticked-off lady. And she has weird powers. She can do things with Chi'karda. For all we know, she's messing things up pretty bad out there."

"Yeah," Lisa replied, her eyes staring at a spot in the distance. She looked slightly dazed. Sato had to remind himself that all of this was new to her, no matter how many times she'd heard about it. To really understand it, to really *know*, you had to experience stuff like this yourself.

They sat in silence for a while. Then Lisa said, "I can't imagine how scared Kayla is." A tear trickled down her cheek. She sniffed and squeezed her nose with her thumb and forefinger. "I won't be able to live if something bad happens to her."

Sato couldn't help but feel her sorrow. It made him think of the days and weeks and months he'd spent bawling his eyes out after Jane killed his parents. Why did there have to be so much evil in the world? Why couldn't people like Jane realize the pain they inflicted or understand the end results on everyday lives? How was it possible to have such a complete absence of compassion? He couldn't possibly hate Jane any more than he already did, but he felt his rage and thirst for revenge spring up anew.

"We'll find your sister," he said, hoping the promise didn't sound too empty. "We'll find your whole family, and we'll make Jane pay for whatever she's done. It's the only thing I live for now."

Lisa looked at him, her eyes red and wet and surrounded by dark, hollow circles on her face. "Thanks."

Something hummed deeply behind Sato, and he noticed Lisa look sharply over his shoulder, surprise transforming her face. The floor vibrated slightly as well.

He spun around to see what had happened.

Mothball was standing there, looking as surprised as Sato felt.

⟨~~⟩

It took a minute or so for Tick to gather himself, remembering that he'd seen many strange things since receiving his very first letter from Master George and that this was just the next in a long line of oddities. He pushed away the shock he felt, ignoring the impossibility of what he saw before him. So a big oval of silver-blue light was talking to him with hundreds of different faces mouthing the words. Big deal. He had to respond.

"How do you know my name?" he asked, proud that the words came out with no squeaks or stutters.

When the entity responded, its face started out as a teenage girl with long hair but had morphed into an old man by the time the short phrase was finished. "We have been observing you and your Realitant friends."

"Really?"

"Yes," said a woman who changed into a man.

Tick was completely fascinated. "What are you? I mean . . . *who* are you?"

The glowing apparition was quiet for a moment, though the faces continued to change at the same rapid pace. Finally, a wise-looking, ancient woman appeared to speak the words, "They call us the Haunce."

CHAPTER 27

✳

SOULIKENS

The entity paused after revealing its name, as if it wanted Tick to respond. But Tick had questions buzzing around his head like flies swarming a lightbulb, and he couldn't settle on just one. So he sat there, slack-jawed and silent.

"Do not be afraid," the many-faced apparition said. "We are as close a thing to a ghost as you will ever see, but we are much kinder than the storybooks make us out to be. It takes considerable effort to gather ourselves into something strong enough to appear visually to those still alive. We would never do it simply to scare someone. It would be ridiculous."

If Tick had flies buzzing a moment earlier, now

they had become an army of bees. *A ghost? Appear visually to those still alive?* What was this thing?

He decided to make a statement that encompassed all of his confusion in three short words. "I don't understand."

A smile appeared on a girl's face, glowing silvery blue. When the face transformed into a middle-aged man, the smile was still there. "We would not expect you to. Sit and listen. We will explain."

Tick had never heard a better idea in his life. He nodded his head emphatically.

"Good." The Haunce's orb of light expanded then retracted, as if it had taken a deep breath. The ever-changing faces spoke. "We are here because terrible things have happened in the Realities over the last few hours. When it became apparent that we must reveal ourselves, we chose you. The reason for that choice is something we may not have time to explain, but we shall see."

Tick didn't say anything, but he scrunched up his face in confusion, hoping the entity would change its mind. Whatever this ghostly visage was, why would it have chosen *him* of all people to appear to? Tick wanted to know the answer to that question very badly, but he forced himself to remain silent and listen intently as the Haunce continued speaking.

"We come to you now because enormous and catastrophic disturbances have shattered the barriers of the Realities. We know this because we are *part* of the barriers, interwoven into the Chi'karda that has served to bind the Realities together and build the wall to keep them apart. If we had not acted quickly, we might have been destroyed and the memories of billions upon billions of lives would have been obliterated. But we escaped before the worst of it happened."

The Haunce paused, flashing three different faces before a weary-eyed man with a short-cropped beard appeared and spoke. "We never would have thought it possible that someone could harness, much less control, the dark matter as the woman named Mistress Jane has done. Even we do not understand its properties to the fullest. And yet, she has unleashed it, annihilating the bonds between the Realities and sending them to drift apart from one another. What she does not understand is that soon the fragmenting will begin. In *every* Reality. A human body cannot survive when separated into pieces; the Realities are no different. What she has done will lead to the end of everything as we know it. The end of existence."

Tick felt a leprous lump growing in his belly. Although he didn't understand the nitty-gritty details, not to mention any of the logistics or complex science of what the Haunce was describing, he was smart enough to connect the dots. Mistress Jane had said from the start that she was going to sever the Fifth Reality and destroy it. From what the Haunce had just said, Tick suspected Jane must have accidentally enacted her diabolical plan on every last Reality.

And then Tick had another thought, perhaps the worst thought to ever cross the pathways of his mind. What if *he* had done this? What if his little exercise in throwing a trickle of Chi'karda into the black tree, into the dark matter that made up the Blade of Shattered Hope, had somehow disrupted Jane's plan? What if, by trying to help, he'd made it worse—infinitely worse? His more rational side had told him he wasn't ready to try something so foolish. Why hadn't he listened?

The lump inside him grew, filling his body with acid. He'd spent the last few months trying to ensure he never repeated anything like what he'd done in Chu's mountain palace. But if he'd just helped destroy every last Reality, that made the fiasco with Chu's Dark Infinity and Mistress Jane look like a food fight. Panic and worry consumed him.

"Atticus," the Haunce said. "We can feel your thoughts. We can feel your mind and see this dark path which you choose to walk. You must stop. Immediately. You do not understand even the slightest parcel of the whole."

Tick was staring at the floor. He didn't remember looking away from the Haunce, but he returned his gaze to the glowing entity at its words. He sensed some hope, maybe some redemption, in what it had said.

A young woman stared back at him, her face full of compassion. Tick wished desperately she could stay, that her face not change. But a few seconds later it slipped into an older man, the kind look not as reassuring on him.

"We are soulikens, Atticus," the Haunce said. "Do you know what that means?"

Tick shook his head.

"We sense in your memories that you have recently come to understand the heart of the human body and how the power of electricity is vital to its life-giving properties. Without electricity, the heart would not pump. If the heart did not pump, blood would not flow. And if the blood did not flow, there would be no life."

Tick nodded, surprised by this turn in the conversation, but intrigued.

"Most people do not understand that electricity is a natural phenomenon," the Haunce continued. "Much of its uses are unknown and immeasurable to scientists. Similar to how Chi'karda is not understood by most quantum physicists in the Realities, except for those who have joined ranks with the Realitants. Electricity is the key. Electronic pulses. Electronic imprints. They intertwine with almost every function of your mind and body, creating permanent stamps in the fabric of

Reality—of time and space—that represent the person from whence they came."

The Haunce paused, and Tick realized if he moved one more inch forward, he'd fall out of his chair. After an interminable few seconds, the glowing pool of faces continued.

"*That* is what soulikens are, Atticus. They are your imprints on the universe, and they can never be erased. They pool together every second of your life, collecting and gathering and forming into something that is undeniably as much you as . . . you. That is what we are. We are the soulikens of billions of people, a bank of memories and thoughts and feelings. We give life to the spaces between the atoms and neutrons and electrons. We give life to the universe of quantum physics. We give life to Chi'karda."

Tick stared at the morphing faces, completely and utterly engrossed in every word.

But then the faces frowned, the endless eyes filled with a deep sadness.

"What's wrong?" Tick asked quickly.

The Haunce wiped away the frown, but it still looked unhappy. "It works both ways, Atticus. The Chi'karda also gives us life. One cannot exist without the other. Mistress Jane has severed the Realities from one another, destroying the bonds between them. And when the fragmenting begins, when all of Reality begins to fall to the lasting and eternal grip of entropy, so will we. Everything will end. Everything."

Tick didn't know how to respond. Impossibly, he almost felt as if his grief and worry for this collection of ghosts was as strong as his concern for his family. He was starting to understand that what Jane had done would not only kill all those living today, but also all those who had lived in the past. It would be a holocaust of all time and of all people, of all thoughts and ideas and memories. Everything would be wiped away into the oblivion of dark matter.

The Haunce spoke again, snapping him back to attention.

"But not all is lost."

"What do you mean?" Tick asked.

"We believe there is someone who can save us. Save the Realities."

Tick had the horrible feeling he already knew the answer, but he asked anyway. "Who?"

The Haunce glowed brightly. "You."

CHAPTER 28

✳

COME TOGETHER

Sato and Mothball stared at each other for what seemed like a full hour, eyes locked, eyebrows raised. She was filthy from head to toe, her hair hanging in ratty strings to her shoulders. Sato kept thinking she'd disappear any second, sure that he was having a hallucination. The staring became almost comical. Especially when she broke into a grin and simply said, "'Ello."

Hearing her speak snapped Sato from his trance. "Mothball! What are you doing here? Where are we? What happened to everyone else?"

Mothball limped forward, eyeing Lisa as if she'd just noticed Tick's sister was there. "No idea what's 'appened. Felt like I've been nappin' for a full week, just woke up, and 'ere I am in a ruddy place that can't possibly exist. How long you been 'ere?"

Sato realized he had no clue. "I . . . don't know. Maybe an hour? I wasn't here very long before Lisa showed up. By the way, this is Tick's sister."

Mothball couldn't hide her surprise. "What in the name of the Grand Minister is Tick's wee little sis doin' 'ere?"

"Nice to meet you too," Lisa said in a deadpan voice.

"So sorry," she said quickly, holding out one of her gigantic hands. After Lisa shook it, Mothball continued. "Just surprised, is all. What are the ruddy chances of us meetin' 'ere with you?"

Lisa shook her head. "You think you're confused? Guess how I feel."

Sato felt it too. Everything seemed to have gone completely insane. He turned in a circle, throwing his arms up to gesture at their strange surroundings. "Where could this possibly be? What is it? Why would the three of us—"

Before he could finish, that same humming noise vibrated through the air, this time coming from a spot directly in front of him. At the same time, a dark blue square of marble rotated on an unseen axis, completely turning over until what had been the bottom was now the top, though with dark-red squiggly lines scratched across its surface. As soon as the tile settled into place, a person appeared on the marble square, instantly flashing into existence.

It was Mothball's mom, Windasill.

Sato swore right then he was done being surprised.

Mothball ran to her mom and pulled her into a massive hug as Windasill looked about in confusion.

"Don't worry," Mothball said after stepping back. "None of us know a ruddy thing, but thank the heavens we're together. Mayhaps the old man'll show up soon, he will."

"It was so dreadful," Windasill said after giving her daughter the kindest smile Sato thought he'd ever seen. "The shaking, the lightning. Last thing I remember, a bolt of energy came straight down on me head. Burned like the dickens, it did. Then it was dark, like sleep. I was barely aware. Next thing I know, I'm 'ere. Mothball, what's going on, dear?"

"Don't know." She shrugged and looked at Sato.

"Me, neither," Sato murmured.

"Does anyone at least have a guess?" Lisa asked. "Come on. You guys are Realitants, right? At least take a wild stab at it."

Sato was impressed with Tick's sister. She was no-nonsense, levelheaded. Brave. Tick had once made her out to be a smart-aleck pain in the rear. Maybe hard times had brought out her inner strength.

"Well?" Lisa said.

"If I 'ad to make a guess," Mothball said, folding her arms as her eyes revealed she was frantically trying to come up with an answer. "I reckon I'd say that . . . well, me instincts tell me that . . . if that lightning was . . . mayhaps it could've been . . . if you think about it . . ."

Luckily, another humming sound saved her. Sato looked to his right just in time to see a light green, marble square settle into place after rotating. An instant later, Rutger appeared, sitting on his bum in his black pants and black shirt, looking as frightened as Sato had ever seen him.

"What happened?" he yelled, scrambling to get his short legs under him. He looked so much like a huge ball pitching back and forth on two sticks that Sato worried what Lisa would think. He'd grown quite fond of Rutger, despite the constant teasing, and he always worried when the short man met new people. But Lisa seemed completely at ease, and his esteem for her went up another notch.

Before anyone could answer Rutger's inquiry, another humming sounded. Sato didn't look around in time to see the marble rotate, but about forty feet behind him, Tollaseat had appeared.

Windasill's shriek of delight had barely pierced the air when there came another humming. Then another. Then another. Sato was spinning in circles trying to catch sight of all the flipping tiles. People appeared each time, people he didn't know. Most of them were tall like Mothball and obviously from the Fifth. Hum, hum, hum—the sound blended together into a resonating vibration that strangely soothed his nerves.

Suddenly it was like musical popcorn. More and more and more marble slabs spun in ninety degrees all around him, changing colors as they did so, while a stunned, often dirty, sometimes injured person winked into existence on top. Sato finally quit trying to take it all in and instead focused on Mothball, then Rutger. Both of them were gawking at the strange sight around them, but Lisa was staring straight at him.

She raised her eyebrows in an unspoken question.

"You know I don't know what's going on," Sato said. "Let's just hope none of these people are maniacs bent on killing us."

"I just don't . . ." She trailed off, her eyes focusing on something past Sato's shoulder. They widened in surprise, then shock, then a huge smile wiped the anguish and confusion off her face.

"What?" he asked, already turning to see what she'd discovered.

Lisa shrieked with joy, brushing past him and sprinting toward a group of shorter people—compared to the Fifths, anyway—a heavyset man, a brown-haired woman, and a little girl.

It had to be Kayla. And Tick's parents, too.

Sato hurried after Lisa, feeling a rush of excitement at meeting Tick's family, somehow putting out of his mind that they were all standing in an impossible place with no explanation of how they'd gotten there.

Lisa reached her family and practically tackled Kayla, pulling her into a tight embrace and twirling her around. Their mom and dad soon joined in, a group of entwined arms, jumping up and down and laughing. It was one of the sweetest things Sato had ever seen.

When he reached them, he stopped, wondering if maybe he should've left them alone to their reunion.

Lisa saw him and broke apart from the vise of her dad's arms. "Mom, Dad—this is Tick's friend Sato." She reached out and grabbed his arm, pulling him closer for the introductions.

"I'm Edgar," her dad said, taking Sato's hand and shaking it vigorously. "I don't know where we are or how we got here, but I'm honored to meet one of my son's partners in crime."

"Nice . . . nice to meet you," Sato managed to mumble. Everything suddenly felt like a dream.

Tick's mom pulled Sato into a long hug, then looked at him as she squeezed his shoulders. "I'm Lorena, and it's an honor indeed. Atticus told us about your parents and what happened to them. I was so sorry to hear the news. Your mom and I were dear, dear friends for many years. But after I left the Realitants, I had no choice but to lose touch with her. It has been one of the biggest regrets of my life."

Sato raised his eyebrows. "Why'd you have to do that? Why couldn't you stay friends?"

Lorena looked at the ground for a second, a flash of fear on her face. But then she returned her gaze to him and her eyes were filled with resolve. "Because Jane said she'd kill me if I ever contacted a Realitant again. She was scared I'd tell them about the Thirteenth Reality before she was ready."

CHAPTER 29

✳

THE ONLY HOPE

Tick spent a long minute simply staring at the shifting faces of the glowing Haunce. Their eyes stared back, full of scrutiny and concern, waiting to hear his reaction to the pronouncement that Tick was the only one who could save the Realities from ripping apart and ceasing to exist forever. No pressure, right?

He decided to show how much he'd grown up in the last year or so. "Okay. I'm not gonna sit here and waste time. It's hard for me to believe I could do anything to stop or reverse what Jane's done. But you obviously know what you're talking about—I mean, you're a billion ghosts crammed into the space of a water heater. That's a lot of brains. So what am I supposed to do?"

The Haunce laughed just as its face morphed into that of a young woman with dark eyes. The sound was like electronic music. When the face changed to an old man with a mustache, the Haunce began speaking again. "No brains here, Atticus. At least not physically. But our combined knowledge is here all the same, stored on countless imprints of soulikens. But there will be time for school lessons later. You are correct that we should not waste any more time. We must get to the heart of the matter, and quickly."

Tick nodded, half-fascinated and half-terrified of what he was about to hear.

The Haunce continued, the faces forever shifting. "Atticus, we have been observing the Realities for many years—living them, breathing them, *being* them. We exist in the boundaries and seams that keep the Realities together and apart, united but separate, all things balanced as they should be. At times, we have intervened, but only in extreme cases of need. Never before has the need been so great as it is now.

"The seams are splitting. Dark matter is consuming them, triggering chain reactions of heightened entropy and introducing fragmentation on a level never seen. We believe there is only one way to stop it."

"How does it involve me?" Tick asked.

The Haunce's current face—a boy, maybe only ten years old—frowned at the interruption, then the expression smoothed away like rippling water. "As we said, we have been observing the Realities for countless centuries. And in all that time, there have been only two people with a concentration of soulikens and Chi'karda levels similar to ours. You are one of those people, Atticus. And Mistress Jane is the other. We do not yet understand how the two of you came to possess this power or why you both came to exist in the same period of time. But it will take your combined powers to reverse what has happened today."

Tick had to bite his lip. He wanted to shout a million questions, refute the Haunce's words. If saving the Realities depended on him *and* Jane—depended on their cooperation—then the battle was over before it had begun.

The glowing orb of the Haunce flexed, as if taking a deep breath. "We must rebind the seams of the Realities and restore stability to the inner workings of quantum physics. To do so, we will need to harness an unprecedented amount of Chi'karda. And to do that, we will need four components."

The Haunce paused, and Tick felt the agony of each passing second.

"In all of the Realities of the Multiverse there is a place where the Chi'karda levels are exponentially higher than at any other place. So concentrated, in fact, it makes the Realitant headquarters in the Bermuda

Triangle look like a spark of static compared to a lightning storm. You and Mistress Jane must join us there."

"Is it the place in the desert?" Tick asked. "Where Jane had that black tree? The dark matter, the Blade of Shattered Hope?"

The Haunce—now showing the face of an older, homely woman—slowly shook its head. "No. Jane chose that spot because it best fit her needs for linking the different elements of the Blade. Because she had an Alterant of herself in the same place in all thirteen Realities, it was more a matter of the substance of the Blade than it was of Chi'karda."

"Then where do we have to go?" Tick was saving the biggest and most obvious question for last: How in the world would they get Jane to cooperate with them?

"There's a place in the Thirteenth Reality where . . ." The Haunce faltered. The face of an Indian woman, the red dot on her forehead looking almost black against the blue glow of her skin, wore a look of complete sadness. "It is a place of atrocities and horror. We are sorry; it is hard for us to talk about it." Another long pause.

Tick didn't know if he wanted to hear the answer. After millennia of observing the world and all the things humans had done—both good and bad—the Haunce was having difficulty talking about a place to which Tick had to go. The thought was terrifying.

The Haunce finally continued, the look of sadness now draped across the face of a young Asian man. "We do not know why evil things have always been drawn to this particular spot in the Thirteenth Reality. There have been thousands upon thousands of deaths there—perhaps millions. The Chi'karda levels created by those tragedies is unsurpassed."

Tick swallowed a big lump, then took a guess. "It's where Jane's castle is, isn't it?"

The eyes of a little girl met Tick's. "No. Not there. Somewhere much, much worse."

Tick waited.

"The place we must gather," the Haunce said, seeming to have recovered its composure a little, "and where you must bring Jane, is . . . the Factory."

"The Factory?" Tick repeated.

The Haunce nodded. "Yes. It is the place where Jane manufactures her creatures. Her abominations. It is a hideous, wretched place full of death and tortured souls. But also the site of massive amounts of Chi'karda."

"And what do we do once we get there?" Tick asked. He was trying not to think too much about what a creepy and horrible place the Factory must be. "Assuming that we somehow convince Jane to come with us and do what we ask, I mean."

The pulsing, silver-blue orb of the Haunce moved several feet across the floor and back again, as if pacing, deep in thought. "The task you and Jane must do is simple. Both of you need to concentrate and summon every ounce of Chi'karda you can. Gather as much as you can, and then you must channel to us. Our job will be to harness the power and combine it with the Chi'karda that already exists within the Factory."

The Haunce quit pacing and took another one of those deep breaths. "Once we have gathered enough power, we will bleed the Chi'karda through the cracks of space and time, binding the seals of the Realities that are currently rupturing. Quite honestly, the task could destroy us, but we believe we can save the Multiverse before that happens. Before we ourselves cease to exist."

Tick didn't know what to think. The whys and hows didn't matter so much at the moment, and he couldn't pretend to feel a pang of potential loss at hearing that the Haunce might die in the act. Especially if the Haunce's sacrifice would save thirteen entire worlds—and his family. But still, hearing it all poured out so short and sweet when so much was on the line was dizzying.

"Do you have anything to say?" the Haunce asked, now showing the face of a pretty girl about Tick's age.

"Not a thing," Tick responded. "I don't know what else I can do but trust you. If you say we can do this, then let's do it. I guess the first thing is to figure out how to get Jane to play along. I'm sure once we tell her what's about to happen, she'll have to. I mean, how could she want everything to disappear, including her? That'd be beyond stupid."

"We can only hope." The Haunce morphed into an old woman. "There is one final thing to say before we begin. You must know that a lull has occurred in the fragmentation of the Realities. For the moment, they are safe. And so is your family. But . . ."

Tick felt a thrilling rush of joy as he realized that somehow he'd known all along that his family was safe. The relief lasted only a second before being tempered. "But?" he repeated, thinking, *What now?*

The face of a small boy responded. "But we have only thirty hours until the fragmentation begins again. And when it does, it will not stop until all that we know ceases to exist."

PART 3

——— ✳ ———

THE FIFTH
ARMY

CHAPTER 30

✳

A BOWL OF DEBRIS

Sofia lay on her back, staring at the twilight sky of the desert, the deep blue just beginning its fade to purple. No clouds. A throbbing pain pulsed somewhere inside her skull—something had knocked her out. Something had hit her in the head during the chaos right after Tick disappeared.

Tick disappeared!

She forced herself into a sitting position, groaning at the thunder of pain it ignited. She coughed, a dry rasp that hurt her throat. She needed water. Badly. The natural rock formations of Jane's secret spot still surrounded them, though several chunks had broken off and tumbled to the dusty ground during the earthquake. The tables and screens and computers used by Jane's people lay scattered and smashed, strewn about like abandoned toys. The air smelled burnt.

Twisting her head around, she searched for signs of her friends. She felt a fleeting moment of panic when she didn't see them at first, but it quickly vanished when movement under a collapsed table caught her attention. Master George, his nice suit filthy and torn, was wiggling his way out from under the heavy slab of the table. Paul sat a few feet from him, his arms wrapped around his knees, staring into the distance with a blank expression.

"You guys okay?" Sofia asked.

"They all vanished," Paul said, not bothering to look at her. "Jane first, and then everyone else right after. Zip, zip, zip. Zippity gone, just like that. Left us here to die, I guess."

"I'm actually quite surprised." Master George grunted. He finally freed himself from the confining rubble and stood up, dusting himself off. "She went to all that trouble to kidnap us, and then she simply ran away? Odd."

Sofia disagreed. "I don't think it's that weird. Somehow Tick winked away, or someone took him, whatever. But without him, she didn't have what she needed anymore. It's *his* family she took, after all."

"It's not even that," Paul said in a subdued voice, still staring at the rock walls like he'd been hypnotized.

Sofia scooted a little closer to him. "What are you talking about?"

"Look at that." Paul finally blinked and pointed to the middle of the depression where the black tree—the Blade of Shattered Hope—had been. It was gone, replaced by a small crater. The ground was blackened and charred, some of the desert sand actually glistening where the heat had transformed it to glass. "I think something went wrong with what that freak Jane was trying to do. Really, really wrong. She doesn't care about us anymore. She ran away to try to fix whatever it is she messed up."

Sofia stared at the dark scar of a hole and slowly nodded as she thought about what he'd said. Paul was right. The earthquake had been horrible, and all of Jane's people had run around screaming, falling down, and crawling over each other as they looked for a way to escape. Things had obviously not gone according to plan.

"That certainly sounds reasonable," Master George said. "What I wouldn't give to know what exactly happened here today. All that nonsense about dark matter. Perhaps it wasn't quite rubbish after all."

"Dark matter," Paul muttered in disgust; Sofia shared the sentiment. "I don't give a patooty about any of that stuff right now. All I want is a chance to put my hands around Jane's neck and squeeze."

Sofia felt her eyebrows rise in surprise. "A little violent this evening, aren't we?"

Paul looked at her for the first time since she'd come to, and she couldn't help but lean back a couple of inches before stopping herself. His eyes were full of fury and hatred. There was no sign of the normally lighthearted, joking Paul.

Sofia felt a deep anger inside of her, too. "Just kidding. I'd like to do that myself."

Master George walked over to Paul and offered a hand. "All in due time, Master Paul. All in due time. For now, we need to find water—or we won't live long enough to put our hands around a sandwich, much less Mistress Jane."

Paul ignored the offer of help, but did stand up, his face still tensed in anger. Sofia pushed herself up as well, and the three of them began searching through the debris. Jane's people had to have brought plenty of food and water if they planned on being out here for any significant amount of time. It took only a few minutes to find the stash.

Several coolers with bread, meat, fruit, and big, glass bottles of water—most of which had been packed tightly enough that they hadn't broken in the chaos— had been wedged between a toppled table and some large computer equipment.

Sofia drank half a bottle of water, trickles of the liquid splashing down her cheeks and onto her clothes. Even though the water was warm, she was sure she'd never tasted anything so refreshing in her life.

They didn't dare eat the meat, but the bread and fruit seemed okay, and soon they were all sitting together in one of the few spots clear of wreckage, enjoying their odd little meal. The sun had sunk even further, the shadows from the towering rocks stretching all the way across the desert bowl. Full darkness would be upon them soon.

Sofia hated the thought of being in the middle of a desert in the Thirteenth Reality at nighttime. "Guys, this is great to eat and rest a little, but what're we gonna do next? It'll be totally dark soon."

"We'll probably get eaten alive by fangen," Paul said, neither his voice nor his face revealing any sign that he was kidding. "Jane's probably already sent some out here to hunt us."

Sofia wanted the old Paul back. "You're real great to have around when things get rough," she said. "You really know how to look on the bright side."

Paul shrugged and took a big bite of an apple, wiping the juice on his sleeve.

"There are much worse things than fangen," Master George said with a doomsday voice.

Sofia stared at him, surprised and curious. He returned her look, his eyes squinting despite the fading light. When he said nothing, she finally asked, "What makes you say that?"

Master George glanced at Paul, then looked away toward the western wall of the bowl, now draped in shadow. "Our spies have learned a lot about Jane's extracurricular activities these past months. She has a place called the Factory, located in one of the heaviest Chi'karda spots ever discovered. Word is she's created things far more hideous than her precious fangen. Far worse. More vicious by a long shot."

"What are they?" Paul asked.

Sofia found it hard to believe something could be worse than those flying, snarling, diseased, sharp-toothed monsters.

"She hasn't brought them out for full usage yet," Master George said. "We've caught only bare glimpses and heard rumors. But her work in using nature to create nature has gone beyond anything you or I could dare scrape up in a campfire tale. Evil, evil things. We think she is also working to isolate the soulikens of . . . very bad people from the past."

Soulikens. Sofia had heard the word before, but she'd never pursued its meaning because of countless other things that seemed more important. Master George continued before she could voice her question.

"I haven't told you much about soulikens, because I myself didn't know enough. But I've spent every spare second since we last said good-bye researching the phenomenon. It might be the most fascinating thing I've ever studied—everything from the fundamentals of natural electricity and its role within human biology to old tales and rumors of ghost stories."

"Well, what *is* it?" Paul asked in an impatient voice. "What's a souliken?"

The sun seemed to finally disappear for good in that moment, the sky darkening as if all the light had been frightened away. When Master George turned his gaze to Sofia, she almost gasped out loud at how creepy he looked with the angles of his face deep in shadow.

"Soulikens are your eternal stamp on reality," he said. "They are the means by which you'll haunt the world far after you've rotted to dust and bone."

And then, for some odd reason, the old man laughed.

CHAPTER 31

✳

MAKING PLANS

Thirty hours?" Tick asked, hating how that sounded both long and short at the same time. "We have only thirty hours to save the entire universe?"

The silver-blue glow of the Haunce flared a bit then subsided. "Thirty hours or thirty years—it would not make a difference. There is not much we can do to prepare, and it might even be worse if we did have the time to try. The problem will be convincing Mistress Jane to cooperate. Once you accomplish that, all that will be left is our attempt to rebind the Realities and reseal the barriers."

Tick felt a bubble in his stomach as he shook his head in disbelief. "Once *I* accomplish it? You really think Jane is gonna trust me for even one second? You'll have to talk to her, not me."

The face of an old man frowned back at him. "We are sorry, Atticus. Our ability to appear in this form is extremely difficult to maintain. Once we leave here, neither you nor anyone else will see us again until the moment we make our attempt. The task of having Jane join us is entirely up to you."

Tick didn't say anything for a minute, trying to process the new information and its potential ramifications. He felt an incredible amount of pressure draped across his shoulders like an iron shawl.

Finally, he said, "Okay, look. I don't know how I can possibly do that. I'm not even sure I understand what it is I'm supposed to do. But you said something about my family being safe. I need to hear about that right now. How do you know they're okay?"

A woman with a big nose responded. "As Jane was building her cache of dark matter and assembling her Blade of Shattered Hope, we watched carefully. We normally do not interfere with the realm of living humans. It is not our place. If Jane had destroyed the Fifth Reality, we would have been shocked and horrified, but we would not have stopped her. However, when the chain reactions that could end all existence were ignited, we no longer had a choice."

Tick groaned on the inside, doubly annoyed. Both

at the long non-answer about his family and the fact that the Haunce would sit back and let an entire world be destroyed. "What does this have to do with my family?" he asked.

An annoyed buzz sounded from the ghostly creature. "We hope your impatience will serve you well since we will have little time left together. No more interruptions. We will not be able to appear in this form much longer."

The glow changed into three faces before Tick finally nodded.

"Good," the Haunce continued. "When the barriers began to break and the seals began to split, we knew immediately what we must do. We winked you here to Reality Prime, where we would be able to discuss things in private. We also winked your family away from Jane's prison, as well as a number of people from the Fifth Reality who were located in the area of your Realitant friends—Mothball, Rutger, and Sato. They are together in a special holding place we created long ago—a sort of way station that exists in a quasi-Reality that only we know about."

"What about—" Tick stopped himself, not wanting to interrupt again.

"Your other friends?" the Haunce asked. "Sofia, Paul, and your Realitant leader, Master George?"

Tick nodded.

"They are in the Thirteenth Reality, where you last saw them."

Tick couldn't remain silent any more. "Why didn't you take them to the same place as my family?"

The face of the Haunce flowed from an ugly woman to a pretty one, then morphed into a man with beady eyes. "They remain in the Thirteenth, because that is where you are going. You will need their help. You will be together very soon, though you will not have much time for happy reunions."

"Okay, so what do I need to know?" Tick asked, surprised at how steady he felt. He was ready to have this whole mess done and over with.

⌒

No one had spoken since Master George's explanation of soulikens. Sofia continued to sit still, staring at the dark shadow of a wall standing a few dozen feet from her. The sounds of the desert were soft and faint—an insect here and there, the sigh of the wind, sand scratching across rock.

When Paul spoke up, it startled her. She hoped he hadn't noticed her jump.

"Soulikens," he said. "Basically you're telling us that throughout our lives we create these freaky electronic imprints on the world that never go away but hang around us like a fog, building and building until it kind of becomes our ghost. Is that what you're telling us? That ghosts are real?"

"If you could see on a quantum level," Master George responded, "you'd see an aura of energy around you and others that very much resemble exactly that. A ghost."

Sofia felt a little creeped out. "Then I don't wanna see on a quantum level. I hate scary movies, and I hate ghosts."

"Now who's the cheerful one?" Paul asked.

"You rubbed off on me."

"I love scary movies. Especially the ones where lots of people die."

Sofia couldn't help but feel happy that the old Paul was starting to come back. "Call me crazy, but I prefer my movies to have the slightest hint of intelligence."

"When all this is over," Paul said, "check out *Steve the Slashing Monkey* and tell me that movie doesn't *bleed* intelligence."

Sofia couldn't stop before a snort of laughter came out.

"I knew it!" Paul yelled, his voice echoing off the rock walls. "I knew I could make you laugh!"

"You two are driving me mad," Master George muttered. "I believe I'm quite ready to get some sleep."

"But what're we gonna do?" Paul asked him. "Can't

you get someone to wink us out of this stinkin' place?"

"Sorry, old chap. If someone hasn't winked us by now, then there's obviously been a break in communication. Jane brought us here, remember, and her shield must still be working. And I don't have my Barrier Wand. I assure you, Sally's doing his very best to find us."

Great, Sofia thought. They had to spend the night in the middle of the desert, with no telling how many creatures of Mistress Jane lurking about. *Just great.*

"Well," Paul said, "at least it's not cold. I bet we can find some soft sand to snuggle in, Sofia. You in?"

Sofia leaned closer to him and smacked him on the arm. It felt so wonderful that she did it again.

Paul jumped to his feet and ran away, snickering as he rubbed his sore spot. "Man, for a chick who's a scaredy-cat of scary movies, you sure do know how to punch."

"I was glad you'd gotten over your sour mood," Sofia responded as she started looking around for her own place to get some rest, feeling with her hands mostly. "But now that you're back to normal, I kind of miss the grumpy Paul after all."

"I love you too."

She'd just found a nice spot of open sand when a slight thump in the air sounded behind her. It was barely noticeable, and she almost felt it more than heard it. She whipped around to see what had happened.

A shadowy figure of a boy stood between her and

Paul, a hump of a backpack on his shoulders. When he turned and faced her, the starlight revealed his face just enough.

"Tick!" she cried, scrambling to her feet and running to him. Paul reached him just as she did, and they all joined in a group hug. When she finally pulled back, she said, "What happened? Where'd you go?"

"And how'd you get back here?" Paul added.

Master George joined them. "Atticus! Speak, man, speak!"

Tick laughed a little, though it didn't hold much humor. "Calm down, guys. It's a long story, and we don't have much time to talk. We have to get moving. I'll tell you everything on the go."

"Get moving?" Sofia asked, feeling a slight chill. "Where are we supposed to go?"

"Some place called the Factory," Tick answered. "It's full of Mistress Jane's little monster pets. But don't worry. We have a billion ghosts to help us out."

CHAPTER 32

*

REUNIONS

Tick didn't want to waste a single minute. When the Haunce outlined the plan for what they needed to do to stop the fragmenting of the Realities, one thing bled through all the others: they needed to hurry.

Tick had less than thirty hours to get to the Factory, convince Mistress Jane to help—after getting her there in the first place, of course—then summon all the Chi'karda he could to help the Haunce rebind the barriers of the Realities.

No problem. Then why did he have the terrible feeling that nothing would go right along the way?

Sofia, Paul, and Master George stood in front of him in the darkness. The starlight was not strong enough to reveal their faces, but Tick could imagine the looks of surprise and confusion.

"Seriously," he said. "We need to go. We're gonna be winked in five minutes."

"Whoa," Paul said, his upraised hands mere shafts of shadow. "I'm not takin' a single step till you elaborate on this whole ghost business."

"A *billion* ghosts," Sofia added. "What was that all about?"

Tick was about to answer when Master George made an unpleasant harrumphing sound.

"What?" Tick asked.

"You met the Haunce, didn't you?" the old man responded. Tick could barely see him shaking his head. "I've met it only once in my life, and if I ever do again, you can bet your bottoms I'm going to have a word or two with it about holding back vital information about soulikens and all that."

Tick felt a flutter of confusion, but Sofia spoke up before he could.

"The Haunce? What's that? And why would it know everything about soulikens?"

Tick's confusion increased. "You guys know about soulikens?"

"You mean *you* do?" Paul responded.

Tick nodded even though he doubted they could see him. "The Haunce told me about them."

"What is the Haunce?" Sofia shouted.

For some reason a chuckle burst out of Tick. "We sound like the dumbest people who've ever lived." He remembered the urgency of what they had to do. "But come on—we really need to go. The Haunce wants us to stand at the spot where the Blade of Shattered Hope tree thingy was."

"Why?" all three of them asked in unison.

"He—*it's* going to wink us closer to the Factory. We can sort things out once we get there. Come on—can you tell where the Blade used to be?"

"Over this way," Paul muttered. "Doesn't sound like a good time to start doubting Superman Atticus Higginbottom."

Paul's shadow moved past him and started walking toward the central area of the dark stone walls surrounding them. Tick followed and heard Sofia and Master George right behind him.

Tick tripped twice over debris and stepped on things that clanged and snapped. The place must've gotten really messed up after he'd been winked away.

Paul finally stopped in an open spot and turned to face the rest of the group. "Pretty sure it was right about here. But be careful—some of the sand turned into glass shards."

Tick felt the crunch under his shoes, smelled something burnt. When they were all standing in a circle, he reached out and took Sofia's hand, then Paul's. "The Haunce told me we need to hold hands. It's easier that way."

Tick was glad they didn't argue. Sofia took Master George's hand, and then the old man took Paul's. Standing there in the dark desert with the slight breeze sighing as it passed over the towering rocks, Tick felt a major case of the creeps, like they were about to begin a séance.

"Okay!" he shouted. "Wink us away, Haunce!" The words sounded incredibly stupid, but he wanted to get this part over with. He had no idea what to expect once they got to where they were going.

Before this last thought even fully formed in his mind, the tingle shot across his neck and down his spine.

It had been a strange hour for Sato.

There'd been the reunion of Tick's family—without Tick, unfortunately—as well as hearing more details about Mrs. Higginbottom (a.k.a. Lorena) and her brief stint as a Realitant. Sato had been amazed to learn that she and Mistress Jane had been partners of a sort in exploring and seeking out new Realities, and they'd been together when the Thirteenth was discovered. They'd realized that something was special about it right away, and how odd properties of Chi'karda ran rampant there.

It was the first time Jane had started to show the dual signs of her thirst for power and her edge of obsession with the idea of a Utopian Reality. When Jane threatened Lorena if she dared tell anyone about their discovery, that had been the last straw. Lorena decided to call it quits, realizing she wasn't cut out for that kind of life—namely being killed by a crazy woman.

Sato eventually drifted away from the Higginbottoms. He suspected they probably wanted some time to themselves to bask in the joy of being together again. And, he admitted to himself, it hurt to see such a thing. It painfully reminded him that he'd lost his own parents, and that such a get-together would be impossible for him. It hurt, and he left them before it became unbearable.

But that's when things had really gotten strange for him.

There were several hundred people from the Fifth Reality in the strange space, all of them winked in from the general location of where Mothball's parents lived. How that had happened was beyond anyone's guess, but they'd mostly gotten over their shock and just generally reveled in the fact that they were still alive.

Or, Sato figured, at least they hoped that was the case. The bizarre place to which they'd been sent didn't seem like anything in the normal world. Maybe they *had* died and been sent to an afterlife. Who knew? Sato didn't want to think about it until he absolutely had to.

Once all the people from the Fifth settled in, they began to notice him. They began to see the resemblance he had to their recently assassinated Grand Minister. His Alterant. And now they surrounded him completely, a huge crowd of giants, all of them staring at him, waiting for him to speak. But he refused, sitting cross-legged with his chin resting on his closed fists. Mothball had to get him out of this. She had to do something! If not her, then her parents.

But they seemed to be enjoying the spectacle, along with Rutger. The four of them sat outside the crowd somewhere—he'd lost sight of them a good half hour earlier.

Sato buried his face in his hands and groaned, hoping everyone heard the scream of frustration barely veiled within it.

The first thing Tick noticed was that the air was much cooler, laced with a wetness almost as thick as mist. Then he saw the tall, looming poles of shadow all around them—trees. Lots and lots of trees.

They were back in the Forest of Plague—the place they'd come a year ago on a mission to steal Mistress

Jane's Barrier Wand. This time they'd be going in the opposite direction; the Factory lay due east, according to the Haunce.

Tick felt the reassuring grip of Sofia's and Paul's hands in his own. "You guys okay?"

"Still in one piece," Master George answered from a few feet in front of him. Tick couldn't see his face very well. In fact, he couldn't see much except for the trees and the dark shapes of his fellow Realitants.

"Fine," Paul grumbled. "At least it's not hot here. My pits are in desperate need of some deodorant."

Sofia sighed. "Pleasant as always."

"Okay, so where are we?" Paul asked.

"Yes, Atticus," Master George added. "No more time for hasting about until you answer some questions. Where are we? What's behind all this?"

Tick felt surprisingly calm despite the clock winding down inside his mind; he didn't have the heart to look at his watch. He knew the calm wouldn't last long. He knew terrible things lay ahead.

"Tick?" Paul prodded. "Speak up—can't hear ya."

"All right, listen," Tick began. "I'll explain everything, but then we gotta get going. Jane screwed up the whole universe with her dark-matter tree—that stupid Blade of Shattered Hope. The barriers keeping the Realities whole and bound together are fragmenting, breaking apart. Right now there's a lull, but the

Haunce says in twenty-something hours from now, it'll all snap, blow up, disintegrate. In no time at all, everything will cease to exist. That's how the Haunce put it."

"I feared the worst," Master George whispered, a deathly rasp. "However, this is beyond even what I cooked up in my head. But if the Haunce told you as much, then it's true."

Tick nodded despite the darkness. "It thinks we can fix the problem somehow, but it'll take me, Mistress Jane, and the Haunce itself together in the biggest Chi'karda spot in all the Realities. Which is this Factory place a few miles to the east of here."

"Oh, goodness gracious me," Master George said. The others stayed silent, maybe too shocked for words.

"Anyway," Tick said, "we can talk more about the details, but the Haunce wants me to do a quick job first." Tick reached into his pocket and pulled out the short metal message tube Master George had given him earlier. "First, it wants me to send an important note to somebody—wink it, actually."

"Wink it?" Sofia repeated. "You mean . . ."

Tick held up the tube between his thumb and forefinger, barely able to see the silver shine of its smooth surface. "Yeah. The Haunce wants me to wink it with my so-called powers. Called it . . . *practice.*"

CHAPTER 33

SENDING A MESSAGE

Tick finally remembered that he'd packed a flash-light before leaving his house. He swung his backpack off and pulled it out, then clicked it on. The light reflected off the silvery surface of the metal tube, making it look like a valuable piece of jewelry.

"Atticus," Master George said as he moved closer and put a hand on Tick's shoulder. "Listen to me carefully. I want you to describe what the Haunce looked like. Once I'm absolutely sure this all came from our strange and powerful friend, I promise I won't doubt another word you say."

Tick let the flashlight tip downward until it illuminated the leaf-strewn forest floor. "It was a big, silver-blue oval of pulsing light, with hundreds of faces replacing each other in the middle of it, their mouths forming the words as it talked to me. Creeped me out big time."

Master George nodded as his eyes focused on the ground. "Indeed. Indeed. It's hard to put into words what it means that the Haunce visited you, Atticus. There's no longer any doubt that there is something special about you, something extraordinary. Especially if the Haunce thinks you can wink this message away without the use of a Barrier Wand."

"Yeah, well, we'll see," Tick said. He shone the flashlight under his chin to make his face look scary. "You both can think I'm special all you want, but let's see if I can actually do it."

"You *are* special," Paul said, not bothering to hide his sarcasm. "You're so special."

"He *is*," Sofia snapped. "Be quiet and let him concentrate. Do it, Tick. Show him. Show us what you can do."

Paul snickered, evidently thinking his joke was hilarious. "I'm just playin', man. Sheesh. What's the note in there say, anyway? And who are you sending it to?"

"It's for Sally—" Master George began, but Tick cut him off.

"No, it's not."

"What do you mean? You changed it?"

Tick shone the light on the silver tube still clasped in his other hand. "Had to. The Haunce said we had no chance of getting all the Realitants together in time to help us. They're spread all over the place, dealing with the earthquakes and junk that happened when everything went wrong."

"Then who's it for?" Sofia asked.

"It's a note for someone who already has a bunch of people gathered, ready to fight the first bad thing that walks in front of them." Tick paused, needlessly adding drama to the revelation, just for kicks. "It's for Sato."

⌒

Sato ignored every word spoken to him and every tap on his shoulder until he heard the voice of Lisa.

"Sato?" she asked. "You okay?"

He looked up to see she'd maneuvered her way through the tightly packed crowd. She stood in front of him, leaning down with her hands on her knees, looking at him with concern creasing her pretty face. The fact that she cared one whit made him feel a little better.

"I guess so," he replied. He swept his eyes across the tall people of the Fifth who were packing in tighter and tighter around him, still gawking and pointing. "I just don't know what they want. I'm not who they think I am—they have to *know* that! What do they expect me to do? Pretend I'm their leader raised from the dead?"

Lisa knelt down, the movement causing her blonde curls to bounce on her shoulders. "We all thought it was kind of cute until you put your head down and ignored them. Why don't you come over and sit with my family? Maybe that'll make them leave you alone."

Sato shook his head slowly as he considered her offer. How stupid was this? These people fawning over him were the least of his worries. Where were they and how were they going to get out of there?

"Sato?" Lisa asked. "You want me to—"

"No, no, sorry," he said. "I was just thinking that we need to figure out what's going on around here. I need to talk to Rutger and Mothball. Figure out if we can get in touch with the other Realitants somehow."

Lisa nodded. "Okay, sounds good. Why don't you . . ." She paused, looked around quickly, then focused back on him. "Tell you what—I'll get their attention so you can sneak off or something."

"Get their attention? How're you gonna do that?"

Lisa straightened, rubbing her hands together as if planning something evil. "I can be a brat when I need to be—ask Tick. I'll think of something brilliant to make them leave you alone."

Sato stood to join her, wincing at the gasps of anticipation his action elicited from the crowd. "Okay, fine by me. Good luck with that." He started through the crowd of Fifth citizens standing between him and his Realitant friends.

"You people listen up!" he heard Lisa shout from behind him. "Sato will be right back. He has to, um, go use the bathroom."

Sato stopped for half a second, thinking, *That is the best she can come up with?* But then he pushed on, making his way toward Mothball and Rutger.

⁓

Tick did his best to explain what the Haunce had said about Sato and the others being taken to some kind of way station anomaly in the Realities for safekeeping. But it was kind of hard when he didn't really understand it himself.

"What *is* this place?" Paul asked. "*Where* is it?"

"I don't know!" Tick practically shouted, though he toned it down to a rough whisper on the last word. They couldn't risk Jane's creations finding them yet. "All we care about is that they're all safe—including my family, thank goodness—and that the Haunce is gonna move them very soon. Which is why I need to hurry. As soon as I get this note winked, we'll have time to talk about stuff while we walk toward the Factory." Annoyed, Tick pointed the flashlight in Paul's face. "Okay?"

Paul reached out, flailing with his hands. "All right, dude, get on with it!"

"Yes, Atticus," Master George pitched in. "I'm very anxious to see what you're about to do. Quite anxious indeed. And when we're done, I'd love to hear more about this hideaway spot in the Realities you mentioned."

Sofia reached out and lightly punched Tick in the arm. "We'll leave you alone, now. Do your thing. I can't wait to see it."

Tick had a sudden rush of terror. He had no idea what he was about to do—or even where to begin. The Haunce had left him with some parting words of advice—mainly about envisioning a conduit between him and Sato and opening an imaginary slice through space and time. But mostly, he was supposed to sit back and let his power do its thing. He needed to believe in it and let the Chi'karda take his vision of need and manifest it for him.

His mind knew what it wanted. His heart did as well. He had all the power he needed, waiting for a spark to set it boiling. All the ingredients were there, even if he couldn't lay out the scientific formulas on any chalkboard no matter how many times he tried. It was all there. The need, the ability, the power.

He just had to set it in motion.

He just had to believe.

"Tick, you waitin' on something?" Paul asked.

Sofia shushed him. "Seriously, Paul, shut up!"

"Sorry," he whispered.

Tick barely heard the exchange, but realized he was standing completely still, staring at some dark point in the distant woods. Giving his head a little shake, he knelt down on the ground, feeling the prick of a twig. Then he heard it snap, along with the crunch of leaves. He placed the flashlight on the ground, still lit, and brought the silver tube up with both hands to look at it, turning the thing slowly between his fingers.

Now or never, he told himself.

Now or never.

He closed his eyes, took a deep breath, and urged a sea of calm to wash across his body. He thought back to his two main encounters with Chi'karda, the times when he'd actually been able to see it visually.

Sparkling, orange clouds of mist.

Heat.

Raging, burning heat.

Something flickered inside him. He'd found the spark. It grew, warming him from the inside out. Surprisingly, it didn't terrify him. It felt more like comfort.

He squeezed his eyes tighter and threw all of his concentration into his thoughts. In the amoebas of darkness swirling there, he tried to form a picture of Sato. Different images kept flashing in his mind, different faces. Tick tried harder. The face of his friend wavered, then held. Unbelievably clear, it was like a photo had been implanted in his brain. Tick almost opened his eyes in shock.

But he controlled himself, focusing on keeping the picture clear. Sato. He thought of the silver tube, clearly told . . . who?—himself? maybe the Chi'karda itself— that he wanted that tube to dissolve into the quantum realm, travel through spacetime, and reach his friend.

The heat increased, forcing beads of sweat to break out all over his skin. He didn't dare look, but he knew that misty swirls of orange were floating around his body, lighting the darkness of the forest with an eerie glow. He held on to that vision of Sato and on to the precise and clear thought of what he wanted to happen.

Then, not quite sure if he was doing the right thing, he formed words inside his mind.

The silver tube. To Sato. He waited. *Now.*

As a tingling wave sent goose bumps bursting out all over him, he felt the weight of the tube disappear from his hands. He heard Sofia and Paul gasp. Master George shrieked with excitement like an old woman. But Tick didn't truly believe it until he opened his eyes and saw for himself.

The tube was gone.

The message had been sent.

CHAPTER 34

THE WAY STATION

Sato never thought he'd be so happy to see Rutger.

"Why, you look a little uncomfortable!" the short man shouted when Sato finally made it through the crowd to his Realitant friends and Mothball's parents. "I was, uh, just about to come out there and rescue you."

"Yeah, I'm sure you were," Sato muttered.

"They've all taken quite the likin' to you, they 'ave," Mothball said, an enormous grin revealing her big, yellow teeth.

Those two were enjoying this ridiculous scenario way too much, and it was really starting to annoy Sato. "What am I supposed to do? We've all been winked to this psycho place, and those people act like I'm gonna save them or something. Just because I look like their murdered leader. What am I supposed to do?"

Tollaseat and Windasill were holding hands, looking on with pinched up grimaces as if they were embarrassed by the whole affair. Tollaseat reached out—and down—to pat Sato on the shoulder. "There, there, little man. Don't take it the wrong way, and don't be feelin' any pressure 'cause of this lot. We're all a wee bit scared, and a familiar face gives a lift, it does. Even I'll admit you seem like the natural person to take charge 'round these parts."

Windasill laughed, a sound that held nothing but kindness—no hint of mockery or condescension. "Reckon I ruddy agree with me love on that one. Can't you just pretend to lead a bit? Give 'em all a good talkin' to? Bring 'em straight out of the doldrums, you would. I'd bet me own two ears on that."

Sato knew he had to quit whining. Their problems were piling up by the minute, and—

An object appeared in front of his face—instantly, one second not there, the next second there—a small, elongated stretch of shining silver. He barely had time to see it or register what it was before the tube of metal fell. He reached out to catch it, but he didn't move in time. The tube smacked onto the weird marble floor and bounced with a couple of clings and clangs before rolling several inches and coming to rest next to Rutger's foot.

No one moved for a couple of seconds. Sato could tell they were all staring at the mysterious—and magical—visitor just as he was. He finally gained his wits and leaned over to pick up the tube, turning it this way and that for the others to take a look.

Sato was about to ask what it was when Mothball blurted out, "That there's one of them fancy message tubes from Master George."

"Open it!" Rutger yelled, jumping up and down in excitement—maybe reaching a grand height of three millimeters off the ground. "I knew he'd find us! I knew it! Don't you worry, we'll be out of here . . ."

He trailed off, a troubled look coming over his face.

Sato had been relieved to get the tube, but now worry swept over him. "What's wrong?"

"Well, I just . . . It's . . . well." Rutger cleared his throat. "It's just that if he could send us this message, why didn't he just wink us out of here?"

"Got plenty of worries without lookin' for fresh ones," Mothball said. "Open the ruddy thing, Sato, and see what the old man has to say."

"How do you do it?" Sato asked. He knew George often sent message tubes like these out before, but Sato had never helped him with them or even seen one up close.

"Just pull the ends apart," Rutger said with an annoyed huff.

"Well, excuse me for not being a message-tube wizard," Sato griped. Shaking his head, he gripped the two rounded ends of the tube and pulled in opposite directions. A seam appeared and expanded until he held two separate pieces. A rolled up piece of paper slipped out and dropped to the floor.

He snatched it up and unrolled it, so eager his hands were shaking. The tightly coiled note sprung closed twice before he finally got it under control enough that he could open it and read its handwritten contents. He'd barely started before Rutger yelled at him to read it out loud.

"Okay," Sato said, surprisingly not annoyed at the interruption. He cleared his throat and started from the beginning. "'Dear Sato. This is Tick. Mistress Jane did something really bad, and every last Reality is going to roll over and die unless we do something about it. You were taken to that place you're in by, well, I can explain all that later. You're safe for now. But a few hours after you get this, you're gonna be winked to the Thirteenth Reality. All of you. I need you to convince everyone there to come help me.'"

Sato paused for a big breath and looked around at his friends, all of whom stared back with wide eyes.

"Keep going!" Rutger snapped.

Sato did. "'There's a place called the Factory. Mothball should know about it. It's where Jane creates her fangen and some new things that are worse. I'll be there in a little bit with Master George, Paul, and Sofia. With any luck, we'll be working with Jane to fix the Realities. Yeah, long story, but we'll need her help. Anyway, once we're done, there's no way Jane will let us go. That's where you guys come in.'"

Sato saw Mothball shake her head back and forth, but he chose to ignore her for now and kept reading. "'The people of the Fifth are known as warriors—even those who don't do it as a profession. Somehow you and Mothball need to organize them and convince them to come rescue us. The Haunce—don't ask—also says there are lots of children we'll need to save while we're at it. Sato, you have to come! Be ready so when the Haunce thinks the time is right, it can wink all of you to the Thirteenth.'"

Mothball was quietly groaning now—almost wailing—but the note only had a few more sentences. Sato finished up quickly. "'I know you have a ton of questions, but there's no way I can explain everything in a stupid note. I hope you can trust me. The Factory, Sato. The Factory. Come and get us. And just so you know it's me: remember how mad you were that I saved you twice? Well, it's payback time. Tick out.'"

Sato stared at those last couple of lines for a few seconds. A trickle of doubt had entered his mind upon first reading the note—anybody could've sent the note. But now he knew it really was Tick. The tone, the phrasing, the reference to their exchange after Sato had been freed from Chu's Dark Infinity device—it was Tick, all right.

Mothball let out a sound like a bear with its foot caught in a trap.

Sato looked at her and saw something awful and afraid in her expression. "What's *wrong* with you?" he asked.

"The Factory," she replied in a whisper. "Master Tick's spot-on when he says I should know all about it. Know far too much, I do. Sorry to be a pussycat, but if that's where we're goin', then I'm a might scared, that's all."

Rutger nodded, his face a full shade paler than it had been before Sato had read the note. "She's right. Our spies in the Thirteenth have told us all about that nightmare place. I can't imagine what Tick's gotten himself into, but if he really is headed for that place of horrors, then we have no choice but to go after him. Just like he asked for. Even though it terrifies me just as much as it does Mothball." He leaned back to look up at his friend, a ball tilting on a pivot. "In fact, I'm pretty sure I've never *seen* you scared before."

"Hogwash," she mumbled back.

Sato hadn't known her nearly as long as Rutger had, but he'd definitely never seen her so afraid—at least nothing even approaching the way she looked now, pallid and sweaty with dead eyes. "Well, what *is* the Factory?" he finally asked. "Why is it so awful?"

"Tell him, Mothball," Rutger said. "Tell him what they told us."

The tall Realitant's eyes flickered down to her friend, then to Sato. She stiffened her body and held her head a little higher, composing herself. "Well, there's the obvious bit Tick mentioned. Factory's full of Jane's hideous creations, guardin' every last inch of it. But that's not the worst part. Not worst by far, the way I reckon it. What chills me bones is to think of what we'll see if we get *inside* the ruddy place. Things unnatural and evil. Things that just might cure us of sleepin' till we drop dead of it."

"Like what?" Sato asked, his curiosity mixed with a chilling fear. "What are they doing in there?"

Mothball pulled her long, gangly arms behind her and clasped her hands as she stared down at her own feet. "They take animals and . . . meld them with other animals, usin' the mutated powers of the Thirteenth's Chi'karda. Meld 'em right together into things you wouldn't dare tell 'round a campfire."

Sato held his breath.

Mothball's head snapped up so she could look him square in the eyes. "But that ain't the whole of it. Learned somethin' brand-new few weeks back, we did.

Somethin' that'll make your heart shrivel and scream."

Sato swallowed. It felt like a dried clump of dirt went down his throat. "What?"

Tears leaked from both of Mothball's eyes. "Kiddies," she said, her voice cracking. "The animals only be tests. She's done captured a bunch of kiddies and plans on usin' 'em soon as she's good and ready."

CHAPTER 35

✳

DARKNESS OF THE WAY

Tick couldn't believe what he'd done. Even after some time to think about it, his mind still couldn't accept it. He sat on the forest floor, absently ripping apart leaves from a nearby bush, surrounded by darkness and cool air.

He'd winked something away. All by himself. After all the strange episodes leading up to that moment—the reappearance of the letter Kayla had burned, winking his group from the Thirteenth back to Master George's headquarters, the near-catastrophe in the Fourth Reality—he'd finally used Chi'karda on his own terms. He'd controlled it and used its power to wink—a thing the Realitants thought only a Barrier Wand could accomplish.

He'd done it all by himself.

"Told ya you were superhuman," Paul said from behind Tick, startling him.

He needed that jolt because he didn't have time to sit and contemplate. He looked down at his watch and clicked the little light—it'd been at least ten minutes since he sent the message to Sato. At least, he *hoped* he'd sent the message to Sato.

He pushed off the leafy bed of the ground and stood up, turning the flashlight back on as he did so. The others all stood closely together, examining him. Only Paul was smiling.

"What?" Tick asked. "I told you what I was going to do."

"Yeah, you did," Sofia said. "But . . . it was kind of spooky to watch. You're really weird, Tick."

He knew her well enough by now to recognize the compliment. But what did she mean about the spooky part? "Why? What happened? What did it look like when I did it?"

Sofia glanced at Master George—who nodded once, slowly, then at Paul—who let out a little burst of a laugh—then back at Tick. "Little streams of orange light spilled out of your eyes and ears and then swirled around the silver tube until it disappeared. You didn't see that? You were staring straight at the thing like you'd been possessed by forty demons."

Tick felt only a little bit of shock—not so much at the orange light but the fact that he hadn't noticed it. "No, I didn't see it. Maybe I was concentrating too much. But when Jane pulled the Chi'karda out of me when we were under Chu's palace, that's what it looked like. Orange light—kind of like a fog or mist."

"No, well, kind of, I guess," Sofia responded. "It was more like ribbons of orange, something you'd see twirling off a cheerleader's baton."

"Interesting that it's orange," Master George said. "I wonder why we never see Chi'karda manifest itself that way when we use a Barrier Wand. Something tells me it's related to the souliken discovery—though I'm far from understanding everything about that."

Tick's mind started processing what the Realitant leader had said, thinking it through and analyzing. He'd spent so much time the last few months studying science that such thinking had become second nature. But he forced himself to stop. They had to get moving—they were already behind schedule!

"Man, what are we doing?" he said through a groan. "We have to get going. Now. Come on." He took a step, but then stopped, frowning. "Wait, any of you guys know which way is east?"

Master George pointed over his right shoulder, but Paul cut in. "Wait, man. You just did something crazy, like magical. Shouldn't we talk about it, figure out what and how and all that, so next time you can do it again? Maybe even better?"

Tick was tired of saying it, but he repeated himself anyway. "It'll have to wait—we need to go. Now. Just trust me."

"Fine," Paul said, turning toward the direction Master George had indicated. "But you promised to explain things as we walked. Start talking."

"Okay," Tick said. He shone the flashlight ahead of him, revealing an endless expanse of trees and brush, then walked forward, his every step crunching twigs and leaves. He moved past Master George, and the others followed right behind him. The strain from winking the tube away had worn off, and he felt the chill of the air like a sprinkle of fine mist. Being on the move again would feel good.

They'd gone about fifteen feet or so, and Tick figured now was as good a time to start talking as any. His friends deserved an explanation—even if Tick didn't understand everything himself.

"So, the Haunce is like this big sack of people's memories and personalities and thoughts," Tick said. "It told me that every time we have a significant event in our lives, it leaves an electronic stamp on Reality, and those moments collect and become attached to us. That's what a souliken is. Seems a lot easier to just call it a ghost."

"I think I like *souliken* better," Sofia said. "I'm not a big fan of ghosts."

"Wuss," Paul muttered. "Ow!"

Tick heard the punch on Paul's arm that he'd fully expected.

"Doesn't matter right now," Tick said. "What matters is that the Haunce is a collection of millions and millions of soulikens, and it acts like a guardian of the Realities. Sort of a gatekeeper or a watchman. Whatever. But we gotta trust it."

"Yes, indeed," Master George added, his voice already a little winded as they tramped through the forest. "The Haunce has the Realitants' highest respect—there's no doubt in this matter. What the Haunce says, we should do."

"Okay," Paul said. "So what is it we're gonna do?"

Tick walked around a huge oak then settled back in on the course his instincts marked as east. "Well, ultimately the Haunce, me, and Jane are going to link and use our . . . power"—how he hated using that word!—"to rebind the barriers of the Realities that are falling apart."

"Yeah, ultimately," Paul said, a major hint of doubt in his tone. "But something tells me we're not gonna like hearing what you keep avoiding—what we have to do to *get* to that point."

Tick winced. Paul had hit at the heart of the matter.

"Um, yeah, you're probably right on that one."

Tick felt Paul's hand grab his arm as Paul forced him to stop and turn around.

"What!" Tick shouted way too loudly. But then he remembered what the next stage of the plan was and that being quiet didn't quite play into it. Now that he had to tell them what the Haunce wanted, he was terrified of their reaction. They weren't going to be very happy.

"Come on, dude," Paul said, almost pleading. "Don't make me give the corny speech about how we're all part of a team. Tell us what's going on."

Tick shook Paul's hand off his arm, but then nodded. Paul was right. He had to tell them. "Sorry. Obviously I've been avoiding that part."

Paul folded his arms disapprovingly. "Yeah, obviously."

"Come on, Tick," Sofia said. "Just tell us real quick."

Master George put his hands on his knees to catch his breath, not seeming to care one way or the other.

Tick thought furiously for a second. It hadn't sounded so bad when the Haunce had told him about this part. But then again, they'd been tucked away safely in Tick's home at the time. He decided to just get it over with. "Jane has a new creation—something called a Sleek."

He expected everyone to repeat the word or start

asking questions before he could continue. Instead, they all just stared at him, waiting.

"Once she had the fangen all figured out and perfected, she moved on to other creatures. And from the sound of it, always nasty and terrifying creatures. No big surprise there. But she always works with a purpose. The Sleeks are what she created to guard the Factory. And, um, we're getting really close to the place where they'll be hunting through the woods."

Tick saw fear flash across his friends' faces, and seeing that made him feel even more scared. "The Sleeks sound really, really awful. The whole purpose of their existence is to hunt down anything that's not supposed to be in these forests. They're tall and thin when seen straight on, but most of the time they're impossible to see clearly. They have ten times the strength of a fangen, and they have almost magic abilities using Chi'karda. The Haunce said they're wispy and fast, almost like living smoke mixed with wind. And once they catch sight of you, forget escaping. No way, according to the Haunce. But don't worry—there *is* some good news."

"I'm having quite a hard time seeing the *good* news in any of this," Master George said.

Tick looked at him. "Well, there is. Kind of. The Sleeks aren't allowed to kill what they hunt down. Mistress Jane wants to interrogate any intruders."

"Oh, no," Sofia said. "Don't tell me . . ."

"You've gotta be kidding," Paul added.

Tick was relieved they'd gotten it before he had to say it, but he did so anyway. "You guessed it. The Haunce wants *us* to find *them*. We have to let the Sleeks capture us."

CHAPTER 36

THE SPEECH

Sato sat alone, his heart like a dying filament inside a lightbulb, about to burst and flame out at any second. What Mothball had said—about Jane planning to use human kids for her creations—horrified him like nothing ever had before. He knew a lot of bad things had happened in the history of the world, but this had to top it.

Killing was bad enough, but . . . what was the word Mothball had used? Melding. Jane was melding animals together . . .

He slammed the door on that thought. His mind had already slipped close to an edge overhanging a dark and awful abyss from which he didn't know if he could escape. He needed to keep it together. Hold on to the anger, sure. Let it fester and boil inside him until he had no choice but to go forward in a rage and do what he had to do to stop what the witch was doing. But he couldn't allow himself to sink back into that dark place which had once haunted him every day after seeing his parents murdered, burned alive by Jane herself.

He shook his head, slammed another door in his mind. Looking around, he saw that the people of the Fifth were gathering around him again, though a bit more timidly than before. They must have seen the anguish on his face, enough to scare them a little.

But that look of awe still clung to their expressions, their eyes filled with something he could only describe as hope. Which was good. Ever since reading the note from Tick—and *especially* since Mothball's revelation about the Factory—he'd been heading down a path toward a decision. He didn't even quite know if he consciously controlled this path, but every part of him walked along it.

He was going to do exactly what Tick asked. Somehow.

The tall people of the Fifth inched closer and closer, surrounding him on all sides. Sato craned his neck to look through the scant open spaces to where Lisa and the rest of Tick's family huddled far outside the crowd, still seeming to revel in their reunion and the good news that Tick was alive.

Mothball and Rutger had told them about the note—all of it. Now wasn't the time to hide anything from anybody. Sato knew that the Higginbottoms also had mixed feelings, and more reason than ever to worry over their son. Just another twist of the path Sato traveled. Just another reason to make things happen, no matter what.

"Excuse me, good sir," a soft female voice said close to his ear. Closer than he felt comfortable allowing— he wasn't ready yet!

He looked up, ready to snap at whoever had invaded his space. But it was an old woman, as tall as Mothball and just as gangly, leaning over him like a wind-broken tree. She had a gentle, pretty face, and Sato's anger quickly slipped away.

"I'm sorry," he said. "You all keep asking me the same thing, and I can't answer it any differently. I'm not the guy you think I am." He returned his chin to his fists, his eyes to the floor. How was he going to do this?

"We don't rightly think that anymore," the woman answered. "We're not a bunch of dumb lugs, ya know. But there's somethin' right special about you, there is. And we want to 'ear from ya, that's all. Not too much to be askin', now is it?"

Sato took a long, deep breath. He had to do something, get the ball rolling. Sitting there with all of them gawking like kids at a zoo would drive him crazy if it went on for another minute.

"Fine," he said, sighing as he forced himself to stand. The old woman smiled, her grin revealing that she only had about half her teeth, and those remaining were dark yellow. But still, she had a pretty face, despite its age and wear and tear. Somehow, she was keeping him polite and levelheaded.

"Give us a speech," she whispered to him, still leaning down considerably. "We could all use a bit of uppity-up, no matter the source. You've got the looks of one who can do that right nicely. You do, really." She winked at him then stood straight, a good foot taller than Sato.

Sato looked away from her and around at the crowd. Many had taken a seat—especially the ones closest to him. Those farther back stood, arms folded, staring at him expectantly. There had to be at least three or four hundred people packed all around him. He slowly turned in a circle, taking it all in as he tried to think of something to say. The whole lot of them grew quiet.

You can do this, he thought to himself.

"I know why you guys are so fascinated by me," he said, wondering if he could've possibly started his speech with anything more stupid. He doubted it. "I know I look a lot like the kid who was your ruler until those crazy Bug soldiers assassinated him."

This caused an uproar, people shouting and yelling things all at once, many of them throwing their arms up and shaking their clenched fists in anger.

"Boo to the Bugaboos!"

"Death for the Bugs!"

"Drown the clowns!"

"No rest till the pests' death!"

Sato didn't think it was possible, but he felt even more uncomfortable. He held his hands up, palms out, trying to shush them. Finally, they quieted. And he started talking; where the words came from, he had no idea.

"I'm not the same person as your leader who was killed. It's really hard to explain, but I'm from a different world—one that's a lot like yours but . . . different. Maybe it's not so hard to believe if you just look around at this weird place. But none of that matters. I know why you want me to be your Grand Minister. Everyone wants a leader, someone to look up to. But I don't know if I could ever really be that person."

A surge of complaints started to explode from the crowd, but Sato cut the noise off by swiping his hands back and forth. "Just listen to me! We all need something here, and I think we can help each other."

"What's that then?" the old woman asked, her right eyebrow cocked high. "What can we do for ya, lad?"

Sato was thinking on the fly, caught up in the moment. He was *feeling* it. "I know Mothball. I know her family. I know that the people of your world are fighters. You're warriors. Am I right?"

A hearty shout of cheers rang through the air, fists pumping toward the endless gray sky of nothingness above. A surge of heat and electric energy filled Sato's veins.

"The first thing we have to do is get out of this place. I have a very good friend who's in a lot of trouble, and if he dies, we all might die. I need your help to go after him, to help him, save him. We also need to stop something that a very evil person named Mistress Jane is doing—the sickest, most horrific thing I've ever heard of. We'll give you all the details soon enough— I think we have a little time yet. But if you do this— if you'll help me and . . . fight for me—I'll make a promise to each and every one of you."

Sato paused, scanning the crowd, in awe at how every eye was trained on him. Complete silence settled across the strange place. Even Mothball and Rutger stood rigid, mouths slightly agape, probably wondering who'd possessed Sato's body.

"If you'll go with me," Sato said, the rush of adrenaline inside sounding like an ocean's roar in his ears, "and fight to help my friend and stop Jane, then I promise to go back to your world with you and lead the war against the Bugs. The endgame of all endgames. We won't stop until we wipe them from existence. All of them! We will fight. And I swear, we will win!"

The roar that filled that impossible place made Sato want to take a step backward and cover his ears. He did neither.

He stood tall and yelled right along with the warriors from the Fifth Reality.

CHAPTER 37

✳

SHIVERS

The sounds of the night-darkened forest were starting to get to Tick as he and his friends slowly made their way eastward.

Besides the normal buzz of insects going about their business, a wind had picked up, something that seemed impossible based on how many trees crowded their pathway. Limbs and branches swayed and scratched against each other; leaves rustled; small animals jumped and ran through the bushy ground cover. Eerie mating calls moaned through the air, and every once in a while a cat-like thing screamed far in the distance. It all added up to give Tick a major case of the shivers.

He'd tried his best to show a brave face when telling the others about how the Haunce wanted them to be caught by the Sleeks. It had seemed a practical matter—the best way they could get into the Factory and possibly face-to-face with Jane. And the others had reluctantly agreed to the plan after wasting five minutes arguing about it. Master George had proven to be the voice of reason that cut through the obvious hesitancy to do something so scary.

But now, trampling their way through the spooky woods, his flashlight beam stabbing the darkness ahead, getting closer and closer to something that was created by and for evil, Tick felt a different kind of fear than he'd ever experienced before. A thick terror sprinkled his skin with chills and surged in his throat, like a balloon had been shoved down there. With every crick and crash of broken twigs and crushed leaves as his companions and he walked forward, he had to fight the urge to look around, searching for an enemy he knew was coming for him.

Instead he forced himself to look ahead, to keep walking and dodging his way through the tightly packed trees until the attack came. He held on to the fact that they wouldn't have to fight or run this time— they just had to give up and be taken prisoner.

"Tick," came a soft whisper from behind him. Sofia. "Have you seen or heard anything weird yet?"

Tick turned to look at her quickly before facing

forward again, not missing a step. "We don't really need to whisper," he called out, louder than he needed to. "It kind of defeats the purpose of what we're doing. And no, I haven't really noticed anything too weird yet."

"Nothing too weird?" Paul repeated. "Some demon cat is being eaten by Satan out in the woods, screaming its fool head off. I'd call that weird."

Tick had to suppress a snicker, a fleeting break from the fear that had been suffocating him. "It's probably just a deer or something that broke a leg."

"A deer? Never heard anything sound like that on *Bambi*."

Master George spoke up. "My guess would be that we're getting quite close to the area where these guardian creatures roam and hunt. Based on what I've learned from Mothball's, er, reports."

George cleared his throat in an embarrassed sort of way, and Tick's suspicions shot up enough to make him stop walking. He turned to face him. "You just said 'er' and cleared your throat. What aren't you telling us?"

Paul and Sofia stopped as well and faced Master George. Tick held the flashlight so that the beam pointed at the ground, but the glow was enough to show a tight look of worry on the man's face.

"Really should keep walking, don't you think?" he said, trying to smile but somehow making himself look even more uneasy. He feebly pointed toward the direction they were heading.

"What's wrong?" Sofia asked.

"Yeah," Paul added. "You look constipated all of a sudden."

Master George folded his hands together—they'd been twitching slightly at his sides. "Our Realitant spies have recently been providing Mothball with information on the Factory."

"And you didn't say anything?" Sofia shouted. The echo of her voice seemed to hang in the tops of the trees for a full five seconds.

"Calm yourself, goodness gracious me," Master George snapped back, Sofia's outburst having brought back some dignity to his face. "We need to go there no matter what I know, and I was merely waiting for the right time to speak on it. But, if you must hear it now, what I have to say will only make our reasons for going forward even stronger."

"*What?*" Tick asked, not bothering to hide the impatience that came out in his voice.

Master George kicked a bush near his feet. "Oh, how it angers me. This, more than anything she's ever done. Jane is stealing children from towns and cities across the Thirteenth Reality and keeping them in the Factory. We suspect she is planning to use them somehow to create her abominations at the Factory. She's currently using her powers of Chi'karda to deconstruct various animals on a quantum level and put them back together again to serve whatever purposes she's dreamed up with her evil mind. *Horror* is the only word I can think of to describe such a thing."

The Haunce had told Tick about this when discussing the overall plan, but the reality of it hadn't hit until he heard his boss explain it in such stark terms. An emptiness expanded inside Tick, a void that should've been filled with a long list of terrible emotions but instead felt numb.

"She can't be that sick," Paul said. "She can't be."

"I'm afraid our sources are very reliable," Master George said. "I believe what happened to Jane in the Fourth Reality"—he shot a nervous and quick glance at Tick—"has driven her past a point from which I can't imagine anyone could ever return. Her life has been consumed by hatred and evil, encompassed by a delusion that she can still find her Utopian Reality and bring an endless peace to the universe. Bah! She'll have every last one of us dead. The woman's insane, I tell you. Insane!"

Tick had a disturbing thought pop into his head. "Well, I guess if we can't stop the Realities from going kaboom, at least Jane won't be able to steal any more kids."

"Don't let your mind wander down that path," Master George said, stepping closer to Tick. He put a hand on his shoulder. "Instead, let's focus on accomplishing what the Haunce has sent you to do. Once done, we'll stop Jane's madness *and* free the children."

Tick looked at Sofia, then Paul. Both of them had stern faces, made all the harsher by the sharp shadows from the flashlight. "What do you guys think?"

"What do you mean?" Sofia asked, an edge to her voice. "What do you *think* we think?"

"No," Tick said. "I just . . . does this change anything? We knew we had to get in there and convince Jane to help us. After we do what the Haunce wants . . ." He didn't know how to finish. Despite what George had said, every potential pathway that flickered inside Tick's mind seemed to head for disaster.

"Dude," Paul said in his gimme-a-break tone. "This only makes it clearer. Crazy Jane can do all the hokeypokey stuff she wants, but if she's messing with little kids now . . . we gotta get in there and stop it. Simple as that."

Sofia was breathing as if this latest news had pumped up her adrenaline. "And Sato will come—just like you asked him to in your note. We can do it, Tick. You'll save the universe with your fancy powers, then we'll get the kids out, then we'll burn the whole place to the ground. Let's go!"

She didn't wait for a response but marched off into the dark woods, toward the east. Paul stepped in line right behind her.

Tick looked at Master George. "Guess I'm not in the lead anymore."

"Well, I think they could use your flashlight. Let's go, Atticus. Lots to do."

Tick nodded and started walking, shining his light up ahead so his friends could see. As they made their way forward for the next few minutes, the shadows leaping with every movement and the eerie sounds of the forest haunting the cool air, Tick realized his earlier choking fear had disappeared. It had transformed into impatience, an eagerness, even.

Sofia stopped, holding her hand up to signal them to do the same. Paul almost bumped into her, letting a branch loose as he caught his balance. It hit Tick square in the nose, but Sofia cut off his cry of complaint before it got started.

"Quiet!" she snapped in a harsh whisper, finally lowering her hand as she looked back at them. "Something just . . . whisked across our path. Up ahead."

Ice began to fill Tick's chest again. He stepped to the side so he could shine the light forward without his friends being in the way. He saw gloomy, towering trees and thick bushes and ivy, all the greenness muted and pale. The shadows stretched and retracted as he swept the area, but nothing out of the ordinary came into view.

"Hear the silence?" Master George whispered from

behind Tick, startling him. His voice seemed louder than it should have, and Tick realized why. All those creepy sounds they'd been hearing earlier had cut off. Completely. The sudden quiet reminded Tick of being outside after a heavy snowstorm back home—all sound sucked in by the cold, white stuff.

Tick caught a glimpse of something flashing toward him from the right—a wispy trail of fog that he barely saw. He imagined he could see the faint image of a head and a long body, an outreaching hand, when sharp tingles pricked the skin along his forearm, making him suck in a breath.

There was a popping sound, and then the flashlight went out.

CHAPTER 38

✳

SMOKY EMBRACE

The needle pricks vanished. Tick instinctively held up the flashlight to take a look, but the darkness was too complete; black engulfed everything. He flicked the switch back and forth. Nothing. Then he shook it.

Shards of loose glass tinkled together and fell to the ground. The lightbulb hadn't burned out; something had smashed it, making it useless.

"Tick, dude, what happened?" Paul whispered, though it sounded like anyone within a hundred miles could've heard him.

"I don't know." Tick looked around but couldn't see a thing. He remembered the ghostly image of what he'd seen from out of the corner of his eye. Those long, smoky fingers of fog reaching out . . .

Leaves crunched a couple of times where Sofia had been standing.

"Sofia!" Tick shouted, a boom in the silence that echoed off the tree branches.

"I'm fine," she whispered back harshly. "Sheesh. I'm just feeling my way toward you." Another couple of steps, more twigs breaking. "I heard glass break—how did you smash your flashlight?"

Tick could see the shadow of her figure right in front of him now. He reached out and found her shoulder. "Okay. So, I was standing there, and then I saw something to the right. Something like a trail of fog. But it was kind of shaped like a . . . like a stretched-out human with really long arms and fingers. Then it felt like a hundred needles stabbed my arm, and something popped, and the light went out. It's broken."

"Wait a second," Paul said as he also took a couple of tentative steps toward Tick and Sofia. "What did you see again?"

"I guess it must've been a Sleek. Kind of smoky and long, looked human-like. What do you think, Master George?"

Silence answered him. Chills swept over Tick. He looked in the direction where he'd last heard George's voice. His eyes were already adjusting to the darkness, but he saw nothing except the tall, dark shadows of trees and more trees.

"Master George!" he called out, wincing at the loudness of his voice. Again, no answer.

"Those creepy things took him," Paul said in a fierce whisper. "And we're next!"

Sofia shushed him then spoke in a quiet voice. "That's what we *want* to happen, remember? We just have to—"

A twig snapped to Tick's right, silencing Sofia. A few leaves rustled in the same spot. The swell of chilling panic crept up Tick's chest as he looked in that direction, straining his eyes to see.

Something stood there, a dozen or so feet away, its shadow splitting the space between two huge, towering trees. Thin but man-shaped, the thing had to be as tall as a basketball standard. The edges of the shadowy figure wavered like a reflection on water, ripples of darkness running up and down. The slightest glint of silver shone where its eyes would be, and something about the light—maybe the hue, maybe the angle—made the creature look very angry.

"Who—" Tick's voice caught in his throat. "Who are you? Are you a Sleek?"

The thing's silver eyes flared brighter for just a moment, but it was long enough to reveal more of its features. Streamers of dark smoke were packed tight and swirling through and across each other, compressed together to form the tall body that stood before them. Tick thought they looked almost like worms being held back by some invisible force until they could be unleashed to seek out food.

But the face was different. It didn't seem to be made of the smoky substance. It looked . . . human. Real skin, though misshapen and scarred. Every cell in Tick's brain screamed at him to run.

The light of the creature's eyes dulled again, throwing the tall figure back into shadow.

"Ask it again," Paul whispered.

Tick didn't know if he could bring himself to speak. Sofia saved him.

"What are you waiting for?" she yelled. "We know you're a Sleek, so get it over with! Quit standing there all spooky, you haunted-house wannabe!"

Tick looked over at her, wishing he could see her face. Sometimes her bravery completely stunned him.

A noise from the creature pulled Tick's attention away from Sofia. A whispery, raspy sound. Harsh and guttural. It continued on for several seconds, but if the thing was trying to communicate, Tick didn't understand a word of it. The metallic glow of those silver eyes seemed pinpointed on him.

The Sleek quit talking, leaving them all in an eerie stillness. The sounds of the forest remained silent, as

if every living creature had long since run away. Then everything changed in an instant.

A wind swept through the woods, sudden and violent. A torrent ripped at the trees, sending leaves shooting through the air like flaky bullets. Tick threw his arms up to protect his face, catching a glimpse of the Sleek's silver eyes flaring again before they disappeared altogether. Darkness took over, leaving the world black and consumed by the rushing sound of wind.

Sofia screamed, the screech of it barely begun before it whisked away into the distance, fading and gone. Something had taken her. Paul yelled several terror-filled words, but Tick only caught his name. Then a scream even higher-pitched than Sofia's rang out, followed by a thump and the crack of a broken tree branch. The sounds of a body being dragged quickly across the forest floor were soon swallowed by the overpowering wind.

Sofia—gone. Paul—gone. Master George—gone.

Leaves and small twigs pelted Tick's body. The howling wind ripped at his clothes and hair. He risked a peek, lowering the arm he held tightly across his upper face, but he saw only darkness in front of him. Flecks of debris hit him in the eyes, making him squeeze them shut. He rubbed at them with his other hand, then opened up again.

He let out a cry of terror when he saw two silver

lights right in front of him, looking out of a hideous, mangled face. With a swirl of black smoke, the Sleek grabbed him by both ankles and squeezed them like a metal rope cinched tight enough to break skin and crush bones. His feet flew out from under him as the Sleek pulled. Tick's back crashed to the ground. Then his whole body jerked forward, dragged across the rough forest floor.

Master George knew what was happening the instant the tingle first sprinkled across the back of his neck. Someone at headquarters had finally locked on to his nanolocator and was winking him back to the Bermuda Triangle station. Sally, probably, having likely broken a hundred things in the process before finally figuring out how to do it.

And Master George knew what he had to do.

As soon as the dark forest vanished, replaced by the inner workings of his cramped Control Room with its bright monitors and blinking instruments and metal piping, he threw his hands up and started shouting.

"Don't wink the others! Don't wink the others! Don't wink back Atticus or the rest of them!"

Big Sally—dressed in his usual plaid shirt and overalls—stood at the main computer, a Barrier Wand clasped in his huge hands. The look on his perplexed face was almost comical, and somewhat pitiful as well.

"I's waitin' on that brain a'yorn to figger it out anyhoo," the burly man said. "'Bout chicken-fried my noggin gettin' you here as it was!"

Master George finally felt a bit of calm. "Excellent work, Sally, excellent work! We mustn't wink the others back quite yet—they have a very important task to accomplish first. But we need to get to work straightaway." He walked past Sally and headed toward the door.

"What's on that mind a'yorn?" Sally asked as he set the Wand down and followed George.

Master George reached the door and entered the hallway. "We've got things to collect before we move out. As many weapons as possible . . . and nanolocator patches—we'll probably need hundreds of patches. We must hurry!"

"Where you reckon we're goin', then?"

"We're going to meet up with Sato at a place called the Factory. We have to rescue Sofia, Paul, and Atticus." Master George turned to face Sally. "Not to mention a lot of children."

CHAPTER 39

✳

THE SURGE

The wind in the forest stopped suddenly, cut off like a giant door slamming shut. Tick could hear the scrape of his body against the leaves and scattered debris underneath him. Things poked and scratched. His shirt ran up to his shoulders, leaving his skin exposed and vulnerable. Pain lit through him. The Sleek's grip didn't loosen; if anything, it tightened as it pulled Tick along.

He tried to look at it, but saw nothing except the occasional glimmer of silver light reflecting off tree trunks. He tried to pull himself up, crunching his abs as he reached for his legs, his ankles, but the speed and roughness of the way was too much. He fell back, his head slamming against a fallen log just as he popped over it.

Scratches and scrapes, bumps and bruises. Tick felt the warmth of blood trickling in his hair, wetting his entire back. The sounds of crunching leaves and snapping twigs as his body was dragged across them filled his ears. Darkness surrounded him.

His instincts had him reaching for Chi'karda before his mind formed the thought. Wrapping his arms tightly around his body, he rolled to his side, trying to give his back a break and let his shoulder take some of the abuse. Then he forced himself to close his eyes, searching and probing for the heat of the power within him.

There. A spark.

He reached for it with mental hands and grabbed it, squeezed it, embraced it. Quicker than ever before, the Chi'karda burst through him, filling his body with a raging burn. It pulsed and throbbed. Tick felt like it was about to explode out of him, devouring first his flesh and then the forest in flames. Tick heard the woods around him shake, heard the same odd bee-buzz sound from months ago when he'd unwittingly unleashed his power in fear, wreaking havoc with molecular structures, melding trees and other things together. The same had happened in Chu's mountain building.

Tick knew he was losing control.

He screamed and opened his eyes.

The first thing he noticed was that he'd stopped

moving. An orange cloud of sparkling mist surrounded him, illuminating the forest. The Sleek had released his ankles and stood several feet away, its silver eyes wide and bright, maybe out of shock. Tick could see the thing's body clearly now—the seething tendrils of black smoke that coiled and wrapped together to form the elongated body, the hacked-up face, the wispy trails of its fingers.

Tick was trembling, his hands balled into fists. He didn't feel pain anymore, only the surge of Chi'karda threatening to scorch him and everything around him. His jaw clenched as if it had locked closed forever. He wanted to kill the Sleek. Chase down the others and kill them. Rescue his friends. Run away. He almost boiled with the desire.

With a scream of rage, he jumped up and pounced on the Sleek, grabbing it by the neck just as it tried to break apart and whisk away. Tick slammed the creature against the closest tree, knowing he shouldn't be able to do this, knowing that he was somehow using the Chi'karda to make the Sleek maintain its structure and solidity. The thin neck of coiled smoke felt like shifting sands under his fingers, churning and slipping but staying in one place.

Tick squeezed, feeling the neck crackle, as if it *were* sand and hardening to glass. That creepy, cackling whisper of a voice escaped the Sleek's mouth, saying things Tick couldn't understand. But it seemed desperate and terrified, the sound of it chilling.

The buzzing sound intensified above them. Chi'karda blazed inside Tick. The orange mist swirled around him like a tornado of fire. A wind picked up, seeming to blow from all directions at once, though it did nothing to the cloud of Chi'karda. Tick felt as if the entire world were about to melt into a pool of lava.

He squeezed the Sleek's neck even harder.

Something tried to click inside Tick's brain. Tried to tell him that he'd forgotten the whole point of what he'd come here for. That in the pain and terror of being dragged through the forest, he'd let his anger take over. That he'd lost it, completely lost it.

And yet . . . he was controlling the Chi'karda more than ever before. He was controlling it! Kind of . . .

"Tick!"

A voice. A girl. From somewhere to his right. He barely heard it. He didn't want to look, didn't have time to look. The Sleek was almost dead, and then he could go after the others. Maybe he could experiment with Chi'karda, see what he could do with it. Strike out with it somehow? Maybe shoot beams of fiery lasers? Yeah, that'd be awesome.

"Tick!"

The voice was too loud to ignore this time, despite the ripping wind and blazing heat inside him, the buzz of things disintegrating and re-forming above him. He knew he was doing things to the trees again, but he didn't care.

"Tick!"

He snapped out of his delirious daze and looked over to see Sofia standing close to him. The smoky tendrils of a Sleek's fingers were wrapped around *her* neck. Paul was next to her, also in the custody of a Sleek. The orange glow of Tick's power made the Sleek's silvery eyes look angry and red.

"Tick!" Sofia shouted. "You can't do this! Remember why we're here in the first place!"

Tick didn't quite feel like himself. He'd let the burning power of the Chi'karda consume him and take over his bad parts—the anger, the temper, the thirst for revenge—and part of him had liked it. "You're just saying that!" he yelled over the noise of the wind and the buzzing. "You don't want them to kill you, so you're trying to stop me! Well, *I* can stop *them!* Look at this!"

He let go of the Sleek and took a step back, gesturing with his arms like a magician. The orange cloud swirled around him and through his fingertips, around his arms and legs, curling, almost caressing. Fire raged inside him. He turned, pointing at the wooden formations surrounding them. Dozens of trees had been blown apart on a quantum level and put back together again like a series of haunting sculptures crafted by a lunatic.

Tick couldn't believe it. He was close to understanding how it all worked, close to *really* being able to control it. So close. And he had no idea how—it was just . . . instinct.

He turned back to face Sofia and Paul, their necks still ensnared by the cuffs of smoky fingers. "I know I'm a little bit weird right now," he said. "But check it out. If I can really do this—"

"Dude, you gotta save it," Paul said. "You're freakin' me out here, man. You've got the crazy eyes."

Sofia tried to step forward, but the Sleek yanked her back. She let out a choking cough then said, "Tick, he's right. Something's wrong—on a lot of levels. Just let it go and stick to the plan. Let the Sleeks take us to Mistress Jane. Okay, Tick?"

Tick dropped his eyes and held out his hands to look at the glowing orange mist of Chi'karda swirling around his arms and through his fingers. Hunger burned within him almost as strong as the power itself, a fierce desire to wreak havoc on Jane and the rest of his enemies. But somewhere in the nooks and crannies of his mind, he realized that something wasn't right about the way he felt. Something on the cusp of evil.

"Okay," he said, barely a whisper. Then louder, "Okay."

He closed his eyes and imagined the cloud of sparkles retracting, absorbing back into his body. He pulled it all inside, then let it go, releasing it to whatever place it lay dormant in the quantum realm, where it would wait for him to snatch it up again. When a refreshing coolness rushed through his body and filled the void left by the Chi'karda, he had the thought that he'd just extinguished himself.

He opened his eyes and noticed the stark silence and darkness of the forest. Sofia, Paul, and their spooky captors remained still, staring at him. He could just see the two sets of wide eyes and four pinpoints of silver.

"All right," he said, amazed at how incredibly thirsty he was. "We'll go with the Sleeks, nice and easy. But this time we're walking. Don't make me mad again."

CHAPTER 40

FRAZIER'S GOOD NEWS

Mistress Jane wasn't happy. Everything had gone horribly wrong today, and the only thing that could make her feel better was for someone to pay the consequences. Anyone. Whether or not they were actually at fault for the debacle was a minor point she didn't care too much about at the moment.

She sat at the window of her room in the Lemon Fortress, looking out at a land covered in night, no moon to break up the darkness. The earthquakes and shattering lightning storms had finally stopped, though the damage they'd caused would take months to repair and rebuild. It was a miracle the castle still stood at all. She wondered if it was foolish to be up here. Who knew what had happened to the foundations and inner structure—the whole thing could collapse at any moment.

Her foul, foul mood darkened to black.

What had gone wrong? After months of preparation, the tireless, tedious work required to retrieve and alter the dark matter into the form she needed, the time to find and secure every single one of her Alterants in the major Reality branches—after all the planning and sacrificing and risking . . .

It had all gone wrong in an instant. The Blade of Shattered Hope had failed her.

That was the worst part. The second worst part was the fact that she didn't really know *why* it had failed. The Higginbottom boy had done something—she knew that much. But her instincts told her that his meddling alone had not caused the catastrophic change in direction. His trickle of Chi'karda had not ruptured the connection of the Blade, causing its apocalyptic damage to explode from its course and spread throughout each and every Reality and the barriers between.

No, it wasn't just him. She'd . . . missed something, done something wrong.

There—she'd admitted it to herself. But it didn't make her feel any better. It made her feel worse. Angrier.

Maybe, just maybe, the Blade could've overcome this fault if the addition of Higginbottom's usage of power had not occurred. Yes, maybe.

And that was enough for her. She had a focal point on which to exact her vengeance. Not that she really needed anything to make her hate the boy any more than she already did, but still, it helped.

The knock she'd been expecting finally rapped at her door.

"Come in!" she yelled.

She heard a thump then a small scrape. The big door was stuck because of the shifting of stones from the earthquake. With barely a thought, Jane dissolved the wood particles into the air to allow Frazier to enter the room. Once he was inside, she put the door back together again.

"I have news," her most faithful servant said.

A fire roared in the brick hearth, a luxury Jane loved even as the coolness of winter faded into spring. She pulled a few sparks out with her power and lit the huge candles scattered throughout the room. The glow showed an eagerness on Frazier's face that lifted her hopes.

"Have a seat and tell me what you've learned." She pointed to the chair across from her. "I don't have to tell you how . . . disappointing further bad news would be at the moment." She let the expression on her mask turn to anger for a second before bringing it back to smooth calmness.

Frazier nodded, the barest hint of a smile flashing across his face as he walked over and sat down on the edge of the chair next to her. "I think you'll like what I have to say."

"Then get on with it."

"Yes, Mistress." He leaned forward, his elbows on knees, hands clasped. "Over the last few hours, we've sent people to all the Realities to gather as much data as possible. We, um, had to send out quite a few, because they kept dying in all the chaos. More than half, actually."

Jane's first instinct was to snap at Frazier for wasting time about such an unimportant detail, but she kept her cool. "Yes, a worthy sacrifice, I'm sure. Whatever it took to learn what we needed."

"Yes. Yes, of course. Anyway, the devastation we saw here was universal. Massive earthquakes, catastrophic storms, tornadoes, you name it—it all happened in each and every Reality. Lasted for a good hour or two. Killed, um, millions of people." His eyes flickered to the floor at this last part.

"Feel no shame, Frazier. Remember, we knew there would be collateral damage in our mission for Utopia. For Chi'karda's sake, if the Blade had worked today like it was supposed to, six *billion* people would've died! What's a few million? Keep your focus! We don't have time to mourn the losses along the way." In truth, she felt a constant, choking swell of guilt, but had learned to accept it and live with it.

Frazier composed himself and continued his report.

"We know the destruction was widespread throughout all the Realities. But it seems to have stopped, everywhere. Maybe we've avoided the complete meltdown you feared."

"'Meltdown'?" Jane repeated. "That seems too sweet a word. What worried me was that we'd set off a chain reaction that would wipe us all from existence. I still sense something wrong in the air, in the Chi'karda, like a bubble that's about to burst. Don't be too confident that we're in the clear just yet."

"At least it's calmed down for now. That first hour or so, I was ready to accept my fate and make my peace. I don't know—I feel like we're good now. I think we're going to be okay."

Jane scoffed at him. "You trust your instincts over mine? Not a smart way to go about things, Frazier. What you're feeling is just the natural relief after a close call. We are not safe yet—trust me on that. If you're going to be my right-hand man, I need you to stay pragmatic and sharp and not fall for whimsical feelings of comfort and safety." How she hated being mean to this man, but she could never restrain herself.

"I understand, Mistress. And I promise we haven't let down our guard in the least. Our people are winking back and forth, constantly giving updates. If anything bad starts up again, we'll know right away."

"Good. What else? I have a feeling that smile you

couldn't keep off your face walking in here wasn't for this alone."

Frazier grinned enough to show his teeth. "Observant as usual. You always know—"

"Get on with it."

"Yeah, sorry. Um, well, I think I have some news for you that none of us could've expected this soon."

Frazier paused, staring into the eyeholes of her mask like a lover. His confidence and courage shocked Jane. Surprisingly, it didn't anger her, only made her more eager to hear what he had to say.

"Word has come from the Sleeks guarding the forest at the Factory. They've captured three Realitants. They're not quite to the Factory yet, but one of the Sleeks rushed to get the news to us. The prisoners will be locked up and ready for you to interrogate by the time you arrive, I'm sure."

Jane felt a pleasant tingle wash across the severely damaged skin of her entire body—something she hadn't experienced since the Dark Infinity incident. She didn't know she still had the capability for such things—for pleasure.

Almost forgetting herself, she leaned forward like an eager schoolgirl wanting to hear about a boy she liked. "I know what you're going to say next. I know who they've captured, or you wouldn't be so excited. Tell me I'm right, Frazier."

He laughed, surprising her again. "You are. Higgin-bottom and two of his friends. We got 'em."

Jane leaned back in her chair, then realized her mask had transformed into a giant smile. She quickly erased it, but that's how she felt. When Atticus had disappeared back at the Blade tree, she'd had a thousand troubling thoughts flash through her mind. The worst one was that the Haunce had gotten involved, and if that had been the case, very bad things could have happened. But there had to be another explanation if the Sleeks had captured the boy again so soon, so easily.

So . . . easily.

Her brief elation vanished. "Frazier, why in the world would those people come to the Factory? Why come to the Thirteenth Reality at all? Something's wrong here."

Frazier's face so quickly melted into distraught panic that Jane felt sorry for him. "I . . . don't know, Mistress. I . . . but . . . if we have them, does it matter? We caught them. Whatever they were trying to do, we stopped them!"

Jane stood up. "It's too easy, too simple. Tell the Sleeks to guard them with every creature they can spare. I want every weapon on the grounds gathered—send more if necessary. Search the entire area. Something is wrong!" She pulled up the hem of her robe and started marching toward the door.

"What . . . where are you going?" Frazier called from behind her.

She swiveled sharply to look at him, her mask full of rage. "No more chances, no more mistakes. The boy must die—he's too dangerous! We'll have to be careful so as not to accidentally ignite the powers inside him. But I'm going to kill him till he's dead, dead, dead!"

She felt a trickle of insanity—and relished it.

CHAPTER 41

✳

AN INTERESTING GATE

Tick's display of power must've made an impression on the tall, wispy Sleeks. They didn't make a sound as they moved through the forest, and they had even let go of their prisoners' necks, letting them walk freely as long as they stayed on course. And they came nowhere near Tick himself.

Dawn had finally hit the world, making everything in the forest look dull purple. While the extra light made the journey easier, it also reminded Tick of how long it had been since he'd last slept, and exhaustion weighed on him like soggy clothing. He knew they must be close to the Factory. He couldn't help but hope that once they got there, they'd throw them in a prison cell where he could get at least a little rest before Jane showed up and they had to do their magic tricks to save the universe.

He'd tried twice to speak to Paul or Sofia, but neither of them would respond, flickering their eyes at the Sleeks as if scared of the consequences. Tick guessed he could understand their hesitation, but he felt no fear of the creatures anymore. It was odd—their creepy look alone should've made him shudder with chills every time he looked at them, but his episode earlier with the surge of Chi'karda had pumped him full of confidence.

Those things weren't going to mess with him again. Right that second, he thought nothing in the world would ever mess with him again. His rational side tried to tell him that he was being stupid, but he pushed it away, wanting to enjoy this feeling of invincibility for a little while longer.

The air around them brightened suddenly, a combination of the trees thinning out and the sun rising higher by the second. Tick looked up and saw the sky for the first time in a while. A flat layer of bumpy clouds panned across most of it, the eastern edge outlined in fiery orange. Something smelled really awful, growing more pungent as he thought about it. He was pretty sure he'd never been around a rotting animal before, but for some reason that's exactly what the odor made him think of.

He shot a glance at Paul, wrinkling up his nose.

Paul returned the sour face, then waved his hand back and forth in front of his nose.

Tick returned his attention to the path ahead of him. The Sleeks refused to walk in front of him, instead pointing every once in a while with a rasping, hoarse croak. Tick just loved it—the things were scared of him. Scared of *him!*

Shut up, Tick, he told himself. *Something's wrong with you.*

He knew he didn't have time to worry about it, but he felt like he'd ingested rotten milk into his system. There was a taint of . . . evil coursing through his veins. Maybe using Chi'karda—and letting it consume him and take over his emotions, his anger—had a price to it.

He shook it off. Things were changing up ahead.

They stepped past a last bunch of trees into a wide open, muddy space, void of any vegetation. A hundred yards or so away stood a tall, jagged wall of lumber, the thick pieces thrown together as if by accident. The wall ran in both directions for at least a mile before curving out of sight. The only break was a large gate made of twenty or thirty black iron bars, the upper tips ending in spikes. Heads of fangen and other monsters had been impaled on each and every spike.

Tick shuddered. Weren't fangen and other creatures *created* here? Then it hit him. Just as you might see several auto models displayed in front of a car factory, so were the products being shown off here.

Tick continued walking without missing a beat, each footstep squishing in the mud, his eyes fixed on the heads on the gate. He wanted to remember them for later, for when he would need something to give him incentive to stop what was going on here. Everything about the Factory disgusted him, and for just a second, he felt a flare of Chi'karda ignite inside him. He put it down and kept moving.

He didn't break his gaze until they'd crossed about half the open area. He wanted to see what the Sleeks looked like in full light. They still walked right behind Paul and Sofia, their tightly wound coils of smoke looking blacker than ever. Their bodies were impossibly long and drawn out, little puffs of dark fog bleeding off them with every step. They wore no clothes and looked like nothing but a ragtag doll made of old, dirty rope. Their silver eyes were the only things that broke the monotony; they flared just as brightly during the daytime as they had in the night.

Tick caught Sofia's eyes, then Paul's, silently telling them that this was it, things were about to get interesting. As he swiveled his head back toward the approaching gate, he wondered about the Sleeks. What were they? Had they been created here in the Factory? Mistress Jane had used her powers to set this all up. Was it something

Tick could learn if he wanted to? Surprisingly, the question intrigued him and, for the briefest of moments, excited him. The thought chilled his heart.

Yeah, something's wrong with me, he thought. He caught a powerful whiff of something totally foul, making words like *rotten* and *decay* pop into his head. Pinching his nose shut with two fingers, he took the last few steps until they were standing just in front of the looming iron gate. Oddly, the only thing he could see through the bars of the gate was a grove of trees.

"All right, Sleeks," he said. "What now?"

One of the smoky creatures walked ahead of him, seeming to float along, then clasped its smoky fingers into fists and leaned forward as it screeched out a breathy series of harsh words, completely indecipherable.

"That guy needs a cough drop somethin' awful," Paul said, the first time he'd spoken in a good hour or two.

"How do we know Jane will come here to see us?" Sofia asked. "For all we know, she could just tell them to kill us and be done with it."

Tick winced at the thought, but he had confidence that wouldn't happen. "She'll want to know what I did to ruin her black tree thing. That, or she'll want to rub it in our faces before she slaughters us herself. She'll come, don't worry."

The Sleek moved to stand with its companion behind Tick and his friends. Tick turned his attention to the gate, feeling each breath draw in and out as he anxiously waited for the thing to swing open.

A low rumbling noise seemed to come from everywhere at once, like the sound of cranked-up machinery. The ground vibrated, then intensified to an outright shake, making Tick's feet almost bounce in the mud. He warily took a step backward, then a few more. Paul and Sofia did the same until they were about twenty feet from the iron bars. The gate remained closed. The sound of thrumming machinery grew louder.

"Seems like a lot of work just to open a stupid gate!" Paul yelled.

Tick nodded but didn't respond, his gaze riveted ahead, the anticipation making him feel waterlogged in his chest. His concentration was so focused on the gate itself that he didn't notice what was happening at their feet until Sofia shouted for them to look down.

A huge section of the muddy ground was shifting, the front edge right in front of the gate lowering, tilting on a fulcrum in the middle of the section. Tick and his companions rose as the other end sank like a giant seesaw. The angle steepened at an alarming rate, approaching forty-five degrees before anyone could react.

"Get—" Tick began, but couldn't finish, his feet slipping out from under him.

He fell on his butt and scrambled to hold on to

something, but his fingers found only wet, slippery mud. He looked up, frantic, and saw a big chunk of black smoke heading for his face. It hit him like a hard shot from a firm pillow, and then he was sliding toward the gaping hole that had opened at the foot of the gate.

He slipped through the slimy sludge, Paul and Sofia right next to him. Down, down, until they reached the edge and plummeted into dark, empty air.

CHAPTER 42

✳

STRIPS OF FIRE

The fall lasted only ten feet or so, but it was the longest and worst second of Tick's life—a terrifying second when he felt like he'd either drop forever or be smashed to a bloody pulp far below. He barely had time to curl into a protective ball before he slammed into a dirt-packed floor. He felt the wind knock out of him and heard the grunts of his two friends. He only peripherally noticed the section of ground above them slam shut with a metallic clang, leaving them in complete darkness.

Groaning, he rolled over onto his side, knowing he'd been lucky to avoid a broken bone or worse—even though at the moment, his whole body hurt.

"You guys okay?" he called out.

"Fine," Sofia answered.

A few seconds passed, then Paul said, "I think I broke my spleen."

"What?" Tick forgot his aches and pains and sat up.

"I'm kidding, dude. I'm fine. I don't even know what a spleen is. Does *anybody* know what a spleen is?"

Tick spoke before he knew what he was saying. "It's a highly vascular lymphoid organ between your stomach and diaphragm." He paused. "Sorry. Been reading a lot of science books lately."

"I already knew that," Sofia said.

"Yeah," Paul replied. "I'm sure you did, Miss Italy. What do you think happened to Master George?"

Tick got to his feet, the jarring pain of the fall starting to fade for the most part. "He's probably being held somewhere else. This can't be the place they want to keep us. Why would they have a prison cell right below the gate?" He held his hands out, trying to feel for anything in the darkness.

"I bet it's a trap," Sofia said. "Ya know, for people who come here who aren't supposed to. Like us. Makes sense to have it below the spot they'd most likely come to if they wanted in."

Paul must've been exploring, too, because he bumped into Tick. "Oops, sorry." He patted Tick on the shoulder then walked in a different direction. "I don't know, Sofia. Maybe it's just a marker or something, and the way you actually get into the Factory is to come down here."

Before Tick could say anything, a loud clang filled the air, and a source of faint light made him look to his left. A huge door had swung open, and a dark figure stood in the widening crack, mostly in shadow because the glowing, orange light source was behind him. Or her. Or it. Tick couldn't quite tell yet.

The door opened all the way until it came to rest flush against the wall, their visitor standing alone in the doorframe. Something was odd about the thing, and when the light behind it flared brighter, as if someone had stoked a fire, Tick got a good look for the first time.

It was man-sized and man-shaped, but any other comparison to a human being ended there. The creature had no eyes, no nose, no mouth, no ears. Its arms were stumps without hands. Winding strips of what looked like thick cotton covered every inch of the thing's body, protruding from the skin, moving and swaying back and forth like flags in the wind. Each strip was about a foot long, and they shot out from the body as if charged with static electricity.

"What . . . who . . ." Sofia began but didn't finish.

Tick and Paul remained silent.

The creature turned its head, looking without eyes at each of them in turn, its odd strips whipping the air like they were trying to escape and fly away.

A rush of chills ran along Tick's arms and shoulders.

A female voice came from somewhere down the tunnel, echoing and bouncing its way to them like scurrying bats. The voice was strong, but whispery. Scratchy. Creepy. It said only two words.

"Firekelt, burn."

In that instant, Tick remembered the water monsters that had tried to kill his mom and dad. Jane had called them *waterkelts*. *Kelts* must be some term she used for her new creations. And if this one was a *firekelt*—

Bright, flaring light cut off Tick's thought.

Each strip of cloth on the creature's body from head to toe ignited into searing hot fire, like a thousand old-fashioned wicks soaked in oil. Flames licked out in every direction, the blazing ribbons whooshing and spitting and hissing so that the monster looked like Medusa with fiery snakes.

Intense heat radiated from the firekelt and washed over Tick in waves as he backed away, Sofia and Paul right by his side. Sweat beaded on Tick's forehead, dripping into his eyes.

The creature took one step toward them, sudden and quick. Then another. The strips continued licking at the air like tiny solar flares, raging with fire but not burning up in the least.

"What do we do?" Tick shouted.

"Got a bucket of water on ya?" Paul responded.

"It won't hurt you," said a voice from behind the flaming monster, that same scratchy voice that had instructed it to burn in the first place. Tick guessed it was Mistress Jane, and when she spoke again, he had no doubt. "Firekelt, extinguish."

A great swooshing rush of air swept through the door and swirled inside the big room. It intensified, seeming to come from all directions at once and gusting back and forth like a hurricane. Tick instinctively reached out and grabbed Paul for support, feeling as if he were about to be swept off his feet. Sofia joined them, and they huddled together in a strange group hug.

The wind tore at the firekelt, whipping its flames toward Tick and the others. The odd wicks flapped tightly, parallel to each other as they tried to tear loose from the body of the creature. The fires flared brighter at first, but then flickered and sputtered under the enormous pressure of the windstorm. Each flame traveled down the course of the strips until they reached the ends, holding on for dear life. The creature waved its arms in frustration, helpless. Then the final small blazes winked out, throwing the room back into relative darkness.

The wind stopped without warning. The sudden silence that descended almost popped Tick's ears. Hesitant, he let go of his friends. He looked at the firekelt, mostly in shadow again because of the faint orange light still coming from behind it.

The creature stood tall, defiant. Each flameless wick began to move about again as if a slight breeze still remained.

Mistress Jane spoke again, her raspy voice making Tick want to cough and clear his own throat. "The firekelts are mostly used for lighting purposes only. You'll have to pardon my desire to show them off—I'm quite proud of my creations. Now, feel no alarm when it lights up again. Firekelt, burn."

Sparse flames ignited on the tips of the wicks then worked themselves brighter and brighter, consuming the cloth-like tentacles for several seconds until they were fully on fire again. The light seemed even brighter this time; Tick finally had to look away, splotches of afterglow in his vision.

From the corner of his eye, he saw the firekelt turn away and walk out of the room, taking most of the light with it. Then the robed and hooded figure of Mistress Jane replaced the creature, standing in the doorway, the front of her completely in shadow. She clasped a tall staff made of wood in her heavily scarred right hand.

"Welcome to the Factory," she said, as sincerely as a tour guide. "I'm sorry our last meeting didn't go so well. I promise things are going to be different this time. Yes, things are going to be very, very different."

CHAPTER 43

✳

THE FIFTH ARMY

Sato had finally asked all the people from Mothball's Reality to sit down, cross-legged, so he could actually see them as he spoke. Even then, the tops of their heads came to the middle of his chest, which made it all the more absurd that he was suddenly their leader. But there they were, rows of soldiers sitting on the checkered marble-like stone of this bizarre place, all eyes upon him.

After a long break, he'd reassembled the group. He had no clue how long it'd be before Tick—or whoever—winked them away. Or even if it was really going to happen.

No, he believed it. Tick's voice had been alive in that note, as had the urgency he felt. Something big was about to happen, and Sato had to get these people ready to help with it.

"You gonna stand there all day or talk to us?" said Rutger, sitting in the front row, just a few feet from Sato.

"Hold on! I'm thinking. If you wanna get up here and lead this army yourself, then do it!"

Instead of being taken aback, Rutger nodded, as if in approval. As if he were proud of his own son standing up here. This annoyed Sato greatly.

Next to Rutger were the Higginbottoms—Mom and Dad, Lisa and Kayla—the four of them having not separated an inch since being reunited. Of all the things that worried Sato about what was coming up, Tick's family was Number One. They obviously couldn't fight—not with Kayla to care for. They protested, of course, when Sato had pointed that out earlier, but even then it was halfhearted. Their first priority had to be keeping Kayla safe, and going off to battle wasn't the best way to do that. But Sato didn't know what else to do with them.

He realized he was staring at the family; Mr. Higginbottom tentatively waved at him. Sato shook his head slightly and tried to save himself by smiling. *Okay*, he thought, *I have to get on with this*.

He returned his attention to the waiting rows of Fifths. "I guess it's time for my big motivational speech. We could be winked away from here at any second to the Thirteenth Reality, where very dangerous stuff is going to happen. I hope you're all a little more aware of things like winking and other worlds by now—I know Mothball and her family have been around talking to you all about it. Well, none of that matters much. All we need to care about is that we're going to a bad place, and we need to save some good people and a lot of children."

He was relieved to hear a low rumble of positive responses—"Yeah," and "Let's get 'em," and "Ruddy ready, we are"—along with vigorous nods and shaking of fists. These really were a warrior people—Sato would never doubt it again. How the Bugaboos had lasted this long against them, he had no idea. Of course, they came from the same stock, he supposed . . .

"We've got no weapons!" someone shouted from the back, breaking into his thoughts. Then another person called out, "Don't even know who we're ruddy fighting! Or what!"

Instinct told Sato what he needed to say in response. If their confidence was going to be solidified, it needed to come from within. "Good questions! So, are you saying we should give up? Not even try? Throw in the towel?"

A chorus of angry denials thundered through the vast space, a deafening roar backed by red faces and pumping fists. Some even stood, looking as if they might charge Sato and wallop him for even suggesting such a thing.

"No, I didn't think so!" he yelled as loud as he possibly could. The Fifths quieted. "We'll fight with our hands and our feet, with sticks and stones! We'll fight with our elbows and knees! Whatever it takes!"

A shocked silence greeted this last part. Mothball finally said from her spot, "A bit much, but I like your spirit, I do." A few chuckles rose from the crowd.

Sato would have none of it. "I don't care if it's a *bit much.* If you guys wanna take this as a joke and treat me like a little kid, then fine! But we don't have weapons, so we have to be willing to *do* terrible things to *stop* the terrible things we're about to see! Are you willing or not?"

Impossibly, the chorus that greeted him was even stronger than before, piercing his eardrums with a needle of sharp pain. The roar went on and on, and this time every single Fifth stood up, arms raised to the sky, shouting and screaming. Sato let it go on, looking around with a stoic face, accepting their display of devotion.

When it started to die down naturally, he lit into them again. "When this is over, when we've gone to the Thirteenth and rescued our friends, when we've destroyed this unnatural and evil factory of creatures, we won't stop. We'll go back to your world, we'll gather more people—the greatest army the world has ever seen—and we'll wipe the Bugaboos from existence!"

More shouts, more cheers. Sato kept going, trying with all his might to increase the volume of his already strained voice.

"We are the Fifth Army! Say it with me! The Fifth Army!"

He raised a fist to the sky and screamed the words, ripping his throat to pieces. "The Fifth Army! The Fifth Army! The Fifth Army!" His soldiers shouted the words along with him, a sound so loud it seemed to shake the strange floor upon which they stood.

Sato stopped, knowing he'd need his voice in the hours to come. The others didn't quit, however, and kept chanting as if they never planned to stop.

Rutger stepped to Sato's side. "Nice work. Now what?"

"Now we wait for the call," Sato said. "It's coming, and when it does, we'll be ready."

⁓

Lisa watched the pep rally with mixed feelings—a whole barrage of them.

Her parents sat to either side of her, Kayla in her lap, the four present members of the Higginbottom clan clasped in an awkward but wonderful hug. Despite having everything in their world turned upside down, Lisa felt safe at the moment. But deep down she knew the feeling was fleeting, and there were a thousand and one things to worry about.

Sato's speech had really shocked her. He'd seemed quiet for one thing, and then to suddenly stand in front of this crowd of human giants and speak so loudly and convincingly was quite a thing to see. She thought his speech was a little bit on the cheesy side with a few roll-the-eye moments, but that's what you needed for something like this. Overall, very impressive.

But still.

What could they do? What could a few hundred people—even tall, gangly, gimme-some-blood warrior giants—do against this psycho lady Mistress Jane? And more importantly—personally, selfishly—what was going to happen to Lisa and her family? They couldn't go to this Thirteenth Reality place and fight. The idea was ridiculous. She almost laughed at the picture of herself running around like a chimpanzee trying to jump on bad guys and, what—bite their ears?

Plus, there was Kayla to think about. Lisa and her parents had already decided that the battles and the mysteries and the monsters should be left to the Realitants—including her own brother, Tick. For the rest of the Higginbottoms, staying away from danger and protecting Kayla was all that mattered. They couldn't do much else, anyway.

Could they?

Lisa hugged Kayla a little tighter to her chest.

The Haunce floated in eternity.

The Haunce floated in the spaces between the spaces, in the darkness between the light, the light between the darkness. It floated in the smallest of the small and the largest of the large. It was everywhere and nowhere, up and down, left and right, big and small.

The Haunce floated and watched, its countless soulikens observing and communicating on a scale no individual human could ever understand.

The lull in the catastrophe Jane had started was almost over. The slipping and cracking and shattering of the Barriers would resume soon. And then it wouldn't stop until all was lost.

Atticus had reached Jane. They were together in the Factory.

It was time.

The Haunce floated—and watched.

Then it acted.

First, remembering the most human of emotions—compassion—it sent the family of Atticus back to their home. There, they would be safe, as long as everything went according to plan.

Once done with that—a thing that took less than a nanosecond of time—the Haunce winked Sato and his makeshift army to the Thirteenth Reality.

PART 4

✵

CHI'KARDA'S POWER

CHAPTER 44

✳

TALKING WITH
THE DEVIL

Tick and his two friends followed Mistress Jane down a long tunnel dug into the bedrock beneath ground, the hissing flames of the firekelt the only sound and light. No one spoke, no one asked questions, no one made any threats against anyone's life. Tick rattled his thoughts with each step, trying to come up with the best way to talk to Jane about what needed to happen and to convince her that they needed to put their heads and powers together to stop the Realities from imploding.

But he didn't know what to say or do. Was he supposed to wait for the Haunce to show up? He sure hoped so, because he didn't have the first clue how to go about things.

They turned a corner around a jagged edge of dark stone, Jane and her fiery creation a step ahead of them. But Tick stopped. He felt and heard the same womping sound he'd experienced back in the woods near his home, right before finding Jane in his basement. Right before this whole mess started.

Womp.

There it was again—a faint but definite pulse of energy, the vibration of horns and bees.

Womp.

Paul and Sofia took another couple of steps before noticing he'd quit walking.

"What's wrong?" Sofia asked.

Jane noticed as well, turning around to face them. She tilted her wooden staff forward as though about to strike him with some magical spell. The wavering splashes of light from the dancing firekelt flames turned her red mask the hue of wet blood.

Womp.

"Why have you stopped?" the robed tyrant asked in her painful, raspy voice. "Don't even think of trying anything—there's more Chi'karda coiled inside this Barrier Staff than you've seen in all your prior glimpses combined. I programmed it especially for you, Atticus Higginbottom. It's set to unleash its fury on you the second you even breathe a wisp of the power."

Womp.

Tick felt each and every energy pulse like a wall of water crashing over him. "I just . . . I just keep feeling surges of Chi'karda. Why?" He ignored her threat about her Barrier Staff; they had bigger problems to solve before he could worry about himself.

Jane hesitated, her mask void of expression, probably mulling over whether he was being sincere or trying to trick her. Finally, she said, "You and I are very sensitive to the ripples of energy triggered by Chi'karda, Atticus. I think it's something you picked up since growing more in tune with the power inside you. Get used to it, or it'll drive you crazy. Especially in the Factory, where it's constantly churning. Now come on—I want to show you something."

Womp. This time the pulse did feel a little more distant, like a constant breeze that he'd grown accustomed to. Or maybe more like breathing—you realize it's happening only when you think about it.

"Jane . . ." Tick began, wanting to bring up the subject of his mission and get it over with. But the words lodged somewhere down his throat.

"You will call me *Mistress* Jane," she said with a flare of anger on her mask. "After the horrible things you've done to me, I would think you could at least find a smattering of respect for your elders. For your superiors."

Tick didn't care about his pride anymore. He didn't even feel an ounce of fear for this woman. The only thing that mattered—that throbbed in his mind like a beating heart—was what the Haunce wanted him to do.

"I'm sorry. *Mistress Jane.* Whatever. We'll do whatever it is you want us to, and we'll see whatever it is you want us to see, but we need to talk first. Something really bad is about to happen, and I . . . we . . . need your help."

Jane's face melted into a slight frown, a look of curiosity on her mask. She took a few steps toward him. "I can tell you're not lying. What are you talking about?"

Her response surprised Tick, and something told him that the only reason she didn't fly off the handle was because she already suspected the truth. He played for that angle. "You have to know that things really went screwy when you tried to destroy the Fifth Reality with your dark matter Blade of Shattered Hope. Well, things are worse than you think. A lot worse. You made the Barriers unstable and ignited a whole bunch of bad stuff that's gonna end up wiping us all away. We have only a few hours until we'll all be dead—thanks to you."

Jane didn't answer for a long time, her eyes concentrating on Tick, her hand gripping the odd staff. Tick wondered if maybe it just looked like wood but was actually something else. She'd called it a *Barrier Staff* . . .

She finally spoke. "How could you know these things, Atticus? What kind of trick—"

"It's not a trick!" Tick yelled. "You're supposed to be the grown-up here! Act like it! The Haunce rescued me from you—and it told me all this stuff. Your Blade of Shattered Hope did something really bad to the Realities, and we have one chance to fix it."

Her red mask sharpened and tightened into a fit of rage; she visibly shook.

Tick knew he had to save himself, and quickly. "I'm sorry—just please listen to me! If I'm lying, you can do whatever you want to me, I swear. I promise I won't even touch Chi'karda. Just please listen."

Womp.

There it was again, the first time he'd noticed the energy pulse in several minutes. Jane had been right— he was getting used to it.

"You dare stand there," Jane said, "looking at me with that pathetic little innocent face of yours, and tell me this? That the Haunce visited you? Spoke to you? You expect me to believe such nonsense? You almost had me until you took it that far. Your capacity for evil was proven quite well back in the Fourth, but to lie like that . . . amazing. Do you even have a conscience?"

Tick sucked in a few dry breaths, frustrated into silence. He wouldn't have guessed she'd believe him right away, but her tone and arrogance made it seem as if she wouldn't even consider the truth. He finally snagged some words and forced them out.

"Seriously, Ja—Mistress Jane? You're seriously going to act like that and not even hear me out? Are you so full of yourself that you'd risk the whole universe?" He threw his arms up then slapped the sides of his legs. "Unbelievable. Fine—do what you want. The Haunce'll be coming here soon anyway. Maybe you'll believe it then."

Jane walked toward him again, not stopping until she stood only a foot or two away. Her yellow robe glowed in the firelight; her now-stoic mask shimmered and glistened. Her scarred, metal-pocked hand gripped the Staff tightly, the bones seemingly ready to burst through the taut skin.

"Look into my eyes, boy," she whispered, a sandy croak of sound.

"I already am," Tick replied, standing as straight as he could and holding on to the small amount of courage he'd scrounged up from within. "All I can see are little black holes with no life in 'em."

"You . . ." She made an odd squeak like someone holding back tears. "If it weren't for you, things would be so different. I could've stopped Chu and used his technology for good. I wouldn't be scarred and hideous from head to toe. Do you have any idea how hard it is to lead when people can't even glance at you? Do you have any idea how humiliating it is to look like a monster? And if it weren't for you, the Blade would've functioned perfectly, and we'd be on our way to a

Utopian Reality. But no, you've ruined everything. You've ruined my . . ."

She stopped and shook her head slightly. "No. I won't say that. You've made things difficult—no doubt about it. But you haven't ruined everything. You haven't ruined my life. Do you know why, Atticus? Because I won't give up. I'll overcome it all, and in the end, I . . . will . . . win. I promise you."

Tick momentarily lost every bit of hatred for the woman. Every bit of frustration and angst. The only thing he felt was pity. And the familiar pang of guilt for what he'd done to her.

"Mistress Jane," he said. "I'm sorry. I'm sorry for what I did in Chu's building. I promise I didn't mean to. I swear."

"You're sorry, you promise, you swear. Too little, too late, as they say." She started to turn from him.

Tick reached out and grabbed a fold of her robe. She spun and knocked his hand away, glaring at him. "Don't . . . touch . . . me!"

Tick stepped back, trying to shrink into the wall behind him. A spark of Chi'karda flared inside him, but he pushed it away. Something about that tall staff gripped in her hand terrified him. Plus, this was no time to battle her—he had to win her over.

"I'm sorry," he said again, trying to throw as much humility into his voice as possible.

Jane touched the top edge of her staff to Tick's head, then pulled it back. "I'm not a fool, Atticus. I'll listen to what you have to say. But first, you will come and see the Factory. I want you to see my gift to science. I want you to see me change the world."

And with that, she turned away and set off down the tunnel.

CHAPTER 45

✳

SPLITTING UP

One second, Lisa had been sitting on the cold, hard floor of the magical nowhere place, Kayla gripped in her arms. The next, she felt a tingle shoot down her back, and their surroundings changed completely. From light to dark, from vast and open to close quarters. She sat on something soft. Kayla was still in her lap, Mom on her left, Dad on her right.

"We're home," her dad said, squirming to stand up. "We're home!"

Lisa knew he was right before he'd said it the second time. The faintest glimmer of dawn—or twilight?— shone through the curtains of their living room windows. She saw the worn-out armchair her mom always sat in to wait for them after school, the piano, the crooked arrangement of family photos on the wall.

Dad stood in the middle of the room, slowly turning with his arms outstretched like that lady in the wildflower-strewn mountain field in *The Sound of Music*. Though he looked a lot more ridiculous. Lisa laughed, which sent Kayla into a fit of giggles.

"I think we've officially had the strangest day in the history of our family," Mom said, leaning back on the sofa with her arms folded, smiling at Dad. "But I have to say, I'm a little offended that whoever is in charge doesn't think we could help out in this fight of theirs."

Dad toppled a bit, obviously having grown dizzy. He collapsed into the armchair, its springs groaning in complaint. "Come on, dear. We're not cut out for that stuff. Especially with Kayla and Lisa to think about. Let the Realitants do their job—and I'm sure Tick'll be home safe and sound before we know it."

Lisa agreed about Kayla, but felt a little swell of self-defense spring up inside her. "Hey, speak for yourself, Dad. I could've helped Sato. Put me in a room with this Mistress Jane witch, and I'll show her what bony knees and sharp nails I have."

Mom reached over and squeezed Lisa's knee. "That's my girl. Maybe old Master George will be knocking on our door for you once this is over." She looked down at the floor, her smile fading. Then she seemed to catch herself and brought it back, returning her gaze to Lisa.

"What, Mom?" Lisa said. "What's wrong?"

Her mom had a second of surprise on her face, probably chagrined that she'd been caught. "Oh, well, it's nothing really. I guess I just feel a little ashamed that I quit being a Realitant all those years ago."

Lisa thought long and hard about that. She gave Kayla a squeeze before gently pushing her over to sit with Dad, who took her into his arms while his eyes darted back and forth between Lisa and Mom.

"What's goin' on in those heads of yours?" he asked.

Lisa reached out and took her mom's hand, helping her stand up. "Dad, Mom and I are gonna play a big part in all this. Somehow. Aren't we, Mom?"

Mom stared at her with glistening eyes. "Why . . . yes, Lisa. Yes, I think we are."

"Good. Let's be ready when the time comes."

***

Sato had known it was coming—hoped it was coming, anyway—but he still felt a thrill of shock when the winking tingle scooted across his neck and back. He instinctively started to yell at the people of the Fifth to get ready, but of course, by the time any words popped out of his mouth, they'd already arrived at their location.

They stood in a big field of drying mud. The morning

sun had just lifted over a forest to their left, its brilliance cutting through the last leaves and branches at the very top. To their right was a huge wall of stacked logs, stretching in both directions until they curved away and disappeared. The air smelled truly awful, like a rotting dump.

Sato had a few horrible seconds when self-doubt hit him as he looked back at his army. Most of them were gawking left and right at the place to which they'd come, many patting their chests and arms in disbelief at the seemingly magical experience of having been winked there. Sato didn't know what he'd been thinking—how could he lead an army? He had zero experience, zero training, zero confidence. What was he supposed to do? Yell "Charge!" and start rushing the fence? The whole idea seemed ridiculous all of a sudden.

The Fifths appeared to be gathering their wits a lot quicker than he was. Sato watched as they stood in rows, composed and standing at attention, waiting for him to give a command. They really were warriors. They really did consider him their leader.

Buck up, he told himself. *When this is all over, then you can sit down and have a good cry about it.*

"Okay, listen up!" he yelled. Rutger, Mothball, and her parents were standing right in front of him in the very first row. He exchanged glances with his two fellow Realitants, relieved to see there'd be no teasing. Time for business.

When the Fifths had quieted and all the attention turned to Sato, he continued. "We don't know what to expect, what kind of defenses they have, who's watching us—anything. Jane could send a whole pack of fangen or who-knows-what at us any second now, so we need to get moving. I want us to split into three groups: left, right, middle." He pointed as he spoke. "Middle group stays here, close to the fence. Rutger, you and I will stay with them."

The short man nodded, his face scrunched up as if considering whether he'd gotten a good assignment or a bad one.

Sato pointed to the left. "Left group, you guys go around the perimeter that way. Right group, go that way." He pointed in the opposite direction. "I want you to run as quickly as possible while still being able to keep a good lookout. With any luck, you'll make your way around that wall and meet up on the other side. Then come back here. We'll decide what to do based on what you learn."

As the Fifths separated into smaller groups, Sato started doubting his first major decision. What if they were attacked? What if, by splitting up, they'd weakened themselves too much? What if the groups never hooked back up again? What if . . . what if . . . what if?

He shook it off. He couldn't do anything until he knew what they were dealing with, and it seemed too dangerous to send individual spies out to scout the area. He was sticking with his decision, and that was that. He had nothing but his instinct.

"Okay, then! Go, already!" He shooed them like dogs, and immediately made a mental note that he probably shouldn't do that ever again.

But they didn't seem to mind. Mothball, her parents, and the rest of their group sprinted toward the right, heading for the fence. Once they were right next to it, they took off running alongside it. The left group did the same thing but in the opposite direction. Those ordered to stay put gathered tighter around Sato.

Rutger stood right next to him and reached up to poke him on the upper arm. "I'm proud of you, Sato. Have to admit, I didn't wake up this morning thinking I'd see General Sato by the end of the day, but here we are. Don't worry—worst thing that can happen is we all die."

Sato grumbled, not in the mood.

Rutger kept talking as if they were sitting down for a nice picnic. "I'm really happy about how it worked out. You need someone cranky to lead like this, and . . ."

Sato tuned him out, searching for signs of guards or visitors. He couldn't see very well over the tall Fifths, so he stepped out of the crowd, scanning the area with his eyes. The day was fully bright now, not a cloud in the sky.

A quick movement in the woods caught the corner of his eye, like someone had poked their head out to look around, then pulled back again, hiding. But when Sato focused his attention on the spot, he saw nothing but trees.

Sato pointed at three Fifths, one by one. "You, you, and you," he said, making another note to learn these peoples' names. "Come with me."

Rutger finally realized he wasn't being listened to. "Hey, what's going on?"

"Just be quiet," Sato replied. "Let's go."

He moved away from the rest of them with the three Fifths he'd chosen right on his heels. Keeping his eyes glued to the spot where he'd seen the movement, Sato ran for the forest. He'd made it about halfway to the tree when a figure darted out from behind it—an oddly shaped, wispy thing. It seemed to fly through the air like a ghost, quickly disappearing deeper into the dark woods.

Then other creatures did the same, darting out from behind at least a dozen other trees that lined the boundary between the field and the forest. They were all like living, flying shadows, gone before Sato got a better look.

He stopped and held up a hand. "Those had to be some kind of spies or guards. Now Jane or whoever's in charge of this place definitely knows we're here. I hope I didn't—"

A commotion from behind cut him off. He turned to see Rutger excitedly pointing toward the far bend of the wooden fence to the right, where the group of Fifths that had gone in that direction was already coming back, marching along through the slippery mud.

"Something's wrong," Sato half-whispered. "They shouldn't be back yet."

He headed in that direction, running as fast as he could, determined to meet up with them and see what was happening. He'd only gone about a hundred feet when he noticed several of the Fifths working together to carry large wooden boxes. Also, two newcomers were with them, looking very out of place. Sato almost fell down, already knowing what this meant and feeling like they'd won their first victory.

It was Master George—his Barrier Wand in tow—and Sally from headquarters.

More importantly, Sato was sure the boxes they carried had weapons inside them.

CHAPTER 46

A VERY BAD SMELL

Tick, man," Paul whispered to him as they followed Jane down the seemingly endless tunnels. "What's going on? Is she for real about that staff of hers? Is it some kind of Barrier Wand on steroids?"

Tick shrugged his shoulders. "I don't know. But I can't risk anything right now. We just need to stick with her and wait for the Haunce to come, I guess. Don't do anything to tick her off!"

"Tick her off," Sofia repeated through a half-hearted laugh. "That has meaning on so many levels, it's ridiculous."

Paul snickered. "I gare-on-tee you could take her, Superman. I'm not worried."

Tick rolled his eyes even though the others probably couldn't tell. He wasn't in the mood to talk to anyone, much less hear the junk about his powers. Despite what had happened so far, he felt no more like a superhero than he would a bird if someone glued wings on his back.

Jane reached a large shiny, metal door, big silver bolts lining the edges. It seemed almost too modern for the cavernous feel of the tunnels through which they'd been walking forever.

As they approached the door, Tick felt an increase in magnitude of the womps—the rhythmic pulses vibrating his teeth and skull.

Jane turned around to face them. The firekelt stood slightly ahead of her and to the left, and the light from its flames illuminated her perfectly. She spoke in her desert-sand voice.

"I don't know what you've heard about the Factory, but you're about to witness it firsthand. I'll admit that my pride has gotten the better part of me today. I desperately want to show this to the three of you—especially you, Atticus. Otherwise I wouldn't bother with the extra protection of my Barrier Staff and would've killed you already. Your lingering presence in the Realities is beginning to disturb me. Greatly."

"So you're gonna show us your evil factory and then kill us?" Paul asked, his tone full of the usual sarcasm.

"What is this, a bad James Bond movie?" Jane's mask didn't show any anger. Tick thought she probably didn't want to give Paul the satisfaction. "Please, boy. What you're about to see will be so above your mental capacity and intellect that even if you escaped, you'd barely be able to describe it, much less share any of my secrets. Just consider this a whim of mine. Nothing more."

"You said you'd hear me out," Tick said. "We don't have time for this!"

"Patience, Atticus. A short trip through my house of wonders, and then you can talk. Now, if you don't mind, I'll be the only one talking from this point on."

"Could you maybe drink some cough syrup first?" Paul asked.

This time Jane's mask did fill with rage as she pointed the upper tip of the Staff at Paul. An instant later, his entire body lifted up from the ground and slammed against the wall. He tried to scream, but nothing came out—only a slight gurgling in the bottom of his throat. His face turned purple with pain, and his hands squeezed into fists.

"Stop it, Jane!" Tick yelled, unable to stop the surge of Chi'karda that ignited inside him. "Leave him alone!"

Jane pointed the Staff at Tick; Paul dropped in a heap of arms and legs onto the floor. "Don't even think about it, Atticus. Pull your Chi'karda back, right now!"

Tick closed his eyes for a second, calming his heart. The spits of lava flaring in his chest puttered out, cooled. He still breathed heavily, though, as he looked at Jane once again. "You didn't have to do that to him."

Paul groaned and shifted his body. At least he seemed okay.

Jane's mask still held on to its anger. "I don't like him. He's a smart aleck. Tell him to keep his mouth shut." Her face melted back into the void as she turned toward the silver door once again.

Sofia immediately moved to help Paul to his feet, being more gentle than Tick had ever seen her before. Paul hunched over slightly, his face maybe forever locked into a grimace of pain, but, surprisingly, he said nothing.

Sofia looked at Tick and mouthed the words, "We're dead."

Tick shook his head adamantly but didn't say anything. Movement from Jane grabbed his attention.

She placed her right hand on the center of the silver door. Shocked, Tick watched as the metal seemed to liquefy at her touch. Jane's hand sank into the gray goop up to the wrist. A second later she pulled her hand back out again. Tick expected the metal surface to ripple like a pond, but it didn't, solidifying instantly instead.

Then, with a great rumbling sound, the entire door

slid to the right, disappearing into the rock and revealing a very modern-looking hallway ahead of them, with white tile floors, fluorescent lights on the ceiling, and glass windows on the walls.

"All the doors in the Factory have a Reality Echo," Jane explained. "That means it's actually a combination of matter taken from more than one Reality, visible in each place but absolutely impossible to open no matter what you do. Explosives, tanks, the strongest battering ram ever made—none of it would work. Only the pre-approved cellular structure of those previously recorded by my people can do it."

She looked at them over her shoulder, her mask alive with arrogance. "Even I wouldn't be able to use my powers to dissolve the material without an extraordinary amount of effort. The door is literally in different Realities simultaneously—therefore, nothing existing solely in this one could make it move. Reality Echo. Impressed?"

Tick nodded before he could stop himself. He was impressed.

Paul let out a low whistle, a small but telling sign to Tick that Jane hadn't killed his spirit completely, not yet—Tick hoped not ever.

"The door is nothing compared to what you're about to see," Jane said, a hint of giddiness in her voice. "Follow me."

She entered the brightly lit hallway, her shoes—hidden beneath the folds of her long robe—tapping on the tile floor. Tick hesitated a second before following, terrified of what horrors they might be about to see, not to mention the worry eating at him about the Haunce and what they were supposed to accomplish. His chest tight with every breath, he stepped through the doorway along with Paul and Sofia.

The first section consisted of offices—normal human people dressed in normal human clothes tapping away at computer keyboards with monitors, printers, and servers everywhere. Several odd-looking machines were also scattered about the desks, similar to the machines they'd seen back in the desert. But nothing too out of the ordinary. If Tick didn't know better, he would have thought it was an accounting business.

"This is where data is analyzed," Jane explained without turning around. She kept walking. "It's also where oversight of the melding processes takes place—a tricky operation that needs tight supervision."

Melding processes? Tick thought. She acted like she'd said *cereal production* or *car manufacturing*. How could she be so callous?

They came to another massive metal door exactly like the first one. Jane shoved her hand into the silver goop, and soon this one opened up as well. A rancid smell of decay surged through the door like an infested wind. Tick and his friends coughed and sputtered, covering their noses. Tick tried to breathe only through his mouth, but then he tasted the air, which was even worse.

"What is that?" Sofia managed to choke out.

"It's the smell of progress," Jane said as she entered the barely lit hallway on the other side.

Tick, despite the putrid smell, despite his queasiness, couldn't help but feel extremely curious. The surging, throbbing pulses of invisible power emanating from the open door pounded his senses.

He followed Jane into the stinky darkness.

CHAPTER 47

✳

WEAPONS OF MASS COOLNESS

Sato kept trying to dampen his emotions, stay levelheaded, but a new surge of confidence swelled inside him. For the first time, he felt like they were a real army with a real chance.

Now they had weapons.

The reunion with Master George and Sally had been thrilling but brief, exchanging barely a dozen words before they turned their full attention to the large wooden boxes. The Fifths looked like their eyes might pop, they were so excited and intrigued by what Mothball and Sally started pulling out of the crates, George explaining their uses in his very sophisticated voice, Rutger butting in now and then to say how cool this or that was.

The usual: boxes of Ragers—those little balls of compacted static electricity that exploded on impact in a display of destructive lightning. Some Shurrics—large guns of sonic power that devastated with sound waves.

A couple of new things as well: Squeezers, which were grenades full of tiny but extremely strong wires. When it exploded, the wires shot out and latched on to whatever was closest, then immediately retracted and curled up, no matter what the material. Very nasty results.

Finally, there was the Halter. A thin but sturdy plastic tube that ended in a cone, with a simple trigger on one end of the tube and a small cartridge on the other. Each cartridge equaled one shot: a spray of tiny darts spread out and injected its victims—potentially dozens if it hit a group—with a serum that immediately paralyzed them for hours. It was a variation of what Master George had created for Sofia to stop Tick's madness at Chu's headquarters. Very effective.

Ragers, Shurrics, Squeezers, Halters. Plenty to go around.

This could be fun.

The other group that had gone exploring returned about a half hour after Master George's arrival, saying they found nothing but a very long, encircling wooden fence, with only one exception—a gate of iron bars. The only thing they could see through it was a small grove of trees and nothing they did would open up the

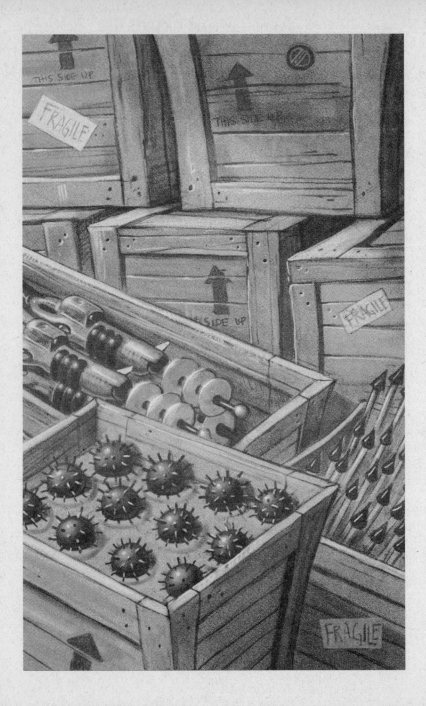

gate or make someone appear. So they'd come back, relieved to see why they hadn't met up with the others on the far side.

Once the weapons had been passed out and the wooden boxes thrown into the forest to hide them—though they were probably being spied on anyway—the entire Fifth Army gathered around Sato. Time for business.

"Okay," Sato began, his voice raised. "Seems like we've got no choice but to climb over that stupid fence. It's probably about thirty feet high, but there are plenty of handholds and footholds, so it shouldn't be too hard. I'm just worried about what might be waiting for us when we pop our heads over the edge. Once we have a good, solid group of twenty or so right at the top, we'll throw volleys of Ragers and Squeezers to clear the way, and then we'll send the first group over to cover with Shurric fire while the rest of us enter. Sound good?"

Rutger tapped Sato on the arm. "What about me? Don't see myself rolling up the side of that fence very easily."

Sato had to hold in a laugh—he didn't want to embarrass his friend. "I think you, Sally, and Master George should use the Wand to go back to headquarters, monitor us, and wink us out when we're ready."

The look of relief that washed over Rutger before he quickly wiped it away made Sato like him more than ever. George stepped closer, pulling a yellow envelope from the inner pocket of his suit coat.

"Goodness gracious me," he said, ripping the envelope open. "I almost forgot the most important part." He pulled out a handful of square pieces of paper—no more than an inch on each side—then shook them on his flat palm for everyone to get a look.

"What are those?" Sato asked.

"Nanolocator patches." George poured the square pieces back into the envelope, then pulled a single one out and held it between his thumb and forefinger. "There are hundreds here, and all you need to do is slap this against the skin of any person. The microscopic nanolocator will immediately slide off the patch and onto the subject, at which point we can wink them away. If we're looking to rescue children from this miserable place, these patches will be our best shot."

Sato was amazed and thrilled. Solutions to his two biggest concerns had been opened up for him—how they'd fight without weapons, and how they'd herd a bunch of potentially injured, suffering children safely away while fighting Jane's monsters. Everything was in place.

"This is great," Sato said, ignoring that small part in his brain that said it all seemed too easy. Meeting whatever waited inside the Factory would probably cure him of that, and quickly. "You guys wink back to headquarters now. We'll take it from here."

George handed him the envelope. "Best of luck, then. There are plenty of those patches, so be sure to put them on everyone here first—except you and Mothball, of course. We already have you pegged. We'll have all the information we need back in the Control Room, and we'll be watching closely, I assure you. Sally will be at the Grand Canyon HQ with Priscilla Persephone from the Seventh to help with the children—we'll send them directly there."

"Just call me Papa Sally," the big man said. "Might even read dem squirts a story or two 'bout the old days on the chicken farm."

"Sounds good," Sato said. "Now you guys get out of here—time's wasting. I mean . . . please, whatever."

George hardly seemed to notice. He made a few adjustments to the Barrier Wand, had Rutger and Sally put their hands on it, and then the three of them disappeared. A few oohs and aahs escaped the Fifths.

Sato handed the envelope of nanolocator patches to Mothball. "Pass those out. We climb the wall in five minutes."

⌒⌒⌒

After sending Sally off to the Grand Canyon, Master George got straight to work at the Bermuda Triangle headquarters, walking around the mesh metal walkways of the confined and claustrophobic structure, pointing left and right.

"Rutger, I want every computer in this building set up in the Control Room. I want the Big Board lined up and ready to go with monitoring all those nanolocators. Put a call out to all Realitants—if they can make it here to help, so be it. With all the destruction, they may be needed elsewhere, but make them aware of our plans, anyway."

Rutger waddled to keep up, saying, "Okay," after every instruction.

"We need to help Sally and Priscilla set up a refugee camp at the Grand Canyon. They'll need beds and clothes and doctors and who knows what else! We also need to come up with a contingency plan—so many things could go wrong. And we—"

"Master George?" Rutger asked.

"Yes?"

"I got it."

"Good, then. Let's get moving!"

Rutger cleared his throat. "Could you, um, at least make me a sandwich while I'm doing all this work? I'm starving."

CHAPTER 48

∗

THE FACTORY

The dark and smelly hallway, its walls made of black stone, wet and slimy, went about fifty feet before it came to its first window. Tick could see it just ahead of Mistress Jane when she stopped and turned to face them, but he couldn't tell what was behind the window. A sick anticipation poisoned his veins. The firekelt was behind them now, throwing their giant shadows along the floor like flat creatures of the night.

"What we do here," Jane began, "is the coordination of my lifetime's work in the fields of science with the special characteristics of the mutated Chi'karda in the Thirteenth Reality. We use bio-engineering, genetic restructuring and manipulation, and chemistry. But without the special touch of . . . shall we say magic? No, that's such a dirty word. It's all semantics, I guess. But without the special power of the Thirteenth's Chi'karda, all of this would suffer from a missing link."

She raised her arms, the robe fanning out like a fallen angel's wings. "But here, where I've put it all together to showcase the greatest scientific achievements of all human history—here is where the revolution of the Realities has begun. Here is where we begin our journey to a perfect place for all mankind. In a thousand years, they will look back and say it began with me. Now, watch and learn. Watch and let yourself feel wonder."

The mask on her face showed something like ecstasy, the black holes of her eyes actually widening for the first time Tick could remember seeing. She looked completely crazy.

"Amazing how humble you are," Sofia said. Tick was glad she spoke and not Paul, because he might not have survived the punishment a second time around. "If your intentions are so pure, then why do you care so much about taking all the credit? Sounds like a power trip to me."

Jane lowered her arms, her look of rapture melting into a glare. "Don't judge me, you spoiled, rich brat. Always had everything you wanted, always pampered, always safe. Always judging those less fortunate than you. Don't . . . judge . . . me." These last three words came out so enflamed that Sofia took a step backward and didn't respond.

"Now," Jane said in a much nicer voice, though laced with an icy insincerity. "The three of you will step up and look through the first observation window. You will say nothing, and you will not look away. You will not close your eyes. I, also, will remain silent, letting you get a good look before I explain what it is you're witnessing." She stepped to the far side, opposite the window, and gestured toward it with her Staff. "Now come."

Tick and his friends exchanged quick glances, then stepped forward until they stood together in front of the large glass square. Tick felt the struggle of each and every breath as he leaned forward, the window mere inches from his nose.

He looked. His mind jumped to full capacity trying to take in and understand all that he saw.

The room he observed was about forty feet square and dimly lit, mainly from four pale yellow panels on the ceiling. Three beds occupied the middle of the floor, lined up to form the edges of a triangle, the closest bed empty and parallel to the window. In the center of the triangle stood a hunched over monster of a man at least eight feet tall with his back to them. He wore black clothes and had no hair on his head. His massive back was covered in a tattered shirt, and the skin beneath the ripped clothing was wet with bloody gashes. The man didn't move anything but his arms, typing away at what Tick assumed was a computer on the other side of his gigantic body.

Tick turned his attention to the very different occupants of the other two beds, which lay at angles to either side of the workman. A large, odd-shaped tube, maybe ten inches in diameter, snaked from rafters in the ceiling and connected to the two bodies at the chest—right over the heart—linking them together. The left bed contained a large raven—black as oil and two feet tall. The bird barely moved; every few seconds its wings twitched, making Tick think it must be awake on some level and suffering horribly.

A good-sized black bear occupied the bed on the right side. It was bigger than the bed and looked underfed and abused, lying there as if asleep, its big paws occasionally twitching. The bear was also strapped down, that tube arching out of its chest to the rafter above before continuing across the ceiling and then back down to the bird.

Tick focused on that tube. It didn't seem to be made out of artificial material—it looked . . . alive. Like skin. Blue veins ran throughout the long object, just underneath the pale, translucent material, pulsing and changing shades from dark to light to dark again. The ends connected to the raven and the bear looked as if they had grown there like a natural extension. There was no sign of stitches or staples.

Two beds with two bodies. A bird and a bear. Connected by some kind of bio-engineered, monstrous-looking tube. The third bed was empty.

What did it all mean? What horrific thing was Jane doing to these poor creatures? Tick's hands shook; he reached out and pressed his fingers against the lower sill of the window to steady them. Out of the corner of his eye, he noticed that Paul and Sofia had actually clasped their hands together.

The third bed. What was the third bed for?

Jane spoke from behind them, her voice soft and low. Never before had it sounded so evil as it did then.

"What you see here—and more important, what you are about to see—is a miracle of science and technology that today's doctors and scientists can't even imagine, or wish for, or dream about. It's simply beyond their wildest spheres of possibility, beyond their capacity to comprehend. And even if they could, they'd never be able to make it happen. Not unless they were here and had a hundred years to figure it out."

"I think what you really mean," Tick said, throwing all the hatred he could into his voice, "is that they wouldn't be evil enough to do something like this. You're sick, Jane. Totally psycho. I don't feel bad for what I did to you anymore." He shouldn't have said it; he knew that. Not yet. Not until things with the Haunce were worked out. But he couldn't stop himself.

"I told you not to speak," Jane said in a completely calm voice, as if she hadn't heard his actual words. "Say one more word before I allow it, and I will hurt Paul. I promise."

Tick looked back at her. She stared at him, waiting for his response, practically begging him to call her bluff. He fumed, his breathing stilted. Luckily Paul didn't say anything. Finally, using all of his willpower to show restraint, Tick simply nodded. No more words. No more apologies.

"This first observation room is relatively early in the process," Jane said, in her tour guide voice, as if she hadn't just threatened bodily harm to Paul. "The genes and blood and cells haven't been consumed yet, haven't been . . . processed. The next room down the hall will show you what these two subjects will look like in about twenty-four hours. On we go."

She set off walking, her Staff tap-tap-tapping on the stone floor.

Tick followed, hating how she'd called the animals "subjects." Hating every single thing about this horrible woman.

When the next window came into view up ahead, Jane spoke again, over her shoulder. "I hope you haven't eaten in a while. What you're about to see is amazing and wonderful, but might be a bit disturbing."

CHAPTER 49

✳

THE MIRACLE OF BIRTH

Sato had wanted to climb the wall himself, but Mothball made it clear that wasn't an option. She said they couldn't risk having their leader shot in the eyeball with an arrow to start things off. Sato grumbled, of course, but in the end he sent up a crew of six Fifths to peek over the top edge. He got back at Mothball by not letting her go, telling her she had to stay by his side as his second in command. When she grumbled as well, he had to hold in a laugh.

"Ready the Ragers and Squeezers!" he yelled when the six tall soldiers—Sato had decided to start calling them that—reached the point where all they had to do was pop their heads up to see the other side.

"Gotcha, Boss," Tollaseat said, his hands full of Ragers. His wife, Windasill, stood next to him, her hands full of the black, wire-filled grenades called Squeezers. Sato had told Mothball's parents they were supposed to stay near him as well, to be used for long-range action like this.

"You guys ready up there?" Sato called out.

Instead of speaking, the three men and three women above simply gave him the thumbs-up, a sign that was evidently universal.

"Okay. Tollaseat and Windasill will throw the cover weapons on my count of three. As soon as you hear the first round of explosions, pop over and climb down as quickly as possible. Start firing those Shurrics, and the rest of us will be right behind you."

Another round of thumbs-up.

"One. Two. Three!"

Mothball's parents brought their hands low then flung them toward the sky, letting go at the right moment to send the weapons flying up and well over the top of the wooden fence and the waiting Fifths. A few seconds later, the clatter of the weapons raining down on the other side was immediately followed by the ripping static thumps of the Ragers exploding. Then came the Squeezers' metallic clanging and sounds of wires whizzing through the air. All muted and distant, but loud enough to be heard clearly.

"Go!" Sato yelled. "Go now!"

The six soldiers were already on the move. They grabbed the very top of the fence and swung their legs over, the bulky Shurrics already gripped in one of their hands, ready to start firing. They disappeared from sight.

Sato started climbing the wall after them. "Go! Go! Come on!" He didn't need to say it—every last Fifth was already scaling the clunky wood face of the fence.

Just before Sato reached the top, a soldier's head suddenly popped back over, looking straight down at him. It was a woman, and she had a puzzled look creasing her skinny face.

"What's the matter?" Sato asked.

"You need to see this," was her response. She disappeared once again.

Sato clambered up the last few feet to look over the edge. He'd had ideas of what to expect inside—barracks, groups of creatures, large weapons ready to fire, a creepy hospital-looking thing that was the Factory. But he froze in confusion at what he saw below him.

Other than the grove of trees that grew close to the iron gate, there was nothing. Absolutely nothing.

From where he perched on the fence, looking left and right and forward all the way to the other side of the fence—barely visible in the distance—he saw nothing but dirt and mud and a few trees. Not one

building, not one creature, not one person other than the soldiers he'd sent over.

Dirt and mud and trees.

Sato turned to Mothball, who was right next to him and looking as bewildered as he felt. "Are we sure we came to the right place?"

~~

Tick wanted to look away. Every single cell in his body wanted him to look away. Every notion of normalcy and human decency and right-and-wrong screamed at him to look away—that this wasn't something a boy like him should witness.

But he stared through the window in disbelief that Jane could really be this evil.

The room was identical to the first one—three beds lined up in a triangle, the odd, skin-like bio-tube, and a creepy man in the middle, his back turned, typing away at a computer. As before, the closest bed was empty and the left and right beds had occupants. But that's where the similarities ended and the true horrors began.

Another raven lay on the bed to the left—or what used to be a raven. The poor thing that lay there now barely resembled a living being. It looked like a corpse, its emaciated body sucked dry of fat and water, the feathers gone, yellowed skin clinging to its bones. The bio-tube still grew out of its dead chest toward the ceiling.

Tick turned his attention to the right bed, where a panting wolf lay clinging to life, the other end of the tube shaking with each desperate breath. Most of its black-gray fur had fallen out, littering the bed and the surrounding floor like some kind of haunted barber shop. Diseased skin stretched taut over the dying thing's bones.

And then there was that third bed. Empty. Waiting. For what?

When Jane spoke, Tick flinched, startled. "The needed materials have been fully exhumed from the subjects at this stage. They've been collected, filtered, sorted out, and reconfigured. All done with an intense heightening of the scientific process made possible by our special version of Chi'karda. The sweet sacrifice of these two noble creatures is about to conclude in an even greater achievement than their separate lives could ever have accomplished. And one day we'll be ready to use human subjects. I've already gathered many worthy candidates— children with the spark of Chi'karda strongly within them. Soon the possibilities will be endless."

Tick's hands compacted into tight fists. He felt like the skin might burst, he squeezed them so tightly. Trickles of Chi'karda burned within him. It took every bit of his willpower not to explode, do whatever it took to kill this insane, evil woman.

"Ah," she said with an intake of breath, a sick burst full of joy. "It's just about to happen. Keep watching, keep watching!"

Tick didn't want to. He wanted to run and hide. But some sense of duty made him stay where he stood, eyes focused, ready. He needed to know the truth—all of it—if he was ever going to stop Jane.

Movement at the top of the room caught his attention. He looked up to see a huge growth blossoming out of what he'd thought was a normal ceiling, but could now see was made up of the same material as the bio-tube. Bulky and bulbous, an orb grew out and downward, swelling until it was only a few feet above the tables, centered around the empty bed closest to Tick. Another growth shot out of the first one, a thick, squat tube that pulsed with life.

This second growth lowered down until it was directly above the empty mattress, then its end split open, pieces of material curling out and away like the petals of a flower. Gooey slime dripped out and sloshed across the white sheet, followed by a dark lump of a thing, squirming and kicking out its long legs. Before Tick could get a good look, the monster bounded off the bed and skittered across the floor, disappearing behind a large, boxy computer in the corner.

The man monitoring the situation from the middle of the room moved to chase the creature down, a nasty-looking instrument in his hands with metal rods and sparks of electricity shooting into the air.

Tick couldn't take it anymore. He turned around and leaned his back against the warm glass window, folding his arms. He pushed away the bubbling flames of Chi'karda in his chest.

"I know what you're thinking," Jane said, her mask set to something that looked like a teacher speaking to a student. "That I'm horrible. That I'm evil. That I'm a monster myself."

"Yeah, you witch," Paul said. "That's exactly what we're thinking."

Tick tensed, worried Jane would retaliate. But she kept talking. "However, you aren't blessed with the same perspective that I am blessed with. You don't share the vision of what the Realities will become. I need these creatures to carry out my orders, to help me defeat my enemies, to help me achieve my purposes. In the end, no one will disagree that it was worth the bumps along the road. That, as they say, the ends justify the means."

"Bumps along the road?" Tick asked, surprised at how tight his throat felt, how hard it was to get the words out. For now, he had to put aside the shock and disgust of what he'd just seen. "You're not even worth arguing with anymore. But you promised to hear me out about something. We need to talk, and we need to talk now. Things are gonna get really bad any second."

"Yes, I know," Jane said back in a whisper. "I've started to sense it. Something is wrong—"

She didn't finish because the entire tunnel seemed to jump three feet into the air then drop again, throwing the four of them to the ground. The whole place continued to shake, the groans and cracks of shifting rock thundering in the air. The glass of the window shattered, raining pieces down upon Tick, who knew in his gut what was happening.

The Haunce had predicted it: the final devastation and destruction before the Realities ripped apart and ceased to exist forever.

The end had begun.

CHAPTER 50

HOLES IN THE GROUND

Sato and the Fifths walked around the flat, muddy ground of the wooden fence's interior, kicking at occasional rocks and looking for anything that might give them a clue as to the purpose of the place.

"Why would they build a huge fence around dirt fields?" Sato asked Mothball, who walked beside him, mumbling about how time was a-wasting.

"Has to be a reason," she answered. "Whoever it is been winkin' us 'round like pinballs must know what they're doin'. We're in the right place, we are. I feel it in me bones. Just need to use them brains of ours."

Sato knelt down and dug in the mud, throwing handfuls to the side. "Maybe your dad was right. Maybe it's all underground, and there's an entrance somewhere in here."

"Can't imagine they'd have to dig their way in every ruddy time," Mothball said, but squatted down to help him. Soon they were a good two feet into the soft earth.

"I know a door wouldn't be under here," Sato said. "But if we hit a hard surface, at least we'll know there's a building underneath."

He glanced up to wipe the sweat from his forehead with his sleeve and stopped. The Fifth Army soldiers had spread out all over the place, following his example by digging in the ground. Sato rolled his eyes and got back to work. These people had gotten a little fanatical in their loyalty to him.

He was all the way to his elbows in greasy mud when the tips of his fingers finally brushed against a rough, hard surface. Spurred by adrenaline, he dug faster, throwing out huge chunks until he had cleared away several square inches of his discovery—a dark stone. Disappointed, he pulled out of the hole and sat back on his haunches.

"What's bitten your buns?" Mothball asked, looking up from her own pathetic excavation.

"I thought I'd found something," he muttered. "Something man-made. But it's just a big, buried rock."

"Must be a mighty big-un, then. Looks like I've found me own slice of it." She pointed toward the bottom of her hole.

Sato crawled over to her and looked down at the swath of bumpy, dark rock. His heartbeat picked up its pace. "You think maybe Jane's built something down there made out of this stone? Wouldn't surprise me, now that I think about it—her castle looks like it was made a thousand years ago. Why would her factory be any different?"

"Want us to keep diggin' around, do ya?" Mothball asked, eyebrows raised.

Sato got to his feet and cupped his hands around his mouth to shout the order, even though his people were already doing it. His first word didn't make it out of his mouth before the ground beneath him lurched, throwing him on his back. As he scrambled to regain his feet, the earth continued to shake, knocking him down again. Then again.

"Earthquake!" Mothball roared.

The ground moved and jostled and jumped. The world around Sato looked as if he was viewing it from a shaking camera, his vision blurry and bouncy. He concentrated on the ground directly below him, settling his feet into the mud so he could stand up and figure out what they should do. He balanced himself, holding his hands out as he slowly stood, swaying back and forth to avoid falling.

The soldiers of the Fifth appeared as if they were dancing, leaning to and fro, stumbling this way and that, falling into each other then away again. The quake increased in intensity, shaking everything. Sato couldn't think of one reasonable order or command to shout. What did you do against Mother Nature?

An earsplitting crack fractured the air, like the sound of an entire mountain shattering. A jagged piece of dark stone erupted from the mud about forty feet in front of Sato, thrusting up from the ground like a primitive knife. One of the Fifths had been standing on the spot, and he rose twice his height into the air before tumbling off, a bloody gash on his left leg.

To Sato's right, a huge gap in the ground opened up like the yawn of a sleeping giant; several soldiers screamed as they plummeted into the darkness below. More rocky pillars jutted up from the dirt, and more holes appeared out of nowhere, the crack of splitting stone like hammers on nails. All the while, the world shook and trembled. Still, Sato didn't know what to do. Everything had gone to complete chaos, and he had no idea how to gain back control.

He'd barely noticed Mothball sliding away from him when he felt the ground disappear beneath his own feet. He fell into an abyss, an embarrassing squeal escaping his throat when he landed on top of his tall friend ten feet below. He heard her grunt as she pushed him off. He rolled across dark, wet stone, barely lit by the sky peeking through the long, jagged hole in the roof above them.

Something furry and strong grabbed both of his arms.

He shrieked again as it dragged him into the deeper darkness until he could see no more.

～◯

The tunnel was breaking apart, splits and cracks and rocks falling. Everything shook.

Tick had fallen on top of Paul, who grunted and squirmed to push him off. Sofia lay just a few feet from them, not moving. Somehow Jane still stood upright, using her Staff as a brace in one hand. She had her other hand raised, fingers outspread, and Tick realized she was using her powers to create a shield around them, the larger pieces of debris disintegrating before they hit anyone.

"Sofia!" Tick yelled over the sounds of splintering stone. "Are you okay?"

She moved, filling him with relief. When she turned to look at him, trying to smile to show she was okay, he noticed she had a long gash on her forehead— the guilty rock lay right next to her. She must've been hit before Jane had created the shield.

"Come on," Tick said to Paul, grabbing him by the shirt. Losing balance with each movement, they managed to scoot their way to Sofia. Tick looked up at

Jane. "This is what I was talking about! The Haunce said we had to work together to stop it!"

They bounced in the tunnel like they'd been thrown down a steep mountainside. Jane's mask showed no expression.

"Jane!" Tick yelled. "We can't stay here. We have to get out of here and figure things out!"

"Call me *Mistress*," she said, but without conviction. Tick wouldn't have been able to understand the words if he hadn't heard her say them before. He couldn't believe she'd worry about such a stupid thing right then.

"Mistress Jane!" he screamed at her.

She seemed to snap out of whatever trance held her, her mask transforming into a look of concern. Her voice boomed as if she used a microphone. "We need to get above ground—to the dirt fields on top of us. Nothing to fall on us there."

"Then do it!" Tick called back. "How do—"

He cut off when she gripped the Barrier Staff in both hands and thrust it toward the cracked ceiling of the tunnel. Its upper tip slammed into the rock. A bright burst of white fire made Tick shut his eyes and look down. A new sound overwhelmed the cracking and splitting of rock around them: pounding ocean waves and the familiar shifting of sands. He'd heard that noise before—when his own powers had heightened entropy and dissolved matter.

When he sensed that the brilliant light had died down, he looked up. Jane had created a massive hole that led directly to open air and cloudy skies above them. The cavity was round and smooth, as if it had been carved by the strongest lasers in the world. Before he could fully process it, he saw her grip the Staff in both hands and hold it horizontally, like someone readying for a quarterstaff fight. Then all four of them suddenly shot up from the tunnel, an invisible force lifting them through the gaping hole and into the outside air.

Tick didn't have the time or energy to wonder about how she did it. They flew like the fangen he'd seen at her castle, out of the collapsing rubble underground, across fields of dirt and mud which had pillars and jagged triangles of rock jutting through the surface. She found a safe spot just outside the large wooden fence they'd approached from the forest an hour or so ago. They landed with a soft bump, and the magic ride was over.

"Whoa," Paul said. "We don't even have wings."

Tick thought it was a perfectly absurd thing to say at the moment.

CHAPTER 51

✳

FLIES IN THE BISCUITS

Sato squirmed and kicked and twisted his body as the monstrous, furry thing dragged him across the rough stone floor. He couldn't see a single thing, the darkness complete. Scratches and burns lit up his skin like biting flames. Even with the movement, he could tell the place around him still shook from the never-ending earthquake.

He decided to still himself and save up his energy for one concentrated effort to escape from the creature. He calmed his body and legs, trying to relax despite the pain. The thing continued to pull him through the black, cool air. After several seconds, Sato went for it.

He thrust up with his pelvis, at the same time planting

both feet and pushing off. Tensing his arms, he twisted his body as violently as he could, trying to flip over onto his stomach. The last gasp effort worked—the creature lost its grip on him and Sato heard it trip and tumble across the stone.

Sato scrambled to his feet and ran toward the sound, knowing that he didn't have time to pull out any weapons, that he'd have only one chance to surprise the monster and attack it. His foot hit a soft lump of something, and Sato pounced, falling on top of the creature. He felt around with his hands, squeezing the thing's body between his legs as it thrashed around, trying to throw him off. Sato felt fur and sweat. Sharp claws grazed across his upper arm, his shoulder.

He found the neck, gripping it with both hands, and squeezed. Eventually, the thing slowed its attempts to escape. And then it stilled completely, one last gurgled gasp of a breath escaping, the smell of it awful and rotten.

Sato fell off the creature, scooting away frantically until his back found a hard wall. He pulled his legs up to his chest and wrapped his arms around his knees as the dark place continued to shake and rattle around him. Rocks and pebbles rained from the ceiling, pelting his head. A sudden urge to quit—to forget all about his army and his promises and all the horrible things that were happening—almost consumed him, almost made him decide to sit there and wait to die.

But he couldn't give in. He pushed his fear away and slammed that door closed.

Trembling, terrified, and blind, deafened by the sounds of cracking rock, Sato somehow got to his feet and started running.

⁓

Master George had to stop every once in a while and force himself to take deep, pulling breaths. The Control Room was abuzz with alerts and flashing indicator lights. Sato and his army had somehow been scattered, seemingly running around—and, inexplicably, up and down—like hornets with a busted nest.

Rutger came running in from the other room where he was doing his best to monitor TV stations around the world. "It's all started up again! Earthquakes everywhere. Lightning storms in some places. I don't know how much longer the networks will be able to keep broadcasting."

"Dear me, dear me. It's begun, just like Atticus said it would. At least he and his friends are still together—though they just moved a great distance rather quickly. Not sure how that happened."

"We're going to have our own worries," Rutger said, looking down at the clipboard in his hand, charts and graphs filling the first page.

Master George groaned, not needing yet another fly in his biscuit. "What is it, Rutger?"

"All these quakes are gonna send a tidal wave right down on top of us."

<hr />

The muddy ground rumbled and grumbled around Tick and his friends. The trees of the forest were only a hundred feet away and shook like grasses caught in a wind. Every few seconds a loud crack filled the air as the wooden fence split from the raging quake.

At least nothing was falling on them from above.

Tick got to his feet, wobbling back and forth. The deep mud around his shoes actually helped him keep an uneasy balance. Jane stood nearby, her face blank, swaying with the earth's movements as she grasped her Staff with both hands. Tick decided to get it all out in a rush, leaving her no time to talk back until he was finished.

"Ja—" He stopped himself. "*Mistress* Jane. The Haunce is supposed to come here any moment. Then we all have to work together to somehow fix whatever it is you did to the Realities. If we don't, everything's gonna be destroyed, and every single person in every single Reality is going to die. So we need to make a deal—we need to put aside our fight and do what the Haunce wants us to do."

She didn't respond, only stared at him with those black holes she called eyes.

"Are you even listening to me?" he yelled, unable to restrain himself. "*You* did this! Now we have to make it better, make it go away. What good is it to you if we all—"

"Don't insult me, you stupid child!" she screamed back at him, her face transforming to anger so quickly that Tick didn't see the usual flow of red metal. "I'm fully aware of what's going on. Of course I'm going to do whatever it takes to fix it. You think I'd be foolish enough to jeopardize my plans over something so . . . human as pride? Now stop your arrogant spouting, and let's get on with it. Where is the Haunce? Where are we supposed to meet that big cloud of electrical waste?"

Her insults and tone didn't faze Tick in the least. "I don't know. It just said I needed to come here and convince you to help. We had to meet here because for some reason, the Chi'karda is stronger here than anywhere else."

"Of course." A particularly strong bounce in the ground made her stumble backward. "That's why I built the Factory here. And why I'm able to do the miraculous things you just saw."

Tick just happened to look at Sofia as she rolled her eyes, then literally bit her lip to keep from saying something smart. As for him, he didn't know what to do. He'd come to the right place; he'd convinced Jane she needed to help. What now?

A few minutes passed. No one spoke, only observed the world shaking and cracking all around them. Tick didn't know when exactly he'd dropped to his knees on the ground, but having the lower half of his legs firmly entrenched in mud sure helped his balance. His thoughts drifted to his family, to his Reality, to what horrible things must be happening there and the terror the people he cared about must be feeling.

Before his heart completely melted into a pool of pity and anguish, he snapped his mind away from it all. None of it mattered. Nothing mattered unless he got the job done right here, right now.

A stiff wind picked up out of nowhere, blowing swirls all around them, pulling at their clothes and hair. Tick squinted his eyes against the flying grit. A few jagged streaks of electricity abruptly knifed through the air in a spot just a few yards away from the group. The thin lightning bolts fired back and forth, collapsing in on each other as if they were trapped inside an invisible sphere. Then it all collapsed into a blinding ball of whiteness, hovering above the ground.

Tick looked away, a big bright spot in his vision. He heard a loud thrum of energy combined with the snaps of popping static. Surges of that now-familiar womping Chi'karda washed over his body in waves of tingles and vibrations. When he finally blinked his vision back to normal and returned his gaze to the spot, the glowing silver-blue orb of the Haunce floated there, its many faces alternating rapidly.

It spoke in a deep and resonating voice, its face changing from an old, wrinkled woman to a young boy as it did so. "It is far worse than we feared. Millions are dead already. Come, hurry. In thirty minutes, the universe will no longer exist."

CHAPTER 52

✳

CREATURES IN
THE DARK

Screams up ahead. Some human, but most unnatural, almost demonic. Explosions. Thumps of sound more felt than heard. Ragers and Shurrics, most likely.

Encouraged, Sato moved toward it all, keeping his right shoulder close to the rock wall, doing his best not to fall down at every lurch of the earthquake. The air had brightened slightly, but he still could barely see. Here he was supposed to be leading a great army in their very first battle, and he'd somehow ended up all by himself, nowhere near the action. He would've felt guilty if he had the time or energy to worry about such things.

Rapid footsteps approached, accompanied by grunts

and gurgly breathing. It sounded like a whole pack of Jane's creations coming straight for him. Sato reached into his pockets and pulled out a Squeezer grenade in one hand, a Rager in the other. He crouched down and backed into a natural alcove in the stone, hoping not to have to use the weapons until the monsters were past him, hoping they wouldn't notice him.

His wish came true—mostly. At least thirty creatures ran by in a storm of heavy footfalls and flying sweat. Sato could see only their outlines: hunchbacked wolves walking on their hind legs. He shuddered and had to fight not to close his eyes and act like a little kid wishing they were just nightmares that would go away.

The last one of the group stopped as its companions kept moving. Sato held his breath and tried to shrink into the stone at his back. The odd creature sniffed several times and pivoted its muzzled head back and forth. Sniffed again. And again.

Sato didn't move, only tightened his fingers around the grenade, ready to throw it directly at the monster's chest and run if it came to that. The creature took a step toward him, then another. Sniffed again. Made a low, wet, rattling sound somewhere deep in its throat. Another sniff. Sato could see its outline plainly; it was just a few feet away. He could only hope the thing had poor eyesight or wasn't expecting something huddled near the ground.

It took another step toward him, sniffed, and let out its growl again.

A sharp barking sound rang out from where its companions had gone. The creature in front of Sato barked back—a horrible, horrible sound—before it turned in a slow circle, giving the area one last look, sniffing again and again. It took two slow steps away from Sato then turned and ran after the others.

When the monstrous thing had finally been swallowed by the inky gloom of the tunnel, Sato got back to his feet and threw the two projectiles as hard as he could after it. He didn't wait to see the result, but sprinted in the near-darkness in the opposite direction, toward the still-clanging sounds of battle. A few seconds passed before he heard the Squeezer's boom and the clatter of flying wires behind him, followed by the electric-tinged explosion of the Rager. Inhuman screams pierced the air, flying through the tunnel like a wind full of death.

Sato kept running.

⟯

The Haunce obviously didn't think there was any time for manners.

"We need to get rid of the boy and girl. We do not need them." Its eyes—set in the face of a middle-aged man with a huge nose—darted at Paul and Sofia. "And if they stand too close to us when we begin, they will explode."

Nervous pangs, almost painful, bit and poked at Tick's insides. Luckily, his friends didn't seem to think they should argue the point.

"So what do we do?" Paul asked, kneeling on the ground on all fours struggling to keep his balance.

Tick had an idea. "Master George!" he yelled as loud as his sore throat would allow. "If you somehow made it back to headquarters, wink Paul and Sofia back!"

"Wait!" Sofia snapped. "We should stay here, go find Sato. Help him rescue all those—"

Too late. She and Paul disappeared.

<hr />

"—kids!" Sofia barely got the word out before she collapsed to the hard metal floor of Master George's headquarters in the Bermuda Triangle. Going from an earthquake to the steady surface totally threw her off balance.

"Whoa! Hey!" This from Paul. "How'd you do that so fast?"

She looked at him kneeling next to her, mud caked all over his pants, then up at a grinning Rutger. "Yeah, how did you know what Tick was saying?"

Rutger looked like a proud parent. "You kids still have a lot to learn. I was monitoring your nanolocators more closely than anyone else's, and we can pick up the vibrations in your larynx when you speak. How do you think we kept such good tabs on you when you were being recruited?"

"You guys seriously creep me out sometimes," Paul said. He got to his feet and wiped at the mud on his clothes. He held out his hands, a disgusted look on his face. "Don't you think we deserve some privacy?"

Rutger scoffed at him. "We only monitor in emergencies. Now quit your boo-hooing and come with me to see Master George in the Control Room. We have some serious problems."

Why didn't Sofia feel in the least bit surprised?

As soon as his friends vanished, Tick made his way closer to the Haunce, stumbling left and right through the mud. The cracks of the nearby wooden fence splitting and tumbling filled the air.

Jane lifted off the ground and floated the few feet over to their visitor, landing with a squish in the soft earth just as Tick reached a spot right next to her. They both turned their attention to the Haunce.

The ghostly creature showed the face of a young

434

Asian boy. "We know the two of you are bitter ene-mies. We have observed you both from afar with the utmost interest. Your base and childish actions have disappointed us many, many times. We know that in your hearts, you both want to kill the other." Its face morphed into a pretty lady as it paused.

Tick, shocked by this odd opening statement, looked at Jane, but she didn't return his gaze, her mask blank, her eyes focused on the Haunce. Tick glanced back at the silvery glowing face, now an old man. "Yeah, you pretty much nailed that one."

The Haunce's voice rose in volume, sounding almost excited. "It is time to put that aside. We can-not let trivial matters interfere with what we are about to do. Your hatred, your anger, your ill-fated desires—they must disappear. Now. Do you both understand?"

Tick nodded, though he couldn't imagine actually accomplishing such a thing. He hated the woman next to him more than he'd ever known it was possible to hate. But he did try to slide those thoughts and feelings behind the angst of what was now more important. He would do whatever the Haunce told him to do.

The Haunce's eyes focused on Jane, waiting. Tick noticed in his peripheral vision that she gave a very slow but obvious nod. Just once.

"We can only hope," the Haunce said through the lips of a hideously ugly man, "that after this experience—

if we succeed—you and the rest of the living will remember how close you came to never living again. That you will learn how to live appropriately. That you will learn to see life as the gift that it is."

Tick couldn't help but feel a deluge of impatience. Now didn't seem like the best time for a lecture from a big, fat ghost. They needed to get on with it!

The Haunce's current face trembled, its eyes narrowing as if it had realized the same thing and was refocusing on the task at hand. "The minutes are ticking away. It is time to begin. What you are about to experience will feel very . . . odd."

Tick swallowed the giant lump in his throat. He felt such a powerful swell of nervousness in his chest, he thought for sure his heart had been crushed. But then the Haunce turned into a face that looked so much like his mom he almost fell backward. The lady smiled, and the smallest trickle of peace washed through Tick's insides.

It didn't last long. A blinding white light came from everywhere at once, the mud and forest and fence and blue sky swallowed by its brilliance. A loud buzzing sound filled his ears.

And then he felt himself explode.

CHAPTER 53

✳

ETERNITY

Sato was thankful for the growing light as he ran through the tunnels, sick of that terrified feeling of blindness in the dark. But it was greatly tempered by the increasing sounds of horror from up ahead. Screeches, mostly from creatures he knew couldn't be human. Cries of pain from those that were. Explosions and cracking rock.

When he turned a corner and saw the full spectrum of battle in front of him, he couldn't help but stop. He stared at the scene, having second thoughts about his self-imposed calling for the hundredth time that day.

A massive chamber that looked to have once been some sort of underground atrium for Jane's Factory now looked like a tornado had touched down. Chunks of earth and stone littered the floor, some taller than a grown man. Patches of open sky broke up what had once been a painted ceiling—murals of Bible stories and famous moments from history. In his quick scan he noticed half of Noah's ark and a scene of Abraham Lincoln sitting in the theater where he had been shot.

On the floor, dozens of Fifths fought a variety of Jane's creations, outnumbered twenty to one. At least. But the advanced weapons of the Realitants seemed to even the score. Still, he saw with a pang to his heart that several of the tall soldiers lay dying or dead.

Squeezer grenades exploded on the left and right, downing a whole slew of hairy, fanged beasts, all of whom fell to the ground squealing and squirming from the attacking wires. One of the Fifths shot her Halter tube, sending a spray of darts that immediately paralyzed five or six four-legged things with wings flapping their way through one of the holes in the ceiling; they plummeted to the ground and crashed with a sickening crunch. Thumps from Shurrics pummeled the air like the beating of silent drums. Every time a shot hit its mark, a creature went flying until it smashed into a wall.

Sato watched the battle with an odd mixture of feelings—guilt that he wasn't out there, an urge to run and join them, terror at the thought of doing so, pride that his little army fought so strongly and bravely—were maybe even winning. Mostly though, it reminded him of what horrible things Jane was doing here by using innocent animals to create those hideous beasts—and soon she would be using children.

He knew what he had to do. He knew his place. There'd be plenty of time in the days and years ahead to lead men and women into battle. But for now, he had to leave the very capable Fifth Army to the fight. He had to find those kids. He had to find them and save them.

He was about to turn around and start searching the complex when Mothball appeared out of the fray, running straight toward him. She pulled up, sucking in huge gulps of air. Then she patted a bulge in the side of her shirt.

"Been . . . waitin' on ya . . . I 'ave," she spit out between breaths. "Got a whole . . . mess of them . . . nanolocators in me pocket."

She didn't have to say another word. Sato was grateful for the help.

"Let's go," he said.

⁓

Tick floated in emptiness in a realm he didn't understand.

He hadn't felt any pain when his body erupted into billions of tiny parts. It had been more like a wash of tingles spreading across a warm, glowing sensation. Really pleasurable, actually. But now a sense of panic set in as his mind tried to comprehend the impossible thing that had just happened to him.

He could barely articulate within his own thoughts what his five senses were experiencing. He saw spinning lights, orange globes, streaks of blue and silver—all on a canvas of the deepest black he'd ever seen. It was like he floated in the depths of unexplored outer space. That same buzzing sound surrounded him, mixed with something that reminded him of waterfalls. The air had a slightly burnt odor to it. Without understanding how he knew, he realized that he didn't exist in his usual human form anymore. He had become . . . part of the things that he witnessed around him.

And yet he was still Tick. Still had the cognitive functions of his brain. Still kid enough to simultaneously think this was really cool and also really scary.

The Haunce spoke, and its booming voice made those peripheral sounds dampened and dull. Tick couldn't see the collection of ghosts—just heard it with ears he didn't have at the moment.

"Atticus. Jane. Nothing we could have said beforehand could have prepared you for what we have done to you. For that reason, we said nothing. With time running out, we must begin our attempt to rebind the barriers of the Realities, to seal up the cracking splits and seams, to make the universe whole again. In the end, we promise we will do everything in our power to return you to your prior forms."

Tick didn't like the sound of that. If they succeeded, there must be a chance he'd never make it back to what he'd had before. Maybe he'd have to float here for the rest of his life.

"Where are we?" he asked, though he had no idea how he did it with no tongue and no mouth, no audible words. It was more like he'd projected his thoughts. "And what did you do to us. What are we right now?"

"Yes." It was Jane's voice, but not her voice. "I think we deserve to know what we've volunteered for."

When the Haunce spoke again, Tick heard real emotion in its voice for the first time: impatience. "We have mere minutes, do you understand? It would take us a hundred lifetimes to explain the complexities of what and who and where you are right now. You are in the depths of space, in the smallest of smallest quantum realms, on the infinite path, in the past, present, and future. All at once. You are a trillion miles long and an atom's width short. You are here and there and everywhere. You are, quite simply, joined with eternity. One day you will understand. Perhaps. But for now, you must do what we say, or everyone and everything will die!"

Tick listened in awe, hoping Jane would shut up and do the same.

The Haunce continued, sounding a little nicer. "The true power of Chi'karda lies not in scientific formulas and complicated theorems and atomic mapping. No. It lies within the heart and mind and spirit. It lies in the power of the soulikens. The two of you have more Chi'karda concentrated within you than any two humans we have ever observed. Far more. We still do not understand why this is so with Jane. Atticus, you have it because every one of your Alterants has died, and their soulikens have transferred to you. Why that happened, we do not know for sure."

If Tick's face had existed, he would've scrunched it up in confusion. But he remained quiet.

Jane didn't. "I thought you said we had no time to waste."

"Silence! Every word we speak is vital. You need to know that the Chi'karda is magnificently potent and powerful within both of you. Almost violently so. You must know this so you will have the confidence that the task you are about to perform will indeed accomplish our mutual goal of saving the Realities. Do not try to understand how or why. The breakdown of the intricate and infinitely complex background of it is for us to worry about. The two of you will use your powers in a way that your minds best decide to present it to you symbolically."

The Haunce paused then, maybe to let its words sink

in. Tick didn't quite understand—not at all, actually—but he knew better than to resort to any childish antics when everything was on the line. He'd only move forward and do what he was asked to do.

"The two most powerful and effective things in the universe are the human mind and Chi'karda," the Haunce continued. "They will now work together within you to present what we need in a way you will best understand it. Trust your instincts and accomplish the task. That is all. By doing so, you will put the pieces in place to heal the breaches in the Barriers. No matter what, trust what you see. No matter what, do what is asked of you. No matter what. Do you both understand?"

Tick's first instinct was to nod, but nothing moved because there wasn't anything to move. So he verbalized again. "Yeah. Yes. I understand."

"Jane?"

She didn't answer until a few seconds passed, probably trying to save a little face, a little power. "Yes. I understand."

"Then let the process begin," the Haunce pronounced.

CHAPTER 54

✳

WORDS ON A TREE

Again, Tick could never have explained to any-one what happened next. The swirling lights and glow-ing orbs and colored streaks suddenly twisted around him like a pyrotechnic tornado, spinning and spinning until he wished he could close his eyes or look away. Dizziness filled him, those pleasurable feelings of float-ing and tingles and warmth gone in an instant.

Everything blended into one bright, all-encom-passing light around him, joined by a rushing sound of wind and roaring trains. Tick felt a pressure, small at first then building, as if his parts had been thrown into a compressor and were being squeezed back together. It had just started to hurt when it all stopped, instantly. The light, the sounds, the heavy force.

He felt nothing. He saw only darkness.

Then things began to change.

One by one, his senses picked up new impressions. He heard a soft wind blowing through the branches of trees. Cold prickled his skin as he suddenly felt that same cool breeze, felt the crisp air all around him. The strong smell of pine trees filled his nose as he pulled in a deep breath. He licked his lips, tasted salt. The bottom of his feet pressed against something—he was standing—and they were cold, too.

Wind. Nose. Lips. Feet.

Tick had been put back together. But why the darkness?

Idiot, he chastised himself. His eyes were closed.

He opened them and took in another burst of quick breath.

A forest surrounded him, a thick layer of freshly fallen snow making the whole place a winter wonderland. Huge trees—mostly pine—towered above him, their branches heavily laden with the puffy white stuff. Tick glanced down to see his feet buried clear up to the ankles. Some of the snow had melted, and his socks were wet, his toes beginning to freeze.

He looked around at the tightly packed trees that went on in every direction as far as he could see. He slowly turned in a circle, taking it all in. The place was beautiful and reminded him of the woods near his home in Washington, though this forest seemed even larger and more widespread.

He'd turned about ninety degrees when he noticed a piece of paper stapled to a thick oak tree just a few feet away. The paper didn't seem wet at all, which meant someone had to have put it there recently, and several lines had been written on its surface. Curious, he stepped forward, slogging through the snow until he reached the mysterious note, now only inches from his eyes.

He began to read but didn't get very far before he knew exactly what it was.

A riddle.

Mothball's flashlight unfurled a spooky path in front of them.

Sato felt like he'd been soldiering with her for years. They slunk their way through the still-shaking tunnels and hallways of the Factory like old pros, anticipating each other's movements as they tried to use their four eyeballs to look in every direction for potential enemies. So far it seemed as if all of Jane's creatures had congregated at the main battle.

Shurrics cocked and gripped in their hands, they

searched and searched. They had to find where these monsters kept the kids.

When they reached a T, Mothball shone her flashlight both directions.

Sato asked, "Left or right?"

She didn't answer, but instead held a finger up to her lips to shush him.

Sato nodded slightly and listened. The faintest sound floated through the cracking and roaring of shifting stone around them. He strained his ears to hear it, even closed his eyes for a second. A whimper. A cry. Moaning. Sobbing. After a few seconds, the sound cut off abruptly with a terror-filled shriek. Then silence.

Sato met Mothball's dark gaze. "That way for sure." They went to the left.

⁓

Sofia sat next to Rutger, fascinated by all the blips and numbers and graphs and charts and squiggly lines on the computer screens. She didn't know what all of it meant yet, and Rutger didn't seem too keen on teaching her with everything that was going on.

"Okay," he said. "I hope this doesn't offend you, Sofia, but what I really need most from you is to run messages back and forth between me and Master George in the Control Room."

It took all of her power not to growl at him like a wolf. No time for wounded pride. "Why don't you have all this junk in the same place?"

Rutger snickered like she'd told a joke. "It used to fit," was all he said.

"At least tell me what you're doing and what he's doing."

Rutger waved his chubby little hand in the air; Sofia had no idea why.

"He's in charge of organizing the rescue of the kids at the Factory. The Barrier Wand's hooked in and set up to wink the nanolocators from the patches we gave Sato and his army. Sally, Priscilla, and a few other Realitants have set up shop in the Grand Canyon. That's where the kids will be winked to. Not enough room here."

"And your job?" she asked.

"Two main things. We're tracking Tick and Mothball and Sato and his army. I'm also tapped into the meteorological reports and ocean monitoring stations. I don't think there's any doubt—we're going to get hit by a massive tidal wave from one of these earthquakes. Not if, when."

Sofia had been studying the screens as he spoke, and her eyes finally focused in on something she should've noticed from the very first. Sato and Mothball and the others had lots of information scrolling and blinking beneath their names. But not Tick.

His screen was blank from top to bottom. Nothing but black space.

She pointed at it. "What's up with Tick?"

Rutger let out a long and dramatic sigh. "Well, Master George says he expected something like this, but it still makes my feet all itchy."

Sofia felt something shrivel inside her. "What do you mean? What's wrong?"

"According to this, Tick's nanolocator is dead."

⟨⟩

Tick couldn't believe it. A riddle.

Now he understood what the Haunce had meant when it said that somehow the healing of the Barriers would be presented to each of them in a form that would seem familiar. Symbolically. Tick thought it was almost like a video game—solving the riddle would be like maneuvering the joystick and pushing buttons on the controller, the complex processes and codes and circuits translating those movements into what he saw on the TV screen.

A riddle.

If anything had defined his journey so far as a Realitant, it had to be riddles.

And here he had another one. A doozy.

Concentrating, he read through it one more time:

Look at the following most carefully, as every line counts:

Be gone in times of death's long passing.
Henry Atwood sliced his neck.
Hath reeds knocked against thee?
If our fathers knew, then winds, they blew.
The sixth of candles burned my eyes.
Horrors even among us.
Leigh tries to eat a stone.
The canine or the cat, it spat.
Pay attention to the ghoul that weeps.

Your number's up, and it is missing. Wary the word second.
Shout out your answer.

A new line suddenly appeared at the very bottom of the page, the space blank one second, then filled with several words the next:

The universe ends in 11:58

And then, as impossible at it seemed, the written time at the end of the sentence started changing, ticking down like a digital clock.

11:57
11:56
11:55
11:54

Tick already had the riddle memorized. He closed his eyes and started thinking.

CHAPTER 55

✳

AN UNEARTHLY SHRIEK

Sato heard more of the chilling sound bites over the now all-too-present quaking noises as he and Mothball stumbled their way down the tunnel and closer to a light source up ahead. Sato heard whimpers and cries for help—all of them the high-pitched voices of children. Anger stirred within him, almost completely obliterating the fear and trepidation he'd been feeling. And all the while, the threat of the entire Factory collapsing on top of them loomed over their heads—literally.

They came to a stony bend where the light grew stronger. Mothball stopped and crouched on the shaky ground right at the edge, her head just a few inches below Sato's. He leaned against the wall beside her, his gut telling him they were on the cusp now of discovering the true horror of this place. He sensed the fear around the corner, as if the kids' tears and sweat evaporated into a noxious cloud that poured through the opening he couldn't see.

Mothball dared a peek. "Gotta be it," she whispered. "Monster or two just 'round the corner, guardin' a door. Lug a Squeezer, we should."

Sato reached into his pocket and pulled out one of the small grenades in answer. "I'll throw it. Soon as it pops, let's charge in shooting the Shurrics."

Mothball nodded then returned her attention forward, gripping the Shurric firmly, its business end pointed away, ready to shoot. Sato stepped away from the wall so he could have the right angle, then tossed the Squeezer around the corner.

It bounced off the far wall then hit the floor with a clang, disappearing from sight as it bounced forward. Seconds later it exploded, sending out a spray of small metal rods. Many of them clinked against the stone, but a few found their marks with a deadly thud. Two or three creatures howled an unearthly shriek.

"Go!" Sato yelled.

He moved to run around the corner, keeping Mothball to his right. He was about to pull the trigger of his Shurric when he saw two bear-like creatures sprawled on the ground, unmoving. A small lamp stood on a table, its glass broken in two places but still lit. Two chairs had toppled over, along with the guards.

Sato looked at the wooden door they'd been guarding. "A Rager ought to—"

Heavy thumps from Mothball's Shurric cut him off, like invisible lightning and soundless thunder—felt, more than heard. On her third shot, the door exploded with a spray of splinters, flying away from them several feet before falling into some kind of abyss. Sato waited and watched, but he never heard the wooden shards hit anything below.

He exchanged a puzzled look with Mothball then warily crept toward the gaping doorway—he didn't want a sudden uptick in the never-ending quake's strength to send him over the edge—his Shurric armed and ready. He reached the threshold of the door and saw that the other side had no floor, only a sheer drop-off with no bottom in sight as far as he could tell. He slowly leaned his head out to get a better look.

They'd reached a vast, round chamber, at least one hundred feet in diameter, that tunneled toward the depths below, narrowing into a hole of blackness far, far down. Along the walls of the chamber were countless rectangular compartments, alcoves set deeper into the stone and open-faced. Inside those compartments were filthy mattresses with thin, ratty blankets. And on top of those nasty beds lay the most terrified-looking children Sato had ever seen.

∽

"Oh, no."

Rutger hadn't spoken in a while, and Sofia realized she'd kind of fallen into a daze, worried about Tick and what it meant that his nanolocator had died. And why Master George seemed to think that was okay, or at least expected.

"What's wrong?" she asked.

Rutger turned away from the busy computer screens, scratching his nose as he stared at the floor. "It's a big one. A really big one."

"What is?" Sofia insisted, almost reaching out and shaking his shoulders.

Rutger looked at her, the usual sparkle in his eyes gone. "A massive tidal wave. Bigger than anything I've ever heard of. It's completely destroyed several monitoring stations. And I know enough to see it's gonna hit us dead-on!"

Sofia choked on several attempts to ask the obvious questions, but finally managed to speak. "When? How long?"

"Thirty minutes."

∽

7:32
7:31
7:30
7:29

Tick had given up on the closed-eyes thinking bit. It wasn't working. Not at all. The lines of the riddle didn't make any sense whatsoever. None.

Something told him there was a visual aspect to it. Something in the first and last line appeared to be instructional, not part of the riddle itself. He forced himself to pretend he didn't have it memorized and read it from beginning to end once again.

Look at the following most carefully, as every line counts:

Be gone in times of death's long passing.
Henry Atwood sliced his neck.
Hath reeds knocked against thee?
If our fathers knew, then winds, they blew.
The sixth of candles burned my eyes.
Horrors even among us.
Leigh tries to eat a stone.
The canine or the cat, it spat.
Pay attention to the ghoul that weeps.

Your number's up, and it is missing. Wary the word second.
Shout out your answer.

5:47
5:46
5:45
5:44

His mind continued churning, pressing, scrambling, processing. There was definitely something visual about the riddle.

Look carefully.

Every line counts.

Your number's up. It is missing. The word second.

Look. Line. Counts. Number. Missing. Second.

His thoughts honed in on those six words. Somehow he knew they meant everything.

There were a lot of things Sato didn't understand as he stood on that dangerous ledge, staring at the curved walls of cubbyholes filled with children. He had questions aplenty. Like why they were kept in such an odd location, why there weren't any ladders, how the children were used in the first place, where they came from. Plenty of things to wonder and ponder and feel disgust over.

But with the whole Factory shaking and ready to collapse at any second, there was only one thing that mattered: getting the nanolocator patches on every kid in sight.

"Divvy them up," he told Mothball, holding out his hand. "We don't have much time."

"Got no ladders or steps," she replied as she put a huge handful of the patches into his hand. "Got no rope. Whatcha ruddy thinkin' we'll do, fly around like birdies to save 'em?"

Sato slipped the square pieces of paper into his pocket and gave her a glare so hard that she took a full step backward. He was instantly filled with shame, but he said what he felt anyway. "Yes, Mothball. We'll fly if that's what we have to do."

Without waiting for a response, he turned until his back was to the abyss behind him, his toes balanced on the former threshold of the door. He crouched down, then let himself slip over the edge.

CHAPTER 56

✳

WHAT IS MISSING

Sato put his hands out, letting the pads of his fingers and palms scrape along the surface of the stone wall as he fell. He focused his concentration so he would be ready for the first opportunity to grab on to something. Fighting off the terrifying panic, he felt as if each nanosecond seemed to beat out a long rhythm.

Bumps and cracks and knobs of rock tore at his skin, but his attempts to grip them proved worthless. The dark surface of the wall suddenly lightened, and he found himself staring into one of the rectangle cubbyholes at a small boy curled up into a ball on his ragged mattress, shaking from the earthquake or bodily ills, or both.

Sato threw his arms forward, hitting the lower floor of the compartment with a terrible bite of pain. His downward movement slammed to a momentary stop, but then he was slipping again, desperately grasping with his fingers for anything to hold on to. A curl of loose blanket, a moist wrinkle of mattress—gone as soon as he touched them. He was just about to fall completely away when his right foot landed on a jutting outcrop of rock; a jolt shivered through every nerve.

Crying out from the pain and shock of his sudden stop, he was still able to take advantage of the moment and adjust his grip on the lower flat edge of stone with his arms. Breathing heavily, Sato couldn't help but pause to make sure it was really true—that he'd really stopped himself from plummeting to his death far below. Hanging there, he looked up to see Mothball looking down on him from twenty feet above.

"A might risky that was," she called out, though a huge smile draped her homely face. Before he could respond, she reared back and took a giant leap to the side, sliding down the stone face as he had done until she caught the next compartment over—with a lot more grace and fewer bruises and scratches, no doubt.

"You think we can do this?" Sato asked, climbing up into the inset hole. The chamber still shook around him, but he'd almost gotten used to it, his body adapting to its movements.

"Like ya said," Mothball responded. "We'll ruddy fly if we have to."

Sato scooted close to the boy sitting there, his arms wrapped around his knees, his eyes filled with a hope that almost broke Sato's heart. The boy wore a dirty shirt and shorts, his hair messed and greasy.

"You okay?" Sato asked. "We're here to take you away. Save you."

The boy didn't answer, but the slightest hint of a smile graced his face.

"This is gonna surprise you, but in a few seconds you'll be far away from here." Sato took one of the nanolocator patches out of his pocket and slapped it on the boy's bare leg.

An instant later, the kid disappeared.

1:45
1:44
1:43
1:42

Tick couldn't help but stare at the dwindling time as it ticked toward the annihilation of the entire universe. His mind wanted him to waste his brain power wondering how all of time and eternity could be dependent on him solving a stupid riddle. He pushed the question away again and again. Pushed away thoughts of what Jane and the Haunce were doing and whether his efforts would matter anyway.

1:21
1:20

"Stop it, Tick!" he yelled to the empty forest. "Think!"

The answer floated just outside his sphere of concentration. He was almost there.

Every line counts.

Counts.

Nine sentences that made no sense at all or seemed to be related to each other in any way.

Number's up.

Number.

0:46
0:45

Sweat soaked his forehead, his armpits, his hands. The cold air did nothing to help.

0:40
0:39

Wary the word second.
Second.
Second word.

0:31
0:30

It all came together so instantly, so unexpectedly, that he felt a lump explode in his throat, racking him with a coughing fit. As he hacked the air through his sore throat, he focused on the words of the riddle. His eyes played tricks, making the answer appear as if the letters themselves had magically changed to help him out. He finally quit coughing and couldn't believe now that he hadn't seen it all from the very beginning:

Look at the following most carefully, as every line counts:

Be gone in times of death's long passing.
Henry Atwood sliced his neck.
Hath reeds knocked against thee?
If our fathers knew, then winds, they blew.
The sixth of candles burned my eyes.
Horrors even among us.
Leigh tries to eat a stone.
The canine or the cat, it spat.
Pay attention to the ghoul that weeps.

Your number's up, and it is missing. Wary the word second. Shout out your answer.

0:10
0:09

The second word of each sentence contained at least part of the numbers he was supposed to look for. To count. And yes, a number was missing.

0:04
0:03

Tick sucked in a quick breath of air then screamed as loudly as possible.

"Five! The answer is five!"

The forest around him sucked away into blackness as once again he exploded into trillions of pieces.

CHAPTER 57

✳

FROM BAD TO WORSE

Sofia followed Rutger into the main Control Room, where Master George was waving his arms like the conductor of the world's largest symphony. Despite all their troubles crashing down at once, a small snicker escaped Sofia. She quickly coughed to cover it up, but Paul—sitting nearby with worry on his face— noticed and broke a half-smile that looked more like a wince.

"George!" Rutger barked. "Most of the earthquakes have stopped, but it's too late for that wave. It's gonna be here in fifteen minutes!"

Their leader shot them a quick glance then returned his gaze to the rapidly blinking screens in front of him.

"My heart can barely stand this confounded predicament!"

"What's the latest with Sato?" Rutger asked as he and Sofia moved closer.

Master George pointed to a series of purple lines that kept appearing then disappearing. Unlike the indicators for Sato and Mothball above them, these had no names attached. "They're doing it. They're doing it! We've already winked ten children to the Grand Canyon, where Priscilla and Sally have several doctors on hand."

Rutger let out a sigh that sounded like he'd lost every ounce of hope. "We won't survive it," he said in a tight whisper.

"What's that?" Master George asked, finally giving his full attention to his partner.

"The wave. There's no way we can survive it. It's too big. We . . ." Rutger looked at the floor.

"What? Spit it out, man!"

"We have to leave. This location—and us with it—has zero chance of making it through the wave's power. It'll rip our cabling technology to shreds, then pick us up and slam us into shore. We have to leave."

Sofia felt that shrinking sensation in her gut again. She half-expected Master George to argue, to say it would be okay, maybe express disbelief or babble about how life's unfair. Instead, he accepted the truth and immediately moved to what needed to be done. Sofia was impressed.

"Then we can only hope they reach every child in time—we don't have things properly set up at the Grand Canyon to wink them in from that location. We'll wait here, monitoring the situation and managing the nanolocator patches. At least we have a bit of good news—if the earthquakes have stopped, then Atticus and Jane must've done their job."

Sofia's heart lifted, but then she remembered their own problem. "What about the wave?" she asked, her eyes meeting Paul's, sharing a look that said so much with no need for words.

Master George puffed his chest out and folded his hands on his belly. "The four of us will wink away the second before it hits. It's time for us to be very brave."

Tick found himself back in that outer-space-like void of lights and streaks and glowing, brilliant orbs. He couldn't feel his body, didn't understand what or where or anything else. But he knew they'd done it even before the Haunce spoke to them.

"Through your efforts and power, we have healed the Barriers of the Realities. We will send you back now. Your worlds are not destroyed, but they have still seen great, great devastation. The healing of such things does not rest in our hands. We say farewell."

The universe spun. Everything changed, and Tick felt the pressure of crushing diamonds.

～○～

Sato put everything out of his mind. The fear. The soreness of his entire body. His hunger, his exhaustion. From somewhere deep in his cells and molecules and tissue, he sucked out the adrenaline he needed to keep moving.

From one inset compartment to the next, he jumped. They were about four feet apart side to side, a little less up and down. Each and every time, for one frightening second, he thought he wouldn't make it and instead would plummet to the unseen depths far below. But so far he'd landed each and every time, gripping and pushing and pulling, squirming his way to the children without falling to his death. Mothball was doing the same, working the other side of the stony, rounded chamber.

He spared a glance for the latest kid he'd found—a shaky, pale girl whose eyes were open and focused on his. "Don't worry," he said. "We're here to rescue you." He'd always wanted to say that to someone.

He slapped a nanolocator patch on her arm, no longer waiting to watch as the kids vanished from sight, winked away by Master George. Already on the move, he crouched on the far end, ready to leap for the next hole, when he noticed two things at the same time that made him pause.

One, the shaking and quaking had stopped completely.

And two, he heard the distant sounds of flapping wings and a chattering, cackling chorus of grunts and squeals coming from below. He looked down.

Several fangen—those horrible creations of Jane's they'd fought at her castle when George sent them to steal her Barrier Wand—were flying through the murky darkness, coming up toward him.

Sato jumped to the next compartment.

〜〜〜

Tick blinked, dazzled by the light of the sun directly overhead. He stood in the mud just outside the broken and jumbled heap of wood that had once been the fence surrounding the Factory. Mistress Jane stood right in front of him, her expressionless red mask only inches from his face.

For the briefest of moments, he forgot that she was his bitter, bitter enemy.

"I can't believe we did it," he said, not ashamed of the childlike wonder in his voice. They had, after all, just saved the entire universe. "All I had to do was solve a riddle—seems crazy. What did the Haunce make you do?"

Jane's mask broke into a smile so full of genuine kindness that Tick wondered if the whole experience had maybe changed something inside her. "Isn't it wonderful, Atticus? What does it say about our species that you and I could put aside our hatred for each other and work for the greater good? We should both feel very proud."

Tick let out an uneasy laugh, not sure how he felt about the way she was acting. "It's definitely pretty cool. So . . . you didn't answer my question. What did you have to do? How did you do your part?"

Jane's mask kept smiling. "Ah, yes. It was quite an amazing thing. The Haunce had me work through my master plan for how to achieve the Utopian Reality I've always wanted. What an invigorating experience it was to focus my mind and faculties in such a heightened, rushed state of anxiety." She moved even closer to him, almost touching.

Tick didn't know what to think. Maybe she—

A burst of pain exploded in his stomach, a wrenching, twisting stab of fire and needles. He stumbled back two steps and looked down. The hilt of a large knife jutted from his abdomen, a dark red bloodstain soaking his shirt, spreading.

Choking and sputtering a cough, he raised his eyes to Jane, whose now-angry mask matched the color of the growing stain around the knife.

"My plan started with something just like that," she said.

CHAPTER 58

*

FAMILY

Tick fell to his knees, both hands gripped around the hilt of the knife, his hands wet with warm blood. He didn't dare pull it out. Clumpy fluid lodged in his throat, cutting off his breath along with the panic that choked him. He tried to suck down air through his nose, but it ended in a cough every time. Bugs of light swam in front of his eyes.

He couldn't speak. He didn't know what he'd say if he could.

Jane crouched down to the ground, the mud caking her robe. "Subtle. That's what I told Frazier. I knew I had to wait until the right moment when you weren't on guard and ready to strike back with your Chi'karda. A

472

knife deep to the stomach—such a simple and beautiful thing. So old-fashioned. It's almost impossible to find help in time. You're dying, Atticus. Tick. Nothing can help you now."

Tick collapsed to the side, and a fresh, striking burst of pain burrowed through his entire body, as if the knife had sprouted steely vines that coursed through his insides. On the outer rim of his consciousness, he realized he'd never come close to understanding the fear of dying. Death had never truly seemed real. And now it was here, ready to drag him away like a stolen bag of gold.

Jane leaned over until the cool metal of her mask touched his ear. She whispered, "The rest of my plan is for the good of mankind and the Realities. Except for one thing, one item on the list—revenge, Atticus. Revenge. I want your last thought in life to be this: to know that I will hunt down each and every member of your family and kill them. Your friends as well. I'll kill them just like I did you. Good-bye."

She stood up, though Tick could barely see her. His vision blurred, dark specks swirling like a cloud of stinging gnats. He felt his life slipping away, a physical dwindling as if he were made of sand and it was slowly leaking out of a puncture in some outer skin. He thought of soulikens and how those small and permanent stamps of electric pulses and energy might be the very thing he felt seeping out of him into . . . wherever they went. His Alterants' soulikens had come to him, according to the Haunce. Maybe now they would go to that odd, ghostly creature of eternity.

Jane was walking away, stabbing her Staff into the mud.

Tick hated her.

Life was running away from him. He closed his eyes, wondering if he would ever open them again. What he saw appear out of the patchy darkness was Kayla. And Lisa. His parents. Paul and Sofia and Sato. He saw them as if he looked at a TV screen.

The Chi'karda exploded within him.

No build-up this time. No slow burn that escalated like stoked flames. It was an absolute detonation of power. His whole body became a conflagration, a perfect and consuming inferno of force and might. He didn't know he'd done it, but he was suddenly standing. A tornado of orange, fiery air swirled around him. He heard himself speak as if he were an outside observer.

"Jane, you're not going anywhere."

CHAPTER 59

FISTS OF CHI'KARDA

The fangen attacked Sato just as he landed on his twentieth compartment. Sharp claws dug into his shoulders and yanked him backward. Sato spun, swinging with a fist. He made contact, thumping the creature's face. With a horrible shriek, it let go and fell away, its thin, translucent wings flapping weakly.

Sato knew there were more fangen, that this would be a tricky task indeed. He quickly stuck a nanolocator patch on to the tiny boy shivering on the stone then moved to jump to the next rectangular hole. He was in midflight when a fangen swooped in and grabbed him, pulling his body out to the middle of the chamber, its legs wrapped around him as it tried to bite his neck.

Sato clutched the top of the creature's head by a tuft of diseased-looking hair and pushed its gaping mouth full of teeth away. Then he punched it, slipping around its body in that moment of weakness so he was on the thing's back. They hovered over the abyss.

"Take me back to that hole!" Sato screamed in its ear, pointing to the place he'd been going. "Take me now, or I'll snap your neck!" He wrapped his hands around the thin pole of the fangen's neck and started squeezing.

The creature had to have some instinct to survive, some will to live. Making sounds like a strangled banshee, it flew toward the place indicated. Sato jumped off and into the inset compartment as soon as he was close enough. He pivoted and kicked out, connecting with the fangen's stomach. It squawked and pulled back, choking and coughing.

Sato pulled out a patch and stuck it to the little girl next to him. He readied for the next one. Nothing about this was going to be very easy. He jumped.

⟋⟍

Womp. Womp. Womp.

Surging throbs of Chi'karda sent waves of energy thumping away from Tick. He could feel its vibrations in the air, in the ground, in the forest behind him, shaking the deepest parts of the wood in the trees. His senses had heightened, almost unbearably so; the smells of mud and pine, the feel of the breeze, every sound amplified tenfold, the crisp clarity of his vision. It all felt wonderful and terrible at the same time.

Jane had stopped when he told her she wasn't going anywhere, probably consumed by curiosity. And, Tick hoped, a little scared. She turned around to face him, standing about thirty yards away.

"You can't handle that much Chi'karda," she said; Tick heard each word as if she'd spoken it directly into his ear. "It'll burn you to a crisp if you don't let it go. Release it, Atticus. Or you'll kill countless others along with . . ."

She faltered, her mask shifting downward just slightly, but enough to show she was looking at Tick's stomach. His eyes fell to see what had caught her attention, and he almost cried out in shock.

The wooden hilt of the knife smoldered, slowly inching its way as if by magic out of his skin. The long blade followed, glowing a hot red. The whole area sizzled like a cooking steak, small wisps of smoke rising from the wound. The knife finally came all the way out and fell to the ground with a thump and another sizzle as it hit the wet mud. Tick watched in shock as the slice in his skin healed back together in a matter of seconds. He felt an intense burning where the wound had been, stronger even than the Chi'karda raging through his entire body.

His dad had once told him how he'd seemed to defy death several times as a kid. What it all meant, Tick didn't know. Maybe his ability over Chi'karda went way further than he ever dreamed or hoped.

He looked back at Jane, quickly wiping the look of surprise from his face. "I'm getting control of it!" he shouted. "And you know I'm more powerful than you are! Give up. Now. Or I'll blow you up along with everything else in the Factory."

Jane's fingers tightened around her Staff. "You're an idiot child, Atticus. I wanted to kill you with subtle ease and avoid the destruction you might inflict if you let loose your chaotic abilities. But I'll do it this way if I have to. I'll never sleep in my bed again until I know the Realities are rid of Atticus Higginbottom. You're about to die, boy. I hope you've enjoyed your short time alive."

Tick's anger built with every word she said, and he couldn't take it anymore. He collected his power by thinking it, imagined what he wanted in his mind, like gathering a mental snowball with mental hands. The Chi'karda burned and roiled inside him, resisting as he compacted it tighter and tighter, compressing it into a dangerous and unstable sphere of pure energy. He saw the fiery orange cloud seeping back into his skin, like smoke in reverse.

Straining with the effort, he spoke through his trembling concentration. "I think I'll keep living." With a terrible scream, he threw his coiled power—all of it—at Jane.

A boom like a thousand strikes of lightning shook the world around him. Mud and dirt exploded from the ground in a straight path to Jane, as if it were a crowded minefield and every last mine went off at once. A visible wave of orange-tinged air slammed against her body, throwing her twenty feet into the air. She flew backward until she landed far on the other side of the broken wooden fence, her Staff broken into several pieces.

Tick had no idea how he did what happened next. But he willed himself forward, wanting to be by her side instantly, faster than he could possibly run. He was out of patience and knew he had to finish her off. In a dizzying instant, he suddenly stood right next to her, looking down at her as she struggled to stand. With a distant thought, he realized that he'd just winked himself.

He reached down and grabbed Jane by the folds of her robe, communicating with his powers of Chi'karda without talking, almost without thinking. He easily lifted her up and held her over his head. Then he threw her at the forest. She sailed several hundred feet through the air, arms and legs flailing; a piercing shriek ripped from her lungs. Tick watched as she finally slammed into a large oak tree and crumpled to the ground below it. She didn't move, a twisted heap of arms and legs.

Tick drew in deep, ragged breaths as he looked around him. He saw the hole in the ground that Jane had created to pull them out of the underground Factory, as well as a much larger gap with broken and jagged edges that had probably been caused by the earthquakes. He winked to the edge of it and looked down to where people from the Fifth Reality were fighting Jane's creatures. Tick saw and heard the sights and sounds of battle, the clashes and the blood and the screams. He wanted to destroy the Factory, level it, crush it, disintegrate it.

"Master George!" he yelled, knowing the man was listening in somehow. "Get them out! Get them all out!"

CHAPTER 60

✳

TEN KIDS

Tick wants us to wink them out!" Rutger yelled.

Sofia watched as Master George's hands flew furiously to turn dials and flip switches, type on the keyboard, adjust his Barrier Wand. "How much time until the wave hits us?" he asked in a tight voice.

"Three minutes!"

"We'll hold out until the last second. We must save every child we can!"

Sofia looked down to see that Paul had grabbed her hand. She squeezed back, terrified and hating how helpless she felt.

"Winking away the Fifth Army now," Master George said, sweat flying off his ruddy, bald head as he worked. "But not Sato and Mothball. Not yet."

"Two and a half minutes," Rutger said, his voice loud but sad.

Tick saw the tall people of the Fifth Reality suddenly disappear, winked away. The creatures they'd been fighting looked around in shock, growling and spitting.

Thankful that Master George had heard him, Tick had to assume that everyone was gone now. He hoped that George had also saved the kids Jane planned to use in her horrific experiments. He had to destroy the Factory now, before any of those monsters escaped. Then he'd finish off Jane and end this nightmare forever.

He closed his eyes for a brief moment, mentally gathering the streams and coils of Chi'karda, pulling it all in.

Then he fell to his knees with a scream, throwing his arms forward as if he were flinging his powers at the scene below him. His Chi'karda unleashed itself on the Factory, destroying everything in its fiery, angry path.

Sato's entire body ached like never before. Worse than when he'd gone through the agony of having Chu's Dark Infinity plague and being bound with ropes by Master George. His arms and legs screamed with weariness and hurt, begging him to stop.

But he didn't. He kept jumping from compartment to compartment, slapping the nanolocator patches on kid after kid, moving on before he even saw them be winked away. All the while, he'd fought off the relentless fangen with punches and kicks. He'd even poked one in the eyeball and sent it screeching away.

Mothball did her part on the other side of the vast, round chamber, leaping with more ease than Sato because of her height advantage. They were almost done. Sato could see the last row of inset rectangles just below him.

He landed in the latest cubbyhole, pulling out a patch before he even settled. A pretty girl with red hair lay curled in a ball, eyes lit with fear. He stuck the patch on her and turned to move on. Just as he did, a great explosion sounded from above, and the entire chamber started shaking again. Huge chunks of rock and metal fell through the air, cracking and clinging as they hit the sides along the way.

It had all started again. What went wrong! He dared not pause to think about it.

He punched a fangen just as it appeared, kicking

it and punching again. The hideous thing backed off.

Sato jumped, ignoring the increased danger of debris and quaking. He landed in the next compartment and reached for a nanolocator patch.

～

The Bermuda Triangle headquarters building trembled and groaned.

"Thirty seconds!" Rutger yelled. Despite the terror and worry she felt herself, Sofia couldn't help but feel bad for the poor little man. With his face flushed and sweat pouring off his skin, he looked like he might drop dead any second. "It's already straining the cables to the max—they're going to snap! We have to go! We have to go!"

Master George continued his frantic, feverish work. "Blasted! They're still working hard. It must mean they haven't reached everyone yet."

"Time's up!" Rutger said, pounding his fist on the desk. "Or we'll all die with them!"

Sofia felt a storm of different feelings and emotions rip through her heart: fear for her life, fear for Sato's life, sorrow for the kids. She squeezed Paul's hand even tighter and waited, holding her breath. The building shook even harder now, groans of twisting metal hurting her ears.

Master George swore, something Sofia never thought she'd hear him do. Then, "Fine. Let's finish this thing."

He started tapping buttons.

⟋⟍

The entire chamber was about to fall down around Sato. The shattering cracks and thunderous rumbles of crumbling stone had risen to a deafening roar. Just after placing a patch on the latest kid, he looked across the way at Mothball and saw her staring back at him through the rain of debris. Her eyes said it all.

They could die here if they didn't get winked out immediately—who knew when the shaking would stop, when things would settle. But then, almost at the exact same time, they both slowly nodded. They wouldn't leave—not until they'd saved every last prisoner.

Sato broke eye contact first and scooted to the edge of his current cubbyhole. He did a quick scan and counted. Ten kids. There were ten kids left. Five for him, five for Mothball.

He coiled for the jump, but just as he pushed off, he felt a quick and cold tingle shoot across his neck and down his spine.

"No!" he screamed. But it was too late. The chamber vanished around him.

Sofia barely had time to notice they'd winked into the Grand Canyon sitting room, barely had time to feel the relief of solid ground under her feet, when Sato and Mothball appeared right in front of her. The two of them looked like zombies, filthy and scratched and worn.

"No!" Sato yelled, twisting around on his feet, as if looking for something. "Send me back! There were ten more! Ten more!"

Master George appeared through a doorway, his face cramped with a tight smile. "The children should be down in the valley. Ah, Sato, Mothball, thank goodness you're—"

Sato ran to the man and grabbed him by the shirt. "Send me back! The whole place is falling down—they could die! There were ten more of them!"

Master George shook his head back and forth. "I'm . . . I'm terribly sorry, Sato. It's far too late— everything was set up back in the Bermuda Triangle station. I simply can't send you back from here. I'm very sorry."

"You have to!" Sato's arms shook with fury or exhaustion. Probably both. "You have to send me back! We didn't get them all!"

"It's impossible," Master George whispered sadly. "Quite impossible."

Sato slumped to the floor. Sofia looked over and saw Mothball had collapsed on a couch, her eyes closed, tears leaking out from beneath their lids. Paul moved to crouch beside Sato and put a hand on his back.

Sato shook it off. "We left ten kids! Ten!"

Sofia joined them, sitting on the other side of Sato. "But think of how many you saved. And the others might escape in all the chaos."

She and Paul pulled Sato into an awkward three-person hug. He resisted at first, but then finally collapsed into Sofia's arms, sobbing.

"Think of how many you saved," she repeated.

CHAPTER 61

✳

COLLISION

Tick stumbled away from the collapsing Factory, sucking the power of Chi'karda back inside him. He felt the flaming heat of it burn his insides. It had taken only three waves of it to destroy the complex. The sounds of crunching and cracking and splintering filled the air as the ground sank, swirling like a whirlpool of mud. He'd begun the chain reactions of destructive entropy that would leave the place as nothing but sand within minutes.

The earth began to give beneath Tick. There was no way he could outrun the collapse. With a thought, he quickly winked back to the forest where he'd thrown Jane's body just minutes ago.

She still lay in a heap at the bottom of the oak tree, but her arms were moving, and Tick heard her groan. His heart sank. He'd hoped she would be dead from the collision, because he dreaded the prospect of having to do anything more to her. His initial anger and adrenaline had subsided, and the reality of the situation was hitting home. If he finished what he'd set out to do, it meant he would have to end it, right here, right now.

He had to do it, no matter what. Unchecked, she could and would murder millions and billions of people. She'd already proven that. Tick had to finish it.

He stepped toward her.

The ground exploded under Tick, a wave of invisible force lifting him off his feet and throwing him backward. Before he could gather his wits, his back slammed into the soft ground, knocking the air out of him. He pushed himself up onto his knees, gasping for breath. If the mud had been dried and hard, he could very well have broken his spine.

When a rush of air finally filled his lungs, he jumped to his feet. Jane stood a few yards away, both of her hands outstretched, palms facing him. Tick reached for the Chi'karda that still churned within him.

"Wait," she said. "Wait. If we keep at this something really bad will happen."

Tick didn't waste time with words. He pushed a surge of Chi'karda straight at her, hurling it like a volley

of sun flares. The power hit her, twisting her body up into the air and back down to the mud where she slid thirty feet and smacked into the base of a tall pine.

Tick switched gears, concentrating on the trees around her. Using his mind as commander, willing what he wanted to happen, he made a dozen trees around her dissolve, the wood bursting into a swirl of tiny particles. They flew around her in a brown tornado, encircling her like a swarm of muddy bees. Then he made them collapse, sealing the wood back together like he'd done before several times now, though unconsciously.

With a loud smacking sound, followed by cracks and groans, a large mass of twisted wood formed around Jane, trapping her inside. Crushing her.

Tick doubled over, his hands on his knees, pulling in rapid breaths. The mental effort of doing such a thing made him feel as though he'd run ten miles in a sprint. He glanced back up at the hideous structure of coiled tree parts. No way she survived that. No way.

The thought had barely formed when the entire formation exploded, chunks and chips of wood flying out in all directions. Tick fell to the ground and covered his head with both arms. He felt the prick of splinters, the whoosh of bigger pieces flying right over him. When it seemed as though the worst had passed, he looked up and saw Jane standing there, her arms once again outstretched.

"Atticus, we have to stop this!" she yelled.

Tick jumped to his feet. She was trying to trick him; he knew it. He threw another blast of Chi'karda at her; she blocked it with a visible bubble of solid air tinted orange. The concussion wave bounced back and knocked him to the ground, jolting the breath out of him once again. As he struggled for air, he clawed to gather another pool of his power, knowing she'd probably finish him off while he was down.

But when he staggered to his feet, she only stood there, her mask surprisingly showing concern, not anger.

"Atticus, stop," she said in her scratchy, painful voice. "Give me five minutes to explain!"

Tick felt a rush of anger just as he pulled in a long, blissful breath. "It's too late, Jane! I can't let you go one more day killing and hurting!"

A ball of power filled him, almost bursting his chest. He unleashed it, threw it all at Jane.

Her shield formed again, resisting his attack. Tick was ready for the rebound of force this time, and he leaned into it, fighting it with his own strength. He let all his fears and inhibitions fall away, all his caution. She seemed to be getting stronger, and he knew he had to go for it. Screaming, he searched and probed his inner mind and body for every last trickle of Chi'karda, channeling it and throwing it at Jane.

She fought back. A wind tore through the air as

the crackle of electricity and booms of thunder filled the world around them. Streaks of orange swirled and kicked; bursts of fire ignited here and there like ribbons of flame; the trees in the forest bent unnaturally away from them; mud and chunks of wood took flight, swirling like loose paper in a tornado. As Tick and Jane fought, their battling powers looked like two stars colliding, white and brilliant and blinding.

Tick hadn't stopped screaming. The world rushed and burned around him. He couldn't see. Life seemed to be draining out of his body. He didn't know how much longer he could last. A trickle of despair dented his heart. He pushed harder.

Somehow he heard Jane yell the words, "We have to stop!"

"No!" Tick shouted back in a ripped shriek that tore through his burning throat. He pushed harder, flinging his whole life at her.

A sound like the world splitting in two pierced his ears, his brain, his every nerve.

And then, in a sudden instant, everything stopped.

All light disappeared. Tick felt himself flying through a dark and silent wind.

Time stretched on, blank and quiet. Eventually, he felt nothing.

CHAPTER 62

✳

THE DETOUR

I can't believe my own eyes."

Tick barely heard the words. A man. His voice was soft, but slightly . . . menacing, like small, sharp-nosed worms, slowly working their way into Tick's brain, needling and hurting. The world around Tick was still dark.

The stranger spoke again. "Atticus Higginbottom and Mistress Jane. Together, with me, at last."

Tick felt himself blinking, felt tears in his eyes, felt pain coursing through every inch of his body. But still nothing—blackness.

The man wouldn't be quiet, and every word throbbed in Tick's skull. "I have no idea how it happened, but I can't say I'm not pleased. It'll be nice to have some help.

I'm sure between the three of us, we can get out of here."

Tick kept blinking and finally saw a faint smudge of light against the darkness.

"Where . . . where are we?"

Jane. It was Jane. She sounded even worse than usual.

The man chuckled, a horribly unpleasant sound. "You're safe and sound, Mistress. No worries. Plenty to eat around here. Plenty of everything."

The light grew in Tick's vision. Increased its pace of brightening. Shapes began to form.

"I . . . warned him," Jane said, her voice filled with resignation, as if she'd just accepted a horrible truth. "I . . ." She didn't finish.

Something clicked, and suddenly Tick could see everything. Gasping, he sat up, ignoring the bolts of pain that shot through his body. He sat on a beach with a perfect blue sky hanging overhead and crystal-clear water lapping against the white sand. An enormous and endless ocean stretched to his right, a forest of palm trees to his left. Mistress Jane lay flat on the ground, several feet away, her mask cracked and tilted.

And sitting cross-legged next to Tick was Reginald Chu. The man who'd once ruled the Fourth Reality. The man who'd tried to rule all Thirteen with his Dark Infinity. The man who'd been sent to—

"Welcome to the Nonex, Atticus," Chu said. "I hope you're ready to help me get the heck out of here."

EPILOGUE

✳

THE MISSION

Sofia sat between Paul and Sato on the couch, her arms folded, her foot tapping. Sally and Priscilla, both of whom had been in charge of collecting and helping the children rescued from the Factory, sat across from them, looking down and as quiet as everyone else. Mothball was on the floor, leaning against the bricks of the fireplace.

Master George and Rutger finally entered the room, their faces grave.

"I believe we finally have our report," Master George announced, looking down at a stack of papers clasped in his hands. "The members of Sato's Fifth Army are mostly safe and accounted for, having lost only"—he cleared his throat—"seventeen lives in battle. It looks like Sato and Mothball rescued ninety-seven children in all, and they are currently receiving the very best in treatment from Realitant doctors."

"We lost ten of them," Sato mumbled under his breath. It was the first thing he'd said since winking away from the Thirteenth.

"Why . . . yes, Sato. Yes, we did." Master George paused, his eyes showing so much love for Sato that Sofia felt tears moisten her eyes. "The damage from our latest affairs is quite catastrophic. Every single Reality has suffered, and the recovery will take years. The worst by far is the Thirteenth, where . . . the final conflict inflicted utter devastation. It will take some time to discover just how much."

Sofia spoke up. "What happened to Tick?"

"Yeah," Paul said. "Out with it."

Master George nodded uncomfortably. "Yes, yes, we're all very concerned about Master Atticus and what has become of him." His voice squeaked on the last three words; a tear spilled down his cheek. "I'm afraid we have quite troubling—and confusing—news."

Sofia's heart froze; her breath stopped.

"I can't say I understand it," he continued, fidgeting with his papers. "His nanolocator started working again once his business with the Haunce was complete. But then . . . it just . . . well, it reported back something we've never seen before. Rutger, you tell them. I can't bear to say another bloody word." He threw the papers on the floor and stomped out of the room.

Rutger took a moment before finally speaking.

"According to our system, Atticus Higginbottom has ceased to exist."

～～～

Lisa had just fallen asleep—after a long time of trying to do so—when she felt someone shaking her by the shoulders, gently. She opened her eyes, ready to scream out in panic, when the sight of her mom silenced it. The glow of the moon shining through the window lit up Lorena Higginbottom's face, making it look somehow kind and fiercely determined at the same time.

Lisa knew she was up to something. "What's going on?"

"Keep quiet and follow me," her mom whispered. "Don't make a peep—you know your dad will wake up at the sneeze of a mouse."

Confused but intrigued, Lisa shook her grogginess away and got up from bed. Then the two of them tiptoed out of her room, down the hall, then down the stairs, both keeping to the silent spots as best they could. Before long, Lisa's mom had led her all the way down to the basement.

After flicking on the light, Lisa repeated her earlier question. "What's going on?"

Her mom walked over to a dusty corner of the large room and dragged a couple of boxes away from the wall, then crouched down. "I know both you and I have been feeling like we want to help. To finally do our part in this whole mess. Especially now that my son"—she faltered, choked back the usual cry that had come so often since Master George had sent word that Tick was missing—"is nowhere to be found. I think it's time we took a little of our own action."

Lisa nodded, feeling the same swell of emotion, knowing she couldn't speak without cracking. But she agreed. Agreed wholeheartedly. She wanted to *do* something. She wanted to act.

Her mom gripped a panel of the unpainted wall, and to Lisa's surprise it came loose. She lifted out a large square and placed it on the ground. Swirls of dust puffed through the air. In the dark recess behind her, an object glinted.

"You've been hiding something down here?" Lisa asked.

"Yes. Though I never, never, never thought I'd have to use it again." She leaned over and reached into the secret compartment.

"What?" Lisa asked, moving closer to get a better look. "What is it?"

Her mom pulled out a long, golden tube with dials and switches running down its sides, then held it up. "It's a Barrier Wand, sweetie. It's gonna help us find my boy."

THE VOID OF MIST
AND THUNDER

This one is for the Storymakers.

You know who you are.

ACKNOWLEDGMENTS

I can't believe the series has come to an end. It's been a long and sometimes tough journey, but I'm so proud of the story and thankful to the people who helped push it through to the finish. Particularly Chris Schoebinger and Lisa Mangum. Without them it absolutely never would have happened. Much appreciation to all my other friends at Shadow Mountain too.

As always, I'd like to thank my agent, Michael Bourret, for his tireless work.

Thanks to Liesa Abrams and all the good folks at Simon & Schuster for believing in the series enough to take it to a larger stage. Here's to many more people discovering the adventures of Tick and the other Realitants.

PROLOGUE

✳

A VERY SPECIAL BOY

It was all about the soulikens.

Master George sat in his study, the lights dimmed, Muffintops purring in a corner, the first light of dawn's birth still an hour off. He stared at the wall as if the most fascinating thing in the Realities had been stapled there for him to see whenever he wished, but it was only a knot in the wood of his paneling. A knot that had two eyes and a mouth if you looked at it just right, and for some reason it reminded him of a boy named Atticus Higginbottom.

Atticus. Tick. The young man who changed everything.

The boy who'd disappeared from existence.

It was a shame. More than a shame. It was a downright tragedy. Master George had never ached in his heart so much for someone lost. Right when they'd finally begun to understand why the boy had such extraordinary powers, why he was able to harness and use Chi'karda as if he were himself a Barrier Wand—and a powerful Wand at that, even more so than Mistress Jane, who had a unique and tragic story of her own—he was gone.

But none of that really mattered anymore. It wasn't the *reason* George missed Master Atticus so much. He missed him—ached for him—because the boy had become like a son to him. So innocent, yet brave. So genuine. Such a kid, but so grown up. Oh, how he missed that dear, dear boy.

He was a wonder.

Sato had completed the mission George had asked of him. He had visited each Reality and searched until he had found the same thing in each one: a grave for the Alterants of Atticus Higginbottom—the boy's "twins" in the other twelve Realities. Never before had such an odd coincidence occurred, where only one version of a person remained throughout all the Realities. They'd never know if there was some deep cosmic reason behind it, or how it had happened.

But one thing was for certain: every one of those Alterants' soulikens had traveled to and collected within the body of the one remaining Atticus who had lived in Reality Prime. It had changed his structure, his makeup, his quantum mechanics. He was full of Chi'karda, filled beyond measure with the powers that bound and controlled the universe. Filled beyond anything mankind could ever hope to recreate or dream about.

He was lost now, gone from existence.

There'd probably never be another quite like him, in far more ways than one.

George called for Muffintops. He needed to hug a friend.

PART 1

* * *

THE NONEX

CHAPTER 1

✳

A GASH IN THE FOREST

The forest smelled of things dead, things rotting.

Jacob Gillian paid the stench no mind, walking his merry way along the narrow path that threaded through the tall oaks and pines like a dried-out stream. Of course, the reason he paid it no mind was because he'd lost his sense of smell thirty years ago in an unfortunate spice sniffing contest. His grandson, Chip, had to tell him that the place stunk like a three-week-old dead rat stuck under the pipes.

The two of them had been hiking side by side for well over an hour, knowing full well that something horrible had happened deep within the dark woods. Exactly *what* had happened was still a mystery, and the reason they were out there. Jacob had heard the awful sound of ripping and shredding and booming. Chip had smelled the nose-wrinkling stench. Those two things together spelled trouble, and by golly, the source behind it needed finding out.

Jacob and his grandson had moved into the boonies after Chip's parents had been killed in a train collision near Louisville. Ever since then, they'd learned to live with little and less, loving the wild freedom and exhilaration of being smack-dab in the middle of nowhere. Their closest neighbor lived a good thirty miles down the poorly maintained state road, and the nearest town was forty miles in the other direction. But that's just how Jacob liked it, and the life had seemed to grow on Chip as well.

One day they'd return to civilization and start learnin' Chip on the ways of society. But for now, there was time. Time to heal, time to grow, time to enjoy. Time to have time.

"I think I see something up there, Grandpa," Chip said, a little too enthusiastically, considering the circumstances that had brought them out into the woods.

"What is it?" Old Jacob couldn't see much better than he could smell.

"There's a bright patch. Seems like it goes all the way up to the sky!"

"On the path or off it?"

Chip grabbed Jacob's hand and started hurrying down the little ribbon of beaten leaves and undergrowth. "Just to the right of it. We're almost there!"

Jacob followed along as careful as he could while still keeping up with Chip's eager steps. Warning bells rang inside his mind, but he did what he'd done since the day he'd stepped out into the humid fields of Korea as a soldier—he ignored them. Curiosity always won out in his book, and courage came as naturally as a nice belch after dinner.

They'd just rounded a bend, skirting past two mammoth pines that looked like brothers, when Chip suddenly pulled up short. Jacob ran right past him, almost yanking his grandson's arm out of its socket when the boy didn't let go. But then Jacob saw what had stopped the kid, and all he could do was stand and stare. He felt Chip's sweaty hand slip out of his own.

Fifty yards ahead of them, a swath of the forest had been wiped from existence and replaced by a brushstroke of . . . something else. Starting deep in the ground and shooting all the way to the sky was a wide gash in reality, a window to another place. Jacob could see part of a beach, the deep blue waters of the ocean beside it, a sun where there shouldn't *be* a sun. The time was almost noon, and the *real* ball of fire was directly overhead. It was as if someone had clawed a rip in the reality of this world and replaced it with another.

"What in the great dickens are we lookin' at?" Jacob whispered.

"Grandpa?" was all Chip managed in reply. His voice shook with equal parts confusion and terror.

"I've been from one end of this world to the other," Jacob said, not sure if he was talking to himself or to his grandson. "And I've never seen a thing like that in my life."

"Let's go home."

"Home?" Jacob tore his eyes away from the spectacle and looked down at Chip. "Didn't you hear what I just said? This is a once in a lifetime opportunity! Let's go check her out."

Jacob took Chip's hand once again, and they started marching closer to the impossible vision of another world streaked across their own. They'd come to within twenty feet when a person appeared on the beach, stepping into the picture from the right edge of where reality had been torn apart.

It was a lady, though Jacob could only tell that from the ratty, filthy dress she wore; a hood was pulled up over her head. A red mask, seemingly made out of metal, covered her face. The expression on the mask was one of anger.

She saw them just as they saw her, and she stopped

to stare, the features of the mask *shifting* to create an expression of absolute shock.

Jacob took a step backward before he realized what he was doing.

"Who are you?" the woman asked, her voice raw and scratchy, like it came out of a throat scarred with acid. "Do you know how this happened?"

Jacob's mouth had turned into a bucket of dust, and he couldn't remember how his tongue or voice box worked. He tried getting words out, but nothing came except the slightest hint of a croak.

Surprisingly, Chip spoke up. "Lots of bad sounds came from over here, and the whole place is stinky. Me and my grandpa were just trying to see what happened."

Such bravery from the kid meant Jacob had to speak. He found his voice. "Where you from, miss? Um, if you don't mind me asking."

The lady's mask melted—literally, by the looks of it—into a frown. "I'm from the Thirteenth Reality. Where are you?"

Jacob swallowed a lump the size of his big toe. "Um . . . Kentucky?"

Before the lady could respond, her image and everything around her suddenly spun into a tornado of colors that quickly merged and transformed into a mass of gray. It swirled and swirled, picking up speed and creating a wind that tore at Jacob's clothing. And then the sound of terrible thunder seemed to come from everywhere at once, shaking the forest and splintering Jacob's skull with pain.

When the spinning mass of gray mist expanded and took him, he had the strange thought that although he certainly wasn't a cat, curiosity had killed him all the same.

CHAPTER 2

*

A FORMIDABLE FOE

Mistress Jane winked herself a thousand yards down the beach as soon as the first sign of trouble appeared with the strange gash into another reality. She'd been talking to an old man and his boy, just beginning to wonder if she dared try to step through and escape the Nonex, when the whole thing collapsed into a spinning vortex of gray mist. It was all gone now, the echoes of the detonating thunder that had accompanied its short but catastrophic end just now rumbling away to oblivion.

Interesting. That was all she could come up with to describe what she'd witnessed. Very, very interesting. She had the faintest spark of an idea as to what had actually happened. It gave her something to contemplate while trapped in her bizarre new world.

She turned away and resumed her long walk down the never-ending beach. The salty breeze coming off the ocean waters stirred her robe, and she wished she could take off her mask and feel the wind against her cheeks once more. But it hurt to remove the thing, and even if she did, the result would be disappointing. The nerves of her skin were mostly burned away, replaced by the particles of Chu's Dark Infinity weapon. She felt things in a different way now. Not unpleasant, necessarily, but not the same.

Chu. Reginald Chu. Why did she have to think of the man?

She'd spent the last week with him and that upstart boy Atticus Higginbottom. In the Nonex, there was nowhere else to go. They were on an island that sometimes seemed small and other times, gigantic. Nothing made sense in this place. You could begin eating a piece of fresh fruit and have the thing turn rotten before you finished. Fish flew through the air, and birds swam underwater. Trees shifted in the night—or what passed for night. It had been three days since the sun last set below the horizon. Everything here was wrong.

Not to mention the bad company. Chu was nasty—always grumpy, always degrading in how he spoke to her, always arrogant. Atticus was nice enough, considering the three of them were bitter enemies, one to another, but he had his own kind of arrogance, as if his innocence and goodwill were tangible things that floated around his body, pointing out how everyone else wasn't worthy to be in his presence. The boy made her ill. And angry. And thirsty for revenge.

But none of that mattered right now. None of it. They all had the same goal at the moment, and that was to get out of the blasted nowhere they currently called home.

A flicker of movement to her right caught her attention. She stopped just in time to see the boy come out from behind some trees, carrying some stray wood. He dumped it on the ground.

How sweet, she thought bitterly. *He's making a campfire. What a Boy Scout.* Same team or not, they all tried to keep their distance from one another as best they could.

When Atticus noticed her, a look of sheer disappointment painted his features. This both hurt Jane and made her angry.

"Where's Chu?" she asked, as though the boy were her servant and not her mortal enemy.

Atticus shrugged. "I don't know." He knelt on the ground and started arranging the logs in an orderly pyramid.

"You find some matches I don't know about?" Jane asked. "If you think I'm in the mood to help—"

The logs burst into flame, all of them. An instant bonfire.

Atticus stood up, gave her a glare. But then his look changed to guilt, as if it were against his nature to be mean. Then he smiled, which made Jane angrier.

"Altering the physical state of wood from a solid to a gas?" he asked with another shrug. "You think I can't do that by myself? Come on. That's as easy as lighting a match, Mistress Jane."

He didn't wait for a response, just turned and walked away, disappearing back into the woods.

Igniting fire. Such a simple thing, really. And yet, for some reason, it terrified her to see the boy do it without any obvious effort whatsoever. She flopped down onto the sand, staring at the waves as they lapped onto the beach, and tried to ignore the icy fear trickling through her veins.

Atticus—the boy known as Tick—was a foe to be reckoned with.

Jane had been sitting on the beach for hours, staring out at the wondrous ocean that wasn't really an ocean, when suddenly the horizon jumped up and down. The water turned from blue to green to black, then froze into ice, crackling; then it was hot and boiling. A fish popped out of the shifting water and spread its fins like wings, hovering a few seconds before exploding into a spray of rainbow-colored sparkles. Lightning shot down from a cloudless sky and hit the water, creating huge splashes of something dark and thick, like oil. She looked down at the sand, and within a matter of seconds, it had changed color three times.

Par for the course in this place that seemed beyond the realm of the physics she understood so well.

She'd just lifted her gaze back to the ocean when a thump of sound shook the air and the ground, a thunderclap that made her bounce off the sand. She threw out her arms for balance and searched the beach for any sign of what had happened.

The sound thumped again. Then again. The land around her shook, but this time didn't stop. The trees behind her trembled; several were uprooted and fell, crashing against each other. Dots of light fell from the sky, vanishing before they hit the ground. Farther down the beach, pillars of stone shot through the sand, rising up until it looked like they had their very own Stonehenge to explore. The ocean froze, then cracked into a million icy pieces, exploding upward a hundred feet, then falling again like a rain of crystal. The sand nearby swirled in little tornadoes, the funnels spinning faster and faster.

Suddenly Chu was by her side, having sprinted in from the shifting woods. He collapsed next to her when another jolt of sound and quaking shook the world.

"This is madness!" he shouted at her. "Things are becoming more and more unstable!"

Jane wanted to argue with him—that was always her instinct—but she knew he was right. First, the strange gash in the air earlier, peeking into another Reality. And now this, a sudden uptick in the strangeness that was the Nonex. She nodded at Chu.

The thumps of noise stopped. The land grew still. The pillars that had risen on the beach slowly sank back underground. The ocean liquefied, glistening and smooth. The small funnels of spinning sand stopped, collapsing with a dusty poof. All seemed still and quiet.

Thoughts and plans were forming inside Jane's head, but they weren't solid enough to describe. Like an epiphany in another language, the ideas still needed to be translated, but they were there all the same.

Reginald Chu had a look in his eyes that made her think his mind had spun in the same direction as hers.

"Together," he whispered, his voice still loud in the sudden silence. "If we can work together, then I think there's a way for both of us to be happy in the end."

CHAPTER 3

✳

ONE LAST TRY

I t's hot, Mom."

Lorena Higginbottom looked over at her daughter as they trampled through the woods. The girl did have a few strands of hair matted against her forehead, like squiggly little worms. "Well, the fall weather should be here soon."

"I'm so hot my *sweat* is sweating."

"That doesn't make sense, dear."

"I know."

They'd visited these woods in eastern Washington every day for the last week, stomping their way along the same path often enough that a solid trail was beginning to appear, making the journey a little easier.

Lorena had the straps of a duffel bag looped over her shoulder, its contents consisting of a single item. An extremely important, rare, expensive, incredibly-difficult-to-create item that she'd guard with her life, if necessary.

The item was long, solid, and heavy, with a brass shell lined with dials and switches. A Chi'karda Drive was housed inside it—a complex network of chips, wires, and nanotech that could literally alter reality itself.

It was a Barrier Wand.

And the only hope she had of finding her son.

"If it doesn't work today," Lisa said as she ducked under the low-hanging branch of an oak tree, "I think we should try something else."

"Can't argue with that," Lorena responded. "I wanted to do this without getting George and the others involved, but we might not have a choice."

The two of them stepped across the forest floor, *cricks* and *cracks* filling the air along with the pungent smells of pine needles and bark and something else that wavered between sweet and rotten. Sunlight broke through the canopy of leaves and sprinkled the ground with golden drops.

"What do you have against Master George anyway?" Lisa asked.

Lorena almost stopped walking, but she caught

herself and kept going. Did she really want to talk about her feelings toward the leader of the Realitants right now? They were so complicated. "Nothing at all," she finally said, a simple enough response.

"Come on, Mom. I know there's something. I'm not quite as stupid as Tick always says I am."

"Tick says no such thing!"

"Mom, answer the question." Lisa pushed her way past a small branch and seemed to make no effort to keep it from swinging back and smacking Lorena in the face.

"Ouch!"

"Sorry."

Lorena heard the girl snicker. "I'll get you back for that, young lady." She was glad her daughter couldn't see the sudden smile that sprang up, but it couldn't be helped. Lisa's playfulness was a welcome thing indeed.

"So . . . answer the question."

Lorena had no choice but to address the touchy subject. "As I said, I have nothing against that man whatsoever. If I did, not in a million years would I have let Atticus continue working for him and his merry group of heroes. It's just complicated."

"Then why haven't we contacted him? Why aren't we working together with him? He knows a lot more than we do!"

Lorena kept her doubts about that to herself. "I

may be out of practice, but I'm no dummy when it comes to the Realities, you know."

Lisa stopped and faced her mom. "I know, Mom, but don't you think we could figure this out a lot faster if we had their help?"

"Maybe." Lorena stepped closer to Lisa and reached out to grip the girl's shoulders. "But I have my reasons. Number one, George has a heart of gold, but he can be reckless when times get . . . tense. That's okay usually—but not when my son's life is on the line like this."

"And number two?"

Lorena gathered her thoughts for a second before answering. "The world's in shambles, Lisa. All the natural disasters, all the deaths, all the homeless and sick, all the damage. And who knows what kind of permanent damage the other Realities have experienced. George and the Realitants are going to have a lot on their plate, and to be honest, I wouldn't be able to blame them if Atticus wasn't their top priority."

"What? How can they—"

"He's one boy, Lisa! One life. The Realitants have to worry about billions of others."

"Then what are you saying?"

"I'm *saying* that even though George claims he's going to do whatever it takes to find out what happened to Atticus, I can't put my full trust and hope in that. We need to take it on ourselves to get this done. Do what *we* have to do, and let them do what *they* have to do."

Lisa pursed her lips, obviously considering it all for a long moment. "Maybe it helps that two groups are coming at it from different directions. Only one of us needs to find him."

"Bingo." Lorena did her best to smile, but for some reason, her heart couldn't make it feel genuine. Once again, speaking of the world and the trouble it was in had soured her mood; everything seemed worse since her son had vanished.

"So we go to the spot," Lisa said, "and we try again."

"Bingo times two."

"And if it doesn't work today, then we try something else."

"Bingo times three."

"Okay." Lisa turned around and started walking again.

As Lorena followed, she thought for the millionth time that she was crazy to involve Lisa in this quest. Yes, she was endangering yet another of her children, but she couldn't help it. Lisa was bright, and upbeat, and funny. Brave. And the girl loved her family as powerfully as Lorena did. She needed Lisa. Edgar—bless his heart—wasn't the right person to help her now. And someone had to be with little Kayla.

Lorena *needed* Lisa. Desperately. She couldn't do this alone. Lorena would just have to do whatever it took to keep the girl safe until they figured things out. Until Atticus was back together with them all.

~⌒⌐

They reached a clearing about twenty feet wide, their recent visits and footsteps and sit-downs having flattened the grass considerably. A circle of thick pines bordered the spot, the tree branches stretching to the sky far above. Lorena saw a squirrel scurry its way up one of the trees, dropping an acorn in its haste.

Lisa slipped off her backpack; she'd been in charge of the food because Lorena had to carry the heavy load of the Barrier Wand. They'd done this every day, and sharing a nice lunch put some cracks in the heavy dome of doom and gloom that hung over their mission. The two of them sat down in the middle of the clearing, facing each other.

"You want the turkey or the ham?" Lisa asked as she pulled out the sandwiches.

"Turkey. That ham's been doing something awful to my stomach."

"Thanks for sharing, Mom. My hunger just doubled."

"Sorry, dear."

They chomped through the meal, and then it was time to get down to business. Lorena unzipped the duffel bag and pulled out the hefty shaft of the Barrier Wand. The scant drifts of sunlight that filtered through the leaves glinted and winked off the shiny golden surface as she maneuvered the thing until she held it directly in front of her folded legs, its bottom end sunk into the debris of the forest floor. She looked past the Wand at Lisa.

"It's a thing of beauty, don't you think?"

Lisa shrugged. "Maybe the *first* time I saw it."

"Oh, I never tire of it. Maybe it's knowing the unimaginable power that's coiled up inside of it. I'm a scientist, and yet it still feels like magic to me."

"A cell phone would be magic if you showed it to somebody a hundred years ago."

Lorena felt a burst of pride at the statement. "Well said, Lisa, well said. Just like Arthur C. Clarke."

"Who?"

The pride bubble burst a bit. "Never mind."

"Let's do this thing."

"Yes. Let's do. I'm going to crank up the Chi'karda Drive to its highest level. We've got nothing to lose."

Lisa didn't answer right away, and Lorena saw a flicker of deep concern in the girl's eyes.

"Don't worry, Lisa. I don't think it can hurt us. I'm more worried about it doing damage to the Wand itself."

Lorena didn't know if that was the total truth, but it was close enough without planting even more worry inside her daughter.

"Go for it, then."

Lorena spent a minute or two moving the dials and switches of the Wand, adjusting and flipping and turning each one until she was satisfied that its power was at maximum and that it was locked onto Atticus's last known nanolocator readings.

She eyed Lisa. "This is it. If it doesn't pull in that boy now, it never will. If you hear a loud buzz in your head or feel like your fingers might fall off, don't be alarmed."

"Of course not." The slightest roll of Lisa's eyes made her look half bored and half amused, but Lorena knew that fear still lurked behind it all.

"Want a countdown?"

"Mom!"

"Okay, okay. Here we go." She reached for the button on the top of the Wand and pushed. The click was surprisingly loud, as if the entire forest and all its creatures had quieted at the same moment.

Nothing happened. At first. Then a low hum seemed to rise up out of the ground, along with a vibration that tickled Lorena's legs, made her shift and scratch at the underside of her thighs. The noise rose in volume and depth, like giant tuning forks and gongs had been struck, the sound ringing all around them. Lorena's eardrums rattled, and a pain cinched its way down her spine.

The world around them exploded into a swirl of gray mist and terrible, thunderous noise.

CHAPTER 4

✳

CONCERNS

Master George stood at the head of the table. He and the other Realitants were in the conference room of the Grand Canyon complex. George hadn't sat down since the meeting began, and he didn't know if he could. Sitting seemed like such a casual gesture, something done for rest and relaxation. How could he do that when the world—the *worlds*—were in such utter chaos?

"Been runnin' our lips for thirty minutes, we 'ave," Mothball was saying. Her stern expression made George incredibly sad. She hadn't smiled since Master Atticus had winked from existence. "And still not a fla-min' thing done. Need to make some decisions, we do."

"Darn tootin' right," Sally added, the burly lumber-jack of a man also looking gruffer than usual. "Get dem plans a'yorn hoppin' so we can quit gabbin' at each other. I'm downright sick of these here chat-and-chews."

Now it was Rutger's turn to speak up. "Look, you bunch of grumpy fusses—"

"That's enough," George interrupted. He hadn't needed to say it loudly or harshly. His little friend of so many years cut off and didn't argue. "Thank you. Just let me *think* for a second."

He looked around the room at Sato, Paul, and Sofia—the only other Realitants in attendance. Those three looked like youngsters who'd been thrown into the horrors of life far too early. And like people who'd lost a dear friend. Both of which were true. They sat slumped over, staring at the table, their faces turned toward the ground.

The other Realitants—people he'd worked with for countless years—couldn't afford to come to the meeting. They had too many problems to deal with in their own areas of responsibility. For now, this small group was all George had.

"Listen to me," George finally said. "I know that Master Atticus is on all of our minds. His . . . loss has put us on edge, and I don't believe we've said one nice thing to each other since he disappeared. But the world is in crisis, and we *must* meet our responsibilities. There are things we can do to help."

To say the world was in crisis was the understatement of the year. When Mistress Jane tried to sever the Fifth Reality with her new tool of dark matter, it had sent ripples of destruction throughout the universe, almost destroying it. Atticus seemed to have saved the day—or at least delayed the ultimate end—but the aftershocks were devastating.

Tornadoes, earthquakes, fires. Everywhere. Millions of people dead. The governments of the world were desperately trying to keep things under control and reach out to the hungry and wounded scattered all over.

Paul cleared his throat, and everyone looked at him. But before he spoke, his expression melted into something full of misery, and he sank back into his seat. Sofia reached out and squeezed his shoulder.

"Master Paul," George began, but he found himself empty of words. He suddenly lost every ounce of leadership he'd ever had in his bones. Despair threatened to swallow him whole.

Sato—who was usually rather quiet—suddenly shot to his feet and slammed a fist down on the table. "Snap out of it!" he yelled. "We all need to snap out of it! Quit moping around like babies and start acting like Realitants. If Tick were here, he'd be ashamed of us."

He sat down, but his eyes burned as he gazed at each Realitant around him in turn. "I've got an army. The Fifth will do whatever they're asked. Just say the word, and we can get started."

George realized he was staring at the boy, transfixed. A spring of encouragement welled up inside him. "Thank you, Master Sato. I think we'd all agree that we needed that."

"Just make a decision. Do something. Or we'll go crazy."

George nodded then straightened his posture, his strength returning. "You're quite right, Sato. Quite right. Enough of our talk. Let's go around the room and make assignments. It is indeed time to get to work. If something comes up that seems more important, then we'll change those plans, but getting to work is our number one priority. Mothball, you first."

The giant of a lady looked as if a little bit of life had been breathed back into her as well. "Alright, then. I'll start winkin' me way from one end to the other— not just in Reality Prime but all of 'em. Start makin' reports and such. We don't know much, now do we? Not with the communications so bloomin' shot."

"Excellent idea," George said. "We need to determine exactly what's happening or we'll never know what direction to take in the long run."

"Your middle name Danger all a sudden?" Sally cut

in with his booming voice. "You plan to hightail it this way and that all by your lonesome, do ya? Not on my tickety-tock watch, you ain't. I'll go with Mothball."

George loved the idea. "Perfect. Plans settled for two of us. Rutger, I think we both know what you need to do."

The fat little ball of a man shifted in his seat. "Um, well, I'd be happy to go on an adventure with my fine two friends, but . . . I seemed to have sprained my . . . elbow. Yes, yes, it's giving me quite the fits lately . . ."

"Master Rutger, please." George struggled to keep from laughing. "We all know very well that we need you here. Our instruments that survived the disasters have been reporting strange anomalies across the Realities. We need your keen researching mind devoted to solving that puzzle."

Visible relief washed over Rutger's features, but he tried to hide it with his words. "Oh, well, I guess you're right, then. Pity. I would've gladly risked further injury to my elbow to help Mothball and Sally."

"I have no doubt of it."

"Didn't know you could even see your elbow," Mothball muttered. "What with all that natural padding."

"Well, at least mine don't jut out like pelican beaks!" Rutger countered. "Try gaining a pound or two so we quit thinking a skeleton rose up from the dead to scare the willies out of us."

"Well, I would, now wouldn't I, if you bloody let us have a bite or two at supper before you gobbled it all down that fat neck of yours."

"Ah," George said through a sigh. "This is more like it. If you two are going at it with each other, then at least *something* is right in the world."

"What about us?" Sofia asked. It was the first time she'd spoken since the meeting began, and her soft voice was sad but strong. These new Realitants had life in them yet. "Our families are fine—we've checked on them, visited them—so we can do whatever you need us to do now."

"Yeah," Paul added, a little more spirit in his face too. "I can't sit around this place one more second, listening to Rutger brag about his cooking and telling stupid jokes."

George looked at Sato. "And you?"

The boy folded his arms across his chest. "I said I'm ready. And my army is too."

"Okay, then." George thought a moment. There were countless things that needed to be done throughout the Realities. Where to start? "Sato, I want you to go back to the Thirteenth Reality and destroy the remaining creatures that Jane manufactured at the Factory. We need to make sure that world is safe and back to the way it was meant to be."

"Done," Sato said immediately, without the slightest hint of fear.

"And . . . us?" Paul asked.

George put his hands on the table and leaned forward. "You two are going to pay a visit to a very old friend of mine. She lives in the Third Reality, and we can only hope that she doesn't eat you for supper when you arrive."

CHAPTER 5

✳

SQUISHY GRASS

Lisa screamed when it happened, but she couldn't hear her voice over the terrible sounds of thunder that pounded the air like detonating bombs. One second she'd been sitting in the forest, looking at her mom and the Barrier Wand, hearing a hum and feeling vibrations in her legs. The next, she'd been whipped into a tornado of swirling gray air, spinning, the world tilting all around her. The noises pounding her skull. She tried to find her mom—at least *see* her—but there was nothing. Only a gray whirlpool of smoke.

And then it ended. Abruptly.

Lisa's body slammed onto soft, squishy ground.

She immediately felt moisture seeping through her clothes and jumped to her feet—which was a bad idea. Her mind was still recovering from whatever she'd just been through and dizziness twirled inside of her until she fell right back down. She was lying on a huge field of grass, saturated with rain. Heavy clouds hung in the sky above her, making the day seem dark.

Her mom was close, the Barrier Wand in her lap. She sat up and stared at Lisa, dazed.

"What . . . ?" Lisa began.

"I have no idea," her mom replied. "All I did was try to latch on to Atticus's nanolocator and pull him in. It shouldn't have sent *us* somewhere else."

"Well, unless we went back in time to before trees grew in Deer Park, it sent us *somewhere*. We were sitting in the woods about three minutes ago."

Lisa hated the feeling of the wet grass soaking her pants, so she tried standing again, this time much slower. Her legs wobbled a bit, and the endless sea of grass tilted a few times, but soon she was steady.

She turned in a slow circle, taking in the view of the place to which they'd been winked. Super green grass stretched in every direction, running down a slope toward a stream that splashed and sparkled as it cut across a rocky bed. On the other side of the stream, trees dotted the land, growing thicker and taller until

543

they became a huge forest. There was no sign of civilization anywhere.

"Mom?"

"Yeah?"

"Where in the world are we?"

Three hours of searching didn't answer that question.

They walked together to the stream, crossed over at a narrow spot where large rocks jutted out of the rushing waters, then explored the other side. They eventually made their way to where the trees thickened into a dark, ominous forest. They'd found no clues or signs of life—human, anyway—and when they stood at the wall of pines and oaks, it was almost as if they were stopped by an invisible barrier.

"Why can't I get myself to go any farther?" Lisa asked.

Her mom's answer didn't help. "Because we're in a strange land, and there might be hideous monsters in there."

"Good point. Let's just walk around the edge of it; maybe we'll stumble across something eventually."

"As good a plan as any."

They set off, Lisa right behind her mom, who

still hefted the golden rod of the Barrier Wand in her hands.

"Tell me more about the old days," Lisa said. The clouds still churned above, dark and heavy, but it had yet to rain again. At least the air was nice and cool.

"The old days?" her mom repeated.

"Yeah. You used to be a Realitant. How'd you go from that to being a stay-at-home mom? Seems kind of lame."

"Lame? You wish you had a different woman stomping around the house telling you what to do?"

Lisa snickered at the image. "No, you're way too good at it. It's just . . . being a Realitant seems so cool and adventurous. What happened to make you give it up?"

The land started to rise up, and the walk was getting a little harder. Lisa saw the crest of the rise a few hundred feet ahead. She hoped they'd see something there. Something helpful. Her mom still hadn't answered.

"You awake up there?" she asked her.

"Oh, I'm awake. I'm just thinking about your question. It's more complicated than you know. It's making me remember a lot of things, and I'm not even sure where to start explaining."

"How'd you join them? How'd they recruit you?"

Her mom laughed softly. "It wasn't much different

from how they recruited Atticus. Some letters, clues, and riddles. It was kind of easy, actually."

"How long were you a member?"

"About four years, maybe a little longer. It wasn't all the exciting adventure you think it was—and nothing like what our poor boy has gone through—except for . . ." She trailed off, and there was something dark in her words, like the storm that brewed far above them.

Lisa pushed her. "Except for what?"

"I wasn't actually there, but I was still technically a Realitant when . . . when Sato's parents were killed. Mistress Jane had been getting more and more suspicious. Acting weird. And it all came to a head that night, when she started using the powers she'd stolen from the Thirteenth. She crossed a line, and Sato's mom and dad paid the price for standing up to it. Nearly all of them there that night did."

"What happened?"

"Jane burned that poor boy's parents to death." She said it so simply, but the words were horrible enough. "I didn't know the world could be so evil. I wanted out. I'm ashamed in many ways—for abandoning the Realitants, abandoning my friends—but I don't regret it. There's a difference, you know. I chose my family, and I've never once regretted that."

Lisa felt guilty, like she'd stirred up feelings her

mom didn't deserve to have. "Well, Tick and I are glad you did. And think about it—if you hadn't done such a good job of raising him, he would've been a stinky Realitant instead of a *good* Realitant, and he wouldn't have saved the world. See? Makes perfect sense."

"You're a sweet little thing," her mom replied.

"Yeah, I know. I've gotta have *some* way of making sure I stay your favorite."

They reached a sudden rise in the slope that was steeper than before, which made Lisa feel even stronger that some kind of revelation waited on the other side.

She trotted ahead to pull even with her mom, who hadn't slowed a bit. "We better be careful," she whispered. "There might be something over this hill that we don't want to see us."

Her mom nodded. "You've got the caution of a Realitant. Maybe old George will make you one after we save Atticus and bring him home."

"Maybe. Come on."

Lisa dropped to her knees and started crawling up the steep rise. Her mom crawled right next to her, holding the Barrier Wand awkwardly on her shoulder.

"You want me to take a turn with that?" Lisa asked.

"No, thanks. I made this one, and I want to keep it nice and close right now."

"When did you make it?"

"I'll tell you later."

They reached the top of the hill, where the land flattened for a couple of feet then dropped again, plummeting down another slope to the land beyond. When she saw what awaited them, Lisa forgot she was supposed to be careful, and she poked her head up, gawking so that anyone within miles could see her if they looked hard enough.

In the middle of a flat plain, there was a castle. Half of it had been destroyed, with stone and rock and wood collapsed in heaps around the edges of the destruction. Black figures crawled over the ruins like ants.

"What *are* those things?" Lisa whispered.

Her mom answered in a deadened voice. "Creatures of the Thirteenth Reality. Creatures of Mistress Jane. Just as Atticus described them." She turned to Lisa, her face pale. "How did we end up *here*?"

CHAPTER 6

✳

POOR MR. CHU

Tick sat on a rock and stared at the ocean.

Though it wasn't any normal ocean. The color of it changed about every three minutes, going from blackish-blue to red to orange, morphing in waves as though someone flew along the surface, spilling huge buckets of food coloring. Fish leaped out of the waters, but sometimes land animals did as well. Deer. Lions. Elephants.

The Nonex made no sense whatsoever. And things seemed to be growing even more unstable lately, sharp upticks in the madness. Like the thumping sound and earthquake attack of the day before. It was all a mixed soup for the senses, and it was beginning to make Tick want to hit somebody. Namely a grumpy, arrogant man named Reginald Chu.

Tick hated the man. Far more than he hated Mistress Jane, for whom he still felt an enormous amount of guilt—he'd scarred the woman for life, after all. And despite her evil ways, she'd shown moments where she doubted the path she'd chosen. If anything, Tick had driven her more toward the darkness.

But Chu was different. The man seemed crazy, and crazy wasn't an excuse for being bad. Every single thing he said or did pointed to one thing for him—power. Dominating others. Ruling. Just the other night, the three of them had been sitting around a fire, talking about theories on how they could make it back to Reality Prime. The conversation hadn't lasted ten minutes before Chu went off about how they needed to hurry, take some risks, because he might be losing his stranglehold on the Fourth Reality. With all the destruction and chaos happening, he feared someone else might be trying to take over what had once been his.

Tick had stared him in the eyes and told him to shut up. And Chu did. Which made Tick feel like king of the world, at least for a little while.

Jane and Chu were scared of him; Tick had no doubt about that. He'd shown them that he had more control of his powers over Reality and quantum physics—lifting firewood, igniting fires, making the sand leap into the air and swirl into shapes—than ever before. One time, as a joke, he levitated Chu, spinning him in a circle a few times. Even Jane had laughed, and when Chu came crashing back to the ground with a loud flump and a grunt, Tick had expected the man to be enraged. But instead, he simply stood up, brushed himself off, and told Tick he hoped the boy would come work for him some day, that a boy with such power was destined to do great things.

That was Chu, though. Always thinking about power. Always planning his next step to world domination. What a big, fat jerk. Tick didn't like the feeling that such hatred gave him—like his insides were rotting—but he couldn't help it.

There was the crack of a broken twig in the woods behind Tick. He turned to see Chu leaning out from behind a tree, staring at him.

"That's kind of creepy," Tick said. "Spying on a little boy like that."

"Spying?" Chu replied. "What exactly am I spying on? You sitting like a frog on a log, staring at nothing? We're wasting time. Jane agrees with me."

Chu walked out of the woods and approached Tick, coming to stand next to him. Tick didn't bother standing up or offering to slide over for the man to sit down.

"What exactly would you want me to be doing right now?" Tick asked him, returning his gaze to the ocean, which had turned a pinkish color. "Building us a log cabin so we'll have a place to mope about while we're stuck here?"

"We need your power, and you know it. Jane is willing to take some risks. You should be too. We're all getting a little crazier with every passing day. We need to *do* something!" The man's voice had risen with each word until he was shouting.

Tick stood up and faced him. "I know. We'll do it when I'm ready. I trust my instincts a lot more than I do your mad desire to get back and stomp on people. *Chill*. Please."

Chu looked utterly stunned, and it was a beautiful thing to see. Tick had to hold back the smile that wanted to leap across his face. He almost felt sorry for Chu, and decided to throw him a bone, out of guilt.

"Tomorrow," he said, sitting back down. "We'll try something tomorrow."

CHAPTER 7

TRICKS ON THE BEACH

Things had changed for Tick when he battled Mistress Jane outside the Factory in the Thirteenth Reality. They'd changed drastically.

He'd been driven by pure and absolute desperation. He'd done what he needed to do for the Haunce, healing the damage done by Jane that would've ended Reality and the universe. And when he'd had to fight Jane afterwards, he'd known more than ever that death was his reward if he messed up. Though maybe he'd learned some things from the Haunce that he hadn't realized.

When he and Mistress Jane were going at each other like two wizards settling a centuries-old spat,

Tick's mind had been focused on his Chi'karda like never before, channeling it, funneling it, *understanding* it. He didn't really know how he knew—he could never sit down and write a book about it or explain it to someone—it was like walking or running or breathing. Things just clicked, and suddenly he *knew* how to do it. His body and instincts and mind all worked together to use the Chi'karda and manipulate the world of quantum physics. He felt like a magician. A magician of science.

And it was *fun*.

Now it was early the next day, when he'd promised Chu they'd try to get out of the Nonex, and Tick had spent the morning out on the beach, practicing his new abilities. He had stacked three logs vertically, end to end, pointing toward the sky. He used his mind and pushed out with his senses, touching the strings and pulleys of the unseen particles of science. Carefully, he moved one, and then another one. The tower stood thirty or forty feet in the air.

"Impressive," Chu said. "Really. Can we get on with it and do something that actually matters now?"

Tick suddenly had an image pop in his head of Chu's giant mountain palace, and how bad things had gone there. That was where Tick had hurt Jane, where he had almost died. Sofia had risked her life to save him. Remembering it again made Tick angry.

He shifted his thoughts and pushed his Chi'karda. The stacked logs flew through the air and shot toward Chu like spears. He cried out and started to run, but Tick was one step ahead of him, turning the logs vertical again and slamming them into the ground in a circle around Chu. He was in a prison, the logs thick enough and close enough together that he couldn't squeeze between them.

"Stop acting like a child!" Chu screamed, facing Tick with rage burned into his expression. "Take these things down! Now!"

Tick looked over at Jane, whose red mask had tilted up slightly in a smile. Her yellow robe and hood stirred in the slight breeze of the day, and images of her past deeds popped into Tick's mind as well. He almost used his Chi'karda to throw some things at her, too, but remembered that she could fight back.

Maybe it *was* time for Tick to quit acting like a brat. He didn't feel like himself lately. They needed to get out of the Nonex. Not just for his own life, but so he could see what was going on back at home. His family and friends could be in danger, maybe even dead. The thought made his heart sink. He'd already tried winking a message to them, but it didn't work.

"Atticus," Chu said, obviously trying to remain calm. "Please. I don't want to interfere with your powers. I'm not an idiot. But I know you want to get out of this place just as much as I do. I can't go back and change the past, but—"

"Shut up!" Tick yelled. He didn't know where all this anger was coming from. "I don't want to hear any lame apologies from you. We all know you're planning to go right back to doing what you do if we get back to the Realities. Well, guess what? I'm not going to let you. So keep that in mind."

Before Chu could respond, Tick exploded the logs, breaking down their substance into millions of tiny splinters and swirling them away in a cloud of wooden mist. He purposefully let a few splinters nick Chu in the face and arms. The man cried out again and gingerly touched the sore spots. Guilt immediately racked Tick, mixed with a little bit of satisfaction.

"Tick," Mistress Jane began in her scratchy, painful voice. "Preach all you want about what we've done in our past. But look at yourself. You're heading down the same road. Maybe you should have waited until you could control your power before you started judging others. Power is a . . . powerful thing. I don't know how else to put it."

Her words made Tick even angrier. "Don't you dare say that. I would never—*never*—use my power to hurt other people like you have."

Jane's mask smiled broadly. "Then what did you just do to Reginald?"

Tick looked sharply at the man, who had several spots of blood on his face and arms. He wanted to get defensive, explain that he was just giving Chu some of his own medicine, but a small part of him knew that Jane was right. No one was born thinking they'd rule the world someday. It developed in baby steps, a slippery slope. He had to be careful.

"He deserves every bad thing that could ever happen to him," Tick said, defiant. "But I won't do something like that again. I promise."

"Yeah, right," Chu responded, glaring at him. "You just wait, kid. Wait until you start to feel the joy of being stronger than someone else. You'll be working beside me before you turn twenty years old. That's a guarantee."

Tick looked at him without answering.

"Let's get to work," Jane said. "Nothing matters if we can't get back to the real world."

Tick felt a little lost right then. A little confused. And scared at what might happen when they started messing with Reality on a big scale. He decided to set everything aside and quit thinking for a while. They had nothing to lose, and he could deal with his feelings about what Jane had said later.

"Okay." Tick pointed down the beach at the campfire that had become their central meeting spot. "Let's go sit down."

"And we're not standing up again until we're in a different Reality," Chu said as he started walking that way. "I can't stand one more day in this place."

Tick and Jane exchanged a glance. She said nothing, her mask melting into a blank expression, and Tick wondered what was going on inside her head. He shrugged, and then the two of them followed Chu to the campfire.

They sat on the stumpy logs they'd brought out on the first day, circling the small flames that spit and hissed as they burned. The fire smelled good, and Tick remembered campouts with his family. The memory hurt his heart, and he swore to do just as Chu had said. They needed to get out of the Nonex.

"We've talked for hours about every theory in the book," Chu said. "Time to put up or shut up, as they say. What are we going to try?"

Tick had listened to every conversation they'd had in the Nonex, and he understood most of them. Master George had made him study pretty much every science book ever written. But none of it seemed to matter right then. The only thing he trusted was his instinct.

He realized Jane was talking, but he'd completely tuned out. Feeling a sudden boldness and certainty, he interrupted her.

"I know what we need to do."

CHAPTER 8

ONE QUESTION

Paul had been waiting for this day for a long time. A mission for the Realitants for which he was in charge. Of course, Sofia probably thought *she* was the boss, and he'd let her keep thinking that, but he knew the truth.

This was Paul's time.

Master George had ushered them into his little office, where they sat on a small couch, and he was perched on a wooden chair with his Barrier Wand balanced on top of his lap. He had a grave look on his face, which was business as usual since the whole world had fallen into chaos.

"Are you both ready?" the old man asked.

Paul nodded.

Sofia cleared her throat. "Of course we are. But you haven't really told us much about what we're supposed to do."

Their fearless leader pursed his lips, looking as if he had a whole bunch of nasty thoughts in his head that he didn't want to share. "The Third Reality is one we haven't charted very well, and, given recent events, we've lost all other means of communication with the Realitant we originally sent there. She can be quite . . . difficult, and she's made it clear that supervising the Third Reality is her job and her job alone. I need you to find her and ask her a very important question."

"You said something about her wanting to eat us," Paul said. "This chick a wolverine or something?"

"No, no, no," Master George grumbled. "And I highly suggest you not say such things to her when you meet. And most certainly, I recommend you not call her a . . . what did you say? A chick?"

Paul shrugged. He wasn't worried—he'd have this lady cooling her jets with some of his simple charm and good looks. No biggie.

"I think I'll do the talking," Sofia muttered. "Don't worry."

"Her name is Gretel," Master George continued. "The woman has a nasty temper, the worst I've ever seen. She makes Mistress Jane look like a princess on a pony. And she's been a bit . . . at odds with me for some time now. But she's brilliant, and I plan to send you with full means to communicate back to me through your nanolocators. Your first task is to reach her. Make sure she is calm. And then ask the question."

Paul thought the whole mission seemed a little strange. "What's this big question we're supposed to ask?"

Their leader hefted the Barrier Wand in his hands and studied it, though his gaze was distant, as though he was trying to stall for time.

"Well?" Paul pushed.

"You may not understand it, but I need you to say these exact words to her. Are you ready? Though short, I've taken the liberty of writing it down on pieces of paper I've slipped into your packs."

"Sheesh," Paul said. "Just spill it already."

"Here it is," the man said, looking very serious indeed. "Six words: *May I please use your bathroom?*"

Paul was still snickering about the ridiculous question when the old man winked them to the Third Reality. Master George had refused to explain any further, saying that those six words were all they needed to know. They'd be sent to a place near a path. Follow the path. Find a house. Knock on the door. Ask the question: "May I please use your bathroom?"

Easy peasy.

Well, worst-case scenario, they'd be able to utilize the facilities before heading back.

Paul and Sofia stood on a soggy, muddy trail that cut ahead of them through marshland and swamp. The air was muggy and seemed to stick in Paul's lungs when he breathed, and the heat made it worse. They'd only been there for half a minute, and he was already sweating head to toe.

Trees rose up out of the black waters of the swamp, moss and vines hanging from their branches. There were the sounds of frogs and crickets and a million other bugs and creatures, and a fragrance that was an inch short of disgusting. Rotten eggs and burnt toast.

"Let me get this straight," Paul said. "This lady could live pretty much anywhere in the thirteen Realities, and she chose to live here?"

Sofia had her annoyed look set firmly on her face. "Do you even listen when Master George talks? He said that she was sent here to study this Reality. That's why she lives here."

"And this whole world is a swamp? I'm pretty sure they have a mountain or two somewhere. A sweet forest dig. A *desert* would be better than this."

"I just hope Master George didn't send us here so we'd be out of the way."

Paul snorted. "You kidding? He probably figured we'd drunk a ton of water, so here we are—waiting to ask if we can use this lady's bathroom."

"I wonder who died here, or how many," was Sofia's reply.

Sometimes she chose to ignore his comments as her best line of defense. Paul didn't mind. "Maybe there was a battle or something. It sure isn't a graveyard."

"It looks like the path starts here and goes in that direction." She pointed down the long trail, which wound its way through the nasty, steaming marshland.

"I bet we get bitten by mosquitos the size of my dad's truck."

"Probably."

"We'll get malaria and die."

"Probably."

"Okay. Let's go."

They reached Gretel's house about ten minutes later.

It was the exact kind of place Paul expected would be in the middle of a swamp. Old, moss-covered wood, the sideboards of the small cottage warped from too much moisture. Faded, worn paint that used to be white. A screen door that was half off its hinges. A porch that looked like it was about to collapse. The biggest trees they'd seen yet surrounded the place.

Paul had sworn to himself that he wouldn't make any Hansel and Gretel jokes since he'd first heard the woman's name from Master George, but he couldn't resist.

"We forgot to drop pieces of bread on our way here."

Sofia gave him a fake courtesy laugh. "I was waiting for that."

"Comedy never works when it's obvious."

Sofia flashed him a smile that *wasn't* fake, and Paul broke out in goose bumps. He hoped she couldn't tell. He started walking toward the porch to hide it.

When he reached the steps of the porch, he couldn't help but hesitate. It seemed as if their feet would crash right through if they dared take one step on the old, rotten boards. But before he could take that first step, the front door tore open with a bang. The screen that had barely been hanging on fell off completely. It clanged against the porch, bent and torn.

An old, old woman stood in the doorway, a huge knife in one hand and a pistol in the other. Paul yelped and backed away. He ran into Sofia, and they both collapsed to the soggy ground.

Gretel moved forward, the boards creaking under

her feet. She had gray hair springing in all directions, a face as wrinkled as a newborn pup, and a tattered dress that looked as if it hadn't been washed in years. But her body seemed strong, solid. Especially the fingers gripped around those two weapons.

"How dare old Georgy Porgy send two *rats* here to nibble on my cheese," she said, her voice low but somehow full of venom. "I told him what would happen if he did that. I sure did. Death, true and true."

The old lady lifted her pistol and aimed it at Paul's face.

CHAPTER 9

✳

A DUSTY ROAD

Whoa! Whoa! Whoa!" Paul shouted, holding his hands up as he got to his feet. Sofia did the same next to him. "You haven't heard why we came yet!"

Gretel cocked the old silver pistol and took a step forward. She kept the barrel pointed directly at Paul. "Don't need hearing your nonsense, boy. I'm here for a reason, and that reason is more important than two pipsqueak babies begging for their lives on my lawn."

Paul's immediate instinct was to tell her she was crazy for calling the mud and weeds on which they stood a lawn. Luckily, Sofia spoke up before he could, as calm and collected as a sheriff in an old Western movie.

"You want to shoot us, Gretel? Go right ahead. But you'll need to answer our question before you do."

Her words took the lady aback a little, as it did Paul. Was this really the time to ask if they could use her bathroom? Then again, Paul thought it was the dumbest thing he'd ever heard come out of George's mouth anyway.

"A question, you say?" Gretel responded. "You say you have a question for me?"

"That's right," Sofia said. "Just one. May I please use your bathroom?"

The old woman swung her gun away from Paul and pointed it off somewhere in the distance. She pulled the trigger, and a boom rocked the air and smoke puffed up from the gun. Gretel spun the pistol on her finger like a cowboy and smiled, her teeth looking like they'd chewed one too many chicken bones throughout the years.

"Yes, you may, my darling," she said. "Yes, you may. Do come in."

Sofia glanced back at Paul, who shrugged. They both headed up the steps of the rickety old porch.

Mothball had always prided herself on being a nice, genuine person who could see the good in everyone.

Yes, she loved to tease and rib, but deep down she had a heart of gold, soft and snuggly and warm. At least, that's what she liked to think.

But Sally irritated the living jeepers out of her. How in the bloody tarnations had she ended up with him on this mission? The man was like a walking bullhorn, he was.

"So, Miss Purty Legs," he said as they walked down a long country road in the Twelfth Reality. "Whatcha thinkin' this old bag of cornfeed's gonna help us with?"

"Don't know as yet," she replied. "Just hopin' I can hear a bloody word that comes out of his mouth over your yappin' tongue. No offense, of course."

Sally bellowed his deep, booming laugh. "None taken, missy. None taken. You should be used to yappin' after hanging out with that friend a'yorn. Rutger could talk the ear off an elephant."

Mothball couldn't help it—she laughed too. Sally always knew how to make her smile eventually. "The wee little fat man can talk, no doubt about it."

"Anyhoo, why we startin' with this farm boy again?"

Though she could swear she'd already explained this to him, Mothball did so again. "He's not really a Realitant, but he's a friend of ours. Lives out in the boonies so as he can keep tabs better without worryin' over communications and such. Watches over the world, he does. Has every satellite and radio and cell service you can dream up in this quaint little Reality. We pay him right nicely, too. He'll know what the goings-on are about."

"Goings-on are about?" Sally repeated. "What the heckamajibber does that mean?"

"We need to find what's the trouble here. We're on a research mission, silly bones. Clean out them bloody ears, would ya? Master George explained it all right nicely. Gathering information, we are."

"Well, I sho 'nuff knew that! I'm just tryin' to figger out how you people speak in them fancy lands a'yorn."

"I know the feeling," Mothball muttered under her breath.

They reached a dusty old mailbox on the side of the road with the word "Tanner" printed on the side in faded black letters. A long, gravel driveway cut through a cornfield before disappearing into a grove of trees about a half a mile away.

"Here we are," Mothball said. "He's waiting for us I 'spect."

Thankfully Sally didn't say another word as they started walking down the long driveway.

Rutger sat in front of his huge screen, reviewing all the data he'd gathered from the instruments spread throughout the Realities. The ones that had survived the destruction, anyway.

He missed Mothball.

Yes, she was a tall sack of bones who took every chance she got to make fun of him. But she was also his best friend, and he hated thinking of her out there without him, especially considering how dangerous things had become. A world suffering from chaos that you *can't* help breeds chaos that you *can*. The thieves and looters and murderers would be out in full force now that the police, firemen, and other authorities were occupied with search and rescue.

Of course, Mothball was a tough old bear. She'd be fine.

He began scrolling through the data—everything from weather reports to measurements of quantum anomalies in atmosphere particle waves. The data was haywire, still settling from the massive disruptions caused by that red-faced Mistress Jane and her attempt to sever the Fifth Reality from existence. What a disaster that had been, saved only by the inexplicable powers of Master Tick. However, it seemed as if saving the universe from one final and all-ending catastrophe had created lots of smaller ones.

Something caught his eye.

He zoomed in to take a look at one of the measuring stations located in an old forest in the Third Reality; a box of instruments had been left there almost a decade ago. There'd been an absolute *flurry* of activity there just a couple of days earlier, spiking the Chi'karda levels through the roof. And then it had ended abruptly, going from immeasurably high to zero in an instant. Rutger read through it all, trying his best to interpret what it could mean.

He noticed that the information had an attachment: a photograph. Many of the instrument boxes had cameras installed nearby, but Rutger was surprised to see that something had been taken and sent before whatever had happened to end the data flow. The box had to have been destroyed eventually.

He was so anxious that his fat fingers hit the wrong key twice, but he finally opened up the attached picture.

There were trees—lots of them. And down the middle of the photo, a gash, as if someone had painted over the forest scene with an image of a beach. And on that beach was Mistress Jane, looking toward the camera with her menacing red mask. Over her shoulder, standing a ways behind her in the sand, was another figure.

Rutger quickly zoomed in, leaning forward to get a better look. His gasp echoed throughout the entire Realitant headquarters.

It was Tick.

CHAPTER 10

✳

PROBING

The air around Tick hummed.

He, Chu, and Mistress Jane had been holding hands for more than an hour, eyes closed, the campfire slowly dying. Tick could barely hear the last flickers of its flames over the thrumming sound that came from the Chi'karda that burned between the three linked humans. Anyone who might have observed the group from afar would have seen a massive cloud of tiny orange lights, a fiery mist that churned and boiled around them.

Chu, of course, had no power whatsoever over the realm of quantum physics. He had never known any kind of power unless it was manufactured with technology. But Tick and Jane were a different story. They both had control over the mysterious force that ruled all existence—Jane, because she'd been forever melded with the largest Barrier Wand ever created, and Tick, because of reasons no one had quite figured out yet. Master George had merely said he was on to something that might explain it and that it involved soulikens.

But they'd never really had a chance to talk about it, had they?

Tick couldn't allow his mind to wander. He pushed away the thoughts trying to barrel their way in and focused on the task at hand. Escaping the Nonex.

Jane and Chu had agreed to his plan without argument. It seemed they both had grown desperate to get out and were willing to rely on Tick's idea. He had, after all, worked directly with the Haunce and saved the entire universe.

And that's what Tick was banking on. Mistress Jane had channeled her Chi'karda—every last drop that she could muster—into Tick for him to use as he needed. Tick had gathered it in, mixing it with his own until he had more of the natural force around him—and within him—than any human should be able to endure. A few weeks ago it would've killed him instantly.

But he had learned so much.

The Chi'karda raged. It was pure power, collected into one place like a newborn star ready to explode with heat and energy. But Tick kept it at bay, probed it, felt it, soothed it in some way. The feel of it was pure and clean, like an inferno burning inside his chest.

He didn't know exactly what he was looking for, but he had a good idea. A sense more than anything. Tick felt like someone was standing right behind him, just inches away. His eyes couldn't see them, but he knew someone was there all the same.

The Haunce had taught him a valuable lesson. Reality spoke to you in interesting ways—not in the formulas and equations of mathematicians and scientists, nor in the dry, lengthy descriptions found in dusty old textbooks. Reality was on another level altogether, at one with our minds. It spoke to you in the best way your own self can speak back. And that's what Tick wanted as he probed things he didn't understand with the power of Chi'karda.

He was looking for a riddle.

Lorena Higginbottom knew her stuff.

She'd suspected from the very second they'd appeared on that rain-slicked grass that her Barrier Wand had winked her and Lisa into the Thirteenth Reality. Something about the smell and feel of the place had been her first clue. The big forest—with no signs of technology or civilization around—had been her next clue. And then, when they'd stumbled up to the top of that ridge and had seen Mistress Jane's ruined castle, any remaining doubt had vanished.

She knew that castle because she'd been there before. Just once. But that had been enough.

Now it was a collapsed shell of its former self, broken and crumbled. Fangen and other creatures swarmed what still stood, but they were too far away to know exactly what they were doing. But if she could help it, Lorena wouldn't take her daughter one step closer to find out.

They'd sneaked back down the hill until the castle was out of sight and entered the outskirts of the forest they'd been trying to avoid. They needed cover, and time to think. The dark depths of the woods chilled her, though, and she kept a wary eye out for intruders.

"So what are we going to do?" Lisa asked. They'd been whispering back and forth for a while now, but no solid plan had solidified yet.

"Well, like I said," Lorena answered, "my first instinct is to get ourselves back to that place we winked into and get out of this scary Reality."

"But?" Lisa prodded.

"But there has to be *some* reason we were pulled here. I was trying to isolate Atticus's nanolocator, pushing the

Chi'karda levels to the extreme, and somehow, instead of bringing him to us, it brought us here."

"But why?"

Lorena had to refrain from giving her daughter an impatient look. "Well, dear, that's what I think we need to figure out. If we just wink back home, we'll never know."

Lisa opened her mouth to answer, but she didn't say anything as a sound came from deeper in the woods, like the whoosh of wind blowing through an open door.

Lorena searched the darkness between the trees but saw no sign of movement. The strange noise stopped after several seconds.

She and Lisa didn't say anything—they didn't need to. They were in the Thirteenth Reality, after all, a couple of miles from Mistress Jane's castle. Caution had already been strong, and now things were on full alert. They both stood up, slowly and quietly, reaching out to take each other's hand. Lorena held the Wand in her free hand, ready to club something if she had to. The Chi'karda levels weren't quite high enough to wink away from where they were.

Something crunched up ahead. Twigs cracked on the ground. Then again. And again. There was no sign of the source of the sound, but it was coming closer.

"Just step away," Lorena whispered. "Quickly now."

They faced the forest as they began to walk backwards, their footsteps also crunching through the underbrush. Lisa's hand was shaking, and sweat slicked her palm. The noises continued, but Lorena *still* couldn't see who was approaching. The mystery stranger picked up its pace, heading for them. The time for caution was gone.

"Run, Lisa!" she barked. "Run!"

She turned and yanked on Lisa's hand, pulling her along as she sprinted for the grassy hill outside the fringe of the woods.

Their pursuer picked up its pace to catch them, but then the sound of footsteps abruptly ceased, replaced by that whooshing sound again. A wind rose up into the air and over their heads, the noise of it making Lorena scream and look skyward.

When she saw what hovered above them, she cried out again and collapsed to the ground, pulling Lisa down with her. She rolled onto her back and stared at the thing that had come after them.

It was a creature with slanted, burning yellow eyes, its body made of what looked like ropes of gray smoke, coiled together to make a long body with arms and legs. It flew through the air, darting back and forth above them like a hawk examining its prey. Another smoky creature flew out of the forest to join its haunted companion. They circled, their yellow eyes leaving streaks of light in the air.

Lorena was frozen in place, squeezing her daughter's hand and holding the Wand to her chest.

The two wispy creatures abruptly flew down to the ground and grabbed Lorena and Lisa by their arms. Gripping them strongly, they lifted them to their feet with a painful jerk. And then they started marching the two terrified ladies back toward the slope of the hill.

Back toward the castle.

CHAPTER 11

✳

A POND IN THE SNOW

The stairs hadn't broken when Paul walked up them, nor had the porch collapsed, potentially dropping them into a heap of spiders and snakes and rats. There'd been a lot of creaks and groans, but he and Sofia had made it to the front door and through it unscathed.

The inside of Gretel's home looked nothing like the outside. As soon as Paul stepped through the door, he knew that the dilapidated exterior of the shack was a disguise, something to make thieves and thugs figure they might as well not bother. He and Sofia stood in a lushly carpeted living room with fancy furniture—all leather and frilly carved wood—and portraits of grim-looking people on the walls. A fire crackled in a brick fireplace, and the air smelled of cinnamon.

"Nice place you got here," Paul said. "I'm glad you didn't shoot us or stab us before we got a chance to check it out."

Sofia elbowed Paul in the ribs. "Thank you for inviting us in. That's what my rude friend meant to say."

Gretel looked back and forth between her two visitors, her tongue cocked inside one of her cheeks as she examined them. "George and I've always had an arrangement. You kids understand? What I'm doing here is too important to let any jackawillie barge in here and mess with my stuff. He promised to never tell anyone that the password question was a test, and to never give it out unless it was serious business. Serious, serious business. I reckon we have things to talk about."

Sofia nodded. "Yes, we do."

"I don't think we know *what* we're supposed to talk about," Paul said. "Could you help us out with that?"

The old lady grinned again, showing her gnarly teeth. "George wouldn't have sent ya with that question unless it was something particular. The whole reason I'm here in the first place. And let me guess—*you're* here because of the earthquake I had."

"Yes!" Sofia answered.

Paul suspected that the lady didn't know the extent of the damage to all the Realities yet; she obviously wasn't communicating with anyone on a regular basis. "How bad was it?" he asked her.

"Shook me right out of my bed, I can tell you that. Ruined my dream about Clark Gable, too. I was half in a tizzy, grabbed my gun and shot a bullet straight through my roof. Thing *still* drips. Don't listen to that nonsense about how duct tape can fix anything and everything."

Paul was really starting to like this woman. "Who's Clark Gable?"

"Never you mind. Now have a seat, enjoy the flames. I'll be back with some warm milk and cookies." She started walking toward the kitchen.

"You *do* know it's really hot outside, right?" Paul asked as he and Sofia took a seat on a leather couch. They sank half a foot into the deep cushions.

Gretel turned to face them. "Yes, son. But I'm old, and old people get cold even if they're in a desert. Plus, the things we're going to talk about today are gonna chill us right to the bone. I think we both know that."

She slipped into the kitchen before they could respond.

⌒⌒⌒

Tick was in a trance.

He felt like an oracle from ancient times, going through a ritual to call down the rain. He still held hands with Chu and Jane, but he was barely aware of it. Eyes squeezed shut, he saw only a dark swirl of orange and black in his vision, and the air hummed heavily with the power of Chi'karda. His skin prickled with chills and sweat at the same time.

He'd been at it for hours, poking the depths of Reality with his senses, looking for something to represent a way out of the Nonex. He felt like an astronaut in deep space, slinging himself from one galaxy to the next, sending out probes to see if he might capture the right data he needed. He'd been on the verge of giving up—his muscles aching, his mind exhausted—when he finally found what he'd been searching for.

A doorway. A portal in the darkness, framed by that eerie orange light.

He mentally flew toward it. The opening expanded, growing larger and larger as he approached. Everything was symbolic now, and he went with what came. His body—his conscience, his imagination, his thoughts—catapulted through the portal, and suddenly the air exploded with light. He closed his eyes. He no longer felt the hands or presence of his two partners, even though he knew they were still there. Until this was over, Tick was on his own.

His feet touched a hard surface, and within his mind, he opened his eyes again.

He stood in a field of white snow. The sky above

him was a piercingly clear blue, and the sun shone down with all its power, reflecting off the whiteness with a brilliant light that he'd first felt when entering the portal that had brought him here. He turned in a circle and saw that there was absolutely nothing in any direction. Just flat land and snow as far as he could see.

If anything could symbolize the Nonex, this was it.

There was one thing. Off in the distance, maybe fifty feet away, he thought he saw something blue—a bruise on the endless sea of white. He headed that way, his feet crunching and sinking slightly in the cold stuff below him with every step. There was no wind, but the coldness of the air bit into his skin, as if someone had just flicked on his senses with a switch. He looked down at his clothes and saw them magically transform from what he'd been wearing by the fire back on the beach to a huge parka and heavy pants and boots. Gloves and a thick wool hat on his head completed the transformation. Much better.

As he got closer to the spot of blue, it grew in size, but not just because he approached it. It literally *grew*, expanding outward like a drop of food coloring on a paper towel. Tick stopped and watched as its leading edge came toward him, then stopped at his feet. He could see that it was frozen water, but the icy lake seemed unnatural, as if it were made up of that nasty colored stuff used to create small ponds at the miniature golf place.

Tick dropped to his knees, knowing this was what he was supposed to do. Crystals of snow plumed out from behind him, dancing across the surface of the deep blue ice. Somehow they avoided a portion of the lake, forming a perfectly white rectangular frame. Tick knew what would happen before it did.

The rectangle flickered like a television coming to life, and then a moving image appeared on the ice, replacing the blue.

Tick leaned forward, placing his hands on the outer edge of the cold, frozen lake. What he saw stopped his heart for three full seconds. His mom and his sister, marching toward a huge wall of broken stone. They were led by two creatures that he'd run into before—long, gangly things that seemed to be made from coils of solid smoke.

Sleeks.

CHAPTER 12

✳

CREATURES

Lisa had felt terror before. When she and Kayla had been taken to that strange house with those strange women and the earthquake had hit. The storm of lightning and thunder. That had been her first true taste of fear.

And now she was experiencing it again.

The creatures that had taken her and her mom were ruthless and brutal as they dragged the two of them down the slope and across the grass to the broken castle. Their grip was hard and their pace furious.

They walked along a stream, the rushing water sparkling and glinting in the sunlight, the sound not doing a thing to help soothe Lisa's nerves. She remembered Tick telling the story of his first visit to the Thirteenth Reality and the battle that had been fought here with the fangen. At the time, she could never have imagined that one day she'd be in the same place, in the same kind of trouble.

"What do you want with us?" Lisa's mom asked for the twentieth time. And for the twentieth time, the creatures said nothing.

Lisa looked at the Barrier Wand that was still in her mom's clutches, surprised that one of the monsters hadn't taken it from her. If she remembered Tick's tale completely, the castle of Mistress Jane was another hotspot for Chi'karda, so her mom would need only a free minute to switch the dials and instruments and wink them out of there. They just needed the right opportunity.

Finally, they approached the ruins of the once-grand structure, the stream disappearing under a stone wall. Now that they were closer, Lisa could finally get a good look at the different types of creatures that had been crawling all over the crumpled and half-standing walls of the castle. Some matched Tick's description of the nasty fangen: blackish skin, splotchy green hair, giant mouths full of spiked teeth, thin membranes of wings stretching out from their backs. There were others. More of the smoky-rope kind that had captured Lisa and her mom. Some that were small and hunched and charcoal gray, like grotesque statues come to life. Some that looked like a cross between an alligator and a bull, with massively strong arms. They all blended together into one display of horror.

And their purpose was obvious. They were trying to rebuild the castle, stone by stone.

Their current captors stopped them by one of the more solid sections of the ruins, about thirty feet from where the stream slipped under the wall. A huge wooden door stood next to it—or what used to be a door. Now it was mostly shredded, chunks and splinters hanging off around the edges. Darkness lurked behind the opening.

The monstrous pair threw Lisa and her mom to the ground in front of the door. The two of them immediately crawled to each other and huddled together, the Barrier Wand snuggled between them, its surface hard and cold. Lisa's mom started slyly turning the dials and switches.

The creatures floated up into the air and flew over to the wall of the castle, their wispy figures like streams of smoke whipping through the wind. They landed on the hard stone and used their long arms and legs to crawl up its side, mixing in with the rest of the other dark and twisted creatures.

"Get us out of here," Lisa whispered to her mom.

"I'm working on it." Her hands slowly turned a

dial until it clicked. "But I don't want them to notice. And I'm not even sure I want us to wink out of here just yet."

"What? Why?"

Her mom looked disappointed. "After all we went through to get here in the first place? There has to be a reason that Chi'karda and Reality pulled us here when we tried to grab Atticus. Maybe we're on his trail or something. Or maybe we're being guided to his nano-locator, and this is a stop along the way."

Lisa was a little ashamed for wanting to hightail it out of there, but being dead wouldn't help Tick much either. "Or maybe we're about to be eaten for dinner by all of these monsters."

"Maybe. Don't worry your little heart, girl. I have the Wand all set, and if worse comes to worst, I'll click the button and wink us away. We can start all over again. From the beginning. Without any hope."

Lisa groaned and rolled her eyes. "Okay, Mom. I got your point loud and clear."

There was movement in the darkness behind the shattered door, and a figure appeared, like a shrouded ghost. Lisa wanted to get up and run, but she kept her eyes focused on the person who approached. As the figure came into the light, Lisa could see a robe made of a coarse, off-white material, its hood pulled up and over the face, hiding it. Two hands emerged from the arms of the robe, the fingers folded together in front. Lisa had expected the hands to be gnarled and ancient, but the skin looked young and healthy.

A woman's hands.

The robed stranger walked to where Lisa and her mom sat. She was tall and thin, and the image of her hooded head gave her a commanding presence, like an ancient oracle or druid.

"You can wink away if you wish," the lady said, her voice a hollow ring. "But I ask only that you allow me to tell you one very important thing first."

"What is it?" Lisa's mom replied, cautious.

The woman reached up with those young hands of hers and pulled back the hood of her robe, revealing a homely, stoic face framed by short, black hair. She had a nose that pointed straight out like a carrot.

"We brought you here," she said, "because you're trying to find Atticus Higginbottom. And so are we."

CHAPTER 13

✳

WORDS ON ICE

Tick's heart had dropped upon seeing his mom and sister captured by Sleeks, and he almost beat his fists on the ice where their images appeared, thinking he could break through, dive through, and save them somehow. He yelled to them as they were brought to the foot of Jane's now-broken castle and thrown to the ground, though he knew it was pointless. Full of desperation and rage, he could only sit there and shake. Helpless.

The screen—the rectangle of frozen pond—suddenly flickered, and the scene disappeared, replaced by a few lines of written words. Before he even read it, he knew it was some kind of riddle, and for some reason, it made him mad. He screamed and *did* hit the ice, cursing Reality for playing such ridiculous games with him. His family was in trouble, and here he was, forced to solve a silly puzzle again.

But on the other hand, he was good at it. The fabric of the universe understood his mind and was trying to help him. Was trying to form its complexities together and present to him a solution in a way he could best grasp it. Just like what had happened with the Haunce.

Tick gained control of his emotions and forced himself to read the words.

The smallest thing begins to grow
It needs no light, it needs no glow
This thing, it fears the weakest breath
And yet it cannot embrace death
The greatest man or bull or steed
Or queen or doe or stinging bee
Eats it, smells it, drinks it some
And one day it they will become

Tick sighed. He'd hoped the riddle would be easy, that the answer would jump out at him. But no. Of course not.

He started thinking.

"My name is Mordell," the woman said to Lisa and her mom. She sat on the grass next to them, her legs folded beneath her flowing robe, her back straight, and her hands settled on her knees. "I am a Lady of Blood and Sorrow, a new order started by our master, Mistress Jane, to serve her in the quest to create a Utopia for mankind. To bring eternal happiness to humans once and for all. We bear our name of despair to teach the world that we will do anything, make any sacrifice, to bring this Utopia to pass. We are servants only."

Lisa felt queasy as Mordell spoke. She seemed to have a blank stare as she recited her mantra, as if it had been beaten into her since she was a kid.

"Why are you looking for my son?" Lisa's mom asked. She had the Barrier Wand gripped in one hand, the other hovering above the button on top. Lisa also had a hand on the device. They could wink away with one click.

"Because we know he is with our master," Mordell replied. "We believe that they disrupted the fabric of Reality by using such astronomical levels of Chi'karda that they were ripped away into the Nonex."

Mom gasped, and one of her hands flew up to her mouth.

"The Nonex?" Lisa repeated. That didn't sound very good. "What's that?"

Her mom looked over at her, her face somehow

showing even more worry than it had before. "We don't know much about it, but it's a place that both exists and doesn't exist, trapped somewhere between the dimensions of Reality. Sort of a no-man's-land, where your mind is the only thing keeping you alive. They say it's where you go if you ever meet one of your Alterants."

Lisa had the thought that her mom was a true scientist, unable to stop herself from breaking it down to textbook explanations despite knowing her own son might be trapped there. But her eyes held deep love and concern still.

Mordell continued. "Mistress Jane has been training us to understand the ways of Chi'karda. It flows here in ways it does not in the other Realities. We've brought every one of our kind from the stations we've established throughout the Thirteen Realities. Even as we speak, they are gathering inside the Great Hall of the castle behind me, which by fate, survived the destruction."

"What are they doing?" Lisa asked.

Mordell's eyes focused on hers for the first time. "We are meditating, probing the universe, seeking any sign of Atticus or Mistress Jane. We must find their nano-locators or sense their presence. We have to be ready to snatch them if they appear, as *soon* as they appear. Right now, it's as if they have been wiped from Reality."

Lisa's mom didn't seem surprised, as if she'd given

up doubting anything anymore. "And how did you find us? Did you wink us here?"

"We have the data on your son's nanolocator. In our probing, we saw you looking for him. And then you were captured by the Great Disturbance that has plagued the Realities ever since our master disappeared. We rescued you from it and brought you here so that you could help us. We're no longer enemies; we have the same purpose."

Lisa's mind caught on those two words: *Great Disturbance*. The lady had said them as if they were the name of a place or a person. She asked what it meant.

Mordell looked into her eyes once again. "We call it the Void of Mist and Thunder, and if we don't find a way to stop it, the lives of our master and your brother, and the quest to build Utopia, won't matter. Because every last person in the Realities will be dead."

Lisa and her mom looked at each other, dread hanging in the air like soaked curtains. How did you even follow up something like that with questions? There were too many to know where to start.

Mordell stood up in a move so graceful that Lisa didn't even notice until the woman was on her feet.

"Come," the Lady of Blood and Sorrow said. "There will be time for explanations later. Right now we need you to join us in our meditations and help us probe the universe until we find those we seek." She turned and started walking toward the broken door of the broken castle.

Lisa knew there'd be no discussing this with her mom. They both got up and followed the strange woman into the darkness.

CHAPTER 14

WATCHING TV

Mothball was thankful something had finally gone right in her life. Klint Tanner had given her a cup of hot tea as they sat down in his living room to talk about the world and its problems. The news was going to be rough and depressing, she knew it, but at least she had some tea to warm her bones and settle her nerves.

Sally had asked for chocolate milk, which embarrassed Mothball to no end. Especially when the buffoon asked if he could have a straw to "sip it up with." Oh, she liked the man well enough, she supposed, but how he'd become a Realitant, she'd never know.

Tanner sat down in a chair opposite them, a remote in his hands. There was a huge television on the wall,

597

bigger than any Mothball had ever seen in her life. Of course, they didn't do a whole lot of that sort back in the Fifth Reality.

Tanner was a scrawny man with mussed-up hair and whiskers on his chin. But he had sharp eyes, and he took his job seriously.

"I've put together a hodgepodge of what's been going on lately," the man said after everyone was settled. He clicked the remote, and the television buzzed to life. "I'd say sit back and enjoy the show, but I don't think you will very much. It's not pretty."

"Oh, doncha worry, son," Sally said, his straw pinched between his fingers as he slurped his chocolate milk. He looked like an overgrown two-year-old kid in overalls. "Back where we work, we sho 'nough used to things that ain't purty. Ain't that right, Mothball?" He laughed, a booming sound that could only be described as a guffaw.

Mothball wanted to slug him; she knew very well he was talking about *her*. But then again, Sally wasn't the handsomest cat in the litter, so maybe he was poking fun at himself as well. "Right as rain, you are," she said. "But I'm sure you were a cute wee one when you were born and all. Been downhill ever since, it 'as."

Sally laughed again.

"Shall we, um, get on with it?" Tanner asked.

598

"Yes, indeed," Mothball replied. "So sorry for my partner, here. A bit cracked in the skull, he is."

Tanner smiled, but it was a haunted one. "I'm afraid you're both going to lose your appetite for laughing soon. The whole world is in one big heap of a mess. Fires, riots, rebellions, anarchy. Looting and murders. Like I said, it's not pretty." He pointed his remote at the television and clicked it again.

A horror show came to life on the big screen.

～⌒⁀～

Paul had never understood why people liked to drink warm milk. He'd heard of it before, but it always sounded nasty to him. Warm *chocolate* milk, maybe. But take out that brown stuff and he wanted no part of it. Milk was meant to be ice-cold, especially when washing down some cookies.

At least those were yummy. Oatmeal and raisin.

Gretel was sitting in her chair, eating and sipping along with Paul and Sofia, but she'd yet to say anything about . . . well, anything. Paul still had no idea why they were there, which was why all he could think about was how much he didn't like warm milk.

Sofia cleared her throat. "We really appreciate you letting us in, but I don't think we have a lot of spare time on our hands. I'm sure Master George wants us to learn what it is you have to tell us, and then get back to him."

Paul felt like he needed to add something. "Yeah, let's get on with it." He winced on the inside. That had come out a little harsher than he'd meant it. "I'm dying of curiosity here. Ma'am." He threw that in there to sound polite.

Gretel took the last bite of her cookie then drained her cup of milk. She placed her dishes on a small table beside her. "I understand your impatience, but you're going to have to bear with me a few moments longer before we get to *my* part of this story. First, I need to hear yours."

Paul wanted to groan and kick something, but he kept himself still and quiet.

"What do you mean?" Sofia asked.

Gretel shrugged as if it were obvious. "I haven't had one squirt of communication with the Realitants—or civilization at all, for that matter—in more than a year. I'm no longer what you'd consider 'active,' and informing me of the latest has to be on the bottom of George's to-do list. So I need to get caught up on everything that's been going on."

"Everything that's been going on?" Paul repeated. "That's like asking us to give you a quick wrap-up of the Civil War. You have any idea how much has happened in the last *year*?"

"Well, actually, no, I don't. Which is why I need you to tell me about it." She folded her hands in her lap and raised her eyebrows.

Paul looked over at Sofia. "You tell her."

Sofia had impatience stamped all over her face, and she started speaking immediately, as if she didn't want to waste one more second. She began in the only place that made sense—how she, Paul, Tick, and Sato got recruited by the Realitants—and then she flowed into the problems they'd had with Reginald Chu and Mistress Jane. On and on and on she went, speaking so fast it gave Paul a headache trying to keep up, but eventually she got to the part about Jane trying to sever the Fifth Reality from existence and almost destroying the entire universe instead. She sounded like she was telling someone how to make breakfast.

Finally, she finished.

Gretel didn't say anything at first; she just kept looking at Sofia as if she needed some time to absorb all the things she'd been told.

"Well?" Paul asked to break the awkward silence. "What do you think? Things as rosy as you pictured, living out here in your swamp palace?"

The old woman looked sharply at him, her expression turning grave. "Son, what you've just described to me is far, far worse than I imagined, even in my worst nightmares after the earthquake that hit this place. I think I finally understand why George sent you to me. Come, we need to enter my safe haven."

She stood up, her eyes distant, and gestured for the young Realitants to follow. Paul and Sofia exchanged uneasy glances then joined Gretel, leaving the comfy living room with the warm fire and entering a cold, uninviting room with shiny steel walls. There was a bare light in the ceiling that flickered and a large safe in one corner of the room. Gretel shut the door behind them with a heavy, ringing thud; Paul spun around to see that it was also made of steel like the inside of a bank vault.

Gretel spun a wheel-handle and clicked a big lock. Then she walked over to the safe in the corner—a big, black square—and started turning the large combination dial. Paul stared, wondering what in the world they were about to see.

As Gretel continued to work at the safe's mechanism, she spoke over her shoulder. "I don't call it the *safe haven* for nothing. It's a haven for my safes. A safe within a safe. What I'm protecting here is very important."

Paul asked the obvious question. "What is it?"

There was a loud click, and then the door of the safe swung open. Paul and Sofia stepped forward to see what was inside. It was an old, tattered, dusty shoebox. Gretel pulled it out and set it on the floor. Carefully. Then she sat right beside it, folding her legs underneath her like a teenager. Paul and Sofia sat next to her on the ground. Paul's eyes stayed glued to the box. He was so curious he almost reached out and opened the lid himself.

Gretel flicked both of them a knowing look. Then she lifted the warped lid and flipped it over. Inside the box lay a small cube of gray metal with a green button on top. The old woman lifted up the cube and held it out for everyone to see.

"Push this button," she said in a mesmerized voice, almost like a chant, "and the Realities will change forever. For good. Or for evil."

CHAPTER 15

✳

THE LADIES OF BLOOD AND SORROW

Tick sat in the snow in the meditative pose of a Buddhist he'd seen once on TV—his legs crossed under him, his arms resting on top of them with his fingers pushed together and pointing upward, and his eyes closed. Couldn't hurt, he'd thought.

He'd been trying for at least a half hour to push all other thoughts from his mind and focus on the riddle he'd seen written on the ice. But he was having a hard time concentrating. The words floated in the darkness of his thoughts, visible in his mind's eye as white letters on a black background. He ran through the lines, letting the skills he'd developed for this sort of thing take their natural course as his brain digested and regurgitated the riddle again and again:

> *The smallest thing begins to grow*
> *It needs no light, it needs no glow*
> *This thing, it fears the weakest breath*
> *And yet it cannot embrace death*
> *The greatest man or bull or steed*
> *Or queen or doe or stinging bee*
> *Eats it, smells it, drinks it some*
> *And one day it they will become*

Tick sat in the wind and the cold and relaxed, doing what he did best.

Thinking.

Lisa and her mom followed Mordell down a long, cold passage under the hard stone of the castle, walking along the dark waters of the stream that rushed by. Lisa knew this was the place Tick and his Realitant friends had barely escaped from during their first harrowing trip to the Thirteenth Reality. Imagining them at that time—Tick and the others desperately waiting for the Barrier Wand to kick in and wink them out, while hordes of bloodthirsty fangen beat down the walls and came after them—sent chills across her skin. It made her feel incredibly sorry for her lost brother, and made her love him more than ever before. Tears welled up in her eyes.

She knew what had happened next. The Barrier Wand didn't even have a Chi'karda Drive inside its golden case at the time—Mistress Jane had secretly removed it—but Tick had displayed his unbelievable power over Chi'karda, using his powers to wink everyone to safety on his own. There had been signs and hints his whole life that there was something special about him, but after that day, the Realitants knew it for sure.

Tick was a wizard. A silly word, but that's how Lisa saw him. Sure, Master George claimed Tick's power could be scientifically explained—or someday would be—but Lisa didn't care about the specifics, the nitty-gritty details. Her brother was magic, he was special, and they needed to find him so he could do great things for the world. For *all* the worlds.

The passageway led through an arch to the right and into a small chamber carved out of black rock. Mordell silently led them through the opening and into the room that had absolutely no decoration or furniture of any kind. The only light came from a single torch that burned and hissed in a sconce on the wall. About twenty other women sat upon the hard ground in a circle. One break in the ring was vacant, and it was just big enough for the three newcomers to sit down.

"Even though its size is humble," Mordell said in a solemn voice, "we call this the Great Hall because its purpose is grand. This hallowed place is where the Ladies of Blood and Sorrow come to show our respect and devotion to Chi'karda and to renew our commitment to seek a Utopia for all mankind." She looked at Lisa and her mom. "Your presence here is allowed by my invitation only. Please, sit."

She motioned toward the empty spot in the circle. Lisa and her mom, holding hands, went over and sat down on the smooth surface of the black rock floor. Her mom cradled the Barrier Wand in her lap, and Lisa noticed that her finger hovered over the trigger button at the top.

Lisa took a moment to study the circle of women, all of whom were dressed in the same off-white, coarse robes that Mordell wore. The Ladies each had a meditative, almost blank look on their hooded faces. It was creepy in the scant light.

Mordell sat down next to Lisa. "We all know of the nature of this room in which we have gathered," she began. "The Great Hall, birthed by the will of our master, Mistress Jane herself. For reasons we may never learn, the Thirteenth Reality is more focused with Chi'karda's might, more concentrated, more plentiful in its power than any other world. And this hallowed place is the heart of that power, which is why our master built her castle on this land and carved the Great Hall in this rock. Using the methods taught to us by She Who Tamed the Fire, we will now join hands and probe the universe together. And when we find our master—and her companions, if possible—we must unite to bring them back here."

"'If possible?'" Lisa asked, not liking the sound of that one bit. Maybe they were using Tick as a means to an end and were planning to dump him as soon as they found Jane. And what was with all the fancy mumbo-jumbo talk?

Mordell turned to her, not looking pleased by the interruption. "You've spoken out of turn, girl. This is not allowed in the Great Hall."

Lisa refused to be intimidated by this servant of the woman who'd tried to kill Tick. "I just want my brother to come back safely too. Make sure he does."

Mordell considered her for a moment then finally nodded. "I give you my word that if it's possible in any way to do so, we will. But understand that our master is our first priority, for the sake of you, and your children, and your children's children."

Lisa thought of a million nasty things that she

wanted to say, but she kept her mouth shut. She could only hope now. She squeezed her mom's arm, who gave her a nod and a look as if to say, Don't worry. *Tick can fend for himself.*

Mordell returned her attention to her counterparts sitting in the circle. "We have with us today the mother of Atticus Higginbottom—yes, we know who you are—with a Barrier Wand constructed by her own hand. She has locked onto the nanolocator of her son, which will serve to benefit us in our search. The Wand's presence alone will aid us. Now, we must all take hands, including our visitors'."

Lisa had no problem grabbing her mom's hand, but she was a little wary of taking one of Mordell's. She clasped her fingers around those of the woman, which were icy cold and felt brittle, as if they'd collapse into a heap of powder if Lisa squeezed. So she didn't.

"Let us begin," Mordell announced. "Close your eyes. Grasp the Chi'karda that flows within this room. Reach into the Realities—reach into the universe."

The Ladies of Blood and Sorrow began to hum. Lisa was the last to close her eyes, but before she did, a spray of orange light started to glow within the center of their circle.

Tick didn't know how long he'd been sitting in the icy snow, next to the icy pond, feeling the icy wind. But he felt it all the way to the core of his bones, and icy was the only word to describe it.

He didn't let it faze him. He thought, concentrated, and focused on the riddle. He knew the fabric of Reality was at his fingertips, waiting for his mind to organize a solution in the way he best understood. The complexities of the universe had been laid at his feet in the form of a riddle.

When the pieces of the puzzle finally clicked into place, the answer hovered within his thoughts, a word as clear as if it were written on a sign hung in front of his face.

Dust.

He opened his eyes and whispered the word to the biting wind, which whisked it away and carried it to whatever ears needed to hear it.

A few seconds later, the world around him was ripped apart, exploding into a horrifying display of noise and light. Tick screamed, but no one heard the sound. Not even him.

CHAPTER 16

✳

A RUSH OF VIOLENCE

Lisa was beginning to feel uncomfortable.

The rattling buzz in the room had grown to an unbearable pitch, vibrating her skull and shaking the walls and floor of the Great Hall. The rock creaked and groaned, as if the walls might burst apart and spray them with tiny fragments. It took all of Lisa's willpower not to open her eyes or scream or run away. Even through her closed eyelids, she could sense the bright orangeness of what she knew was the power of Chi'karda.

The Ladies of Blood and Sorrow continued to hum, and Lisa heard a slight rustling, as if the women were swaying back and forth in their trancelike state.

What they were doing, she had no idea, and she certainly didn't know what she could do to help. But she felt the vibration of power inside her body, and there was definitely something big happening.

She squeezed her mom's hand, and her mom squeezed back. Something hard and warm—almost hot—touched Lisa's forearm. She opened her eyelids to the slightest, smallest crack to see what it was. Her mom had moved the Barrier Wand closer, wanting to show her that it was heating up for some reason.

Yes, something big was definitely going on.

⁓

Tick's body was flying through a fog.

Lightning and thunder flashed and boomed all around him, streaks of white fire crossing the gray, misty air, barely missing his body. The horrible sounds rattled his head, pierced his ears painfully. He felt the sense of flying in his stomach and head, but there wasn't a great rushing of wind blowing at him. His skin was cold one second and hot the next. Even his vision would go haywire—everything turning into a grayish blur then coming into focus again, the edges of the lightning bolts sharp and clear and brilliant. It was as if his senses had a loose connection to his brain.

He tried to quell the rising fear and panic that

threatened to consume him. He had no idea what was happening or where he was, much less how he could use his newfound powers to help the situation. He was hurtling through a void of nothing, surrounded by an angry, powerful storm of energy.

He twisted his head left and right, trying to see any sign of Chu or Mistress Jane. They were nowhere near him, according to what his eyes told his brain, but on some deep, deep level, he felt as though he were still holding their hands. That maybe the storm was simply an illusion and nothing more.

He continued his flight. Nausea filled his belly. He tried to speak, but his voice was lost in the noise of the chaos around him. He had the horrible thought that maybe this was how he'd spend the rest of eternity— that maybe the Nonex, in the end, was nothing more than this.

Tick flew through a void of mist and thunder.

Mistress Jane didn't understand what was going on, and nothing on earth caused her more distress than *uncertainty*. She was a scientist, blood and bone, to the very core of her soul and mind. A scientist. And being here, surrounded by a world of mist and lightning and sound, she didn't have the slightest guess of what was going on. It made no logical sense. And that made her angry.

She looked to her left, though all movement was strange in this inexplicable void. Her senses told her she was moving at great speed, yet she felt no rush of wind. And her surroundings didn't seem to shift at a pace that made sense with the movement of her head.

Reginald Chu was a few feet away from her, keeping an even pace. His eyes were still closed, and he held his hands out before him like Superman. But he didn't look peaceful or asleep. His face was pinched, like someone waiting to jump off a bridge with a bungee cord. Sweat trickled down his brow, giving Jane even more evidence that their motion through this fog didn't match the physical effects on their body.

Jane knew Tick had done this somehow. He had vaulted them from the Nonex and thrown them into a place that was obviously even worse. Maybe she'd made a huge mistake trusting him to help her.

She closed her eyes and reached into the void with her senses, reaching to take back her Chi'karda from Tick's control. Surprisingly, it was there, waiting. She filled her body with the power, sucking it in, keeping it at bay until she needed it. Kept it there like a bomb waiting for a lit fuse.

The Great Hall had continued to buzz and vibrate, the Ladies humming, the orange power of Chi'karda burning the air with energy. Lisa could only sit and wait, though it was agonizing.

Mordell suddenly spoke up beside her with a voice that easily cut through the other noise in the room.

"We've found her! We've reconnected with her nanolocator! Reginald Chu is there as well. We need everyone to focus. Begin to pull them back."

The woman paused, and Lisa didn't dare ask the obvious question. Not because it had been forbidden, but because she was terrified of the answer. Mordell answered her anyway.

"There is, unfortunately, no sign of the boy, Atticus Higginbottom."

CHAPTER 17

✳

FINDING TICK

Lorena knew something was happening with her Barrier Wand, and it wasn't just that the Drive within it was helping pool the power of Chi'karda for the Ladies of Blood and Sorrow. Something else was at play. The metal surface was hot, almost too much to touch now, and the Wand had a hum of its own.

Mordell's words had been like a death sentence. Lorena had suspected the truth from the start, and the people here obviously had different priorities than she did. They wanted Jane back, at any cost. Even if the cost was the life of Lorena's son. And she didn't plan to let that happen.

Breaking her handhold with both Lisa and the

stranger to her left, Lorena opened her eyes and straightened the Barrier Wand in her lap. She quickly ran through the dials and switches, adjusting and evaluating, making educated guesses since she was in such an unprecedented situation. Sweat poured down her face.

"What are you doing?" Mordell shouted, the echo ringing along the walls and ceiling of the black, rocky room. "Rejoin hands this instant!"

Lorena gave the woman a nasty glare. "Back off, lady, or you'll be seeing and feeling a lot of blood and sorrow today."

A quick glance at Lisa showed that her daughter was smiling.

⁓

Tick felt something tugging on his heart.

Not like despair, or love, or missing someone. It was a literal tug, as if someone had sunk a hook into his heart and cinched it tight with a strong rope. And then the rope started pulling.

He cried out, feeling a fire ignite within him that scorched his insides with pain. He clutched his chest with both hands, gripping his shirt and pulling his fingers into tight fists, pressing on his sternum. It did no good. The pull on the rope was getting stronger.

It hurt so bad. The gray mist swirled around him;

lightning bolts exploded through the air as the thunder thumped and boomed. His body continued to fly through it all.

And his insides screamed with pain.

⁓

Mistress Jane knew something had changed. She felt a presence within her, as if some other soul had joined with hers, trying to fight her for occupancy. She looked at Chu, who was still close to her, just as his eyes opened. He'd felt it, too.

He yelled something at her. His words were utterly lost in the deafening noise of the storm around them, but she could read his lips: *Save me.*

Jane thought of the Ladies of Blood and Sorrow and the things she'd trained them for. The endless possibilities they could accomplish within the Great Hall of her castle, where Chi'karda gathered so powerfully. And finally, something logical clicked into place for her. The Ladies had combined their efforts, pooled all their power, and had reached out for her nanolocator. Tick had pulled them out of the Nonex into some no-man's-land barrier between it and the rest of Reality. Just close enough to reestablish contact.

Jane smiled, knowing exactly what expression was on her red mask: joy.

Chu reached out a hand to her, his mouth still moving with unheard words. Fear enveloped him, and sweat covered his face even more than before.

Jane felt ashamed for him. Embarrassed by his weakness. But she knew what the man was capable of. And they'd come so close to partnering before. So close. Until the boy Tick ruined everything, including Jane's body.

Chu—her partner. Utopia—her mission. She twisted her body, straining to reach out with her arm.

Mistress Jane took Reginald Chu's hand.

***

Lisa watched as her mom worked furiously over the Barrier Wand, adjusting the instruments, fine-tuning them with the slightest of movements. The Ladies around the circle had continued their efforts, ignoring the mutiny of Lisa and her mom. Mordell and the woman who'd been sitting next to Lisa's mom had simply moved closer until they could reseal the ring of held hands in their magic circle. Maybe they figured they could deal with the turncoats later.

"Mom, what are you doing?" Lisa asked. She'd been scared to interrupt her mom's concentration, but she couldn't wait one more second.

"I've almost got it." She had her tongue pinched

between her lips, and sweat trickled down both sides of her face. "I can't believe it, but his signal is there. Before it wasn't *missing* so much as showing that he didn't exist anymore. But he's there, no doubt about it."

"Really?" Lisa tried not to let her hopes leap to the sky.

"But it's so weak. So weak. I'm trying to latch on, trying to pull him closer. But I don't dare try to fully wink him in yet. His body could literally tear apart and turn into an atom soup."

Lisa's heart dropped. "Mom, please get him. Mom, please." She'd never realized until that moment how much she loved that stupid brother of hers.

"We will, baby," her mom said. "I swear it."

The buzz and hum and orange light of Chi'karda filled the room like a nebula.

Things started to change around Tick, even as the pain inside his chest grew worse, like needles piercing his heart. His shoulders shook from the ache of trying to muffle the sobs that wanted to escape him, but he tried to push aside all the pain and focus on his surroundings.

The gray mist had thinned out, allowing his vision to reach much farther away. The bolts of white fire shooting through the air had not ceased at all, and he saw more of them than ever—a rain of lightning that continued for miles and miles. Violent sounds shook the gaseous world and continued to hurt his ears and splinter his brain with the worst headache he'd ever experienced.

And in the distance, coming straight toward him, were . . . *things*.

Dark objects. Huge objects. They looked like bulky chunks of broken spaceships, destroyed and shredded, hurling through empty space. There were dozens of them, flying through the gray air, rushing in. As they got closer, Tick could no longer tell if that was true or if he was actually hurtling toward *them*. But then he saw that they were less like spaceships, and more like floating mountains torn from their foundations—the edges rocky and broken, the centers filled with vegetation and trees.

He didn't understand why, but he felt a weighty sense of dread, and not just from the prospect of smashing into the stony chunks of land. There was something ominous about those massive rocks, like they were alive and wanted him dead.

The nearest one was only a few hundred feet away when hundreds of vines shot out from the nooks and crannies of the rock's craggy surface, like an army of snakes striking out at a predator. Their tips tapered to a point. The vines coiled in the air then came for Tick.

Lisa jumped when her mom suddenly cried out, a sound that was impossible to tell whether it was good or bad. She was tight-faced and sweating as she ran her hands up and down the Barrier Wand like it was some kind of musical instrument.

"What's going on?" Lisa asked.

"I'm latched to him," her mom responded. "I just can't seem to wink the boy in."

CHAPTER 18

✳

CORDS OF LIGHT

The vines flew through the air, coming at Tick as if they were magnetized ropes and he was a big piece of metal. He'd been sort of complacent since being pulled into the massive gray void, watching and observing, wondering what Reality was going to do to him now that he'd solved the riddle his consciousness had presented in his mind.

But the vines looked deadly, the massive structures of rock and vegetation were hurtling toward his body, and he had no more time to sit back. He'd mastered his control over Chi'karda. It was time to use it.

The ends of the first vines reached him and quickly coiled around his arms and legs. They cinched tight and jerked him forward even faster, throwing his body at the rock from which they'd emerged.

Tick struggled against the strength of the ropy chains, looked at the jagged granite chunk rushing up at him, and tried not to panic. He relaxed his arms and legs, letting his body go limp. Reaching down, deep inside his heart, he found the spark that had become so familiar to him, that burning flicker of flame that he knew he could ignite into an inferno.

Pure power exploded away from him, streaks of orange light and fire. The surge of Chi'karda slammed into the massive rock, detonating it into a million splinters of stone, which Tick whisked away with a single thought. Like a flinty cloud of smoke caught in a gust of wind, it flew to the right, gone from his vision. The vines that had imprisoned him were incinerated; not a single trace was left.

But there were dozens more of the floating mountains, and each one had more of the vines popping out of their surfaces, pointy ends focused on Tick. He took hold of his power, pulled it all back within his chest, sucking it in like a great vacuum. Then he used his eyes and mind to start destroying.

Looking this way and that, he hurled streaks of Chi'karda outward with each glance. They shot forward like streams of fire, arrows of might, smashing into each of the massive hunks of stone, dirt, and vegetation. The flying structures exploded, obliterated into dusty clouds that whipped away like the first one had. Tick barely had time to make sure he'd succeeded in destroying one before he had to look at the next threat.

Explosion after explosion, he destroyed them. Reaching with all his strength, he was able to send the Chi'karda beams farther and farther out, killing the vines as soon as they came into view.

Without warning, and just as he began to feel like he might get out of the mess, everything changed as quickly as one wink of his eye.

The endless gray sky disappeared, along with the fog of debris from the countless erupted balls of rock. Blackness replaced it, a sea of stars in the background, as if he floated in the deepest realm of outer space. His sense of movement also stopped, jarring him at first. Pulling in a deep breath, he heard the sound of his own gasp and felt his insides twist until he regained his equilibrium. All was silent as he hung there in the empty void.

Several seconds passed. Then each one of those pinpoints of light around him stretched out into a long beam of brightness, all of them pointed at Tick and moving at a blistering speed.

Lorena stood up, her mind so focused on the Barrier Wand that it felt as though she'd become one with it. The orange light of Chi'karda filled the room, blinding her vision. She couldn't separate what the Ladies of Blood and Sorrow were doing from the power generated by her own efforts with the Wand. She'd never experienced anything like it. She wondered if this was how Tick felt when he was controlling the Chi'karda directly. She'd quit adjusting the dials and switches without even realizing it.

And then she remembered. She was in the Thirteenth Reality. Things were different here.

Lisa was at her side, keeping quiet—bless her heart—but a quick glance showed that the poor girl desperately wanted to know what was going on. Lorena went back to the business at hand, knowing she couldn't risk breaking her concentration. She couldn't put it into words or offer up a scientific explanation, but she had control over Chi'karda like never before, a link to Tick that she wasn't going to let go of. She was going to bring him home.

Even if she had to die doing it.

At first the arrows of light made Tick feel as if he were in a spaceship that had shifted into warp speed, about to blast to another part of the galaxy. But he felt no sense of motion, and the angles were wrong. As he twisted and turned in the void, he saw long lines of pure whiteness stretching toward him from every direction, like strings of perfectly straight lightning. And he didn't need a manual to know that their purpose was not to brighten his world so he could read a book.

The beams kept coming.

He could easily shift his body, even move away if he wanted to, but there was no point. The things were heading for him no matter where he looked. Unless he winked to another place, those long strings of white were going to reach him. Besides, where would he wink? *Could* he even wink out of the void? He felt surprisingly calm, confident he could deal with the problem.

The first needles of light reached his body.

Just like the vines, they wrapped around his arms and legs; some slipped across his chest, others slithered along his ribs and side and along his back. He fought at them by flailing and kicking out, but it did no good. The Chi'karda he'd gathered before still swelled inside of him. He lashed out with the power, but *that* did no good either. It was as if the ropes of light were without substance until they needed it to serve their purpose, gripping tightly to his body.

There were dozens of the ropes, then hundreds, thousands. They bled together into a brilliant display of pure white light, covering every inch of his body. Only his head remained free, and he twisted his neck to see what was happening, trying to squirm out of it.

The bindings tightened, squeezing the air out of his lungs, but curiously, Tick felt no panic. His breathing remained even. The white ropes kept coming, flying in like eels until they hit his body and wrapped around the other coils of light. He'd become nothing but a head, sticking out of a blinding ball of brilliance with tendrils of light leading away from him in every direction.

Tick knew he couldn't let it keep going. He closed his eyes, pulled in more and more Chi'karda, filling his body and soul. He felt as if his insides were on fire. Still he kept at it, the power rushing into him like a falling deluge of scorching lava. He found himself liking it, loving the burn and surge of adrenaline, the power that filled him. He let it build, knowing he needed to unleash it but not wanting to. The earlier sensation of being tugged by a strong cable was still there, but it didn't hurt anymore.

The beams of light quit coming, but it didn't matter. He was wrapped neck to toe, unable to move a single muscle. The trailing ends of the ropes stretched out from his body in every direction, as if he were stuck in the middle of a giant spider web. All was silent and still, the light blinding.

The cords around him suddenly grew taut, then began to pull at his limbs and torso. Trying to rip his body into pieces.

CHAPTER 19

FIGHTING THE VOID

At first Tick didn't feel the pain.

The power of Chi'karda within him burned so hot, so fierce, that he was unaware of all else except for a distant tugging sensation. Like he'd been thrown into a crowd and they were using his arms and legs as a wishbone. But the pain intensified, began to hurt. Bad. The pulling on his heart came back, too, as if two separate forces wanted to completely obliterate his body.

He screamed and released the power that had been building within, unleashing the Chi'karda with a mental burst of a detonation.

The bright whiteness of the ropes that had captured him was dimmed by the brilliance of orange light as

Chi'karda erupted out of him. Streams of it shot from his body in arrows, and a cloud swelled from his skin, bulging underneath the cords like a burrowing animal.

The ropes held, pulling at him and continuing to jerk at his limbs and squeeze his middle. Pain stabbed at his joints and muscles. The pleasurable burn of power had been replaced by a different kind of fire, an agony that hurt worse than anything he'd ever experienced.

He screamed again and sent waves of Chi'karda crashing out of him, focusing on the strings of frozen lightning as if the whole thing were a video game, his mind the joystick. Orange flames struck at them, disintegrating half of them in one swoop of power. Tick's body snapped to the left, flying through the air as the severed ropes found life again, coming back at him and trying to reattach their ends to his arms and legs. He held his breath and continued the onslaught of Chi'karda, firing away at everything in sight.

Sprays of pure whiteness erupted in tiny explosions like bursts of electricity out of a live wire as his power severed more of the cords. More and more and more of them. His mind worked relentlessly as he tried to destroy the things attached to him while at the same time keeping the others at bay. He floated in that strange outer space, throwing flares of energy at anything that moved. The mix of white and orange was brilliant and blinding, almost making him lose his focus.

His body ripped free from the bindings.

Tick quit aiming then and simply threw all his power out in wave after wave, destroying whatever dared come at him. Explosions of light and sound. The black air trembled; his skull rattled; his skin seemed to vibrate on his bones like they might slip free of his body. He was completely blind; the whole world had gone white and hot. There was wind and thunder and the smell of ozone and burning charcoal. It all added together into a chaotic jumble of anarchy, driving Tick insane as he continued to thrust outward with the power of Chi'karda as fast as he could gather it. He didn't know what else to do, and he was scared to stop.

Something tugged at his heart again. He felt it despite the madness all around him—that sensation of strings being pulled, of being yanked from the inside.

His body suddenly jerked away from the explosions of energy and flying white cords of lightning. He flew through the blackness of that place that had seemed like outer space, the raging battle he'd been fighting gone in a flash. Things changed around him. Instead of darkness, there was a blue haze, splotches of green and brown and red flying past him. Chunks of gray rock appeared, coming at him like a rain of meteors.

Tick used his mind to control his flight, dodging and flipping and accelerating to avoid the rocks. As he approached the biggest one, a jagged stone the size of a bus, he had to slam on his mental brakes, coming to a stop right before he smashed into the thing. This caused the tugging inside him to intensify, sending shocks of pain throughout his nerves.

He reached out and felt the hard surface of the rock. He crawled along it to the other side, then jumped off it by pushing with his legs. His body once again catapulted through the strange-colored air, and the hurtful tug on his heart lessened enough that he could bear it.

Things changed once again.

He dove into a thick liquid, almost like a gel. Cold wetness soaked his hair and clothes and skin as his perception changed. He could sense up and down, everything shifting around him until it felt as if he were near the bottom of a deep ocean, swimming upward even though his arms and legs did nothing to make it so. He tore through the dark waters.

There was just enough light raining down in wavering rays that he could see creatures coming toward him. Long, powerful leviathans that swam with their back fins beating against the current like the tail of a dolphin. But these monsters had arms and burning red eyes, and Tick knew they wanted to grab him and stop him from reaching whatever was tugging him forward.

The monsters reached out, swimming in all at once. Clawed hands reached viciously for his body, snatching and scratching as their fingers tried to gain purchase.

Tick lashed at them, swinging sluggishly through the thick liquid as he continued his ascent. The creatures kept pace with him, trying their best to grab hold of his limbs or clothes. Kicking and squirming, he spun his body to make it harder to catch, and when one of the creatures latched on, he fought it off. He couldn't see much of their faces—they were all shadows and angles—but their red eyes burned like rocks of lava.

Two of them grabbed his legs, wrapping their arms tightly around one each. They squeezed, and their claws dug into his skin. The unseen forces still pulled him toward some unknown destination through a place he didn't even understand.

He burst through the surface, the two creatures still holding onto his legs as he rocketed toward a bright blue sky. The jellied water cascaded off them in blubbery droplets, and Tick looked down to see the faces of the monsters clearly for the first time. They weren't human at all: their bodies looked like sharks with arms, and their heads were smooth and glistening. Their eyes seemed to glow even brighter.

They flew toward the sapphire sky far above, but the weight of the two creatures and the pain of their claws and desperate clutches were making the journey unbearable. Tick punched down, smashing his fists into those odd faces. There was a piercing, awful screaming sound, but they held on. Tick punched again and again, those horrific cries ripping through the air, louder each time. He slammed down his fists once more, and they finally let go, dropping to the swiftly receding waters below them. He watched as they fell, listening as their screams slowly faded.

Tick continued launching toward the sky.

He looked up, a prickling sensation covering every inch of his body now, not just his insides. Forces pulled at him, like a magnet pulling a chunk of metal or Earth's gravity pulling a skydiver. Except he was flying up, heading toward a dome of brilliant, blinding blue.

Tick hurt. He'd been hurting for what seemed like days. But the closer he got to the blue wall of the sky, the more pain ripped through his body. He screamed like he'd never screamed before, the wind ripping at his face.

And then he hit the sea of blue, and it all went away.

PART 2

---✳---

THE VOID

CHAPTER 20

✳

HUGS AND KISSES

Tick's eyes were closed.

He opened them up and blinked a few times. He lay on a hard surface, and above him he could see the grooves and lines of a ceiling carved from black rock. Faces peered down at him, women in robes with the hoods pulled up over their heads. The women were old, and several of them made a circle around his spot as they looked at him with both wonder and fear.

"Hey," Tick said. His body ached from what he'd just been through—the flying and Chi'karda-laced battles, the plunge through liquid, the sharklike creatures, the lightning ropes, all of it—but not nearly as bad as it *should* have hurt. He felt almost at peace, though more confused than he'd been in a long time.

And then there were the sounds of commotion, people being pushed out of the way, calls of his name from two female voices that he recognized. *More* than recognized. Voices he knew as well as the sound of his own.

Lisa's face appeared above him first, then his mom's. Tears streamed down their faces as they came at him, pulling his body into hugs. Stunned, he hugged back, both of them in his arms, *their* arms wrapped around his shoulders and neck, his mom kissing him over and over on both cheeks. Somehow he managed to sit up, and they huddled for a long, long moment before anybody even spoke. Tick was overwhelmed, a part of him thinking it was all an illusion, terrified it might be and that he'd wake up any second. But sobs shook him as he fiercely hugged his mom and sister, a reunion that he'd begun to think might never happen.

Finally, his mom pulled back, as did Lisa. They both wiped tears from their eyes and cheeks.

"What . . ." Tick began, but his words were choked up in more sobs. Embarrassed, he wiped his own tears from his face.

"Happened?" his mom finished for him. "You're wondering what happened?"

"Uh, yeah," Lisa replied. "I think we'd all kinda like to know that."

Tick had begun to compose himself, and he suddenly felt like he needed to stand, get some fresh air, breathe. He got to his feet and looked around. The old women in their robes and hoods had backed away, gathering into groups of two or three and staring at him with questioning faces. They all stood in a small chamber carved from black rock, a place Tick had never seen before. He noticed a Barrier Wand lying on the floor by one of the slightly curved walls.

Looking at his mom, he said, "I think I could write down a million guesses of how I got here and be wrong every time. Where *are* we?"

She smiled in response. "There's a lot to tell. But that's an easy question to answer. We're in the Thirteenth Reality, in Mistress Jane's castle, in a room she calls the Great Hall."

Tick almost fell down. "The Thirteenth? Mistress Jane's castle?"

"Or what's left of it," Lisa said.

One of the strangers walked over to stand next to Tick and his little group. She had a long face and seemed to have an air of authority about her. "I'm happy to see that you've been pulled back from the Nonex, Atticus Higginbottom. I assure you that we tried as hard as we could to do so ourselves. You have my apologies. I'm sure our master will want to meet with you as soon as she's recovered."

Tick listened to the words coming out of the woman's mouth, getting more confused with each one. Finally, he just said, "Huh?"

She eyed Tick's mom, an eyebrow raised. "We will take our leave. You can do all the explaining you'd like to the young man. I haven't the time. But I'm sorry to say we'll be taking your Barrier Wand until further notice. Mistress Jane would not be happy if we allowed you to leave before she's spoken with you."

"Now just wait one minute, Mordell," Tick's mom replied. He was still wondering what the lady had meant by "your Barrier Wand." And why they were in Jane's castle. And how he'd gotten there. And lots of other stuff. "You have no right to do that after we helped you!"

Two of the other women grabbed the Wand that had been lying on the ground. It was slipped under a robe and gone from sight just like that.

"Hey!" Lisa shouted. "Give that back!"

Mordell spoke in a calm voice. "You're no longer considered enemies of our master. That's your reward for helping us. But we have plenty of creatures outside these doors that will ensure you do as we ask. Please don't push our hospitality. Wait here, and we'll return for you shortly. We'll also have food and drink brought to you."

Tick didn't feel like he knew enough about the situation to argue or help, but his mom was fuming, and Lisa had her arms folded and a red face.

"Mom," Tick said, "I'm not sure what's going on, but if we really are in Jane's castle, we better do what they say until we figure things out. Plus, I'm dying to hear how we all got here. Just let them go for now."

His mom visibly relaxed, as if she was relieved to have the burden of the decision taken from her shoulders. "Okay." She turned to Mordell. "Leave us alone and let us talk. And bring us that food." The hint of command in her voice made Tick want to hoot and holler like he was at a football game. This was his *mom*.

A smile crept up Mordell's face. "I've already said we would do the two things you ask. All things are done under the will and might of our master. Your food will be here within the half hour."

After a slight bow of her head, she and the other women shuffled out of the room.

They sat in a small circle as they spoke, sharing each other's tales. When they were finished, Tick knew *what* had happened, but not how or why. It was all crazy.

"So that bunch of old ladies winked in Jane and Chu, but were going to let me die out there?" he asked.

643

"I can't believe I actually helped us get close enough to be saved, but then would've floated around in the outskirts of the Nonex for the rest of my life. That place wasn't fun, let me tell ya."

Tick's mom shook her head, looking half sad, half angry. "Jane and Chu appeared at the same time, lying on the same spot you did. The women didn't know that you were the one who'd opened up a doorway so they could reach them in the first place. Not that they would've done anything to return the favor— who knows?—but as soon as those two appeared, the almighty Ladies of Blood and Sorrow were done, totally ignoring our pleas to keep helping us so we could pull you in."

"Where did they go?" Tick asked. "Jane and Chu."

Lisa spoke up. "Mistress Jane marched off, her fancy red mask all scrunched up in anger. You'd think she'd have been happy after all that."

"And Chu?"

Lisa glanced at their mom, who provided the answer. "He had a crazy look in his eyes. He said he finally knew how to 'finish his plans.' I think that's how he put it. Then he disappeared, winked away before the Ladies could stop him. Maybe he had people waiting for his signal to reappear back in the Realities."

Tick swallowed, realizing with a lump in his throat that *he'd* been the one who'd provided the opportunity for Reginald Chu—one of the most dangerous men in the Realities, who'd proven he wanted nothing but power at any cost—to come back from a prison he could've never escaped alone.

"Maybe I shouldn't have done that," Tick whispered.

CHAPTER 21

✳

RAPPING AT THE DOOR

Master George lay his head back on the pillow, almost ashamed at how good it felt. He and Rutger had been working tirelessly for hours and hours, searching through all the data and reports from Mothball and Sally. Things were looking grim. Everywhere.

But the worst of it was what they *didn't* know. The disastrous results of Jane's meddling with dark matter had done something to the Realities. Something terrible. A lasting, lingering effect that they didn't quite understand yet. It had to do with links between the dimensions that weren't supposed to be there—rifts in the fabric of Reality appearing out of nowhere and killing people. Reports of gray fog and lightning and terrible thunder. George could scarcely hope they'd be able to *understand* it, much less do anything about it.

But even the greatest minds needed rest. Even his. The lights were off, the bed soft, the pillow even softer. Muffintops—the best cat ever—was snuggled against his chest. If he could just sleep for one solid hour. That would do wonders for his—

Someone started pounding on his door, solid thumps with a squeezed fist, by the sound of it. George yelped, and Muffintops screeched, clawing him as she dug in her claws then jumped onto the ground. George's heart was practically lodged in his throat. The knocking continued without stopping.

Of course, it could only be Rutger.

"What *is* it?" George yelled from his bed. "Rutger, stop that incessant pounding! This instant!"

Rutger didn't stop, and was, in fact, saying some muffled words that George couldn't hear over the knocking. Sighing, he flipped off his covers and headed for the door, his disappointment at missing a nap over-shadowed by dread. As excitable as Rutger was, he wouldn't be making this much fuss unless something bad had happened.

When George ripped open the door, Rutger almost fell down as his arm swung forward for another rap on the wooden door that was no longer there. He righted himself and looked up at his boss. George's heart lifted when he saw the huge smile on the little man's face.

"What *is* it?" George asked. "Goodness gracious me, you just about gave this old bear a heart attack!"

Rutger was breathing heavily, and he fought to control it. After starting and stopping several times, he finally got the words out, "Master Atticus is back! Tick is back! I've spotted him in the Thirteenth Reality, safe and whole and sound!"

George sucked in a gulp of air. "You're certain? No doubt?"

"Really? You really have to ask that?" Rutger's round face showed mock offense at first, but then he grinned.

"No, my good man, no, I don't. So, where is he then? Why haven't you winked him here straightaway? I want to see the boy!"

Rutger's smile vanished. "I tried. Something's blocking me. I think Jane must be keeping him in the Thirteenth Reality as a prisoner."

Master George's hands squeezed into fists at his sides. "Not this time. Jane is *not* going to interfere with us this time. Contact Sato. He and his army are already in that Reality."

Rutger turned to move, but George stopped him with his hand. "And get the others, too. We *need* to be together. Master Atticus could provide us just the lift we need. Finally, things are looking up."

Rutger smiled, then hurried off to follow his orders, his frantic waddle down the hall making Master George very proud indeed.

⟿

Tick, his mom, and Lisa had grown quiet, all talked out about the craziness of pulling Tick back from the Nonex. Now they sat with their backs against the black rock of the wall, the Great Hall empty and dark. A tray of dirty dishes and crumpled napkins sat on the floor next to the wall. Mordell had kept her promise to bring them something to eat. As well as her promise to keep them prisoner. Occasionally a fangen or another creature would pass by the opening to the chamber, just to make sure they knew leaving wasn't an option unless they wanted to be ripped to shreds or eaten.

Tick had been feeling guiltier by the minute. What had he done? How could he have been so selfish? He knew he needed all the Chi'karda he could summon to break free from the Nonex, so he'd used Chu and Jane. But he hadn't thought ahead to the fact that he'd be bringing the two worst enemies of the Realities back to their realms and giving them the opportunity to wreak havoc once again.

How could he be so stupid! He should have sacrificed himself and stayed in the Nonex, knowing those two monsters would be prisoners for the rest of their existence. He'd broken them free—or, at least helped it get started—just so he could come back, live his life, see his family again. The guilt ate away at his insides and made his stomach feel full of acid. And, of course, his mom could tell. She was a mom, after all.

"Atticus Higginbottom," she said, breaking the silence that had grown like a living entity, filling the room with something even darker than the air. "I know what you're thinking over there, and I want you to stop immediately. Do you understand me?"

Tick looked at her and tried to hide the despair that crawled inside of him. "What? I'm fine."

"You're fine, huh? And I've got bananas growing out of my ears. Nonsense, son. I know it's hitting you that Jane and Chu are freed from the Nonex. But it's not your fault. Who knows? Maybe they would've figured out a way to escape on their own eventually. It's what they do, how they got to where they are. They are masterminds, deceivers, manipulators, schemers. And *they* would've left *you* behind. The choices they make in life are not yours to bear. You did the right thing saving them. Maybe . . . maybe they'll change. Realize their mistakes and make them right."

Tick laughed, shocking himself just as much as the others. "Mom, now I *know* you're just trying to make me feel better. You heard for yourself what Chu said before they winked his power-hungry behind out of here. And Jane *had* her chance to become good. I ruined *that* when I melded her body to several pounds of metal. For somebody who was recruited to help the Realitants, I've sure done a great job of messing it all up."

His mom's eyes had welled up with tears, and she came over to sit next to him. She tried to pull him into her arms, and at first he resisted, but then he figured he could use some good old-fashioned mom-love and hugged her back. Fiercely.

"Listen to me," she whispered to him. "I'm your mom. I love you more than any human has ever loved a child before. Do you understand that?"

Tick nodded but didn't say anything. He was trying to hold back the tears.

Lisa was a few feet away, looking down as if she didn't feel like she had a right to hear this conversation.

"You did the right thing, Atticus," his mom continued. "Can you imagine—keeping a boy away from his mom? From his dad? From his sweet sisters? You did what you had to do to come back here, because you felt our love pulling you. You felt it across the universe and all the Realities and the barriers of the Nonex, because it's that powerful. You had no choice, son. Love is more powerful than Chi'karda, and you had to obey its call.

We need you. Your family needs you. Nothing could keep us apart. Nothing will."

"Okay, Mom." Tick didn't really know what to say, but he squeezed his mom even tighter, not caring if he seemed like a two-year-old kid. "Thanks."

"And one more thing," she said. "You didn't just bring back two bad guys. You brought back *you*. Someone who has more power over Chi'karda than anyone in history. Even Mistress Jane. The Realities need you, Atticus. They need *you* more than they *don't* need them. Clear?"

"Clear."

Her words really affected him. Lying around feeling sorry for himself wasn't going to be the answer. He needed to be ready to take action. He swore to himself that he'd be prepared. He'd study and learn and practice. And if the day came that either one of his enemies tried to hurt the worlds again, he would stop them. He swore it.

"I love you," he whispered to his mom.

The shuffle of feet drew their attention to the entrance of the chamber. Mordell, the long and lanky Lady of Blood and Sorrow, stood with her hands folded in front of her.

"I supposed you've had your time to rest and eat," the woman said. "But it's over now. At least for Atticus. Mistress Jane would like to see you, boy. She says it's high time you two spoke about the Fourth Dimension."

CHAPTER 22

✳

A RIBBON OF SHINY SILVER

Sato stood atop the rock that jutted from the hilltop, allowing himself to finally enjoy a moment to himself. The land fell away in all directions, flowing with green grasses and thorny shrubs and leafless trees. Autumn had come to this area of the Thirteenth Reality, and there was a bite to the air that made Sato shiver. Far below him was a river that cut through the valley like a shiny silver ribbon, disappearing into a forest and the mountains beyond.

Somewhere along that river was the castle of Mistress Jane.

It had taken only a couple of days for his army to clean up the few scattered creatures left behind at the evil lady's Factory, otherwise known as the house of horrors. It was where Jane had used her frightening mix of science and magic to create mixed breeds of animals. Humans had been next on the list for her experiments, until the ones she was holding prisoner had been rescued by Sato and the Fifth Army.

All of them but ten.

Sato would never know the faces of the ten people he'd had to leave behind when the destruction became too much. Ten people left to die, crushed by stone and earth. He couldn't blame Master George and Rutger—they'd done what needed to be done. If Sato and Mothball had stayed to rescue those last few people, there would have been twelve dead bodies instead of ten. But that didn't change the fact that their loss haunted him day and night. If only he had been a little faster . . .

But here he was. Back in the Thirteenth again. They had hunted down any creatures of Jane's they could find around the ruins of the Factory, and something told him that any that were left were heading for the castle. He knew he was right after having received word from headquarters that Tick was now imprisoned there, along with his mom and sister.

Tick's sister—Lisa. Sato kind of liked that girl.

He shook his head, ashamed of himself. What a stupid thing to think at the moment. First of all, he couldn't believe that Tick was back, safe. *There* was a story he was dying to hear. And second, he hated to hear the words *Mistress Jane* again. Hated it. She'd killed his parents, burned them alive, right in front of his young eyes. He dreamed of it every night. The only silver lining was that maybe he'd finally get his chance for payback—at *his* hand, not Tick's.

A voice behind him interrupted his thoughts. "Master Sato, we're waiting for word on what we do next."

Sato turned to see an enormously tall man with thin features, his black hair hanging in straggles, his face gaunt, his clothes raggedy. But Sato knew that no one should ever make assumptions based on the appearance of these warriors from the Fifth Reality. They could break a man in half with two fingers.

He especially liked this one, Mothball's very own dad. "Gather them up, Tollaseat. We're marching for the castle. For Tick. For *Mistress Jane*."

~~~

Tick didn't put up much of a fight. With Jane's monsters hovering around outside the Great Hall, Mordell looking as if she'd bite anyone who gave her any trouble, and—most of all—out of pure curiosity, he decided to calmly walk with the old woman to where Jane waited for him.

They'd come out into the long underground

passage that went along the river, the same place where Tick had used his own power to wink himself and his friends away from the fangen attack during their first visit to the Thirteenth Reality. More of those creatures lined the wall now as he and Mordell walked past them, their thin wings folded in, their fang-filled mouths closed, their yellow eyes glaring at him. Tick felt a nauseous chill in his gut.

It wasn't long before he began to see the extent of the castle's destruction. Walls had caved in. Huge chunks of rock had been torn loose from the ceiling and crashed to the ground, breaking the stone floor and creating spider webs of cracks everywhere. It got worse the farther they went; soon they were walking through a maze of debris. Tick looked in horror at some spots that appeared as if one puff of breath would cause the whole structure to come tumbling down on top of them.

They eventually reached an arch that exited into a dark staircase, narrow steps spiraling up to heights Tick couldn't see. Dust covered the steps, but the walls seemed solid enough. Mordell didn't say a word the entire time, just led him toward the upper reaches of the castle.

Tick was out of breath when they finally came to a wooden door.

Mordell stopped and looked at him with a grave face. "These are not the usual quarters of our master.

The destruction caused by"—her eyes narrowed, and Tick knew she'd been about to say that it was all his fault—"the Great Disturbance made quite an impact on our grand castle. Mistress Jane takes her place here until all can be repaired. Wait until I beckon you to enter."

She rapped lightly on the wooden door three times. A few seconds later, it opened, and another woman in a hooded robe stared out at them. She nodded then allowed Mordell to step inside, shutting the door in Tick's face.

Tick was tempted to knock on the door himself— or better yet, just open it up and waltz inside. He wasn't nearly as scared of seeing Jane as he'd been in the past; his progress in the powers of Chi'karda had given him more confidence than ever before in his life. Forcing patience on himself, he stood and waited, knowing that Jane would probably make him wait awhile just to anger him.

He was right. At least fifteen minutes went by while he stood and stared at the walls and steps of the staircase. But just in case Jane was spying on him somehow, he refused to show his frustration or annoyance. He merely waited.

Finally, the door swung open. Mordell was standing there.

"In normal days, our master would disintegrate the wood, inspect you with snooper bugs, make a show of her great powers. But she says she is tired and weak, and that she expects understanding from you. Times are not as they once were."

Tick was surprised by the woman's words and shocked that Jane would dare show weakness, much less admit it outright. Not sure what to say, he shrugged, doing his best to act like it meant nothing to him either way.

"Then come." Mordell swung the door wide, and Tick stepped into a small chamber that led to another opening. Beyond that was a sparsely furnished room with a couch and a few chairs, a small window looking out on the fading light of day.

Jane was lying on the couch, the hood of her yellow robe pulled up over her head, her red mask set in a blank expression. With one of her scarred, withered hands, she motioned for Tick to sit down on a chair near her. He did so, wondering anxiously what she wanted to talk to him about.

"The Fourth Dimension," he said first, skipping the formalities. "This lady says you want to talk to me about the Fourth Dimension. Why?" His voice was naturally curt and devoid of feeling when he was around this woman. What kind of a person had he become to feel such things?

Jane sat up straighter and looked at him through the eyeholes of her mask. "You did something terrible, Atticus. Something really, really terrible."

CHAPTER 23

✳

JANE'S TALK

Tick didn't need one more thing to feel guilty about, and for once he'd been taken by surprise. Here he was, in the castle of Mistress Jane, the woman who had planned to suck the life out of human children and use it to create monstrous creatures, and she was telling him that he'd done something terrible.

"And what exactly is it that I've done?" Tick asked.

Jane grunted as she swung her legs around off the couch and placed her feet on the floor, sitting upright. Her artificial face still had no expression. "My castle, Atticus. It's not a pretty sight. My beautiful room atop the palace is now nothing more than a pile of rocks crushed on top of other rocks. My castle—other than a few spots like this one and the Great Hall—lies in ruins. Most of my servants were killed. My most faithful and trusted servant, Frazier Gunn, is nowhere to be found. My body is weak, and my mind is tired. And here I sit before you now."

Tick didn't see where this was going at all. "What does that have to do with me?"

"My point, Atticus Higginbottom, is that I'm not in any mood to fix the problems you've created for the Realities. Not in a mood at all."

"Tell me, what horrible thing did I do again?" Tick was surprisingly curious.

Her mask melted into a frown. "When I used the Blade of Shattered Hope, Atticus, I was trying to do something that would benefit humanity in the long run. You saw only the short-term point of view—the destruction of an alternate reality—but it was a vital step forward on a journey toward a final and perfect Utopia. Eternal happiness for the rest of mankind's existence. You did *not* understand!"

Tick's anger flared. "Don't sit there and preach to me! There's not a rational person alive who would call anything you've done *good*. You'd have to be totally insane, which I think you *are*. So I guess it makes sense."

"Insolent boy," Jane muttered harshly, like an expelled breath of frustration.

"And you still haven't told me what I did that was so terrible."

"You cracked open the Fourth Dimension!" Jane yelled, standing on her feet as she did so. "You've unleashed a force that we hardly understand! And for all your noble talk about saving people, you've done the worst thing possible! The very energy that created the universe is now on the verge of exploding outward to do it all over again."

Her red mask was pinched in vicious anger, her eyebrows slanted like crossed swords. And her scarred hands were squeezed into fists as she breathed in and out heavily. "I knew it as soon as I got back. I've always known there was a link between the Chi'karda here and the mysteries of the Fourth Dimension. Your battle with me, and the unprecedented amounts of Chi'karda we unleashed, broke that link, Atticus. Every single one of the Realities is in an enormous amount of trouble. All the earthquakes and tornadoes and destruction will seem like the good old days soon enough."

Tick realized with a sinking stomach that Jane was telling him the truth.

"Look, I have no idea what you're talking about," he said. "Just sit down and relax. Neither one of us is going anywhere."

"Sit down and relax?" Jane repeated, as if he'd told her to eat a live rat. But she sat down anyway, folding back into the soft cushions of her couch. "There's no time for relaxation, boy. I first suspected something was wrong when we were in the Nonex and I saw the rift in the air that led to another world. Another Reality. For that rift to reach the Nonex, I knew it wasn't as simple as a pathway between worlds. It had to be something much deeper. And then there was the incident with the earthquake and the subsequent uptick of craziness."

Tick knew that the Nonex was a place where a gorilla could suddenly erupt out of the sand, then turn into a moth and fly away. All kinds of unexplainable stuff happened all the time, but Jane was right. The craziness had ratcheted up considerably right before they escaped.

"You do remember the rip in the air I saw?" Jane asked.

"Huh? Oh. Yeah. I do."

"There was a boy and his father, or perhaps his grandfather, in a forest, looking back at me. And I knew something was off about it, something danger-ous. I backed away, and just in time, too. A terrible storm of gray mist and thunderous lightning exploded within that rift, destroying whatever was close by on both sides of the rift. You saw what the area looked like afterwards."

Tick remembered. It had reminded him of TV

footage of a tornado's aftermath. "So you're saying that what you saw was the Fourth Dimension?"

"A better way to put it is that I saw what comes *out* of the Fourth Dimension. The Void of Mist and Thunder. It's always been a rumor, a myth—pure speculation. Until now. I believe the Void is a living thing, but without conscience. The complete and pure power of creation. All it wants is to escape its prison and consume everything in its path. It's mindless and hungry."

"How do you even know about it? You already have a name for it, but you never told anyone about it. Why not?" Tick felt sick inside. Here was yet another thing that had gone wrong. And somehow it linked back to being *his* fault.

"I'm old," Jane said. Her red mask had returned to a blank expression, but Tick knew anything could set her off. "I've researched the origins of our universe in hopes of making it better. That crotchety old George and I worked on this project together, years ago. Trust me, I'm sure he's figured out what's going on by now and is sweating a river."

"What *is* the Fourth Dimension?" Tick asked. "I still don't really get it." He hated admitting that to her, but he had no choice.

"Well, you know what 3-D is, correct? Three dimensions?"

"Yeah."

"Well, the Fourth is named that because it's a step beyond anything we understand in terms of vision and . . . placement. Three-D is exponentially greater than 2-D. And the Fourth is infinitely greater than 3-D. The power of the Void is much, much greater than any kind of energy we know in our own dimension. If unleashed, it will consume this world like food and use it to recreate another. And all of us will die along the way."

Tick almost wanted to laugh. "You're really clearing things up."

The mask flashed to anger. "Stop it. Now. None of your childish sarcasm, do you understand me? What I'm talking about is very serious. More deadly than even my Blade of Shattered Hope. *Do you understand?*" She shouted the last question, making Tick lean back in his chair. "It was your meddling with that Blade that ripped open the Fourth Dimension in the first place!"

"Okay, I get it." Tick was scared, but he didn't want to show it. "But this isn't the first time you've tried to work with me. The last time ended with you trying to choke me to death. Remember?"

"Oh, Atticus." The anger and spirit seemed to drain straight out of Jane, her shoulders slumping and her mask melting into another frown. "Do you still really believe I was trying to kill you that day? We had to stop

Chu, and at the time, hurting you was the only way to get you to release your Chi'karda. You couldn't do it at will like you can now."

Tick looked at the floor. Jane confused him so much. She seemed to have some good in her, but she'd also done some terrible, awful things. But could he really blame her completely after what *he'd* done to *her*?

"I don't know what to do," he said quietly. He was tired of thinking. "I just don't."

"Atticus," Jane said, her raspy voice quiet, like a small clearing of the throat. "I'm not going to sit here and pretend that you and I are best friends. I resent you for what you did to me, though I know it was partly out of your control. I know you hate me. And I'm not making any promises to stop fighting for a Utopia for mankind. When this issue is dealt with, I'll continue with my mission. I will do whatever it takes."

Tick looked up sharply. "You will, huh? You'll go right back to destroying entire worlds and throwing little kids into awful experiments? No skin off your back, right?"

Jane pounded a fist on her knee. "Yes! I will do whatever it—"

Her words were cut off by the door slamming open, the entire room seeming to tremble. Jane and

Tick both shot to their feet to see who had come in.

It was Mordell, and her face was pale with fright.

"The Fourth Dimension has torn open outside the castle," she announced in a shaky voice, as if she had to avoid shouting to preserve the dignity of her order. "The Void is attacking our creatures."

CHAPTER 24

✳

FOG AND THUNDER

Lorena had been holding Lisa in her arms—the girl had finally dozed off—when she heard the terrible sound in the distance. It was like a great, rushing wind, with cracks of thunder splintering it. And then she heard the screams. Unnatural screams that she knew came out of the mouths of Jane's creatures.

Lisa's head popped up immediately, her chance at slumber gone. "What *is* that?"

"I don't know, sweetie." Lorena's heart picked up its pace, and a swell of panic bulged in her chest, making it hard to breathe. If something was making those awful monsters scream, then what would it do to *them*?

She heard the scuffle of feet running along the

passage outside the Great Hall. Grabbing Lisa's hand, she stood up, and the two of them went over to the arched exit to investigate. The two fangen that had been assigned to guard them were gone, and dozens of creatures were frantically scurrying past the opening, *away* from the shattered door that led outside to the castle grounds. Any noise of their passage was drowned out by the sounds of thunder crashing and booming, which were getting louder.

"What on *earth*?" Lorena whispered, barely hearing herself. She looked at Lisa, whose eyes were wide and scared.

"It sounds like a storm!" her daughter yelled to her. "But how could it be hurting all those people?"

"You mean *creatures*." Lorena shook her head. "It has to be something more than a storm."

"Let's go look!" Lisa shouted.

Lorena frowned at her, thinking her daughter had surely gone nuts. That, or she was still young enough to let curiosity overrule common sense.

Lisa pulled her mom closer and spoke into her ear. "If it's not just a storm, and if it's hurting the *bad* guys, then it must be on *our* side. We need to find out who or what it is and let them know that Mistress Jane has Tick!"

Lorena had started shaking her head before Lisa even finished. "No way!"

"But this is our chance! No one's guarding us!"

"No way," Lorena repeated. But then she peered into her daughter's eyes and saw that courage had replaced the fear to a degree. Motherly pride filled her chest and made her change her mind. "Okay, maybe just a peek. But we stop when I say so. Do you understand?"

Lisa smiled, a pathetic little effort. "Okay. I promise."

Like two spies, they slipped out of the Great Hall and ran down the passage alongside the internal stream, toward the broken door and the gray wall behind it.

⌒

Sato pulled up short when he saw the strange anomaly appear right in front of the castle. They'd been marching for several hours, the sun sinking toward the forest on the horizon, the Fifth Army like a slow-moving tsunami behind their leader. Sato had promised them that one day soon, they'd return to the Fifth Reality and take back their world from the Bugaboo soldiers who'd gone insane and ruled with crazed minds.

But for now, the army was pledged to help the Realitants get things back in order. And before even that, Sato wanted to see his friend Tick again. See him safe and sound.

They were cresting the rise of a hill, the land sloping below them toward the castle, when Sato saw something that made no sense, made him doubt his own eyes. Made him wonder if they'd been working too hard and his mind was on the fritz.

Starting at a spot about fifty feet above the ground, close to the ruined castle itself, the air seemed to rip apart like a burst seam, the blues and whites and greens of the world replaced by a stark and empty grayness that spread in a line toward the grasses below. Lightning flickered behind the torn gash in reality, and even from where he stood a mile or so away, Sato could hear the rumbles of thunder. Not just hear it—the noise made the ground tremble and his head rattle.

Tollaseat stepped up beside him. "There's been rumors of the like, there 'as. Fabric of the world rippin' apart and whatnot. Sendin' out destruction for the poor blokes who might be standin' nearby."

Sato nodded. He'd heard some of the soldiers whispering about it, but seeing it in person sent a wave of unease through his bones and joints. There was something terribly unnatural about it, and he knew it meant trouble.

"What should we do, sir?" Tollaseat asked. His voice revealed a trace of fear, but Sato knew the man and his fellow soldiers would storm the odd thing if he asked. Which he did.

"We need to know what that is," Sato said, hearing the strong command in his own speech. "And we need to save Tick. One mission has become two."

Tollaseat clapped him on the back. "We'll roll it up and bottle it, we will. Take it back to old Master George with a wink and a smile."

"That we will," Sato agreed. "Let's move out."

The Fifth Army started marching down the hill.

⁓

Tick felt weird following Mistress Jane down the long, winding staircase. He felt weird about being around her at all. He was pretty sure two mortal enemies had never acted like this before, trying to kill each other one week, then chitchatting about the world's problems before scurrying down some steps to investigate a bunch of noise and fog the next.

He *was* curious. Was it a coincidence that the Void Jane had spoken of—this beast of the Fourth Dimension that represented some kind of pure and powerful energy—would attack her castle just as they had begun to scheme against it? Or did it have more of a mind than Jane thought?

They reached the bottom of the stairs and stumbled out into the main passageway, which was flanked by a narrow river on one side and the castle's interior stone wall on the other. It was a scene of chaos. Creepy chaos. Dozens of Jane's creatures, mostly fangen, were running pell-mell along the pathway, many of them wounded, some falling into the water. If the creatures started chasing him, he thought he'd die of fright before he could even think to use his newfound powers. But they all just kept fleeing, heading deeper into the castle.

Jane stopped to assess the situation, looking in the direction from which all of her creatures had fled. Tick did the same, but all he could see was a gray light. A rumble of something loud and booming came from there.

"Come!" Jane yelled, sprinting toward the odd light and the noise. Her robe billowed out as she ran, and her hood fell back, revealing the scarred horrors of her head, where her hair had once grown healthily. Feeling another pang of guilt, Tick followed her.

⁓

Lorena pulled up short about a hundred feet from the jagged edges of the broken door, stopping Lisa with an outstretched arm. No matter how much bravery they'd found, the loss of caution would be absurd. They could see better now, and Lorena wanted to understand what they were running toward.

A mass of churning gray air hovered behind the

wide opening of the doorway like clouds that boiled before unleashing torrents of rain. Streaks of lightning sliced through the grayness, illuminating the world in brilliant flashes of white fire. The thunder that pounded the air was deafening, making Lorena's ears feel as if they were bleeding. All the fangen and their cousins had either fled or lay on the ground around the door, battered and dead. Which made her wonder what she and Lisa thought they were doing coming this close to the danger.

The booming sounds stopped so suddenly that Lorena's ears popped, and the silence was like cotton that had been stuffed in her ears. There was the slightest buzz of electricity in the air, and the gray clouds behind the door were now full of tiny bolts of electricity, a web of white light. Lisa was about to ask something, but Lorena shushed her. Things were changing.

The churning, smoky cloud began to coalesce into sections, filtering and swirling, as if some unseen hand had begun to shape the substance like putty. Soon there were gaps in the mist, the green grass and blue sky shining through from beyond. The gray fog continued its shaping until several dozen oblong sections stood on end, scattered around like a crowd of ghosts. Then heads formed as the misty substance solidified into slick, gray skin. Arms. Legs. Eyes full of burning fire.

Oddly enough, they were roughly the shape of some of Mistress Jane's creatures that Lorena had seen fleeing. Though these were bigger and more crudely formed.

The one closest to Lorena started walking toward her.

CHAPTER 25

✳

THE VOIDS

Sato was about a hundred yards away, Tollaseat and the rest of the Fifth Army right behind him, when the mass of fog and lightning in front of the castle started to shift and take shape. *Dozens* of shapes, bigger than most men, were continually refining themselves, their edges sharpening, until they looked like Mistress Jane's creatures. Arms, legs, wings, the whole bit.

Sato realized he'd stopped without meaning to.

"What bloody kind of business is that, ya reckon?" Tollaseat asked him from behind, a deadly whisper that fit the mood.

"I have no idea," Sato answered. "But there can't be anything good about it. We need to get there. Come on!"

Sato burst into a sprint, and his soldiers followed, their feet pounding on the grass like the hooves of a hundred horses.

Tick rounded a bend and finally came into view of the busted door through which he'd been before, a long time ago. Outside of it, dozens of gray shapes that roughly resembled Jane's creatures stood in the fields beyond the castle walls. He couldn't quite compute what was happening—they looked *similar* to what Jane had created, but they were also bigger, and . . . *different*. More humanoid.

The few figures in the front were walking forward, through the door. Their eyes shone with brilliant displays of fire, as if they were windows into a furnace. Tendrils of lightning shot across the surface of their slick, colorless skin.

Then Tick saw two people standing between him and the oncoming creatures.

"Mom!" he yelled, breaking into a run to reach her. "What in the world are you doing out here?"

She turned to face him, as did Lisa, and Tick's heart broke a little when he saw the fear in their eyes and expressions.

"We're trying to figure out . . ." his mom began to

shout, but didn't finish. She pulled Lisa behind her and came toward Tick until they met. "It hardly matters. What are those things?" She gestured to the briskly walking gray people about fifty feet away.

Mistress Jane joined Tick, her red mask staring with a slight look of awe at the oncoming ghostly figures. The fire of their eyes reflected off the shiny, wet-looking surface of the red metal covering her hideous face.

Tick felt a shiver of panic, but he knew he had to put on a brave front for his family. "It has something to do with the Fourth Dimension breaking into our Reality. It's pure energy, so maybe it can take things from our world and recreate them. Don't know, though. Come on."

He pointed down the passageway. The creatures were coming straight for them, marching with purpose. Their faces had no distinctive features—just eyes full of flame. Their arms and legs bulged with gray muscle, and their shoulders and chests were broad, but the wings—on those that had them—were misshapen and barely hanging on. Trickles of electricity continued to dance across the surface of their skin.

The Voids—that's how Tick thought of them, no other word coming to mind—had reached them and stopped. Now fully inside the castle, they lined up in several rows that reached back dozens of feet. There had to be at least fifty of the things. Eyes of fire, gray skin charged with lines of white lightning. But they were still now, staring at Tick and the others.

Mistress Jane spoke in a whisper. "The Fourth Dimension is even more powerful than I thought. What has it done to my sweet, sweet creations?"

⁓

When the gray creatures started entering the castle, Sato's urgency picked up even stronger. Tick was in there somewhere, and these things looked like nothing but trouble.

He sprinted harder, hearing the thumping of his soldiers at his heels. They reached the torn land where the spinning mass of gray air had churned up the soil and ruined the grass. Sato ran across it, taking care not to trip over the divots and chunks of dirt. The inside of the castle was dark, but an eerie orange light shone from somewhere. Sato wondered if it might be coming from the faces of the creatures themselves, but they all had their backs to him at the moment.

Sato stopped at the threshold of the huge entrance and held up a hand. Tollaseat and the others stopped on a dime, and not a peep came from anyone.

The gray monsters had quit walking, and they

huddled close together, watching something on the other side. Sato couldn't see over their heads.

"Come on," he whispered.

Trying his best to make no noise, skulking on the front pads of his feet, he moved forward, approaching the back of the pack. He was about ten feet away when one of the creatures turned around sharply to face them. Sato was shocked to see that the thing had two wide eye sockets filled with flickering, hot-burning flames. It was like the inside of its head was a forge, ready to heat up some iron for sword-making.

"What in the name of—" Tollaseat started, but further movement by the gray man cut him short.

A mouth was opening in the gray face, the gap also full of fiery flames, red and orange. It expanded until the upper edge almost touched the eyeholes, an entire face looking in on an inferno. The creature's long, thick arms ended in stumps that looked way too much like fists coiled in anger. But then the gray man stopped moving. He held that strange, menacing pose with its oven of a mouth stuck in a huge yawn.

Sato didn't know whether he should attack. He knew nothing about this enemy, or whether it really was an enemy. And if it was, he didn't know what kinds of power it had to fight them back. But he had to do *something*.

As he slowly took a few steps toward the creature,

Sato's right hand reached down inside his own pocket and fingered one of the cool, round balls that were nestled in there. He pulled one into his grip, then out of his pocket. It was a Rager, its trapped static electricity bouncing to get out and destroy things.

The gray man started to growl, like a whoosh of air had ramped up the fire in his head.

～～⌒⌒

Tick had been thrilled when he noticed Sato and his Fifth Army come marching through the broken door, many of the soldiers holding Shurrics, those deadly weapons of sound. Sato disappeared from sight—he was shorter than the Voids standing outside—but the heads of people of the Fifth Reality rose above the creatures, and their faces were mixed with awe and excitement. Not much fear.

All of the Voids had opened their mouths wide, fire raging within, their faces slightly angled toward the ceiling of the passage. Their arms were rigid at their sides, stumpy fists on the ends, wilted wings hanging off their backs. A low groaning sound came from the rear of the pack, like the roar of an airplane's engine as it started up.

The whole scene reminded Tick of a standoff in an old Western movie, and he didn't like it one bit.

"Mistress Jane," he said. "If you've got some advice, now would be a great time to share it."

The robed woman stepped forward, seemed to assess the situation for a few seconds, then turned to face Tick. Her mask had no expression, but the roaring, growling sounds were getting louder and louder.

"I don't know how to fight this kind of power," Jane said. "The Fourth Dimension has obviously taken my creations and turned them into a weapon of some sort."

She'd barely finished her sentence when one of the Voids in the front row ejected something from its mouth—a beam of pure flame, fiery and steaming, like a spout of lava shot from a hose. It flew up, then out, then came down and headed straight for Jane's head.

CHAPTER 26

✳

RAGERS AND
SQUEEZERS

As Tick dove forward, his shoulders smashing into the side of Jane and tackling her to the ground, somewhere in the back of his mind, he was aware that once again he was saving a person who'd devoted her life to doing evil things. No matter her intent. They crashed to the ground, and Tick felt a hot streak fly above him, almost enough to singe the hairs on the back of his neck.

He rolled off Jane in time to see the short stream of liquid fire sail past the rest of the crowd and hit the wall on the other side of the stream. Instead of splashing like lava, the fire sparked and burst into tiny explosions, crumbling some of the stone. Chips of rock rained into the water. But the weapon—or whatever it had been—left no trace, evaporating into the air with a puff of steam.

Jane and Tick jumped back to their feet, and everyone faced the Voids. Their mouths were still open in firing position, but none of them were doing anything just yet.

"Could it have been a warning?" Tick's mom asked. "Is there any way we can talk to them? If they're really from—"

"They *are* from the Fourth Dimension," Jane interrupted. "And talking to them would surely be a waste of time. I can't imagine they think like us, talk like us, see the universe like us. Our comprehensions of the Realities are probably as different as those of a spider and a redwood tree."

"Or more like a human and an ant," Tick murmured. "Maybe we're nothing more than something they need to step on."

Jane shook her head slowly back and forth. "We need to kill them, plain and simple. Atticus, prepare yourself. Pull in your Chi'karda, boy."

Tick felt a rushing behind his ears, his heart thumping. He turned to Mordell and made sure he avoided eye contact with his family. "Take . . . please take my mom and sister somewhere safe. Please."

"Atticus Higginbottom!" his mom said, planting

her feet and propping her hands on her hips. "We can do just as much—"

Another one of the Voids shot a stream of flame and lava from its mouth. The fire sliced through the air toward the wall then curved, swinging around to head for Tick's group. Everyone collapsed to the ground—Tick yanking on his mom and sister's clothes—just as the deadly cylinder of bright red and orange flew over them and splashed into the wide stream next to the passage. Sparks and shoots of fire went everywhere as the water boiled and hissed for several seconds. Then it ended.

Tick grabbed his mom and looked her in the face. "Let me do this, Mom. You need to keep Lisa safe. Let me do this!"

Another burst of fire and lava came shooting through the air. This time it was Lisa who shoved Tick and his mom out of the way. The fiery stream slammed into the floor where they'd been lying. Sparks showered onto Tick; he swatted them off his shirt and stamped out the little fires around him.

"Mom!" he yelled. "You have to go! Jane and I can fight them off!"

There was no more argument. Mordell helped his mom and Lisa get to their feet, and then the three of them sprinted back down the passageway, heading for some place Tick hoped would protect them. Maybe the

Great Hall. He turned back to the Voids in time to see another stream of fire erupting from a creature's mouth. The lava shot forward in a violent burst, as if the thing wanted it to reach the three fleeing women.

Tick acted without thinking. He triggered something in his heart, deep within his chest, and pulled something out with his mind and soul. A spinning cloud of orange sparkles ignited into existence around his body, and he threw some of it at the flying barrage of fire and lava. They met in midair and erupted into a fireworks show, sparks dropping and dancing on the ground. But it had worked, and Lisa and his mom disappeared around the bend, with Mordell on their heels.

It was Jane and Tick now. They exchanged a glance that somehow said, *Here we go again. Enemies working as allies.*

They stood side by side and faced the army of gray men, the Voids from another dimension. Tick wanted to say something but kept his mouth shut and waited for the battle to begin.

⌒

Sato had pulled back his men and women, funneling them through the broken door and onto the flattened grasses outside the castle. Three of the gray men had fired spouts of flame and lava at his army, and one of the attacks had hit home, enveloping a giant woman named Erthell in fire. Two of her companions had thrown her into the river to put out the flames, and then stayed to help her back onto the bank.

Sato wasn't running away either. Without any kind of shield to protect themselves, he wanted to fight back from cover. He and several other soldiers lined up against the wall outside the entrance to the castle, Shurrics at the ready. Even more soldiers stood right behind them, ready to jump out and throw Ragers and Squeezers—the nasty little grenades with metal hooks that contracted into whatever they hit—at the enemy to cause distraction and pain.

"Ready the volley!" Sato shouted. "As soon as they fly and ignite, we start pounding them with sound. Ready?"

"Ready!" came the roar of their reply. Tollaseat was on the other side of the broken door, and he flashed Sato a wild grin.

"Now!" Sato commanded.

Little balls full of dancing electricity and dozens of Squeezer grenades flew out of his soldiers' hands, catapulting through the air toward the lines of gray men. At the sight of the volley, the creatures started shooting bursts of lava and fire from their mouths, squirting pure heat in all directions. Some of them hit home, incinerating the Realitant weapons on contact. But some of the weapons got through and exploded, working their magic.

A couple of Ragers hit the ground several feet in front of the first of the creatures, cracking into the rock and collecting debris like shavings to a magnet. It happened so fast, but the process never stopped wowing Sato. The little balls rolled forward in a burst until they weren't little anymore, becoming great mounds of earth and stone that crashed into the unsuspecting gray men, throwing several to the ground and rolling over them. The ones that died seemed to explode into gray mist and were whisked up into the air, forming a small cloud. Jagged bolts of lightning crackled through the gray masses.

A few of the Squeezers made it through as well, exploding when they hit anything solid, their little metal clips flying in all directions. When they made contact with the gray skin of the creatures, the grenades' sharp, needlelike ends contracted and squeezed. The monsters roared with pain, flames leaping out of their mouths. The entire castle rumbled from the awful sound of it. One of the creatures was hurt badly enough that it dissolved into mist and flew toward the circling cloud like its companions had done. Several clouds hovered above the castle now.

"Fire the Shurrics!" Sato yelled.

He and his fellow soldiers aimed and obeyed, shooting out blasts of pure sound waves at the creatures. The leading edges of the waves, heavy thumps that were felt instead of heard, flew forward until they slammed into a few bodies of the gray men. Most of them erupted into mist and rose to join the other lightning-laced clouds. But there were still plenty more creatures to fight, and Sato kept shooting.

He caught a glimpse of the battle raging on the other side. Streaks of sparkling orange and thick, gray bodies flew in all directions. Their screams were like the roars of a blacksmith's forge.

Sato fired his Shurric at the enemy.

CHAPTER 27

✳

BEAMS OF FIRE

The battle had begun slowly once Tick's mom and the others were gone. The few shots of fire and lava from the mouths of the Voids were easily blocked by Jane or Tick, taking turns as if they'd done this for years. There seemed to be more action on the other side of the creatures, where Sato and his army had obviously started attacking with some of the Realitant weapons. Tick recognized the sounds of Ragers and Squeezers and that skull-rattling thump of a Shurric. And there were weird cloud shapes of gray mist hovering near the ceiling above—tiny bolts of lightning dancing within.

But then things close by changed.

The entire front row of Voids closest to Tick opened

their glowing mouths even wider, and pure flame poured out, gushing with lava and brilliant yellow light. There were at least a dozen perfectly cylindrical geysers of fiery material coming at Tick and Jane like a mass of thick snakes.

Tick threw all his focus into the Chi'karda that burned within him and sent it out in waves to crash against the oncoming heat. There were spectacular explosions and sparks and hisses of flame raining to the ground, bouncing like yellow raindrops. He had to keep his eyes open against the blinding light in order to see what was coming and where to aim his powers. Spots swam in his vision, purple blotches and streaks of black.

He wiped his hands across his face and blinked hard several times. Still the streams of pure fire came at him, and he blocked them, destroyed them. Jane was doing the same, but it was taking every bit of their effort. The point at which Chi'karda and Void-fire met and exploded was getting closer and closer to where Tick stood. He needed to change tactics, shift the advantage.

With a scream and an almost violent push of Chi'karda from his body, he ran forward, blasting away at anything dangerous that came in sight. His sudden movement seemed to take the Voids by surprise; several of them quit shooting their deadly venom. Tick narrowed his eyes, focused all his energy on the bodies of the Voids, and threw his power at them. An almost solid wall of orange sparks erupted from him like a wave, flying forward until it crashed into several gray men. The orange power swarmed around the Voids, picking them up and tossing their strange forms into the air, sweeping them away like a giant with a broom. Those strange, furnacelike screams tore through the building; the ghostly sound gave Tick the creeps.

He turned to see Jane copying his method, running forward and bringing the attack to the Voids. A wave of Chi'karda shot out from her and sent even more of the gray humanlike creatures toward the ceiling like tossed bags.

Several spouts of Void-fire suddenly came shooting at Tick from the untouched creatures next to the far wall. Without time to react, he dove for the ground and rolled, feeling the impact of the fire hitting the ground near his back. Sparks and chunks of rock sprayed into his skin, needles of pain that made him roll harder and faster. As he spun, there was suddenly a drop below him—the hard floor vanished, and he was in open air. It was like time had frozen just long enough for him to realize that strange fact.

He plunged into the ice-cold waters of the castle river. The freezing liquid bit at every one of his nerves.

He gasped for air as he began to right himself and swim back to the stone edge.

Something grabbed him by the ankle and pulled him under.

～

They were making progress.

Sato called on his soldiers to enter the castle proper, firing away with their weapons as they advanced. The enemy's numbers had been cut in half at least, the gray bodies collapsing into a mist of smoke before swirling up to the high ceiling to form yet another lightning-laced cloud. It was like a storm had gathered in a false sky and rain would fall at any second.

Gray creatures still catapulted up from the ground left and right on the other side of the fray, and Sato began to feel confident they had turned the tide. He kept firing, slamming the sound power of his Shurric into one creature after another. Beams of molten fire continued to shoot all around him; one came straight at Sato, and he dove and rolled to avoid it. He jumped back to his feet and kept fighting, as did the rest of the Fifth.

He heard the sound of splashing to his left. He risked a quick look and saw that Tick was flailing in the water of the river, trying to make his way to the edge. He seemed disoriented, or like he'd forgotten how to swim.

"Cover me!" Sato shouted to his closest soldier.

Sweeping his weapon left and right as he ran, Sato booked it to the river's edge, wary of any arrows of fire that might come his way from the gray men. But the battle seemed almost over—he could see that witch, Mistress Jane, using her powers to destroy the same enemy he fought. That made a million questions tear through his mind—almost made him stop running. Mistress Jane. He couldn't possibly accept that she was on his side.

"Sato!"

He looked down to see Tick's face in the water, his hand reaching out for him. He was still thrashing as if he might drown.

"Tick!" Sato shouted as he got to his knees, leaning over to see if he could grab his friend's hand. Tick was about five feet from the river's edge. "Swim over here!" He looked behind him every couple of seconds to make sure nothing came at him that might dissolve his head in lava.

"Something's got my foot!" Tick yelled. "A tentacle, maybe! It's wrapped around my ankle!"

Sato leaned a little farther out and was almost able to grab Tick's hand. "Just . . . come a little closer!"

Tick didn't answer, just kept beating at the water

with his arms. His body moved a couple of inches, but his hand was still out of reach.

Sato inched forward, his knees now extending past the edge, straining to clasp . . . those . . . fingers.

He made contact and squeezed his fist around Tick's and pulled, snapping his friend almost a foot closer. But then Tick jerked to a stop, almost causing Sato to tumble into the water. Something definitely had hold of Tick and wasn't letting go without a fight.

"Kick your body to the right!" Sato yelled as he pulled his Shurric around and took aim. The thing was heavy and hard to hold steady with one hand, but the noise and chaos of the battle still raged, and there was no one to help him. He risked another quick glance behind him and saw fire and gray bodies flying through the air.

Tick was doing his best to follow the order. Sato, with a shaking hand, pointed the Shurric at a spot that seemed clear of his friend and pulled the trigger. A soundless thump rocked the building, and water shot up in great spouts as if a meteor had just splash-landed. Tick suddenly tore loose and swam forward, almost leaping out of the river.

Sato dropped his weapon and grabbed Tick by the torso, pulling him the rest of the way. They collapsed on the ground, both of them soaking wet, sucking in and blowing out deep breaths.

Sato remembered that they could be incinerated

at any second. He flopped over onto his stomach and surveyed the scene. Even in the last few seconds, everything had changed drastically.

There wasn't a gray creature in sight. To his left, Jane was standing stiffly with her arms held out in front of her, looking as haggard as any person Sato had ever seen. Her shoulders slumped, and she was struggling to breathe. Her mask was tilted on her exposed, scarred head, and its expression showed pure exhaustion. To his right, the Fifth Army appeared even more disheveled. Bodies lay scattered on the floor, many of them horribly injured or dead. Those standing seemed like wilted flowers, hoping for water and sun.

Sato's eyes wandered upward. Dozens of tightly wound clouds of gray mist hovered by the ceiling, lightning flicking and striking both within and between them. He was about to get to his knees, order everyone to flee the castle, when all the clouds suddenly collapsed into one, like some sort of separating membrane had been whipped free. The entire mass began to spin, a whirlpool of thick, gray mist churning in the air. A funnel formed in the middle and started lowering toward the ground. A breeze picked up, grew stronger, whipped at Sato's wet clothes.

Something terrible was about to happen.

"Run!" he screamed. "Everyone get out of here!"

CHAPTER 28

＊

A MIGHTY WIND

Tick was sopping wet. And freezing cold. His ankle hurt from whatever weird creature had been gripping it, trying to pull him under to his death. He was exhausted from using Chi'karda to defend against those beams of fire and to fight back at the Voids.

But something odd was happening above him. His relief at seeing that the Voids were gone lasted all of two seconds. Looking up, he saw that the small, electricity-filled clouds from earlier had grown in number until they'd gotten too big, collapsing into one giant, churning mass of gray. As the funnel cloud began to lower to the ground, the wind picked up measurably, making his already wet skin grow even colder. When

Sato screamed for everyone to run, Tick didn't waste any time pondering the command.

He jumped to his feet, feeling the sogginess of his clothes, the weariness of his bones and muscles. Sato grabbed him by the arm and pulled him along as they ran together toward the giant door with its frame of broken wood.

The wind was increasing in speed by the second, whipping the air in a frenzy. Tick's clothes flapped like flags on a speedboat, almost hurting his skin, and it felt as if every one of his hairs might rip out and fly away. The spinning funnel of the gray tornado descended rapidly as Tick and Sato ran, and Tick saw Mistress Jane standing on the other side of it all, motionless.

Her body disappeared behind the tornado as its leading point crashed into the stony floor. Lightning arced and arrowed through the cloud, the rattles of thunder sounding like detonations, deafening. The moment when storm met stone was violent, as if the cloud had been a giant fist of steel smashing down, shards of rock vaulting toward the ceiling from the shattered surface. The entire castle jolted, the floor jumping into the air and crashing back down again. Tick sprawled across the floor, still dozens of feet away from the exit. Others fell all around him, and tiny splinters of stone flew through the air, smashing into people.

Tick felt pinpricks of needles on his cheeks and threw his hands up to protect his face. Struggling against the wind and the still-shaking castle, he stumbled to his feet and leaned forward, making it several steps before he crashed to the ground again. He caught sight of the funnel that continued to twist like a giant drill digging into the hard earth below the layer of stones it had already destroyed. Rock chips flew in all directions, and with a broken heart, he realized that even more bodies littered the ground, many of them still moving, still trying to get up.

Like him.

He couldn't let this destruction continue. He had to *do* something. It had yet to become his instinct to use Chi'karda, to use his powers to fight instead of running away. But how? How could he fight a giant tornado filled with lightning?

His mind focused on the air around him, on the particles, molecules, atoms. Surrendering to his instincts, he created a wall, a shield from the count-less chips of rock flying through the castle like tiny daggers. The wind suddenly decreased, and he saw the rocks bouncing off an invisible barrier inches in front of him. He stood up, his fists clenched, his brain working in overdrive. The exhaustion that had been consuming his body seemed like a distant memory as the pure fire of Chi'karda burned inside of him, raging as strongly as the winds that swirled around his shield did. Speckles of orange swam along his skin and thickened into a cloud, but it didn't obscure his vision. He was looking at the world through different eyes now.

The tornado of gray mist spun, churning like it was digging a hole to the other side of the earth, thickening at its core. Debris spun out from the ground and was caught in the mighty winds until everything was a fog of dust and stone.

Tick needed to help those who hadn't been able to escape. Sato was on his back, his face cut up, his eyes wide as he stared at Tick in disbelief as if he were a freak.

Tick's heart almost broke at the sight, but he knew what he had to do. He threw his hands out, threw his thoughts as well. Sato's body suddenly leaped from the ground and flew like a tossed football, tumbling end over end and out the broken doorway. Tick swept his vision and his hands across the passageway, doing the same thing to each person he saw, whether alive or dead. Body after body catapulted into the air and went sailing through the exit, ripped from the ground as if a giant string had been attached to them, yanked by a puppet master. Tick didn't know how he was doing it, but he did it all the same. Instinct ruled his powers now.

He sent the last few people flying out of the castle. He didn't know if they'd land safely out there, or if they might break bones, or worse, but he knew they'd die if they didn't leave this place; that was all he could do.

When he was finally alone, he turned to face the massive cyclone of fog, its bolts of lightning flickering down the edges and smashing into the stone. It was almost like the energy from the bolts was trying to help dig the hole even wider. Thoughts rushed through his mind then, wondering if he should just turn and run. The people were safe; they could run or wink away and let this thing do whatever it wanted to do to Jane's precious castle.

She appeared to his right.

Wind tore at her robe as she inched along the far wall of the passageway, her back to the stone as she moved, her red mask tightening into an expression of fear as she stared at the tornado ripping apart the ground. Water had been sucked up into the churning funnel as well, sending a spray of mist in all directions and adding an odd blueness to the gray core. Jane was soaked.

A terrible thought hit Tick. What if this thing really didn't stop? What if the Fourth Dimension kept throwing all of its power into the Realities, growing and growing until it consumed everything? A spinning mass of material as big as the universe? He had to sever the link. Somehow he had to stop this; he knew it without any doubt.

He put out his hand toward Jane, manipulating the world with his thoughts. Her body jumped up into the air and flew toward him, landing right beside him. The look of shock on her mask gave him the smallest bit of satisfaction.

"What are you doing?" she yelled over the terrible noise.

"We have to stop this thing!" he shouted back. "We have to break the link!"

Jane's mask wilted at the suggestion. "I don't know if I can do it! I'm spent, Atticus! I have nothing left in me! I need to rest!"

Tick had to hide his shock. For her to admit to that . . .

"We have to try!"

Jane stared back at him through the eyeholes of her mask. Then she gave him a reluctant nod.

The two of them turned toward the tornado and held out their hands as if they were going to walk in and embrace the spinning thing.

"Try to collapse it!" Jane yelled. "Throw all your Chi'karda into collapsing its mass then we'll blow it apart! We have to hope that ends it and seals the breach into the Fourth!"

"Okay!" Tick screamed, his heart pumping. The power was an inferno inside his chest, and he was ready to unleash it. "Let's do it!"

He pushed his hands toward the spinning beast and released the Chi'karda that had been building and building. Streams of orange fire exploded from his fingertips and into the tornado, getting caught in the spin. Jane was doing the same. Soon the gray funnel was colorful and bright; the lightning was more brilliant and sharp, the thunder louder.

Tick screamed with the effort as he pushed more and more of his powers at the Fourth Dimension, trying to envision what he wanted, trying to make it happen. His body began to shake, his muscles weak. Chi'karda poured from him and Jane in spouts; the streams were almost the same color as what had come from the mouths of the Voids.

Now everything was shaking—the ground, the castle, his skull. The funnel of the tornado was white-hot, blinding. Impossible noises erupted from its form, and the wind was torrential, ripping away the shield Tick had built around himself.

He screamed again and threw all of his strength into the storm.

There was a sudden concussion of pure energy that ripped away from the tornado like the blast of a nuclear bomb. Tick felt his body be jerked into the air, and then he was flying. What remained of the castle exploded, every last brick of it cracking apart and flying right along with him.

He didn't hit the ground until he'd been thrown a thousand yards. A chunk of rock landed on his head, and all he knew was pain.

CHAPTER 29

✳

JOINTS AND EARDRUMS

Lorena held Lisa close, and it broke her heart to feel the trembling of her daughter's bones. The girl had always been strong-spirited and tough, but no one could be expected to hide their fear after the last few days of their lives.

Mordell had brought them back to the Great Hall, whispering something about its natural powers and it being the best place to protect them. They found the farthest corner of the chamber carved from black stone and huddled together while Mordell sat nearby; she had a look on her face as if she wanted to be closer but had to maintain her dignity as a Lady of Blood and Sorrow. There wasn't much for the three of them to do except be scared and listen to the sounds of battle.

They were distant, but terrible: the swooshing of fire, screams of pain, shouts of command. Soon it all changed to a great, rushing noise, like wind passing through a narrow canyon, or a tornado. The screams intensified. And then the worst sound—breaking rock. It wasn't the loudest noise, but it made the entire castle quake and tremble. Lorena felt the vibration in her joints and eardrums.

She'd never felt so helpless. Her only son was out there, fighting something that seemed impossible. Something that shouldn't exist. And to add to it, he was fighting alongside the woman who'd tried to kill him and countless others. Atticus was putting his faith in a madwoman. It took every ounce of Lorena's will-power to not run back out that door and try to help her boy—she almost itched from the desire. But she had Lisa to think about. And Edgar and Kayla back home. Atticus could take care of himself—he'd proven it over and over.

And so the battle raged on, the sounds of fire and wind increasing in volume. Lorena could do nothing but sit and hold her daughter and imagine all the awful things that might have happened, or might be happening, to her sweet, sweet son.

Everything changed again in a moment. An instant

so terrible and horrifying that Lorena knew she'd never sleep again without it haunting her nightmares.

It was an eruption. A detonation. A thunderclap of sound and movement that shook the Great Hall as if it were nothing but an empty cardboard box. Lorena and Lisa both screamed as they flew across the room, smacking into Mordell and rolling another few feet before coming to a stop. The air was filled with the noise of cracks and booms, as if the entire castle had exploded and collapsed in on itself.

Lorena threw away her caution and scrambled to her feet, trying to set aside the panic that thrust itself through her nerves. She grabbed Lisa by the hand, lifted her to her feet, and ran to the exit of the Great Hall, swaying back and forth as the floor continued to tilt and pitch. She'd just stepped in front of the doorway when she stopped, her heart plummeting. Rock and stone and brick had collapsed into a heap, blocking the arched opening completely. Dust choked the air.

Mordell's voice from behind Lorena made her jump and spin around to see the woman standing there, impossibly looking even more grave than before.

"The Great Hall has survived," the Lady of Blood and Sorrow said. "But I'd guess nothing else has. We're trapped."

Sato was lying on his stomach, his hands held over his head to protect himself from the debris that had been raining down for several minutes. Every inch of his body had been battered and bruised by falling rocks, but luckily, his skull had been spared for the most part. It'd been rough going since everything went haywire inside the castle.

Not to mention the fact that he'd been thrown through the air. Twice.

First when Tick used his powers to pick him up and whip his body out of the castle. Saving him. And second when the castle suddenly exploded, a wave of pure energy erupting from its core and tossing him and the rest of his army hundreds of feet away like they were nothing but dried leaves. That had saved him again, because if he'd been any closer, he probably would've been crushed by larger chunks of stone from the destroyed castle.

And so, he was alive.

He pushed himself to his knees, groaning from the aches and pains that riddled his body. He was woozy too, the dusty grass beneath his knees seeming to bob up and down like the surface of the ocean. What little energy he had, drained right out of him, and he collapsed again, but at least he was able to spin himself a bit and land on his rear end. He could see the rubble that had once been the great castle of Mistress Jane, the woman who had killed his parents.

What had been half-destroyed before now lay in utter ruins. A giant heap of crumbled stone and wood and plaster. Pieces of the castle lay scattered outward from the main body all the way to where Sato sat and beyond, reaching the forest that wasn't too far behind him. But as satisfying as it was to see the carnage, he felt a tremor in his heart for what still pulsed and throbbed in the middle of the destruction like a beating heart.

The tornado of mist still churned where it had been, with nothing but open sky above it. Except it wasn't much of a tornado anymore.

It was a seething, roiling mass of gray, its billowing surface frothing and foaming before turning back in on itself, leaving little wisps of fog streaming out like some kind of dreary decoration. Lightning continued to flash and strike in huge bolts of brilliant white, the thunder rumbling across the ground and echoing off the wall of trees behind Sato. The mass was probably fifty feet wide and a hundred feet tall. It was still moving in a circular motion, but not as intensely as a tornado anymore. It was like a living thing, devouring the air around it and ever growing, slowly.

Members of the Fifth Army were scattered all over the field, groaning and rubbing their eyes and stiffly testing their joints, looking for injuries. Sadly, some weren't moving, and Sato felt the heavy weight of leadership once again. He'd led people to their death.

Something caught his eye as he scanned the area—a body that lay lifeless but wasn't as big as the others. A boy.

Tick.

A blister of alarm popped in Sato's heart as he leaped to his feet and started running, finding strength from some hidden part of his soul. He dodged and maneuvered around soldiers, his eyes focused on his friend, who wasn't moving a muscle, not even a twitch. Sato didn't know if he could take another death of someone so close to him. He was ashamed that he didn't feel quite the same about his army fighters, but this was different. Tick had become not just one of his closest friends, but a symbol of everything the Realitants stood for.

Sato jumped over a prostrate woman of the Fifth then slid onto the grass like a baseball player, coming to a stop right at Tick's head. The first thing he noticed was that his back was rising and falling, ever so slightly. Tick lay on his stomach, his arms spread out awkwardly, as if he'd landed and conked out immediately. But he wasn't dead. Thank the Realities, he wasn't dead.

Sato reached out and gently shook his friend's shoulders. No response.

He grabbed him by the arm and carefully rolled him over onto his back so he could get a good look at him. His eyes were closed, his clothes ripped and filthy, his skin covered in dirt and soot. But most troubling was a huge gash on the side of his head, blood matting the hair down like dark red gel.

"Tick," Sato whispered, trying to fight back the tears that wanted to pour out. Why? Why did everything in their lives always have to be so terrible?

"Tick," he repeated. Then he picked him up and slung him over his shoulders, grunting under the weight. He began to walk, though he had no idea where he was going.

CHAPTER 30

✳

COMING TOGETHER

Paul walked through the twilit forest of the Thirteenth Reality, Sofia and Rutger to his right, Mothball, Sally, and Master George—using his Barrier Wand like a cane—to his left. No one said a word as they picked their way through the bush and bramble. The massive concussion of sound they'd heard a few minutes earlier was enough to silence anyone for a week. Paul forced his thoughts away from the terrible possible explanations for that sound and concentrated on moving forward.

Ever since he'd returned to the Realitant headquarters, he'd been dying to know what in the world the little button in the box Gretel had given them was for.

Old George had sent them to Gretel for a reason, had given them a secret password for a reason, had wanted that box with nothing in it but a plastic green button for a reason. But neither he nor Gretel would tell him what it was supposed to be used for. Phrases like "a need-to-know basis" and "you'll find out soon enough" were thrown around. But that didn't satisfy Paul.

Not one bit.

Oh, well. They had much bigger problems on their hands. There was trouble here in the Thirteenth Reality, and any notion they'd had of getting rest and relaxation was out the window. Master George hadn't needed to tell them that when he said they'd all be winking there to regroup with Sato and find Tick. The situation was surely dangerous.

Paul smiled. It was as if his brain was so used to bad stuff that it wasn't allowing him to focus on the best piece of news he'd ever received in his life. Tick was alive. Tick was back. Now they just had to figure out this mess and get him home safe and sound.

The woods had slowly thinned over the last hundred yards or so, though the air up ahead seemed slightly murky, like a dust storm had passed through recently, which seemed impossible for a place so green and vibrant with life.

"Shouldn't we pick up the pace a little?" he asked the small crowd of Realitants.

"No need for haste, my good man," came the not-surprising reply from Master George. "Our old friend Jane might have placed a few traps along the edge of the forest. Won't do us much good to run willy-nilly right into them and spring the things."

Paul was annoyed. "Won't do us much good if we show up and everyone's dead, either."

"Don't talk like that," Sofia said. "He's going to be fine."

Paul heard a deadness in her voice that scared him. He realized that she had already begun the process of accepting that just because Tick was back and alive didn't mean he was okay or safe. Paul didn't look at it that way. If their friend was back, he'd figure out a way to get out of any mess thrown his way. The guy was a freak of nature—in a good way.

"I mean it," Sofia added.

"Sorry," Paul muttered. "I'm just anxious to see him. Help him if he needs it."

She nodded but didn't say anything.

They finally reached a point where the end of the woods was visible, and all of them saw it at once. A person with a body slung over his or her shoulders, stumbling at the last line of trees. Even as Paul watched, whoever it was fell down and out of his view. For the first time, he could focus on the scene beyond. And it was like a scene out of an old war movie.

Dust-choked air. Bodies littering the ground, many moving sluggishly to get up, some not moving at all. Countless chunks of rock and wood strewn about the grassy fields. And past all of that, the closest edge barely in sight, was a big pile of ruins and rubble. Paul had been here before so he knew what it was—Mistress Jane's castle, completely destroyed.

Sofia broke into a run, her feet crashing through the weeds and twigs of the forest floor. Before Paul could follow her, she stopped like she'd seen a big snake. Then she was yelling.

"It's Tick and Sato!"

Tick's head felt like the end of a stubborn nail that refused to go into the wood straight. Like a hammer had pounded on it, bent it, yanked it straight, then pounded it all over again. He was barely aware of someone picking him up, then later falling again. He tried opening his eyes, but the light was like a sunburst right in front of him, stabbing and making the ache in his skull even worse.

Now he lay face-first on a ground that was prickly with twigs and pine straw. He groaned a couple of times to make sure whoever had tried to help him knew he wasn't dead, but even the sound of that went off in his head like clanging church bells. A sudden burst of nausea filled his gut.

Please don't throw up, he thought to himself. *Oh, please don't throw up.*

He heard noises then, shouts and the cricking and cracking of footsteps. It all became a painful blur to him, and he figured it didn't matter much anymore. He hurt, and that was that.

Someone rolled him onto his back, and that was the last straw. He jolted to his elbows and threw up to the side. When he finished, he flopped back flat to the ground and grimaced as a fresh wave of agony punched its way through his skull and down his spine.

"Tick?" said a soft voice. A girl. It took him a few seconds to recognize Sofia's voice, and his heart lifted. "Tick, are you okay?"

He wanted to tease her that she'd just asked him the dumbest question in history, but he figured that raising his voice—even talking at all—would hurt too much. So instead he mumbled something. Not even a real word, just an acknowledgment that he'd heard her. He still refused to open his eyes, terrified of the light.

He heard a crunch of ground covering right next to him and figured someone had knelt there.

"Master Atticus?" That was definitely George,

and his heart lifted a little more. "Goodness gracious me, boy. What on earth has happened here?"

"Yeah, man. Quit napping down there and talk to us."

Paul. The relief inside Tick was swelling more by the second. At least his friends were safe, and he wasn't dead. Things could've been a lot worse.

"Really, Paul?" Sofia said. "Even now you have to be sarcastic? Look at that nasty gash on his head. We're lucky he didn't bleed out."

"I'm sure he wanted to hear that," Paul muttered back.

"Sato, what happened?" Master George asked.

Sato too? Tick thought. This was too good to be true. Maybe he was having one of those dreams where you see all your friends and loved ones before you died. That thought jolted him back to reality.

He sat up, the pain like strikes of lightning in his head. "My family. My mom. Lisa. Where . . ."

The pain and nausea were too much. He passed out again.

Lisa was starting to accept the fact that she was about to die.

It surprised her how easily the realization came.

Although she felt a terrible sadness, it wasn't really about death itself. It was more about not seeing her dad and Kayla and Tick before she went. At least she had her mom.

They'd been silent for so long now. After a couple hours of trying to move the rocks and debris that blocked their exit from the Great Hall, they'd finally given up. Almost nothing would budge, and the one chunk of stone they were able to move was instantly replaced by several more from above. There was no sign of daylight in any of the cracks. What an awful way to die. They'd either starve or suffocate.

With cheerful thoughts like those, she'd resigned herself to sit with her mom, holding each other as they waited for the inevitable.

She was just thinking how stuffy the air had become when she heard a scrabbling sound near the exit, as though an animal was trying to burrow its way through the stack of debris. Then there was a crunching, some cracks, and the hollow scrape of stone against stone. Dust billowed out from the mess as rocks began to shift and collapse. Lisa didn't know what to think, but refused to let herself feel any hope as she waited to see what was happening.

Finally a huge section of the rubble shifted and slid away, leaving a huge gap, choked with dust. A robed figure appeared, hunched over and filthy. Mistress Jane stepped into the room, the light from the lone torch barely reflecting off her dirty red mask.

Mordell lost every ounce of her usual reserved demeanor. "Master!" she yelled. "Master, you're alive!"

"For now," she said in her raw, scratchy voice—it sounded weaker than ever. "Come. We have a lot of work to do."

CHAPTER 31

FROM HEAD TO TOE

Whadhen Tick came to his senses again, the pain in his head had lessened a bit. The tiniest, tiniest bit. But the nausea was gone, and it didn't seem like the whole world would swim away from him at any second.

Someone—he didn't know who—helped him sit up. Groggy and dazed, he waited a few seconds before opening his eyes. The light had faded considerably, the orange glow of sunset settling somewhere to the west beyond the trees. The others were sitting around him on the edge of the forest; they could see the long fields of grass, littered with rubble and debris, that led to the utter ruin of what had once been the mighty castle of Mistress Jane. He could just barely see the slowly spinning mass of gray mist that still churned within it. He looked away. He didn't want to look at it or think about it.

He couldn't believe all the people sitting around him. It was like a reunion too good to be true. Mothball, with her scraggly hair and her clothes hanging off her skin-and-bones body, her face lit up by a smile that seemed almost out of place in the gloom of their situation. Rutger, his round body nestled next to her like a fat penguin. Master George, dressed up as always, though his suit was wrinkled and dirty, with a Barrier Wand laid across his lap. Sally, sitting cross-legged in his plaid shirt and overalls like a lumberjack waiting for an order to start cutting down the trees around them.

And then Tick's three best friends, sitting in a row, staring at him like they expected him to give a speech. Sato. Sofia. Paul. They were dressed as if they'd just gotten home from school, but worry etched lines on their faces. Tick didn't know if it was the fading light, but they looked older. They definitely looked older.

And then an emptiness hit him again, hard. It was like he was looking at a portrait of his life, and a big chunk had been ripped out. His family.

A wave of despair almost made him pass out again. "My mom and sister," he said, hearing the panic in his own voice. "I told Mordell to take them somewhere safe. Any idea what happened to them?"

Everyone in the group looked at one another; they didn't need to say anything.

"We have to go look for them," Tick said, starting to get up.

Master George reached out and put a hand on Tick's shoulder, gently making him sit back down. "Atticus, none of us even know what *happened*. The castle is completely destroyed, and Sato's army is just now recovering and counting up their losses. Before we can help you or find your family, we need to know what we're dealing with. A few minutes more won't change their plight. In fact, the more informed we are, the more we can help them. Do you understand?"

Tick didn't. For some reason, he was angry. "I'll go sift through every one of those stones by myself if I have to."

"You mean they were *inside* the building when it collapsed?" Master George's face paled.

Tick stood up. "*Yes*, they were inside. And if you haven't noticed, there's a big tornado right in the middle of all that mess. Maybe growing closer to my mom and sister right now."

"Which is exactly why we need—"

"No!" Tick yelled. "No."

He was lost and confused by the worry that ate away inside of him, but he didn't care. He got to his feet and started marching toward the ruined castle, ignoring the pain that lanced through his body from his skull to the bottoms of his feet.

⁓

Lisa didn't like what Jane had gone on to say about the Fourth Dimension and the all-consuming Void it had unleashed. She assumed that it would consume her too. But Mistress Jane had said little else—including whether or not Tick was safe. Instead she had rested for a time, eyes closed, until she was ready. Then she started using her fancy powers to move and shift more of the rubble so they could get out of the destroyed castle. Lisa watched, fascinated.

The woman's robe was a mess, caked with grime and dust, ripped in countless places. Her hood hung off her head like a discarded flag, revealing a scarred mass where her hair should've been, the skin red and raw. Lisa knew she was supposed to hate Mistress Jane—the crazy lady who'd killed people and done evil, evil things—but how could you not feel sorry for someone who looked so miserable and probably felt even worse?

But nothing seemed to faze Jane. She held up her wounded hands like Moses parting the Red Sea, and sparkles of orange flew from her body in sprays of bright mist. Grinding sounds filled the air as rock and stone moved at her will, shifting and flying and breaking apart. Dust clogged the air, but she used her power to whisk that away as well, obviously needing to see what she was doing.

After several minutes of this show, Lisa was expecting to see daylight spill into the room, but it never happened. She had no clue what time it was, and her heart dropped a little to think it might be in the middle of the night. She'd never wanted to see sunshine so desperately, and she was dying to get out there and see if her brother was okay. To see if he'd survived whatever force was trying to "eat this world," as Jane had put it.

Her mom reached out and squeezed her hand as if she'd sensed the thought. "I'm sure he's okay. He has to be. If this witchy woman made it through, I'm sure our boy did too. Don't you worry."

Lisa looked at her mom and forced a smile. "Yeah, I'm sure you're not worrying one bit. Are you?"

"Of course not." She grinned back. "Okay, maybe a teensy tiny bit."

Mistress Jane stopped what she was doing. The fiery orange cloud sucked back into her like something shown in reverse on video, and she lowered her hands. The woman's shoulders slumped as if she'd used every last ounce of her energy. Now that the rock and stone had quit grinding and cracking, Lisa heard another odd sound. Like a rushing wind, with a hum and bulge of power behind it. It reminded her of the heavy thrum of machinery, as if somewhere around the corner was a manufacturing plant still trying to work its way through the landfall of a hurricane.

Mordell had stayed very quiet through the whole ordeal, but now she walked up to Mistress Jane and gently put her hands on her boss's shoulders.

"Are you alright, Master?" she asked in a voice Lisa barely heard over the noise coming from outside. "May I help you sit down?"

Jane turned around, and her mask showed no emotion at all. "My friends. My creatures. I . . . What did the Void do to them?"

Lisa thought that was a strange thing to say and exchanged a confused look with her mom, who shrugged her shoulders slightly then spoke. "What do you mean, Jane? After everything that has happened, the abominations you created are the only thing you're worried about? Do you even care in the slightest that my son could be out there, hurt or dead? *Do you?*"

Lisa's mom had grown angrier with every word and had shouted the last question. She visibly huffed like a bullied kid on the playground.

But Jane seemed to have no reaction. Maybe she was just too weary. "I fear for your son, too, Lorena. I do. But you could never know what it's like to stand here and not sense the presence of hundreds of your own children. The Void took them . . . transformed them somehow."

Lisa's mom took a furious step forward and stopped, as if she realized how crazy it would be to threaten this woman who'd done the magical things they'd just witnessed. "I could never know? You stand there and say I could never know? I have an actual child out there, and you're talking about things that were created only to hurt and kill others."

Lisa had never seen her mom so mad.

Unfortunately, so was Jane. Her red mask pulled back into a fierce expression. "How dare you speak about them that way! You have no inkling what you're talking about! I won't stand for this disrespect!"

Lisa knew her mom was about to do something stupid. She quickly grabbed her arm and pulled her back. "Who cares what she thinks, Mom? Let's just get out of here and—"

There were several soft thuds of something landing on the ground nearby, and Lisa heard her mom gasp. She quickly turned around. Several people had jumped down from the piles of rubble to join them, and the one standing closest sent a wave of something indescribable through Lisa's body, filling her heart and making it beat rapidly.

She and her mom ran to Tick and pulled him into a hug so tight she might have feared for his life if they all weren't laughing and crying so hard.

CHAPTER 32

✳

TALKING ALL AT ONCE

Tick didn't know if he'd ever felt such a burst of pure emotion. As he hugged his mom and sister—both of them seeming to have a contest on who could squeeze him the hardest—he was crying one second then laughing the next. It was as if he'd lost his mind and all the control that went with it. But the feelings surging through his body were so strong, he didn't quite know how to handle it.

All the things he'd been through recently flashed across his mind: being taken by the Sleeks, the ordeal with the Blade of Shattered Hope, the terrible battle with Mistress Jane at the Factory, and then the short time he'd been in the Nonex, wondering if he'd ever see his family again. When they'd first been reunited in the Great Hall, he'd been too dazed to fully appreciate what it meant to be back together again. But now— especially after thinking they might have been crushed by the collapsing castle—it had hit him all at once.

Finally, reluctantly, he pulled away and took a step back. And the first thought he had when he looked at the tear-lined faces of his mom and Lisa was that they were still missing two important pieces.

"Dad," he said. "Kayla. I wish we were all together. Do you think they are okay?"

His mom nodded. "We left them at home, and I'm pretty sure Edgar wouldn't dare venture out with all the problems going on. They've got plenty of food, and the house wasn't hurt in the earthquakes."

"We need to hurry and get back to them," Tick said. "Make sure they're okay and let them know we're all safe."

His mom simply nodded and smiled, fresh tears squeezing out of her eyes.

Lisa reached out and patted him on the shoulder. "Good thing you had such an awesome big sister all those years, huh? Or you'd probably still be bawling your eyes out somewhere, too chicken to save the universe."

"Yeah, something like that." Tick rolled his eyes, then remembered with embarrassment that there were people standing around gawking at them. Master George, Mothball, Sally, Rutger, Sato, Paul, and Sofia. Mistress Jane, her robe in terrible shape, her exposed head as bad as ever. And Mordell, who looked like she'd just drowned her own puppies in a bathtub.

George was leaning on his Barrier Wand.

"Can you wink us back to my house?" Tick asked the Realitant boss. "I could do it myself, but I'm a little spent." He smiled wearily.

His mom spoke up. "We've got our own." She stared sternly at Mordell. "What did you do with it?"

The woman shook her head.

"Lost in the rubble, I take it?" his mom responded. "Do you have any idea how long it took me to build that Wand? How much it means to me?" Her voice rose, and her face reddened.

"I'm terribly sorry," Mordell replied.

Tick felt he should ask when and where and how his own mom had created a Barrier Wand, but nothing surprised him anymore. She could tell him all about it once they were home. He decided he had the strength after all. "It's okay, Mom. I can wink us back. I've done it before, but now I know how to actually use the stuff that makes me a freak."

"Hey," Paul chimed in, "I'm the only one here allowed to call you that."

"He's not a freak," Sofia said. "You're just jealous."

Everyone started talking at once, then, as if a cork had been popped off and permission had been given to converse freely. Mothball and Rutger were next to Tick, speaking over each other to say how happy they were that everyone was safe. Tick's mom was arguing with Mordell about the lost Wand. Lisa was trying to calm their mom down. Master George and Sally were discussing their options, and Paul and Sofia wanted to butt in and have Tick to themselves, but Mothball and Rutger would have none of it. Even Sato seemed to be talking to someone, but Tick couldn't tell what was being said or who it was.

"Silence!"

Mistress Jane's voice boomed throughout the room, echoing back and forth unnaturally off the carved black walls as if she'd used Chi'karda to make it happen. It sliced through everyone's conversation instantly. The Great Hall fell quiet, the only sound that of the churning, rushing noises caused by the spinning mass of whatever had come out of the Fourth Dimension.

Tick stared at her, ashamed that he was too scared to disobey and curious about what she was going to say. He readied himself, pooling the Chi'karda within him in case the woman tried to do anything questionable.

"How can you all stand here like all is well in the world?" Mistress Jane asked, her mask covered by disappointment and disbelief. "Kissing and hugging and crying with joy? Making jokes and making plans for reunions? Am I the only one in this room who is aware of what's happening just a few hundred feet from here? Do any of you have even the slightest inkling of what's at stake?"

"We need no lectures from you," Master George said. "Nor your hypocrisy. You're the only one in this room who deliberately and maliciously tried to destroy an entire Reality—and almost destroyed all else in the process. The entire universe, according to the Haunce."

Jane waited with a condescending look of patience on her mask until Master George was finished. "Don't blame me, George. If you and your so-called Realitants hadn't interfered, my Blade would've done its job, and we'd be on our way to creating the Utopia we so desperately need. But instead, we were put on a course that led to this. To rips in the fabric of Reality. A breach to the Fourth Dimension. Say all you want that Atticus and the Haunce saved us, but I say that all they've done is make things worse."

Hearing that made Tick blister inside with anger. "Oh, really? What could possibly be worse than destroying the entire universe? Care to explain that, Jane?" He stressed her name, spitefully refusing to include her title.

She stared at him. "The universe would not have needed saving if you hadn't tried to stop me in your arrogance, boy. And now what we have is an entity that no one truly understands—not even the Haunce. The Void will grow and strengthen. It will spread throughout my world and then the rest of the Realities. It will inflict pain and suffering the likes of which you couldn't comprehend. Better that we had all ceased to exist at the hands of the Blade of Shattered Hope."

Now it was Tick's turn to stare back. If she was telling the truth, what did the past matter anyway? What did their terrible history with each other matter? He felt a sinking in his gut that almost made him sit on the black stone floor.

"I want everyone to listen to me," Master George said. "And I want you all to listen very carefully. There's quite a bit of anger in this room. And we stand on the ruined grounds of a castle that represents the bitterest of enemies to me and my organization."

Mistress Jane's mask shifted, suddenly and violently, to a look of outrage. But George held up a hand and, miraculously, Jane didn't say anything.

"But," the old man continued, "I'm asking each one of us to put all of that aside. Including—perhaps especially—myself. Jane, you know very well that you and I have countless reasons to despise each other. But this threat you've spoken of . . . I believe it's real, and my good associates here have gathered numerous pieces of evidence. We all knew there'd be terrible destruction as a consequence of . . . recent events. But there's something much deeper going on. And animosity toward each other will only increase our speed along this path to eternal death."

Tick became aware that his mouth was hanging open. It'd been awhile since he'd seen Master George like this—so formal and full of speeches—but there was so much to process in the few sentences he'd spoken that Tick's reactions couldn't keep up with it.

The old man continued. "Jane, I don't even need to ask my fellow Realitants this question, but I must ask you. Are you willing to put aside your grievances—and your personal aspirations—to work with us until we can solve this problem?"

Jane's mask had smoothed back out to a neutral expression. "You insult me with every word that comes out of your mouth, George. Implying that I could actually say no to such a request. Implying that I could be so selfish as to—"

"Answer the question!" Sato suddenly screamed. He'd been still and quiet before, but now his face burned with hatred. "It was a simple yes or no question!"

Mistress Jane slowly nodded her head, and a little smile broke out on her mask as if she wanted to wound Sato by showing that she wasn't fazed by his outburst.

But when she spoke, her response was the last thing Tick had expected to hear.

"It's not *me* you should all be worried about. We're going to have a major obstacle to any plans we might have to stop this thing."

"What are you talking about?" Master George asked.

Jane's smile vanished completely. "Reginald Chu."

CHAPTER 33

✳

A CROSSROADS

*C*hu? What does he have to do with this Fourth Dimension problem?" Tick asked.

Mistress Jane sighed, a croak of a sound that reminded Tick of what he'd done to her throat and the rest of her body when he'd thrown the Dark Infinity substance at her in Chu's palace. It seemed so long ago, and he never would've guessed that all of their lives would stay so intricately connected.

"I know him," she said. "I know the way he thinks, and the way he lusts for power. I also know he's a very, very smart man. I'm sure he's back in the Fourth Reality, studying and watching and gathering data just like George has been. He'll know about the breaches in Reality, and eventually he'll come to the same con-clusion we have made about the Fourth Dimension—that *it's* been breached, unleashing the Void. And then there's the final thing I know all too well about him: his arrogance. All of these together will spell our doom as surely as the mass of gray fog that churns atop my once-great home."

"What do you mean?" Tick asked at the same time as at least three of the others. He exchanged quick glances with Paul and Sofia, both of whom looked as worried and as curious as he felt. Sato kept his angry gaze focused on Jane.

"You've witnessed yourself what Chu will want," Jane said. "The power of the Void is massive, and Chu will see it as nothing but an opportunity. A chance to harness a new source of energy that could be the last piece to his puzzle that will allow him to rule us all. I won't waste our time with defending *my* actions any-more, as noble as they are and as beyond comprehen-sion for you as they may be, but we can all agree on Chu's motives. He wants power, and he wants all of it. He wants to rule the rest of the Realities along with the Fourth. I find it ironic that his world is numbered the same as this . . . thing that threatens all of us. Chu will not *fear* it. He'll embrace it until he figures out how to control its energy for his own use."

For some reason, Tick thought back to one of his

first experiences with the strangeness of his new life. The Gnat Rat that had been hidden in his closet. That creepy mechanical thing full of robotic gnats that had stung him and sent him to the hospital. Even though Master George had sent the robot as a test for Realitant recruits, Reginald Chu had invented the device. The man had been a thorn in Tick's side ever since.

"I agree that we have many problems, indeed," Master George concluded. "Jane, I won't stand here another minute and debate morals with you. The Realitants have a job to do, and you can either work with us or against us. Make your choice."

Jane shook her head. "I most definitely do not have a choice, and you know it. It's my world where this entity has begun its massacre, and it'll be my world that gets consumed *first*. I'll work with whomever I need to in order to stop it. Not to mention the fact that you need me and my knowledge. You could have asked a little more humbly, but yes, I will help you."

"More *humbly*?" George repeated. "Your *world*? The very fact that you . . . oh, goodness gracious me. Never mind. We are all in agreement then?" He looked around the room, gathering nods from his Realitants. Tick gave his when the glance came his way.

Their leader nodded. "Good. Each one of us will put our animosities aside, our grievances, our petty wishes for revenge, and work together. Though none of us truly understand what this new threat is"—he held up a hand when Jane began to protest—"some know more about it than others. And we all know it's very, very grave. We'll begin work immediately. No rest, I'm afraid. No vacation, no relaxation. The world leaders will have to deal with the aftershocks from our . . . most recent troubles on their own." His eyes darted to Jane for the briefest of moments.

Tick could think only of his family. "Okay, then. I'll take my mom and sister back home, and then I'll meet you at the headquarters. The Grand Canyon one, I guess?"

Master George looked hesitant for some reason, fumbling with his words a bit before simply giving a quick nod of his head.

"Sounds good," Tick replied, wondering what that had been all about. "We better leave before that tornado starts making creatures again."

"First smart thing I've heard yet," Paul agreed. "Let's get out of this stink hole."

Tick turned to face his mom and sister, sweating from the thought of winking them all back home. He was pretty sure he could do it, but there was always a risk. He thought about asking Master George, but the man only had Tick's nanolocator reading, so they'd have to take the actual Wand with them when they winked. That wasn't going to work.

"Alright," he said, pushing everyone else and their problems out of his mind. "Let's hold hands while we do this."

His mom didn't budge. "Atticus, we're not going back home."

"What do you mean?"

She looked annoyed, like the answer should have been obvious. "We played a big part in bringing you back from the Nonex. Am I right or wrong on that?"

Tick knew where she was going and hated it. "Definitely right."

"I was a Realitant once. I built my own Barrier Wand. I just risked my life—and the life of my daughter—to bring you home safely. And if you think I'm going to let you out of my sight again, you're sadly mistaken. Not to mention the fact that Lisa and I are both capable of helping out. You're going to need every single body working on this that you can get."

Tick looked at her for a long time. He knew he couldn't let this happen. He couldn't. He'd never be able to focus on what needed to be done—and *not* focus on how dangerous it might be—if he had his family around. He'd be able to think only of them, saving them, protecting them. He could *not* let them stay.

"But what about Kayla? She's what matters most right now. I—*we*—need you to go back and make sure she and Dad are okay."

His mom folded her arms together in a defiant gesture. "Your *father* is perfectly capable of taking care of our sweet little princess. Don't insult him like that. Lisa and I are staying, and that's that."

"Mom, you—" He stopped. There was no arguing with that look in her eyes. But he also knew what needed to be done. He was racking his brain for the words to say when someone tapped him on the shoulder. He looked to see the weathered, reddened face of Master George.

"Yeah?" Tick asked.

"I, er, wondered if I might have a moment with you."

Tick wanted to leave so badly. "Can I figure this out first?"

"Only a moment," the old man interrupted. "I need just a few seconds of your time. Please." He held out a hand and raised his eyebrows. "Please." The windy, rushing sound of the Fourth Dimension cyclone was like the pulse of a rising tide on the beach.

"Okay." He gave a look to his mom and then joined Master George over by the wall farthest from the entrance to the Great Hall.

"What's going on?" Tick asked him. "I need to get them back safely before I can do anything else."

The Realitant leader's voice dropped to a whisper. "There are urgent matters at stake here, Master Atticus. Quite honestly, we don't have the time for you to go home right now. I need you, and I need you immediately."

"Just let me get them—"

"No." His face was tight, his voice curt. Tick had never seen him so insistent. "There are times when you must remember that your power doesn't put you in charge. Do you understand? You've sworn your services to the Realitants, and I'm giving you an order."

Tick sighed, feeling lower than low. "Okay, then. Yes, sir."

He turned away from his boss and looked squarely at his mom and sister, both of whom stared right back. Tick's mind spun, calculating. He felt the gathering force within his chest.

"I'm really sorry, Mom," he said.

Then he winked her and Lisa back to Reality Prime.

CHAPTER 34

DIABOLICAL PLANS AGAIN

Reginald Chu sat in a chair, looking out a window that had no glass.

The chair was inside a structure that could barely be called that—it was nothing more than a few panels of wood nailed together with a makeshift roof of plastic thrown on top. The floor was nothing but the sodden rot of an old forest floor. And the single window existed because one of the stray pieces of wood used for the hut just so happened to have a hole in it. The air was hot and steamy, seeming to rise from the moist earth as if a pool of ancient lava rested somewhere beneath the ground.

It was a far cry from the offices he had enjoyed

the last time he'd been to the Fourth Reality. This had been his home, the world he had ruled single-handedly. Until the Realitants came. Until Mistress Jane betrayed him and helped push the Higginbottom boy to the madness that had demolished his entire headquarters, which had been shaped by the most advanced technology possible into a literal mountain of glass and steel. But Chu Industries was like the great phoenix of legend. Its shell had been destroyed, but the spirit was about to rise again from the ashes.

A surprisingly low number of people had been killed that day. Many of his top executives survived. And since that fateful day when he was catapulted to the Nonex by the unfortunate meeting with his Alterant—that slimy, weakling of a science teacher—the cogs and wheels of his great empire had been turning. Planning for his return. Putting the pieces of the puzzle back into place. Watching for the first sign of his nanolocator.

And now he was back.

But he didn't want anyone besides his closest staff to know about it. Not yet. That was the reason he was in the middle of a forest, miles from the temporary location of Chu Industries, in a hut cobbled together by two idiots on the bottom of the payroll. Two idiots who had been taken care of as soon as their work was done. He relished the discomfort of the pitiful makeshift office they'd created for him. He needed the shack. It reminded him of how great his power had once been, and it motivated him to find that power once again.

There was a tapping—three hits—at the ugly slab of wood that served as his door. Reginald waited. Another three. Then two. Ten seconds passed. Five taps. Chu reached below his chair and pushed the button on the tiny device that had been taped there. The shack may have looked harmless, but if anyone tried to enter without his permission, they would've been completely incinerated by the automated lazbots hidden in the trees.

"Come in, Benson." He knew who it was because only one person had been taught the code that had been used on the door. There was something incredibly dopey about the man, but Benson was faithful beyond anything Chu had ever witnessed. So faithful he'd almost died on several occasions.

Just as he'd been instructed, he waited until Chu repeated the command—"Come in, Benson"— before finally slipping inside the small hut of discarded wood.

"I'm ready to give you a full report," the man said nervously, which pleased Chu. At Chu Industries, there was no room for error.

"What did you find out." Reginald always spoke

his questions as statements. They were commands for information, not requests.

"I spoke with every department head," Benson began, his eyes cast to the floor and his hands folded before him. A servant, through and through. "In almost every way, we're back to full strength. Everything from personnel levels to supplies to research and development. Most importantly, the underground facility is only a few weeks from completion. This time your mountain will be a real one, boss."

"Benson."

"Yes, boss?"

"Don't ever call me 'boss' again."

"I'm sorry, sir. I just wanted to show some respect— show who's the, um, boss."

Reginald stood up. He figured there was time for one more lesson before the real data started pouring out. "Benson. I think you would agree with me that neither I, nor you, need any reminder whatsoever that I am your boss."

"Yes, sir. Of course, sir."

Chu sat back down. "Good. I won't interrupt you again. Tell me everything. Especially about the findings concerning the Fourth Dimension."

Benson started talking, and as more time went by, the more quickly he spoke.

True to his word, Chu didn't say one thing or

present one inquiry. A half hour later, he knew exactly what he needed to do and how to do it.

Within six months, Chu Industries would no longer be a company. Or an empire.

It would be Reality itself.

CHAPTER 35

✳

A SIGHT OF GRAY

We should never have let her go," Rutger said. "Someone a lot bigger than me and a lot stronger should have stopped her."

"Maybe someone a little less roly-poly, I'd say," Mothball quipped.

They all stood on the hill that led to the forest, looking down in the early-morning light upon the ruins of the castle and the great, slowly churning mass of gray air that still raged in the middle of it all. Sato's army was assembled nearby, observing as well. The invading, mysterious entity below hummed and buzzed and growled as it spun, crackling when tendrils of bright lightning shot through its surface. Tick watched in awe, knowing the thing had almost doubled in size since he last looked at it from a safe distance.

The Void of Mist and Thunder. Pure power, according to Mistress Jane. How could they rely on her information about what was happening? Well, that was an easy answer—they *couldn't*. They needed to get back to headquarters and begin their own research.

"I'm just saying," Rutger continued, "never in a billion years should we have trusted that woman. Not in a trillion."

No one really argued with the butterball of a man because what he kept insisting was so obviously true. Soon after Tick had used his own hold on Chi'karda to wink away his mom and Lisa—something he'd hear about for sure in the future—Jane had used hers to wink the rest of them to this spot of temporary safety. The rumbling, machinery-like noises of the Void had grown louder and louder; the ground had begun to shake as its mass crept closer to the Great Hall. They'd needed to get away.

But then she'd gone on about how she needed to do her own part in all of this, and that she'd meet up with them soon enough, when both sides had made some progress. Master George had been furious, his usually red face growing closer to pure scarlet as he lectured her on how this problem needed all of their heads together, and then . . . she was gone. Without a word, she winked away, one second there—disheveled and scarred and exhausted—the next second, gone.

And so, a smaller group of Realitants stood in the chilly air of dawn, watching with empty bellies as an unknown force of gray fog began devouring the universe.

Typical stuff for people like us, Tick thought. Simple job. Hopefully they'd be done in time to beat rush hour tonight and get home for an early supper.

He snickered at his own lame joke.

"Telling jokes in your head over there, sport?" Paul asked him. He stood next to Sofia, and neither one of them seemed to think anything was even remotely funny about their current situation.

"No. It wasn't that kind of laugh. It was more like the we're-definitely-going-to-die-so-why-even-bother laugh. You know."

Paul actually broke a smile, a genuine one, even. "Oh, yeah. Like in the movies. The bad guy always giggles before he gets pushed out a plane or something. Or right as the axe starts swinging down."

"Uh . . . yeah," Tick said with a sarcastic nod. "Something like that."

"Rutger's right," Sato cut in, curt and abrupt. "Every single one of us was stupid to let Jane leave. We should've shackled her to a tree—something. Now we have three enemies to worry about—Jane, Chu, and that . . . thing down there."

Master George sighed, looking about as weary as Tick had ever seen him. "Sato. Rutger. My good men. I understand your concern, but I assure you, there's no way we could have stopped her. Like Master Atticus, she has herself become a Barrier Wand and has power beyond what we even think. I believe there was honor in her once, and I know she couldn't possibly want the end of her own world—as she puts it—to come about. We'll have to trust that she is off doing something that will truly help the cause."

Sally suddenly spoke up. He'd been so quiet, it seemed as if he wasn't even around, despite his huge stature and ridiculous clothes. "I trust that snicker doodle of a woman 'bout as much as a hen can toss a rooster barn. Cain't believe she was ever one a-yorn, ole George. Just cain't believe it nohow."

"She was," their leader said through another heavy sigh. "She most definitely was. And, sadly, one of the best we ever had. Who knows what might have been if she hadn't been assigned to the Thirteenth Reality? Power corrupted her like mold condemns a building. Slowly, but certainly. As it grew inside of her."

"So?" Sofia asked. "What do we do now? What's first?"

Master George pulled in a deep breath, sticking his chest way out and adjusting his filthy suit. "Some of us are going back to the Grand Canyon in Prime.

We need to put our thoughts together and make sure we understand everything we can. We need to *understand* before we can do anything to stop this madness."

"Some of us?" Tick asked. "Who *isn't* going, and what are they doing instead?"

George gave a tired look to Sato, and Tick knew he was about to ask his friend to do something dangerous. "Sato, my good man. I want you and your army to stay here. I need you to research this business about the creatures of Mistress Jane being transformed by the Void somehow. I believe there may be something extremely important to learn there. We also need someone close by to observe this . . . monstrosity and report back regularly on its progress."

Tick expected to see a flash of disappointment in Sato's features—he was missing out on a chance to go back to safety, shower and eat, rest up—but instead, he stood a little straighter and gave a stiff nod.

"Okay," he said simply. "That's what the Fifth and I will do, then."

Tick was filled with an unexpected sadness. They'd all just been reunited. He walked over to Sato and held out a hand, fighting to make sure he didn't let a stray tear leak out somehow.

Sato took his hand and shook it, squeezing it hard. "Glad to have you back, Tick."

"Yeah. Good to be back. Glad to see you alive. I know you saved a lot of kids that day at the Factory."

Sato's hand dropped to his side; Tick felt the blood rush back in his own. "We had to leave a few behind."

Tick didn't know what to say to that.

"But . . . it's good we could save the ones we did," Sato added. He looked at Master George knowingly, as if they'd had a conversation about it countless times.

"Yeah," Tick responded lamely. "Well, looks like there's gonna be a lot more to save. You think we're up for it?"

Sato smiled, something so rare that Tick almost took a step backward. "My Fifth Army will save so many people that the Realities will get sick of us. Jealous they couldn't have done it themselves."

Tick forced out a laugh. "I doubt that. Well, good luck, man. I'm sure we'll all be back together soon enough, fighting this Void thing somehow. Sound good?"

"Yeah. Sounds good."

Tick was pretty sure he'd just had the lamest conversation of his life, but he hoped that Sato knew how he felt in his heart. The others came over and said their good-byes, including a very long one between Mothball and her parents that included some very disturbing wailing along with the tears.

When everyone was done, Tick gathered with

Master George, Sally, Mothball, Rutger, Paul, and Sofia. The Realitants. They used George's Wand this time, winking away from the cyclone of the hungry Void from the Fourth Dimension.

Tick knew they'd be back.

PART 3

* * ✳ * *

THE BLUE RIVER

CHAPTER 36

A NAP ON THE COUCH

Mistress Jane was beyond exhausted. She felt a deep, aching weariness like nothing she'd ever felt before in her life. Her arms, her legs, her chest, her bones, her nerves, her veins. Her brain and head and skull. She was just so tired. And it seemed as if every last souliken she'd ever owned had drained out of her over the last couple of days. She needed rest. Desperately. Food and sleep.

Which was exactly why she couldn't handle another single minute with those buffoons who called themselves Realitants. She'd fed them what they wanted to hear about helping them against the Void and Chu, but she had her own ulterior motives. If it weren't for

Atticus Higginbottom, the Realitants would have absolutely no reason to even stay on her radar. But that insolent boy changed so many things. Everything.

She was in a place no one would have ever guessed. In an apartment—an ordinary, drab, dusty old thing that hadn't been lived in for years—located in the middle of New York City, Reality Prime. It had been the first place she'd ever rented on her own, and where she'd fallen in love so long ago. Where she'd completed her studies and first dared wink herself to other realities with the Barrier Wand she'd made with her own hands. It was here, sitting on this same frumpy couch, where she'd first had the thought that the Thirteenth Reality might change her life and, eventually, all of Reality itself.

The place had been rented and paid for ever since. Cleaned every so often by a maid. Jane couldn't bear to get rid of it, not after all the memories born within its humble walls. And, with her castle destroyed, her body depleted, and her future in doubt, she didn't know where else to go except to this place that had once been home.

She lay back on the couch, pulling her tattered robe around her body like a blanket. As horrible as she felt, being here brought her the smallest bit of comfort.

Her life was at a crossroads. The plan she'd had to essentially destroy and rebuild the Realities from the ground up had been foiled. She'd accepted that.

Perhaps it was a little easier to take since immediately afterward, there'd been the threat of spending the rest of eternity in that awful, awful Nonex. Making it back safely had been a breath of fresh air that took the stink off the failure that had led to it.

But life could be so ironic sometimes. Now there was something beyond her control that threatened to annihilate the Realities. If the Void succeeded, that may be that. Destruction with no hope of rebuilding. Although, deep down, she didn't believe it. There was always a solution. Always a way. *Everything* was an opportunity. She and Chu had made a bargain in the Nonex. A plan to see both of their destinies fulfilled. The breach of the Fourth Dimension had at first seemed to put that plan on hold, but now she wasn't so sure. Not so sure at all.

Beneath her mask, she smiled. All she needed was a little rest. The growth of the Void would take some time. She could use a couple days of eating and relaxing and healing.

A couple of days of scheming.

Mistress Jane fell asleep.

⁓

Tick waited in the conference room; he was the first one to get there. Master George had said they could take exactly thirty minutes to shower, rest, and gather their wits. Rutger was supposed to be putting together a meal for them all—something Tick couldn't wait to get his hands on. That little guy could *cook*. Tick's stomach rumbled and bounced and gurgled, desperate for anything. Even a slice of boiled cabbage sounded good right then.

He was still worried about his mom. And Lisa. And Kayla. And Dad. He should've ignored George's curt command and gone home really quickly to make sure everything was okay. But then again, maybe not. If he was going to be a Realitant, then he needed to act like one. He'd have to trust that they'd—

He stopped. Suddenly and absolutely, he felt like he'd made the biggest mistake in the world. This was his *family* they were talking about. His family. How silly that he couldn't just wink back to Deer Park really fast, check on everybody, then make it back here. How could his peace of mind and the safety of the four most important people in the universe—to him, anyway— be relegated to the bottom of the stack? In fact, it made him mad. How could Master George expect that of him?

Tick stood up and looked at the door. No one was even there yet. He was supposed to sit and wonder about his own family while everyone else took their time primping and relaxing. The last hour or so suddenly seemed absurd to him. He'd sent off his mom without asking her! Sent away his sister! All so Master George could rest assured that his number one weapon was close by and ready for service.

Forget that.

Tick closed his eyes, focusing and pooling his power. Then he winked himself to the woods that ran along the road to Deer Park. He winked himself home.

⌇

Rutger huffed and puffed as he carried the stacks of plates down the hallway. Why Master George didn't buy him some kind of rolling tray to make this easier was beyond him. Of all the Realitants to be carrying heavy plates full of hot and scrumptious food down the length of hall between the kitchen and the conference room, he was the *least* qualified. But every time he pointed that out to the boss, the old man just said it'd probably be awhile before another event, and that next time, he'd help Rutger personally.

Of course, that never happened. The buzzard always had something more urgent to attend to until the very second. By then, Rutger was all done. Even his best friend, Mothball, would magically disappear when the time came to transport the food. And what food it was.

Savory thrice-baked potatoes. Succulent steak with mushroom sauce. Crisp, bright green asparagus soaked in butter and lemon juice. Freshly baked rolls with honey butter. He expected to hear many, many, many compliments after the meal. The anticipation almost made him forget that the entire universe was on the cusp of being devoured by a giant gray fog. Well, it wouldn't happen *today*, at any rate.

Paul and Sofia were there when he brought in the first round. They offered to help, but he declined, suddenly liking the idea that he did it all himself. Sally was there the next time. Then Master George. Mothball popped in after he'd brought in the last of the meal, giving him an "Oh, would ya need some 'elp there, little man?" He just gave her a knowing look and continued about his business, making sure everything looked nice and pretty on the table. Steam rose to the ceiling, and the smells made his considerable belly ache to be fed.

When all was set, he rubbed his hands together, feeling very satisfied indeed.

"Well," he said, "looks like we're ready to partake. All we need is Tick."

"Forget that," Paul said. "He must've gone outside or something—he left the dorms way before I did. And I didn't see him anywhere. Let's dig in!"

"Absolutely not!" Rutger roared. "After all he's done for us? I won't hear of it. We'll wait until he gets here."

Paul grumbled something unintelligible and put his chin in his hands, staring longingly at the delicious, mouthwatering food—in Rutger's humble opinion, of course.

Master George slowly stood up, then leaned forward and put his hands on the table, a grave look on his face. "Goodness gracious me," he whispered. "I know exactly what's happened."

"What?" Rutger asked, hearing the whine in his own voice. He didn't want anything to ruin this fine meal.

Their leader closed his eyes for a moment before opening them again. "I believe we have a rogue Realitant. Tick has run away, against my orders. And at such a time as this." He puffed out his chest, his face sunken in disappointment. "I guess I can understand his decision, but I certainly hope it doesn't come back to haunt us."

CHAPTER 37

A NICE
MORNING STROLL

Sato couldn't remember the last time he'd had a full night's rest. And what a strange time to do it.

After the other Realitants had winked away, he'd led his army—now only a few dozen strong—in a full march around the perimeter of the ruins of Mistress Jane's castle. He didn't really know what he was looking for or wanted to find, but they'd searched all the same. And saw nothing unusual—except for the everpresent, massive gray cloud of mist and lightning that spun in the middle of the ruins, growling as it got bigger and bigger. Sato guessed by the end of the next day that it would cover every last inch of fallen stone.

It had grown dark by the end of their long walk,

and he'd given his soldiers the entire evening to get some sleep. Tollaseat had seemed the most appreciative, though he never would've admitted it. But the way he collapsed on the ground and started snoozing said it all.

Now it was early morning, and the world was full of that purple, chill air that comes right before the sun begins to show its light. Sato had slept soundly and peacefully, and when he woke up, he'd felt refreshed and filled with strength. As he sat and stared out at the distant horizon, determined to catch the moment when the sun *did* pop over the edge, he thought about what Master George had said. The old man thought there was something to the fact that all the creatures of Mistress Jane had disappeared somewhere, then reappeared in some altered state out of the Void.

Sato hadn't thought much about it at the time, but there was something weird about it. When he'd first caught sight of the castle, hordes of fangen and other nasty creatures had been crawling all over the surface of the structure and its grounds. And Sato had also seen some of them fleeing when the weird breach in Reality had first split the air. But there should've been more creatures. Many, many more. Where had they all gone? And why weren't their bodies strewn all over the place if they'd been killed? There'd been some bodies inside the passageway by the stream, but none anywhere else. Had they been . . . cloned? Transformed? What?

The more Sato thought about it, the stranger it seemed. Well, it was his job to find out the truth, and he meant to do it. He was glad to have a specific task to keep himself occupied.

He stood up and stretched, allowing a big, loud yawn to escape that sounded like a demented ghost.

"Get your bones all nice and rested, you did, I 'spect?"

Sato turned to see Tollaseat, who was stretching and yawning himself. "Slept great, actually. I've been thinking a lot about what we're supposed to be doing for Master George. About the creatures and how they all disappeared."

"Been thinkin' myself, I 'ave," the giant man said. "Remembered you tellin' us all about how them nasty little buggers were runnin' toward the middle of the castle when the mess started and all. Well, mayhaps we should be lookin' there? Only checked the roundabout yesterday night, we did."

Tollaseat was right. Yes, they'd walked around the entire ruins of the castle, but Tick had told everyone that the fangen and all their ugly cousins had been screaming and sprinting deeper *into* the building. Why would they have done that with the whole thing about to come down?

"You might be on to something," Sato said. "Why don't you and I go take a look before everyone else wakes up?"

"Could use a nice mornin' stroll, I could."

The two of them set off again for the destroyed home of Mistress Jane. Sato tried to ignore the huge, churning cloud of gray fog and lightning in the middle of it, but that was one task that proved impossible.

⁓

Tick stepped out of the woods near his home just as the sun tipped over the horizon and spilled bright morning light across the old, cracked road that he'd walked down a million times before. He was still disturbed by the long swath of broken, mangled trees he'd seen in the forest. They were leftover from the time he'd let loose his powers without even realizing it. Dissolving and reconstructing mass in his panic. He'd wanted to forget those episodes, but maybe it was a good reminder that he had a vast amount of power inside him. He needed to make sure he kept learning how to control it.

As he set off down the road toward his neighborhood, he started feeling the inevitable guilt. Master George had been very stern in ordering him to return to headquarters with the other Realitants and to save this reunion for another time. But it made Tick mad. His family was the most important thing to him right now, and he needed to make sure they were safe. He'd tried to wink directly to his house, but the pull of the deep Chi'karda pool in the forest had brought him there instead—exactly where he'd first seen Mothball disappear so long ago. It felt like a lifetime ago.

So this wouldn't quite be as quick of a trip as he'd hoped. He imagined his leader and his friends sitting in the conference room, waxing on about what a poor example Tick had shown. What a bad Realitant he was. How selfish he was. But a few hours wouldn't matter. Plus, he was pretty sure Paul and Sofia would defend him no matter what.

Tick suddenly filled up with cheer at the thought of seeing his family again. He broke into a run down the long, straight road.

Reginald Chu was scanning through a few more of the data reports Benson had wired to his reading tablet when there was an abrupt pounding on the wooden slab he called a door in his makeshift office. He almost dropped the device from the shock of the interruption, and half of him was angry, the other half relieved no one had seen his embarrassing reaction.

It took him another second to realize that the number of knocks—as hard and frantic as they were— matched the first part of his secret code. After a pause, the knocks started again. Chu quickly reached down and deactivated the lazbots.

"Oh, come on in, already!" he shouted.

Benson slipped through the door, looking as nervous as ever; trickles of sweat ran down both sides of his face.

"What, pray tell, could be so urgent?" Chu asked sternly.

"The boy. Atticus. For some reason, he left the Realitant headquarters and is all alone. I know it's earlier than you expected, sir, but this is too golden of an opportunity. We have him tracked and know exactly where he is! With no one around him to fight off!"

Chu stood up. "Amazing—what a fool that kid can be. But let's not forget, he doesn't really need an army with all that Chi'karda boiling inside his body. We'll have to tread carefully."

"He's heading toward his house, sir. He might be alone for only a few more minutes."

"Oh, please," Chu said with a laugh. "It'll be even easier if he's surrounded by his family. He'll be . . . more distracted."

"Whatever you say, boss. I mean, sir."

Chu hardly noticed the slip. "But maybe haste is best. Ready the Bagger. We leave immediately."

CHAPTER 38

✳

A TENSE CONVERSATION

The conference room had been silent for at least five minutes.

Paul kept fidgeting in his seat, worried about Tick and wishing he hadn't left. All his friend wanted to do was check on his family—they all did. How could anyone blame him? Just because Tick was a freak and could actually travel on his own without a Barrier Wand didn't make him a monster. If Paul could do that fancy trick, he'd be on a beach in the Bahamas sipping lemonade and waiting for the world to end.

Oh, forget this, he thought. Time to speak up.

"Hey, Tick will be back soon. Quit looking so sad."

Everyone in the room was staring at the table or the floor like hypnotized zombies. Sofia seemed distraught, and Mothball looked even more sullen than usual. Rutger was eating, the little stinker, but that was probably just how he dealt with things.

"You don't understand, Master Paul," George said. "I could see the rebellion in your friend's eyes, and I knew he was tempted to do things that he wasn't even thinking about yet except on a subconscious level. I knew he'd see his family, remember the horrors he's been through, and begin to think selfish thoughts. Feel tempted to stay with them, run away, keep them safe. How can we have our Realitants run off willy-nilly when we need them the most? He shouldn't have gone. I'm terribly sorry to say it."

Paul understood but didn't want to admit it. "How can you blame him for winking away really quick just to check on his family? I'm sure he'll be back any second. You're making too much of it!"

George slammed his hand down on the table. "I will not have you speak to me this way! I am your leader and I demand respect! We're on the cusp of something that could kill every single living person in every Reality! Each of us have higher callings than running off to check on mums and dads!"

He stopped, and the entire room fell dead silent. Even Rutger had frozen with a piece of steak halfway to his mouth. Paul's anger had vanished, replaced by pure shock. He'd never seen *this* before.

"I know I sound harsh," George finally said in a much calmer voice, "but I feel as if our organization has slowly gone down the pits, so to say, since Jane embraced her evil ways and Lorena Higginbottom decided to leave our ranks. We used to be disciplined and strong and willing to sacrifice all for the greater good. But now I can't even convince any of our members to leave their homes and come to help us. We've fallen apart, I swear it."

The old man suddenly slumped down in his chair and buried his head in his hands. Paul half-expected him to sob, but he just sat there, perfectly quiet and still, for a long minute. Then he looked up, and his face was as determined as Paul had ever seen it.

"Never mind all that," George said. "We have a job to do, and I expect us to do it. If I have to go it alone, I will. And if . . . *when* I defeat the Void of the Fourth Dimension, I'll build the Realitants from the ground up. I stake my life on this promise to all of you."

Paul blinked, not sure what to say.

"Ya won't be alone s'long as my heart's still tickin', you won't," Mothball said. "I'll be by your side to the bitter end, warts and all."

"Me too," Rutger added. Then he finally finished off his bite of juicy steak.

Sally wasn't about to be upstaged. "Ya'll ain't havin' all da fun, I can promise you *that*."

"Paul and I—we're in too," Sofia said. She shot Paul a look that said he better shape up. But something in her eyes let him know that she understood his frustrations about George's reaction to Tick leaving.

Paul groaned. "You guys know very well that I'm not quitting. But after all that Tick has done, I think it's really lame to just snap your fingers and accuse him of being a traitor. It's about the most unfair thing I've ever heard."

"It wasn't a snap of my fingers," George said sadly. "Master Atticus chose to go against my direct order. If my words were harsh, I apologize. But I don't want someone by my side in the very last battle of these worlds who might turn his back on me."

"Tick would never do that," Paul said in a low growl. "You know it. He just went for a quick trip to check on his *family*."

"Sorry to be the one to point this out," Rutger said, "but he hasn't come back yet, now has he?" His eyes darted around the room as though worried he'd said something wrong. "But no one likes the boy more than me. I hope you'll be a little forgiving, Master George."

The leader of the Realitants nodded slowly. "We will deal with him how we must, I assure you.

However, I already have a very bad feeling that we may not see him for a while. A very bad feeling indeed."

Tick's heart lifted when he passed a clump of trees close to the road and saw the turn into his neighborhood come into view. He'd been lightly jogging and now picked up his pace to a full sprint, eager to run up the steps of his porch and rip the door open. He knew everyone would be there. Safe and sound and happy. He knew it. He was completely ignoring the small part of him that worried something horrible had happened. That they *wouldn't* be there. Or worse.

This was why he had come. He needed to know for sure. Master George was probably ranting and raving by now, but he'd deal with that when he got back. Soon. He was just about to reach the street, less than thirty feet away, when he heard a loud noise from somewhere above him.

It was a bang, instant and piercing, like the clang of two giant iron pots. Times a thousand. Tick was so startled that he cried out and fell to the ground, rolling off the road and down the slight decline. He came to a stop in the dirt, on his back, looking up to search for what could have possibly been the source of such an awful sound. He saw a blur of flashing light and something silvery and long above him, accompanied by a great whooshing sound, like the thrust of rockets. Wind tore through the air and ripped at his clothes, sending dust and pebbles scattering down the slope.

Holding up his forearm to shield his eyes, his vision finally cleared enough to see the thing that had suddenly appeared in the sky over his head. It was a thick rectangle of silver metal, roughly the size and shape of a coffin. Its surface was smooth, without any seams, and the lights that flashed around it made no sense to Tick, as if they were being created by invisible protrusions from the flying object. Whatever it was, the push of air from the silver coffin was like a hurricane blast, growing stronger as it hovered in the air.

Then it slowly descended toward Tick.

He flopped onto his stomach, got his hands beneath him, and pushed up to jump to his feet. He slipped and slid as his arms windmilled, fighting to gain his balance on the small hill. He'd just gained solid purchase when there was a clicking sound right behind his ears. The noise sent a burst of terror through him, though he didn't understand why, and he burst into a sprint, not even taking a chance to look back.

He'd only gone a few yards when a thin cable of something strong slipped around his stomach, coiled tight, and ripped his body up into the air.

CHAPTER 39

✳

A REBOUND OF POWER

Tick's initial shout turned into a strangled grunt as the cord pinched into his stomach and he vaulted away from the ground. His body doubled over as he grabbed the ridged metal of the thing that had captured him— it felt like a wire on an old telephone pole. He twisted and kicked with his feet and tried to pull the thing loose, to no avail. He continued to rise, the sight of the road replaced by the tops of trees, all of it making his head spin and his stomach flip. Giving up on the cord, he tried to turn so he could see what held him.

The blocky silver rectangle was pulling him along, the metal cord coming out of a hole just big enough for it to fit. There was a moment where everything seemed to freeze, and Tick searched his mind for a possible explanation of what was happening. If anyone was watching from below, what else could they think except that a UFO had zapped down from outer space to steal the first human they could find in order to perform experiments? It was all just so . . . odd. Tick was surprised at how little terror he felt now—much less than when he'd first heard that clicking sound.

Because he remembered that he had an untapped amount of power inside his body.

He closed his eyes and let the Chi'karda flow into his chest, into his heart and nerves and bones and muscles. The surge of it was like a rushing river, somehow cold and hot at the same time, filling him with a rapturous clarity and a sense of being unstoppable. Like he could crush mountains or drink up the entire ocean and spit it back out. He wanted to roar and pound his chest. When he opened his eyes again, the familiar orange mist spun around him and clung to his skin, particles of light bouncing along his clothes, untouched by the wind.

With both hands, he grabbed the trailing length of the cord that connected his waist to the boxy contraption that flew through the air. He wrenched his body around until he'd twisted enough that he faced the long cube of silver. After pulling in a deep breath, he blew out the power that had boiled and churned inside of him, letting it flow like an open faucet, throwing every ounce of power at the box that had captured him. A great rushing sound filled his ears, and the world blinded him with orange light.

A thunderclap shook the air, along with a massive jolt of power.

Tick was suddenly plummeting, his hearing deafened, his senses completely out of whack. It was like he'd been flooded with numbing drugs. On some level, he felt the tops of trees scratching his back, felt the cord still cinched tightly around his waist, but his vision had gone from orange to bright white, and he could hear absolutely nothing. The pulse of his blood was a pounding in his head, a thump-thump-thump that he could only feel, a vibration that rattled down his spine.

He was still being pulled along. Somehow he knew that. The branches weren't suddenly gone—nothing tore at his clothes or bit at his skin. His eyes darted wildly, trying to see anything but the whiteness that seared his sight. The calmness and sense of invincibility from earlier completely vanished, replaced by a fiery panic that lit up his nerves. What was happening to him? He couldn't see, couldn't hear. He barely felt the motion of flying through the air or the metal rope wrapped around his middle. How could all that power he'd thrown at the long, silvery coffin not have freed him and dropped him to the forest floor?

He didn't know what else to do but try again. Though weakened from whatever had happened the first time, he concentrated on his internal self, pooling the Chi'karda once again. It came as only a trickle, a weak stream of power that barely made a splash compared to what it had been before. It had no form or substance. It couldn't take shape. It wasn't strong enough for him to do anything with it. And he still couldn't see.

His panic erupted into anger. Rage tore through his body and weakened some of the dam holding back the Chi'karda. He screamed and tried again, pulling on whatever lever he sensed that controlled the link between him and the Realities. The surge came, rushed through him like a flood, filling him with relief as strong as the power itself.

Still flying through the air, still attached to the cord, he didn't wait, didn't allow himself even a second to enjoy the swell of pleasure. He threw everything he had at the object holding him captive.

This time he didn't hear the thunderclap at all, just felt it. A thump of violence that jarred his bones and rattled his skull. The blinding light around him brightened even more, intense with heat and pressure. The rope around his waist jerked forward, pulling his body along with it. A sprinkle of pain cut through the numbness, making him reach for his back. But his fingers were numb too, and he felt nothing there. All was blunt and dull and lifeless. Nothing made sense anymore. His brain began to shut down.

His hearing came back just long enough for him to hear that clicking sound again. Then everything exploded in a rush of movement, and darkness engulfed him.

～～～

Chu needed a break from his run-down excuse for a temporary office. Maybe a permanent break. He hated the little place, and he missed the power of being in charge, of being *seen* as the man in charge.

Reginald Chu stood in the newly built laboratory, leaning against the railing as he stared down at the massive chamber. It was seven or eight football fields wide and at least three tall. Big. Really, really big. Even larger than the chamber inside the mountain palace, which Atticus Higginbottom had brought crumbling down right before Chu was sent to the Nonex. Tick. The little rat.

But Chu's people had already been working on this new facility and had even picked up the pace, hoping that someday their leader would return. They were loyal and smart. Benson led the security details, but the real geniuses were Chu's engineers and scientists and physicists. He'd gathered more brain power into one place over the last thirty years than anywhere else in all the Realities. His men shared his goals. Most of them didn't care what the end result might be—let Chu rule the world, other worlds, whatever—as long as they kept getting the funds they needed to do the research that kept their old hearts ticking.

And now they'd built the largest research facility in history. This chamber was only a small part of it. It went on and on and on. And the most amazing thing about it was that the complex had been built entirely underground. It was simply awesome.

And it was time for Chu to finally move back in. He'd had his moments of reflection and his moments of appreciating what had been taken from him. But things were going to move, and move fast, now. Below him, his workers were finalizing the very device he planned to use to harness the immense power of the Void that had escaped the Fourth Dimension.

Right on cue, his earpiece buzzed. It was Benson.

"We got him, sir. The Bagger worked like a charm."

"Excellent," Chu replied. "Let Mistress Jane know at once."

CHAPTER 40

✳

A PULSING LIGHT

Sato picked his way along the top of the rubble, knowing that he could slip to his death at any second. The ruined stone and brick and wood and whatever else Jane had used to build the place lay stacked on top of each other like some kind of fragile toy, ready to collapse at any second. Something shifted with every step, and Sato kept thinking he couldn't possibly feel his heart leap any stronger, but it seemed to do so every time.

The gray mass of spinning air was only a few hundred feet to his left, and that certainly wasn't helping his nerves. Cracks of thunder shook the air and made the debris beneath his feet tremble, and as hard as he tried, he couldn't stop himself from looking over every few seconds at the brilliant displays of lightning. The Void itself was downright creepy. It had a steady roar and a chilling movement to it that made Sato feel as if it were alive and hungry.

And it was growing steadily. Half of the castle ruins had been swallowed by the entity, and its pace of expansion seemed to be increasing. If they were going to learn anything about what had happened to Mistress Jane's creatures, they'd need to figure it out fast.

Tollaseat tapped him on the shoulder, making him almost jump out of his skin. "What if that blimey thing decides it wants to take a bit of leapin' at us?" Mothball's dad asked. "Takes a fancy at throwin' a lightning bolt or two our way?"

"Then duck," Sato replied. "You're welcome to go back if you want."

Tollaseat laughed, a booming sound that drowned out the thunder and rush of wind for a few seconds. "You make a grouchy grump, you do. Or is it a grumpy grouch?"

"Just keep looking." Sato had enjoyed the tiny reprieve from the noises of the Void, but knew he couldn't admit it. He needed to keep his game face on now. Be a leader. "You go that way, and I'll go this way. But not too far off. We need to be off this big pile of rocks in an hour."

"Can't come soon enough," the man mumbled.

Sato turned his back to him once more and started gingerly walking over the rubble again. According to their best guess, they were currently over the section the fangen and other creatures had been running toward, but everything looked the same from the outside—broken and dusty. Keeping his arms out for balance, he walked across the crooked stacks of stones, looking through the gaps and cracks for any sign of . . . he didn't know. Something.

A few minutes later, he spotted it. Far down below the debris, just visible through the layers of stone, he saw a glowing blue light that pulsed every two or three seconds, flashing more brilliantly before fading again to a dull glow.

"Hey!" he shouted. "Come over here and look!"

Tollaseat's face lit up with excitement, and he started lumbering his way over to where Sato stood. The man was so much taller and bigger than an average man, and Sato feared he'd crash down in a cloud of dust and rock chips at any second. But he finally made it and raised his shoulders in question.

"Down there." Sato pointed.

Tollaseat put a big hand on Sato's shoulder and leaned in to take a look. Sato flexed his leg muscles to keep his knees from collapsing under the added weight.

"Well, I'll be," the man said, the glow from below

reflecting in his large eyes. "Take me spine out and tickle 'er up and down! What in the blazes you reckon that is, sir?"

Sato looked at his friend and best soldier. "I don't know. But this can't be a coincidence. Those nasty things of Jane's were running this way, and then they all seemed to vanish, only to reappear later. And now there's a flashing blue light shining in a place that doesn't use electricity."

"Right, you are. Can't be two toads bumpin' tongues on the same fly, that's for sure."

"Huh?" When Tollaseat opened his mouth to answer, Sato cut him off. "Never mind. Let's get down to that thing. Time's running out."

He planted his feet as firmly as he could then bent over to lift a piece of rock directly above the odd blue glow. He chucked it to the side, the crack of it hitting the rubble barely audible over the noises of the Void.

In the shadow of the huge gray funnel of mist filled with lightning and thunder, Sato and Tollaseat started digging through the ruins of Mistress Jane's castle.

Paul was curled up in his bed—or the bed he'd been given at the Grand Canyon headquarters—staring at the wall. He'd never felt so low in all his life, and there'd been some freaky, scary moments over the last couple of years. But right that second, he just wanted to sink into the mattress, fall asleep, and never wake up again. Everything had gone so wrong.

How could the whole world—scratch that, the whole *universe* and every single Reality within it—be in so much trouble? *Again?* Mistress Jane and her fancy schmancy Blade of Shattered Hope had almost set off a chain reaction that would've destroyed the universe. Paul didn't care about the specifics, but he knew that Tick had saved them all. Yeah, he'd been sucked away into the Nonex, but deep down, Paul had known the kid was okay and that he'd find his way back somehow. Or, at least, Paul had told himself that.

But now all this? Some big gray cloud called the Void from the Fourth Dimension was eating away at a planet? And then Jane said it would keep on going once that was all done. And then Tick had to make it worse by running off against Master George's wishes. Which wasn't so bad to Paul—what was *bad* was the fact that Tick hadn't come *back*. And Rutger couldn't get a lock on Tick's nanolocator. The Realitant system kept saying that it was blocked, a thing that had obviously bewildered and bamboozled everyone listening.

Not Paul. To him, the news had just made him sick to his stomach. He'd insisted on leaving, going to his room. *Sorry, so sorry, but I don't feel so well.* Which was the absolute truth. They were supposed to take care of Chu and Mistress Jane then have fun exploring other worlds for the rest of their lives. It wasn't supposed to be like this. Paul wanted to shout at the top of his lungs. Maybe pound on some walls while he was at it.

He sat up.

He had to do something. Master George and the others had talked and talked around the conference room table and had come up with absolutely nothing to show for it. Except that they were going to keep researching, keep tabs on things, blah blah blah. Paul couldn't stand the thought of all that wasted time and energy. A big glob of *fog* was eating away at Reality, and his best friend had gone missing.

He had to do something, and he had to do something now, or he'd go completely nutso bat-crazy. Ignoring the ache and nausea in his belly, he slid off the bed and opened his door, stepping out into the hallway. It was right then that an image of a box popped into his head. A little metal box with a green button. And Paul knew exactly where Master George had placed it.

He started walking in that direction.

CHAPTER 41

✳

ILL REUNION

When Tick opened his eyes, the face of Reginald Chu was staring back down at him. It was a face that had once meant so much to him—this terrible man was the Alterant of Tick's beloved science teacher, one of the greatest people ever. It was crazy how two opposites could look so much alike.

Tick was surprised at how little panic he felt. The ordeal that had happened near his home had been terrible. The movement and disorientation from whatever it was that had captured him had caused him to faint. He'd eventually awakened on a gurney of steel in some kind of bright washroom, reeking. He almost gagged from his own smell. He'd barely been conscious enough to have the thought, however, before someone pricked him with something that made him doze off again. His last memory was of a big hose washing him off before the darkness took him away.

And now, here he was again. Waking up. He could feel clean, fresh clothes on his skin. He could see lights in the ceiling. And the ugly, smug face of Chu peering down at him as if he were nothing but an insect specimen.

"Don't even think about reaching for your Chi'karda," the man said. "Before I say anything else, I'll warn you on that front. Do you understand?"

Tick stared at him but said nothing. His mind went back to his failed attempts to escape from that weird silver coffin that had captured him. Twice he'd tried to destroy the object and free himself by throwing out his power, only to have it rebound and practically fry his brain. He still didn't really understand the whole strange turn of events.

Chu continued. "I can see the light of understanding in your eyes. I'm sure you remember when you and Jane came to Chu Industries, invited by yours truly. I wanted the best for my Dark Infinity project, and I knew there had to be something in place to block your Chi'karda levels. Well, obviously it didn't work then—now did it? You destroyed my entire building and ruined Jane's body for life."

"Maybe I'll do it again," Tick responded. His confidence was returning, and he still felt no real fear, despite the situation.

"You're missing my point. Once again your arrogance is preventing your brain from processing my words. I'm reminding you of the measures I had in place because they have been improved upon. My people are very clever, and you would be wise not to try anything. You felt what happened when you tried to use your force against the Bagger."

"The Bagger?" Tick repeated. He lifted his head up and saw that he was lying on a small bed with several metal cords wrapped around his body, holding him down. The cords were much thinner than the one that had sprung from the long silver box and grabbed him by the waist, but seemed to be made from the same material.

"It's an invention of Chu Industries that I have neither the time or the desire to explain. It uses technology that lies beyond terminology you would understand anyway. But the key is that it was armed with my anti-Chi'karda recoil mechanism. And it worked. Sorry to test it on you—I'm sure you don't appreciate being the guinea pig, considering you could have died. What a pity that would've been."

This supposedly grown man was acting like a child, and it annoyed Tick to no end. "Maybe you can just *tell me why I'm here.*"

Chu's head pulled back ever so slightly, as if he were surprised that Tick would take such a tone considering his obvious disadvantages. "Don't mistake bravery for stupidity, boy. With all the people I've crushed or pushed aside in my lifetime quest to rule the Realities and make them better, it should be clear that I have many, many enemies. But no one comes close to being a target of my sheer . . . animosity as you do. Mr. Higginbottom, I despise you—there's no other way to put it. And your margin of error with me is as thin as a red blood cell. Do you understand?"

"*You* despise *me*?" Tick asked, incredulous. "How do you think I feel about you?"

"I'm sure the feeling is mutual. But it hardly matters now that I have such complete control over you. I suggest you take a more humble approach."

But Tick wasn't done sharing a piece of his mind. "And what's all that garbage about making the Realities better? All you want is power, and you know it. You don't care about anyone but yourself."

Chu's face flashed with anger, and he leaned in closer to Tick. His bad breath wafted to Tick's nose and made him want to squirm out of the bed. "You shut that mouth of yours, do you hear me? Shut your mouth and show me some respect. You could never possibly understand me or my motives. I'll do what needs to be done, and no one can stop me. Yes, I may have a petty streak in me, and I may have done a few things that I might not be proud of, which is unfortunate for you because when I'm done using you, I'm going to dispose of you in a way that brings me a great deal of satisfaction. It's something you can start looking forward to."

Tick lashed out, but the restraints held his arms in place. He was furious and had never wanted to hit another person so much in his life. But he slouched back down onto the bed, knowing he couldn't be stupid enough to try anything with his power over Chi'karda. He'd just have to be patient and wait for the right opportunity to come along.

But at least he had his words. "You're a pathetic man, Chu. How can you even look yourself in the mirror tonight after standing there and talking like that to someone who's not even fifteen years old yet? Pathetic and sad."

Chu, of course, did the most maddening thing then. He laughed as he straightened back up to stand tall. "Don't goad me on, kid. You can yap all day if you want about how young you are, but we all know the power that's trapped inside your child's body. And we all know why."

Tick paused, surprised by the odd statement. Even though he hated to let go of his anger, he had to know what the man meant. "What . . . why . . . why what?"

Chu raised his eyebrows. "Don't play dumb with

me, boy. Reginald Chu knows all—or at least what he cares to."

Tick started to sit up before he remembered the restraints. Groaning in frustration, he closed his eyes then opened them again. He needed to find some humility. "I'm serious. I don't know what you're talking about."

"This is unbelievable. How could he keep you in the dark about this?" Chu looked at him in disbelief. "I'm talking about why *you*, of all people, have this incredible ability to manipulate and control Chi'karda. Don't tell me that old man George hasn't explained it to you yet. He knows. He went well out of his way to confirm it."

Tick was dumbfounded. "*What* does he know?"

Chu folded his arms and peered down at him, slowly shaking his head. "Soulikens, Atticus. It's all about the soulikens."

CHAPTER 42

*

POOR LITTLE CENTIPEDE

Sweat poured down Sato's face, and it wasn't just from the effort of digging through and tossing aside the countless broken stones that had lain between him and the source of the glowing light at his feet. He was nervous because the massive storm of the Void was growing louder and bigger, its shadow looming over him, Tollaseat, and the dug-out pit in which they stood. They needed to figure out this anomaly and get away from there.

He got down on one knee and inspected the source of the light. It was a slit in the floor, about three feet long and a few inches wide. Although it wasn't really *in* the floor—it was more like the rip in Reality he'd

seen before when the gray fog had first appeared beside
the castle walls. Blue light shone from behind the odd
crack in the air, so intense that it was hard to look at
it directly. There was nothing else there, as if it were
a small window into a river of radioactive material or
something otherworldly. The light continued to pulse,
flashing every few seconds so brightly that it was
blinding.

"How're we s'posed to figure what she might be?"
Tollaseat asked. The man was too long and gangly to
try to squat down next to Sato. "Took a bit of work, it
did, gettin' down this far. T'would be a mighty shame
to go back empty-handed, now wouldn't it?"

Sato thought Mothball's dad had an uncanny gift
for saying a lot of words that offered no help whatsoever. "I don't know. Just let me think for a second."

He did try to think, and that didn't help either. He
wasn't a scientist. Somehow he'd become the captain
of an army, for crying out loud. But he knew without
any doubt that this small spit of shining blue light had
something to do with . . . something.

Out of the corner of his eye, he noticed a centipede creeping along a broken slab of stone. Testing
some theory on the edge of his mind, he picked up the
poor little thing and tossed it into the slice of pulsing
light. The bug disappeared in a tiny burst of white
electricity, tiny jagged bolts skittering across the blue

surface before dying out. There was no sign of the critter.

"Well, ain't you a cruel one," Tollaseat chided him from above. "What did that wee bugger ever do to you?"

Sato stood up, letting out a big sigh as he did so. "I was just putting him out of his misery. Pretty soon this whole place will be eaten up by . . . whatever that is out there." He jabbed a thumb in the direction of the tornado, then gave one last glance to the blue anomaly. "It was just an experiment. I thought maybe something would happen. Look, I have no idea what to do here. We'll just have to describe it to Master George and see what he thinks. Come on, let's go."

The two of them started up the pile of rocks they'd burrowed out of before. Sato was halfway to the top when he heard a horrible roar, like something half-mechanical and half-animal. It was followed by shouts from his soldiers.

His heart sank, and his first thought was, *What now?*

He picked up the pace and scrambled the rest of the way, almost falling twice as pieces of stone tore loose or broke off. When he reached the peak of the debris, he balanced himself and stood up, Tollaseat right beside him.

Something monstrous was crawling out of the churning mass of the Void's huge tornado. It was big and long, with lightning arcing along its gray skin. With a terrifying dawn of awareness, Sato realized that the thing looked like . . .

It looked like a *centipede.*

⁓

Paul was just about to slip into the laboratory of the Realitant headquarters when Sofia spotted him from down the hallway. *Great,* he thought. He'd almost made it.

She ran up to him. "What in the world are you doing? I looked all over for you. Master George is *not* happy."

"Hey, it's not my fault those idiots can't figure out what we're supposed to do next."

"Idiots?" she repeated. "Really? You're calling *them* idiots?"

"Very funny. Look, I might not be the smartest tool in this workshop, but at least I don't think it's okay to sit around fiddling my thumbs. I think it's high time you and I figured out something on our own."

Sofia rolled her eyes, but he saw some compassion in there too. She was trying to keep everyone happy on both sides of the fence. "Paul, you know very well that not a single person here is fiddling their thumbs. The rest of them are analyzing data, talking to other

Realitants, and researching. They're trying to learn more about the Void and its energy so we can beat it. I was just coming to find you to help. We need every set of eyes."

"I'll tell you what the Void is," Paul said. "It's a big gray tornado that's getting bigger the longer we stand around here. We need Tick to go in there and . . . do whatever it is he does. Our *friend* is obviously in trouble, and that should be our number-one priority. Getting him *back*."

"And you really think Master George disagrees with that?" She folded her arms. "They can't latch onto his nanolocator. Mothball went to Deer Park but saw no sign of him. His dad said he never showed up. We can't go looking behind every rock and tree in the universe."

"Oh . . . oh, man." The news made Paul wilt inside. "There's gotta be a way to find him."

Sofia sighed. "Rutger will keep scanning for him, hope he pops back onto the radar."

"Tick should be our—"

"—number-one priority. I know! Don't you think I'm worried like crazy too? I just think we should all work together, not sneak around like this. What are you doing here anyway?"

Paul couldn't keep a secret from her, not now. "I came for the box."

"The box?"

"The box."

Her mouth was slightly open, her expression saying that she had no doubt he'd gone nuts. "And why are you going for the box?"

"Because I'm going to push the green button."

"No, you're not."

"Yes, I am."

"We don't even know what it does yet!"

"George does, or else he wouldn't have made us go get it." Paul reached out and opened the lab door. He'd seen their leader put the box into a cabinet drawer, even though the old man had tried to keep it a secret. The drawer wasn't a safe, though. It didn't have a lock or anything. Maybe George thought if the box was hidden in a place people wouldn't suspect, it might be safer.

"Paul, don't."

He ignored her and stepped into the room. When she didn't reach out and yank him back by the collar, he knew he had her. Times had grown desperate, and it was time to *do* something desperate. Before either one of them could change their minds, he ran over to the cabinet. She followed right on his heels. Paul ripped open the drawer.

The drawer was empty.

"I thought you might come looking for this," a voice said from behind them.

They spun around to see Master George at the lab door, bouncing the box with its little green button in his right hand. At first Paul thought that Sofia might've betrayed him, but one glance at her showed that she was just as surprised—and disappointed—at their leader's arrival.

"I just wanted to . . ." Paul began, but didn't know how to finish.

"Yes, I know," George said. "You just wanted to help, I'm sure. I guess it's time we had a talk about this very special device. It's time I told you about Karma. And then it may very well be time to push this button."

CHAPTER 43

✳

ONE WITH REALITY

Chu had refused to say another word after announcing that it was "all about the soulikens." Tick knew soulikens were imprints of energy created by life and memories and thoughts. Stamps of life on Reality. They accumulated throughout one's existence until their signature hung around them like an aura. The Haunce—the most amazing creature Tick had ever met—was made up of trillions of soulikens.

Tick had an idea of what Chu meant. Most of his Alterants—if not all—had died at some point. Maybe their soulikens had somehow bled to him. Maybe that could explain the powers he had. He'd never wanted to talk to Master George so badly.

But that would have to wait. The gurney on which he lay had been rolled out of that hospital-like room by a man and a woman dressed in blue scrubs then down a long hallway and into an auditorium with rows and rows of chairs and a stage. Draped behind the stage was a huge screen of white material. The workers pushed him about halfway down the aisle then raised the back of the bed so Tick was able to sit up. His arms, legs, and torso were still fastened tightly down by the thin cords of metal. And his Chi'karda was still being blocked.

Chu had walked the entire way beside them, silent and brooding. He dismissed the blue-clad man and woman, leaving him and Tick alone inside the auditorium. The room was barely lit and cold; it was about as uninviting a room as Tick could imagine.

He looked at Chu, but the man was staring at the large screen, his hands folded in front of him. For at least two minutes he said nothing, which drove Tick batty. But he refused to say anything either, because he knew the man was waiting for him to do so.

Finally, Chu gave in and spoke. "Have you ever seen a fire, Atticus?" He still stared ahead, not turning to face Tick.

It certainly wasn't the question he'd expected. "A fire? Of course I've seen a fire. I've *made* fire. You saw me do it in the Nonex."

Chu seemed unfazed, in full business mode.

Eerily, he reminded Tick of the other Mr. Chu, his science teacher, when he was about to begin yet another lecture that he thought would change his students' lives forever.

"So then, you have, in fact, seen a fire before?" the man said.

Tick wasn't going to be baited into anger. "Yes. I've seen a fire. Many times."

"Then you know about matter changing from one form to another. In your own experience, you've seen—and caused to happen—a solid molecular structure turn into a gas. Wood to flame. There are countless other examples of the physical makeup of one substance *changing* into another substance. Water evaporating, the decay of leaves, and so on and so forth."

Tick nodded. He had to admit he was intrigued, and he had no choice but to listen anyway.

"You're going to help me do that, Atticus. You're going to help me harness the power of Chi'karda and the Void that is escaping from the Fourth Dimension. And then you're going to make me—and Mistress Jane—one with them."

Tick felt an unpleasant flutter in his chest. He couldn't find any words. Chu was talking about something beyond evil, even though Tick didn't understand it fully yet.

The man finally turned and faced him, and there was something fanatical in his expression. "*One*, Atticus. You're going to make us *one* with Reality. The universe will never be the same."

⌒⌒⌒

The creature was as big as a bus. Bulky and thick, with dozens of legs protruding from its gray-skinned body. Sato watched in sick fascination as the monster birthed itself out of the spinning mass of the Void then lumbered its way across the remaining span of castle ruins toward his army. The giant centipede's skin was slick with wetness, arcs of lightning flashing along the surface.

Sato was reckless as he jumped and ran over broken stones and bricks, knowing he might break an ankle at any second. But this centipede creature from the Void was heading straight for the Fifth Army, and he wanted to be there to help fight it. As he picked and leaped his way along, frantically looking for the next spot to land a foot before he jumped again, thoughts tore through his mind. This couldn't be a coincidence. He'd thrown the bug into that blue light, and soon after, only only only a monstrous version of it had emerged from the Void. Earlier, gray monsters that looked like creations of Mistress Jane's had come out of the tornado—most likely after having been sucked into the blue light.

And it scared him that the one place the newest creature decided to go was to a campsite full of people, which meant it could probably *think*. And that it wanted to kill and destroy. At least, he assumed so. A few seconds later, his suspicions were confirmed.

One of the many legs on the creature suddenly ripped off the main body, spinning away like a boomerang, headed for the center of Sato's army, which was gathering for battle. The shaft of gray fog flew through the air about forty feet then suddenly erupted into flames, brilliant and yellow. It struck one of Sato's soldiers, a man standing bravely at the head of the front line, who'd just been pulling up his Shurric into a firing position. There was a violent explosion of sparks and fire that started but stopped almost instantly, leaping out then collapsing in on itself. It was so bright that Sato stumbled and fell, smacking his upper arm on a sharp stone.

With a grimace, he quickly looked back at the front line—amoebas of light dancing in his vision—but saw nothing. The poor man had been incinerated.

Sato heard the shouts of battle as his soldiers surged forward to fight, charging the creature as it continued to come at them. He scrambled to his feet, wincing from the pain in his shoulder—there would be one terrible bruise there before long. Tollaseat was there, helping him get up. The man said nothing, but there was a mix of sadness and fear in his eyes.

Noise filled the air: the rushing roar of the Void's spinning cloud, the cracks of thunder, the battle screams of his soldiers.

The Void monster crashed through the last part of the castle debris, landing on the ground dozens of feet from the charging Fifth Army. It righted itself and shot off another one of its legs, a three-foot-long stub of gray fog that spun through the air until it erupted into flames like its predecessor. The twirling missile of fire slammed into the body of a man, causing an explosion just like before. When the sparks and pyrotechnics collapsed again into a tiny spot and disappeared, there was no sign of the soldier.

Another leg flew off of the creature, doing the same trick. Spinning, erupting into flames, flying toward a soldier. This time it a was a woman. She was ready, though, and held her ground. She lifted her Shurric and, with patience that Sato couldn't believe, took the time to aim and fire her weapon at the heart of the incoming attack. The thump of pure sound wave was too deep to be heard, but Sato felt a rattle in his bones. The force of power slammed into the spinning projectile and ruptured it, sending small spits of flame and sparks in a million directions. But no one was harmed.

Sato grinned. They could do this. They *could* beat this thing.

He picked up his pace across the ruins, watching as his army attacked the creature with everything they had. The creature was dead by the time he got there.

CHAPTER 44

GOOD AND EVIL

Master George had taken Paul and Sofia to a small, private room located in the deepest part of the headquarters, far below the surface of the Upper Rim of the Grand Canyon. Unmarked, it could've passed for a utility closet. It held only a table and four chairs, nothing else.

"I come here sometimes when I need a bit of time to myself," the old man said wearily after they'd taken their seats. He held Gretel's box in his hands under the table. "And to be quite frank, I'm at a loss right now. I can barely face my dear old friends, Mothball and the rest. I've always felt as if I have known the direction to take, even in the most dire of circumstances we've faced. But not now. I'm at a loss, indeed. It's no wonder I wanted to hide in this room. I very much appreciate you taking refuge along with me."

Paul looked over at Sofia. Had the geezer really given up?

Sofia reached out and patted George's shoulder. "Everything kind of took a crazy turn," she said soothingly. "But we'll figure things out."

"Yeah," Paul agreed. What he really wanted was to find out more about the box. And the button. "So can that box do something to help? Are we really going to push the button?"

Sofia shot him a glare. "Seriously? I guess there's only room enough in that brain of yours for one thing at a time." She winked, then, taking away the sting of her words.

He felt a nice flutter inside. "I'm just saying. Things are messed up beyond belief, and we went on a special mission to get that box, so it must be important. We need all the help we can get, don't we?"

Sofia didn't answer at first, just looked back at Master George. "He's right. It might be time to do something a little drastic."

Their leader nodded slowly as he stared at the table. "I couldn't agree more, Sofia. I fear we've come to a place in our journey where we need something a little . . . beyond the regular means. We know so little of this Void from the Fourth Dimension that I'm afraid we need your minds and skills more than ever. We can't rely on Mistress Jane to teach us about the threat that churns inside the Thirteenth Reality. At least when we faced the Blade of Shattered Hope—and the Dark Infinity weapon before that—there was a path before us. Possibilities. Like I've said, this time around, I'm at a bitter loss. You two need to step it up."

Paul couldn't help the impatience that wanted to burst out of him at the seams. "So . . . then what are you saying?"

George pulled his hands up from his lap and placed the small metal box on the table in front of him. The green button was like a beacon, and Paul had to resist the urge to reach out and push it right that second.

"This is your assignment," George pronounced. "But before I tell you about this box, we need to talk about a very important subject. Very important, indeed. It's something that is almost as beyond our understanding as this Void that plagues us presently. And that subject is . . . Karma."

He'd said that word earlier, but now it had a haunted, foreboding ring to it. Paul leaned forward, eager to hear more.

"There's a reason talking about this makes me . . . uncomfortable," George continued. "I'm a scientist, and I know both of you are well aware of that fact. I'm a scientist above all else. And that means that everything I live for is grounded in a solid foundation of tested theories, facts, and proofs. Many of the things you've seen and experienced since being recruited—goodness gracious me, that seems like decades ago—may appear to be magic to many people. To *ordinary* people. But my favorite two words, *quantum physics*, have always been able to explain it all. *Kyoopy*, I believe it's been coined before."

He paused, a look of blissful contemplation on his face. But then he shook his head and snapped out of it. His expression grew very serious. "But this . . . this is something that is a little less certain. A part of our cosmos that is beyond our capacity to comprehend fully. Or beyond mine, at any rate."

"Karma?" Sofia asked.

"Karma," the old man confirmed.

"Everyone knows what that means," Paul said. "Basically, what goes around, comes around. Right?"

"To put it simply, yes." George looked down at the box then back at Paul. "The notion that the universe pays back what people deposit is something that has been a part of human culture since the beginning of recorded history. Be a good person, do good things, and then good things will happen to you eventually. Be a *bad* person, do *bad* things . . . well, then quite the opposite. One way or another, your actions always

come back to you. Repayment of what you've dealt. Almost every civilization has believed in the concept in some form. *Karma* is just the most commonly used word to describe the phenomenon."

Paul was fascinated. "And this button has something to do with it?"

George nodded, holding up the box as if inspecting it for flaws. "Yes, it does. There have been those in our ranks who believe Karma is a scientific principle as rigid as gravity. And, *like* gravity, they accept it one hundred percent, even though they can't quite explain why it happens or how it works."

"They?" Sofia repeated. "You mean you don't believe in it like some of the others?"

"It's as I've said. I have difficulty accepting something that's not grounded in solid scientific principle and analysis. But the gravity example is a good one. No rational person could possibly argue that gravity doesn't exist, despite our inability to understand it fully. Likewise, evidence of Karma is rampant. And it's possible—and strongly believed by some, in fact—that it can be gathered and manipulated, just like Chi'karda can be with the Chi'karda Drives we have inside our Barrier Wands that power them and make them work."

"So that's what this box is?" Paul asked. "A . . . Karma Drive?"

George looked at him, his eyebrows lifted in slight

surprise. "Why, yes, that's *precisely* what it is, Master Paul. Precisely. This box was built by a small group of Realitants, led by Gretel, with some extremely speculative and revolutionary technology. It took them a full decade—exhausting work. Two of the members of the team went mad and had to be discharged from our society. But Gretel believes strongly that she and her team were successful, and that they've created a mechanism that will harness Karma and concentrate it for one purpose. Just like a Barrier Wand."

Sofia reached out to touch the box, but George pulled it away. "No, no. We must be very careful how we decide to proceed in this matter."

"Karma's a good thing, right?" Paul asked. "Let's just push the button and hope for the best." Even as he said it, he knew he couldn't possibly sound *less* like the scientist he was supposed to be. But he was mostly joking. Mostly.

"My good man, use your brain. After all that effort and work, no one has ever pushed this button before. Gretel believes that the power will swirl and coalesce around the one who holds the box, infusing them and their surroundings with Karma to use for whatever purpose the bearer may need."

"Well," Paul countered, "I'd say we're in pretty bad shape, so maybe now is a good time to try it. You're the one who says you don't really know what to do about the Void. Let's push the button, and then maybe Sofia and I can figure out how to use the power."

George pulled the box back into his lap. "You haven't understood what I've told you if you think we should be so hasty. Remember what Karma does. I believe you said it this way: 'What goes around, comes around.' In a way it magnifies, significantly, good or evil."

"Yeah? So what?" Paul pushed, a little sarcastically.

"That's all very well if the power latches on to something good." George pursed his lips and shook his head dramatically. "And I daresay the both of you are as good as it gets. But if it somehow got into the hands of someone *evil*, then we'd all be in very much trouble, indeed."

CHAPTER 45

✳

BRAINPOWER

The Void was a monster now.

Sato and his troops had retreated to the edge of the forest, watching the gray mass continue to grow.

There was nothing left of Mistress Jane's castle. The churning, spinning cloud was now two or three miles wide, its edges a chaotic dance of lightning and boiling tendrils of gray mist. The vortex was probably half a mile tall, blocking out the sun. Thunder pounded the air, and the darkness of a heavy storm cast a gloomy mood over everything.

No one could have felt it any deeper than Sato. There were things to learn here. Terrible, awful things.

He had to talk to Master George, tell him about the centipede experiment.

"Tollaseat!" he called out.

The man was a few dozen feet away, but came running. When he pulled up at Sato's side, he looked haggard and exhausted.

"Yes, Captain?" he asked.

Sato took one last glance at the growing Void, hoping he'd never have to see it again. How were they supposed to fight such a thing? They needed brainpower.

"Let's get everybody deeper into the woods," he said, hearing the defeat in his own voice. "I'll contact Master George and have him wink us somewhere safe. We're done here."

*

Tick lay in the dark, staring up at a ceiling he couldn't see. Chu had put him in a room with no windows and then turned off the lights. Just to make him angry, probably. Just to show him who was in control. It obviously still rankled the man that a teenager had more power than he did.

What a mess. Tick's chest hurt from holding in so much stress and despair. He longed for those few moments after escaping the Nonex, seeing his mom and sister, thinking that maybe all would be right in the world again. How wrong he'd been.

As if the Void weren't enough of a problem, he'd been captured by a man insane with the lust for power. Chu had explained to him a few things, had even shown him a video feed using a Spinner on the screen in the auditorium. It basically boiled down to one simple fact: Chu wanted to harness the incredible amounts of energy he believed emanated from the Void currently devouring the Thirteenth Reality, then use it to *meld* himself—and, evidently, Mistress Jane— with Reality itself. It sounded similar to what Tick had accidentally done to Mistress Jane—melding *her* with Dark Infinity—so long ago.

Chu claimed that once he'd accomplished that task, it would be easy for him to stop the Void and force it to return to the Fourth Dimension. Then he and Jane would use their godlike powers to rule the Realities in a way no one would have thought possible. It was such an impossible idea that Tick couldn't even grasp it. And he highly doubted those two actually trusted each other. Each one of them probably thought there'd only be one left to rule in the end. Each one probably saw the other only as a means to an end.

But Tick was scared. He knew better than to underestimate Reginald Chu. The man was psycho, but he was a scientist through and through. There was no way he'd pretend he could do magical things. If Chu thought this scheme was possible, then it probably was possible. And that turned Tick's fear into terror.

He tried to rest up. He needed to be ready when the time came to act.

CHAPTER 46

*

A LITTLE HELP, HERE

Mistress Jane was exhausted. Not physically— she'd gotten plenty of sleep over the last couple of days inside her apartment—but her mind was spent from all the research. Every waking moment, she had been poring through her old notes, her computer files, her books. She needed to know everything about the Fourth Dimension, and the Void that had once been trapped within it, before she went to Chu's rebuilt headquarters.

She'd winked herself to a lonely mountaintop in the Thirteenth Reality, a place where she'd come before to meditate and scheme. Two things she did very well and needed to do now. But the main reason she'd chosen the location was so she could see the latest developments of the Void that had ripped her beloved castle to pieces, and, by the looks of it, had proceeded to eat the remains as well. The enormous spinning cloud of gray mist looked almost peaceful from this far away, the thunder just a low rumble rolling across the land. But she knew the Void was terrible, without compassion.

It would grow. And it would destroy. And once this world was gone, the other Realities would follow. The energy and power of the Void was a thing of awe, a thing that would make most people cower and shake with fear. But not her. She'd had her moment of doubt, and it had passed. Now she was here, facing the beast that threatened to destroy everything she'd devoted her life to. She faced it, and saw only opportunity now. Opportunity to build the Utopia of which she'd always dreamed.

Power. Energy. Unlimited.

There was a way to capture that, to harness it. To divert it from its current path and use it for better purposes. But she needed help, at least for now.

Yes, with some help, she could do great things with this Void of Mist and Thunder. This Void that represented the pure power of creation. Great things indeed.

It was time to reunite with Reginald Chu and Atticus Higginbottom.

Paul was pretty sure he could've talked Master George into taking a risk and pushing that green button, but they were interrupted. Rutger, waddling and sweating like never before, burst into the room, his words spilling out between ragged breaths.

"Good grief . . . people!" he shouted. "Why . . . it took me . . . forever . . . to find you!"

George shot up from his chair and asked what was wrong. Eventually Rutger managed to say that Sato had made contact with headquarters, asking for a good spot of Chi'karda in the Forest of Plague. Rutger, with the help of Mothball and Sally, had been able to wink Sato and the rest of the Fifth Army out of the Thirteenth Reality, and now most of them were down in the valley of the Grand Canyon, washing in the river, eating some much-needed food, resting, and recovering.

Paul sat with Sofia on the couch in George's office, waiting for the old man to return with Sato and the other Realitants. They needed to hear the entire story, and their leader said he wanted to wait until everyone was gathered to do it. But Paul had heard enough of the tidbits to have a sickness in his belly. The Void growing bigger, more soldiers dying, something about a blue light that turned things into monsters.

Yeah, none of that sounded too good.

Sofia's knees were bouncing.

"Hey," Paul said to her. "Chill. We're going to figure out all this junk. You'll see."

She stopped moving, and her face flushed red as if embarrassed. "I'm not nervous."

"Yeah, right."

"And you're not? You just want to *chill*, huh?"

Paul shrugged. "I have a good feeling about this box and its button. About the Karma thing. I mean, that's the definition of Karma! The Realitants have always been good, trying to do what's right. And now things are going to come around for us. We're going to get some help from the cosmos, or Karma, or whatever you wanna call it. All we have to do is push that button."

Sofia scooted away on the couch to face him, flashing her standard glare. "Seriously? You think the world's so simple that you can push a button on a tiny box, and everything will be all better? You thought you were smart enough to join the Realitants?" She folded her arms and looked away. "Unbelievable."

It surprised him how much his feelings were hurt. "I'm just trying to show some hope here. There has to be a reason for that box, right? It's supposed to scientifically channel Karma matter. But to me, it's Karma that we even have it in the first place. What's wrong with a little hope? Geez."

Sofia was suddenly at his side, pulling him into a

fierce hug, crying into his shoulder and shaking with sobs. When he recovered from his shock, he hugged back, patting her uncertainly.

"It's okay," he said. "Somehow it's going to be okay. Trust your old Uncle Paul."

She pulled away and laughed over her sniffles. "*Uncle Paul?* Please don't ever call yourself that again." She wiped at her eyes and nose then cleaned her hands on her pants, which somehow made Paul like her just a little bit more.

"You can call me whatever you want."

"Oh, man, I'm so embarrassed. I can't remember the last time I broke down like that."

"Please, girl," Paul said. "You've been the toughest one out of all of us. Or did you forget your little jaunt through Chu's mountain building while the whole thing was falling down, saving Tick, then pulling him out at the last second? You can cry all you want—no one's gonna say boo."

"It just all hit me at once." She'd stopped crying, fully composed just like that, but with puffy red eyes to show for it. "Seems like we can't get ahead before the next bad, awful, terrible thing happens. And now Tick's missing. *Again.* And we still don't know how to stop this stupid Void of Mist and Thunder."

Paul had absolutely no idea what to say to make her feel better. Or how to make *himself* feel better. "I just . . .

I don't know. Tick can take care of himself—I'm not as worried about him anymore. Maybe he just wanted to be with his family for a while. Or if he's in trouble, he'll get out of it. As for our other problems . . . well, all we can do is hope for something. Right? Karma. A breakthrough. A brilliant idea. Maybe the Fourth Dimension will call and make the Void go home."

Sofia laughed again. "I vote for that last one."

She'd just spoken when the door opened and Master George came through, Muffintops perched on his shoulder like a parrot on an old sea pirate. Paul didn't know if it looked creepy or hilarious. Mothball came next, then Rutger—his face red from the exertion of coming up from the canyon floor, even though it was mostly via elevator—then Sally. Finally, Sato, who had cleaned up and eaten but still looked like he'd been dragged down a mountain by a billy goat.

Sofia jumped off the couch and gave him a hug. He didn't respond much, his eyes cast to the floor.

Man, Paul thought. *That is one haunted dude.* "Hey," he said. "I'm glad you made it back safely."

Sato gave him a weary look, and it was obvious that he wanted to say something, but he held it back and took a seat on one of the plush chairs. The others did the same as Master George went over and lit up the fire. The guy loved his fires. Then he turned to face his small group of Realitants.

"My dear friends and associates," he announced gravely. "I'm afraid that our deepest fears regarding the Void have only skimmed the surface. It's now time for action, and we're all going to do our part. But there's something we need to do together before we split up."

"And what's that?" Paul asked.

George looked at him for a long moment. "I believe with all of my heart that I've found the two people I trust most with the power of Karma. We're going to push your favorite button, Master Paul. And we're going to do it this very minute."

Paul realized he was smiling.

"And then," George continued, "I'm going to trust you and Sofia to figure out what to do with its power."

CHAPTER 47

✳

I AMAZE EVEN MYSELF

A light went on, blinding Tick even though he had his eyes closed. After opening them on instinct, he had to squint until he finally got used to it. A shadow crossed his vision, then there was the scrape of a chair across a tile floor then the settling sounds of someone getting comfortable. Tick could finally see that it was Chu sitting next to his bed. Tick had to twist his neck uncomfortably to see him because of the restraints holding down his arms and legs and torso.

"What do you want?" he asked, trying to sound angry but having lost all of his spirit after being held captive in a dark room for hours. He'd been tempted to try his powers of Chi'karda, but he couldn't quite bring up the nerve. The memory of what had happened to him the last time still scarred his thoughts.

"It's almost time for us to act," the man said calmly.

Tick looked back up at the ceiling so his neck wouldn't hurt, and because he couldn't stand the calm expression on Chu's face right then.

"Jane will be here soon," Chu continued.

"To act, huh?" Tick asked. "We're just going to grab some ropes, lasso the Void from the Fourth Dimension, mix it up with some sugar in a glass, then let you drink it? Piece of cake."

Chu remained unfazed. "That's a very unscientific way to put it, but I guess it's not too far from the truth. Great things, Atticus. You're going to be a part of great things in the next couple of days."

"You *do* realize this is crazy, right?"

"There have been those throughout history who have misjudged brilliance for madness. I can assure you this is not the case. Most men simply can't comprehend the speed and level at which someone like myself utilizes the functions of my brain. It's something I've grown to appreciate and admire about myself."

Tick laughed—he couldn't help it. "You didn't really just say that."

"How can anyone not admire greatness?" Chu asked in a sincerely astonished voice. "Can I help it that the greatness is within my own being? No, I can't. I don't deal in such things as pride and humility. I'm a scientist, and things are as they are. No more, no less."

"You keep telling yourself that," Tick muttered.

"If you're done with childish discussions," Chu said sternly, "then perhaps we can move on to the important matters at hand."

"Do you really think I'm going to help you?" Tick asked. It really did baffle him. "I might be a little shy right now about pulling out my Chi'karda, but when push comes to shove, you *know* I'm going to do whatever it takes to stop you."

"I have ways to change your mind. But I don't think I'll need them. By the time we're ready, I think you're going to do exactly what I ask. Voluntarily. You'll *want* to, in fact."

Tick decided to quit talking. It was pointless, and the man was probably trying to manipulate him anyway. *Let him think whatever he wants,* Tick told himself. He knew that in the end, he'd die before he let Chu follow through with his schemes.

"Silence," the man said. "Maybe that's the best thing for you now anyway. You can shut your mouth, but not your ears. Nothing like a . . . *captive* audience. There are a lot of things I need to—"

whomp

A thrumming vibration shook the air, cutting off Chu's words.

Tick instinctively tried to sit up, but the metal cords dug into his skin, and he slammed back onto the bed again. That sound, that tingle in the air . . .

whomp

Chu had frozen, his face caught in a look of childish fear.

whomp

Tick had heard this noise before. *Felt* it before. He'd been walking on the road that led to his house in Deer Park when a wave of power and sound and feeling had reached him. It had been coming from his house, and when he'd run home, he'd discovered Mistress Jane in his basement, scheming very bad things.

whomp

"Does she always have to make such a grand entrance?" Chu whispered, having lost all of his bravado from a minute before. Tick thought the woman must still scare him, even though she'd obviously agreed to work with him.

whomp

The sound was getting louder, the vibration stronger. Things in the room rattled.

"It's Jane, alright," Tick said, seeing an opportunity. "She told the Realitants how dangerous you are. She'll betray you the second she doesn't need you anymore."

WHOMP

This time, the entire room shook as if struck by an

earthquake. A cabinet in the corner of the room fell over, tossing supplies everywhere. Chu stood with his arms outstretched, as if he could ward off the threat.

"You can't trust her!" Tick yelled at him. "Let me go so I can help!" He almost felt ridiculous—it was obvious he'd say anything to be released.

WHOMP!

This time the sound and vibration was followed by a hissing noise, like sand running down a metal slide. Tick looked over at the door to see it *dissolving*. He'd seen Jane use the power of Entropy before; he'd done it himself too. The particles of the door decayed toward chaos and vanished, leaving an empty hole. Mistress Jane stood in the hallway, wearing a new robe, its hood pulled over her head, hiding the red mask in shadow.

"Impressive," Chu muttered under his breath.

Jane stepped into the room then reached up and pulled back her hood. The scarred tragedy of her head looked pitiful, but the mask held no expression.

"Sorry I'm late, Reginald," she said in her raspy voice. "But I'm excited for the three of us to be working together again. And so soon after our last adventure."

CHAPTER 48

✳

BOX IN A CIRCLE

For some reason, Master George had decided to sit on the floor, something Paul had never seen the old man do before. It didn't seem proper for such a gentleman in a fancy suit, but he'd done it, and so the rest of them had followed his lead. The room was barely large enough for the group to fit between the couches and chairs—and the roaring fireplace at the head of it all.

But there they were. George, sitting with his legs crossed. Mothball next to him, her long, gangly legs somehow folded up into an impossibly small spot. Then Rutger, perched precariously as though he might roll away at the slightest push. Sally sat by him, looking like a lumberjack taking a long-needed break. Sato was next, all business. Sofia and Paul completed the circle, and Paul kept having the urge to reach out and take her hand. He fought it off, but kind of hoped she was feeling the same way.

A complete circle of Realitants, sitting on the floor.

The Karma box, with its enticing green button, sat on the carpet in the middle.

"I'm sad that Gretel couldn't be here with us," Master George said. "She was needed in the Third Reality. But I've decided to put my trust in her findings and research and . . . this invention . . . at this time of dire need. The box will channel the Karma that she so dearly loved to study, and once we have it within our grasp, I believe we'll be able to figure out the best way to use it."

He shot a glance at Paul, then Sofia, then at the stack of Gretel's notes piled next to them. Paul was thrilled that the two of them were being entrusted with something so important.

"I need everyone in this room to understand the gravity of the decision I've made," George continued. "Karma is nothing more than a concept. A theory. Even those I deemed experts on the mysterious substance were making educated guesses at best, dreamy wishes at worst. But they are people I trust implicitly. I believe their educated guesses may be more reliable than the most researched, documented theories of the world's renowned scientists. In my heart, I believe this complicated device is going to do something extraordinary. And that it will help us."

"Then let's get on with it," Paul muttered, trying to lighten the mood. "Time's a wastin'. Isn't that what they say?"

"Better to waste time than people's bloomin' lives, it is," Mothball countered drily, her eyes not even looking up from the floor.

George cut in before Paul could respond. "I wouldn't take this risk unless I thought the risk was worth it. I fear we've reached a time of desperation, and if we wait much longer, the damage may be too great to reverse. Especially with the troubling observations Master Sato made in the Thirteenth Reality."

"Sofia and I will figure out what to do with it," Paul urged. His hands were sweaty with anticipation. "Please just push the button. *Please.*"

"I need everyone here to—" George began.

Rutger cut him off. "Boss. You're stalling. We wouldn't all be sitting here on the floor like kids at bedtime if we weren't committed. The boy is right. Push the button. We can trust Gretel that it will work."

"Very well."

George fidgeted in his seat, wrung his hands and cracked his knuckles, then wriggled some more. No one said a word, and Paul leaned forward. Their leader finally reached out and picked up the small metal box, gingerly, as though it were a bomb that might accidentally go off. He placed it on the floor again, right in front of his crossed legs.

"Here goes nothing," he said. "Now, something I chose not to share with you, Master Paul, is that only two people in the Realities can push the button—me and Gretel. The device was built to read our DNA signature before it will compress. I must say, I'm quite proud that you didn't fail my test and try to do it yourself."

"Oh," was all Paul said in response. Relief filled him from top to bottom.

"But once it's pushed," George continued, "I want you and Sofia to take it and keep it with you at all times as you study the power. The Karma will be focused on the source—the box itself—and, therefore, on whoever holds it." He waited for Sofia's nod. Then Paul's. "Right. Here we go, then. May the Realities smile upon us on this troubled, troubled day."

"And Karma," Paul added.

Master George reached a hand to the box, pressed his thumb against the top of the button, waited a second, then pushed it all the way down.

CHAPTER 49

✳

BENDING AND WARPING

There was a very distinct *click* when the button went down. It was louder than it should've been, it seemed to Paul, the quick bang echoing off the ceiling of the room. There were no other sounds but the crackling of the fire. Everyone else was too busy holding their breath to make a noise, waiting to see what happened.

Master George had a wide look of expectation on his face, his eyebrows raised to their fullest. He slowly and carefully removed his thumb from the button and pulled his hand back into his lap. The button didn't pop back up but instead remained inside the box, so that only the green circle of its top was visible. He handed it to Sofia.

"Hide this away," the man said. "Guard it with your life."

She nodded. "I feel something tingling across my skin."

Paul felt it, too, just barely. He strained his ears to hear anything and his eyes to see anything. Sometimes Chi'karda presented itself in the form of an orange cloud or misty sparkles. He wondered if Karma would do the same sort of thing. He hoped so—he wouldn't be able to stand it if all he felt was this tingle, no visible confirmation that something was happening. He stared, and listened, and felt with his other senses. Waited.

"I don't think it—" Rutger began to say, but he was quickly silenced by shushes from the others in the room. Chagrined, the little man seemed to roll up into a tighter ball.

Master George held up a hand, palm out. "I believe something else is happening."

There was a light rumbling in the distance, like the growl of thunder in an approaching storm. Paul and the others looked at each other with wide eyes. He wondered if they were as spooked as he was. He had a shivering chill going up and down his spine, as if someone had just said they'd seen a ghost walking down the hall and they were all now waiting for it to appear at the doorway.

The rumbling grew louder, and then the room began to shake. Just a slight tremor at first, barely noticeable. Paul put his hands on the carpet and felt a vibration that shot right up his bones. It strengthened until there wasn't any doubt that something unusual was happening—the windows to the balcony rattled, and the picture of Muffintops that hung over the fireplace suddenly fell off its nail, crashing onto the floor. The glass in the frame broke.

Master George let out a little cry of surprise and struggled to his feet. Mothball helped him up as her long bones straightened out to stand up as well. Paul got up, he and Sofia leaning on each other for support. The shaking had escalated to an all-out earthquake, the floor jumping up and down as the walls seemed to bow in and out. There was almost something unnatural about it, as if the room was bending and stretching in impossible ways. He looked at the balcony, where the glass in the windows appeared to have had melted into a liquid, bubbling inward then back out again toward the canyon.

An uneasy feeling replaced the immediate panic from the quake. If this was the good Karma Paul had hoped for, then he wanted to go back in time and throw that box in the river.

The room swayed side to side, up and down, with no sign of stopping. The small group of Realitants had so far stood together in a daze, balancing, maybe hoping it would end. The distant sound of thunder had been replaced with something more sinister: a long, shrill whine like the high-pitched whistle of an old steam train. But intermixed with that were more disturbing noises that cut in and out—moans and groans and screams that weren't quite human.

Paul was beginning to feel dizzy and queasy, and not just from the jolting movement. He was sick that maybe he'd talked George into doing something terrible.

As if on cue, their leader finally took charge.

"Keep hold of each other!" he shouted over the increasing noise. "I don't think—rather I *hope* this isn't related to the Karma box. I'm quite sure of it. I believe we are experiencing a disturbance like the ones that have been happening since the incident with the Blade of Shattered Hope. I want to look outside, see what's going on. But we mustn't separate! Does everyone understand?"

The scene was absurd. The whole room was shaking and bending and warping in impossible ways, and the Realitants looked like old daredevils trying to balance on a high tightrope. But they all nodded their assent and held hands with each other: Mothball, Rutger, Sally, Sato, Sofia, and Paul, all in a row. Mothball held on to George as he started making his way to the balcony.

As they stumbled toward the sliding glass door, everything intensified. The walls bubbled in and out more deeply, the sight of it so disorienting that Paul was starting to wonder if maybe they'd been drugged or something. The floor bounced and rippled, making it impossible to walk a straight line. If they hadn't been holding hands, each one of them would've been sprawled across the carpet. And the noises, awful and disturbing, were also increasing in pitch and volume. It was like a soundtrack for a haunted house, moans and groans and squeals.

George reached the door and paused. With the glass bending and warping, it seemed impossible that it could slide open. But he reached out anyway, grabbed the handle, and pushed all of his weight onto it. The door opened easily, sliding all the way to the left—even as it continued to ripple in crazy ways.

The old man turned and shouted back at them over the terrible chorus of sounds. "I've never seen anything quite like this! Something is *wrong* with Reality!"

"Ya think?" Paul murmured, but he was pretty sure no one heard him. What had they done? What had pushing that button done to Reality? It couldn't be a coincidence.

George turned back to the balcony, which looked like something seen through a sheen of water. It definitely didn't seem like a safe place to go right then, but

George walked out onto the wavy, bouncy surface of the balcony floor, still holding hands with Mothball behind him, reaching out with his other hand to grab the railing. It was as shifty and rippling as everything else, but it had to be better than nothing.

When he touched the railing and took hold of it, an odd thing happened. Beginning at his hand, a distinct bulge of warped Reality shot up his arm and through his body like a wave of energy. It went down his other arm then hit Mothball, doing the same thing to her. The ball of power proceeded to go through every single Realitant like a snake swallowing a base-ball until it passed through Sofia and shot up Paul's arm. He almost let go of Sofia's hand but didn't. He felt nothing more than a tickle and a surge of static electricity along his skin, his hair shooting up on end. But then the energy traveled down his other arm and disappeared.

Master George was still clasping the rail of the bal-cony, and even that was a weird sight. The rail was moving, wavering like a mirage, but the old man's arm seemed to be solid. Two things happening at once? That wasn't possible. George faced the open air of the canyon, and looks of confusion passed down the Realitants. Clearly no one understood the anomaly that had passed through their bodies.

"Everyone!" George snapped, his voice muted

against the awful noises that still haunted the air. "Everyone up here to have a look! Quickly, now!"

The motion of the room—the entire building, in fact—was still intense, jumping and rippling, an earthquake mixed with hallucination. But Paul and the other Realitants fought against it and surged forward, through the open door to the balcony. They crowded close, maneuvering so that each person could look over the railing and see what Master George saw.

Two seconds earlier, Paul had thought there was no way things could get worse. But he'd been terribly wrong. He stared out at the valley of the Grand Canyon and forgot all about the rocking movement around him.

Slicing its way through midair, running between the tall, rocky walls, was a floating river. Just a hundred feet or so above the raging waters of the Colorado River, there was a wide, bright gap of intense blueness. It was long and stretched in both directions, as if a giant knife had cut through Reality and the wound bled glowing blue blood. It was the same blue glow that Sato had described dropping the centipede into.

"The Fourth Dimension has ripped open into this Reality!" George shouted.

People started falling from the rent in the air.

CHAPTER 50

✳

ODD COUPLE

There'd been a very long talk.

Tick lay there awkwardly, feeling like a spectator at a silent film, as Jane and Chu whispered with each other. His face was tense, and hers—the mask—showed no expression at all. On and on they talked, but Tick couldn't hear a word they said. He was getting closer and closer to giving in to his instincts and just unleashing his Chi'karda with every bit of strength he had. How could it be any worse than letting Chu do whatever he wanted with him?

Finally, Tick couldn't take it anymore.

"You two need to listen to me," he said, trying to sound more patient and reasonable than he felt. "Bad things are going on, and we all know they're getting worse. It's just like in the Nonex. We can't fight each other until we make things right again in the Realities. I promise not to fight if you will."

Tick didn't like saying the words; he didn't *want* to work with Jane or Chu, but maybe he had no other choice. He wished he could find a way to get out of his restraints so he could use his Chi'karda again.

Both Jane and Chu looked over at him. Jane's mask actually pulled up into a slight grin.

"Let me go," Tick pleaded. "I swear on my family I won't try anything. I won't hurt anybody. And I'll stay here while we talk everything out." He winced at that last sentence. Now he was trying too hard.

"Pipe down while the adults talk," Chu said. If he'd said it angrily, or meanly, Tick would've been okay with it. But he said it like he actually thought of Tick like a child, and that boiled his insides. He almost felt steam coming out of his ears.

"Please," Tick said. "You know I can help."

Chu looked back at Jane as if he hadn't heard him. "Ever since this . . . *opportunity* presented itself in your Thirteenth Reality, my people have been working on a device that can harness the power of the Void, adapting it. We can do it, Mistress Jane. We can become one with it. We can *meld ourselves* to Reality. Just like we discussed. Things have come to fruition faster than we could've ever dreamed."

Jane nodded her head slowly. "Don't double cross me, Chu. I'm warning you."

Something snapped inside of Tick. It was like a bunch of valves had been holding back the flow of Chi'karda inside him, and they all broke at once. The power almost burst out of him, but somehow he grabbed it at the last second, held it at bay. But he couldn't keep the words from tumbling out.

"That's enough!" he yelled. "I swear, if you two don't stop acting like I'm not here, I'm going to let it all out, no matter what happens. It's like a dam over here, and it's about to break! Take these straps off of me. Now!"

His heart raced, and he could feel his limbs shaking, the blood rushing to his head and face. Heat ebbed along his skin, as if his pores were straining from exertion, the orange might of Chi'karda trying to burst through.

"Let me go!" he shouted.

He saw a flash of fear in Chu's eyes before the man tried to hide it. Jane was no longer smiling. But neither one of them moved.

"Let me—"

He didn't finish the sentence. A sudden jolt hit the room, shaking it so intensely and violently that all other thoughts vanished from Tick's mind, as instant as the flip of a light switch. The overpowering surge of

Chi'karda disappeared as well, making him feel empty and scared. The room slammed toward the side, then sprang back the next second. Chu and Jane both fell down, sprawling over each other in a tangle of arms, legs, and the folds of her yellow robe.

It all happened so fast, like a speed bump in time. The room had barely stabilized before it began to shake again, this time more steadily, growing in strength. Chu and Jane were scrambling to get to their feet, reaching out to hold on to Tick's bed. Things fell off the shelves, rattled across the floor. Tick was helpless, holding on to the sheets as if they'd give him any protection—the straps held him down as firmly as ever.

And the Chi'karda really was gone. Completely. He even reached for it again, wanting to feel its power and comfort, but it was like something had blocked it *within* him. He couldn't find a single trace.

He was looking at Chu when everything in the room went completely crazy. Walls started bubbling outward, and the floor looked as if it had turned into liquid, waves running through the tile without breaking them. The bed jumped up and slammed back down again, and Jane and Chu lost their balance, sprawling out on the rippling floor once more. The ceiling bulged in the middle, as if water were collecting there. None of it seemed physically possible.

And then the horrible sounds started.

CHAPTER 51

✳

HOLDING HANDS

Paul had never seen Master George move so fast.

The old man seemed to lose thirty years in age once he spotted the frightening and impossible sight of bodies falling from a long, blue rent in the air. He turned on his heels and bolted back through the balcony door, pulling everyone else along with him as best he could. They eventually all made it—struggling against the disorienting sights that continued to warp and bend all around them—Sofia and Paul at the tail end. The Realitants were still holding hands, helping each other as they took turns losing and regaining their balance.

"We must get down there straightaway," George called over his shoulder as he headed for the hallway.

"After a quick detour to grab my Barrier Wand, as we may have to get ourselves far from this place."

Sofia stopped, and everyone looked back at her. "You guys go. I need to head to the operations center. I can feel . . . it. I can *feel* the Karma. I think if I can study Gretel's notes—the whole team's notes from that time—I can figure things out."

"I'll help you," Paul added immediately. He felt it too. Even as Reality broke up all around him, he felt a power like electricity trickling through his veins.

Master George looked proud, shockingly not offering one ounce of protest. "Rutger," he commanded. "Take them there at once. Give them access to everything. The others—with me."

Paul's heart leaped as Sofia grabbed the notes from the floor. They followed Rutger, fighting to keep their balance the whole way there.

Chu's face was pale with terror.

Tick didn't understand it. He'd thought the man was brave and ruthless, but now he looked like a toddler who'd lost his mommy at the shopping mall. He swayed on his feet as the entire room shook and wobbled, his eyes darting this way and that in a steady flare of panic. Jane was close to him but seemed much calmer as she mildly took a step when needed to keep herself from falling to the floor again.

And then there was Tick. Strapped to the bed, unable to even touch the slightest bit of his Chi'karda. The madness of everything seeming to have lost its solid structure was made ten times worse by the sounds of moaning and wailing that flew through the air. That, and the fact that Tick couldn't do anything, not even run.

"You've gotta let me go!" he yelled at Chu, hoping to take advantage of the man's obvious terror. "Something really bad is happening, and I can probably help stop it! Take these stupid things off of my body!"

"He's right," Jane said.

She didn't shout the words, and Tick barely heard them, but Chu looked at her as if she'd gone crazy.

"You can't be serious!" the man yelled. "You've seen what he can do! He'll escape before we can count to three! You know that we need this boy's power for our plans! He has to be contained until we're ready!"

"And *then*?" Tick asked. "You think at the very end I'm just going to agree to do whatever you want?"

The disturbing sounds of people in pain and dying and suffering swirled through the room, joined by the creaks and groans of the building that shook around them. Everything in sight was twisted and bent, moving in impossible ways. Nothing made sense.

Jane's mask remained expressionless as she stood

there, trying to keep her balance. She looked back and forth between Tick and Chu. Back and forth, as if pondering some monumental decision.

Tick kept his eyes on her, feeling so helpless he thought his chest might implode from the rage and panic trapped inside him.

"Reginald," she finally said, her raspy voice somehow cutting through the cacophony of haunts that floated in the air. "We need to leave for a few minutes to talk privately. We'll come back and get him when we're ready for his contribution."

Chu nodded absently, his eyes showing that his mind was lost in deep thought.

"What?" Tick yelled. "What are you talking about? This is crazy! You guys have to let me go!"

Jane held out a scarred hand to Chu, and he took it. Both of them were still fighting to maintain their balance amidst the quaking, but managing well enough. Hand in hand, swaying, they walked to the door of the room, opened it, then exited into the hallway. Chu swung it closed behind them.

Leaving Tick all alone.

⁓

Paul was shocked he hadn't fallen down yet, or tripped over Rutger. The entire headquarters shook like a baby's rattle, and Paul's brain was feeling like the stuff on the inside of the rattle. He stumbled left and right as he tried his best to move forward at a sharp clip. The three of them reached the data center, where Rutger was king. The short man pushed his way past Paul and Sofia and entered the room first, turning on lights and flipping the switches on monitors and machines.

"We'll get to the bottom of this," Rutger said, all business now that he could actually contribute again. "It's always in the numbers. Always."

He climbed up onto his specially-made raised chair and focused on the largest screen in the room, which was several feet wide and already filled with flashing data and colors. Sofia stood right behind him, Paul at her shoulder.

"O . . . kay . . ." Rutger said slowly, drawing out the word as he quickly scanned the data splattered across the monitor. Paul did the same, but he knew the other two would come up with something interesting before he did.

Right on cue, Rutger started in with his findings. "Chi'karda levels are extremely low in a three- to four-mile radius around the canyon headquarters, and the pocket appears to stretch along the river in both directions—probably in line with that blue streak of . . . whatever we saw in the air. There's also some kind of reading for a substance that our sensors can't identify. It has mass, and it's everywhere. My goodness, it's *everywhere*. But . . ."

He spun around in his chair and looked up at the others. "I'm not sure I can . . . I mean . . . it'll take me some time, but . . ."

Paul knew the man was probably ashamed that he didn't immediately know the explanation for the foreign force that permeated the air around the Grand Canyon. But Sofia latched on to the answer right away, excitement shining in her eyes.

"It's Karma, Rutger. It has to be!"

CHAPTER 52

✳

DOWN BELOW

Going down the elevator had been just about the scariest thing Mothball had ever done. The long ride to the bottom of the canyon floor had been riddled with sudden jolts and constant shaking, and even an unexpected drop of twenty feet or so that made everyone scream. Sally may have been the loudest, as shrill as the youngest girl on a roller coaster.

And those sounds. Like a crowd of people with the plague, waiting on death. She wanted the sounds to end, no matter what. Being in the tight confines of the elevator car made it that much worse, the noise amplified and echoing off the walls, ceiling, and floor.

Mothball had never felt such an instant rush of

happiness as when they thumped onto the bottom and the doors of the lift slid open. Sunlight spilled in, though even the brightness of it looked somehow . . . *off*, like everything else. As if the light was too yellow, too disproportionate to the shadows it created.

Master George slipped through the opening as soon as the elevator doors opened wide enough, holding his Barrier Wand before him like it was a weapon. On the trip down, he'd done his best to examine the device and make adjustments to the dials and switches that ran along its one side. The button at the top—the one that would initiate the Chi'karda Drive and wink them to somewhere that was hopefully a lot safer—looked so enticing to Mothball that she almost reached out and pushed the ruddy thing herself.

They filed out of the elevator and stumbled their way along a narrow section of towering red and orange rock, finally emerging into the vast expanse of the canyon floor. Things looked just as wild there, but on a grander scale. The mighty cliffs that rose up from the rugged valley wobbled and bent and bubbled just as much as the walls inside the headquarters had, but the terror of the sight was magnified. If those cliffs cracked and crumbled, it'd be the end of the Realitants. And the end of the members of the Fifth Army, who bustled about the banks of the river, looking up at the one anomaly that outshone the rest.

The long rip in Reality ran the length of the valley, disappearing at both ends, and hovering in the air at least a hundred yards above the ground. It shone with a glowing blue light that pulsed every few seconds, its luminescence flashing more brilliantly before fading again.

And what Mothball and the others had seen from the balcony was still happening—odd-looking bodies were falling from the blue gash, but none of them had reached the canyon floor yet. About halfway down, they were whisked away—as if caught in a stiff wind or the gale of a hurricane—toward the cliff walls on both sides of the canyon. They perched by the hundreds on jutting rocks or held on to crevices in the stone with gangly arms and legs.

And they weren't human.

⌒

Tick had finally closed his eyes, unable to take one more second of the troubling sights all around him as he lay helpless, strapped to the bed. But there was nothing he could do with his ears. Unable to use his hands to cover them, he had no choice but to listen to the awful wails and moans that streaked through the air and pounded his senses. It was as if he were in some experiment run by a madman to see how much he could scar a kid's brain for life.

He tried his best to focus his mind on other things. On the odd exchange between Jane and Chu before they'd left him alone. She'd obviously been scheming inside that head of hers and had come to a big decision—something that obviously didn't involve him yet. He hated to admit it, but he felt as if he had to place some hope in Jane, that she might turn back to those feelings she'd expressed before to him of wanting to do good. Tick didn't see how it was possible to survive this mess unless she joined forces with him against Chu and all the weird things going on with Reality.

But the sick feeling in his stomach told him the chances of that happening seemed awfully slim. There'd been something sinister about the way she'd been looking back and forth between him and Chu right before they left. And the words she had said—and the way she'd said them—made it sound as if she was up to no good at all. Maybe she'd finally slipped past some threshold from which she'd never come back. Maybe Mistress Jane was finally evil through and through.

The door popped open to reveal Chu. His face was draped in shadow, but there was something about the way he stood in the midst of the shaking that told Tick that the man had moved past his panic attack and was back to business. His next words, shouted over the terrible sounds, removed all doubt.

"We're putting you back in the Bagger, boy. Time to go for a little ride."

～

Sato was finally getting his spirits back. He'd been in a daze since leaving the Thirteenth Reality, trying to come to terms with everything that had happened. But ever since George had pushed the button on that weird little box and the world had turned into a freak show, he'd slowly awakened back to his normal self. And now his first concern was the army he called his own; they were in obvious danger from the nightmare that had ripped open in the sky above them.

He ran forward a few steps, squinting against the sun to look at the creatures that had flown out of the blue gash and attached themselves to the side of the canyon cliffs. They were dark and gray and gangly, almost humanoid . . .

And then it hit him. They were too far away for Sato to get the greatest of looks, but he knew what they were. The remainder of Jane's creatures, transformed by the Fourth Dimension, were here.

Even as he had the thought, the gray monsters started scampering—and flying—toward the floor of the canyon.

CHAPTER 53

OVERRUN

Mothball didn't like the sight of all those gray creatures descending toward them. She didn't like it at all.

"We need to get out of here!" she yelled at Master George.

But the old man was already swinging into action, holding the Barrier Wand up with both hands as he started barking orders. "Sato! Get your army over here, and quickly! We need to pack together into a group, everyone touching someone else!"

Mothball thought Sato had seemed like a new person since taking over leadership of the soldiers from the Fifth Reality. Unshakable, a true leader. But even *he* hesitated, probably in awe and fear of the weirdness of it all. There was a river of blue light running through the sky, the world was shaking, monstrous creatures of the Void were descending toward them, and it sounded like a haunted house at an amusement park.

Sato sprang into action.

As he ran around, shouting and pointing and herding his people toward where Master George stood with the Wand, Mothball and Sally huddled close to the old man. The gray creatures were almost to the canyon floor now, seeming to pick up speed the closer they got.

The army almost made it to Mothball and her group. Sato was in the very back, encouraging and pushing people away from the river toward the canyon wall, when the first wave of Void creatures overran him.

Tick didn't fight it when Chu's lab rats wheeled him out of the small room, down a hallway, and into a large chamber that looked like a massive laboratory. He didn't fight it when the lights started flashing and the banging, whirring noises overcame the now-constant and familiar sounds that haunted the air. He didn't struggle when the Bagger wrapped its cords around him again.

He didn't fight, because he wasn't able to fight. His body was strapped down, and he couldn't feel the slightest trickle of Chi'karda. He was helpless.

All the while, Jane and Chu marched along nearby, whispering to each other and making frantic arm gestures. Tick didn't know what was going on and didn't bother to ask. His heart and will were starting to give up with everything else. He needed to snap out of it, find a spark somewhere. But as with the elusive Chi'karda, he was empty.

At some point it all became too much, and, like before, when he'd been trapped inside this machine that he didn't understand, his mind sped away to a cold and dark place.

There were no dreams in that lonely place.

～～～

Sato didn't scream or cry out for help when the first claw dug into his shoulder. The sharp nails pierced his shirt and raked across his skin, slicing pain through his nerves, but it was the last straw to snap him out of his momentary dazed state and lunge him back into the soldier he'd become. He dove forward, curling into a ball and flipping over at the last second. He kicked out with his feet—landing a solid hit on something soft but solid—then jumped back up to see that the creature had tumbled across the ground. Even as Sato watched, the monster's form dissolved into a swirl of mist and was whisked up toward the sky.

Sato didn't have time to follow the path with his eyes. Dozens more of the scary things were already on him. The closest one leaped into the air—gray wings unfolding like an umbrella—then swooped in, claws reaching for his face. The unmistakable thump of a Shurric pounded the air, and the creature was ripped away before it could hurt Sato. More thumps followed from behind him. His soldiers to the rescue.

Someone threw a few Ragers at the line of fangen and other monsters, mounds of dirt and rock compacting into a giant ball of destruction before it slammed into the creatures. Most of the ones on the ground—those close to Sato, anyway—were annihilated, dissipating back to mist and swimming toward the sky in a streak of smoky haze. The fangen that leaped into the air to escape the Ragers were caught by a ruthless volley of pure sound from the Shurrics.

Sato and his army had survived the first wave of attack.

He wasted no time.

"Get to Master George!" he yelled, waving his arms to direct his soldiers. He didn't stop until every soldier was running. "Form circles around the Realitants! Face them—a hand on the person in front of you! Quickly!"

Faithful and brave, they did exactly as he commanded.

Mothball was amazed at how quickly Sato had assembled his soldiers into a formation of circles radiating out from the center, where George and the Realitants huddled as a group. Each person in the rings placed a hand on the shoulder of the person in front of them. They were ready to wink away.

"Everyone closest to me!" Master George barked when the Fifth Army was settled. The madness around them continued, and more creatures were coming, but Mothball and the others were still and silent. "Put your hands on the Wand! Its power will flow through all who are connected!"

He made a quick couple of adjustments to the dials and switches as the other Realitants reached out and gripped a spot on the cool, brassy surface.

"Do we have everyone?" George bellowed out in a loud voice.

There was a chorus of assents, but no way to confirm it for sure. Mothball knew they'd just have to get on with it and hope they didn't leave anyone behind.

"Alright, then," George said, though Mothball could only read his lips because he spoke so quietly.

The old man pushed the button at the top of the Wand.

Nothing happened.

CHAPTER 54

✳

A HORDE
OF CREATURES

Sato had learned an amazing amount of patience since becoming the leader of an army. But it was being tested like never before now. They'd formed up; hands were on shoulders; they'd all faced the old man like he'd told them to. Why wasn't George pushing the button already? Sato tried to look over the shoulders of the giant soldiers he called his own, but it was pointless.

The creatures were coming.

"What's he *doing* up there?" Sato finally shouted, the frustration ripping through his throat, rubbing it raw. He coughed for a few seconds. There had to be something wrong. Had to be. "Report back to me! Send it up the line! I need to know what's going on!"

The soldiers started whispering furiously to those in front of them. Sato kept his hand on the back of the woman who was crouched before him—she was still almost as tall as he was when he stood up straight—but he took a look behind him to gauge the situation. Void-twisted fangen were flying in fast, and other creatures were splashing through the river and loping across the ground. They had only a few more seconds until they'd have to battle.

"Hurry it up!" Sato screamed, even though he knew it was pointless. He was about to explode with impatience. He remembered their first visit to the Thirteenth Reality, when the Wand they'd stolen from Mistress Jane had refused to work because the witch had taken out the Chi'karda Drive. Those moments waiting for something to happen had been agonizing. Tick had winked them out, showing for the first time what a phenomenon he was. The powers he had.

But Tick wasn't here. And everything had gone nuts all around them.

The woman in front of him leaned forward to hear the message being passed backward, then snapped her head to face Sato.

"It's not workin' rightly," she said simply, as if talking about a leaky faucet.

Sato hadn't really needed to be told. "Yeah, figured that," he mumbled to himself. Then he stood up and sucked in a huge breath, ready to scream orders. The world tilted and shook and bent. "Arm your weapons!"

He turned around to face the horde of creatures coming at them.

～～～

Tick wasn't sure when it ended. Or how much time had passed. But he woke up and looked up at a cloudy, gray sky. He felt a hard, gritty surface beneath him. Jane and Chu stood next to him, peering down impatiently, as if it were *his* fault he'd been out of it for a while. The ground shook, and his vision bent and twisted. Things were still wrong with the world, but at least he was in a different place. Red rock and dusty land, sprinkled with scrub brush and cacti, stretched away from him.

He sat up, not realizing at first that he hadn't been able to do that for a while. Hard, silvery bands were still fastened around his arms and legs like bracelets, but other than that, he was free to move. When all this dawned on his still-foggy mind, shock swam through him, and he looked at Chu sharply, expecting some sort of trick.

The man appeared numb to emotion at the moment, giving a quick nod and scrunching his eyes. All scientist. "The bands will still repress your Chi'karda, boy, so I wouldn't try anything. But I think you'll work with us regardless, once you take a peek over the edge of this canyon."

Chu clicked a remote-control device in his hand, and the bands around Tick's arms and legs sprung loose like coiled wires, popping off him and landing several feet away. On instinct, Tick reached for his Chi'karda, searching for that spark inside of him that was becoming more and more a part of his instincts. As simple as taking a deep breath. He sensed it—could feel it pooling deep inside of him—but barely, as if the pipe between him and the power was clogged.

But he wouldn't have fought back anyway. Not yet. Not until he knew the best route to fixing all the things that had gone bad in the Realities.

He stood up slowly, fighting the imbalance caused by the never-ending quake that rattled the scorched land to which they'd come. He saw the coffinlike silver box that Chu had called the Bagger off to the side, a small opening on one end creating a window into darkness. He swore to understand what the thing was and how it worked some day. But again, not now. Not yet.

Chu was looking at him, his face hard and pinched. But there was also understanding there, as if he wanted to say that things were worse than any of them had imagined and that they needed to work together or die.

Jane stood next to him, her mask a blank expression.

"Something is blocking the Chi'karda here," she said, her raw voice sounding full of pain. "The closer we came to this place, the weaker it got. Neither one of us is completely sure what's going on, but it does remind me of something we'd studied long ago . . ." She nodded to her left, and Tick looked in that direction.

The Grand Canyon. At least, a part of it.

A few hundred feet away, the flat land beneath them ended in the jagged lip of a cliff. Tick only knew this because beyond it was open air and the sight of canyon walls. A sea of stratified rock, layer upon layer, every shade of red and brown and creamy white. Gray clouds churned in the sky, thicker and more erratic over the abyss closest to them. There was a strange blue light reflecting off the bottoms of the boiling vapors of clouds.

"Go and have a look," Jane said, her tone sad and filled with dread. "We wanted you to know what's at stake."

Tick knew he had no choice. Feeling as if someone had draped a hundred pounds of wet cotton across his shoulders, he started walking toward the upper edge of the looming cliff.

CHAPTER 55

LET'S MOVE

Sato fought furiously. Wielding a Shurric provided by one of his soldiers, he aimed and fired the thumps of sound energy at creatures as they came close, barely having enough time to see them catapult away before he had to do it again. And again. The monstrous forms from the Void were relentless and numerous, and they seemed to have no concept of death as they charged in. As each one died, they dissolved into a wispy stream of smoke and shot toward the sky. Up there, they joined their dead in a massive, churning pool of clouds. The bright blue streak of the floating river cut through the gray.

The Fifth Army had spread into battle formation,

still braced in a rough circle around Master George and the others in order to protect them. Many of the fangen—or creatures that had once *been* fangen and had been transformed into something worse—leaped into the air and tried to fly toward the middle, as if they knew the precious lives that waited there. The heart of the Realitants, and maybe the last hope in defeating this indescribable new enemy of Voids and mist and thunder and blue light.

Sato's soldiers kept steadfast, picking off the creatures one by one. But they kept coming.

They kept coming, and there was no end in sight.

⌒⌒

Tick looked down into the valley of the canyon and couldn't believe what his own eyes reported back to his brain. The assault on his senses made him think it couldn't be real. So many things were going on at once, and none of them made much sense. A thick, pulsing streak of blue light cut through the middle of the air like a floating river, running the length of the canyon just as the real river made of water did. A battle raged down there, and it appeared to involve the Fifth Army, judging from the tall human figures standing their ground in a circular formation. They fought creatures of gray, Voids no doubt. When they died, wisps of smoky mist shot up from the ground like ghosts trailing gray rags until they reached—and joined—the churning storm clouds that hung over everything.

Tick reached for his Chi'karda again, and it was even weaker than before. There, for sure. But mostly blocked. He could pull it out if he wanted to, try to use it, but only a little would come out at a time. It'd be pointless. The strangeness of everything around him was also affecting Chi'karda. A scary thought—he already felt helpless enough.

"The situation is even worse than we thought."

Jane's voice made him jump. He turned to see her standing right behind him, the wind whipping at the folds of her hood and robe. Chu was right next to her. Tick had been so engrossed with the haunted vision before him—and the sounds of thunder, so loud—that he hadn't noticed them creep up.

"What's going on?" he asked, hoping for answers but knowing they didn't have them.

"The Realities are being ripped apart," Jane said. "Things have escalated."

"Escalated?" Tick repeated. "I'd agree."

Jane nodded. "This is why you need to work with us. Chu and I can stop this madness. With your help."

"So you guys keep saying," Tick said spitefully. "I'll only promise to help if you promise to quit being so . . . *evil*."

A look of hurt flashed across Mistress Jane's mask, but it vanished quickly. Chu rolled his eyes and chuckled, a sound that was thankfully whipped away by a surge of wind.

"Your word means nothing to me anyway," Tick said, hearing the defeat in his own voice. "I'll do whatever I can to help stop this craziness. But I swear I won't let either one of you hurt more people in the end. I won't!"

Jane looked at him with hard eyes, glaring through the holes of her mask. "So are you committed then?"

Tick wanted to howl mean words at her, but he simply shouted, "Yes!"

"Reginald?" Jane turned her gaze to the man. "Are you ready?"

"Of course."

Jane pointed back in the direction from which they'd come. "We need to get a couple miles out at least, I'd guess. We can't do anything—especially here—until we can find the full strength of Chi'karda. Come on."

She pulled up the lower edges of her robe and started running, a sight that for some reason made Tick want to laugh. Instead, he shot a dirty look at Chu and sprinted after her, wondering if the old man could keep up.

CHAPTER 56

＊

THE FURIOUS
BEAT OF WINGS

We need to make it to the wall!" Sato shouted.

His throat hurt like acid had been poured down his gullet; his voice was raw and scratchy as he continued to encourage and command his Fifth Army. The creatures of the Void kept coming in their onslaught of an attack, threatening to overwhelm Sato and the rest with sheer numbers. But the soldiers kept their composure and maintained their positions, firing Shurrics and throwing Ragers. With every monster killed, another wispy streak of mist shot toward the sky to join the ever-growing mass of storm clouds that boiled above them.

The ground shook beneath them; screams of pain

and anger pierced the air; thunder rumbled and lightning flashed; things bent and twisted and bubbled in unnatural ways. And the gray creatures kept coming—fangen through the air and the others loping and leaping across the dusty canyon floor.

Sato aimed his Shurric at a lanky, six-legged beast with a head that was all gaping jaws and teeth. He fired, then watched the thing disintegrate and swirl into smoke and be whisked away, flitting upward out of sight. He aimed at another monster—three legs, three arms, two heads. Fired. Killed it. Another one—a blur of arms and smoky fur and teeth. Shot and obliterated. Another, then another. The beasts of the Void were everywhere.

Sato was taking aim when claws ripped into his shirt, scratching his skin. He looked up at a fangen just as its claws clenched into a fist and gripped the material, yanking him upward. The Shurric slipped out of Sato's hand. He reached out to grab it, but he was too late. It clattered against the head of one of his soldiers.

The creature flew farther up, keeping a tighter hold on him now with two clawed fists, its membranous wings flapping against the twisty, windy air. Sato flailed with his arms, trying to beat at the beast, to no avail. He changed his focus to the thing's two-handed grip and tried to loosen the claws. They didn't budge.

Sato reached up with his hands and gripped the

fangen's forearms. He held on tightly for leverage, then kicked up with his legs, smashing one of his feet into the beast's face. It wailed a piercing cry and shook his body while it plummeted several yards, almost crashing into the soldiers below. But at the last second, it swooped up again, furiously beating its wings. Sato's stomach pitched and twisted as badly as the morphing shapes of Reality all around them.

He gripped the fangen's forearms again, kicked up with his legs. His foot connected again, and this time he threw his hands at the wings, catching one of them by the thin stretch of skin between two bones. He yanked on it with all of his weight, pulling downward.

The creature shrieked again as they both fell toward the ground once more. This time, they came within reach of two tall soldiers, who quickly dropped their weapons and grabbed the fangen, slamming it to the ground, freeing Sato. And then they took care of the beast.

Sato jumped to his feet, adrenaline screaming through his body.

An odd sound suddenly tore through the air, overpowering everything else. It wasn't just that—all other noises seemed to cease at once, replaced by an overbearing, all-consuming sound that made everyone pause in whatever they'd been doing. Sato couldn't help it any more than the others. He faced the open canyon that towered above him.

A tonal thrum, mixed with a sound like bending metal, rang throughout the valley, giving Sato the strange sense that his ears had been stuffed with cotton. He didn't see anything different or unusual at first, other than both sides of the battle had stopped fighting. The soldiers of the Fifth Army had lowered their weapons, searching the sky to figure out what was going on. Most of the Void creatures had disappeared—when, Sato had no idea. But trails of mist were everywhere, all of them snaking their way toward the clouds.

His gaze lifted; he felt almost hypnotized by the warping and the bell-like sounds clanging through the valley. He was looking directly at the churning gray storm when it suddenly divided into countless tornadoes, funneling down like a hundred gray fingers.

And then Reality itself started to split at the seams.

CHAPTER 57

✳

GASHES IN THE WORLD

Paul's eyes hurt from looking at so many screens in the operations center, and his stomach was queasy from the shaking—though he was getting used to it—but his heart had swelled about three sizes. They were making progress. Real progress. And he could *feel* the power of Karma working inside of him. His mind was filled with images that he knew didn't originate from his own thoughts.

Sofia had worked the hardest of the three of them, searching and reading every last line of Gretel's notes. She looked exhausted and had finally taken a seat across from Rutger and Paul.

"Karma," Sofia said, almost reverently. She held the

gray box with the pressed green button in her hands. "I thought Chi'karda was like magic. Karma's even beyond how we thought the world worked."

"It's pretty cool," Paul agreed. "I think you're right that it's the cause of all the weirdness around us. For some reason, Karma wants things escalated. Like maybe our window of opportunity is going to be short. Whatever it is."

Rutger slapped his thighs. "Are we all agreed on the findings, then? Our theories about what's happened so far, and where we think it's leading us?"

Instead of answering, Sofia looked at Paul. "What do you see in your mind, right now?"

"The place where Jane's castle used to be," Paul said with a smile. They'd had this conversation a dozen times already, and the answer was always the same.

"The Thirteenth Reality," Sofia responded. "Me too."

"Me too," Rutger added.

They all kept seeing the same vision in their heads. Karma was communicating with them. And they knew what it meant.

"Let's run through our data one last time," Sofia ordered.

Tick had jogged or walked at least a couple of miles when everything changed again. At first, it was just an odd feeling, his ears popping, the drop of his stomach. But then a sound like bells and twisting metal filled the air and everything went dead silent for a few seconds; the quiet almost made him fall down, he'd grown so used to his eardrums being pounded. But then a new noise started up, and he and Mistress Jane and Reginald Chu stopped moving and looked back toward the gaping canyon they'd left behind. There was something incredibly mesmerizing about the . . . *music* that floated along the wind.

"What's going on back there?" Chu asked, his voice full of irritation as if all the crazy stuff was putting a chink in his plans. Which was true, Tick admitted.

"It's changing," Jane announced.

Chu scoffed. "Thank you for that scientific assessment."

Tick ignored them both, staring at the massive disk of clouds that spun above the canyon in the distance. Lightning flashed, but no thunder rumbled away from it. The bluish light that shone out of the strange floating river—which was not visible from where he stood—reflected off the bottom of the brewing storm. A buzzy, relaxed tingling went through his body and across his skin. A part of him wanted to lie down and take a nap.

"Atticus," Chu said, his words muffled slightly as if he were outside a bubble. As if they weren't worthy enough to overcome the sweet sounds wafting from the canyon. "What's that look in your eyes? What do you know about what's happening over there?"

"Nothing," Tick said softly, though he doubted they heard him. "Nothing."

Things changed then, so abruptly that Tick stumbled backward, falling to the ground as his eyes widened in astonishment. The slowly spinning mass of clouds instantly transformed into countless towering funnels, the roar of the twisting tornadoes wiping out the peaceful sounds from before. The clouds dropped then, falling like arrows toward the valley floor below. Quick bursts of lightning arced through the gray mist of the funnels, and this time, the thunder was loud and cracking. When the tornadoes vanished from sight beneath the upper lips of the canyon walls, Tick readied himself to stand and pull himself together.

But another sight in the sky made him stop cold. Gashes in Reality ripped open all over the place, streaks of dark and light that tore across the air. Some were a few feet long, others in the hundreds. The ground shook, and the sounds of breaking and cracking rocked the land.

Tick pressed his hands against the hard dirt to steady himself as he focused on the gaps that littered the sky. At first he'd only noticed that they didn't look the same, that they had varying shades of color and light, but as he got over his initial shock and peered closer, he could see that the rips in Reality were actually windows to other worlds.

Through the one closest to him, he saw buildings and cars and people—a city at night. The darkness of the scene made it hard to see much, but there seemed to be a huge traffic jam and people running down the sidewalks. Another gash nearby revealed a field of crops and a farmhouse during the brightness of day. Yet another showed a jungle or rainforest, thick with trees and vines and foliage. All the rents in the sky showed something different: a desert, a mountain peak, a neighborhood with damaged homes, people packed inside a mall—many of them huddled together as if they were cold, several views of lands with broken trees or floods.

Tick's mind was overrun with all the information he was witnessing. He tried to process it, understand it. A blue river of light that hovered above ground, creatures from the Void, Reality looking warped and weird, churning clouds and lightning and tornadoes, rips in the air that led to other Realities, more earthquakes. His Chi'karda being held back from him somehow. What did it mean? What did it all mean?

Someone shook his shoulders and snapped him out

of the trance he'd fallen into, gaping at the gashes in the air. He looked up to see Jane, her red mask pulled tightly into a look of concern.

"We need to get out of here," she said, her scratchy voice somehow cutting through the din of terrible noises that rattled the world around them.

"What's happening?" Tick asked. In that instant he almost forgot all the things he hated about the woman kneeling beside him and holding on to him with scarred hands.

Her mask relaxed into a neutral expression, but with her so close, Tick could see directly into her eyes behind it. And there was cold, hard fear there. She leaned in closer to whisper in his ear.

"I can sense a force here that we studied long ago. A project that I was led to believe had been abandoned because of its danger. Apparently not. And that only makes our mission more paramount."

After a long pause, the noise and shaking and ripped seams in Reality glaring at the forefront once more, she finally spoke again. And even though Tick didn't really know what she was talking about, the icy tone in her voice made his blood run cold.

"It's Karma, Atticus. Karma's been unleashed. And it's only making things worse."

CHAPTER 58

✳

A REASON

Mothball gawked at the tornadoes and the splits in Reality—at a brief glimpse at one of the impossible gashes that showed a boy and a girl running down a beach, a moving image that hung right in the middle of the air—as she and Sally fought to protect Master George from the onslaught, taking him to the wall of the canyon.

The rents in the air—long gashes that appeared to be windows to other Realities—were all over the place, as if the world was a sheet of canvas and someone had taken a sharp knife to it, slashing uncontrollably. Behind each rip was a different scene. Forests and oceans. Cities and farms. Close-ups and faraway views. The people she saw looked frantic and scared, often running from or toward something. It was all a big nightmare.

But at least the creatures from the Void had all vanished. Sato stood nearby, his soldiers lined up behind him, facing the valley floor.

"Those tornadoes are dropping," Sato announced. "I don't know how to fight tornadoes."

Mothball glanced up and saw them, dozens and dozens of spinning coils of gray air. Even as she looked, she felt their wind against her face and clothes. And it was getting stronger. They had maybe two minutes before most of them touched down.

"I don't either," Master George said glumly.

Jane moved surprisingly fast, saying that they had to get farther out of range. She yelled at Tick that they needed Chi'karda so they could wink away before it was too late. The three of them—Tick, Jane, and Chu—ran across the dusty land, ignoring the rents to other Realities that floated magically around them, glimpses into an endless display of worlds and settings.

Tick moved as close to Jane as possible without a risk of his legs getting tangled with her robe as it swished, swished, swished.

"What's keeping us from Chi'karda?" he yelled at her. "We could use it just fine back at your castle!"

"It has to be Karma," she replied without slowing or looking his way. "It's a power that's both unpredictable and immense. If it's suppressing Chi'karda, then it has a reason. Either way, we need to hurry and get where we're going. I think we're almost far enough out."

Tick knew exactly where they were heading. Felt it in his bones. "We're going back to the Thirteenth Reality."

This time, she did turn her head toward him, a look of surprise on her mask.

"Yes, Atticus. We need to go back to the source of it all. To its heart."

They kept running.

CHAPTER 59

✳

WALL OF WIND

Whⁿen the leading tips of the tornadoes touched down on the dusty, rocky floor of the canyon, a wild wind erupted. It ripped through the air, picking up dirt and pebbles as it went, coming at Mothball and the others like a wall. She could barely see through it or past it, but she noticed the funnels of the tornadoes joined together, creating one huge cyclone of gray.

Soon that wall of wind and debris burst over the soldiers then swept across the rest of them. Mothball shielded her eyes as it hit her and the others in the back. The wind was like a solid thing, a bubble of air that had a giving but strong membrane, pressing her against the hard rock of the cliff. George and Sally were next to her, fighting to breathe clean air.

Particles of dirt and dust beat at Mothball's face, scratching across her skin. The fierce wind tore at her hair and clothes, seeming as if its force would rip all of it off and bury them in the solid rock. She screamed, but dust flew into her mouth, choking her and making her cough. She closed her lips and looked to the side. The hurricane blast didn't stop—it just grew stronger and stronger. Pressed her harder and harder against the rock at her back. The world had become a haze of brown, swirling and churning.

It stopped without any warning.

The wind pulled back as if it were being sucked in by the gray cyclone like a giant vacuum. Mothball saw the visible wall of debris suddenly sweep away from her. Before long it was gone, completely, and the churning gray mass of fog and mist was lifting up from the ground. She thought it looked alive, and angry, being sucked toward the sky against its will. Even as she watched, it narrowed and compacted, rising, getting smaller and more tightly woven. Most of the others around her had recovered and were standing or sitting and observing the show. She felt Master George's hand squeeze her upper arm.

"What . . ." she started to say, but stopped. Any question would be pointless. And George certainly didn't try to answer. They watched, together.

A few seconds later, it became apparent what was

happening. The fog and mist of the Void was being *consumed* by the floating river of blue light. Every drop of the gray mist whooshed into the still-throbbing blueness, disappearing as soon as it did so. The long sapphire streak across the sky didn't change or grow thicker. It just kept pulsing, kept sucking up everything in sight. Not just the Void, but sticks and loose stones and any lingering clouds that had tried to stick to the sky. Mothball was surprised that she and the others hadn't flown up with the rest of it.

And then, just like that, the air was clear. The only things visible above them were the strange river of blue light running between the walls of the canyon, and the gashes in the air that were like windows to other worlds. They hadn't moved or changed, and there were probably a hundred of them that Mothball could see, all shapes and sizes. But the ground had quit shaking, and all the bending and twisting of Reality had stopped as well. The world seemed to have gone back to something a little more close to normal.

"I'll be darned," Sally said.

"That sums it up right nicely," Mothball replied.

Master George was straightening himself, dusting off his clothes. The Barrier Wand lay on the ground, dull and dirty. "Let's get upstairs straightaway. I hope Paul and Sofia have learned something valuable."

Even Tick was out of breath when Jane finally called them to a halt. He figured he was younger and in better shape than the other two, but somehow they'd all kept up and together, although Chu was sucking wind, hard. Tick turned back to look at the canyon. There wasn't a sign of any clouds or the gray mist of the Void anymore, but those rips in Reality that looked in on countless scenes and settings from all over still hung in the air like decorations.

"I think . . . we've gone far enough," Jane said, her voice even more raw than usual with the heavy breathing that scoured her throat. "In fact . . . it's odd. I can feel every ounce of my Chi'karda. And I don't think it's because of the distance we ran."

Tick immediately probed his inner self and saw that she was right. His power was there, as strong as ever. "You mean whatever's been blocking it is gone? What do you think happened?"

"Like I said, if it's Karma, the force obeys its own rules. We need to wink to the Thirteenth before anything changes."

Chu looked at Tick with narrowed, suspicious eyes. "I should've kept you in those bindings. We can't trust you now."

"We can trust him," Jane said. "He knows he has no choice but to work with us right now. Ready yourselves— since I'm most familiar with the Thirteenth, I'll wink all three of us there. I want us to be a nice, safe distance from the Void. And we will need time to meditate and regroup."

"My people are ready when you're ready," Chu added.

"One step at a time."

Chu had no response, but right before Jane winked them away from the outer reaches of the Grand Canyon, Tick saw something in the man's eyes that he didn't like. He didn't like it at all.

PART 4

* * *

THE
TRANSFORMATION

CHAPTER 60

✳

ROUND TABLE

Paul had never seen such a captive audience.

Mothball, Sally, Sato, and Master George—Rutger was busy in the operations center—sat at the conference table, looking at Paul and Sofia with wide, though tired, eyes. The group had made their way back up from the canyon floor after the strange events had subsided, discussing what had happened in drained, weary voices. They looked awful—dirty and windblown and scratched and bruised. But thankfully, they were alive, and every last one of them—including those who'd been researching—were eager to talk about what needed to happen next.

"We know some things," Paul said to start it off.

"And we've made our best guesses about a lot of others. But time is short, so I'm going to let Sofia fill you in."

Sofia looked more determined than Paul had ever seen her before. She cleared her throat and started talking.

"This all began when Tick and Mistress Jane had their battle outside the Factory. The Haunce had helped Tick heal the Realities from the disaster that was the Blade of Shattered Hope, but the boundaries and barriers and seams were still really weak. Sealed, yes. But weak. When Jane and Tick battled, using extreme amounts of Chi'karda to do so, they . . . broke things. Things we might not totally comprehend, but were certainly never meant to *be* broken."

"We're talking about the rips in Reality," Paul added.

"Exactly," Sofia continued. "We believe Tick and Jane created a situation in which conduits between Realities opened up. Not only that, but conduits between *dimensions* as well. And ultimately that's what allowed the Void of the Fourth Dimension to begin bleeding through to the Realities themselves. Whatever Tick did to escape the Nonex was kind of the last straw."

"You mean he stirred the dadgum pot once and for all is what yer sayin'," Sally said.

Master George raised his hand like a kid in school. Sofia tried to hide a smile and pointed at him.

"Perhaps the situation would've been much more manageable had the Fourth Dimension not been so . . . agitated. There may very well be a bees' nest outside your open window, but it'll get much worse if you swat that nest with a big stick. I think that's what happened here."

"Something like that," Sofia agreed. "Whatever the explanation, we are where we are. Which brings us to Karma."

There wasn't a sound to be heard in the room.

Sofia took a deep breath. "We need to gather all of our forces. All of them. Load up on weapons and ammunition. And then head back to the Thirteenth Reality. It's what Karma wants us to do. Rutger has already started trying to contact all of our Realitants out in the field."

Paul half expected shouts and complaints. He also wondered if Master George would feel as if his authority had been challenged, but if anything, the old man looked proud. He had, after all, given them the assignment to figure things out.

"I know we're short on time," their leader said. "And I trust you both implicitly. But give us an explanation as best you can."

"Of course," Sofia replied. "For starters, we believe that the blue anomalies seen by Sato in the Thirteenth and the one out in the canyon represent the Fourth

Dimension itself. Conduits for the Void to reach into *our* dimension. And it's a little scary that the blue river outside these walls decided to suck everything back into itself. It's like the Void was reaching out to gain strength and ammunition and has now pulled it all back to its main force."

Paul hated this new enemy. Shapeless, mysterious, seemingly without any kind of mind or conscience. No fear of death or consequences. "Which is why we have to go to the Thirteenth," he said. "That's where it all started, and it probably has something to do with the unique power of the place and its abnormal links to Chi'karda. We think the Void is gathering its forces there until it can unleash an attack we could never stop."

"Which is where Karma comes in," Sofia said. "It's hard to describe it, but I can't get the image of the Thirteenth—the place where Jane's castle used to be—out of my mind. Paul and Rutger feel it too. It's more than just a thought or a daydream. It's almost like something is putting it there . . . *inspiring* us. We're getting better at understanding Karma's power and how it communicates. But we know this: Karma escalated events, put pieces in place, so that we'd all head back to the source of the Void's birth in our dimension."

At that moment, Rutger stepped into the room, his face lit up with excitement.

"I've reconnected with Master Atticus!" he shouted.

"Found his nanolocator! He's just winked to—"

Paul cut him off. "The Thirteenth Reality."

Rutger nodded with a huge smile.

"I guess that seals the deal," Sofia said.

Master George stood up, a fierce and proud look on his face. "My good friends. I'm sure I'm not alone in saying that I'm scared of what awaits us there. And I believe it's quite alright to feel a bit of fear now and then. We can use it as a weapon. But know this—our society was created for such dark times as these. And the Realitants are about to have their most shining moment of all."

Paul's hands clenched into fists, and his heart started to thump.

"Sato," George continued, "go and ready your army."

CHAPTER 61

✳

A GOOD-BYE

At some point while Sato had been upstairs in the conference room, the blue river floating in the air had disappeared. But the rips into other Realities remained. Like slashes in a great invisible curtain, they peeked into countless other places. It gave Sato the creeps.

He stood on top of a big rock in front of his army, staring them down, having remained silent for at least one long minute on purpose. He wanted them to contemplate, to gather their thoughts, to have a last moment of peace. Trouble waited for them ahead. The worst they might ever face. Master George had no doubt that their fate would be settled in the Thirteenth Reality, and Sato trusted the leader of the Realitants like he never had before.

Finally, Sato spoke, his voice rising up to echo off the walls of the canyon.

"I've asked you all to do a lot lately," he began. "Too much. And we've lost some of our soldiers along the way. I'm sorry for the sacrifices you've had to make, for the pain and injuries and suffering. I'm sorry for those who gave their lives. I'm sorry for a lot of things. But I accept the responsibility. It's all on my shoulders. And I just have a few questions for you."

He paused again and took a moment to sweep his gaze across the eyes of the crowd. He was glad he'd stepped up on the rock so he could see them all—their tall, weary bodies and their haggard faces.

"Are we ready to give up?"

The resounding boom of their collective "No!" made his heart soar. Adrenaline pumped through his body.

"Are we ready to quit fighting?"

"No!"

"Do we fear an enemy we don't understand?"

"No!"

"Will we go and fight no matter what fate brings?"

"Yes!"

"Will we fight?" He screamed it now, energy surging through the air like electric charges.

"Yes!"

"Will we win?"

"Yes!"

"Will we win?"

"Yes!"

"*Will . . . we . . . win?*"

"*YES!*"

Sato's chest heaved with heavy breaths. "Then let's go and do it."

⁓

Master George was back in the operations center with Rutger, and he felt a deep sadness in his heart. There was a part of him—deep down, hidden, but there for sure—that was telling him he was saying good-bye to his longtime friend for the very last time. He tried to ignore it, but it was shattering his heart.

"I'm sorry to leave you here," George said. "But I fear we can't win this battle unless we gather all of our forces. Keep trying until you've found them. All of them. Can you do that for me?"

"Of course I can," Rutger said. The short man put on a brave face that hid nothing. "I give you my word that I won't rest until every living Realitant responds and we come to help you in the Thirteenth. I'm already about halfway there."

George nodded slowly, his lips pressed together.

"Good, then. You'll know where to send them—we'll stay in constant contact."

"I know, boss. I know."

George reached out and put a hand on his old partner's shoulder. "My dear Rutger. We've been through a lot together, haven't we?"

"We sure have." He grinned, as genuine an expression as he'd ever shown.

"I . . . just want to thank you for being there for me all these years. I want to thank you for . . . for being my friend. Whatever happens . . ."

Rutger held up a hand. "Not another word, boss. Please. Not another word. It's not needed."

The two of them locked eyes for a long moment, a thousand memories bouncing between them. It was true. They needed no words.

"Very well. Then we'll see you and the rest of the Realitants on the field of battle. Whatever form it takes. Now, I have a lot of winking to do. My Barrier Wand is going to be very hot indeed."

Master George turned away and walked out of the room, hoping Rutger hadn't noticed the tears that had begun to well up in his eyes.

CHAPTER 62

✳

REST AND RELAXATION

Jane had winked them to the top of a mountain, a craggy peak of black stone that had no vegetation whatsoever. Tick had felt the cool rush of thin air when they'd arrived almost an hour ago and hadn't stopped shivering since. Once there, Jane had insisted on taking some time to meditate and prepare herself for the difficulties that awaited. Chu had grumbled, and Tick had asked questions, but she'd refused to say another word.

Tick was glad for the break and for the time to collect his own thoughts. Everything had been such a mad rush. But instead he'd fallen into a restless sleep, shivering all the while. When Chu woke him up with a light kick to the ribs, Tick was instantly awake, and thankful his body had gotten a break.

"It's time we get moving," Chu barked. Tick wondered if there'd ever been a more unlikable person in the Realities. Ever. The man turned his attention to Jane, who was up and ready to go. "Why'd you wink us so far out anyway?"

Instead of answering, Jane pointed to a rise of rock to their left with nothing but cloudy sky beyond. Then she walked toward it briskly, obviously expecting the other two to follow her. Which they did—Chu a little begrudgingly, mumbling something that Tick couldn't hear. They reached the spit of rock that rose about thirty feet above their heads, and began to climb the slope, a gradual one with plenty of handholds and footholds. As they neared the top, Tick heard a noise like the rushing sound of water in a swift river. It grew in volume, becoming a roar when he finally poked his head over the upper lip of the jagged black stone.

What he saw before him, stretching from one side of the land to the other, was something that his brain couldn't compute at first. It seemed impossible, an image he'd only seen in weather reports and videos of massive storms out in the ocean. Miles and miles across, a wide whirlpool of gray clouds slowly spun in a giant circle, an enormous hurricane of fog and mist, with tendrils of lightning flashing within. Thunder rumbled across the windswept fields between Tick and the unbelievable sight in the distance. And even as he watched, he could tell that the storm was growing, as if with every sweep around the churning circle, the vaporous gray air pulsed outward.

The Void looked ready to consume the entire planet.

"Because I thought it'd be a bad idea to land in the middle of the belly of the Void," Jane finally said after everyone got a good look at the beastly storm. "Let's be glad I'm in charge."

"You're in charge?" Chu laughed. "I'm the only one here with the technological means to accomplish what we both want. And you know it."

"We all need each other right now. And that's that."

Chu didn't answer, but his eyes showed a fanaticism that scared Tick. Something was up with the man.

"We *will* capture the power that rages within that storm," Chu said slowly, evenly. "We will harness it and use it to accomplish the greatest feat ever known to mankind. We'll become one with the fabric of Reality, see all things, be able to *do* anything we imagine. My team has it all calculated. We're ready to move, even though we haven't done the testing I'd normally demand."

"My goodness," Tick said. He barely heard his own voice over the increasing sounds of thunder booming across the land. "You've completely lost it!"

"Lost it?" Chu replied with a bark of a laugh.

"Boy, you have no idea what we've planned! When we add the consciousness of my great mind and soul to the infinite power of the Void and then to Reality itself, I'll become like a god. All suffering, all crime, all hunger . . . I can make it end. *We* can make it end. Jane will have her Utopia. Finally."

Tick looked over at the red mask of Jane, which showed no expression. The wind ripped at her robe and hood. She said nothing, which, for some reason, filled him with dread.

"Am I the only one left here who's sane?" Tick finally asked. "We're talking about wild experiments and fantastical ideas when we have a hungry storm out there about to eat everything? Including us, by the way!"

Jane turned sharply to him. "Atticus, you don't understand. You don't."

Just then, not too far away—toward the bottom of the slope of the mountain—a host of people suddenly appeared, winking into existence in a quick series of flashes. Tick's jaw dropped open—it was Master George, Paul and Sofia, Mothball and Sally, Sato and dozens of tall soldiers. They spread out before him like . . . like an army. Tick couldn't believe it.

"It was just as we feared!" Jane shouted at Chu.

The man took a few steps back, a suspicious look on his face, one of his hands reaching for his pocket. His fingers slipped inside.

"What are you doing?" Tick asked.

Chu's voice suddenly boomed through the air as if he were commanding an army through a loudspeaker. "It's time, Benson! Bring them all in. Bring them all. The entire force. The Metaspides, the Ranters, the Denters. It's time for war."

Tick leaped into motion, running toward him, not fully understanding, but determined to stop whatever he was trying to do.

"I'll be right back," the man said with a last glance at Tick.

Reginald Chu disappeared.

CHAPTER 63

✳

A GIFT FROM FRIENDS

As soon as Chu disappeared, Tick had only one thought consume his mind. Reuniting with the Realitants. But he'd barely taken a step when he felt a tingle shoot down his back, and suddenly he and Jane were on the far side of them, off the mountain and between his friends and the churning Void. Jane had winked them there.

The wind tore at their clothes, and the cracks of thunder coming from the lightning within the Void made the world seem as if it were about to split open. Which, Tick realized, was actually happening, in a way. Though there weren't as many rips in Reality as he'd seen back at the Grand Canyon, glimpses to other worlds dotted the air.

"Why'd you do that?" he yelled at Jane.

She stepped up close to him. "No matter what you think, you have no choice but to help me now. Call it a trap if you'd like, but you are out of options. Help me, or the Void will kill everyone. Everyone!"

They stood on grassy fields that had seemed far away just a minute ago. The massive hurricane of the Void churned in a grand circle next to them. It was easily the most frightening thing Tick had ever set his eyes upon.

He knew she'd won. Only he had the power to stop such a horror. "How can I even trust you?" he yelled at her. "I'd be better off doing it alone!"

She leaned into the fierce wind, her gaze glued to the monstrosity in the near distance. She finally looked at him. "And if you succeeded, I'd still do whatever it takes to build my Utopia. Do you understand? You might as well join forces with me now."

Tick glared back. He wanted to ask how she could still be thinking of her Utopia when so much was on the line. But he chose to let it go for the moment. He was going to turn the tables on her. Use *her*, for a change. He'd rely on his instincts, pool their powers just like when they broke out of the Nonex. And somehow he would destroy the Void and sever the link with the Fourth Dimension.

"Then let's do it," he finally said.

"It's the right decision, Atticus!" she shouted. "Be prepared to use every ounce of our Chi'karda once the time is right! Stick together every step of the way!"

Tick nodded, refusing to give in to the fear that wanted to cripple him on the inside. "Then there's only one thing to do."

She nodded, pointing at the spinning mass of the Void. "Walk straight into it."

"Tick!"

He looked back to see Sofia and Paul running straight toward him, sprinting at full speed. Part of him wanted to tell them to go back, to leave him, that it was too dangerous this close to the Void. But he wanted to see his friends. Desperately. He started off in their direction to close the gap.

"Atticus!" Jane shouted. "We don't have time for this!"

"I'll only be a second!"

He ran until they met, and then they were all hugging each other, fiercely, even laughing. Right then Paul and Sofia were his tie to everything that he cared about in life. Seeing them filled him up, something he'd needed so badly. He'd been running on empty for a long time.

"What's going on?" Tick asked them. "How did you know I was here? Why are *you* guys here?"

"No time to explain," Sofia responded, shouting into the wind, leaning close to his ear. "We finally connected with your nanolocator, and . . . we figured some things out. Karma, Tick. There's a thing called Karma that's going to help you. It's made things happen so that we'd all end up here. Right here, right now."

Tick squinted his eyes in confusion. "Karma?"

Sofia put a small bag with a hard, boxy thing inside it into his hands. Paul had tied a string to Tick's wrist before he could even vocalize the questions in his mind. He felt a buzz inside of him, a surge of feeling that gave him goose bumps.

"There are things we don't totally comprehend yet," Sofia said, smiling. Actually smiling. "Take this with you for whatever it is you . . . and she have to do. It's going to work out, Tick. Paul and I know it. Sato knows it. We all know it!"

"But . . ." Tick was speechless.

"We've trusted you a billion times," Paul added. "Trust us now. See you when all this is over!"

He swatted Tick on the back, and then the two of them ran back toward the other Realitants and Sato's army.

CHAPTER 64

*

THE MAGIC SILVER CUBE

It was almost impossible not to stare at it. The massively huge storm of the Void, roiling in a giant circle as lightning cracked and whipped through its fog and mist. A gray, monstrous thing that was growing by the minute. Master George thought he was being more than careful when he'd winked them several miles away from the spot of the once-great castle of Mistress Jane, but they had still ended up way too close for comfort.

At least they had no excuses, now. No time to look and wait and grow more fearful. The nearest wall of the Void was close, and they'd have to start fighting soon. Though *how*, exactly, you fought a storm was anyone's guess. What could they do but try? Follow

911

the path of Karma and buy time for Master Atticus to do what he must and meet his own destiny with the Void. Paul and Sofia had given him the Karma Drive and returned safely.

They were all together now—Sally and Mothball. Paul and Sofia. Sato and his Fifth Army. Only Rutger was missing, having stayed in the command center in order to gather in the other Realitants. It was a rag-tag group, but the best hope the Realities had at the moment.

Sato stepped up to him. "No time like the present."

Master George could tell that the boy wanted to show him some respect, allow the leader of the Realitants to issue the first command. But George was no fool. He was here to fight, as old and frail as he may be, not command. He wouldn't send all these people to their most dangerous task yet without being by their side. Not this time.

"You're in charge now," he told Sato. "Especially since you've fought this . . . thing before."

Sato was trying to hide a look of disappointment on his face. "We only fought the things that came out of the Void. Not the Void itself."

George shrugged his shoulders. "Well, they're bound to be related, connected. I know of nothing else we can do but to take our weapons and attack it as you did the monsters it unleashed. If nothing else, perhaps we can at least stop it from growing. We need to buy time until Atticus can do what he has planned."

"We'll do it," Sato said. "We'll beat it, or we'll die trying."

"Oh, goodness gracious me. Don't talk like that." He patted the boy on the shoulder. "All right, then. Take charge, my good man. I'll be right here fighting with you—though I may linger in the back." He gave him a smile. "And we'll hope that others come to help soon enough."

Sato nodded, a different countenance spreading across his face and demeanor. He suddenly looked like a cold, hard leader. He gave a long, lingering glance at the nearby wall of churning fog then turned to his army and the other Realitants.

"Line up!" he shouted. "Rows of twenty, staggered by four soldiers on the ends!"

The orders were followed, and soon the formation was complete, each person facing the Void. Paul and Sofia, and Mothball and Sally, were mixed into the group, new members along with Master George.

Sato shouted a command that was lost in the wind, but his hand signals were clear enough.

The Fifth Army started marching toward the Void of Mist and Thunder.

Tick refused to tell Jane anything, saying simply that his friends had given him a good-luck charm. He felt the string tightly wound against his wrist, felt the bulk of the box inside the bag. He was doing exactly what Paul had asked him to. Trusting them. He could use all the help he could get anyway.

His eyes stung from the ripping winds that tore across the fields away from the Void, picking up dust and rock and debris along the way. All of it pelted him from head to toe. He wiped at his face and kept going, determined to stay by Jane's side as she marched toward the towering wall of spinning gray fog, leaning into the stiff wind. They were almost there, and the sight of the Void up close was frightening, all lightning and thunder and swelling power.

Jane didn't slow. And neither did Tick. He did look back every once in a while, and it seemed as if Sato's army was massing for an attack on the Void itself, which seemed ridiculous.

Just let me handle this, guys, he thought. *I can do it.*

They were a few hundred feet away, Tick's entire vision filled with nothing but gray mist and flashes of light, his ears numb from the pounding noise, when Chu abruptly appeared right in front of them. Winked in, flashing into existence. He held a large, silver cube about the size of a microwave oven in his hands. The wind pushed his black hair all over the place in a frenzy

and riffled his clothes, but Tick noticed his eyes. They were sane and clear, which, for some reason, scared Tick.

Chu held the metallic box out in front of him. "This is it!" Even though he was obviously screaming, his words were barely audible over the deafening roar of the Void. "The work of more than a hundred scientists! It will change the Realities forever, and I plan to be the guinea pig this time!"

"Get out of our way!" Tick yelled back at him.

"Atticus," Jane said. "We need him, remember?"

"No!" Tick was done being told how things would be done. "Chu, we don't need you; I don't care what Jane says. Get out of my way."

"I have an entire army about to wink in!" Chu responded, shouting his every word. "With all my greatest creations at their disposal! They have orders to annihilate anyone and everyone in the fields behind us unless you do as I say! Don't let their deaths, and the end of the Realities as we know it, be on your shoulders! My plan is the only way!"

"What is that thing?" Tick yelled, nodding toward the silver cube.

Jane didn't let Chu answer. "It doesn't matter!"

"It does! I want to know!" Tick replied. And he did. He *wanted* to know. Something told him it was important.

Chu lifted the cube up a couple of feet, and then he screamed out his words to be heard over the storm of the Void. "It's made of the same matter that binds the universe together. A science that only a precious few understand. We need simply to utilize the almost infinite energy of the Void to break it apart, dissolve it—and *me*—into trillions of atoms. Then, with the power of your Chi'karda—both of yours—we can meld and bind myself to the very fabric of Reality. And Jane, too, if she still wishes. We can do this!"

Tick had been leaning forward, focusing with all his concentration to hear and compute every sentence as it came out of Chu's mouth. It sounded like the ranting of a mad scientist, but Tick knew better. He couldn't underestimate Reginald Chu. There was something here, something unprecedented in human history. And it scared Tick.

He'd have none of it. "Get out of my way!"

"Please, boy!" Chu shouted, sincere pleading in his eyes. "I swear to you, this is real. This can work. My intentions are noble! I can make the Realities better with a human side! We can finally create Jane's Utopia!"

Tick thought the man had gone too far—losing every ounce of the scant credibility he was shooting for—when he claimed he was trying to be noble. Did Chu really expect him to *believe* that?

Tick looked over at Jane, and he saw the most human expression he'd ever seen on her mask. She was torn, through and through. He felt pity for her, then, shocking himself. He could see that the promise of her elusive Utopia had gotten to her.

"Mistress Jane," Tick said, but not too loudly. Working with Chu was the worst idea possible. And yet he had no doubt the threat that the man had made was real. And something—some feeling deep within him—told him what to do.

He lurched forward and grabbed Jane by the arm, pulling her along as he walked toward Chu. Tick grabbed him by the arm with his other hand, letting Sofia's bag dangle from his wrist. Then he broke into a run, dragging the other two along with him, fighting the monstrous winds.

A few seconds later, they slipped through the outer wall of the Void, swallowed by the gray, angry mist.

CHAPTER 65

✳

ENLISTED IN THE ARMY

The noise was unreal. A level that Tick had never experienced before. Loud, pounding, relentless. Gray darkness surrounded the three of them as they walked through the outskirts of the Void. Each flash of lightning was followed immediately by a brutal crack of thunder. Tick figured he'd be deaf within a half hour, if not dead.

At least the wind had stopped. Jane had used her Chi'karda to put a bubble of protection around them, more to prevent being struck by lightning than anything else. It was invisible, but had an orange sheen to it that mixed oddly with the gray, boiling mist that seethed along its edges. It was all so strange, so surreal.

But Tick knew they probably hadn't seen anything yet; it was about to get a lot weirder and a lot scarier.

Chu walked alongside him, hefting that large silver cube. Tick wanted to ask him more questions but didn't have the heart to attempt it. He'd have to scream at the top of his lungs, and who knew if even that would work.

Out of the corner of his eye, he noticed Chu balance the cube in one arm and reach his other hand into his pocket. He opened his mouth to say something— exactly what he'd done earlier when he'd communicated with someone in his own Reality—but an odd expression came over his face, and he seemed to reconsider his decision. He pulled his hand out of his pocket and gripped the cube firmly once again. Was it because of the noise? Or had he changed his mind on something? Decided not to do what he'd planned after all? Maybe the device didn't work in the middle of the storm.

The three of them kept moving, protected by a bubble of clear orange, going deeper into the depths of the gray storm.

The heart of the Void waited.

Master George had emptied the last of the Realitants' arsenal to arm Sato's army for one last battle.

Paul held his Shurric steady, its butt end pressed

against his chest, handle gripped firmly, his finger ready at the trigger. He had Ragers and Slicers in both of his pockets and another Shurric strapped across his back in case the first one ran out of juice. He was ready for battle as they marched toward the wall of the Void. Streams of mist jumped out and swirled back, and plumes erupted from the surface then were sucked in again; the entire storm boiled and fumed. All while lightning danced and crackled within and without.

Somehow he and Sofia had been jostled and pushed about by the much taller members of the Fifth until they found themselves along the back line. It seemed like chance, but Paul had a sneaking suspicion that the Fifths were trying to protect them, since they were young and small compared to the rest of the army. That made Paul mad—even though he couldn't help the small part of him that was relieved. His scared side. His terrified side. He was ashamed of the feeling and swore that when they got into the heat of battle, he'd do whatever it took to prove he wasn't a scaredy-cat chicken.

Sofia was next to him, stepping stride for stride, gripping her own weapon, staring straight ahead. She seemed too focused, or maybe even too lost in thought. Paul had the sudden urge to grab her hand and run away from the danger. Shame filled him again. What was wrong with him? He was a *Realitant*, for crying out loud.

"Hey!"

The sharp bark of a man's voice came from behind him, loud enough to be heard clearly over the rumbling sounds of thunder. Paul stumbled to a stop and turned around, even though the rest of the army kept marching. Even Sofia. A man stood about twenty feet away, dressed in shiny clothes and black boots. He was stocky and had a balding head and a red, angry face. He looked like the kind of guy you'd see in a parking lot and turn around to walk in the opposite direction. Had no one else heard him shout?

"Sofia!" Paul yelled, turning back to look at her. She stopped and saw him, then the stranger who'd appeared, her eyes widening at the sight. *At least I'm not crazy,* Paul thought. "Make sure someone tells Sato!"

As she grabbed at the soldier closest to her, Paul faced the visitor again, who still stood in the same spot. "Who are you?"

The man walked up to him, an arrogant smirk on his face. "I'm from the Fourth Reality. Name's Benson. Who are you?"

"Uh . . . Paul. What . . . why are you here?" Something weird was going on, and Paul hoped Sato would send some people back quickly to help him out.

The stranger smiled, though it was full of anything

but kindness. "I work for a very important man, kid. His name is Reginald Chu. Ever heard of him?"

Paul swallowed, the weirdness of the situation turning to fear. He took a step back and pointed his Shurric at the man. "Don't move."

Benson laughed. "No need to shoot, son. Just letting you know that my boss—he doesn't like me to call him that, which is a shame, don't ya think?—well, my boss said that if I don't hear from him, I'm supposed to come in here and start attacking anything and everything I see. You understand?"

"You?" Paul asked, his finger itching at the trigger. "By yourself?"

"Yeah, me and what army, right?" Benson laughed again, but then his face suddenly creased into an angry, angry look. "Guess what, little man? I *haven't* heard from the boss. Which is very bad for you."

The man snapped his fingers like a magician, and machines started appearing behind him, dozens and dozens of machines and other contraptions, filling the fields.

Paul took a step backward in shock, then another as he scanned the area with his eyes, dazed. But he stopped when he recognized some of the objects lining up behind Benson. A nightmare from what seemed like another lifetime.

Metaspides.

CHAPTER 66

✳

TWO DIFFERENT ENEMIES

Sato's thoughts churned as he marched toward the Void, wind ripping at his clothes and hair.

It had taken all of his willpower not to charge after Mistress Jane when he saw her standing near Tick earlier. His anger toward her had been building for many years, and this time, something inside of him snapped as if he suddenly knew this was his last chance to seek revenge for the death of his parents. When all this was over, surely one of them—either him or Jane—would be dead. And if it was *her*, he wanted it to be at his hands. He had dreamed of it for years.

But something had stayed his hand. Calmed him. Brought a peace that almost didn't make sense. Almost on a subconscious level, he made a decision. And, just like that, all the anger and the hate and the thirst for vengeance went away. Gone. He didn't understand it, but he felt it all the same. He had a calling in the world now. And he swore to never think of Jane again after he watched her disappear into the gray mist with Chu and Tick.

A murmuring behind him interrupted his thoughts. A rumbling of whispers and movement as people talked to each other, leaning close to speak ear to ear. He looked back at his soldiers, wondering what they could be excited about. He didn't see anything on the other side of the tall soldiers who made up his army, when he heard a different sound coming from the Void. A series of thumps and roars, like drums and wind. He quickly whipped around to take a look.

The giant wall of churning fog was only a couple hundred feet away now, and forms of mist were separating from the main cyclone. Pockets of swirling gray air popped out all over the place and coalesced into more human-shaped bodies than any Void creatures they'd encountered before. They formed in the air then dropped to the ground, landing on two feet that were suddenly solid. The ones closest started walking toward the Fifth Army.

On some level, Sato knew that these creatures were people who'd been stolen by the Void, sucked in from who knew where by the pulsing blue substance that was somehow related to the Fourth Dimension. It didn't make sense to him, probably never would. But the Void had turned them into monsters, and now more than fifty had already been created. They were coming toward him, as if they'd zeroed in on him specifically.

He remembered all too well what those things could do.

His army would need to attack hard and fast before the beams of pure flame came shooting out of the creatures' mouths.

He was just turning to face his army and shout commands when Tollaseat interrupted him, something he'd never done before.

"Got major trouble, we do," the giant man said.

"Yeah, I'm pretty aware—"

"No, sir! I 'spect you don't! Not talkin' about the fog things! There's an army of machines revvin' up on the other side of us. Looks a might nasty, too."

Sato lifted up on his toes and saw a few traces of silver and what looked like mechanical arms. He didn't understand it at first, didn't know what was going on. But he knew three things.

His army was small. And surrounded. By two different enemies.

Tick guessed they were about two miles into the massive storm of the Void when everything fell apart. It started with the wind, a visible, monstrous thing mixed with the gray mist. It grew to an unnatural level, so fierce and mighty that the sound of it drowned out the booming thunder. And the bubble of protection created by Mistress Jane finally became worthless.

It stayed intact, but suddenly became a victim of the wind, whipping up into the abyss of the Void with Tick and the other two still inside of it. They smacked into each other, rolled around, tossed back and forth like pebbles inside a bouncing beach ball. Chu's cube flew out of his hands, and its corner hit Tick just above the eye, sending a sharp lance of pain through his skull. An inch lower and he might have been blinded for life. Chu called out, frantically trying to maneuver his way through the chaos to grab his precious device once again.

But movement was impossible for any of them. Tick finally curled up into a ball and quit trying to fight something he couldn't change. He bounced up and down, wincing each time he slammed into Jane or Chu, hating the feel of chins and elbows and feet digging into his flesh and bones. The temptation to unleash his Chi'karda was overpowering, but he held back, realizing that flying around in a bubble was better than getting separated and lost, each of them swept away by the brutal winds.

The shiny orange bubble of Chi'karda hit the ground and rolled. Grunts and shouts and barks of pain filled the air as Tick closed his eyes and squeezed his arms and legs into an even tighter ball. The bouncing finally settled, and everything stopped moving. Tick, filled with nausea, looked up to see that not much was different from before. The orange sheen of the bubble was still around them, the swirling mist of the Void raging on the other side. His first thought was that maybe a particularly strong gust had caught them from underneath to throw them through the air like that.

He saw Chu crawling toward his silver cube. Jane was trying to stand up, obviously woozy, her robe in disarray and revealing her scarred hands and arms.

"We need to move," she said in a hoarse voice that Tick barely heard. "The Void is going to keep trying to stop us. We need to move! Now!"

Tick nodded. Chu picked up his precious device. Jane pointed, making Tick wonder how in the world she could possibly know which way they'd been walking before. But he had no better ideas. They picked up where they'd left off and started moving.

They'd taken maybe ten steps when the ground exploded upward, throwing them all in different directions. The bubble vanished for good.

Benson winked away as soon as his army of machines showed up. Paul couldn't blame him. What good would one human do when you had the kind of technological might Reginald Chu had at his disposal? The metallic machines—some boxy, some round—littered the flattened fields in front of Paul, and each one of them looked ready to kill. The only ones he recognized were the Metaspides, spherical, with long legs and nasty weapons. They had attacked him twice before; they weren't very nice.

The other machines out there were new to Paul, but just as vicious-looking. A big, boxy robot on wheels with two arms that resembled bulldozers but had fists of steel with nasty spikes on the end. Hovering, disk-shaped metal plates that were several feet across and came to a razor-thin edge along the outer circle.

In the long pause that seemed to float through the air like an air-bound virus between when Benson winked away and when the inevitable battle would begin, Paul could see labels on the closest machines. All of Chu's inventions were marked, starting way back with the Gnat Rats.

The bulldozer-robot was called a Denter. And the flying saucer weapons were Ranters. The phrase "Manufactured by Chu Industries" was printed on every machine.

Beautiful, Paul thought. *Just beautiful.* Like fighting

a massive storm called the Void of Mist and Thunder from the Fourth Dimension wasn't going to be a big enough challenge for the Realitants.

The moment felt like an eternity but couldn't have been longer than twenty seconds.

Sofia finally broke the silence. "How did it all come to this? The smallest army ever caught between two impossible enemies."

Paul had never heard such sadness in her voice. That's what hit him with a rush of fear—the realization that they were probably about to die. Not seeing all the machines in front of him. Not hearing all of the terrible sounds of the Void behind him. If Sofia was feeling hopeless, they must be in bad shape.

Paul shot a glance back at the Fifth Army. They seemed confused, milling about as if deciding which front to fight first. There was a commotion on the far side, but it was hard to see over the tall bodies of the soldiers. It all added up to equal one major downer.

"We just have to fight," he finally said. "That's all we can do. Fight until we either win or die. Until Tick does whatever he's going to do. Maybe Rutger will find us some more people. But all we can do—me and you—is fight."

Sofia looked at him with something like awe, which swelled his chest up with pride. She even had the beginnings of a tear in one of her eyes.

"One of these days, I'm going to realize just how much I like you," she said. "Maybe once you're old enough to quit making fart jokes."

He smiled, a ridiculous thing to do when you were about to die. But he did it anyway. "That's a deal right there. I'm gonna hold you to it."

She smiled back.

The machines of Chu Industries started whirring and chirping and revving, a chorus of awful sounds. Then they all moved at once.

CHAPTER 67

✳

A GLIMPSE OF RUTGER

Sato barely had time to assess the situation. On one side of his army, a horde of machines were about to attack with technology far beyond a few Shurrics and the other meager weapons the Fifth had at the ready. And on the other—on his side—at least a hundred gray soldiers were marching toward him, their mouths already beginning to open up. The abyss inside matched the fiery sockets of their eyes. Pure flame and heat.

They had no time to wallow in despair or wish for better days. It was fight or die.

"Attack!" he yelled, as loud as he possibly could. "Slam them with Shurrics before they can fight back!"

A series of thumping concussions rocked the world as every one of his nearby soldiers started firing. Sato felt a quick burst of pride at seeing a dozen or so of the Void creatures obliterated into wispy trails of mist. But more came.

And beams of brilliant fire shot out of their mouths, like a volley of arrows, streaming up toward the sky then back down toward the Fifth Army.

"Take cover!" Sato shouted, but the screams had already begun.

Master George was in the middle of the fray, wondering desperately why in the name of all that was good and green on the earth he'd decided to pretend to be a soldier. He could barely hold the Shurric in his arms, and he didn't know what to do. He stood there, looking to Mothball and Sally for direction. He'd do whatever they did.

The sky was suddenly lit up with streams of fire, coming from the direction of the Void. The sounds of revved up machinery came from the other side, where that nasty ogre Chu had sent some of his inventions. But for what purpose, George had no idea. What in the dickens was going on?

"Whichaway should we be a-fightin'?" Sally asked.

"I'm a bit bamboozled, I am," was Mothball's reply. "Paul and Sofia are back there." She nodded toward where Chu's attack was starting. "I reckon we best go that way."

The two of them charged behind other soldiers, bringing up their weapons to take aim. Master George followed, fighting the temptation to wink himself straight out of there.

Come on, Rutger, he thought to himself. *Don't fail me now. After all these years, don't fail me now.*

⟨⟨⟩⟩

Tick's body bounced, something he didn't think was possible for a human body to do. But he did. With the protection of Jane's Chi'karda bubble gone, he'd flown through the air when the ground erupted from below, then landed fifty feet away and bounced. At least twice. He rolled to a stop, dazed and bruised. The winds were fierce and hard and loud around him, lightning flashing everywhere, the sounds deafening. All was a gray blur; he might as well have been blind.

He got to his knees, then tried to stand up, but the gusts ripped at his body and made him fall again. Back to his knees, he squinted his eyes against the wind. He looked in every direction, saw nothing but the mist and fog of the Void swirling and churning like boiling water.

"Jane!" he screamed, though the sound was caught up and whisked away before even his own ears heard it. "Chu!"

He tensed his leg muscles and tried to stand up once more. He'd just gotten his balance when the surface below him exploded outward again, throwing his body forward. After flipping and flailing, he bounced and rolled again. Every inch of him hurt.

Chi'karda. He needed to use his Chi'karda.

Power filled him at the thought, consumed his insides with alternating waves of hot and cold. Orange sparkles mixed in with the gray that filled his vision. With a thought, he replicated Jane's protective bubble of air. It formed around him and cut off the wind and a lot of the sound. But there were thumps that he felt through the ground. Those eruptions were happening all over the place. And it dawned on Tick what was happening.

The Void didn't want them to find its core, its heart, or whatever represented its essence. The Void was trying to protect itself.

Filled with the raging power of Chi'karda, Tick went in search of Jane and Chu.

Paul tried not to fall apart inside as utter chaos ruled around him. Metaspides cut across the ground with their spindly legs and jumped on top of soldiers, who had to fight with all four limbs to keep from getting hurt. The Denter machines stomped around, shaking the ground beneath them, swinging those massive, spiked arms at anything that moved. The Ranters spun and flew through the air, trying to cut a path to victory.

But the soldiers of the Fifth weren't giving up. Not by a long shot. They fired their Shurrics and threw their Ragers and tossed their Squeezer grenades at the creations of Chu Industries. They battled with their arms and legs when their other weapons failed. It was an all-out war, and Paul found what little bravery he could and did his part.

He slowly moved forward, legs bent in a crouch, sweeping his Shurric left and right to fire at any machine that came close. A Metaspide leaped into the air, came down at him. A quick jerk of his arms, a hopeful aim, a pull of the trigger. A thump of pure sound sent the thing catapulting away.

Sofia was at his side, skipping Ragers in strategic locations. One of them balled up into a sphere of ground and rock and destroyed two Denters and a Ranter in one fell swoop.

But people were dying, getting hurt. The Fifth

Army was getting smaller and smaller. How much longer could they hold out?

Paul shot a Metaspide to his left, a Ranter spinning in from the front, and then blasted a Denter to his right. Sofia threw an entire handful of Squeezers at a pack of machines that had somehow slipped behind them. Paul gave her a quick cheer.

They kept fighting.

⁓

Sato pushed out of his mind the screams that kept piercing the air and invading his thoughts. They were an army. This was a battle. People would die. All he could do was try to prevent as many deaths as possible. He ran across the fields, shooting his Shurric at the creatures of the Void, aiming for any that looked ready to open those mouths of theirs and spit out fire. The other soldiers had caught on as well, taking care to kill the monsters of mist before they sent out streams of flaming heat that were almost impossible to defend against.

A beam of fiery orange came sailing through the air, straight for Sato's head. He dove to the ground, spinning onto his back just in time to see the terrifying flames swoop over his body and land in a patch of flattened grass. It caught fire but was soon put out by his soldiers running across it, looking for something to shoot. Some soldiers tossed Ragers, which proved very effective, often taking out five or six of the Void creatures in one destructive roll.

Sato leaped to his feet and rejoined the fray.

Master George had given up on doing much other than shooting his confounded Shurric weapon when he had a very clear shot. Otherwise he was too scared he might lop off the heads of his own people. He was no soldier, and he had begun to greatly regret thinking he could help. If anything, he felt as if he was a terrible hindrance.

Mothball and Sally fought ferociously beside him, attacking any threat that came close. He knew they were trying to protect him, and it touched his heart. Though if they died doing so, he'd never forgive himself.

The battle raged all around him, an awful experience that made his insides tremble. Beams of fire shooting through the air from Void creatures on one side, horrific machines stomping and scuttling and spinning all over the place on the other. Brave soldiers fighting with everything they had; brave soldiers dying. Shurrics pounding, Ragers smashing, Squeezers breaking apart machines, people screaming.

The battle was everywhere.

There was a squeal of metal against metal next to him, followed by a solid thump and the quake of earth at his feet. He stumbled as he turned to see what had happened then almost fell at the sight of a huge machine, silver and black with dark rubber wheels, appearing at his side. The robot had two huge mechanical arms that ended in spiked fists of steel. George looked in fright at the letters written across the chest of the beast:

DENTER
Manufactured by Chu Industries

He'd barely read the last word when the robot raised an arm up into the air and swung it back down. The metal fist and its spikes dug into George's chest, and then lifted him up and threw him through the air like a discarded piece of trash. Pain erupted through every single cell of his body, a flashing burn of hurt that made his mind want to shut down. He flailed with his arms as he flew, saw blood dripping from his skin, watched as the ground rushed up at him. He slammed down, and every last ounce of breath escaped from his lungs.

He landed in a way that turned his face to the fields beyond the battle, toward a spot that had been empty when the fighting started. But now he saw a sight that lifted his heart despite the pain that ripped through him. A short, round ball of a man, waving his little arms frantically, as if giving orders. Behind him, hundreds—maybe even thousands—of people had appeared, wielding all manner of weapons.

Rutger had done it. He'd found the other Realitants and come to the rescue.

Master George ached like the end of the world. He closed his eyes, wondering if it might be the last time he ever did so.

CHAPTER 68

✳

A DEAD BODY

The Void was throwing everything it had at Tick. He doubted if he'd ever understand how the thing worked—if it was alive or a mindless pool of unchecked power. But it seemed to be thinking now, and it didn't want him to take another step toward the elusive core that made up its heart.

The ground exploded all around him, like the spray from a breaching whale. The bubble he'd created with his Chi'karda did nothing against that, throwing him left and right. He'd get up only to have it happen all over again.

Great spouts of flames and lava rained down from above, like descending angels of fiery destruction. Tick had to stop and focus each time they hit, throwing his power out to keep the shield from breaking down. Lightning split the air in any direction he looked, its sound like a thousand locomotives next to his ears. His head felt numb through and through.

Balls of mist solidified, pounding on his protection like an angry kid trying to break through a piggy bank. Each wallop sent a vibration of pain through his bones, and he threw even more of his thoughts into controlling the flow of Chi'karda. All while the ground continued to explode and throw his body around, all while fire rained from the sky, all while lightning tried to strike its way into any opening it might suddenly find. All with the horrible, horrible noise of the world breaking in half. Tick was rattled, and he knew it. But he forced himself to keep his wits intact, to not let the fear and panic win over his nerves.

He dealt with the chaos, doing his best to keep moving in the general direction he thought Jane had indicated, and relying on his instincts. Relying on some inner sense that he didn't even comprehend. He was just moving now. Moving forward, not backward. Guided by what, he didn't know. But guided by something.

A body lay up ahead, its arms and legs sprawled in impossible positions. Lifeless. A silver cube was perched in a pile of rubble right next to it.

Tick walked up to the spot and stood over the dead form of Reginald Chu.

⤳

Paul heard the shouts and cheers first. Then he noticed that most of the machines had stopped in the middle of whatever havoc they'd been inflicting. His soldiers turned to look at something in the distance.

Haggard, beat, exhausted. That was Paul. His arms and legs felt like rubber, and he hurt in roughly seventy-five places. He'd run and jumped and dodged and dove and shot both of his Shurrics almost to their limit. He'd been hit and swept aside by machines. A spinning Ranter had almost taken his head clean off, but Sofia had saved him with a quick burst from her Shurric. It had been her last charge, because she then tossed the weapon aside and started throwing the few Ragers she had left.

It was a miracle, but both of them were still alive. And now something new was happening. Something was going on.

He ran up to her, grabbed her by the hand. She was filthy and bloody and bruised. But she didn't protest and went with him as they zigzagged their way through the crowd of tall soldiers from the Fifth Reality. It was as if the very air had changed—gotten brighter. The mood had visibly lifted.

He saw why, when they finally made it to a break in the people and machines. Hundreds and hundreds of people—dressed in oranges and reds and browns and blacks and turbans and robes and jeans and sandals and every color and type of clothing he'd ever imagined, and many that he hadn't—were charging the enemies on both sides. Somewhere in the middle of all that, he thought he saw Rutger.

Rutger.

He and Sofia exchanged a glance, then turned to look at the churning hurricane of fog and mist and lightning. It was still growling and angry. Getting bigger.

Then Paul spotted Master George, lying on his stomach.

Not moving.

⁓

Sato had been on the verge of giving up. He hated to admit it to himself, but the truth was the truth. Cold, hard Reality. They were outnumbered, outmanned, and almost out of weaponry. The creatures from the Void kept coming, shooting their beams of flame. The world rocked with thunder and screams.

But now they had help.

A sea of people, dressed in all kinds of clothes, surged forward. They carried all kinds of weapons, some of which Sato had never seen before: red tubes looped around shoulders, connecting a backpack to nozzles held in both hands; long poles with electricity sparking on the end; cubes of blue metal that glowed with a brilliant light. The people came down the slope to join the battle, most of them roaring, eyes aflame. Sato saw Rutger in their midst, cheering them on.

The tide had turned.

Jane limped up to Tick as he stared down at the lifeless face of Reginald Chu. She slipped through the protective bubble of his Chi'karda and put a scarred hand on his shoulder. He turned to face her and saw the mask, which was half-melted. There was only one eye now, half a mouth. Everything else was a smeared ruin of metal. He probably would've gasped from shock if he hadn't felt so numb inside.

"He never had a chance," she said.

Tick looked over at the silver cube, a third of it buried in a pile of rock and dirt. Something had taken ahold of him inside. A presence. An unmistakable feeling in his heart and unexpected thoughts in his mind that he knew weren't his own. It was pure power—a lot like Chi'karda in how he could sense it. Where it had come from, he had no idea. But a clear path had suddenly opened before him. It hurt him—hurt him deeply—but he knew he couldn't stray from it.

Karma. Sofia had called it Karma. He touched a finger to the bag she and Paul had tied to his wrist. Everything in the world was now crystal clear in his mind. He knew his destiny and how to find it.

He walked over and picked up the cube. He turned to Jane.

"I need your help!" he shouted.

She nodded, and he wondered if she felt the power's presence as well. It was like electricity in the air, and warmth in his veins. Unmistakably *there*.

Jane pointed to her right. "The heart of the Void is that way. We're close now."

Tick and Mistress Jane headed for their destiny—and their doom.

CHAPTER 69

✳

BECOMING ONE

The ground trembled and shook as they walked across it. Tick's mind was more focused than ever now, as if some miracle drug had been pumped through his veins. His hold on Chi'karda was absolute.

He was ready for anything.

The winds swept past in torrential gusts, but they did nothing to even stir his clothes. Without hardly thinking about it, his bubble of protection stayed true, as did Jane's. They'd even learned to control the earthquakes beneath them, squashing their force before they could lift their feet off the ground. The Void noticed, and quit trying. Fists of fog continued to form in the mist, pounding at their shields, thumping and bumping. Nothing broke through.

They kept walking. Tick hugged the silver cube to his chest. That unseen presence that had filled him left him with no doubt that the object was vital to what awaited. Everything was about to come to a head.

A brightness began to lighten the air, like the beginnings of dawn. It had a blue tint to it, and it either thinned out the fog and mist or just made it easier to see. But the feel of the air around them was changing. And then it appeared before their eyes. Not gradually, and not from a distance, growing in size. It was suddenly just *there*, as if they'd been catapulted three miles forward without feeling anything.

A thick shaft of pure blue light, blinding in its brilliance. It came from the sky and tunneled into the ground, running in both directions as far as Tick could see. The perfectly round cylinder was at least fifty feet wide, the radiance within its core pulsing like a heartbeat.

Tick squinted and held up his hands, peeking through his fingers. It was impossible to look at the light for more than a second or two, but there was something incredibly beautiful and mesmerizing about its steady beat of flashing brightness. The purity of its blue. The hum and buzz emanating from it. Tick felt it in the air and in the ground beneath his feet. The steady roar and pounding of a thousand waterfalls.

It was energy and life and power, unlimited and

daunting. Tick had to fight to not lose himself to the awesomeness of it all.

"The core of the Void!" Jane shouted.

Tick nodded. He knew that already. Just as he knew what needed to be done. Just as he knew that Mistress Jane would never leave this place, and that he'd never be the same.

He turned to her, finally breaking his trancelike state. "I need your help to harness its energy! I need you to break apart the cube. And . . . me."

Her half-melted mask stared back at him, saying nothing. Showing nothing.

"You know it's the only way!" he yelled. She *had* to know.

"It's going to fight us," she finally replied.

Tick nodded.

She paused again. "You have to promise me, Atticus! Promise me!"

"What?"

The roar of the Void shook the air.

"You know!" she shouted. "You *know* what my heart has always envisioned! It's always been about the end, Atticus. *Tick.* Always the means to the end!"

"Utopia."

"Utopia!" She stepped closer to him, only inches away. "I need your word if you want me to do this. Otherwise nothing matters!"

"I give you my word that I'll devote everything to it. But in my own way."

"Swear it!"

"I swear."

She stared at him a long time before nodding. "Then let's go."

She didn't wait for him to respond. She turned and sprinted for the blinding, brilliant shaft of pulsing blue light. Tick ran after her, hefting the cube in his arms. The Void immediately retaliated.

Things started flying out of the core, all shapes and sizes, some alive and some not. Dozens of man-shaped creatures like the Voids who'd attacked them at the ruins of Jane's castle came first. Their mouths gaped open as soon as they appeared, yawning wide to reveal the furnaces that burned inside. Beams of lava and flame shot out all at once in an organized volley of heat.

Jane stopped to face the threat, as did Tick. With flicks of his eyes, he directed the power of Chi'karda—bursts of brilliant orange—to shoot forth and meet the attack in midair, obliterating the streams of lava before they could fall toward the ground. The two forces met in a shower of sparks and a burst of explosive sound. Jane and Tick swept their gazes left and right, destroying them all. Then they focused on the creatures themselves, wiping them from existence with one brutal assault of Chi'karda. Wisps of fog flew in all directions.

Jane moved forward again, and Tick followed. They'd only taken a few short steps when all kinds of animals made from the same gray substance emerged from the blue core. There were tigers and dogs and snakes and mad bulls. Alligators. Giant scorpions. They mixed together into a crowd of monsters, scurrying about the ground, all of them bent on attacking the two humans close by.

Jane and Tick stopped again and fired away with Chi'karda. The creatures' eyes had that same bright look of flames, vicious and angry. Snakes slithered across the ground; tigers leaped forward; everything came at them.

Tick could feel pressure mounting inside him as he picked apart the unnatural creations with his power. Sweat poured down his face. Every blast that took down one enemy seemed to reveal three more—they just kept coming and coming. Jane's arms were whipping around, back and forth as she aimed and fired, like her hands were weapons. Tick just looked, killing with a glance. Zap, zap, zap. The sounds of explosions and the roar of the core filled the air.

Heaving deep breaths, Tick wiped away all of the enemies on his side then helped Jane destroy the last few on her side. They ran a few steps closer to the blue light.

A massive tree trunk, gray but looking solid enough to smash a truck, came hurtling out of the core, end over end. Tick dissolved it into wispy nothingness with a burst of Chi'karda. Next came a huge chunk of steel and concrete, the jagged and broken remains of an old skyscraper. Jane destroyed it. Cars came flying out. Busses. More trees. Homes, ripped from their foundations. Boats. Planes. Telephone poles.

Now yelling with each blast, Tick attacked the objects coming at him, annihilating them all. Nothing came within ten feet of him. Jane seemed just as strong, throwing her spurts of power out like grenades. Chaos reigned, noise battered the world around them.

Still the core continued to throw things at them, and on some level, Tick understood that the Fourth Dimension sucked things away from the Realities and transformed them into these projectile weapons. All of the matter they were fighting against had once been real and whole in a world somewhere.

He'd had enough. He couldn't keep it up forever. Exhaustion was creeping in.

"Jane!" he yelled. "We need to rush the core! This has to stop!"

She answered by moving forward, still waving her arms as she directed her powers. Tick followed, taking step after slow step as he focused with all his might. One slip, and he'd have a crushed head.

Still enemies flew at them, relentless and unstopping. Huge rocks. Giant Dumpsters. More beasts and man-like creatures. Some monsters shot back with streams of lava flames.

Tick wiped them away with nothing but his thoughts, exploding Chi'karda out of himself. Jane did the same.

They made it to the blindingly bright core, its pulsing blueness as hot as the thrusters on an alien spaceship. Tick couldn't look at it directly. He screamed as loud as he could and sent out one last detonation of pure Chi'karda, obliterating every single gray creature and monster within sight.

And then there was only the light and the roar of the core.

Jane quickly stepped next to him and grabbed the cube from his hands. For an instant, he wanted to rip it away from her, but he knew what she was doing. What she had to do.

"It's the only way!" he yelled at her.

"The only way!" she shouted back. "Atticus Higginbottom! Don't you dare forget your promise! Don't you dare!"

She backed away from him until she was at the very edge of the core, the shaft rising above and below her to infinity, visible as if they stood on a plane of glass surrounding it. Then she turned and thrust the cube directly into the light.

A concussion of sound and power rocked the air, making Tick fall down. Jane's robe burst into fire, and she screamed, an awful noise of things ripping and tearing. Tick had to shield his eyes. He could barely see what was happening, but he knew her entire body was being consumed. She kept screaming. Louder and louder. Then she suddenly turned back to him, her mask gone, her face a mess, her whole form burning. Where the cube had once been was now a spinning vortex of blue and gray and white lights.

"Now!" she shouted with a strangled, ruined voice.

Tick got to his feet and ran to her. He put his hands into the swirling lights. They immediately jumped out and began to spin all around him, growing brighter and thicker, encompassing every inch of his body. He barely had time to see Jane's destroyed body fall backward into the core and disappear forever. Then he was consumed by light and energy and a million other things he didn't quite understand.

Time stretched forward before him. He felt himself breaking apart, dissolving into molecules and atoms. There was a great rushing noise, and there was pain. He suddenly saw the entire universe before him, all at once. He saw the eyes of every person in every Reality, all at once. He saw fields and houses and forests and mountains and waterfalls. Oceans and deserts. But he had no eyes—his body had been ripped apart, thrown to the very edge of existence.

He and Reality—the fabric of Reality itself—were becoming one. The transformation lasted for infinity, yet was instantaneous. He was everything and nothing. Everywhere and nowhere. He was the space that filled the gaps, the barriers. He was matter and antimatter. He was Reality.

Tick had no idea how it worked. Not yet. But he knew that understanding would come soon.

A thought formed in his head. He pictured the core of the Void, the Fourth Dimension, the rips in Reality, and the link between them all. The chaos that reigned throughout all the worlds—even the countless ones that had yet to be discovered—filled him. His consciousness brought it all in, saw it all before him. The things that needed to be healed and the things that needed to be severed. Like the answer to a riddle popping into his mind, he knew how to heal and sever.

With powers no human had ever known before, Tick started fixing the wounded universe.

CHAPTER 70

✳

AN ABSENCE OF SOUND

Paul sat on the ground, holding Master George in his arms. Sofia was there, too, weeping just like Paul. The battle still continued around them, but Paul could tell it was almost over. Most of Chu's inventions had been obliterated by the new armies brought in by Rutger, and everyone had now turned their forces on the monsters from the Void. They were being destroyed almost as soon as they came out of the churning hurricane of mist. But the Void still raged, still grew. How could they ever stop it?

Master George barely had any life left in him. Each breath was a struggle, and his body was well past healing. Their leader was about to die.

The old man sputtered a cough, and his eyes blinked open. They focused on Paul, then Sofia, then filled with tears.

"I'm so sorry," Paul whispered. His heart crumbled inside of him.

"Master George," Sofia said through a lurching sob.

"No . . . no . . ." the man said through another coughing fit. "It's . . . okay. My good friends . . . you'll carry . . . on."

"Why?" Paul asked, feeling a sudden bubble of anger. "Why didn't the Karma work? The Void's still there! And . . . look at you . . ."

Sofia squeezed his arm but didn't say anything.

George reached out and grabbed both of their hands, seeming to gather one last surge of strength. "Oh, but Master Paul. I believe it *did* work. I have no doubt of it. You'll see soon enough."

The leader of the Realitants exhaled his very last breath.

Sato had just begun to feel some comfort. The influx of armies had turned the tide, at least in the short term. Chu's machines were defeated. The creatures of the Void were being destroyed almost as soon as they emerged from the spinning vortex of mist.

Now they just had to pool their resources and figure out a way to attack the—

The Void disappeared. The entire thing disappeared in an instant.

An abrupt absence of sound popped Sato's ears as if he'd just been sucked into the vacuum of space. His brain tried to process what he suddenly saw before him—empty air and distant mountains and fields and sky. Sunlight.

There was no more wind. No lightning. No thunder. No mist. No creatures of gray.

The Void had vanished.

It was gone.

Paul sat in the flattened, ruined grass with his eyes closed, feeling the warmth of the sun against his cheeks, still stunned. Somehow Tick had done it—he'd defeated the Void—but there'd been no sign of him after its disappearance.

The Void was gone. But so was Tick.

The lifeless body of Master George lay a few dozen feet away; the soldiers of Sato's army lined up to pay their respects. Mothball, kneeling next to the old man, sobbed uncontrollably as Sally and Rutger both rubbed her back.

Mixed feelings would be the order of things for a while.

Sofia was sitting beside Paul, and he opened his eyes when she nudged him with an elbow.

"Hey," she said softly. "You okay?"

Paul wondered how to answer that. "I think so. I still feel kind of weird, and sad, and . . . weird. There's no way I'm going to accept that Tick is gone. It has to be like the Nonex or something. He'll find his way back."

Sofia's eyes fell a little, but then she seemed to catch herself, as if she was trying to stay strong for Paul. "I hope so. I mean . . . he made it all go away—the Void, the rips in Reality. He couldn't have done that if he was dead, right? Maybe he's stuck in the Fourth Dimension, battling his way out."

"Yeah. Maybe."

Sofia leaned her head on his shoulder, which made everything just a little bit brighter.

Paul suddenly had a rush of thoughts that he couldn't keep to himself. All his words came spilling out.

"I'm going to be more serious, work harder. Make a bigger difference. Help the Realitants get back to what George was talking about—strong and rigid and organized top to bottom. We'll start recruiting again, find the best of the best. We can build more headquarters, make sure we have a presence in every Reality. I think we should maybe even go public soon, work with governments and universities—make a real difference in people's lives. And I think we should start exploring, see if we can discover and name new Realities. The Fourteenth, Fifteenth, Twentieth, Thirtieth. We've got a lot of work to do, Sofia."

He'd been staring at the empty fields where the Void of Mist and Thunder—and before that, the castle of Mistress Jane—had once stood. But he noticed that Sofia had lifted her head and was staring at him. He looked at her, loved seeing the awe in her eyes.

"I mean it," he said. "I really do."

"I know," she whispered back. "And we're going to do it together, with Mothball and the rest. It's going to be great."

"And fun."

"Lots of fun." Sofia pointed out into the distance. "I think we should build something right there. A branch of the Realitants. Not a gaudy castle—something simple. We should use the power of the Thirteenth like it was meant to be used. Before Jane messed it all up."

"Brilliant idea, maestro." Paul still had a heavy heart, but he couldn't deny the excitement he felt for the future.

Sofia took a deep breath and let it out. "So. We've made some pretty grand plans. What should we do first?"

Paul found a smile. "We'll figure it out tomorrow."

CHAPTER 71

✳

ONE MONTH LATER

Lisa sat on her front porch and stared out at the trees as the morning sun broke through in the distance and lit everything up. She wished she felt that way on the inside. She wouldn't have thought it was possible, but she missed Tick more and more with each passing day. It wasn't getting any better.

He'd vanished from their lives. Again.

But Atticus Higginbottom—her stinky little brother—had somehow stopped the Void before it could destroy everything. Tick had saved the universe. Again.

Despite her worry, she laughed at the thought. It seemed so absurd and ridiculous, and she knew Tick would laugh, too, if he were there. But it was true. Totally true. Tick was a hero for the ages. At least she had that to hold on to.

The front door banged open, and Kayla came sprinting out onto the porch, her head swiveling left and right as she looked for something. When she finally spotted Lisa, a look of excitement spread across her face.

"Come inside!" the little girl yelled. "Quick!"

Lisa was tempted to be annoyed—she'd just gotten comfortable and wanted some time to be alone outside. She wanted time to think about things. How the world was slowly but surely getting back to some sense of normalcy, how people were rebuilding and laying foundations for an even better future. The Realities were sharing information through the now very-public assistance of the Realitants. The universe would never be the same. Things were changed forever.

But she wasn't annoyed. She couldn't be. Kayla was smiling for the first time in a long time.

"Li-sa!" her little sister insisted with a stomp of her foot. "Daddy said come inside right now! Something's in the fireplace!"

That picked Lisa right up out of her chair. The look in Kayla's eyes showed that this wasn't a silly game. The two of them went through the front door and into the living room, where their mom and dad were standing arm in arm, staring at the fireplace. Inside the dark hole within the brick frame were hundreds of orange sparks flashing and snapping, crackling like a fire, though there were no flames.

Lisa stepped up beside her parents and looked at their faces, which were filled with awe. Lorena and Edgar Higginbottom had tried so hard to put on a brave front since Tick had gone missing again, to be strong for Lisa and Kayla. But they hadn't been able to hide the devastating sadness within them. It was in their eyes. Like death itself.

"What's going on?" Lisa asked.

"It has something to do with Tick," her dad replied. "I know that much. It has to."

Lisa's mom patted her husband on the arm. "Let's not get our hopes up, Edgar." Her face showed she wasn't following her own advice.

The dancing orange lights suddenly stopped, winking out of existence. Lisa was shocked to see a piece of paper resting on top of the logs—she was certain it hadn't been there a second ago.

"Grab it," she whispered to Kayla.

Her little sister ran to the fireplace and picked up the paper, took a look then ran to their mom and handed it to her. Everyone crowded around to see.

It was a letter. Lisa's mom read it aloud.

Dear Mom. And Dad. And Lisa. And Kayla.

You're probably wondering right now how this letter was created. Or how it got to you. More importantly, you're probably wondering where I am and what I'm doing. What I've become. There are things in the universe that are beyond our comprehension—I've still got a lot to learn myself. Someday I hope to understand it enough to explain it fully.

Something amazing has happened. A combination of so many things. The soulikens of an infinite number of my Alterants somehow bled to me. Filled me up. The power of Karma was involved. So was the unbelievable energy of the Void from the Fourth Dimension. The inventive mind of Reginald Chu and the sheer will of Mistress Jane. It all added together to make this possible—I've become an entity, like the Haunce, a force to help watch over the Realities.

But the details and the complexities of it all don't matter. Not right now.

This is what matters:

Know that I'm alive in so many ways. That I will always be with you in some form or another. That I'll devote every ounce of my energy to making life better in all of the Realities. Great things await us in the future. But most important of all, know that I love you. All of you. More than the infinite power of Chi'karda and Karma combined could ever express. I love you. I love you guys so much.

I will always be near. Always.

Your brother and son,

Tick

Lisa's mom finished reading, and silence filled the room except for a few sniffles, most of them coming from Lisa's dad.

"Go get Tick's *Journal of Curious Letters*," he said. His voice trembled a bit, but there was a smile on his face and the unmistakable spark of life in his eyes. "It's under his bed. This letter will make an excellent last page to the collection. Don't you think?"

EPILOGUE

THE FIRST MEETING

Paul sat at the large conference table, feeling a little bit as if he'd finally awakened from a long, long dream. Things felt surreal and kind of strange. Different. But good. Mostly good. Today's agenda had an item listed that would never be forgotten. He took a second to look around the room at his fellow Realitants.

There were a few people here he didn't know very well. Not yet, anyway. People like red-haired Priscilla Persiphone, a doctor named something-or-other Hillenstat, or the dude that couldn't speak named Jimmy—the guy didn't even have a tongue. Ew. There were others: Nancy and Katrina and William. A couple more he couldn't remember. All of them had come just in time to save the Fifth Army—along with Paul and Sofia—from being completely wiped out in that last and final battle. So they were definitely his new friends.

And then there were the others. The ones who'd become family.

Mothball, still marked with wounds from the terrible battle in the Thirteenth Reality, but with a smile planted on her long and weary face. Rutger, sitting taller than ever; he'd done the impossible and gathered together all the missing Realitants. Sally, who'd been wearing the same shirt since that fateful day, saying that it'd be bad Karma to put on anything else.

Sato's face was actually a little less stern than it had been of late. Paul knew he was thinking of all the soldiers he'd lost, and the promise he still planned to keep. To take what was left of his army and reclaim the Fifth Reality from the Bugaboos. They'd be leaving soon to do just that.

And Sofia.

Her eyes met his. She didn't say anything, and neither did he, but a lot passed between them in that gaze. The months that seemed like years, the pain and hurt and terror, the thrill of winning mixed with the sorrow of all that had been lost along the way. The ache for those who were no longer there. And an unspoken bond that could never be taken away from them. She smiled, and he smiled back.

And finally, he looked to the head of the table.

To the place where Master George had always sat with his flaky red scalp, his loyal Muffintops on his lap, his three-piece suit, and his Barrier Wand usually somewhere nearby. The old man with the proper speech and the constant twinkle in his eyes. The old man who'd brought them in, trained them, encouraged them. The old man who'd chosen to fight by their side in the end, though he had to know his chances of surviving were slim. Paul had a lump in his throat at the thought, and wished he could say good-bye one last time.

Someone else was sitting in the leader's chair now. Someone very different, having just appeared in a blaze of sparks and the sound of static charges.

A being, roughly in the shape of a human body, a cloudy mix of blue and white light swirling through and around each other, occupied the seat where Master George had once reigned. Little flashes of orange danced throughout the ethereal substance, along with zigzags of bright electricity, like miniature strikes of lightning. The otherworldly apparition glowed warmly and gave off a humming sound. Paul could feel a vibrating buzz in his bones.

There was a face projected on the surface of the

wraithlike figure's head. A familiar face that was smiling at the moment. Tick. It was good to see him again. Oh, man, it was so good to see him again.

Atticus Higginbottom, in a form that no one else in that room would ever understand, leaned forward and put his ghostly elbows on the table.

"Let's get this meeting started," he said.